Praise for Greg Rucka's Novels

KEEPER

"Crisper, tighter and tougher...A keeper as a novel."
—*San Francisco Chronicle*

"Riveting...*Keeper* is full of surprises."
—*Houston Chronicle*

"*Keeper* pulls at the heartstrings and brings tears to the
eyes....A remarkable first novel."
—*Orlando Sentinel*

FINDER

"A memorable novel, dark as a moonless night."
—*Mostly Murder*

"As grit-gray and compelling as life. A-plus."
—*Philadelphia Inquirer*

"The action is nonstop."
—*Boston Globe*

By Greg Rucka

GREG RUCKA

KEEPER

FINDER

Bantam Books

KEEPER/FINDER
A Bantam Book / May 2005

Published by
Bantam Dell
A Division of Random House, Inc.
New York, New York

Bantam Books and the rooster colophon are registered
trademarks of Random House, Inc.

0-553-38385-X

These titles were originally published individually by Bantam Dell.

Printed in the United States of America
Published simultaneously in Canada

www.bantamdell.com

OPM 10 9 8 7 6 5 4 3 2 1

For Art and Bernie

In the new code of laws which I suppose it will be necessary for you to make I desire you remember the ladies, and be more generous and favorable to them than your ancestors. Do not put such unlimited power into the hands of the husbands. Remember all men would be tyrants if they could. If particular care and attention is not paid to the ladies we are determined to foment a rebellion, and will not hold ourselves bound by any laws in which we have no voice, or representation.

Abigail Adams, letter to John Adams, March 31, 1776

■ ACKNOWLEDGMENTS ■

I am indebted to a number of people for their assistance and guidance, not only in the areas touched upon by this novel, but in all that was required to reach this point.

At the Federal Bureau of Investigation: Special Agents John Weis, Bobbi Cotter, and Ernest J. Porter for their patient cooperation in assisting me with my research and keeping me informed as new information became available. Additional thanks to Special Agent Swanson D. Carter, Unit Chief, Office of Public and Congressional Affairs.

Gerard "Jerry" V. Hennelly, President of Executive Security Protection International, Inc. (ESPI, Inc.), who provided guidance and insight into the profession of the "true" bodyguard. My newest old friend.

Others who left their stamp on this work in a variety of ways: Officer William M. Conway, NYPD; N. Michael Rucka and Corrina Rucka; Elizabeth Rogers, NY EMS, Paramedic; Eric Lonergan, NY EMS, Paramedic; David Farschman; The Friday Mid-Day Coffee Klatch—Nic, Mike, and Mark; Daria "Or Should I Say Bridgett?" Penta; Casey Alenson Blaine; Kate Miciak; Peter Rubie; Sid, Frank, Peter, and Leslie.

Special thanks to Nunzio Andrew DeFilippis. Jillian loves Teah almost as much as I love you. May Walter Matusek live forever.

Finally, to Jennifer. She knows why.

KEEPER

CHAPTER ONE

Much as I wanted to, I didn't break the guy's nose.

Instead, I kept both hands on Alison's shoulders, using my body as a shield to get us through the crowd. At six feet and over one hundred and ninety pounds, I'm big enough to be intimidating, even wearing glasses. People normally get out of my way when I want them to.

But the guy stuck with us, even going so far as to lean his face closer to mine. His teeth were the product of either good genes or expensive orthodontia, and the fire was hot in his eyes. He yelled, "Don't let her murder your son!"

Another man pushed a camera at us and snapped a quick photograph, reflecting us in the lens. Over the prayers of several people who pleaded with Jesus to save the soul of our unborn child, I could hear the photographer say, "We won't forget you." Whether that was directed at us or the fetus wasn't clear.

Alison said nothing, her head low and near my chest, one hand around my back, one on my arm. I'd never felt her hold me like that. It almost hurt.

A young black man wearing a safety-orange vest over his T-shirt opened the glass door for us. As we went past he said, "Damn. We don't usually get this." He closed the door behind us, then turned and gave a nod to the uniformed security guard, who buzzed us through a second door, letting us into the ground-floor reception room.

For a disorienting moment we stood there, on the neat checkers of linoleum, still clinging to one another. New faces all around looked back, some embarrassed, some sad, some carefully blank. Eight women, waiting on chairs and couches, and only two of them looked obviously pregnant. One had a baby in her arms. Somehow the child could sleep through all the noise from outside.

A nurse behind the desk said, "Your name?"

Alison let go of me. "Alison Wallace."

The nurse checked a printout on the counter, then nodded. "You want the second floor. Through that door, down the hall, take the elevator or the stairs." She smiled at Alison. "Check in at the counter there." Then the nurse looked at me and asked, "You'll be going up with her?"

"Yes."

"Your name?"

"It's Atticus," Alison told her. "Atticus Kodiak."

I took Alison's hand. We went through the door and down a long hall, past a lounge and several examination rooms and offices. We passed a doctor in the hall and he gave us the same smile the nurse had.

Alison wanted to take the stairs. "I'll get to see the elevator after," she said. She let go of my hand when we reached the second floor, stepping into another waiting room, almost identical to the one on the ground floor but with nicer furnishings. More couches and chairs, magazine racks, coffee tables, a coffeemaker, a television. The walls were painted light blue, with white detailing at the trim.

At the opposite side of the room from the stairway was a glass partition where more nurses were controlling intake. There was a door beside the partition, and I figured it led to the procedure and recovery rooms. Another door on the wall to the right of that had a sign on it reading "Education and Services."

Alison told me to sit down, then went to the partition and checked in. We filled out her paperwork together, and I had to sign a waiver and a release form, not unlike the forms you fill out before getting your wisdom teeth pulled. Alison returned the completed paperwork, and we sat together for another forty-five minutes before the nurse called her name. I gave her a kiss on the cheek before she rose.

"This is the right thing," Alison said.

"I know."

She returned my kiss with dry lips, then went with the nurse. She didn't look back.

Three hours later, and I was still sitting on the same couch, skimming magazines and watching people. Five women were filling out forms, two with men beside them. One of the men was absolutely silent, barely aware of his companion. Another six people were waiting, pretending to read or watch television. Most were Latino or black, but one of the couples filling out forms was white and I suspected they had come from Columbia University. Occasionally a nurse would open the door beside the partition and announce a name, then escort the chosen through the door after checking her clipboard. Many more people had come and gone. They left with paper bags full of educational literature, dental dams, condoms, and tubes of Nonoxynal-9.

Turnaround with the sex-ed crowd was a lot faster, it seemed.

I stood and stretched, crossed to the window overlooking Amsterdam, trying to ease my nerves. This window had a grille over it, and I wondered why they didn't use them on the ground floor, too. It's harder to throw a brick through a grille, after all.

Nearly forty people milled around across the street, held behind a police barricade line by NYPD uniforms. The Federal Access to Clinic Entrances Act of 1994 had been designed to solve this problem, but so far it hadn't worked all that well. The law is considered by many to be unconstitutional, specifically in violation of the First Amendment, and challenges to it occur on a regular basis. As it was, protesters had positioned themselves at every approach to the clinic, and while they did not block access physically, they certainly created a daunting psychological gauntlet for a woman to run. There was no way to avoid them, as we had discovered the hard way. From the window, I saw placards and a couple of poles with dolls impaled on them. The dolls were naked and spattered with red paint. Several people held signs depicting a large cross draped in bloody barbed wire: "SOS" was painted in red in the upper right corner. Keeping well away from this group were other pro-lifers, more moderate contingents passing out pamphlets and singing hymns, their signs citing scripture, or stating, simply, "Stop Abortion Now."

Alison had chosen the clinic on recommendation from her OB/GYN. One of the deciding factors had been the assurance that the Women's LifeCare Clinic rarely had trouble with demonstrators. When we had called the clinic that morning, before coming in, the person we spoke to said that there was a "minor" protest in progress, but that shouldn't discourage us. It hadn't sounded too bad.

I had been willing to turn back when we saw the crowd, more concerned with Alison's peace of mind than anything else. But she had gotten angry.

"Hell with them," she had said. "I'm not going to be scared off by these assholes." Then she patted my arm and said, "Besides, I've got my bodyguard with me."

Her bodyguard, and the father of her child, I thought.

Getting out was going to be worse than going in, because now they knew we had been inside, and for how long. We would come out to more of the same, perhaps worse, and knowing that Alison would be on the far side of a particularly painful operation didn't help my mood. She had made her decision; she was the only person with the right to question it.

I saw a sign with "Abortion is Murder" on it, and swore under my breath.

"You're swearing and that's not nice. Don't swear."

The voice came out of a short, chubby woman, with light brown skin and a face shaped by Down's syndrome. She wore turquoise sweatpants stretched tight over her middle, tiny pink tennis shoes, and a hot-pink sweatshirt on which white cats chased each other around her body. She held a Walkman, but the headphones were off her head, and she was looking at me sternly.

"Don't swear."

"I apologize," I said.

She looked down at her pink tennis shoes and muttered something, then looked back to me and said, "It's all right, you're all right. My name is Katie."

"I'm Atticus."

"Atticus who?" She said it tentatively, pushing hard on the consonants.

"Kodiak."

Katie repeated my last name, tripping it over her tongue. She had a lot of trouble with it, and finally said, "Can't say it. Say it K, 'Cus K."

"That's right," I said. "Atticus K." Over her shoulder I tried to spot a parent or someone associated with her. No one was paying us any attention. Katie smiled and said carefully, "I'm very pleased to meet you, 'Cus." She stuck out her hand and I took it. Her hand was small, warm, and moist. Her fingers barely made it out of my palm, but

Katie shook my hand vigorously, then tugged me toward an empty couch.

"Got to sit down, got to sit down and stay out of the way," Katie said, but she didn't say it to me; she said it to herself. Then she dropped her voice further and said, "Yes, you do, Katie. You know that."

We sat on the couch and Katie fumbled with her Walkman for a moment, but the headphone wires were tangled and she couldn't straighten the cord.

"Can I help you?" I asked.

Katie thought about that, weighing the decision, then said, "Here, fix them." She thrust both the Walkman and the headphones into my lap. The Walkman was a cheap model, functional and without frills, as were the headphones. Both had been dinged about, and the pads on the headphones were ripped, exposing the speakers. I untangled the cabling and plugged the jack into the player. A Madonna tape rested inside.

I handed the player back to Katie and she put the headphones around her neck, then stared at me. Softly she said, "He has brown eyes," and then, louder, "Thanks, thank you."

"You're welcome. You like Madonna, Katie?"

"I like her a lot, 'Cus. She's sexy. Do you like Madonna?"

"Not particularly."

She laughed and pointed a finger at my chest and said, "You're silly. You like Madonna." She was smiling again, but this smile seemed more honest than the one she had used to introduce herself, broad and even. Her teeth were small and yellowed.

"All right. I like Madonna."

"I know! I know that. He's silly. You're silly."

"I think you're silly."

"I am not."

"Yes, you are."

"I am not. Stop it. I am not silly."

"Okay, I'm sorry, you're not silly."

"It's okay, it's okay, 'Cus." Katie played with the Walkman for a moment, opening and closing the cassette door, then said to herself, "Ask him. Ask him."

"Ask me what?"

She jerked her head around to look at me, surprised, and said, "Uh-oh, he heard us." She looked back down to her lap and poked the cassette player with her fingers for a few seconds. Then Katie said, " 'Cus, do you have a, uh, a girlfriend?"

I grinned. "Yes," I told her. "Her name is Alison."

"Oh." She toyed with the Walkman again, then said, "I have a boyfriend. His name is David and he's strong and protects me. But when he gets angry he loses his temper and he gets very mad. He turns into a monster and he doesn't like it, but he gets angry and can't con-con-control himself." She studied me and said, "David loves me a lot, though, he does. Is your girlfriend, is she here?"

"Yes, she is."

"I knew that, I know."

From the street came a roar, voices rising together with glee. I went back to the window. Most of the crowd had converged around a white Cadillac parked on the opposite side of the street, their SOS signs waving.

Katie peeked around my elbow, looking out the window. "Uh-oh," she said. "Uh-oh."

"Do you know who that is?" I asked her.

"Who is it? I don't know who it is."

The Caddy's front passenger door opened and a man got out, blond and short, though the angle made it hard to determine more than that. He began waving the crowd back. Then he opened one of the rear doors and another man emerged, this one a head taller, dressed in a neat summer suit. His hair was black, and he held a megaphone. Katie and I watched as the man in the suit climbed to the roof of his car.

For a moment, he stood there on the roof of the big

white Cadillac, surveying the crowd. Even from the window, I could see he was smiling.

"Oh, no! It's the Loud Man," Katie told me. "He's the Loud Man."

"Yeah?" I said.

"Very loud he's very very loud, 'Cus. Mommy doesn't like him."

I was about to ask where her mother was, when the Loud Man raised his megaphone and began to speak.

"I speak to you of murder," he said.

The crowd murmured.

"Murder again and bloody murder more," the man said. "Bodies upon bodies, broken and torn, filling their trash cans, their Dumpsters, their sinks. Cold metal, sharp metal, the coldest, sharpest things they have ever felt, their second feeling, pulling them from their mothers, from their safety, and warmth, and home."

He stopped, watching the mob soak up his words. In the summer heat, he only made them hotter. When he spoke, his pauses were perfectly placed for emphasis, the whole speech well rehearsed.

He pointed up at our window and bellowed, "Felice Romero, queen butcher of this abortuary, are you listening to me? Every murder is on your hands, every death is on your head, every soul is anchored to yours, and they weigh you, dragging you down to the Pit. Fire, Dr. Romero. Pain, the same pain you inflict on those helpless souls you tear screaming from their mothers' wombs every day!"

He stopped again, bowing his head and dropping the accusatory finger. Softly, nearly in tears, he added, "I give you Ezekiel 16:21, Dr. Romero: 'Is this of thy whoredoms a small matter, that thou hast slain my children, and delivered them to cause them to pass through the fire for them?' "

His head came up again and the crowd made more noise, apparently pleased with his scriptural choice.

"Your daughter, your own daughter. She is precisely the

kind of child you would destroy. You dare call yourself a mother? Dr. Romero, your hypocrisy knows no bounds.

"We remember," he said. "We are witness to your crimes, to every murder committed behind your walls. For the mothers are guilty, surely, that they let you kill in them what the Lord himself has placed. But you prey on that, and your bodies continue to mount.

"We remember each and every unborn child you murder, Dr. Romero. We remember each and every life you destroy. We are the Lord's eyes in this, and we know what you do. We will be the Lord's hands, and we will seek justice.

"We know what you do. And we will have justice!"

I turned away from the window, went back to the couch. Some of the others in the waiting room had gone to the window as well, and they continued to watch. Several looked shaken, and the nurses moved from person to person, speaking softly. If they were trying to reassure, it didn't look like they were doing a good job.

Katie sat back down beside me.

"He's very loud," she told me.

"Yes, he is," I agreed. "Is your mommy Dr. Romero?"

Katie smiled proudly. "My mommy is a doctor and she helps people. My mommy's smart." Then she put the headphones over her ears and pressed the "play" button, and it was as if nothing was happening outside of her at all. She sang along with whatever tune was being piped into her brain. She sang badly, toneless and inarticulate, but without self-consciousness, and when people in the room glanced at her, Katie ignored them, swaying on the couch. While singing, she took my hand and placed it between hers, patting it.

The door beside the partition opened and a young black woman called, "Mr. Kodiak?"

I stood up, slipping my hand out of Katie's. She didn't seem to notice, and continued to sing. I said, "Yes?"

"Dr. Romero would like to speak to you. Would you follow me?"

I started cataloging all the traumas that could have occurred, and in the seconds it took me to move from Katie to the door I compiled a pretty impressive list. The waiver and release forms were in my back pocket, and I found that my recall of all the potential complications was very clear. Alison was in trouble. Alison was in shock. Alison was being taken to the hospital. Alison's uterus had been punctured. Alison hadn't been completely evacuated. Alison was hemorrhaging. Alison had a heart attack. Alison had an aneurysm, a stroke, a seizure.

"This way," the woman said, and I followed her through the door, my heart seriously starting to knock about in my chest. The door swung shut behind us and the nurse led me down the corridor.

"What's happened?"

"Dr. Romero would like to speak with you," she repeated. She wore a cream-colored name tag over her left breast, "Delfleur, R.N." printed on it in blue letters.

The fact that my question had gone unanswered did nothing for my growing anxiety.

The hall ended with doors to my right and left. The right door was marked "Bathroom." The left door was marked "Dr. F. Romero, Administrator." The nurse knocked on the door then said, "Go on in." She turned and headed back to the waiting room.

I took a second, trying to stay calm. Then I opened the door.

CHAPTER TWO

It was a cramped office, with a window looking out at another building across the alley. A densely packed bookshelf ran along the opposite wall. A filing cabinet stood in a corner beside a trash can. Two chairs covered in pale orange fabric were placed in front of a metal desk; on the desk were papers, a typewriter, and a telephone. Framed degrees hung over the bookshelf, one from Columbia, another from Cornell. The room smelled of paper and stale cigarette smoke.

Behind the desk, speaking into the phone, sat a Hispanic woman in her late forties, her short black hair streaked silver. She had a narrow face and dark eyes behind black-framed glasses, and she was marking a paper on her desk with one hand, holding the phone with the other. She pointed her pen at me and made a horizontal swing, back and forth, and for a moment I had no idea what she wanted me to do. Then I turned and shut the door behind me. When I looked back she nodded and pointed the pen at one of the chairs in front of her desk. I sat.

"Yes, I think it's serious enough," she was saying. "No, more than that. . . . Yes . . . that's what I'm trying to do right now . . . the board should cover at least half. . . . I don't know. When I find out I'll call you back. . . . Yes."

She hung up the phone, then rose, extending her hand. "Mr. Kodiak? I'm Felice Romero."

I shook her hand and said, "Is Alison all right?"

She lit a cigarette and sat back down. "Alison's in recovery right now, completely evacuated. She should be ready to leave by the time we're finished."

I exhaled long, and tried to dry my palms on my jeans. "I thought something had gone wrong," I said.

Moving papers around on her desk, Dr. Romero uncovered an empty ashtray. She tipped it into the trash can anyway, saying, "I apologize. Lynn should have said something. No, she's fine. She'll be sore for a while and you two shouldn't engage in intercourse for at least sixty days, but you know that, you already filled out the release forms. I'd recommend reevaluating your method of birth control. Other than that, there were no complications. She was a model patient."

"I see."

Dr. Romero knocked ash into the tray and pushed her chair back, openly studying me. I adjusted my glasses. She took two drags on the cigarette, blowing smoke out of the side of her mouth.

"It's procedure here to ask the patient if they still want to have the abortion before we get started," she told me. "I wanted to know if Ms. Wallace might be having second thoughts, especially considering the crowd outside. She told me that you are a bodyguard and had kept the nuts outside away from her. Is that correct—you are a professional bodyguard?"

"What is this about?"

"I'm sorry, I'm on a schedule and there's been a lot of pressure here with Sword of the Silent out front."

"Sword of the Silent?" I remembered the signs bobbing in the street, their bloody crosses and barbed wire. "SOS?"

"Cute, isn't it?" Dr. Romero stuck the cigarette back in her mouth and began searching through the papers on her desk again. "They've been around for over a week now, ever since the conference was announced."

I was starting to feel exceptionally dim. "Conference?"

She stopped shuffling papers and stared at me. "You don't know? It's being called the Common Ground Conference, to be held downtown at the Manhattan Elysium Hotel in two weeks. Pro-choice and pro-life attendees, lectures, seminars, panels, all designed to stop the escalating violence. I'm one of the organizers." When I still looked blank she added, "Local media has been giving us fairly heavy coverage."

"I've been out of the country," I said.

"Really? Where?"

"I was on a job in England," I said. She seemed to expect me to elaborate, but I didn't. In my work, you don't talk about your clients.

After a second she asked, "How old are you, exactly?"

"Twenty-eight."

"Is that young for your profession?"

"Younger than many, older than some."

"What exactly does a bodyguard do?"

"Personal protection. I came out of the Army's Executive Protection program, served some time in the CID. I've been out about three years. I'm the real thing, doctor, not the kind that gets hired to break the kneecaps of Olympic hopefuls, in case you're wondering."

She laughed curtly and said, "You understand why I'm asking?"

"I understand how you could be confused," I told her.

"How much do you charge?"

"Depends on who I'm protecting and from what. It's rated against the kind of coverage and how many other people are needed. Solo, I charge one hundred and fifty an hour for fieldwork plus expenses, eighty an hour for consultation. But alone I can't do much. Real protection requires more bodyguards."

"If you were protecting two people, twenty-four hours a day?"

"I'd need to know what I was protecting them from before I could plan a detail," I said.

She nodded and handed me a sheet of paper, saying, "That came yesterday."

It was a photocopy of a letter, typed. It read:

To the Murdering Cunt Wetback Doctor—
Hell is waiting for you, bitch. I'll send you there myself, my hands ripping the life out of your cum-filled fucking throat. I'll crack your spic skull, it'll look like the babies you break and pull screaming from their trapped mommas. I know what you do, you fucking bitch. Talk all you want, lie all you want, I know and you'll pay.
I'm going to do it to you. Tie your fucking spic ass down and fucking rip your cunt in two, ram a Hoover all the way in you till you scream for me to stop.
Open your mouth and I'll shut it for you, bitch. And it won't be murder, when I kill you, slut. It's going to be self-defense.
Hell is waiting for you. I'm going to send you there.

It was signed with the same cross-and-barbed-wire crest that currently graced several of the placards outside.

"Who has the original?" I asked.

"The FBI. You're holding a federal offense." She said the last grimly, without mirth. "The NYPD has seen it, too. Detective Lozano at the Twenty-sixth Precinct."

"Is this the only one?"

In response she shoved a stack of paper in my direction. It was easily three hundred pages. "These have all come since the first of the year. We receive them every day. Some are short and to the point—the burn-in-hell variety—others are longer, more passionate and considered monologues urging us to stop our work here. Twenty-three letters in the last two weeks, and I haven't seen today's mail yet. It's gotten considerably worse since my involvement with Common Ground was announced."

"Are they all like this?" I looked back at the letter. It had been typed neatly, no blurs or smudges from correction fluid. Maybe off a computer.

"Content-wise? No. Some are better; some, believe it or not, are actually worse. Especially the more recent ones."

"You have any idea where they are coming from?"

"Sword of the Silent," she said. "Jonathan Crowell. If he isn't writing them, he knows who is."

"Jonathan Crowell? Tall white guy with a megaphone?"

"That's him. Very much of the Pensacola crowd. Following in the footsteps of John Burt, Randal Terry, Paul Hill, those people."

"I've heard of him. I tend to ignore radicals."

"Crowell's not a radical, Mr. Kodiak. He is a demagogue. He's an evil man who's trying to overcome a mediocre life by preaching hate and intolerance disguised with the name of Jesus Christ." Romero crushed out her cigarette. "That's the only reason to target this clinic. Rarely has a white man been so concerned about the reproductive rights available to blacks and Hispanics. But Crowell has targeted this clinic quite specifically. We serve the university, but mostly we serve the rest of Harlem. Single mothers are our stock-in-trade. We deal with reproductive services and education here. Abortions are a very small part of what we do. And for Crowell to target us is Crowell targeting nonwhites."

"He's that clearly a racist?" I asked.

"I'm certain he doesn't think of himself as one," Dr.

Romero said. "But I believe he is, yes." She gestured toward the letter in my hands. "Do you think that is a serious threat?"

"Frankly, no. This sounds more like terrorism than the precursor to an attempt on your life."

"I'm used to terrorism, Mr. Kodiak," Dr. Romero said flatly.

"Who's doing the conference security?" I asked.

"I really don't know. A friend of mine, Veronica Selby, is handling that end of things. Veronica's the primary organizer of the conference, and she's assured me that security will be good."

For Dr. Romero's sake, I hoped she was right. A lot of self-proclaimed security firms are nothing more than fly-by-nights that hand out badges for minimum wage.

She took the letter back from me and looked it over again. "I've lived with letters threatening me, degrading and demeaning me for a long time now," she said. "But this one frightens me."

"I can see why."

Dr. Romero leaned forward, resting her elbows on the desk. "I'd like to hire you. I want protection for myself and my daughter, here and at home."

"How old is Katie?"

She was surprised only for a moment. "Sixteen. You've met her?"

"In the waiting room."

"What do you think of her?"

"She's very sweet," I said. "She talks to herself a lot."

"Imaginary friends," Dr. Romero said. "It makes sense, when you think about it. Very few people actually talk to Katie rather than at her, and she finds communication with them quite difficult, too, I think. The people she speaks to understand her completely."

"I think you'd be better off with official protection," I said.

"I don't trust the police. I've known too many officers

who believe abortion is murder. Detective Lozano himself is antichoice."

"There's the FBI," I said. "Federal marshals, too."

She sighed, leaned back in her chair, and went for another cigarette. I wondered if she had always smoked, or if it was a habit she had adopted in response to her work.

"The agent who's been assigned to us, Special Agent Fowler, is only interested in pursuing the terrorism approach at this time," Dr. Romero said. "He is unconvinced that Crowell or Sword of the Silent is after me. Special Agent Fowler does not like conspiracies." She watched the flame from her lighter for a moment, then set it down on the desk without lighting the cigarette. "Our requests for federal marshals have been turned down, too. We're told they're needed more at clinics outside of New York." Felice Romero reached for the light again, used it, then said, "I want you to do it."

"The protection you want is expensive," I said.

"Give me a figure and I'll call our board of directors. They'll put up at least half. I'll cover the rest. I have money."

I thought about it, making rough calculations in my head. "If I were to do it," I said, "we'd be talking three thousand dollars a week. You can get security guards and rent-a-cops for less, but it won't be the protection you want."

"For that much money, what do I get?"

"Complete coverage, twenty-four hours a day, seven days a week."

She drew on the cigarette thoughtfully, then asked, "When can you start?"

I shook my head. "I recommend trying Sentinel Guards. Ask for Natalie Trent, tell her you talked to me. She can put everything together for you. They're a great firm. Her father runs it, and he's ex–Secret Service."

"Mr. Kodiak, you don't seem to be listening. I want you."

"I am listening, Doctor. But right now I've got other things on my plate."

She dropped ash on her desk, looked at it for a moment, then brushed it into the ashtray with her palm, smearing it across her desk. After she set the ashtray back down, she said:

"Many of the men who come in here with their girl-friends, when they do come, aren't exactly supportive. Most would have seen the mob out front and turned tail. Others would simply wait, bored. Others would wait, concerned. Many wait and grow angry. Sometimes they take that anger out on the women they came in with." She watched the smoke from her cigarette curling toward the ceiling vent.

I could hear the SOS protesters chanting outside. There was no question that Dr. Romero heard it, too.

She said, "Abortion is an emotional issue, not a cerebral one, Mr. Kodiak. It is a damned-if-you-do, damned-if-you-don't decision, and it's a decision impossible to make in this society without hurting someone. This is why no consensus has been reached on the subject and why people are now murdering doctors. It's why Common Ground is so important, because it's a chance for all the voices to be heard, and to be heard without threats or screaming. It doesn't matter to me whether you're pro-choice or anti-abortion, Mr. Kodiak. I don't want some apathetic ex-cop with a beer gut. I don't want lean SWAT team professionals. I want someone who understands that no matter what side of the line you're on, someone always gets hurt. What matters is that you know what it's like to cross that line." She ground out her cigarette and locked eyes on me.

"I'll consider it," I said. "Can I see Alison?"

"She'll meet you in the waiting room," Dr. Romero said, and reached for the phone. She was already arguing with someone on the line by the time I shut the door.

———

Katie wandered over after I'd been back in the waiting room for a few minutes, sitting down beside me on the couch. Without warning, she wrapped her arms around my middle and gave me a hug, saying, "Hello. I missed you."

I patted her back.

" 'Cus, 'Cus are you all—all right? You look sad, he looks sad."

"I'm fine, Katie."

She mumbled something into her chest, then slipped her hand in mine and sat quietly, her legs swinging just above the floor.

Twenty minutes later, Alison came through the admitting door in a wheelchair pushed by Lynn Delfleur. She saw me and smiled thinly, brushing brown hair out of her eyes, turning her head to Delfleur and murmuring something I couldn't catch. The nurse laughed. Sitting in the wheelchair she looked pale and tired, and still beautiful. I let go of Katie's hand and stood up. They came over to me and Delfleur said, "Take her home and treat her well."

"I always do."

"You want me to take you downstairs?" she asked Alison.

Alison shook her head.

"Leave the wheelchair at reception," Delfleur said.

I got behind the chair and took hold of the handles. Katie stood to the side, watching, still quiet, and I said, "It was nice meeting you, Katie."

"Nice to meet you, too, are you his girlfriend?"

Alison nodded.

"He's nice."

"Yes, he is," Alison said. Her voice was constricted and low.

We went to the elevator, and Katie watched us go. After the doors closed I leaned over and kissed the top of Alison's head. She said, "You don't waste any time."

"Well, you know me, I see a pretty girl and go to pieces."

"Can't let you out of my sight," she said.

The elevator stopped and I pushed her down the hall, passing a very young-looking Latina and a nurse as they entered one of the examination rooms. The girl looked at us with hollow eyes.

"How you doing?" I asked.

"I feel sick," Alison said. "I want to go home."

At reception another nurse took the wheelchair while I helped Alison up, and we worked out a way to walk, her on my left side, head on my shoulder, my left arm tightly around her waist. "Slowly," Alison cautioned me.

The security guard, a big black man in a clean white uniform, got to his feet and asked, "You want an escort?" His name tag identified him as "Sheldon Bullier."

"Absolutely," I said.

He picked up the phone and punched two numbers, then said, "Escort out at ground reception."

Less than a minute later the same thin man who had held the door for us on our way in entered the room. He introduced himself as Nate and said he'd lead, and we headed out the door.

The crowd was no bigger than before, but it certainly seemed more hostile, even at their legislated distance. Crowell and the Cadillac were gone. The moment we exited there was a response, people yelling and wailing. The roaming photographer snapped another shot of us as a chorus of "Mommy, mommy, you've murdered me" started. The protesters had the singsong down well, almost sounding like children. But not quite.

Seven men and women fell to their knees on the sidewalk across the street and began praying loudly for the soul of our baby, blocking a young, well-dressed couple, trying to reach us with pamphlets. The man who had harried us on the way in urged Jesus to strike us dead where we stood. We headed down the sidewalk to where I had parked. A voice shouted, "You've let her kill your son. He was your son!"

Under his breath, Nate said, "Freedom of speech."

Alison's hands dug into me, and I felt her tremble and try to pull me closer, and I squeezed her back, gently. We had cleared the safe perimeter, and were maybe another twenty feet from where I had parked her car.

Nate said, "Look out."

Four men and women were rushing toward us. All carried paper shopping bags, and as they reached into them I instinctively shifted my weight, pivoting left, and lifted Alison to put our backs to the clinic. Nate stopped one woman but the other three pushed right past him and came at us, yelling. A bushily bearded man reached into his bag, screaming, "Look what you've done!" but before he could withdraw his hand I'd turned again, loosening my grip on Alison so as to not pull her with me, and putting my shoulder into the man's chest. While I was at it I straight-armed the man beside him. They both reeled backward off the sidewalk, cursing. The bushy beard shouted, "He tried to kill me."

I felt Alison let go of me and turned to see the small black-haired woman who had slipped past screeching, "Murderer, murderer, murderer, murderer, murderer, murderer!" in Alison's face. She had dropped her bag and was shoving something into Alison's hands, and Alison was trying to push her away. Alison's hands were red and wet.

I grabbed the thumb of the woman's left hand in my right, pulling back and twisting hard, sweeping the back of her left knee with my right foot. She shrieked and went down on her rear; the mutilated doll she'd been pressing on Alison fell onto the sidewalk beside her. Red paint spilled out of the doll's cracked head, pooling beside the woman.

Alison was sagging against the wall. Tears streaked salt tracks on her cheeks, and I caught her, pulled her against me, and made it to her Honda. Without letting her go I unlocked the passenger door, opened it, and slid her inside. Then I slammed the door shut, locking it, making a quick scan. The protesters had lurched forward, their shouts shrill and coarse. Nate and I caught eyes and he thumbs-upped and I nodded, and he turned to begin forcing his way back to the clinic.

The black-haired woman still sat on the sidewalk, clutching her thumb, bushy beard trying to help her up. They both watched me, and I stared back hard, and they looked away. I got into the car, started the engine, and pulled out, seeing more people shouting at us in the rearview mirror.

Alison made no sound, her chin pressed to her chest, hair hiding her face, her hands palm-up in her lap, smeared with wet red paint. The front of her shirt had been spattered, too. After a moment she tried to wipe her hands off on her shirt, but then she gave up and sat motionless and silent.

We had been together for just under seven months. Seeing her sitting beside me on the passenger seat, bent and in retreat, burned me. This wasn't her, and I hated it and knew that she did, too.

At a light on Broadway I reached out, touching her shoulder. She shook her head and said, "Don't." The word rode on a single sob, and I withdrew my hand. We made it to her place on Eighty-fourth and I double-parked on the street. With her out of the car, I took the keys from her pocket and unlocked the town house's front door. She allowed me to guide her to the bathroom, then knelt at the toilet and vomited. I held her hair away from her face until she waved me away, then went to park the car.

When I returned, the bathroom door was shut and the shower was running. I went into the kitchen and hunted about for the teakettle. I wasn't overly familiar with the town house. Alison had been occupying it full-time only for the last six weeks, since starting work in the city, and although I'd visited it frequently, I hadn't done any significant exploring. The town house had been purchased by her parents and Alison had the run of it while she lived in Manhattan, on the sole condition that her mother could visit, unannounced, whenever she chose to. I liked her mother a lot. She had chosen to visit a few times and once caught us making love in the kitchen, which was no more embarrassing than being arrested streaking around the mayor's mansion, but no less than, well, than being walked in on by the mother of the woman you are making love with. Linda Wallace had taken it well, certainly better than I had. Currently, Linda was vacationing in France, bicycling around Provence. She would be calling soon, probably; the abortion was not a secret between her and her daughter.

I found the kettle in the cupboard over the oven, and a tin of Earl Grey hidden behind some macaroni in the pantry. I started the water heating and reread my instructions on how to care for Alison. Sleep seemed high on the list right now, and not a lot of movement. When I heard the shower stop I went back to the bedroom to turn down the covers and draw the blinds, then headed to the bathroom.

She called my name as I got there and I said, "I'm right here."

"Can you get my robe, please?"

I got her robe from her bedroom and came back, and Alison opened the door to the bathroom and took it from me without letting me see her. Then she opened the door wide and, clad in her robe, said, "I want to lie down."

"Sure," I said, and put an arm around her, guiding her to her room. There, she disrobed and got slowly under the covers, immediately closing her eyes. I pulled the blankets up around her and she shivered, sinking into the pillow. I kissed her cheek and said, "I'll check on you in a bit. Otherwise, I'll be in the kitchen if you need me."

She mumbled a response as I rose and made certain she was tucked in. At the door I added, "I'm sorry, Alison."

Her eyes opened, and she turned her head to look at me. But her gaze went through me and she stayed silent, and all I got was a small nod before she closed her eyes again.

I shut the door quietly, then went to the sitting room and turned down the air conditioner. In the bathroom I found some cleaning supplies under the sink and cleaned up the red paint smeared on the porcelain and tile. Finished, I found my way back to the kitchen, poured a mug of tea, and drank it sitting at the kitchen table. The air conditioner cycled, peacefully sucking me dry, the refrigerator humming with it. No noise other than appliances, no movement other than air and me, and I watched the steam curling out of my mug. The mug was black with a Star Trek insignia on it. Alison's late father had bought it, I had been informed.

I could cover Romero and her daughter. With additional help, with Rubin and Natalie, and, say, Dale, I could do it. I could possibly even keep them alive, but there are no guarantees in this business. Dale was at least as well trained as I; we had done the Army course together. Natalie had been trained by her father, and was probably better than I at this sort of work. Rubin had learned at my knee. He wasn't professional, but he was amateur in the way that Olympic athletes are amateurs, and we had been close friends forever. Rubin's learning was through osmosis, I supposed, and he had absorbed a lot.

Including me, that'd give us a four-person, twenty-four-hour-a-day, seven-day-a-week rotation. Two people to stay with Romero at the clinic when she worked; two people at her home while she slept; leave one person to stay with Katie during the day. Alternate that, have the remaining person cover Romero's clinic ingress and egress, and the protection would be fine, giving that person room to investigate and perform the advance work, what little would be needed.

I could do that, and thinking about it, I realized I

wanted to do it. If nothing else, I wanted to give back a little of what I'd had to take this morning.

After draining the cup I called Rubin. He took a few rings to answer, and I pictured him in our apartment, dropping his pad and pencils, swearing as he picked up the phone in his room. When he picked up I asked if he was busy.

"Nothing I can't put down; the art's on spec, anyway. How's Alison?"

"She's sleeping. I need you to call Natalie and Dale and have them meet me here, and I need you to bring me my gun. Can you do that?"

"I know Natalie's free, we were going to have dinner tonight. Dale's in your book?"

"Yeah."

"Okay, I'll be right over."

"Don't ring the bell. I'll be watching for you."

I cut the connection and pulled the sheet from the clinic across the counter, thinking. I wasn't committed yet; dialing the number on the page would change that.

"Women's LifeCare, may I help you?"

"My name is Kodiak. I'd like to speak with Dr. Romero."

"Hold, please." Classical music for forty seconds, then a click and, "I'll transfer you."

"Mr. Kodiak? Dr. Romero. Is Alison all right?"

"She's asleep. I think she's fine. Have you contacted Sentinel Guards yet?"

"Not yet."

"I'll take the job," I said.

I heard her light a cigarette before she said, "When can you start?"

"Tonight. We'll pick you up when you leave work and go from there. I'll need to hold a meeting at your place, and two of my people will stay behind and spend the night there. I'd do it but I don't want to leave Alison alone for too long."

"Commendable."

"Starting tonight you've got your twenty-four/seven."

"Who are these other people?"

"Colleagues. I can vouch for them."

"I'll have a check ready for you."

I told her what else I required and she asked a couple of questions and agreed to my terms, and I said I'd see her at six and bring a contract with me. She said thank you, and we got off the phone. As I hung up, I thought I heard Alison murmuring and went to look in on her. She was sleeping, her mouth slightly open, her head tilted and resting on her hair. I watched her from the doorway for a long time.

CHAPTER THREE

We didn't notice her when she came in. Late twenties, maybe, a little plain, looking like every other expectant mother who had entered the clinic in the last week of work. Sitting in the second-floor waiting room, her purse in her lap, her belly showing second trimester, she struck me as odd only because she was Caucasian and alone. Most of the white patients at the clinic came with someone else, a friend or lover to hold their hand. She had been nervous, but I had yet to see a patient who wasn't. Mostly, I put that down to the noise of the SOS protesters outside. So I didn't stop when she came in, but continued back to my office.

Romero had, not unreasonably, explained that she would not allow a guard on her when she was with a patient, and I didn't argue the point. Excuse me, ma'am, just put your legs in the stirrups and don't mind him, he's my bodyguard.

Not good for business, if nothing else.

So, while Romero did her job, I did mine. I had taken over an empty office on the second floor as our on-site command post and, while Natalie patrolled the second floor and Dale watched the first, I did as much advance work as possible over the phone. Truth to tell, there wasn't a whole lot of advance work to be done. Romero's schedule was simple. We had all our alternate routes memorized, our formations down, our communication clear. The only other thing for me to do was try to determine the source of the threats, and I could do only so much of that at the clinic. Mostly phone calls, either to Detective Lozano or Special Agent Fowler. My attempts to set up an interview with Jonathan Crowell at SOS had all failed. I got the feeling Crowell didn't want to talk to me.

So I called Rubin at Romero's apartment to check on Katie.

"How's it going?" I asked him.

"Fine," Rubin told me. "I'm bored senseless and Katie's having the time of her life. She's stolen my sketch pad and is working in charcoals now."

"Any problems?"

"Well, she's got charcoal dust all over herself, but I've managed to keep it off the furniture."

"You're a funny guy," I said. I could hear music in the background, and Katie was saying something.

"No, no problems," Rubin said. "No phone calls, no letters, and no protesters. I just finished checking the mail. It's clean. I really don't think they have her home address yet, Atticus."

"It's only a matter of time. Enough of her life is public record and it's there for them to find. All it takes is one SOS member who also works for the IRS or a bank. Let me know if you see anything suspicious."

"Of course," he said, sounding hurt. "Katie wants to speak to you."

"Put her on."

I listened as the phone changed hands, then Katie said, "Hello, who is this?"

"It's Atticus, Katie," I said, thinking it was a hell of a thing to ask after she had told Rubin she wanted to talk to me. "How you doing?"

"Oh, it's 'Cus, hello. When are you coming home?"

"Not for a while yet. Your mom hasn't finished work."

"Where's my mommy, can I talk to my mommy?" Katie asked.

"I'll see if she can call you later."

"Okay, she's working. We can't talk to her, but we can. Ask her, please, so I can talk to her."

"I will, I promise."

"Okay. David says hi, he says hi, and we'll see you, okay? I'll see you, okay?" she said, and then the phone was back to Rubin before I could answer.

"You'll be coming in at the same time?" he asked.

"Yeah. We'll radio our ETA once we're moving. You're not going too stir-crazy?"

He chuckled. "Hell, no. We've done finger-painting and *Sweatin' to the Oldies* and she's on charcoal now, like I said. After that, we're going to watch some episodes of *The Incredible Hulk*. Romero got them for her on video-tape. As far as I can figure, she can't really discern a difference between Bill Bixby and David Banner, but she sees the difference between Banner and the Hulk. It's sort of cool. Bixby's this consummate nice guy, but if you get him mad he becomes the incredible protector. Super strong, but only doing harm to evildoers."

"There's something to that."

"Would that we all could turn green and frighten our problems away."

"Don't get too many ideas. See you later," I said.

"Cool. Don't get shot," Rubin said.

———

At exactly two o'clock, I performed our hourly radio check. Both Dale and Natalie called in, told me that I was loud and clear. Rubin didn't respond because he was out of range. I went for a cup of coffee in the second-floor waiting room, and was headed back past the nurses' station when I heard sudden yelling and the sounds of metal hitting the floor.

Stupid Things You Think When The Adrenaline Pumps #87: Well, Jesus, Atticus, if you knew this was going to happen, why did you just pour yourself a cup of coffee?

I dropped the mug, running to the noise, and pulled my radio. Just before I keyed the transmitter, Natalie came over the air, saying, "*Room two twenty-three, principal's inside.*"

I pressed the button and said, "En route." Came around the corner, bringing my gun out as I heard Dale call in that he was on his way.

It took maybe another five seconds to find the right door, and that was more than enough time to commit murder, but I couldn't move any faster. I found 223 as Natalie pushed inside, following her into the room.

The woman I'd seen in the waiting room earlier stood behind the examination table, a plastic pop bottle in her hand. The cap was off, and the bottle was half-filled with a red liquid that had been splashed over the equipment, walls, and Dr. Romero. The woman was shouting.

I went for Romero as Natalie went for the other woman. "She's pregnant," I shouted to Natalie. Felice Romero had her glasses off, and the skin that had been protected by them was untouched, although a thick strip of red ran from her dark hair down across her lab coat. I wrapped my arms around her, pivoted, and dropped her outside the room, just as Dale came around the corner.

"Principal's clear," I told him. "Get her secure and call the police." Then I turned back to see that Natalie had the pregnant woman pinned against the wall, one hand on the bottle, immobilizing it. Natalie's right forearm was pressed under the woman's chin.

"You've been marked!" the woman was screaming. "Anytime we want to, butcher! Anytime we want to!"

"Shut the fuck up," Natalie said, "or I will knee you so hard you'll miscarry right here."

The woman shut up. Whether because she believed the threat, or because Natalie had six inches on her and the ability to crush her larynx, I don't know.

I holstered my weapon and then took the bottle out of the woman's hand, setting it down on the counter.

"She got paint on my blouse," Natalie told me.

"You're overdressed anyway," I said.

"It's going on my expense report," she said.

I took the woman's purse and began looking through the contents. "Write it up," I told Natalie. "All expenses will be reviewed."

"Skinflint," she said.

"No free rides," I told her. The purse held a lipstick, a pocket Bible, a hairbrush, five subway tokens, a folded piece of paper, and a driver's license. The license was state of New York, and identified the pregnant woman as Mary Werthin. I showed the license to Natalie, who snorted, then I dropped it back in the purse and unfolded the sheet of paper.

It was a photocopied wanted poster, with a grainy picture of Dr. Romero centered on it. At the top of the sheet were the words WANTED FOR MURDER, and beneath the picture, DOCTOR FELICE ROMERO. At the bottom of the sheet was a list of her crimes. According to the paper, Dr. Romero had murdered over one thousand children.

I kept the wanted poster, putting it in a pocket, then set the purse on the counter beside the bottle.

"I want a lawyer," Mary Werthin said.

Natalie sighed heavily. "Would you cuff her, please?" she asked me.

"I don't know," I said. "You two look so nice together."

"You can't hold me, you're not the police," Mary Werthin said.

I got my cuffs and locked them around the hand that had held the bottle. Natalie backed up, releasing her grip, and I turned Werthin carefully toward the wall, and cuffed her other hand behind her back. Natalie dragged a chair away from the corner and I led Werthin to it. Once she was seated, Natalie went to the sink and ran some water over a paper towel, dabbing it at her blouse. The blouse was white, and the paint had pretty much ruined it. After a few more swipes at the paint, Natalie sighed and threw the towel in the trash can.

I said, "Whose idea was this, Mary?"

Mary didn't look at me. She found a paint blotch on the floor and examined that. After a while she said, "Anytime we want to, we can stop her. This was only a warning."

I looked around at the paint-spattered room. It wasn't as bad as I'd first thought coming in. "You stay with her," I told Natalie. "The police should be here in a couple of minutes. I'm going to check on the doctor."

Natalie nodded.

I picked up my coffee mug and stopped at the nurses' station. I asked Lynn Delfleur to check the appointment book for Mary Werthin. "When did she make her appointment?" I asked.

She flipped pages until she found the name, then said, "Two weeks ago. She came in for a counseling session last week, just before you guys started here."

"She was going to have an abortion?"

Lynn shook her head. "Prenatal checkup. Second trimester."

"You checked her ID when she showed up today?"

"I always check IDs," Lynn said.

"And she did nothing suspicious?"

She glared at me. "Not that I noticed."

I thanked her and continued down the hall.

Dr. Romero was in the bathroom opposite her office, the door shut, Dale standing outside. I'm tall, but Dale is big, with about two inches and thirty pounds on me, mostly muscle and bone. His face is broad and smooth, his Japanese features clear. As I approached he said, "She's unhurt. The glasses kept the paint out of her eyes."

"When that lady came in, you and Sheldon ran her through the metal detector, right?"

He nodded.

"Didn't check the purse?"

"We haven't been checking bags. I assume that's about to change?" He said it without sarcasm.

"Yeah. Go on downstairs, meet the cops when they get here," I told him. "We're holding the assailant in two twenty-three. Her name's Mary Werthin." I handed him my mug. "Dump that for me."

He took the mug with a nod and headed off down the hall. I could hear water running in the bathroom. After a moment, I knocked on the door.

"What?" Dr. Romero asked.

"It's me," I said. "Are you all right?"

"How the hell did that woman get in here?" she asked. "Why didn't you people stop her?"

"Ms. Werthin made her appointment two weeks ago. Lynn checked her ID. There's no way we could have known she was going to pull something like that."

"She could have had a gun," Dr. Romero said.

"No, she couldn't have. At least, not easily. She went through the metal detector downstairs. We haven't been checking bags. We'll start now."

"You're searching bags?"

"We will now," I repeated.

The door opened. The doctor was wearing a black T-shirt, and her hair was wet, but the paint had come off. She put her glasses on and said, "I'm not certain I want that."

"It's your choice, of course."

She stepped past me and across the hall, into her office, motioning for me to follow. I shut the door after me, and sat down in one of the chairs by her desk. Dr. Romero lit a cigarette, and remained standing.

"She could have killed me," she said after a moment.

"She could have."

"You're supposed to keep that from happening."

"Yes."

She turned and looked at me, waiting.

I hated this part of the job. This was the Cold Hard Truth part. I said, "I can't protect you completely. No one can. If somebody really wants you dead, if they've got the patience, half a brain, and a little money, they'll get the job done. It might take them ten years, but they'll do it. No depth of security will keep it from happening, no number of bodyguards, no amount of money. You could move to the Yukon Territory, and if somebody really wanted you dead, they would follow and find a way. There is no such thing as absolute protection.

"What you've hired me to do is to protect you to the best of my ability. My ability is substantial. I work with some of the best people around, and I'm very good at my job. But I can't guarantee you anything. From now on, we will search all bags that enter the building."

"Invasion of privacy," Dr. Romero said.

I nodded. "Yes, it is. But that's your choice. We can risk another Mary Werthin, or I can have every bag searched. No gun is going to find its way in here."

"But there are guns that can be smuggled past metal detectors."

"Knives, too," I admitted. "But both take a lot of money and some connections, and the odds of either of those items finding their way in here without whoever's carrying them attracting our attention are very low. And we're still not certain that the threat against you is lethal. What that woman did reeks of terrorism, not murder."

She struggled with it for almost a minute, finally sitting down in her chair. "All right, search the bags," she said.

I pulled my radio and keyed it, saying, "All units, SOP change: Search the bags."

Natalie radioed a confirmation, followed by Dale, followed by Sheldon.

"That woman . . . she didn't want to kill me," Felice said. "Even what she said, that was just a scare tactic, wasn't it?"

"I think so. She had a wanted poster for you." I took the sheet out of my pocket and unfolded it, placing it on her desk.

She smoked for a few seconds, looking at it. I waited. "Not a good picture," she said finally.

"No."

"You think this came from Sword of the Silent?"

"Possibly."

"I am used to being harassed, I've told you that. This won't work on me. Common Ground is in six days, and I won't be scared off." She said the last more to herself than to me. "I have done nothing wrong."

For nearly a minute Felice was quiet, thinking, and then she remembered I was there, and she ground out her cigarette. "Have the police officers stop by my office, please. I want to swear out a complaint."

"Natalie and I will do that, if you like. It'll keep your name out of it."

She thought about that, then nodded. "All right."

I stood up. "We'll leave at six-thirty," I said. "Call me if you need me."

"Of course."

Mary Werthin was taken away by two of New York's finest, who returned my cuffs to me before they left, having replaced them with a set of their own. After briefing Natalie and Dale on my conversation with Romero, I went to the Two-six to take care of the paperwork and to speak to Detective Lozano.

"You're not doing a very good job," he told me. His black hair was short and receding, and sweat shone on his forehead.

"She's still alive," I said.

"True enough." Lozano wiped his forehead with the back of his hand, then offered me a cup of horrible coffee, and I took it more out of courtesy than need. "She's made a statement," he said. "She says that you and Miss Trent assaulted her. She has no idea where the paint came from."

I laughed and handed him the letters that had arrived in the morning's mail. Four more, all offensive, which brought the grand total to seventeen since I'd begun the job a week ago. Today's batch was relatively tame. Only one threatened Romero's life. The author wrote that he or she would "butcher every doctor" who performed an abortion.

Lozano looked at the stack and made a face, then put them on his desk. "I'll get these to Fowler."

"Anything else on Ms. Werthin?" I asked.

"We put a call in to the SOS offices, and she is a dues-paying member. Doesn't prove jack-shit but it's a connection."

"They collect dues?"

"How do you think Crowell affords his suits?" Lozano shrugged. "Son of a bitch has more money than I do, that's for certain. That's not saying much, admittedly." He scratched his jaw with a chewed fingernail, wiped his forehead again. "Too fucking hot," he mumbled.

"The Feds have anything on her?"

"Fowler is running it, but I doubt they'll find anything. You could go talk to him."

"Where's he at?"

"How should I know? Goddamn feebies. I'll keep you informed," Lozano said.

I took that as my exit cue and headed back to the street, and ultimately back to the clinic.

Lozano had the unenviable assignment of watching the clinic and the protesters on both sides of the line. Special Agent Fowler had pretty much the same assignment, but on a federal level, and the LifeCare clinic was only one of several he was concerned with. Fowler and Lozano didn't get along for a number of reasons, but I supposed the major one was simply that Fowler was FBI and thirty-two, and Lozano was NYPD and late forties. There's a long and distinguished history spiced with plenty of animosity between the FBI and the NYPD. The NYPD looks upon the FBI as meddling, arrogant busybodies who can't use a toilet without executive authorization from Washington, D.C. Conversely, most of the special agents I've met think that NYPD detectives are arrogant, stuck-up bullies who believe an interrogation is simply Twenty Questions played with a baseball bat.

Every threat Dr. Romero or the clinic received got forwarded to Fowler as a matter of course, to be processed by the Bureau labs in D.C. Then the document would be copied and sent to the NYPD. Lozano had told me that this sometimes took a week or more. The FBI kept the originals. Today's letters would be no exception. Lozano didn't like being second, and since it was he who was most frequently on site, I had to grant him the point. Unlike Fowler, Lozano made a point of coming on scene when he heard that something was going down. He had been watching the day I first arrived at the clinic with Alison. Fowler worked out of the Bureau offices, and visited only when necessary.

Dale went for the car at five-thirty. I gave him the extra hour before we had to move Dr. Romero, so he could double-check the vehicle. Dale knows cars; he took the Crash Course when we were at SpecWar together. I went from the Executive Protection Squad to the CID, sort of a sideways transfer, but Dale stayed EPS from the ground up. We were renting a vehicle from Natalie's father, a souped-up Ford that Sentinel reserved for "high risk" clients.

I doubted we would need the bulletproof glass or the solid rubber tires. For that matter, I doubted that someone had wired a bomb to the ignition, but Romero was paying me to be certain.

Dale backed the gray Ford into the alley behind the clinic at six twenty-five, by which time Natalie and I had Romero ready to go. We walked her downstairs, waited while she said good night to the few staff members who were still around. While she did this, I went out to check the alley and talk to Dale.

"Clear," he told me.

I gave the surrounding rooftops one last survey, then unlocked the back car door nearest the clinic. "Two minutes," I told Dale, and went back inside. Dr. Romero had finished her good nights, and was now putting on her Kevlar vest with Natalie's assistance. For some reason, watching the two of them made me think of a bridal fitting, but I kept that observation to myself.

"I hate this thing," Dr. Romero told me as she slipped her coat back on over the vest. "As if it's not hot enough out there already."

"You'll love that thing when it stops a bullet." I handed her back her briefcase and the plastic bag she had put her paint-stained clothes in. "You ready?"

She nodded, and I looked at Natalie, and Natalie nodded. I used my radio and told Dale, "Pogo's coming out." The code name had been chosen by Felice herself, and she looked faintly embarrassed every time I said it.

To Natalie I said, "Go."

Natalie went out the door and headed straight to the Ford while I held Romero back in the hall. Natalie opened the car door, then came back into the building, turned around, and now, with Romero close behind her, went back out. I took up the rear, and then we were all in the car, Natalie, Dr. Romero, and myself, a cozy protective sandwich. I closed and locked our door, said, "Charlie," to Dale, and sat back as he pulled out onto 135th.

"We did Charlie day before yesterday," Natalie said, looking out the window.

Dr. Romero shifted uncomfortably between us.

"Everybody's a critic," I said, and looked out my own window. I'd worked out seven routes for our travel, and each had a call sign, A to G. All of us were absolutely familiar with them. All I had to do was give Dale a letter and he would know which route I wanted to take.

The routes mattered to me because, in my opinion, cars are death traps. If I'd had the people and the money, there would've been four more bodyguards on the road with us, two in a follow car and two in a lead car. All the security professionals I know have a particular paranoia—for some it's snipers; others, bombs. Mine is ambushes. When I'm not working, it doesn't bother me, but when I'm on, I'm very careful about avoiding anything that could be used to set up an ambush. And it's too damn easy to ambush someone in a car.

"I'm clear on my side," I said.

Dale grunted.

"Clear," Natalie said.

"So we're not being followed?" Dr. Romero asked.

"We are most definitely not being followed," Dale told her.

She sighed and wiped sweat from her forehead. "I don't suppose that means I can remove the vest?"

"No," Natalie said.

"Dale, you want to put the air conditioner on?" I said.

He shook his head. "Car's too heavy. We'll overheat."

I looked at the doctor sympathetically. The ride was hard for her, cramped between both Natalie and me. With the New York humidity, the vest, the tension of the ride, and the rotten day she'd had, she had every reason to get pissy. But she hadn't yet. She even managed to not smoke in the car, knowing that the windows couldn't be opened.

I radioed Rubin, told him we were fifteen minutes out. He said he'd be ready.

After a moment, Romero said, "I'm melting, I'm melting."

CHAPTER FOUR

"Mommy, my mommy's home," Katie said, taking the stairs as fast as she could. It wasn't very fast, honestly, but it was endearing as all get-out to watch. She jumped off the last step and flung her arms around Felice's waist. "I missed you, come sit with me, I missed you."

The Romero apartment was a halfhearted trilevel, and we entered at the bottom, the short flight of carpeted stairs Katie had descended from the main level off to our right, beyond the closet. To the left was a small bathroom, the door open and the light on. Rubin locked the front door behind us and headed back up the stairs with Dale and Natalie while I stood with Dr. Romero.

Felice kissed Katie on the forehead and said, "In a moment, sweetie. Your mother wants to change first." She gently stepped out of Katie's grasp and took off her coat, then the vest. She hung both on the coatrack.

Katie put her arms around my waist and said, " 'Cus! I

missed you, too, I did." It was a tight squeeze, and I wasn't ready for it.

"Thanks," I said hoarsely.

Just as abruptly, Katie released me and followed her mother up the stairs. I went up after them onto the main floor, basically a large open cube that served as mostly living room, with couch, table, chairs, and television, and a little bit of kitchen, defined by a counter that jutted out from the wall perpendicular to the stairs. The living room was carpeted the same as the stairs, a lush green, the kitchen tiled white.

Katie had finished hugging Natalie, and now moved to Dale, who looked damned silly with her clutching his thick waist. Dr. Romero thought so, too, and laughed, before saying to me, "I'm going to change. Give me ten minutes before you leave."

"Fine," I told her.

Rubin handed her the day's mail, saying, "All yours."

She nodded and took it with her into the bedroom.

Together, Katie and Dale moved to the couch in front of the television and sat down. Katie released him, quickly shifting her attention to the screen, then began talking, perhaps to Dale, about her day. I heard her mention David.

I checked that the curtains were drawn tight over the sliding glass door that led to the patio. The patio overlooked Fulton Street. Through the fabric, I could make out the sparks of light that shone from apartments in the building across the way.

Rubin was already packing up his art supplies, with Natalie's assistance.

"Where do you want to go?" he was asking her.

"I don't know, I was thinking seafood."

"Whoa, kids," I said. "He's off, you're not. You work tonight."

"I worked last night," Natalie said.

"I know. But it's you and Dale tonight, Natalie. You're off tomorrow."

Rubin gave me the I'm-not-going-to-get-laid-tonight-and-it's-your-fault look. I shrugged. He turned to look at Dale, making his ponytail whip around as he did so.

Dale said, "Not on your fucking life, Rubin."

Without looking away from the television, Katie said, "Don't swear it's not nice, Dale. David, he swore, that's bad."

Dale said, "Sorry, Katie." He looked back at Rubin and shook his head.

"It's okay, it's okay," Katie told Dale.

Rubin transferred his gaze to me.

"I've got plans," I said.

"I hate you," he said. "So I get the night off, and I don't get to spend it with my sweetie?"

"That's right."

"You're a cruel, cruel man, Mr. Kodiak," Natalie said. She gave Rubin a brief kiss and murmured, "Later."

Rubin savored the kiss, then groaned when Natalie moved away to the kitchen to get herself something to drink. After a moment he opened his eyes and looked at me again. "I adore that woman. And I hate you," he repeated.

"Yeah, but it's the good kind of hate, isn't it?" I took a seat beside Katie on the couch. They were watching the news, and I came in on the tail end of a story about a body and an alley. Another pointless death. The police were saying it looked like a mugging, maybe for drug money. Dale switched the channel to MTV.

"How was your day, Katie?" I asked.

"It—it was fun, we had fun and we did drawings. And David helped and Rubin helped and we made pictures, good pictures. And we watched the—the Hulk and had fun, and did you have a good day?"

"It was pretty good," I said.

"Melanie B died," she said, her eyes on the set. "Nobody knows what happened to her, but she died and that's sad."

Dr. Romero emerged from her bedroom, wearing denim shorts and a T-shirt and looking better for the change of clothes and the brief shower she'd grabbed. She lit a cigarette and went into the kitchenette, motioning me after her.

"Who do I get tonight?"

"Dale and Natalie. Rubin and I will be by tomorrow around seven, same as before."

Dr. Romero nodded, then began searching the freezer for something to defrost for dinner. "I'll see you then," she said. "Katie? You want enchiladas for dinner?"

"Enchiladas!" Katie shouted. "I adore enchiladas!"

Felice smiled the way only a mother can smile at her child, then said to Natalie and Dale, "Is that all right with you two?"

They both said that enchiladas sounded grand.

Rubin and I said good night to everyone, then caught the number six train back up to Bleecker. We stopped at the Grand Union a block from our place for some soda, then walked to our apartment on Thompson.

We had a railroad apartment that we paid far too much for. My room was immediately right off the hall as you entered. The kitchen was beyond it, then the bathroom, and then finally the hall opened into one large living room. Rubin's room was at the far end of the apartment, in what was still technically the living room. We had installed a folding wall partition a year or so back to provide the illusion of privacy, but it didn't really work. If he had company for the night, and I ventured further than the kitchen, I heard far more than I needed to.

I put the soda in the fridge while Rubin continued to his room. We had a few bottles of Anchor Steam left, so I opened one for each of us and brought his to him. He had dumped his bag and was already pulling on a pair of cut-offs. I sat on the chair, looking out across the courtyard, and he took up position on the futon with a hairbrush and a couple of comic books. He put the beer on the little table by the television, out of the way of the comics, and began to brush his hair. Rubin is Puerto Rican, and his hair is almost the same light brown as his skin and eyes. We've known each other since we were kids, we went through Basic Training together, and he hasn't had a haircut since we left the service. He's been collecting his comics twice that long.

"You're a hippie artist freak," I said.

"I'm not the one who's got holes in his ear."

"Earrings are cool."

"On pirates," Rubin said. "Not on bodyguards. Makes you look like a . . . wimp."

"I'd rather look like a wimp than a . . . girl."

He laughed, setting the hairbrush down and taking up his beer. "You know, you talk like that, and I know you want me."

"Is it that obvious?"

"This is the nineties. Homoeroticism is hip."

"Except in certain states."

"And those don't count," he said. "You're going to see Alison tonight, aren't you?"

"Uh-huh," I said.

"You're going to see Alison and I am going to stay home alone."

"Uh-huh."

"Is that fair?"

"Nope."

"So you admit it?"

"Uh-huh."

He drank from his bottle, then opened his first comic book. "Have a nice time, you bastard."

"I will," I said, and left hoping that I was telling the truth.

We went for Chinese at a small restaurant off Broadway near her place. We'd eaten there a couple times before and it was beginning to feel familiar. The manager gave us a wave before we were led to a table.

Alison looked good, her color back in her skin and her eyes clear. She was wearing her hair untied, and kept having to brush it back out of her face each time she bent to the plate with her chopsticks. I told her about my day, and she told me about hers. She was working at Oxford University Press that summer, but she didn't think of that as her job. Her job was her band.

"We got a gig," Alison said. "Brownie's, Wednesday after this one."

"Is that good?"

"You don't remember going to Brownie's?"

"Come on, you know me. I don't know from clubs," I said.

"We went last month, saw C Is For Coyote."

"Okay, yeah. They were good."

She poured herself some more tea. "It's a good gig. You going to be able to make it?"

"It'll depend on the job. I'll try, but I can't promise anything."

"How's that going?"

"All things being equal, well. Today was a little out of the ordinary, but I think we're doing all right."

"Good."

I looked at her, realized that she was watching me closely.

"What is it?" I asked.

"What?"

"What's wrong? You feeling okay?"

"I'm fine with the abortion," Alison said.

"That's not what I was asking."

"Oh," she said. She drank her tea, then leaned back in

her chair as the waiter dropped our bill and two fortune cookies on the table. We divided the check, then she took one cookie and I took the other.

" 'Long life and happiness will be yours,' " she read.

"Mine's 'The strongest mind does not dissemble.' More an aphorism than a fortune, I think."

She laughed and said, "At Vassar I had a friend who always tacked on the phrase 'in bed' at the end of her fortunes. The strongest mind does not dissemble in bed."

"Cute."

"Long life and happiness will be yours—"

"In bed," I said.

"Exactly."

We went out onto Broadway, enjoying the night. It was still warm, but the humidity had fallen, and it was good weather for walking. I took her hand and we went like that for a while.

"My mother called," Alison told me. "Sends her best."

"I do the same."

"She wanted to know how we're doing."

"What'd you tell her?"

"I told her that we were fine. Not great, not bad."

I nodded, then said, "I'm sorry I haven't been able to spend more time with you."

She didn't say anything.

"It's not avoidance."

"I know," Alison said. "You're busy. I am, too." We were quiet for nearly another block. Then she said, "Atticus? Do you wonder?"

I knew exactly what she meant. "Once in a while."

"Me, too. More than I thought I would." She squeezed my hand. "Not second thoughts, exactly. But it sort of puts things in perspective. Makes me wonder what exactly I'm doing with my life, that sort of thing."

"And what are you doing with your life, Alison?"

"Right now? Taking a walk."

I dropped her off with a good-night kiss and headed back downtown, getting home a little before midnight. Rubin was in his room, and I could hear his voice, low, and knew he was talking to Natalie on the phone.

I went to sleep after thinking about Katie and Felice, and then Alison, and wondering what sort of father I'd have made.

CHAPTER FIVE

"Katie and I are going to the movies," Felice informed me the following evening.

I was sitting on the couch in their apartment, Katie beside me with her head on my arm more than my shoulder, totally focused on the early-evening MTV lineup. Natalie and Rubin had been granted their much-coveted night off together, leaving Dale and me to provide coverage. Currently, Dale was showering in the downstairs bathroom. It had been a quiet day, and I had been expecting a quiet night.

"You are going to what?" I asked.

"I promised her we'd go to the movies tonight."

"Absolutely not," I said.

Felice adjusted her glasses and frowned at me. "I told her I would take her to the movies," she said.

Katie lifted her head to look at her mother. "Is it the movie? Are we going to see the movie?"

"That's right, honey. Go get your coat."

Katie slid off the couch, cast a last glance at the video in progress, then headed toward the stairs up to her room. She pumped her arms as if jogging, moving as fast as she could.

Wonderful, I thought. Now I get to be the bad guy. "When did you decide you were going to do this?" I asked Felice.

"Last night."

"But you didn't tell me until now."

She lit a cigarette, then crossed out of the kitchen to pick up her windbreaker draped over the back of a chair. The windbreaker was light blue with navy blue piping. She checked her purse before saying, "You would have forbidden it."

"I don't have the power to forbid anything, Doctor. But you're right, I would have advised against it."

"She wants to see a movie, Atticus. It's summer, she's out of school, and she's bored."

I sighed. This wasn't the first time my principal had decided to exert some passive/aggressive resistance to my presence. Nobody likes being told what to do, even if they are paying someone to do so. The situation would be different if we were going directly from the clinic. The apartment still seemed secure, and so far nobody had been following us.

"I'm going to have to call Rubin and Natalie," I said.

Relief washed her features like a breeze lifting a kite. "Thank you."

"If nothing happens, then you can thank me," I said, and headed for the phone.

Natalie and Rubin were at the movie theater in Murray Hill, around Thirty-second Street, when we arrived. Rubin had grumbled when he answered the phone, but both he and Natalie had smiles on as we walked up, and Katie let go of her mother's and my hands to run and give them both hugs, saying, "We're at a movie, we're seeing a movie."

They led her back to us, and then Natalie extended a hand, showing six tickets. "They're seating already," she told me. "We should go on in."

Katie put her hand back in mine, and we stepped up to the line, Natalie leading, and the usher took our tickets and directed us to the appropriate theater. The appropriate theater was down a flight of stairs, and Katie had trouble with the steps. She refused all assistance, saying, "I can do it, I can."

Felice stayed right beside her on the way down, and I could see her resisting the urge to reach out and steady her daughter when she faltered. When Katie made it to the bottom, both of them looked proud enough to burst.

"See? I did it, by myself, I did it," Katie said loudly.

Felice gave her a hug.

The film was an animated Disney feature, one of the new releases, full of color and music, and fairly distracting. Felice was really the only person who paid full attention to it; Katie fell asleep halfway into the movie, snoring gently, her chin pressed to her chest. A subway tunnel had been burrowed through the ground close by, and every ten minutes or so the theater would fill with the rumbling of a train, loud enough to defeat the soundtrack. Katie didn't wake up.

Dale, Natalie, Rubin, and I devoted our time to watching the house, keeping a bead on the audience. There weren't a lot of people at the show, but we did our jobs, and consequently I don't have the first idea what the movie was about.

When the film ended, Felice woke Katie, saying, "Honey? We're going home now. Time to get up."

Katie opened and closed her mouth a couple of times,

tasting sleep, then rubbed her eyes and opened them. "It was a good movie," she announced.

"It was a wonderful movie," her mother confirmed.

Katie nodded, then reached for my hand, and I helped her out of the seat. We started back up the aisle.

"Did you like your movie, 'Cus?" Katie asked.

"I liked it a lot."

"Does your girl-girlfriend, does she like movies?"

"Yes," I said. "Alison likes movies."

"Did she like this movie?"

"I don't think she's seen this movie, Katie."

We had to stop at the stairs again, Katie once more refusing any help, and it took five minutes to get to the top, with plenty of people casting sidelong glances or just plain old-fashioned stares our way. At the top of the stairs, behind the railing, three pack-boys watched our progress. They looked to be in their late teens at most, decked out to look tough. We were three-quarters up when I heard the Alpha of the pack mutter, "God, what's that retard doing?"

He hadn't said it loudly, but the pack snickered. Katie froze on the stairs. Her shoulders rounded in as if to shield her chest, and she lowered her eyes to her feet. Then she held out a hand to her mother, saying, "I need help, Mommy. Help me."

Dale was leading up, and he swiveled his head to catch the Alpha, then turned and started to offer Katie his hand, but Felice stopped him by shaking her head. "You can do it, sweetie," she told Katie.

"Fucking retard," the Alpha said louder.

Katie rocked from her right foot to her left and back, one hand gripping the railing. Over her, Dale made eye contact with me, and I gave him a slight nod. He climbed the rest of the way and positioned himself at the top, maybe ten feet from the pack. His presence was enough to silence them, but the Alpha was now in trouble, looking from Dale to his two pals, then back at us; if he backed down, he lost face, and in front of his pack, it wasn't something he could afford to do.

Katie restarted, one foot carefully placed before the next, and we climbed steadily to the top without stopping. At the landing Felice gave Katie a hug, but she didn't respond, still staring at her sneakers, too aware of the ignorant, mocking eyes on her.

"That was great, sweetheart," Felice told her. She gave Katie another squeeze, then looked at me. "Let's go."

We fell in and moved out to the sidewalk. I told Dale to get the car and bring it around.

"I would prefer to take care of the problem inside," he said.

"I'd like that, too," Rubin added.

"Go get the car," I said.

Dale looked back to the lobby, then headed off. Rubin and I kept scanning the street, while Natalie started talking to Katie about the movie. Katie had begun responding when the pack came out of the theater. The Alpha stopped, looking over at us. He pulled cigarettes from inside his Chicago Bulls team jacket, and I caught a piece of molded plastic, Day-Glo green. He lit his cigarette, thumbed the match.

I met his eyes and made the look hard, hoping that he wouldn't be stupid.

He decided to be stupid.

"You know why retards make good bitches?" he asked his friends. "It's 'cause they're real easy to train, you know?"

Rubin looked for a cue off me. I didn't give him anything, just kept my look on the Alpha.

Katie had gone silent again.

"That one's too fucking fat, though," the Alpha added, inspired.

"You don't want to start anything," I told him. "You really don't want to start anything. Walk away."

"Fuck you, bud. You think I'm scared of you, of some fucking retards?"

Felice spun, said, "Young man, don't you have a store to rob somewhere?"

He looked indignant, bobbing his head back like an ostrich. He took a couple of steps forward, saying, "You talking to me?"

"Stupid and deaf," Felice said, and then she turned her back to him.

Here we go, I thought.

The Alpha looked at his crew and saw that they were watching him, looked back at us, and gauged the situation. He took another two steps forward, saying, "I'll fucking show you, stupid bitch." Then he started to reach into his jacket with his right, and that's when I went.

It took one long stride to get in his face, my right going to his, locking his arm against his body. I put my left hand behind his head, took a handful of hair, and then spun him so he was facing his crew. I yanked back hard with my left, pulling his arm out of his jacket with my right, and then I hopped up, right knee in his back, and drove him to the sidewalk. He hit it hard, his right arm immobilized and his left too busy reaching for me. He smelled like a Laundromat, and I knew why. In his right hand, still held tightly, was a squirt gun, one of the nice, new, pneumatic kinds with a big reservoir. The kind that can squirt twenty feet or so on a good day.

He had loaded it with bleach. One shot to the eyes, and you'd be blind.

The pack started to back up, and then they broke and ran and I looked over my shoulder to see that Rubin had opened his coat to show them his gun.

Alpha was swearing a blue streak, so I pulled back harder on his hair and put more of my weight on my knee and said, "Quiet."

Rubin came around and took the squirt gun from his hand, sniffing at it. "Nasty toy," he said.

"I know," I said.

"Fucker, let me up you motherfucker."

Rubin pointed the barrel of the squirt gun at his face. He said, "Excuse me?"

Alpha shut up.

I leaned my head next to his right ear and whispered, "Okay, asshole, here's the deal. I'm going to let you go. But don't try this shit again on anyone, or you'll end up with a bleach enema, got it?"

He didn't say anything.

"Got it?" I asked again, twisting his hair.

"Got it," he said.

"Good. Now we're going to stand up, and if you try anything, I'll break your neck."

We stood and he didn't try anything.

"Felice, will you and Katie come over here?" I called.

Rubin raised an eyebrow at me. I grinned.

Felice came around, holding Katie's hand, stopping next to Rubin. Natalie was right with them, grinning.

"Apologize," I told Alpha.

"What?"

"Stupid *and* deaf," I said. "Apologize."

He wavered, then took a deep breath and said, to Felice, "Lady, I'm sorry."

"I accept your apology," she said.

I turned his head to Katie. "Again," I said.

"I'm sorry," he muttered.

"No, once more with feeling," I said.

"I'm really sorry, I'm really sorry, please accept my apology."

Katie just looked up at him, and it was impossible to see what she was thinking, what she felt. Then she smiled, and said, "Okay, you're mean. I don't like you, you're mean. Go away."

I let him go, and we watched him run down the street.

Dale returned with the car, and we all went for ice cream before going back to the apartment.

CHAPTER SIX

The bottle flew on a frozen rope, a hell of a throw, shattering against the brick clinic wall two inches from where Dr. Romero's head had been, sending green Heineken slivers dancing to the sidewalk. The glass broke clear and loud, and all the noise, all the people on both sides of the line fell quiet.

Dale had caught the arm movement before the release and shouted, "Bottle——left," and I had taken Dr. Romero down, butting the back of her right knee with mine, collapsing her like an aluminum can. She went down to her knees, her hands coming around to shield her head, with me wrapped about her body for extra protection. Coming back up, I caught sight of the thrower, a squat white man, yelling in victory, his hand raised in triumph.

Natalie spun to cover us, all red hair and motion, and together we half dragged, half carried Dr. Romero to the clinic door where Sheldon thrust out his hand and helped pull her inside. He propelled her efficiently past the security gate, and Natalie followed before he blocked the entrance with his body. I was off the steps and already running across the street past Dale, shouting for him to follow me.

The lines seemed still stunned, little movement and little noise, snagged in the tar of the action. Some of the pro-lifers were backing away, disgusted with their radical cousins. A cluster of people holding NARAL signs were starting to move, but the uniformed police held them back, trying desperately to keep the two groups separate. Throwing the bottle had changed the tenor of the crowd, starting a countdown to contact, and everyone was wearing their anger and indignation like clothes soaked in gasoline. All it would take was a match.

Then I saw the thrower being congratulated by a big blond man in a Columbia University sweatshirt, property of the athletics department, saw the thrower basking in the attention, and I threw the match myself, leaping over the line and into the crowd.

I took the thrower in the side and rode him into the pavement. I heard his skull hit the street, felt the shock of impact rush through him. University was stunned, involuntarily half-stepping back with a gasp. Coming up, I twisted the thrower's arm around his back, heard him cry out, then used that as a handle to pull him upright. University reached in to bear-hug me, and I pivoted the thrower between us and began backing up, shouting at him to keep his distance. University took two steps toward me but the thrower shouted, "Do it!" and that stopped the other man. Dale had a hand on my back, clearing the path behind us.

The police were wading into the crowd, trying to get to us and not gaining much ground. Behind them a news crew circled for position. The mounted spot on the cameraman's unit flashed on, and he pressed in to get a good shot, the reporter with him on point, but both were repelled by a gray-haired woman who thrust a NARAL sign at the camera. An Asian cop took a punch on his shoulder and responded by putting the teenage offender in a head lock. Someone was screaming that she had been assaulted.

"You're in the shit," I shouted in the thrower's ear.

"Fuck my ass, cockbreath," he snarled back.

I twisted his arm until he made a noise, still backing toward the sidewalk. "Fucking coward. You been pregnant?" Someone grabbed my shoulder and I heard Dale grunt and then the touch was gone. "Self-righteous bastard," I said to the thrower. "Who gave you the right? Who gave you the fucking right?"

I felt the curb against my left heel and stepped up smoothly, yanking the man after me. "You're under citizen's arrest," I told the thrower.

"Natalie got a cop," Dale shouted in my ear. "Get him inside."

The news crew made us, then, the cameraman just behind the reporter, and they forced their way to the steps as Dale and I tried to manhandle the thrower through the door. The thrower chose this moment to start resisting again, as the reporter, a white woman with blond hair and pale brown lipstick, leaned forward and started to shout a question at us. The thrower lashed his right foot out before we could react, and Dale almost lost him. The reporter recoiled and dropped her microphone, then swore and tried to take a swing at him but I beat her to it, taking a handful of the thrower's hair and yanking hard back. He yelped like a dog whose tail has been stepped on. Dale fixed his grip on the thrower and we managed him through the door.

The cop was waiting, and without any preamble he spun the thrower back around, pressed him to a wall, and slapped the cuffs on him. I got a good look at his face while the cop patted him down, and then placed him.

"You're Crowell's driver," I said.

The thrower jerked his head toward me, alarmed, then went back to staring at the wall.

"You're shorter in person," I said.

That must have hit a nerve, because he let loose with a torrent of profanity that nearly drowned out the noise from the street.

"Big words for such a little guy," I said.

He tried to go for me; the cop slammed him hard back against the wall and read him his rights. While the officer called for a sector car, the thrower said, "I'll get you, cocksucker."

"Taller men have tried," I told him. Then I turned to Dale and asked, "Where's the principal?"

"Secured. She's okay, no scrapes, not a thing."

"Good."

Through the barred window I could see the police restraining and separating the protesters, running a gauntlet of SOS signs and NARAL banners. Another naked baby doll fell in the street, red paint on its too-pink skin. Feet quickly broke the doll off the coat hanger it had been impaled on.

There were sirens now, but in Manhattan there are always sirens. Placards were falling into the street, forgotten in the melee. Any trace of civility had gone the way of the dodo, and the police were starting to get angry, shouting as incoherently as everyone else.

"What are you charging him with?" I asked the cop, gesturing at the thrower.

"Inciting, felonious assault."

"Tack on attempted murder. He's a member of SOS, and they've been threatening the doctor's life."

The cop blinked at me.

"I'll follow you to the precinct," I told him. "Two-six, right?"

"Yes, sir."

I shook my head and told Dale to stay put, then went to find Romero. The thrower never took his eyes off me.

Felice slumped in a chair in the lounge on the first floor, drinking a cup of tea with both hands around the mug. Natalie stood by the door as I entered.

"Dr. Romero?"

"Two times," she said. "How long have you been working for me, now? Ten days?"

"Ten days," Natalie confirmed.

"And this is the second time someone has attacked me." She looked up from the mug at Natalie and me. "Did you get him?"

"He's under arrest now. I'm going to follow him to the Two-six and talk to Lozano."

"If that had hit my head," Felice said, then stopped. "If it had hit my head and broken, I could be blind."

We didn't say anything.

"My hands won't stop shaking," Felice said.

I looked at Natalie, who said, softly, "I put a lot of honey in the tea."

"I'll be back in a few hours," I told her. "I should be in radio range, if there's an emergency. Otherwise I'll be at the Two-six."

I closed the door quietly when I left.

CHAPTER SEVEN

As far as interrogation rooms went, the one they put the thrower in was pretty run-of-the-mill. One table, bolted down. Two chairs, bolted down. One one-way glass window, dirty. One detective, frustrated.

Lozano worked on him for over an hour, with me watching from behind the smudged glass, and we learned next to nothing except the man's name, and that had come from the computer, not from the suspect.

Clarence Jesse Barry, thirty-three years old, and sporting a yellow-sheet that detailed crimes from criminal possession to attempted rape. It made me wonder if all Sword of the Silent members had such checkered pasts.

The only honest thing Mr. Barry said was, "Get me my lawyer." He said that after Lozano showed him the three photocopied wanted posters for Romero that had been taken from Barry's person before he went into holding. Lozano went after him hard on the posters, and after he'd tried being smart for a while Lozano must have gotten to him, because Clarence played his lawyer card.

At which point Lozano rose and left the interrogation room, circling back to where I stood. He arrived with two paper cups of that awful coffee. We looked through the glass together at Barry. Barry looked at the window and smiled. He didn't look at the wanted posters arrayed on the table before him.

"I am disappointed," Lozano said. He had removed his suit coat, and his white button-up shirt was wrinkled but clean. There was an orange plastic lighter in his breast pocket that showed through the fabric.

"Maybe he wants you to earn your pay," I said.

"Public-spirited asshole, isn't he?"

"You should have said something about his height. He loves that."

Lozano looked at me and grinned. "I'll keep that in mind." He finished his coffee in two gulps, then crumpled the cup and viciously shot it overhand to the trash can in the corner. The cup hit the inside lip of the can with a low ring and dropped inside, and the trash can rocked slightly on the impact.

He said, *"El café es una porquería*. Means, this coffee is for shit. Roughly."

"The gesture communicated the sentiment."

"Good to know a little Spanish," he said. "Say it with me. *El café es una porquería.*"

I said it with him.

"You learn fast."

"I'm a gifted linguist."

"Sure you are."

The door opened into our viewing room and Special Agent Fowler came in, shaking his head and saying, "Dude, sorry I'm late."

"Why break a pattern?" Lozano said.

"Scott," I said.

"Atticus. Detective." Fowler looked at Lozano for a moment, who didn't turn away from the window, then shifted his eyes to Barry. "What'd I miss?"

"He confessed," Lozano said. "Came completely clean. He's writing it up now."

"Uh-huh," Fowler said. He ran a hand through his hair. His hair was straw blond, and he was wearing a subdued blue suit with a white shirt and a navy tie. He had a good tan on, too, and it looked darker than I suppose it actually was against his collar and in this light. He was wearing his glasses, thin-lensed, and he had his diamond stud stuck in his left ear. All in all, he looked just out of high school.

I thought, no wonder Lozano hates him.

"He have the wanted posters on him?" Fowler asked.

"Yeah," I said.

"Brilliant detective work," Lozano muttered.

"Where'd he get them?" Fowler asked.

"He wouldn't say. He lawyered up before you got here," Lozano said.

"What'd you do?" Fowler asked.

"I interrogated the suspect, Special Agent Fowler."

Scott made a face.

"You know what?" I said. "I'm going to go back to the clinic, I think. Check on Dr. Romero. You guys get in touch if anything happens, okay?"

"Of course," Fowler said.

Lozano just grunted in my direction.

Felice was in with her last patient of the day when I got back, so I checked up with Natalie and Dale, told them about the grade-school performances at the precinct.

"No wonder she hired us," Dale said before he went for the car.

"Barry was with Crowell the first day I was here," I told Natalie. "He was in the car with Crowell. Did he show?"

"No. Did you think he would?"

"I don't know. I get the impression Crowell only descends from his heaven every once in a while to stir the pot."

"You talked to him yet?" Natalie asked.

"Can't get through to him," I said. "His office keeps giving me the runaround. He was supposed to call me this morning to set up an appointment to talk."

She frowned. "Some advance work."

"I'm doing the best I can with what I've got. I can't take the time to chase him down, you know that. We need another guard."

"I know a PI we could use for the strictly investigational stuff," Natalie said. "We could ask Felice to put her on the payroll."

I shook my head. "I don't want to do that to her. She's footing half the bill as it is, and despite what she told me, I think it's a hardship. And Felice's been feeding us when we're at her place. I don't want her to have to pay for another body."

Natalie sighed and ran her hand through her red hair. "It's probably best," she said. "You and Bridie would never get along. But you're going to feel really stupid if something happens because we're undermanned."

"I'll feel really stupid whether we're undermanned or not," I said. "Believe me, I'll find a way."

The egress was handled with the same precision as all the previous times. No one shot at us, no one got in our way, and no one followed us, as far as we could tell. We took the Baker route home that evening, which put us on the FDR for ten minutes of the ride. I brought Romero up to speed while Dale drove.

"Barry," she said, frowning. "I've never heard of him."

"He's definitely one of Crowell's."

"Crowell has a lot of people," she said flatly.

"I need to talk to him," I said.

Romero raised her eyebrows at me.

"Procedure."

She tugged at the collar of her Kevlar vest and exhaled down into her shirt. Then she looked back to me and said, "Lucky you."

Katie greeted us exactly as always, hugging the stuffing out of her mother, then me, then Natalie, and finally Dale. Rubin handed the doctor her mail and she disappeared into her bedroom, as had become her custom, while Katie dragged me to the television with her. On the way there I dismissed Dale and wished him a good night.

"Elaine is very sick," Katie told me when we were seated. "She's very sick and she's dying and David can't save her." Then she looked at me and said, solemnly, "It's very sad."

"I'm sorry," I said.

"People die," Katie told me. "Bixby Bill died and Melanie B died and maybe Elaine, too." Then she put both her arms around me and snuggled close, watching the television screen.

Rubin said, "You ought to tell her that you're taken."

I stuck my tongue out at him.

"You staying tonight?" he asked me.

"Just to talk to the doctor after she gets changed. You and Natalie tonight."

He gave me an evil grin.

"Not while you're working, you don't," I said.

Rubin looked hurt. "Do you think I take my duties so lightly that I would risk our principal and her daughter for one night of sordid pleasure?"

I nodded.

"You know me too well," he said.

From the bedroom, Dr. Romero said, "Atticus? Could you come here, please?"

Natalie, Rubin, and I exchanged looks. "Sure," I said,

and extricated myself from Katie's grasp. She didn't seem to mind.

Felice was sitting on her bed, now wearing jeans and a faded Amnesty International T-shirt. Her feet were bare, and she held a sheet of paper in her hand. She looked small and frightened.

"I thought it was a charity solicitation," she said.

I took the paper. It read:

> BUTCHER BITCH—
> ONE BULLET,
> TWO BULLET,
> EACH IN YOUR HEAD.
> BANG BANG.
> YOU'RE DEAD.
> BOOM BOOM.
> DEAD DEAD.
> THERE IS NO SUCH THING AS
> COMMON GROUND.
> JUST KILLING GROUND.
> YOUR KILLING GROUND.
> I WILL HAVE JUSTICE.
> YOU'RE NOT MY FIRST.
> I WILL HAVE JUSTICE.

No signature.

I set the letter carefully on the bed, went back to the bedroom door, and said softly to Natalie, "Call Fowler. We got a letter."

Then I went back to Felice.

"They just won't stop," she said. Her voice was very low.

"I don't want you going to the conference," I said.

She looked at me.

"Hotels are almost impossible to secure, and with only four people I absolutely cannot do it."

"You think that's what—of course. He doesn't want me to speak, whoever wrote it. A man wrote that."

After a second, I said, "I can't protect you at the conference, not as it stands. It's too easy for someone to get a gun or a bomb into a place like the Elysium. And it's already been publicized that you'll be there."

Felice inhaled deeply, then reached for her pack of cigarettes. "I'm going," she said. "I won't be frightened off."

"I can't provide adequate protection there," I said.

"Can't or won't?"

"Can't."

She stared at the pack of cigarettes for a few seconds, then lit one and smoked, watching my face. "You're serious, I've never seen you look this serious," she said.

"The stakes have changed," I told her. "You could have been seriously injured this morning. And it was a stupid thing for someone to do and that worries me. So far, there's been a terror-campaign logic to this. The bottle . . ." I left it unfinished.

But she was right with me. "That was an attack, wasn't it? Testing the defenses, maybe?"

"Yes."

"I'm going."

"Felice, listen to me. It's a hotel, do you understand? Suppose a man wants you dead. He knows you will be there in three days, giving a lecture, sitting on a panel. He checks into the hotel tomorrow, all he has to do is wait, polishing his gun. Do you see the scale? Everybody in the hotel—all the guests, the staff, the temps—everybody must be checked and cleared before you can go. It's impossible for me to do that and to protect you at the same time with just four people."

Felice got up and took the ashtray off her nightstand, tapping her cigarette on the rim. After a moment she said, "I am going to speak at Common Ground. I helped organize the damn thing, and I will be heard there."

I started to open my mouth but she held up a warning

finger. "Let me finish. I agree with you. I don't want to die, Atticus. I won't go to the conference if you tell me it can't be made safe. But I want you to talk to Veronica, Veronica Selby. She's the one who got the hotel in the first place, and she told me that she'd take care of security. Talk to Veronica, and if she can't make you reasonably happy, I won't go." She sat back down on the bed. "Fair enough?"

"I won't take chances here, Felice," I said.

"I know," she said. "And I appreciate that."

Fowler arrived shortly after we finished talking. I got Selby's phone number from Felice and gave the woman a call while Scott talked to Dr. Romero.

The phone was answered on the second ring.

"Hello?" The soft voice held just the slightest southern accent.

"This is Atticus Kodiak calling for Veronica Selby," I said.

"Speaking."

"I'm in charge of security for Dr. Felice Romero, Ms. Selby. I was wondering if I could come and speak with you?"

"Is Felice all right?"

"She's doing well enough."

"When did you have in mind, Mr. Kodiak?"

"I was thinking in about half an hour," I said.

"Oh," Selby said. "Well . . . yes, that would be fine. I'll expect you shortly, then." She told me her address and I copied it down on a sheet of paper. "Please give Felice and Katie my regards," she said.

"I'll do that."

Fowler had bagged the letter and the envelope, though we all knew there wouldn't be any prints. The serious threats always came back from the lab clean. I asked him if he could give me a ride up to Selby's place on Park Avenue, and he said he'd be glad to.

"She told me to send her regards," I said to Dr. Romero.

Romero managed a crooked smile.

"I'll get back to you later tonight," I told her. "You can reach me by pager or at home. Don't hesitate to call."

"I won't," she said.

Katie gave me another hug before I left, saying, "Come back, okay, 'Cus? Come back soon."

Fowler drove well, very legally. Once we were rolling he said, "You're going to hate this but Barry is out. The charges were dismissed."

"What?" I asked. "How the fuck did that happen?"

"Dude, I know. Looks like NYPD blew the paperwork. Barry claims that he didn't understand his Miranda. I think maybe one of the cops on the desk is sympathetic to the cause."

"He's been arrested enough, he fucking knows his Miranda by heart," I said.

"He didn't even say anything in interview to take to trial. But he's out, and I'm sorry, man. I thought you should know."

"I can't believe this," I said.

"It gets worse. He's running with another guy, too, Sean Rich, who came to pick him up. Both are apparently tight with Crowell."

"How is that worse?"

"Rich has a record," Fowler said. "In Florida. Pensacola."

Pensacola, the town with two dead doctors who performed abortions to its name. "Jesus."

"Yeah."

I didn't speak for a few moments, fuming. It had been a righteous collar, and Barry was out anyway. And now it sounded like there was a ringer up from the land of the faux-Christian Nazis. All of that plus the throwing of the bottle; it hadn't been thrown at Romero, it had been thrown at us, to see how we would react.

"Do you think they're really going to go after her?" Fowler asked.

"She's high profile, she's a woman, she's a minority. She's the perfect target. They'll go for her at that conference. Wouldn't you? They know exactly where she'll be, when she'll be, and if she goes down in front of the crowd—you can't buy that kind of publicity. Barry is SOS, we both know that. Crowell's up to something."

"Don't let her attend, man," Fowler said.

"If I don't like the security, I won't, believe me, Scott," I said.

He made a careful turn onto Park. "I don't think Crowell will do it. I don't like conspiracies." He pulled up outside Selby's apartment building. "Don't like conspiracies, and I don't like conspiracy theories at all, man. They're too easy. You're looking for a nut with a gun, not the Illuminati."

"I'll take a conspiracy over a nut with a gun any day," I told him, unbuckling my seat belt. "At least, with a conspiracy, you know where you stand."

He was still laughing when I got out of the car.

CHAPTER EIGHT

Selby's apartment building had the feel of New York when it was still the classiest, most cultured city on earth. Whether or not it is now is subject to debate, but then again, whether it ever was is probably subject to the same debate. The lobby was marble, the fixtures were brass, and the plants were very green. To top it all off, the doorman was dapper, his uniform neatly pressed. He looked like a Royal Guard. He greeted me by name, saying that Ms. Selby was expecting me. I felt horribly underdressed, and acutely aware that I had a gun on my hip.

Selby's apartment was on the second floor, and I knocked on her door and waited. The door was opened almost immediately by a woman roughly my height who allowed me in, shut the door behind me, and offered to take my jacket, saying her name was Madeline. I declined, and she bade me follow her down a short hallway. She motioned me into the room, then turned and left.

The curtains were drawn, and even with the last of dusk giving way to night the sitting room appeared bright and airy. The fixtures were predominantly white, with some green and some blue thrown in. There was an overstuffed couch and a low coffee table, bare, several bookshelves, and a desk by one of the windows, with a PC on top of it. The computer was running, and a screen saver of rain falling over a city skyline played on the monitor. Every so often lightning would flash across the skyline.

On the walls hung two framed posters, both Monets with beautiful fields and delicate sunlight. A wood carving hung over the computer, PEACE in polished mahogany letters, spelled in Greek, Hebrew, and English. There were other pictures of a vague religious nature, but nothing garish. As I stepped into the room I heard the sound of paws scrabbling on a hardwood floor, then saw a golden retriever corner hard from another room and run toward me. The dog passed me and stopped at Selby's feet, turning twice to look at both of us, then lowering itself to the ground.

Veronica Selby sat in a wheelchair, opposite the couch, wearing white pants and a dark blue blouse that looked like silk and comfortable. She was utterly stunning, certainly one of the most beautiful women I had ever seen. The blouse clung to her upper body, revealing the shape of strong shoulders and a proud back. She was on the near side of forty. Her hair was golden—literally—drawn around the right side of her neck and tied with a blue ribbon. She wore a small gold cross on a necklace, and the slightest application of makeup to highlight her blue eyes and her cheeks. With her left hand she stroked the dog behind its long, floppy ears.

She extended her right hand and said, "Mr. Kodiak, I'm pleased to meet you." I heard the soft southern thread of accent in her voice again.

"The pleasure is mine," I said, and shook her hand. Her grip was good, not too strong. She had nothing to prove.

"Please, have a seat."

The couch didn't give much when I sat on it. I said, "I realize that this was short notice."

"I assume this concerns Common Ground?"

"That's right."

"It has my absolute attention." Time was only beginning to work on her. At her eyes were the slightest lines, and her mouth exhibited barely a wrinkle. She would keep her beauty for the rest of her life. "What can I do for you, Mr. Kodiak?"

"Dr. Romero told me that you are taking care of security at the Elysium."

"Yes, I am," Selby said.

"I'd like to know what's being done."

"Felice is still receiving threats?"

I nodded.

Veronica Selby shook her head. "That anyone would do so in the name of God is abhorrent."

"Frankly, I think it's abhorrent, period."

She smiled. "Yes. May I ask—are you pro-abortion?"

I should have realized it when I first saw the apartment, I thought. I had assumed that Felice and Selby were on the same side. But it was being called Common Ground for a reason.

"Yes, I am," I said.

"I see. Yet your job is to protect the lives of the innocent, isn't it?" ·

"That's one way of looking at it." I shifted on the couch, wishing it would give just a little bit.

"I'm curious, you understand," Veronica Selby said. "I've spent twenty years now, off and on, trying to know the minds on both sides of the issue. You're uncomfortable talking about this."

"The issue's not the reason I'm here."

"No, you want to know about the security at the hotel. Fair enough," she said. "I've hired two firms, Vigilant Security and another called Aware, and officers of Midtown North will be present, too."

"And?"

She looked embarrassed. "I'm afraid that's all I've done."

Three days, I thought, and must have made a face, because she said, "I'm open to suggestions."

"Ms. Selby, I've advised Dr. Romero not to attend the conference because I believe there is a substantial chance that someone will try to kill her if she goes. My team and I cannot secure both the hotel and her person at the same time. Felice has agreed not to attend unless I approve the security."

Selby's expression slid, turning to disappointment. "No, please. Felice must be there. She's vital to making this work; it's essential that she attend and speak. Her commitment . . . she's got to be there . . . this may be the last chance any of us gets to talk instead of scream. If she doesn't come, easily half of the pro-abortion groups won't attend either." She moved her chair forward, closer to me, intent. The dog rose and looked at her.

"Please, Mr. Kodiak. You don't know how important this conference is, how desperately I want it to succeed," Veronica Selby said. "You must tell me what I need to do. The conference must be safe, not just for Felice but for all of us."

I was floored, not so much by her words, but by her passion. It had been a long time since I'd heard somebody speak with her sincerity, and, in a way, it was immediately intimate, as if I'd glimpsed something in her others would take years to see.

Selby kept her eyes on me, then suddenly seemed to become self-conscious. The dog put his head in her lap, rolling his eyes at me. Her hands went immediately to his glossy head.

"I can be somewhat . . . intense, I suppose," she said softly. "Forgive me."

"There's no need to apologize," I said.

"Will you tell me, please? What do I need to do?" she asked again.

I took off my glasses and rubbed my eyes. So much needed to be done, so much that I had assumed would already have been taken care of, to make the conference safe. The smart thing to do would be to tell Selby that I was sorry, but Romero wasn't going to show.

That would have been the smart thing to do, instead of being swayed by passion and courage.

I put my glasses back on. "First, you've got the wrong people," I said. "The police are a nice touch, and their help will be appreciated, but they're not in the business of protection. They apprehend for a living, if you see the distinction. Same thing with most security guard firms; you tend to get a lot of ex-cops, or cop wannabes. If they see someone with a gun, their instinct is to go after that person first, rather than to protect the target.

"There's really only one way to do this, and the problem is that to do it right, you need a lot of money—"

"I'm rich." Selby said it simply. "Money isn't a problem."

I absorbed that, then said, "Call Sentinel Guards tomorrow morning. Make an appointment to meet with Elliot Trent, and mention my name. His daughter works with me. He can come to see you, if you like. Tell him exactly what Common Ground is, everything you have planned for the conference, and tell him you've got 72 hours before it happens. You want complete protection. Those are the words to use: complete protection."

"What does that mean, exactly?"

"Sentinel will do as complete a background check on as many attendees to the conference, and as many employees of the hotel as possible, in the time remaining. They'll try to check on all the guests, too, and make certain that none of them is a potential troublemaker. They'll place guards in uniforms and plainclothes, they'll have metal detectors, a command post, even dogs for sniffing out explosives."

I looked at her and then said, "It's got to be done like that, and they've got to do it. Otherwise, I'll advise Dr. Romero not to attend. We're in the hole as it is. This should have been done weeks ago."

"I didn't realize . . ."

"Talk to Trent tomorrow. Tell him to call me after you speak with him."

"I will," Selby said, wheeling over to the computer. She nudged the mouse and the screen saver went off. She opened an appointment book on the screen and began to type. "Will you look this over, please?" she asked.

I got off the couch and looked over her shoulder at the monitor. She'd gotten all the important points of what I'd said, and I told her as much.

"One other thing," I said. "I need a list of all attendees, if you have one. Trent will, too."

"I've got it right here." She opened a document, set it up to print. There was a whine as her laser printer charged and began spitting out paper, and Selby said, "I updated it today. We're at twenty-two speakers, over two thousand registered attendees, but frankly I'm expecting more."

"How many more?"

"Perhaps twice or even three times that number."

"Christ," I said.

She looked at me sharply.

"I apologize," I said. "No offense was intended."

Selby made a small smile. "Taking the Lord's name in vain . . . I'm used to hearing it outside. Just not in my own home."

She gathered the paper from the printer and handed it to me. As I flipped through the sheets, Selby said, "I'll let you know as more names are added."

I was about to thank her when I saw Crowell's name. "Why's Jonathan Crowell on the list?"

"He'll be speaking," she said.

"Are you kidding? That man doesn't believe in common anything."

She wheeled back to where the dog now lay, saying, "Jordan, come here." The dog immediately rose and returned his head to her lap, wagging his tail.

Selby said, "Mr. Crowell's point of view deserves to be heard."

"No."

She frowned. "Everyone who wishes to speak must be heard, Mr. Kodiak. We all have that right. I don't agree with what he does, or what he says. But if Dr. Romero can speak, then he must be given the opportunity as well. That's the whole purpose of this conference."

"That means that SOS will be there," I said.

She nodded. "And they will behave or be expelled. Those are the ground rules for the conference. There will be no screaming tantrums, no accusations."

I wondered how the hell she was going to manage that, but didn't say anything. Barry threw a bottle, and now SOS would be attending Common Ground. Suddenly, my day seemed to be in a serious nosedive.

"He's not that bad," she said. "Crowell, I mean. His rhetoric is that of an angry man, but . . . he sincerely believes that abortion is murder, and I cannot fault him for that."

"You speak as if you know him," I said.

"We've had an acquaintance over the years. He's strained it recently." She looked at her hands, then at me again, the small smile back in place. "I've been lobbying against abortion for nearly twenty years now, Mr. Kodiak. I've lectured all over the country, I've published everywhere I could get accepted. I've even managed two or three books. Through all of this, I've met many people on both sides. I have enemies on my own side and friends, like Felice Romero, on the other."

It struck me that she had more to say about Crowell, but I didn't want to press her. I folded the papers, put them in my jacket pocket. "When you see Trent, make certain you tell him that Crowell and his troops will be there."

"I will," she said. "You're leaving?"

"I've got some other things to take care of tonight."

"Let me show you out, then," Selby said.

"That's not necessary," I said. "Have a good night."

"You as well. Thank you again for coming."

I started for the door and she said, "Mr. Kodiak? Do you think that SOS will really be a problem?"

I stopped and looked back at her, gorgeous in her wheelchair, just as passionate, just as concerned as before.

"Yes," I said. "They really will."

I went straight home, opened a beer, and dialed Romero's number. Natalie answered.

"It's Atticus. I need you to call your father. Tell him that Veronica Selby will be calling tomorrow, and she'll want the works."

"How bad is it?" she asked.

"Oh, it's about as bad as it can be. We're a good three weeks behind."

"No way we can do this, Atticus," Natalie said.

"I know."

She was quiet for a moment. I heard Romero ask her how my meeting with Selby had gone. Natalie said fine, then said, to me, "I'm going to change phones. Hold on." I heard her set the receiver down, then ask Romero if she could use the phone in the bedroom. Felice said yes.

I drank some beer. I knew what was coming, and couldn't fault her. Of all my colleagues, frankly, Natalie's the best. At least as good as I am, and certainly better looking.

She picked up the extension and someone hung up the other phone, and as soon as she felt the line was secure, she said, "You absolutely cannot let her attend. There's no way that Sentinel can catch up, no way they can clear everybody by the day after tomorrow."

"I know."

"Goddamn you, Atticus. I know you and I know what you're thinking. You can't let her do it."

I didn't say anything.

"She's got a daughter, for God's sake."

"I know."

She was quiet again. "Is it worth her life?" Natalie asked, finally.

"It's her life, Natalie. I'll give her the options and let her make the decision."

"You know what she'll say."

"Yes, I do," I said. I finished my beer. I was paying for a lot of NYNEX silence. I took the beer to the sink and washed out the bottle. After I put it in the recycling, I asked, "Do you want out?"

"Of course not," Natalie said immediately. "Don't be an ass. I'm in for the whole op. But it's a mistake, and I would be remiss in my job if I didn't tell you that."

"Will you be able to sell your father on it?"

She sighed. "He won't like it at all. It'll put the firm's reputation at risk. He'll give me the 'She's our responsibility, too' lecture, and he won't be wrong."

"Tell him it's my reputation, not his."

"I will."

"If we can't get Sentinel, we're fucked," I said.

"We're fucked anyway, Atticus. All right, I'll call him, do my best Daddy's-little-girl act. But don't expect him to give Selby a discount. I'll call you back."

"Okay. Don't tell Romero anything yet."

"Talk to you in a bit."

I hung up and stared out the kitchen window for a few minutes, looking across the alley. Then I took off my gun and pager and sat at the table. My gun is an HK P7, hammerless, and its cocking mechanism is in the grip, making it ideal for one-handed use. It's a good bodyguard's weapon, and looking at it, I wondered if I wasn't creating a situation where I'd be forced to use it. I didn't much care for that thought, and looked out the window instead.

There wasn't much happening in the apartments across the alley, just occasional silhouettes against drawn blinds.

Twenty minutes passed before the phone rang. I answered it immediately.

"He said he'll do it," Natalie told me. "He'll cancel his morning appointments and meet with her right after she contacts him. But he told me to tell you that you're an idiot, and you'll be washed up if this goes wrong."

"Have I mentioned how much I like your father?"

"No, and I wouldn't start now. See you in the morning."

"Night."

"Good night."

After making dinner for myself, I called Alison, hoping that I could see her, or at least get her on the phone long enough to talk. She wasn't in; probably rehearsing. I left a short message, told her it was nothing urgent, and that I'd try to reach her tomorrow.

Then I went to bed.

Sleep came fast, and I dropped into my dream cycle like a sinker through the surface of a lake. Veronica Selby was explaining to me that plastic coat hangers were invented by her, actually, to keep women from using them to mutilate themselves. Dr. Romero told her she was way out of line, but she said it in a friendly enough way, and Selby took it well, asking the doctor in return why she hadn't aborted Katie.

"I couldn't," Dr. Romero told her. "I wouldn't have even if I had known."

They talked, and I sat on a black leather couch next to Katie, watching television. Bill Bixby turned into Lou Ferrigno, and together the two of them trashed a clinic held by fat men wearing ski masks. On the screen I saw a child's doll, naked and anatomically incorrect, with its crotch split open. Its crotch had been detailed to look like a vagina, but someone had bored a hole through it, and from within spilled festering, bloody matter, burned and broken chunks of skin that could have been anything from fetal remains to chicken entrails. "She's dead," Katie told me.

Then Felice was being chased by men who all looked like Barry. The many Barrys held paper knives, which they had managed to smuggle past the metal detectors without a problem. Felice stopped running, turning to face them down. She said, "You're all such little men, why are you here?"

Before I could reach her, they descended, the knives rising and falling, until they cut out her womb. The chief Barry held it aloft, presenting it to Crowell as he floated down from heaven on wires. Crowell took it, and said to Felice, "No more children for you."

CHAPTER TEN

The phone was ringing. I heard it in the dream and made for it, climbing desperately, until finally my eyes opened and I jerked up. It was still dark, and I stumbled out of my room and into the kitchen, stubbing my toe on the utility cart while trying to reach the table.

"Atticus, it's Rubin. Dr. Romero and Natalie just left here. The burglar alarm at the clinic went off."

"Damn," I said. "All right, I'll get right over there."

"Okay," Rubin said softly.

It took half a second, and then I recognized the tone in his voice. Doubt.

"What is it?" I asked.

"I don't know," he said. "The phone rang right after they left, and I thought it was the police again, or the alarm company. But nobody was there, they just hung up after I answered. It feels like somebody's probing."

"You want me to come over there?"

"Yes," Rubin said.

"All right, I'll send Dale to the clinic. Give me twenty minutes. Katie's all right?"

"She's in her room, sleeping."

"You checked?"

"Yes. Called the doorman, too. He says nobody he hasn't recognized has come in."

"Twenty minutes," I said and hung up.

I turned on the kitchen light and winced, then called Dale. He got it on the second ring, and was remarkably lucid. I briefed him and he said he'd get there ASAP.

I dressed fast, grabbed my gun and pager, and ran down all six flights of stairs onto Thompson, pulling my jacket on as I went. I flagged a passing cab on Houston and told the driver to get to Gold Street as fast as he could. It was four in the morning and the sky was still dark, the streets still bare, and everything shining in the false moisture of night. The dream still had its claws in me, and I tried to shake them out as the cab popped and swerved its way south.

The driver stopped in front of Romero's building, and I scanned the street before getting out, looking for anything out of the ordinary. There was nothing to see. The driver took his money and the doorman let me through. Rubin was waiting at Romero's door and stepped out of my way to let me inside. I heard him lock the door after me.

The main floor looked fine, and I took the steps up to the third level quickly, found Katie's door, and looked inside. She was asleep in the bed, snoring. The room smelled of perfume and soap.

Rubin handed me a mug of coffee when I got back downstairs. His eyes were puffy, with heavy bags underneath. I took the mug and checked the other rooms, not expecting to find anything and not being disappointed. Then I moved the curtain back from the window and unlocked the sliding door, stepping out onto the concrete patio. Rubin followed me.

The air was cool outside, and helped push the last of my cobwebs away. The coffee was hot and too sweet.

"False alarm?" Rubin asked.

"Maybe." There was movement across the street, a man in a dark windbreaker walking down toward the Seaport. Several lights shone in the opposite building, and movement fluttered the curtains in a couple of windows, people rising for the day or maybe preparing for bed. A homeless person slept on a grate at the corner of the building, unmoving. But mostly the city was still wrapped in night, and mostly there was nothing to see.

"God, I'm tired," he said, rubbing his eyes.

"What exactly happened?"

"Felice got the call about a half hour ago, and she tore out of here. Natalie wanted to call you first, but Felice wouldn't wait.

"I hung up the phone and it rang and I picked it up, and then nothing. Just the click, like I said. Disconnect."

"Anything else?"

Rubin rubbed his eyes again. "I don't know. I got twigged, you know, so I decided I'd take a peek out here . . . and I swear to God I saw someone in one of the windows." He looked at me, and his expression was almost apologetic. "Just standing there, not doing a goddamn thing but staring out, right at me."

"Could you see who it was?"

"Shit, Atticus, I could only see a silhouette. The person could've had their goddamn *back* to me, I wouldn't have been able to tell. Looked like a guy, looked about your size, but I don't know. It doesn't mean anything."

"Which window?"

He extended an ink-stained index finger. "Seventh in from the left on the third floor."

The window was lit, but barely, as if there was only one source of light inside, and I could dimly make out the railing on the fire escape. Curtains or some kind of blind obscured the view, and if anyone was moving inside, they weren't visible. On either side of the window there were no lights, and no way to tell if it was one apartment or several. From where we stood, it looked like someone could establish line of sight into the Romero living room, but their field of fire would have been tight, maybe only five degrees at the most. Move to the right a couple of windows and that field would open up to almost twenty degrees, maybe more.

"This is probably nothing, right?" Rubin asked. "Somebody just got the number and was making a run-of-the-mill terror call? Coincidence?"

The light in the window went out, and I stared hard for a few moments at the darkened square, thinking, then let my eyes lock on the building entrance. After a minute or so a woman left, walking a dog past the dozing doorman under the awning. The woman was using a walking stick, and the dog was on a retractable leash. Both looked old. Nobody else entered or left. "Maybe."

"Maybe what?"

"Maybe it's nothing. We should find out who's in that apartment, though."

"I don't want to start jumping at ghosts."

"We'll verify that it's occupied, that's all. Find out if the name on the rental agreement matches any name that Fowler or Lozano have."

We surveyed the street for a while without speaking. Early office suits were beginning to appear, heading toward Wall Street with briefcases laden with trade secrets and stock reports. The thought, unbidden and unexpected, came into my mind that each person moving now, every light across the way, represented a life or multiple lives.

"It's been going on for so long now," Rubin said. "It seems like we've been doing this job forever."

"Eleven days isn't long," I said.

"For you, maybe. I feel like every day is the same. Not that they are, of course, I know that, and if I try really hard, I can remember that, too. But the fact that I have to try really hard to begin with is what bothers me."

"Have you gotten any sleep?"

"What, tonight? About two hours."

"Go to bed. I'll cover until Natalie gets back with the doctor." I put a hand on his shoulder. "You can only do so much. Get some rest."

"You don't think I'm paranoid, do you?"

"Paranoia is our game, Rubin."

He smiled and said, "See you in a few hours." He started back into the apartment, then stopped. "Katie shouldn't be a problem when she gets up. She's having her period, now, though, so make sure she changes her pads. She forgets sometimes."

I gave Rubin five minutes to settle in before I turned back inside myself, going straight to the house phone and ringing the lobby. Philippe the doorman answered immediately, and I told him what I wanted him to do.

"I shouldn't leave my post," he told me.

"This is a favor for Dr. Romero."

He listened again, then agreed, and I went back out on the patio to watch.

It took him four minutes to lock up, get the coffees, and cross the street. Philippe offered one cup to the other doorman, and they stood side by side for a moment, drinking and talking. Philippe told a joke, with broad hand gestures, and the other doorman laughed. They talked some more, and then the other doorman nodded and went inside, leaving Philippe alone on the sidewalk. His uniform looked pink in the light under the awning.

The other doorman came back, told Philippe what he wanted to know. They shook hands, and though I couldn't see it, I was sure Philippe slipped the other man some money.

I went back to the house phone, and picked it up as it rang.

"The apartment is owned by Mrs. Batina Friendly," Philippe told me. "She shares it with her dog. She's out taking a walk right now."

Which was what I had thought, but it pays to be certain. "How much do I owe you?" I asked him.

"Twenty bucks," Philippe said.

"Thanks."

"No problem."

Dr. Romero had set out two deck chairs on the patio, white enamel paint with orange rubber slats, and after Rubin left I sat in one of them, waiting for the sunrise.

While I watched the street, I wondered what Katie's dreams were like. She wasn't as affected by her Down's as some people I had met, but she was more impaired than others. Talking to her, it always seemed as if we understood intention without sharing language. The only reason anyone assumed her thoughts to be simple and childish was because she had difficulty in communicating. Did she dream about Bill Bixby and the Incredible Hulk? Rubin's frankness about Katie's menstrual cycle had surprised me; it was stupid, but I hadn't realized she would ovulate. At sixteen, Katie Romero was growing into the body of a woman and certainly had the growing desires of one, as well. If her fantasy life was active, who could blame her? Ultimately, she was alone, with no one to share herself with completely, because words would always get in the way.

The sky continued to color, and it was just before six when the phone rang inside. It hadn't been ringing for long, I know, but for a moment my memory had a gap I couldn't fill, and I answered it with the fear and guilt of someone who may have nodded off to sleep.

"Atticus?"

"How's it look, Natalie?"

"Someone tried to crowbar the back door, mangled the locking plate, but didn't get inside. I'm trying to get Felice out of here, but she won't leave until she's positive that nothing is missing. Dale's with her, now. Fowler's coming down, so we're waiting on him right now. How's things there?"

"Quiet. Rubin got a call after you two left, no voice, just a disconnect. He thought it might be a probe, so he asked me to come down here."

"Anything to it?"

"He went to the window and took the glance, says that there was somebody in one of the windows of the opposite building, looking out. He said he thinks it was a male, perhaps my height, but it was all in silhouette."

"What do you want to do about it?"

"I've already identified the apartment, and it seems safe. When Rubin's up I'll head to the clinic. You guys aren't going to be coming back down, I assume?"

"At this rate, no, we'll be staying," Natalie said. "All right, I'll see you when you get here. Any other orders?"

"Keep her safe," I said.

"I am my sister's keeper," Natalie said, and hung up.

Katie started moving a little before seven, coming down the stairs to where I was reading on the couch, yawning. Her heavily lidded eyes looked even smaller, and she rubbed them several times before they appeared of use to her. Her nightgown was yellow with small blue prancing horses printed on it, and it made her look fat. At the bottom of the stairs she stopped and looked at me.

"Where's my mommy?"

"She had to go out."

"The phone, who was on the phone, calling here?"

"That was Natalie. Your mommy's all right."

"I know that, I know she is," she said. She pointed to

the drawn curtains, where daylight was showing. "Breakfast time, what's for breakfast, 'Cus?"

"What do you want?"

"I want waffles, want waffles and syrup."

"Go get dressed and I'll make you waffles with syrup."

"Okay. I'll do it. 'Cus, where's my mommy? Where is she?"

"She had to go to the clinic. She'll be back before too long."

"My mommy works, that's right," she said, turning back up the stairs. "Mommy works so people don't like her because she does a job."

She disappeared into the bathroom above and I stepped around the counter into the kitchen, looking for a skillet or waffle maker. The light in the kitchen wasn't strong enough to cast shadows on the curtains. After some rummaging, I eventually discovered a waffle iron at the back of a cabinet, hidden behind an automatic juicer. It took another few minutes to get everything together for the batter, and I started to worry that the waffles wouldn't be ready by the time Katie was dressed. But the water in the bathroom continued to run, and I had finished a first batch and was working on the second before she came down, wearing baggy jeans and a T-shirt with the cover of Madonna's "True Blue" album printed on it. When she turned I could see concert dates on the back.

"Did you change pads?" I asked.

She looked angrily down at her bare feet, saying, "He shouldn't talk about that. He shouldn't be talking about that, to me. I did. I did it." She looked at me again and said, "I did."

"Why don't you sit down and I'll bring you breakfast."

She headed for the television, in a line across the glass doors, and I said, "Katie, sit at the table, please."

She changed her course without protest, settling into a wicker chair that creaked, then looked to me expectantly. I brought her a plate of three waffles, stacked, and a glass of orange juice. She went for the orange juice first, and when she drank she placed her tongue inside the glass. It seemed a slow and difficult way to drink, but pointing that out seemed petty. If it made her happy, why criticize? I returned to the table with a bottle of Log Cabin and a cup of coffee for me.

"How did you sleep?" I asked.

"Fine. I slept fine." She opened the bottle of syrup and held it in both hands, pouring the contents onto her waffles. She poured a lot of syrup.

"Katie, don't you think that's enough?"

She looked at me, honestly surprised, then said, "Oops, oh no! That's too much!" She turned the bottle quickly right side up and the syrup line suspended between bottle and table turned, too, getting all over the side of the bottle and her hands. "Yuck," she said. "Yuck, oh, oops, yuck."

I started to take the bottle from her but she clung to it. "No, I can do it. I can do it. Get a towel, go get a towel to clean it up."

So I got a paper towel from the roll over the sink, wetted it, and returned to her. The bottle was upright and capped in the middle of the table, still drooling a strand of syrup. Katie was licking her fingers, but she stopped to use the wet towel. She cleaned her hands vigorously. "Elaine died," she told me. "She died all sick and David couldn't help her." She looked down and rubbed the towel over the table, concentrating on the spot where the syrup had fallen. "It's very sad."

"I'm sorry," I said.

She dropped the paper towel and took up her fork and knife. As she cut the first waffle to pieces she said, "It's only a television show."

I used the mug to hide my smile, drinking coffee and nodding at her. "Yes, it is."

"It's only a television show," she repeated. "Elaine didn't really die and Bixby Bill and she can get married now. That's not sad, it isn't."

"No."

She went through the waffles quickly, barely stopping to breathe between bites. When the last scraps were gone, she coated her fork with the remaining syrup and took care of that, too. Finished, she put the utensils back on the plate, saying, "Is there more?"

"Are you sure you want more? It's awfully fattening."

"No, don't get fat. I'm not fat, I'm pretty. Don't get fat," she said. " 'Cus, I don't want anymore syrup."

"How about waffles?"

"No, I don't want waffles. I'm finished. I've got to exercise, after breakfast, I've got to exercise. Can I do my tape?"

"Sure, where is it?"

The tape was a workout video, and I rewound it and started it on the VCR. Katie took her position in front of the television, hands on her hips, grim determination in her eyes. Waffle crumbs stuck to the corners of her mouth, and I pointed them out to her. She thanked me, licking them off, and began her workout while I removed the dishes from the table and started cleaning up. From where I stood behind the kitchen counter, I had line of sight straight to the window. Katie stayed clear of the doors as she exercised. Hers wasn't an efficient workout, but she took it seriously, following the movements as best she could, never once slacking off or taking an unauthorized break.

When the videotape ended she went to the television and switched to MTV, staying on her feet for a few more minutes, dancing to the forced beat. Eventually she sat on the couch, wiping imaginary sweat from her brow.

"Where is he?" she asked.

"Who?"

"Where is he? Where is Rubin, 'Cus? Where is he?"

"He's getting some sleep."

"No, he's not," Rubin said. He was wearing boxer shorts and looked marginally better than last night, a towel in his hand. "He's taking a shower." He went down the stairs to the entry bathroom.

Katie laughed, and announced that Rubin was silly.

We sat together, watching MTV. Katie seemed to have absolutely no musical preference, although the one Madonna video we saw captured her attention completely, and she sang along with it heartily. The video was an older one, I think, but I'm not a real fan of the medium, so I could be mistaken. Madonna paraded in front of incredibly handsome, incredibly well-defined men and women, coaxing them to sexual frenzy. Not only was Katie attentive, she was beatific in her awe.

The phone rang and I went to answer it. It was Lozano.

"Natalie said you were there," he told me.

"What? Hold on," I said and set down the phone, going back to the television and turning it down.

"Use the remote," Katie said.

"Where is it?"

"I don't know, no. Turn it down, he's turning it down. There, who is it? Is it my mommy?"

"No, it's the police."

"It's the police, looking for Melanie B. Is it my mother?"

"Is Dr. Romero all right?" I asked Lozano.

"She's fine. I want—"

"Hold on," I said. "Your mother's all right, Katie."

"Good, that's good that she's all right. The police call when people are dead," she said. She rose and began hunting around the couch. "I'll get the control, the control for the television for you."

"Sorry, Detective," I told Lozano. "What can I do for you?"

"Just wanted to let you know what we've got, which is practically nothing. A unit found a crowbar in the alley, but there were no prints on it. Fowler's sending it to D.C."

"A crowbar?"

"Don't ask me, Kodiak. I just work for the city, not the

Mighty Federal Machine," he said. "You going to the clinic?"

"When my guard here is ready, yeah, I'll be going up-town. He got a call last night that might have been something, but it's looking okay now."

Rubin came up the stairs at that point, freshly scrubbed and wearing clean clothes, and the change had affected his personality. He was smiling, and flicked the end of his towel at me. I failed a halfhearted dodge, turning toward the far wall. He'd have to attack me from behind, and Rubin wouldn't do that.

"Conference is tomorrow?"

"Day after," I said.

"It's going to get worse before it gets better, bud," Lozano said.

"Well, that's just what I wanted to hear," I said, turning back around. Rubin was in the kitchen, drinking orange juice out of the container. He caught my eye and I shook my head and he set down the carton on the counter, hunting for a glass. I heard him ask Katie if she wanted one. She said yes, and continued searching the cushions on the couch.

"It should never have been made legal," Lozano said.

"But it is," I said. Katie turned on the standing lamp in the corner to get more light.

"Yes, it is. And until the law changes—"

The glass door, the sliding portion, shattered and fell, a translucent wall that tore the curtain as it collapsed into the room, pulling the fabric off its runners. Glass hit the carpet intact but burst on impact, singing as it broke. Out of my hand fell the phone and to my left Rubin was dropping the orange juice. The carton hit the kitchen floor bottom first, then pitched to a side. Juice splashed on the tile floor and Rubin's pant leg. The report was next, full and ugly, large caliber. Katie jerked where she was standing in front of the light, beside the couch, just inside what was now the kill zone, and she fell, her chest leading, hitting the side of the couch and then bouncing off it, soft and buoyant, hitting the carpet on her side, and I was diving to her, shouting for cover and police and an ambulance and thinking quite clearly that it was a very good thing, a very good thing, that Lozano was on the phone, because all he had to do was turn around and shout and there would be an ambulance and the police and it would be all right, everything would be all right.

Another report, the second or maybe the third, just after I got to her, and I slipped my hands underneath her shoulders, pulling Katie back to the kitchen, around the counter, and Rubin was helping me, grabbing her shirt, his head low, and I had the awful sensation that none of this was real; it was a practical, a live fire exercise; certainly not real. When we dragged her we smeared a red stain on the carpet, a bloody snail's trail that became wet and shiny on the tile floor. Rubin was crawling out to the phone already, grabbing the hanging receiver and barking into it, scurrying back to our cover as he did so.

Another shot and I heard it punch hard against the counter as I knelt over Katie, her eyes open and filling with tears. She was speaking and I strained to listen while running my hands over her, trying to find the wound. The blood kept coming with a mind of its own.

"My mommy," Katie Romero said, and it was hard to understand her, and it hurt her to make the words, but she kept repeating, "Mommy, I want my mommy, where is she? I want my mommy."

The hole had been punched in her side three inches below her armpit, just inside her right breast, and the blood coming out was candy-red arterial issue, and I covered the wound with my hand, pushing down hard trying to get a seal to stop the bleeding and Rubin was shouting to get an ambulance fucking now, we were taking fire.

And Katie stopped calling for her mother, no air available to do it, and I was still looking for an exit wound, not finding one, wondering where it had gone, if it was still inside. I tilted her head back, my palm on her forehead, and put my cheek beside her mouth and two fingers on her carotid, waiting for air to come out, for blood to move, for a breath. Fifteen slow seconds, certain I counted too fast, and there was nothing coming out, her chest wasn't moving.

With one hand I sealed her nostrils and then covered her mouth with mine. My lips surrounded hers, she had a small mouth, and my seal was absolute. Two full breaths, Katie's chest rising. The air rustled out past my cheek.

"No pulse, no breathing," I said.

Rubin was landmarking, his hands already sliding up Katie's rib cage to find the xiphoid. I gave another two breaths and he starting compressing and I started breathing and that was it, with Rubin quietly saying "One-and-two-and-three-and-four-and-five and—" breath breath, "one-and-two-and-three-and-four-and-five and—" breath breath. Compressions, breaths, and the air wasn't going down, I was tasting waffles and syrup and orange juice and jerked my head back, spitting, turning Katie's head. I opened her mouth and swept the inside with an index finger, scooping out chewed breakfast and clearing her airway, then repositioning her head. Two breaths.

"Continue."

Compress, relax, compress, relax, compress, relax, compress, relax, compress, relax, and two breaths, and again, we weren't perfect, we were going too fast, I knew that, the air was going in and coming out, and again compress, relax, compress, relax, compress, relax, compress, relax. Stop. Check for pulse. One one-thousand two one-thousand three one-thousand four one-thousand five one-thousand no pulse *where the fuck is the ambulance* "No pulse, continue," breath, exhale, breath, exhale, compress, relax, compress, relax *where the fuck is the ambulance* compress, relax, compress, relax, compress, relax, breath, exhale, breath, exhale, and again compress, relax, compress, relax *if she took the shot in the lung where's the exit*

wound compress, relax, compress, relax *two shots or was
it three shots or was it four shots only one shot hit her the
second shot rifle* compress, relax, breath, exhale, breath,
exhale *where am I in the count should I check pulse God
don't let her die* compress, relax, compress, relax, compress, relax, more breaths compress, relax, breath, compress relax breath *ten minutes irreversible brain damage
where the fuck where the fuck where the fuck the door's
locked oh fuck me the door's still locked.* . . .

Check pulse. Nothing, "Rubin, unlock the door, go unlock the door." My free hand took the gun from my hip
and handed it to him. He took the gun so fast I wasn't sure
he had taken it at all, and he got up and went for the door
as I landmarked, above the xiphoid notch, yes and one
hand, seal, breath, compress, over and over and over and
over and over and he was back.

"Door's open. Coming in on breathing," and he moved
to her mouth and I moved over her chest and she was so
small and my hands were so big on that fucking Madonna
T-shirt, a beatific smile and a bloody halo that's not true
blue.

We weren't even checking for pulse anymore.

The paramedics came, a man and a woman, both intent
and aggressive, and the man ordered Rubin away from
Katie's head and immediately set about administering oxygen with a bag-valve mask. They didn't say anything to
me, so I kept compressing while Rubin explained as best
he could what had happened. Over their radios I heard
others and looked up through sweat-stung lashes to see
two uniforms standing just above the stairs, looking confused. One of the cops said something to the woman in
front of me, who was busily setting up a line.

"Shut up," she told him. "Ringers running," she told
her partner.

He nodded and said, "Stop compressing."

I sat back on my haunches, feeling hot and light-headed, watching as he intubated Katie, sliding the tube down her throat like a professional magician; now you see it, now you don't.

The woman had set up the monitor, was now looking at Katie's absence of rhythm on the LED screen. To hook the system up she had sliced Katie's shirt open down the middle, and the bloodstained fabric pulled back to reveal her body, and even with her natural skin color she seemed pale, dying. The monitor confirmed that, and as the woman busied herself with the IV line, pushing first one drug, then another, I bent to resume compressions.

Another ambulance crew arrived, and then they were loading Katie onto a stretcher, and I was being roughly pushed out of the way, into the arms of a cop who started to ask me something I never gave him a chance to finish. I followed the stretcher down the stairs and into the hall, Rubin right behind me. The elevator was locked open and they moved everything inside. Rubin and I took the stairs down to the lobby. One of the uniforms came after us, and Rubin was explaining the situation in broken phrases that sounded ungainly and unknowable.

From the lobby, Katie was rolled to the back of one ambulance, where both paramedics climbed inside. One of the late arrivals, an EMT, slammed the double doors shut and went around to the front of the rig, and Rubin and I followed the other to the remaining ambulance. The driver was medium-sized and white, with black curly hair and black-framed glasses, and he just nodded to us when we started to climb inside.

"Where're they taking her?" the cop asked him.

"Bellevue."

Buckled up, and then the rig was off with a lurch, lights and sirens down the street and swaying onto the FDR Drive, following the other rig as it sped to the hospital.

"Somebody needs to call her mother," I said.

"Lozano said he'd do it," Rubin said.

We arrived at Bellevue only thirty seconds or so after the ALS rig, in time to jump out and follow the stretcher through the double doors on the loading dock down the hall. Katie was on her back, the monitor still running. They had put a second line in her, but both bags now rested above her head on the stretcher, shut down for transport. We followed them down a hall, made a sharp right, and ended up in a crammed narrow route with stretchers stacked to one side. The paramedics barely had room to move, and we stayed well behind, keeping out of their way, but not wanting to lose them. Left and now an open space, still more stretchers, and through electric double doors into the ER, and more stretchers, now with people in them, their feet sticking out from under covers or uncovered. The room had a smell that rammed its way up my nose and made me gag, twisted with the cloying memory of maple syrup, and my stomach heaved, for a second, then retreated.

The medics turned Katie's gurney to the left, in front of a new set of double doors, and a doctor was standing there, wearing sea-blue scrubs and gloves and goggles and barely audible, saying, "This the Romero kid?"

We never heard the answer; they were already inside and it was clear we had come as far as we could. The doors snapped shut on hydraulic coils, locked with hard clicks, and Rubin and I stood side by side, looking through the small glass windows at the eight people suddenly surrounding Katie's body. They moved her off the gurney and onto another table, the medics backing away, and a phalanx of doctors, men and women, some in scrubs, others not, all goggled, gloved, and masked, bent to work. Instruments flashed off trays in gloved milky hands and the sound of machinery, hard and strong, started up. The doctors bent to the task, and it was clear to me, right then, that Katie was dead.

Rubin was covered in blood, all over his shirt and pants, up both arms, a vampire's ice cream sundae. I probably didn't look any better.

Then a nurse told us to move, to get out of the way and go register the patient.

"She's Catholic," I told her.

"We take all kinds."

"No," I said. "She's Catholic."

"I'll get a priest. Go register the patient."

She gave us directions to registration, but they didn't stick. Rubin and I started down a hallway, passing an alcove containing a bald-headed man on a bench, and dodged an orderly who glared at us, then continued on.

"Where are we going?" Rubin asked.

I shook my head, and we turned around, heading back to the nurses' station. Another door through admitting opened as we returned, and Felice Romero rushed in, Natalie and Dale right behind her, and another doctor from the clinic, Marion Faisall. Lozano followed a second later. Dr. Romero didn't see us, going straight to the station and exchanging quick words with the nurse there. The nurse gestured and Felice turned, moving to the Trauma Room doors, but the nurse shouted after her and Natalie moved, grabbing her arm at the elbow. The grip stopped her, and Felice turned back to Natalie, eyes wild and mouth in a silent scream.

Felice saw us, and saw it in our faces. It was as if someone had thrown a solid punch into her stomach, and she began to bend, shaking her head, as if trying to fold into herself and disappear. Natalie and Dale helped her to the alcove, setting her on one of the benches. Dale stayed by her, an arm around her shoulders, head beside hers but looking out, always looking. Natalie made straight for us. Dr. Faisall just stood beside the alcove.

"How?" Natalie asked. Her eyes were terribly cold.

"Sniper," I said. "We did everything we could." My words sounded whispered, and for a moment I doubted that I had indeed spoken at all. But Natalie nodded, looking us both over, then reached for Rubin.

Lozano was looking at me. I left Rubin and Natalie and walked to him. Behind the counter a phone rang, and one of the staff moved to answer it. Fowler had entered, leading another two police officers, and they all stood idly by the ER doors. We were filling the place up. Beyond the doors, somewhere outside the room, people were shouting, and Lozano turned his head to listen, then said, "Press."

"Fast."

"They were at the clinic, saw Romero and company leave with us. How's the kid?"

"She's not going to make it," I told him.

"Don't talk like that, you don't know that."

Lozano didn't know what he was talking about, but there was no fire in me to argue the point.

"You see anything?" he asked me.

"No."

"I'm not handling it; it's not my precinct."

"Fine."

"Maybe your friend did?" Lozano asked. "See something?"

"Maybe."

He pushed off the counter, saying, "I'll ask," and headed for Rubin. He walked carefully, as if disturbing the air in the ER meant the difference between life and death. Rubin and Natalie were against a wall, heads bent toward each other, and Rubin was speaking to her, softly. Dr. Faisall said something to Natalie, and after a moment Natalie nodded, said something in return. The doctor headed toward one of the pay phones on the wall.

The shouting outside died, and an orderly stuck her head around the door. "Can you give me a hand, here?"

she asked one of the uniforms. "They won't take no for an answer."

Fowler snapped, "Keep them out of here." The uniforms clutched, but Lozano nodded and they went out the door. As it shut a rumble of voices started, then snapped off as the latch clicked. Lozano resumed questioning Rubin, but he cast a sidelong glance at Fowler as the officers left the room. An Asian priest arrived, entered the Trauma Room without ceremony.

After a while, someone told me to take a seat.

I didn't.

Thirty-two minutes after we arrived at Bellevue the Trauma Room doors opened and from where I was standing I could see inside, and I knew what the doctor was going to say. He was a black man, well over six feet tall and very skinny, with his scrubs hanging off his shoulders and hips, barely held on by his bones. His hair was covered in a surgical cap, but his goggles, gloves, and mask were off, and as he came out he ran his hand across his forehead, smearing the beaded sweat there. He looked around and then said, "Felice?"

She came out of the alcove, Dale beside her. "Say it, Remy," Dr. Romero said.

"I'm sorry. We pronounced her at eight forty-eight. We did everything we could."

"I want to see her."

He nodded.

I went into the room after them.

She had been covered on the table, and the overhead lights cast harsh shadows in the folds of the sheet, shaped to Katie's body underneath. The floor under the table was littered with discarded wrappings, papers, gauze, tape, some bloody, some not. The rolling carts of shiny instruments weren't shiny, and the dishes the tools had sat in were dark at the bottom, surgical steel coated with body fluids. Clamps, forceps, scalpels, catheters, needles, saws, equipment now dirty with blood and bone stacked on other instruments in more carts. The room had become suddenly empty, and as the doctor and Felice looked at Katie's body, two people came in the other side of the room and began cleaning up. There was a second table, just like this one, but gleaming clean, with instruments ready to go.

Katie's hand jutted from under the sheet on my side. Not really her hand, just her fingers. She had been wearing pink nail polish, the color of bubble gum. A tube disappeared under the sheet by her hand.

Dr. Romero pulled the sheet back to look at her daughter's face. Someone had closed Katie's eyes. Felice put her hand on Katie's forehead, brushing hair back from where it had fallen across the girl's cheek. For a moment her fingers traced the bones in her daughter's face, touching the chubby cheeks and chin. She made a small noise, the sound of a caught animal, shook her head once as if to clear it, and now, stroking Katie's hair, kissed her forehead.

"I love you, sweetheart," she said. "I love you very much."

Then she replaced the sheet over Katie and turned to look at the doctor, who had remained silent and immobile during all of this. She started to say thank you, but couldn't. She took one step, then another.

We caught her before she hit the deck, and the doctor shouted for someone to bring in a stretcher. Together we lifted Dr. Romero onto it, sliding the gurney out into the hallway. As we came out another orderly was coming in, preparing to move Katie to the morgue. The ER speakers blared an impending arrival, traumatic arrest, ETA sixty seconds, and Remy let me go, turning back into the room, heading for the clean table, the next victim.

The doors shut behind him as he entered, and before they closed completely, I caught a glimpse of Katie being wheeled out of the room. Her hand had been tucked back under the sheet and with it the last evidence of her was gone, and all that remained was a cover for the dead and a stack of bloody surgical instruments needing to be sterilized.

CHAPTER ELEVEN

Dr. Romero was out for only three or four minutes, and for her sake, I was sorry it didn't last longer. She was regaining consciousness within a minute of the stretcher being placed against a wall.

Her glasses were off, safe in my hand, and without them to protect her eyes I could read everything in them when she began looking around. Confusion transforming into comprehension and then despair, all as she sat up, Dale helping her, and carefully swung her legs off the side of the stretcher.

"Don't get up yet," I said.

But I needn't have said anything. The sobs tore at her fiercely, muscle spasms that rocked the stretcher and made me fear she'd fall. The casters on the stretcher clicked with her tremors. She reached a hand toward me and for some reason I thought she wanted her glasses, but as I extended them to her she grabbed my wrist and pulled me in, using me as a support to pull herself to her feet, and then she was crying against me. Her shudders shifted into me, her wailing sobs and the pain in my chest getting stronger and stronger, fighting to be let out. No tears for me; I fought that back with everything I had left. No tears yet. Not now and not here, and not when Felice needed to hold on to something, when the something was me.

I couldn't think of anything else to do.

Amidst this and the noise of the ER came another sound, a mob of cameras and flashbulbs, and the sounds of the press being restrained. A door had opened, then closed again.

Natalie spoke in my ear. "We need to move her."

I nodded, not wanting to say anything.

Natalie spoke softly to Dale, telling him to find a route out and get a cab, have it waiting by the loading dock. He moved out of my periphery, and as he did so more movement caught my eye, Rubin coming in closer and something more.

"Sir, I want you to leave," I heard Fowler say. "Leave, now, or I'll have you brought in for harassment."

"I came to express my condolences," said Crowell.

My first instinct was to go for my gun, and my hand was halfway back before I remembered Rubin had it. Felice was turning, looking up at the sound of the voice, and I let her go to see him, standing inside the doors from the Walk-In Clinic, the eyes of the media pressed against the glass staring in. Crowell was wearing a light suit similar to the one I'd first seen him in, drab linen pants and a white shirt with a tan tie, holding his jacket over his arm like a butler waiting to dress his master. Fowler was approaching, Lozano and another officer with him, and as they did so the blond man beside Crowell took two steps forward. He did it with the air and posture of a bully.

It felt like I moved forward easily, as if I stepped on the air and not the ground, and as I moved I told Crowell what I was going to do to him, and why I was going to do it, but to recall the exact words is more than I can honestly do now. I wanted his blood and was going to get it, until Fowler grabbed me and Rubin grabbed me and Lozano grabbed me and everyone told me to calm down, to calm the fuck down.

Not that I didn't feel calm. I didn't feel anything but an almost arousing thrill at the terror in Jonathan Crowell's face as he backed up, slipping behind the other man.

"Atticus, stop it," said Rubin. "Stop it." He slipped in front of me, put both hands on my chest, and pushed back hard, and I stopped resisting but he didn't move me back.

"Scared?" I asked Crowell. "Terrified?"

"Stop it."

"Fucking coward," I said. "Your goon there can't protect you, Jonathan," I said. "You're a marked man. Your time is running out. You're going to die, and nothing you can do will stop that. You happy? You like what you've created? You took a life today, a young woman who could never hurt anyone. Are you proud? How can you fucking sleep at night?"

"Atticus, that's enough." Rubin pushed harder, once, sending me back off his hands until we separated, and I caught my balance, straightened.

"Yeah, that's enough," I said.

Crowell was behind his man, looking out from around the other's blond hair. The blond looked like a beaten pit bull, ready to put the bite on someone, and although I knew it wouldn't happen here, I desperately wanted it to be me. Crowell wasn't saying anything, and Lozano was approaching him, speaking softly, saying that he had some questions that Crowell and Mr. Rich should answer.

"This is not what I have ever been about," Crowell told Lozano. "I am for life and have always been opposed to murder. This is a tragedy.

"I wanted to express my condolences," he said again.

Dr. Romero said: "You wanted to do nothing of the sort. You're here for the reporters, trying to make yourself look big." She walked toward him, Natalie right on her, and for a moment the division seemed perfect, everybody else incidental. Crowell and Rich on one side, Romero and Natalie on the other.

"You're not big. You're nothing," Felice said softly. "You killed my daughter, and you claim to work in the name of God. You did all of this to be big, and all you are is small and narrow and scared. So don't pretend you care what happened to me today, and don't pretend to care about my daughter. Because I hold you responsible. Kodiak is right, you're a murderer and you're scared. Hide behind your speeches, lie as best you can, but you know the truth, and you know this is your work.

"Tiny little man, nothing little man. You call me a butcher and you took a true life today. How can you even compare the two? Go away, little man. Go away and try to make yourself big again."

She stopped in his face, looking up at him, tear tracks shimmering on her and power roaring in her, and nobody could say anything. Crowell's mouth was open as he looked at her, but he didn't even seem to be breathing. Then Natalie took Dr. Romero's arm and turned her, coming eye to eye with Rich, brushing him with an elbow, and the two women walked out of the room.

Rubin and I followed, heading out the door and back to the loading dock.

CHAPTER TWELVE

She was standing in the hall, just beyond the door, facing us. She had raven black hair about her shoulders, almost blue where the light caught it, accentuating the paleness of her skin. She was at least as tall as I, and slim, with strength in her shoulders and a beautiful oval face, strong-jawed with a narrow chin and a small mouth with full lips, and very blue eyes. Both her ears were pierced several times, small hoops and studs, with one hoop high in the cartilage on her left ear. Another hoop, thinner than the rest, was through her left nostril.

Not a reporter, I thought.

Her leather biker jacket was open, and she had a white tank top on beneath it, tucked into faded blue jeans. Her feet were in a pair of well-worn Doc Martens.

Definitely not a reporter, I thought.

The blue eyes flicked over each of us, then settled on me, and she said, "Kodiak?"

"Not now," I said, and continued down the hall.

"Natalie, tell him who I am," she said.

Natalie said, "This is a bad time, Bridgett."

Bridgett said, "This won't sit."

"Later."

"I'll come with you," Bridgett said.

"Like hell," I said.

She fell into step with us, on my right. "I'm a PI," Bridgett said to me. "I've been hired to help you, to investigate the threats."

"By who?" I asked.

Natalie answered that one. "Dr. Faisall wanted an investigator, asked me for a recommendation."

"And I appreciate it," Bridgett said, moving up in front of me and neatly cutting my peripheral vision. "I need to talk to you about Crowell."

"If you don't stop blocking my vision, I'll break your arm," I said.

"Forgive me," she said. "I assume somebody was blocking your vision this morning, too?"

On my left, Natalie visibly flinched.

"Who the fuck do you think you are?" I said.

"Bridgett Logan," she said, pulling her wallet and holding it out in front of me. "I'm with Agra and Donnovan Investigations. My PI license, see? Want to know what's on my driver's license, too? It says I'm twenty-eight, six feet one, my birthday's November ninth, and my eyes are blue."

I said to Natalie, "Keep going, I'll catch up. Keep your radio on." Then I stopped and put a bloodstained arm out to block Logan's progress, and we faced each other for a few seconds while I stood her against the wall. I got a whiff of shampoo and mint off her.

"I need to talk to you about Crowell," she said.

"Not now."

"Then I'll come with you," she said. "I'm working for the clinic."

"No, you won't," I said. "And I don't care if you were hired by the whole governing board of NARAL. I've got a grieving principal to secure and people to debrief, and I can't do it if I'm playing Q and A with private eyes."

"Then I'll come with you and we can do it after," Logan said.

The frustration and rage I felt at that moment were almost unbearable. Here was this woman showing up and implying it was negligence on my part that Katie was dead, having the gall to do it in front of Felice. And she just stood in front of me, eyes met to mine, no sign of backing off. The light caught on the niobium ring through her nostril, reflecting blue.

"They'll leave without us," she said.

"Uh-huh."

She shook her head, then reached in a pocket for a roll of Life Savers. She pulled one into her mouth with her teeth, never taking her eyes from mine, then offered me the roll. Pep-O-Mint. "Have a sweet, stud," Logan said. "Lighten up."

I ignored the roll. "Why don't you just scurry on home, or something, and I'll contact you when I'm ready."

She straightened her back a little more, drawing up to her full height. "Scurry?" she said softly.

I figured that the cab had left by then, so I moved my arm and turned my back to her, started walking to the loading dock. She fell in on my right and asked, "Where'd they take the doctor?"

"I don't know."

"Some bodyguard," Logan said. "At this rate, you'll lose both of them."

I stopped again, and went face-to-face with her, angry enough that it showed. Her jaw tightened.

"This is the wrong time to be pushing me," I said quietly. "The absolute wrong time. My client just lost her daughter, and if you think that means business as usual to me, you're walking with the wrong crowd." I pointed back to the ER. "Crowell's that way, maybe you'd be happier working for him. Otherwise, go away, now. I'll contact you when I am ready. Not a moment before."

I turned from Bridgett Logan and headed down the hall.

The rest of the morning was a confusion after I rendezvoused with the others—a ragged collage of statements given to the police and the Feds, of movement and more movement, trying to find Felice a safe place to grieve. Rubin finally suggested using his studio, and by one that afternoon we had settled Dr. Romero in.

The studio Rubin used was a joint venture with some other artists he knew, an attempt to find work space without having to pay Manhattan's ridiculous prices for privacy. Each artist paid a quarter of the rent, they all had open access, and they all respected each other's space. It was nothing more than a large loft in Chelsea, broken into four roughly equal quadrants. On the north side of the room were four large windows that looked out over the street, and Dale immediately went to those to double-check our security.

The room had an adjoining bathroom and kitchenette, but that was the extent of the space. Dr. Romero moved to Rubin's corner, spiritless and disinterested in what we were doing. After our departure from the hospital she had crumbled again, ignoring us, returning to the pain inside.

I helped her settle, spreading the army blanket that Rubin kept with his equipment. If she wanted to lie down, at least she could be almost comfortable.

"I want to go home," Felice said.

"We can't," I told her. "It isn't secure." Her apartment would have to be cleaned up, I knew, and she shouldn't have to be the one to do it. The bloodstains would probably never come out of the carpet.

"It's my home," she said.

"I know, Felice. I'm sorry."

She turned, looked at me for the first time since we left the hospital. "What did you say?" she asked.

"We can't take you home. I'm sorry."

The blow came up so fast I didn't even think about moving, and then my head was ringing and she was drawing her right hand back again. Her voice was as smooth and cold as a sheet of arctic ice.

"You bastard," Felice said, slapping me again. "You bastard, you're sorry?" Her hand flew again, and I didn't flinch, just felt the blow echo inside my head, and then she was timing her slaps to the words, each one hitting for punctuation, emphasis, and a terrible anger. "You liar, you bastard liar, you said you'd keep us safe, you said—"

Natalie was between us suddenly, and I stepped back, feeling my left cheek burn and blood leak into my mouth. Felice tried to push past Natalie, explaining deliberately that I was a liar, that I had lied, that I had killed her baby. Natalie took her by the shoulders and told Felice to stop.

"Bastard," Felice said, and then pulled away from Natalie. She sat on a stool, looking at the wall Rubin had painted with spray-painted scenes, cops and Latin Kings and life on the mean streets.

Natalie turned to me. She said, "Sentinel has a safe apartment. We can send Dale to get the car and then move her. You want me to call my father?"

Felice was smoking, and that was the only way I could tell she was breathing.

"Atticus? You want me to call my father?"

I nodded, starting to move toward Felice. Natalie put up an arm and shook her head and I stopped. When she was sure I wouldn't move, she went to the phone and started dialing, drawing her red hair back to place the receiver against her ear.

My cheek still burned, and I touched it again, looking at each of my people. Ostensibly, we seemed to be holding up all right, keeping our grief separate from the work at hand.

But Dale was checking the window over and over again, and he's not the nervous type. And Rubin was now sitting on a stool, staring at his bloody hands. And Natalie was trying hard to keep her voice under control while she spoke to her father.

Little things.

"Rubin," I said. "Go get cleaned up."

He kept looking at his hands. Then he nodded, slowly found some spare clothes under one of his palettes, and went into the bathroom. I heard the shower start.

Natalie hung up the phone. "Somebody's already using it," she said. "Some damn brat from Saudi Arabia, and my father won't move him. We can get it sometime tomorrow."

"Did he see Selby?"

"He was at her place when the news broke the story about Katie. Says that Selby took it hard, that she wanted to go to the hospital to see—"

From the window, Dale said, "We've got a watcher."

Both Natalie and I immediately went to him.

"Green Porsche parked on the corner right after we got here," Dale said, indicating it. "A guy got out, wearing a baseball cap, headed around the corner." He looked at me. "Took him five minutes, but he doubled back, just came into the building."

"Carrying?" I said.

"Hands were clear."

"Pistol, probably," Natalie said.

I nodded, drew my weapon. "Dale, keep watching, use the radio." Then I went to the bathroom door and knocked on it, saying, "Get dressed and get out here. Dale needs backup."

Natalie was waiting for me by the door, her Glock out. I looked back at where Romero was still seated. She hadn't moved.

I turned the bolt on the door soundlessly, and Natalie grabbed one of the handles, prepared to slide it back on its runners. The door was metal and covered in flaking gray paint. I backed to the other side of the door and went down to a crouch, then gave her a nod.

She ran the door back with one quick motion and I rolled out as soon as there was room, seeing motion at the end of the hall and coming up with my weapon. I had sighted the dot on the end of my barrel to Bridgett Logan's throat before I recognized her.

Both her hands came up immediately. "Friendly, friendly!" she said.

She had put on a Yankee cap, piled her hair under it, and was sitting on the floor beside the stairs. I kept my gun on her, hearing Natalie move behind me.

"Are you fucking insane?" Natalie asked. "You could've gotten yourself shot."

Logan didn't answer her, keeping her hands up and her eyes on me.

After a moment, Natalie said, "It's all right, Atticus."

I released the handle on my gun, uncocking it, letting air leak out of my nose. Then I got up and holstered my weapon, saying, "Go away." I went back inside.

She followed me in, Natalie behind her. "Kodiak," Bridgett Logan said. "We need to talk."

"I told you, when I'm ready."

Natalie slid the door shut and locked it, saying, "Did you follow us?"

"Him," Bridgett said, gesturing at me. She turned to me and said, "You made it damn hard to do, too."

Dale and Rubin were around Romero, and I gave them a short nod. They backed off the doctor, but not a lot, still wary of Logan.

She said, "Nobody was following me."

"You're certain?" I asked.

"Yes," Bridgett said.

"Good." I pointed at the door.

She shook her head. "You've got me whether you like it or not. I've been hired to assist and to lead an independent investigation, and I need your help." Lowering her voice, she said, "I'm not leaving until we've got things squared, Kodiak. You'll have to throw me out, and I guarantee you, I won't make that easy."

I watched Dr. Romero. She smoked, staring at the floor.

"Are we all right here?" I asked Natalie.

"We're fine for now," she said. "Just go with Bridgett, Atticus. Get home, clean up, answer her questions. Three of us here will be fine."

Logan didn't say anything.

"Okay," I said. "Fine, let's go."

It was Logan's Porsche, a forest-green turbocharged 911 Carrera with a sunroof and whale tail. She disarmed the alarm and unlocked my door, ushering me into the vehicle with definite pride.

"Where am I taking you?" she said, turning the stereo on. Sisters of Mercy blared, and she adjusted the volume to a low roar.

"Thompson, off Bleecker," I said.

She nodded. We hit a light and she pulled her roll of Life Savers again, dropped three in her mouth one after the other, crunching each. Then she killed the roll, popping the last one, sucking this time. She tossed the empty wrapper over her shoulder into the tiny backseat. "Oral fixation," she said.

I nodded and continued to look out the window.

The light changed and we started rolling again. She drove quickly, but with absolute control, using the Porsche perfectly. She used its speed, too, edging eighty at one point on Broadway.

"Have you talked to Fowler or Lozano?" she asked.

"Not since making statements."

"The CSU's report of both the apartment and the shooter's position came back," she told me. "The FBI's leading on the case. They triangulated back to a point of origin for the shots.''

''And?''

''Second-floor fire escape landing. Looks like someone came down from the roof and took the shot from the landing on the second floor. Witnesses have given a description of the shooter: white male, blond or light brown hair, approximately six feet tall. No eye color, strong, broad-shouldered. They're continuing the canvass.''

''Sounds like Barry,'' I said.

''He's a little short for it,'' Bridgett said. ''I'm thinking it's the guy who was with Crowell at the hospital.''

''Rich.''

''NYPD is checking their alibis,'' she said.

''Good for them,'' I said and was silent for the rest of the drive.

I picked up the mail in the lobby, then led Bridgett Logan up the six flights of stairs to the apartment I shared with Rubin. I put her in the kitchen and told her I was going to shower and change.

''Mind if I use your phone?'' she asked, removing her jacket and hanging it on the back of the chair.

''Why not?'' I said and went into my room where I stripped, threw my clothes in a corner, then grabbed my robe. As I went down the hall to the bathroom Bridgett stopped dialing long enough to turn and watch me.

''Can I make coffee or anything?''

''Whatever you want,'' I said and went to take my shower.

The blood on my hands had dried and flaked off, and the two chances I'd had previously to use a bathroom had gotten me only so clean. I stayed under the water for twenty minutes, scrubbing hard, then soaking up the steam. The hot shower felt good. It was midafternoon now, and the day was only getting longer, and I only wanted it to end.

After I had dressed in some clean jeans and a decent shirt, food became a sudden priority. Bridgett was still seated at the table where I had left her.

"Talked to NYPD," she said. "They've got a make on the weapon."

"You want a sandwich?"

She shook her head. "Remington M-seven hundred, thirty-ought-six," she said.

I got two bottles of beer from the fridge and held one out to her. She looked at it and at me, then nodded. I opened both of them, handed one to her, then started to make myself a sandwich.

"They found two intact slugs at Romero's apartment," Bridgett said. "If they find the weapon they'll be able to make the match."

I nodded, and layered mustard on one of my slices of bread. I put the sandwich together, tore a paper towel to use as a place mat, and set my meal on the table. The indicator light on the answering machine was blinking, so I pressed "play" and then cleaned up the kitchen as the messages ran.

Eight messages from reporters, one from Alison, who said, "Atticus? Oh, God, I just heard. Are you okay? I don't know where to reach you and I don't want to use your pager, so if you get this, give me a call, okay? I'm at work until five, and then I'll be in all night. I'm so sorry."

I sat back at the table and picked up my sandwich.

"Significant other?" Bridgett asked.

I nodded.

"You going to call her?"

"I'm going to eat first," I said. The sandwich was good, lean pastrami and thin slices of provolone. I'd found some crisp lettuce on a back shelf and added that to it. I was almost finished when I tasted it.

Syrup.

Maple syrup.

Bridgett asked, "Are you okay?"

I shook my head, gagging, rose to the sink and I spat. The beer didn't kill the taste, even when I rinsed my mouth out with it twice. She had risen, now standing beside me at the sink, and as I hunched over, Bridgett put a hand on my back as I coughed and my eyes clouded with tears. I was certain I was going to vomit; then I was fine and standing up, catching my breath.

"Are you okay?" she asked again.

I shook my head. "Syrup," I said.

"I'm sorry?"

"Katie had waffles for breakfast." I blew a long breath out. "We did CPR on her, Rubin and me. I should warn him."

She hesitated, then put her hand on my back again. I stiffened and she withdrew it, going back to her seat at the table.

For a while I just stood at the sink, thinking about it. Finally I said, "What do you want?"

"I want to see Croweil and I want you to come with me," Bridgett said.

"Why?"

"Two reasons. First, I understand you scared the crap out of him at the hospital. Lozano says that Crowell was in fear for his life. Second, you were there when Katie died, and if he's got an ounce of conscience and he is responsible, he'll be hard-pressed to lie to your face."

"He's the last man I want to see right now."

She seemed to relax a bit, stretching her legs out in front of her with a sigh. She had long legs. "I know. If it's one of Crowell's people that did this, going to see him is a hell of a good way to shake things up."

I gave it a little more thought, then nodded. "Let me make a phone call first," I said. "I'll meet you at your car."

She rose and started for the door. Then she stopped and

looked back at me. "That crack I made at the hospital," she said. "That was cruel. I owe you an apology."

I didn't say anything and she shook her head slightly, then said, "I'll be downstairs."

After she shut the door, I called Alison at work. A co-worker picked up her phone and told me that she was at lunch. I didn't leave a message.

Before leaving I put my weapon back on, feeling the weight of the gun in my hand before saddling it to my hip. On my desk was a manila folder, swollen with copies of all the threats Felice and the clinic had received since Common Ground had been announced. I took that as well, wondering how Crowell would react to them.

Going down the stairs I realized that if Bridgett Logan was right about how Crowell reacted to me, perhaps there was more Common Ground between him and Felice than I had realized.

Both knew fear.

CHAPTER THIRTEEN

"How much do you know about Sword of the Silent?" Bridgett Logan asked me as she guided her Porsche uptown. I had a private address for Crowell on Central Park West in the low nineties, and we had a ways to go before we got there.

"Enough," I said. "They formed in late '88, shortly after Randal Terry and Operation: Rescue made it big in Atlanta. Crowell has boasted that their national membership is over one hundred thousand, but that's probably ten times higher than it really is. They target a clinic in a given city and then use terror tactics to intimidate both patients and personnel. Since the Federal Access to Clinic Entrances legislation was passed in '94 they've had to cool off a bit and get smarter about it, but they're still doing it."

"What kind of tactics?"

"Special Agent Fowler gave me copies of almost fifty

arrest reports from the last six months or so, all of them for suspected SOS members," I said. "They range from illegal possession of a weapon, menacing, stalking, to two members in California who are awaiting trial for attempted murder. Another member in North Dakota is being sought for questioning in the death of a doctor there."

"And none of that has ever been tied back to Crowell?"

"Not as far as I know."

"So he's either very smart or very lucky."

"It would make me a lot happier if he was lucky," I said.

"I'll bet."

I cringed as she shot the Porsche through a collapsing vise made by two cabs on either side of us. Somehow, we made it through the gap unscathed. Bridgett chuckled. "Car like this," she said, "you've got to drive aggressively or it gets mad at you."

"It's very nice," I said.

"Nice?" Bridgett said, her eyes going wide. "Nice? This is a Twin Turbo Porsche Carrera nine-eleven, over four hundred horses of power, all-wheel drive, the works. This animal tops out at over one hundred and eighty miles per hour, zero to sixty in three point seven seconds, and stops on a dime leaving you wanting a cigarette.

"This car is pure sex, stud. It is not 'nice.' "

I let that sink in, looking around at the leather interior, listening to the engine growl underneath the music from the tape deck. It was an amazing car.

"You're a PI?" I asked.

"That's what the license says."

"How the hell can you afford a car like this? Are you crooked?"

Bridgett grinned, flashed white teeth at me. "It's my inheritance from my ma," she said.

"Your mother left you a Porsche."

"My mother was in coach class on a seven-thirty-seven

that crashed and burned in Cincinnati," she said. "She was well insured."

"I'm sorry," I said.

"Yeah, it sucks. Two years now." She found a new roll of Life Savers in a pocket, tore off the top with her teeth, and pulled one into her mouth. These were Wint-O-Green. "What do you know about Crowell?"

"He's in his early fifties, says he went to Harvard Divinity," I said. "I doubt that but haven't checked. Fowler says he's got a record, an arrest in '75 in Wichita for A and B against a woman who worked at the local CBS affiliate. Charges were dismissed. Arrested again three years later in Indiana for firebombing a clinic there. Spent three years inside. He's written two books, both about abortion and the collapse of the American morality."

"A Renaissance man," Bridgett said.

"I suppose."

She didn't say anything else until we had parked across from Crowell's apartment building. Then she killed the engine, and looked at the folder I'd taken from the apartment. "What's that?"

"Copies of the threats sent to the clinic," I said, and handed it to her. She began leafing through them as I said, "They're in chronological order, back to when the conference was announced."

She nodded without looking up. "You going to let Romero go?"

"I have to," I said.

Bridgett looked at me. "They didn't get her this morning, they'll try again, right? They'll try for her there."

"Probably."

"Then don't let her go."

"I can't forbid her from doing anything. I can only advise her against it."

"Hell of a job you've got," she said, and looked back at the letters. I looked across the street, watching the traffic in front of the building.

Bridgett made small noises to herself while reading, whether of amusement or disgust, I wasn't sure. Finally, she said, "There's no sexist like a holy sexist. How do you think these are done?" She gestured at the letters.

"Somebody, perhaps several somebodys, sits around a keyboard and types them up. I think they're done in committee, but I don't know why I think that. They print it out and copy it, destroy the original, then drop the copy in the mail."

"They probably delete the file from the computer, too," she said.

I started to agree, then stopped, and looked carefully at the man entering the apartment building.

"That's Barry," I said.

Bridgett turned to look. "No shit? I wonder where he's been."

"In for questioning?"

She shook her head. "They were done with them hours ago." She took the keys out of the ignition and opened her door. "Coming?"

I nodded and took the file, then got out of the Porsche and followed her across the street. She led without looking for traffic, forcing a Mazda to swerve out of her way. She waited for me on the sidewalk, set the alarm on the Porsche from her remote, then slipped her arm around my waist, and said, "Let's go, stud."

We walked right past the doorman, Bridgett giggling at me and saying, "You're so nasty!" She slipped one hand under my shirt and then licked my ear. The doorman politely averted his gaze, and she clung to me while we waited for the elevator. Inside the car, she punched 14 and, when the doors closed, released me, taking the file with her. "Mind if I hold this?"

I shrugged. "You lick well," I told her.

"And not only ears," she said. "But don't get any ideas."

Crowell was in 14J, and Bridgett Logan knocked on the door twice, hard. We waited patiently, side by side, as we were examined through the eyehole. Then the door opened and Clarence Barry was standing there, a film of sweat on his forehead. He still had on his windbreaker, and for a moment I thought he looked alarmed.

Barry barely acknowledged Bridgett, working hard to intimidate me through posture and eye contact. We locked each other up and his hand drifted a fraction toward the gun on his hip, then returned to neutral at his waist.

"Hello, cocksucker," he said to me. "You're a dead man."

"Just back from hiding the rifle?" I asked him.

Bridgett said, "Boys, boys, not in the hall."

Barry ignored her. "I'm going to fucking do your ass, then I'll waste this bitch," he said.

He was making a serious threat, he meant what he was saying, and the viciousness of his words surprised me. It's frightening to be told by a man carrying a gun that he's going to kill you. But that fear went quickly as our stares lengthened, and suddenly I couldn't take him seriously at all, this childish petulance, the bruises on his face where he had hit the pavement with me on his back, his nose broken from that impact. He was only an ape in a suit, and it wasn't a particularly nice suit, at that. He'd have had better luck trying to intimidate me while sitting on the toilet.

Bridgett said, "My name's Bridgett Logan. I was wondering if I could speak to Mr. Crowell."

"He's busy." He had an accent, hard Appalachian, and when he spoke he moved his right hand over his mouth, maybe reassuring himself that it had indeed worked. A small tattoo of a dagger, green with age, folded between his thumb and forefinger.

"He'll see us. We're here from the LifeCare clinic. We want to ask him a few questions."

"He's not here, bitch."

"Thought you said he was busy?" I said.

"He's busy not being here," he said to me. Then he smiled, pleased with the inventiveness of his answer.

"Mr. Crowell," Bridgett called. "Can I talk to you?"

For a moment we all stood in silence, waiting, then, as Barry started to close the door, a voice said, "Who else is out there?"

"The bodyguard," Barry said.

"Show them in, Clarence."

Clarence would have preferred to show us out, preferably through the window. Somehow he restrained his baser urge and opened the door again. Bridgett went right past him into an open living room, but I waited a moment, simply smiling at Barry. The hate in his eyes was delicious; the resentment foamed inside him. He wanted so badly to hurt me and his master wouldn't let him. I followed Bridgett.

Jonathan Crowell stood in front of a big black leather recliner, and he motioned Bridgett and me to the big black leather sofa that sat opposite it. He gave Bridgett a good look-over before doing anything else, and she gave him one of her own.

"I trust you're not here to beat me up?" Crowell finally asked me.

"Depends on what happens next, I suppose," I said.

He smiled at me, and I thought that I was wrong, that he and Felice had nothing in common at all. He sank back into his recliner and asked, "Then what can I do for you?"

"Where's Rich?" I sat down beside Bridgett.

Crowell raised his eyebrows at me. "I have no idea."

"I got the impression at the hospital that he was your bodyguard."

"No, Mr. Kodiak. I have no need for anyone like you."

"Really? Then what does Rich do?"

His forced gentility slipped. "He's our Personnel Director. And before you ask, I'll tell you exactly what I told the
NYPD and the FBI. Mr. Rich, Mr. Barry, and myself were
having breakfast with an SOS chapter in Yonkers this
morning. None of us murdered little Katie Romero."

"Well, none of you pulled the trigger, at least," I said.

Bridgett shot me a look designed to drop charging ele-
phants. I gave her my best turns-knees-into-water smile. It
didn't work. She said easily to Crowell, "We have some
questions we're hoping you can answer."

Barry came around from behind me, sliding around the
room like an oil spill, shutting the doors and checking for
traps. He moved to stand behind Crowell's chair, trying to
stare at both Bridgett and me at the same time. After a
while he gave up on Bridgett and concentrated solely on
me.

"I've already spoken to the authorities," Crowell said.
He smoothed his tie carefully down along his chest, assur-
ing himself that it was entirely centered. The tie was silk,
striped blue and white on a green background. His shirt
was ivory-white and heavily starched, with French cuffs,
and tucked neatly into tan pleated pants. On crossed feet
hung black leather shoes with pristine soles, as if he had
never touched the ground in them. According to his manner, that was precisely what he wanted you to think.

"This is independent," Bridgett told him. "We've got
some questions about the letters Dr. Romero and the
clinic have received."

Crowell took a sip of mineral water from a bottle on the
table beside his chair and said, to me, "I don't imagine I'll
be of any more help to you than I was to that Mexican."

"Detective Lozano, you mean?" I asked.

Crowell nodded and turned his head to look out the
window at the view across Central Park.

"He's Cuban," I said.

He waved a hand in dismissal. The hand was clean and
sported a class ring from Harvard on one finger. I won-

dered how much it had cost him. "I don't know anything about the letters," Crowell said.

Bridgett opened the folder and set each letter out, chronologically, on the coffee table before Crowell. It took a minute and all the space on the table, and Crowell made a sour face to pass the time. Barry never moved; I'm not certain he even blinked. When Bridgett was finished Crowell looked at them briefly, then out the window. "I've never seen these before."

"Didn't Detective Lozano show them to you?" Bridgett asked.

He considered that, then looked at me again. "Yes, yes he did. And the FBI men, too. I meant, I've never seen the originals."

"So you have seen these before?" Bridgett pressed, the glint of a very sharp edge in her voice.

Crowell stood and walked to the window and stood there, admiring the expensive view. At least, I thought he was admiring the view. He pointed. "The Jewish Museum is over there." He lowered his arm and waited. When he got no response from us he waited some more, then said, "It's all just decay down there. You do know that, don't you? This city is only a small part of this country, but it embodies everything in this nation. Everything here can be found between Maine and Alaska. And it's all falling apart."

"So you have seen these before, Mr. Crowell?" Bridgett repeated. The edge in her voice was clearer now, and the muscles in her jaw tightened after she spoke.

Without turning Crowell said, "And it is falling apart from the heart, from the center. As this city is the center of this nation, this nation is falling apart. As the family is falling apart, so is this city, corrupted, diminished by parasites who refuse God's law. The true values of the American family have been distorted by all those people who now live here, groups with their perverted special interests and their selfish, hedonistic concerns. They are slowly tugging the thread that built this city, unraveling it, and thus the country, leaving us a ruin that may never be repaired."

It was as if he spoke to a huge audience beyond the pane of glass and had forgotten we were in the room. Barry was staring at his back, probably expecting Crowell to sprout wings and a halo.

"I'm right, you know that," Crowell continued. "You never hear about a Christian being arrested for dealing crack. Godless is what we have become, forsaking the Word for our own petty delights. And unless we find God again, we shall be destroyed." He turned and his eyes rested on Bridgett. "Unless our women understand their duty, we shall be destroyed." He looked at me. "Unless our men lead the way, we shall be destroyed."

He turned back to the window and raised both his arms so he looked, in silhouette, like Christ on the Cross. He rolled his head back and said, nearly sobbing, "Unless each and every baby killer is stopped, each and every factory of death is dismantled, we shall all be destroyed. Unless we stop the holocaust of the unborn innocents, we shall all be destroyed. There can be no rest, no hope, no salvation for any of us, until we stop this mad butchery of our own children."

It was grand theater. He didn't move, rigid in his own imagined crucifixion. Bridgett shifted on the couch, making the leather sigh, the tension coiled in her, looking for an out.

Considering the scene Crowell was playing, his apartment was remarkably secular. Only one religious artifact, a large stainless-steel cross wrapped in barbed wire, hung on the wall over the television cabinet. He had two shelves loaded with books, a large easy chair for reading beside them. A well-shined brass lamp stood beside the chair. On the floor beside the coffee table, where Bridgett had moved them to lay out the letters, were hardcover copies of his two books, *Abortuaries and the Death of America* and *Innocence Slaughtered*. Neither copy looked to have ever been opened. I picked up one and looked at the photograph on the back. Crowell looked out sternly at the camera. I put the book back on the floor. The carpet was slate gray, as empty of feeling as the apartment.

Clarence Barry beamed at Crowell's back. Still no wings.

The only emotion worth speaking of was Crowell's, whose arms must have been aching something fierce.

Bridgett Logan said, "So . . . your answer is no?"

Crowell lowered his arms gracefully and spun slowly on the Italian-shod ball of his right foot to face us. "You see," he said, "it is not that I want the blight purged from us with fire and wrath. It is simply that the blight must be purged, and if fire and wrath are the only instruments for the task, then they, of course, must be used.

"Our Lord does not act alone. He acts through us."

Bridgett found her roll of Life Savers and began chewing on one.

"No compromise?" I asked.

He smiled thinly. "One does not bargain with God, Mr. Kodiak. If we are moved to act, then act we must and by any means at our disposal."

"Even if those means are murder?" Bridgett asked, looking at the roll of candy in her hand.

"Man's law is nothing. God's law is supreme. Man can only mock God. Man mocks God's laws all the time. Man means nothing if Man does not live according to God's law," Crowell said. He said it to me. Not once since we had started speaking had he looked at Bridgett. When he chose to answer her, he relayed the answer through me as if I were her interpreter.

"Correct me if I'm way off base here, but isn't murder against God's law?" she asked.

"That is precisely the point," he said to me.

Bridgett's shoulders shifted, and I expected her to throw her roll of candy at Crowell, but she didn't. Instead, she ate another Life Saver.

I asked, "You plan to attend the Common Ground summit, don't you?"

He hesitated for a moment, then nodded.

"The entire purpose of the summit is to find compromise," I said. "By attending, won't you be participating in the mockery you've just so eloquently denounced?"

"We all have a right to speak," Crowell said to me. I think he liked it that I had called him eloquent. "I would be more than a fool if I let such an opportunity to spread my message pass me by without seizing it."

"And that Katie Romero's death has made you all the more visible has nothing to do with it?" Bridgett asked.

"I am not an opportunist," he told me. "I am a servant of Our Lord."

"Your rhetoric's lovely," I said. "Really, it is. And the theological aspects of the debate are fascinating, too, but really immaterial, and neither answers our questions. We're asking you if you know who is threatening Dr. Romero."

He returned to his seat and picked up his mineral water. "I have answered your questions, Mr. Kodiak. But, as God's law obviously means nothing to you, I'll explain it to you clearly. You are not a Christian, and I should know better than to try to appeal to you as one."

"Or to me," Bridgett said. Crowell ignored her. She pulled a new pack of Life Savers from her pocket and began unwrapping them, dropping the foil on the carpet. Barry started at the offense, but remained in place, looking as if he'd love to snap her neck.

"I do not know who is sending those letters," Crowell said. "And if I did, I do not think I would tell you. I do not know who murdered Dr. Romero's poor daughter, but if I did know that, I certainly would not tell you; I would tell the police. And as for the conference, yes, I believe Common Ground is a mockery, and it will surely fail. And that, to completely answer your previous question, is my entire reason for going. I will bring down the house by speaking the truth."

"Did you tell this to the police and FBI?" Bridgett asked.

"I told them something similar," he said to me.

"He told them something similar," I said to Bridgett. "But he didn't tell them the same thing. Because knowledge that a crime is going to be committed, and not telling the police about it, that's called being an accessory."

"It's called being an accessory," Bridgett told Crowell. She offered him a red Life Saver.

"*If* I did know, I said. But I do not." Crowell smiled.

"You wouldn't tell me if someone was planning to murder Dr. Romero?" I asked.

"We're talking about letters, not murder."

"No," I said. "We're talking about murder. Is that what happened? Somebody thought they were shooting Felice and murdered Katie by mistake?"

"Your implication is that I know who shot the girl," Crowell said.

"Very good. That's exactly my implication," I said, leaning forward.

Barry tensed to move, but Crowell kept his eyes on me, and if he was intimidated, he didn't show it. "This interrogation is over," he said evenly. "I have business to attend to."

"The letters come from your group," Bridgett said. "Someone in Sword of the Silent is mailing these letters, possibly several people. That means that someone you are responsible for wants to stop abortion, and thinks that killing Dr. Romero is the way to do it. And maybe that someone murdered Katie Romero by accident this morning. Doesn't that bother you at all?"

For the first time since we'd walked into the room, Crowell's eyes rested on her. Very carefully he said, "If I were to subscribe to your theory, young lady, then my only possible answer would be, yes, it does. Just as it should bother you and Mr. Kodiak that Felice Romero has murdered thousands of preborn children this year. If I am culpable in this thing, then you are equally culpable in that."

He looked at his watch. It had a gold band and looked exceptionally expensive. "You can show yourselves out," Crowell said. "And I expect I'll see you on Saturday, Mr. Kodiak. At the conference."

I helped Bridgett gather up the letters and then we stood and Crowell stood, and nobody offered anybody a hand. We walked to the door and Clarence Barry cut in front of us to open it.

As I went out the door after Bridgett, Barry leaned in to my ear and hissed, "You're dead and you're mine."

The sky had filled with clouds the color of fresh bruises. Bridgett strode right across the street, again ignoring the traffic, and I thought she was going to her car, but instead she went for the stone wall separating the rest of Manhattan on the west from Central Park. She perched on the wall and searched her pockets with one hand, waving me toward her with the other. She started in on another candy, offering me one from the roll. I took it and felt my mouth suddenly cool.

"Tasty, huh?"

"Why don't you smoke?"

"Can't stand cigarettes," she said. "Don't mind the occasional cigar, though, if it's from Cuba."

I looked up at Crowell's windows.

"Well?"

"They're up to something. You didn't catch it, but your boyfriend in there looked more than a little worried when his boss said they had business to do." She looked up at the sky and squinted. "Looks like rain."

"What now?" I asked.

"Crowell's going out, you heard him say it. I want to follow him."

"Good luck. He'll make you the second he leaves. You're not exactly inconspicuous."

She tapped her nose ring. "You'd be surprised."

"If he starts on foot, you're in trouble."

"This is Manhattan. There's always a cab when you need one. It's the law."

"You trying to get rid of me?"

"*You* didn't want anything to do with *me*, remember? You head back to your people, check on Romero." She fished another pocket and came out with a business card and a pen. She scribbled something on the back, then handed it to me. "My home number's on there. Give me a call tonight." The card had Agra and Donnovan on it, her name below, and Investigator beneath that. The agency's address was listed on Fifth, and there were two phone numbers, office and car. She'd written her home number on the back.

"You really should have a backup," I said.

"I'll be fine."

"You're that good?"

"I'm better," Bridgett Logan said, and she wasn't joking.

The discussion became academic because at that moment Crowell and Barry appeared in the doorway, stopping to chastise the doorman. It looked like Crowell was doing most of the chastising, and they didn't seem to have noticed us across the street. Some of the angry notes Crowell hit made it through the traffic to us.

Bridgett saw them when I did and spun on her backside, dropping over the wall and into the park. I felt like an idiot as I followed her. We sat for a moment with our backs to the stone. An empty bottle of malt liquor dug into my leg. At least it wasn't broken glass. I hoped I wasn't sitting in dog shit.

"Should I call you Rockford or Spenser, maybe?" I asked.

"Eat me." She turned and stuck her nose over the wall,

dropping the folder with the letters in it on my lap. An elderly black woman in a pretty summer dress stopped and stared at us as she walked an Airedale along the path. I smiled at her. She smiled at me. The Airedale licked its nose.

"Nice day," I said to her.

She nodded and said, "Looks like rain, though." They continued on.

"Well?" I asked Bridgett.

"They're done with the doorman and now they're talking to each other out front. They didn't see us."

"Oh, goody."

"Wait—wait—a Cadillac just pulled up."

I peeked over the wall beside her. The driver's window was down and Rich was at the wheel. "The third man," I said.

"Looks like Rich," she said.

"Looks like Rich," I agreed.

Crowell opened the front passenger's door and got in. Barry shut the door for him.

I ducked back down as Bridgett lowered her nose and backed up on all fours a few feet until she could stand without being too obvious. "I'm going to go for my car," she said. "Follow Crowell."

"Better hurry."

"Call me, stud," she said, and took off up the path parallel to where she had parked the car. I watched her vault the wall and disappear.

I sat with the folder on my lap feeling stupid. Then I decided what the hell and took another peep over the wall. A bus had pulled up across the street, and I couldn't see either Crowell or Barry, and Bridgett's Porsche was disappearing to the south, so I stood up and brushed the seat of my pants off. They were damp, hopefully with nothing more offensive than water. The bus roared as it pulled away, and revealed no one recognizable in front of Crowell's building. Enough with this, I decided. She's the PI, let her do the tailing.

As I went over the wall and started up to the subway stop at Ninety-sixth Street, the sky opened. By the time I crossed at Ninety-fourth to catch the downtown track none of me was dry, and the folder had transformed into a limp cardboard sandwich. My glasses started to fog, my sneakers squished, and my pants clung to my legs, the seams chafing as I walked. The steps down to the train were cracked tile, slippery and treacherous. I pushed my token in and stepped up to the platform, listening to the water falling down the stairs. My hair stuck against my neck, dripping water down my back, and I shook my head to move things around, but it didn't do much good.

One corner of my shirt was not absolutely drenched, having been tucked in, and with it my glasses became functional again. After putting them back on I shot a look down the tunnel, trying to spot the advancing train. The tunnel was empty.

Waiting behind the yellow line, I looked across at the uptown platform and saw Barry leaning against a pylon, smoking. He was looking at his feet and as he shifted his glance around I turned, trying to conceal myself.

Uptown was the clinic. There was a stop on 135th, I knew; I'd been using it. My gut went tight, apprehensive. Bridgett was supposed to follow Crowell, and according to her, Barry hadn't been pleased about their going out for "business." The odds were he wasn't going to another prayer meeting. On top of that, Barry was a hard case, a son of a bitch, and I wasn't going to give him the chance to throw another bottle, to be party to the murder of another girl. I wasn't going to be scared off by his threats. That wasn't going to happen.

By the time I had concluded all of this, I was vaulting the exit turnstile, charging across the street to the uptown track. Vaulting was stupid, and I slipped when I landed, losing my balance and nearly cracking my head on the tile.

Overcompensating, I used the hand holding the folder to stop me from tipping into the wall, nearly kicking a vagrant as I did so. The folder crumpled with my weight but nothing fell out. The vagrant cursed and then fell back asleep. Water splashed up my pants as I ran up the stairs, looked both ways, and sprinted across the street. The rain was coming down so hard and so fast it seemed to be jumping skyward from the pavement.

From the uptown entrance came the sound of the subway train crushing air out of its way as it entered the station. Down the stairs two, three at a time, I jumped the entrance turnstile, enraging the girl working the change booth. Whatever she screamed was lost in the bulletproof glass protecting her from the rest of the world, and I caught the doors on the train just as they started to close.

The doors met on my left arm, sighed, jerked open again, and let me through.

Thing with New York, most people don't pay attention to anything out of the ordinary. It's not that they don't see it, they just don't want to confront it. So it was with me, standing inside the door, wet and clutching a sodden and torn manila folder, trickling a puddle at my feet. The only person in the car who paid me any mind was a toddler in her father's lap. She pointed at me and giggled. Her father stared straight ahead. The train lurched forward, and the driver announced our next stop as something that might have been Saskatoon, but which I translated as 103rd Street. Using one of the handgrips to steady myself, I looked for Barry. He wasn't in the car.

I'd come in at the south end of the train, and checked that end first. Looking through the connecting door into the other car brought me a pretty full view, but left the near corners vacant. Halfway to the north end of the car it struck me that I was being exceptionally dim. If I was so certain Barry was headed for the clinic, all I had to do was get out at 135th, so I sat down and tried to get my glasses dried again. I succeeded in making the big drops turn into smaller streaks, but that was it.

It was my luck to get an air-conditioned car, too, and by the time we hit 135th Street I was shivering in my wet clothes. Getting back onto the humid platform was small relief turned great when I glimpsed Barry as he started up the stairs. I followed a group of Latino kids out of the station and into the downpour. A bolt of lightning lanced the sky, thunder flowing over it. The kids shrieked, then laughed, joking in a babble of Spanish.

Barry wasn't worried about being followed. He headed straight as a lame bull on a charge to the corner, then surprised me by turning right and heading to Eighth Avenue. Halfway down the block he turned into a diner, and I crossed to the opposite side of the street. He gave no sign of having made me, but from across the street I could barely read the lettering on the diner's window through the rain, let alone see anything inside. After waiting five minutes I crossed over, coming at the restaurant from the right corner of the awning. A steady stream of runoff from the rain gutter doused me as I looked in the window. It had begun to steam up, but it was possible to make out faces inside.

Barry sat at a full booth, his profile to the window, making points to the rest of the group with a meat-tenderizer of a hand. I recognized one other person in the booth, then another when a woman joined them. The woman was the same small, bitter one who had accosted Alison on our way out after her abortion, the one who performed elective surgeries on toy babies. It took a few seconds to be certain about the other one. None other than the bushily bearded man I had straight-armed into the street. He was the hardest to recognize; he had shaved off the beard. Without it, his chin looked naked and soft. I realized as I hadn't when we'd tussled that he was overweight, perhaps by as much as thirty or forty pounds.

Barry produced a small walkie-talkie from his drenched

suit jacket and showed it to everyone at the table. They nodded in complete understanding or agreement, and he keyed it and spoke briefly to the grille.

A much-abused pay phone hung against a building three doors east, but I didn't want to be that close in case anyone came out. Back on the other side of the street was another phone, between a video rental closet and a liquor store, and I dodged cars and cabs and people with umbrellas to get to it. I didn't have any coins other than subway tokens and rushed into the liquor store for change.

The counterman was surly and demanded I buy something. I grabbed a tin of Altoids and gave him a five. He took all the time in the world to make change, and didn't seem to understand that I wanted quarters. While he played with his register, I looked out the door and saw people leaving the diner. As far as I could see, Barry wasn't among them.

"I thought you wanted change, man," the counterman snarled. I went back to him and he gave me my bills first, the change after, coin by coin. I almost asked him if he was on Crowell's payroll.

Barry stood in the doorway of the diner talking to one of his cronies when I stepped out of the store. I put my back to them at the phone. The quarters were clumsy between my fingers. I dialed the clinic and turned around, waiting for somebody to pick up while keeping my eyes on the front of the diner. Barry was heading back inside, and down 135th I could see the troop of Crowell's Christian foot soldiers, doggedly putting one foot in front of the other, heads down in the rain.

But Barry hadn't left yet; he was waiting for something. The diner could have a back door, in which case I was screwed, but I didn't think that was the planned exit. They had done their tricks and thought they were clean. They wouldn't be pulling anything more out of their hats.

"Women's LifeCare, may I help you?"

"Lynn, this is Atticus. Put Sheldon on."

Delfleur put me on hold fast, and I was afraid she'd thought it was a prank call and cut me off. As I waited, Barry emerged from the diner once more, starting a cigarette, using the building to shield his lighter from the rain. Then he went to the pay phone, and with the smoke dangling from his lips, brought out his walkie-talkie again. What I would have done for one now I didn't think about; it was lying on my futon at home.

Barry spoke into the radio, then brought it to his ear to listen to the reply. At that point Sheldon came on the phone. "What's up?"

"What's it look like there?"

He didn't waste any time. "We've got a small group of the moderates, here, you know, offering post-abortion counseling, but they're well outnumbered by SOSers. About one hundred of them out front, maybe more. The back alley's had people moving in and out of it all day; we've got maybe twenty-five there, now. Some are carrying backpacks, sacks, looks like they've got equipment. Building's secure, not a whole lot of patients today, seeing as how the doctor isn't in. We've had people shouting at us all day, since the news broke, you believe it? Feminist Majority is here, too, preparing to counter if anything should happen. There are a few 'We loved Katie' signs."

"Anything else?"

"That FBI guy is here, says they've got intelligence that something's going down. Neither he or I like the Ryder truck that's been parked across the street for the last two hours. Nobody's opened it up yet. We've got some cops here with hats and bats, and there's a VW van unloading more people as I speak."

"I'm looking at one of Crowell's lapdogs right now," I told him, watching Barry pick up the pay phone and dial. "He's just met with a group of protesters and sent them back to the clinic. I don't know—"

"Hold on," Sheldon said. Over the receiver I heard him say, "Keep him on the line—keep him on the line, and use the checklist, and find the FBI dude." He came back to me. "Got to evacuate. Bomb threat."

I dropped the receiver and the folder and sprinted across the street to where Barry was still speaking on the phone.

"—in the abortuary room," he was saying. "It'll blow every fucking one of you into pieces."

Well, maybe Crowell wouldn't be polite enough to roll over when faced with my and Bridgett's double-teaming interrogation, but this wasn't bad, and it was all I needed. Barry caught me reflected in the window as I moved, but too late. Taking his left shoulder with my right hand, I spun him back around, then drove my left forearm up under his chin, pinioning him against the wall. His face flushed, and he started to bring his fist around to punch, but I put my right knee into his stomach. He would have doubled over if I'd let him, but instead my forearm kept him upright and the air came out of him like foul exhaust, bitter smoke and bitter thoughts. His nose was broken from our first dance, when he had kissed asphalt, so it couldn't be easy for him to breathe.

The phone swung on its cable, and I could hear a tinny voice asking if he was still there.

"Bomb threat, Clarence?" I asked Barry, patting him down with my right hand. He was carrying his radio on his hip and I pulled it off his belt and dropped it on the pavement. His eyes darted to it, then back to me. They were opened wide, the small blood vessels revealed above and below his corneas, and his eyes repeated what they'd said earlier: He hated me. "Moving up from just one murder, huh, shithead? Going for double digits, now? Bomb threat? Is it real? Is it real, Clarence?"

He didn't say anything. I kept moving my hand, finding his wallet and dropping that, too. I found his gun, exactly where I'd seen it earlier. It was a semiautomatic pistol, a Smith & Wesson, and it slipped easily from its holster. I brought it around to his stomach, shielding the weapon with my body. We locked eyes and listened to the rain for a second or two before I said, "Nice gun."

My thumb found the safety and I moved back just enough for him to see me flick it off. He did, his eyes going down and then coming back to my face. Hatred turned to terror fed by hatred, and in that moment it could have gone either way—resistance or compliance.

"You wanted a piece of me, that right? How about I take a piece from you, Clarence? You chamber your first round? It's double action, I pull the trigger, you roll the dice." I pushed the barrel hard into his stomach, keeping it pressed there, waiting for his answer.

When he didn't speak I pulled the trigger.

He screamed and his muscles went slack and suddenly I was holding him up in the rain with my forearm and the gun and no help from him.

"Take that as a no," I said.

He couldn't speak, shaking, trying to stand, scrabbling at the wet wall. The scent of urine rose off him, suddenly. I took my grip off him long enough to work the slide on the pistol. The round clicked into place loudly, assured, and there was no question this time. I put my forearm back under his throat and he began to sob as I jabbed him again with the gun.

"Now, don't start crying on me, Clarence," I said.

"It's a fake," he whimpered.

"If you're lying I'll kill you."

"You'll kill me anyway. It's a fake, man."

With the gun as a prod we moved sideways to the phone. I took my left arm off Barry and felt for the phone cord, finding it and bringing the receiver to my ear.

"Hello?"

"Lynn, it's Atticus. Clarence wants to tell you something." I pressed the phone against Barry's face.

"It's a fake," Barry whispered.

"Thank God," I heard Lynn say as I brought the phone back to my ear.

"Call the cops," I said. "We're at a diner on a Hundred Thirty-fifth at Eighth."

When the cops found us we were inside, Barry sitting at the counter, me beside him, his gun off to a side. The manager and waitress, the only people in the place, were concerned until I explained that Barry was a terrorist. Then the waitress spat on him. Barry took it, not moving, sitting in his wet pants, his hands flat on the counter. The manager went outside and came back with Barry's wallet and the radio. Miraculously, neither had been stolen.

Two uniforms led by Lozano showed up and I rose when they came in, backing away from the counter. Lozano came in angry, harried, and said without preamble, "Mirandize him."

The uniforms paused for a moment, unsure which of us he meant, then the younger cop went to Barry, and when Lozano made no protest, his partner followed. The pat down was thorough and slow, and the officer who did it made a lot of noise about Clarence's loose bladder. Lozano glared at me while they cuffed him, read him his rights, and led him out. They read him his rights slowly, taking no chances this time. It was almost satisfying to watch.

At the door, Barry turned, gave me a hard stare, and said, "I'm going to fucking do you."

I blew him a kiss.

"Shut him the fuck up," Lozano told the cops. After the door swung closed with a little tinkle of bells Lozano pointed to the Smith & Wesson on the counter and gave me the evil eye and I shook my head.

Lozano said, "How's the coffee here?"

"Ground fresh daily."

The manager poured two mugs and we sat at one of the booths. Lozano sipped his coffee silently, and I didn't feel the need to say anything, so I followed suit. I took the mug carefully when I drank, fighting my shaking hands, hoping Lozano wouldn't notice. He did, I'm certain, but didn't say anything. After a minute or two, the manager said, "Hey, you, uh, want this gun, here?"

Lozano turned his head and nodded and the manager started to pick it up. "Stop," Lozano said. It was a bark. The manager stopped, then shrugged and went to the pie case, scrubbing at the glass with a rag and not looking at us. The waitress sat down, saying, "Fucking city." When the manager was finished with the pie case he went to clean the stool Barry had used.

"You touch the weapon?" Lozano asked me.

"I took it off him."

"You got a witness?"

"No. But he's got the empty holster, not me," I said.

Lozano looked at the ceiling and shut his eyes, saying, "This is turning into one bitch of a day. They kill the girl, then they pull this." He looked back to the counter, then finished his coffee. "You're sure the call was a fake?"

"Absolutely."

Lozano turned to look full at me, and I tried hard not to look guilty. He raised the mug in his left hand, sticking his arm out as if signaling a turn.

"Fucking city," the waitress repeated, and she walked to the coffeemaker and took the pot from the burner, then refilled our cups. Her uniform was powder blue and she wore white nylons with a run on the inside of her left leg.

"What'd you do to him?" Lozano asked, looking again at the counter.

"Nothing," I said.

"Nothing made him piss on himself?"

"I caught him on the phone making the threat. I took his gun when he tried to fight me. He lost bladder control when he lost the piece."

"You threaten him?"

"No."

He didn't believe me, and his body language made no

bones about that. "Why're you lying to me, Atticus? I thought we were friends, here."

"We are, Detective. I didn't do anything to him."

He sipped some more of his coffee. "How'd you know he's the one that phoned the threat?"

"I heard him. He told me it was a fake."

"Did he? Anybody else hear that?"

"Just me."

"So, you were following this guy? Eight hours after Katie Romero is murdered, you just happen to be following one of our prime suspects, a guy who threw a bottle at Katie's mother? You just happen to be following a guy you already mixed it up with once? Tell me this isn't what it looks like, Atticus."

I explained what had happened, including the meeting with Crowell, to set the stage. I did not tell him about pulling the trigger on Barry. Lozano drank his coffee in silence while I spoke, measuring my words with his eyes on mine.

"Where's the dick?"

"Jeez, Detective. Don't you have a better slang term for a private investigator?"

"You prefer peeper? Where is she?"

"I don't know. She went after Crowell."

"We've spoken to Crowell twice already. You two shouldn't have gone to see him. And following Barry, that's loco. What the hell were you thinking? Why aren't you watching Romero?"

"She's well covered," I said.

"Yeah, but not by you, and that's your job." Lozano finished his second cup of coffee, putting the mug down hard. "You worry me, Kodiak. If Barry says you used excessive force, if I find one single witness, I'll rein you in and I'll rein you in hard." He stood up, pulling his wallet out of his back pocket. He put a five carefully on the table and said, "The girl is dead, and that is rotten, sad action. Don't make it worse."

"Don't forget the gun," I said. Outside, the rain had slowed and the streets were dark and slick.

He stared down at the weapon, snapping on a surgical glove without looking at his hands. Then he took the pistol and dropped it into a paper bag provided by the manager.

"This better not be your way of dealing with grief," Lozano said. "You tell that peeper of yours to come talk to me, get this all straightened out. She doesn't, I'm going to go looking for her."

"I'll tell her," I said.

"You keep your head straight," he said to me, and left.

CHAPTER FOURTEEN

I used the diner bathroom after Lozano left. I stood in front of the mirror, leaning on the sink, for what seemed like a long time. My blood was roaring in my ears.

If Barry had chambered his first round, he would have been dying from a gut wound even as I was staring at my reflection. If Barry had chambered his first round, I would have been on my way to prison, and I wouldn't be coming back for a very long time. If Barry had chambered his first round, I would have murdered him in cold blood while looking in his eyes, and I would have been happy doing it.

The trigger had gone back before I had realized I was pulling it. The hammer had fallen before I knew what I had done. And when the pistol had dry-fired, all I had thought of was racking the slide and trying again.

What I wanted to do was be sick, to vomit in the dirty, cramped bathroom at the back of this tacky diner. I wanted to throw up and get whatever was inside me out. I gagged over the sink, spitting sticky strands of saliva, but succeeded only in getting stomach cramps that pinched me from diaphragm to groin. Nothing came up; it wouldn't let go.

After a while I ran some cold water and splashed my face, melting the tears away. Then I cleaned my glasses and left.

The walk to the clinic was short, the rain tapering from downpour to downtrickle, and I came to the corner of 135th and Amsterdam in time to see protest become pandemonium.

The rain had done nothing to the crowd of protesters. A few had tried to cover up, pulling windbreakers over their heads to shield themselves, but that was all the consideration the weather warranted, except to an elderly woman on the east side of Amsterdam. Holding a sheaf of sodden photocopies in one hand, she tilted her head back and called out something about the cleansing power of God. Her and Robert De Niro.

People were screaming at each other. A chorus of anti-abortionists had started a chant of "Two, four, eight, ten, All you women want to be men." NARAL and the Feminist Majority had trained countertroops, mostly women, from their teens to their forties, arms locked, an immobile line. They countered with, "Two, four, eight, ten, Why are your leaders always men?"

A corps of police officers in riot gear were pushing people back across their perimeter line, their face shields still up, waiting for the order. The actual court-designated property line for the clinic was somewhere in the middle of the street, as arbitrary now as it had ever been. Both groups ignored it freely. The antis had rushed hard and strong, and now were being driven back. Both factions had crossed the line, where the officers held it, looking grim.

Watching the bodies twist and press against each other, I realized how angry I was, and I felt the weight of the holster on my hip.

And I knew I couldn't trust myself.

Parked up on the sidewalk was a large yellow Ryder truck, and I stepped around it, trying to get a look in the back. It was open and empty but for a young man sitting with his legs dangling over the edge. He had a compact two-way radio on his belt. He gestured to the sky and said, "Out of nowhere, huh?"

"Yeah."

"You fall back?"

I nodded.

"You should get back in there. Crowell's coming."

"Really?"

"You bet."

I didn't move for a moment, and the young man continued to watch me. His face was small and soft, and his posture vaguely confrontational. He pulled the radio off his belt and held it against his thigh.

"You're not with us, are you?" he asked.

"Depends. Who are you?"

"Sword of the Silent."

"Ah, no, I'm not with you, then."

"You condone the murder of babies?" He asked it evenly enough.

"There's some debate about that. Calling them babies, I mean."

"All life is sacred. Only God has the right to take life. Baby murderers are no better than common criminals, protected by a godless president who promotes godless laws."

I was tempted to ask him if he was a vegetarian, but instead said, "Crowell teach you that?"

"Our Lord taught me that. He died teaching us all that."

I said, "Actually, I'm Jewish."

He didn't even blink. "Of course. I should have known. And you complain about the Holocaust, while another happens under your nose."

"Been nice talking to you," I said.

"I'll pray for your soul," he told me as I walked away.

A car horn started barking, coming closer, and several people lowered their "Stop the Murder" signs and headed toward the source, the white Cadillac that Rich had driven up outside Crowell's building. It parked illegally just long enough to let Crowell out. The rain had picked up again, and I tried to wipe my glasses off again but gave up and looked past the water drops. I couldn't see either Bridgett or her car anywhere on the street.

The arrival had an obvious effect. Both sides got louder. A lot louder. Crowell emerged from the Caddy, waving nonchalantly, like a movie star at a premiere. Other than a raincoat, he was dressed just as before. The moderates began backing to the opposite side of the street, trying to distance themselves from SOS. Crowell leaned back inside the car and brought out a bullhorn, then slammed the door. As the Cadillac pulled away, he began to speak.

"Dr. Romero," he said, his voice low and crackling. "Dr. Romero, can you hear me? What would you do if you had only five minutes left to live?"

The crowd went nuts.

Son of a bitch, I thought. He knows she isn't here and he pulls this. Her daughter dead hardly eight hours, and he pulls this.

Son of a bitch.

The noise dulled to a low roar, then Crowell said, "Listen to me, now," and the SOS crowd went silent. "Listen to me, now," he said again. "Please, in the name of God and all that Jesus holds holy, please, do not murder any more babies. Stop your slaughter of those silent innocents who die beyond your doors. Your own child today joined the ranks of the fallen, and yet you continue. Oh, dear God, please stop, please do not let her kill any more babies, do not let her murder any more women or their children. Please . . . oh, please."

Everyone was listening and everyone was still. Along the pro-choice line I caught a rustle of movement, some bowed heads speaking to one another, but that was all. The moderates had regrouped at the corner, and were watching the proceedings sadly.

"Beloved, my Christian friends, we are now at a time where our resolve will be most surely tested.

"We all have heard what has happened today. We all know the events visited upon Dr. Romero this morning."

Some people actually cheered. But then Crowell raised his left hand and they again fell silent. Raindrops beaded and dripped from the end of his bullhorn.

"We do not rejoice in this," he said. "As the Lord said to the Israelites on the shores of the Red Sea, these too are my children, and you will find no glory in their deaths.

"We find no glory in the Lord's punishments. Yet we must remain strong, our resolve must not falter. We have all heard of Common Ground. We have heard of the promise of peace through compromise. The events of this day surely speak to such a reconciliation, seductively draw us to more mainstream protests.

"But it is a lie! There can be no common ground, there can be no rest, no peace, no reconciliation. This is a war of absolutes. We cannot just save half a baby, rescue only some of the preborn. It is all or nothing, all or nothing, and what has been visited upon Dr. Felice Romero this day, that is her punishment, and not ours!"

This earned him more cheers and, finally, some aggressive booing and heckling. Crowell didn't seem to mind either reaction. I could see movement at the second floor windows of the clinic, several scared and bewildered faces looking out of the waiting room above.

"This is a house of sin, of horror and torture, of women trapped and bound, held helpless where their children are torn from them. Bloody and broken, these infants come from their screaming mothers. We must never forget this.

"This 'surgery,' " Crowell shouted, and he made the word drip with scorn, "this, 'elective and ambulatory procedure' is murder, bloody, calculated, state-sanctioned murder! It is barbarism, and it is, most of all, a crime against God! And we must never, ever, stop our fight! In the name of God and Our Lord Jesus Christ, we must fight on!"

Crowell's declaration echoed. A counterchant started, not quite on time, and instead of clear words it sounded like garbled tape, chewed and torn.

This was just what his people wanted to hear. They were soaking up every word, assenting, nodding. Crowell wiped rain out of his eyes and said, at first softly, then louder and louder, "No common ground. No common ground. No common ground," until the crowd picked up the cadence of the words, and began chanting them with him. The volume swelled, thunderously loud suddenly, swallowing up the counterchant of *"Choice, choice, choice."* Then Crowell waved his hand once and silenced them again.

"The Lord is vengeful," he shouted. "The Lord is strong. The Lord will destroy that which offends Him. With fire and cleansing wrath, will the Lord purify this place."

Cries from everyone, Amens and Praise Gods and Go to Hells. Men and women exhorted Jesus to right now descend from heaven and smite everyone inside the building. And the crowd was moving suddenly, a great surge toward the clinic doors. I took a step forward.

A window on the ground floor broke and inside the building, someone screamed. Another window shattered, then several, simultaneously. A woman shrieked and fell back, dropping her NARAL sign, blood on her forehead.

During a portion of the Gulf War I had been assigned to

coordinate the protection of a general, and we had been in Tel Aviv when Hussein started dropping SCUDs on Israel. They came at night, the few times they came at all, and they came out of a stillness and silence suddenly pierced by air-raid sirens and people desperate for their lives. There would be nothing, then the sirens, and then immediate movement, people frantically trying to bring loved ones to safety, to save themselves. It was a crowd mentality I had never seen before, people moving ferociously for one reason.

This was worse. This wasn't for survival. These people wanted blood.

Everything I was wanted to move, everything I had ever learned told me to act, to do something. But I stood in the rainfall, on the sidewalk, inadequate, fighting the cold irrational rage of the mob. Lists of options presented themselves to me, courses of action and protection and security, and instead of doing what I was meant to do, what I was trained to do, I dropped anchor and just let myself be beaten upon by the rain.

Crowell was climbing back into the Cadillac, his head low. Police tried to reach him, failing, pinned in by the rushing crowd.

It was as if Crowell's troops had spurs driving them. They threw themselves against the opposing line, the cops, and the clinic building like amphetamine-keyed lemmings. Young kids, just children, were pushed forward into the crowd by their parents, urged to rush the clinic, and some were crying, clinging to their mothers or fathers. Another first-floor window broke.

The doors were holding, nobody was getting inside. The pro-choice line had regrouped and reformed, and was now forging a reinforced cordon, pressing the antis away from the building. With their success, the police seemed to get the upper hand, too, and the massive push turned into fractured fits and starts, kamikaze missions flown by apathetic pilots.

The Cadillac had pulled away, now replaced by emergency vehicles, police cars, an EMS rig. The initial threat was gone, already, but it had been replaced by the death rattle of the assault. Some still resisted passively, and some seemed not to have been involved at all, serenely holding their signs and repeating their rain-soaked litany of hope and salvation.

Entering the clinic was out of the question. Thirty or forty people were still crushed against the door or on the stairs leading to the entrance. I tried to spot faces, again seeing the bushy beard, now ex-bushy beard, as he was dragged by two uniformed officers to the first paddy wagon.

"Hey, stud, can I offer you a cup of coffee?"

Bridgett Logan was beside me. Her hair had been flattened by the rain, and it clung to her face, making her skin seem almost alabaster pale, and her eyes vividly blue. She smiled at my reaction to her, holding the cup out.

The heat from the cup warmed my hands. My fingers looked like flesh-colored raisins, and they began to hurt as I popped the tab on the cover, sipping. The coffee was hot and sweet, a lot of sugar, no cream.

"You like it?"

"It's awful sweet."

"You're a sweetie." She was drinking hers black, the top off the cup, and side by side we surveyed the street together. After a while she said, "How long you been here?"

"Little before Crowell arrived. You?"

"Little after him. Lost him, figured that meant he'd be coming here, booked back. I'm parked at the back of the clinic. Missed Crowell's speech, though. Made it just in time for the floor show."

"You should have heard the monologue. He managed to remove any guilt the SOS crowd might have had about protesting the same day that Katie Romero died."

"Oooh," she moaned, wiping raindrops from her face. "That man just makes my knees go to water."

She drained her cup and crumpled it, and we walked back on the sidewalk, getting against a doorway for shelter. Looking over at the stairs, I saw what the problem was with the entrance. Six people had chained themselves together, wrapping links about their necks, then looping the ends around the banisters on either side and locking them with the standard Kryptonite locks. Bolt cutters just don't work on those things. A couple of uniforms were talking to the group, trying to persuade them to surrender the keys. Then one of the officers went to get the bolt cutters anyway, probably to use on the chains.

"How'd you get here?" Bridgett asked. I told her. I even told her about Barry. When I was finished she asked, "You knew that he hadn't chambered that round, right?"

"No."

She bit her lower lip, eyes narrowing. She shook her head, once, then said, "Where are the letters?"

"Stuck to the sidewalk by that diner. They were a write-off anyway."

"With the rain, yeah. I'll call Lozano, straighten him out," she said. She dropped her crumpled cup in the trash can on the corner. "So, you figure that Crowell's friend Clarence was going to call somebody with that radio of his after he made his bomb threat and tell them exactly when to rush?"

"Yeah, that's what I figure. The attempted break-in last night was probably to make the threat more serious."

"They would have gotten inside while everyone was trying to get out. Nice job, fighting the good fight."

"It's not good," I said. "It's just a fight."

She began searching her pockets and I remembered I'd bought the tin of Altoids with her in mind. I fished it out of my pocket and handed it to her. She took it, saying, "Cool. These things are great."

"Don't let it be said I don't think of you."

After sucking on an Altoid for a few seconds she crunched it between her teeth and said, "You're pro-abortion, right?"

"I'm more pro a woman's right to choose."

"One of those," she said.

"One of those what?"

She sighed. The mint was gone and she took out another one. "Sensitive-fucking-men. Whatever you want, honey. Whatever works for you. It's your choice. Of course it is. Has been all along."

"I'm not following you."

"Men have been behind this thing from the start. It's always been a woman's right to choose. That's obvious, and that's not the problem. That's not what it's about for men."

"So what is it about?"

"Look at Crowell. Look at John Burt, and his boot camp for pregnant mothers in Pensacola. He takes half their welfare checks to cover expenses, you know that? What do *you* think it's about, stud? It's all about power over women. It's all about the fact that men believe they have the right to give women the choice in the first place. That's all it's ever been fucking about." She tossed the mint into her mouth, then said, "Hey! Look at that, the door's clear." She started across the street, her head high in the rain.

CHAPTER FIFTEEN

"That wasn't a rush," Sheldon said. "That was a goddamn riot."

We looked out the broken reception window onto Amsterdam where the rain was falling in waves. Now and then the crackle of police radios carried inside, over the voices and traffic from the street. At our feet glass shards peppered the black-and-white linoleum, and when any of us moved the pieces cracked and popped. Paint, red, tacky and bright, streaked and puddled on the walls, furniture, and floor.

Scott Fowler was speaking in low tones on one of the phones at reception, talking to his supervisor. He had nodded at me once when I came in, but that was it.

Two paddy wagons were outside, prisoners being transferred from one to the other. After the second was filled, a uniform slammed the doors shut and locked it up, thumping the side of the vehicle. It started down the street. I watched the officer walk to the other wagon, now empty, kneeling down near the driver's door to say something to the man who had locked himself to the drive shaft. The gag was getting old; Randal Terry's people had perfected the inventive application of Kryptonite bicycle locks and drive shafts in the late '80s. Someone would have to drill the lock off the man, a dangerous job, considering he had locked himself around the neck. If the drill slipped, the man was dead. Hard to tell if the protester was brave or just stupid.

Lynn Delfleur hung up her phone and said to Sheldon, "Someone should be out to fix the windows in a half hour."

"Fine. I don't think anyone else will try to come inside," he said. To me, he added, "You told us this would happen, that we needed screens instead of bars."

"It would have been too expensive to remove the bars and install grilles," I said.

He shook his head. "It's cheaper to just replace the windows."

I shrugged.

Fowler hung up the phone and said, "Atticus? Let's talk." Then he headed through the door into the staff lounge. I followed him, and Bridgett followed me.

When we got inside he shut the door and looked at Bridgett. When he tore his eyes away from her, he looked at me expectantly.

"Special Agent Scott Fowler, this is Bridgett Logan," I said, feeling very Emily Post. "She's with Agra and Donnovan Investigations, and is being retained by the clinic to pursue an independent investigation."

"Pleasure," Fowler said, offering her his hand.

"Charmed," she said, then crunched her latest Altoid at him.

He lingered on the grip, I thought, but then let go and said to me, "Romero's safe?"

"Yes."

"How's she holding up?"

"Not well."

He frowned sympathetically, then pulled a folded sheet from his jacket pocket. "Came this morning. The original should be in D.C. by now."

I took the paper, unfolded it, then set it on the table so both Bridgett and I could read it.

Another letter.

DOCTOR OF PAIN—
WILL YOU CRY LIKE THEY CRY?
WEEP LIKE THEY WEEP?
BLEED AS THEY BLEED?
WAIL AS THEY WAIL?
DO YOU KNOW THEIR PAIN?
YOU WILL KNOW THEIR PAIN.
YOU WILL KNOW THEIR PAIN.
I WILL HAVE JUSTICE.

And again, no signature.

"And nothing on the envelope or letter, I assume?" Bridgett was scowling.

"Not so far," Fowler told her.

"This would've been sent when?" I asked.

"Local postmark," he said. "Stamped day before yesterday. I know what you're thinking, and I agree. It looks like it's by the same author that wrote the one Romero got at her home last night."

"Still wants justice," I said.

"This was probably sent the day after that other one. I'm sure they're sequential."

"There was another one like this?" Bridgett asked.

"It wasn't in the file," I said. "Never had a chance to copy it. It came last night to Romero's apartment, and Scott here took it straight to the Bureau. But the same phrase was used, that bit about having justice."

"Probably from the shooter," Fowler said. "Nothing

from the lab on that one, either, unless you want to hear about the paper type, so on."

"No, thank you," I said.

Bridgett ran her fingers through her wet hair, ruffling it back behind her ears. "You think that the fellow who shot Katie just did it on the spur of the moment?"

"Huh?" Fowler said.

She sighed and rolled her eyes my way, then back to Scott. "If the guy who wrote this is the shooter, then he took the shot on Katie as opportunity, maybe thinking that she was her mother. Because if he had planned to shoot Dr. Romero this morning, Dr. Romero never would have received this letter, right? Because she would be dead."

"She's right," I said.

Scott's brow creased slightly. "I suppose. Or Katie was the intended target all along."

"That makes no sense," Bridgett said.

Fowler's eyes never left her face. He might as well have been holding a sign asking Bridgett to have her way with him. "Well, perhaps the author knows the shooter," he said.

"Or he may be entirely independent, another nut entirely," I said. "We've got nothing to connect Katie's murder with the guy who wrote this."

"So, no clue as to the identity of the writer," Bridgett said.

"I'm working on it," Fowler said.

I folded the letter again and handed it back to him. "Anything else?"

"Federal marshals are on the way here," he said. "And they'll want to take over the security on Romero, as well."

I shook my head. "After the conference."

Both of them looked at me like I had just fallen out of the sky, complete with halo and harp. "You're joking, right?" Fowler asked.

"No. She's devastated right now, and I won't rotate new personnel in on her while she's grieving and disoriented. I assume the marshals will be at the conference, and I'll be happy to liaison with them, but they're not taking over my principal until Felice is ready for the change."

Fowler threw up his hands. "Jeez, Atticus, you've been riding me for marshals since this damn thing started."

"I know, and I'm glad they're coming in, but I want them kept away from her until I say otherwise. I'll let you know when she's ready for new people."

He didn't like it and didn't bother to hide it. "I'll see what I can do."

"Thanks," I said. "If that's it, then I'm going to head back to Romero and spell some of my people for a bit."

"Fine," he said. "I'll expect to hear from you later."

"You will." I went for the door.

"I'll walk you out," I heard Bridgett say.

Outside, she said, "You want a lift?"

I hesitated, looked at the rain, nodded. "Just make sure we're not followed," I said.

"I can do that."

We got into her Porsche and she pulled out, the wipers sighing against the windshield. By my watch it was a little after six, and the traffic was starting to get thick. I realized that just by the very nature of how Bridgett drove, tailing us would be difficult. She ran lights for sport. With the rain, it was almost a contact sport.

"What do you think?" she asked.

"About?"

"Those letters. You think there's more than one person after her?"

"I expect so. I have no idea how many people want her dead. Looking at that SOS crowd earlier, figure that all of them would love a shot at her."

"Not nice people," she said.

"Well, the SOSers, yeah, I agree. The problem is, they make all the other Right-to-Lifers look bad. They don't deserve that. There are plenty of antiabortion folks who would like nothing more than for Crowell and SOS to dry up and blow away. He's destroying their legitimacy."

"I don't have a hell of a lot of sympathy for their plight." Bridgett said it curtly.

"They have a right to be heard, like anybody else. Crowell's making that impossible."

"Well, there's the conference to give everybody their say."

"Yes, there is."

She didn't reply, and we drove for another twenty minutes or so with both of us checking mirrors. Neither of us thought we were being followed. Still, she parked three blocks south of the studio, just to be safe.

"I'll call Lozano when I get home," she said, flipping off the windshield wipers.

"Find out what Barry said when you do."

"Planning on it." Bridgett pulled a pad from her jacket pocket and a pen, and said, "Lemme have your number, stud." I told her my home and pager numbers, and she said, "I'll call tonight."

"I won't be in until after midnight," I said. "I've got to give my people some time off."

She nodded. "Tomorrow, then."

I got out of the car. The rain had finally stopped. Bridgett pulled my door closed, raised a hand in farewell, and pulled away.

CHAPTER SIXTEEN

I picked up three cups of coffee, some sandwiches, and two packs of cigarettes at the bodega on the corner, then went up to the studio and knocked loudly on the door. After a second I heard Dale shout, "Who is it?"

"Kodiak."

The bolt turned and I heard the bar slide back and then he said, "Go ahead, it's open."

When I ran the door back on its track, his gun was out, held in both hands, barrel pointing about maybe three or four inches from my feet. Dale nodded, released the hammer on his revolver slowly, and holstered while I shut the door again and looked around. It was dark in the studio, the only illumination from the street and the fixture in the bathroom. The light spilled out past the open door onto the floor. Natalie stood against the far wall, and her angle of fire would have cut me to flank steak if she had decided I was a threat. Rubin was standing in front of where Dr.

Romero was lying on a blanket on the floor. She looked asleep.

"Took you long enough," Natalie said. "I was afraid Bridie might've hurt you."

"Bridgett, you mean? She frightens me," I said.

Natalie laughed.

Dale sat on an unfinished stool in the near corner, and I handed the paper bag of groceries to him. "Coffee and sandwiches."

"You always did take good care of your crew," he said softly.

"Lord knows I try," I whispered. "I want you both to go home, get some rest," I told Rubin and Natalie. "Come back at midnight and relieve Dale and me."

Natalie nodded, and holstered her Glock. "She's been sleeping for the last two hours or so," she said, her voice low. "Hasn't said much of anything, hasn't eaten, hasn't used the bathroom. Been smoking too much."

"All right. You might want to call Bridgett when you get home. She can fill you in on what all happened today," I said.

"I will." She went to get her coat.

I told Rubin, "Be careful when you eat. I ended up tasting the memory of Katie's waffles."

He said, "I can't get the taste of orange juice out of my mouth."

"It'll pass," I said.

Rubin shook his head. "I've never seen death like that."

"No." I was trying to think of something more to say, something that would make it better, when Natalie came back, smoothing her blouse and skirt.

"I spoke to Felice about it," Natalie said. "I don't know if it took."

"She's right," I said. "It was my fault. You two get some rest."

Rubin nodded and Natalie shook her head. "You know that's a lie."

"Not to Felice."

She just shook her head again, then went to open the door. Dale set down the bag and drew his weapon once again and I drew mine, squeezing the grip and feeling the gun cock. Nobody was outside, and Natalie and Rubin went through and I approached and slid the door back, locking it.

Dale handed me a cup of coffee, saying, "You want one of the sandwiches?"

"I'm not hungry. Just leave one for Felice."

"No problem," Dale said. He resumed his seat on the stool, putting his feet up on a cardboard box and his back against the wall, his revolver off to his side.

I took my coffee and went over to the window. A police car was going down the block, but didn't seem to be doing anything more than a normal cruise. To my left, Felice Romero slept, curled on the blanket by the radiator, wrapped like a refugee. Someone had put a jacket over her shoulders, and her face was cut in half by streetlight and shadow, stark and angular in repose. I walked around the room once, slowly, looking in nooks and crannies and knowing that if anything had needed to be secured, Natalie or Dale or Rubin had already done it. When that was finished I went back to the window and took a seat on a folding chair, my feet up on the sill.

My coffee lasted almost an hour, and when the cup was empty I crushed it, folded it, unfolded it, tore it, and then, its entertainment value entirely exhausted, threw it out. Sitting post, as Dale and I were, is boring. It takes a lot of concentration and a lot of energy to remain aware and focused when there is really nothing to be aware of or focused on. Thank God the rain had stopped. The only thing worse than standing post in the dark is standing post in the dark in the rain. It's hard to stay awake anyway, but when water is beating a lullaby, it becomes next to impossible.

Around ten Dale got off his stool and headed to the

bathroom. I listened to him urinate and flush and then he opened the door and went back to his seat quietly. Down on the street three men staggered off the opposite sidewalk and into the gutter. After a bit they realized their mistake and mounted the curb again with the effort of the first expedition to conquer Everest. When they disappeared around the corner I sighed, loudly, not meaning to, just trying to oxygenate my body enough to keep from sleeping.

In Rubin's corner Felice stirred. I heard Dale shift on the stool, and I raised my hand to him, waved him back. She sat up, the jacket falling to the floor. She coughed, rich smoker's hacks, then rose, coming over to me. Her lighter flamed in the darkness.

"How long will I have to remain here?" she asked.

"Until tomorrow. We've got a safe apartment, but we may not have access to it until late in the day," I said.

"I don't know where to go." She didn't say it as much to me as to herself. I remembered the blood on the carpet. I knew then that she would sell the place, and I knew she would move somewhere else, maybe outside of the city, maybe outside of the state. It seemed to me that I should share this with her, let her know that I knew and that I understood, but I didn't.

She dragged a chair over the wooden floor and sat in it beside me. A cinder on the edge of her cigarette jumped as she knocked ash into an empty bottle. She put the bottle on the floor between her feet and remained hunched, able to reach it.

"Federal marshals are coming in," I said softly. "They'll want to take over your security."

"Are you quitting?" Felice asked.

"No," I said. "Absolutely not. I'm just saying you have a choice. You can have them protecting you."

"I want you protecting me."

"All right," I said.

"No marshals. You. Natalie. Dale. Rubin."

"I'll tell Fowler."

She drew on the cigarette, then exhaled, blowing the smoke over the cinder and making it flare brighter. When she spoke her voice was low and even.

"I tell you about my husband?"

"After you hired me, yes."

"He's an architect in Albany. We separated four years ago, just about, because my work was hurting his life. People were sending hate mail to his office, accosting his clients. They were parking outside of our house and scaring the neighbors, and he got to where he couldn't take it anymore." She smoked for a few seconds, silently, thinking. At the back of the room, I heard Dale shift again on the stool.

"Not to say that was all that did it," Felice continued. "Marriages have survived worse, but they were better marriages. I used to wonder if Katie hadn't been Down's if we would have stayed together. Maybe without her we could have taken the strain. Probably not. It's not so bad, now, but at first I used to miss him horribly. I'd come home to our apartment and Katie would always ask where Daddy was. She understood divorce, the concept of married people not wanting to be married anymore, but only inasmuch as the television explained it to her. She spent a few months expecting Marcus to return. But she seemed to forget about him pretty quickly. No visits, out of sight, out of mind."

She dropped the cigarette into the bottle, and there must have been some soda or water or something left in it, because there was a sharp hiss and then the cinder went out. She picked up the bottle by its neck and swung it in a small circle, making certain the cigarette was dead. "Do you think he's heard?" she asked.

"I'd think it's likely."

"I should call him."

"Tomorrow."

"Of course, tomorrow. How do you make funeral ar-

rangements, do you know? I've never had to. I suppose
you just call some funeral home and tell them where the
body is and when you'd like it ready by. Give them your
credit card number. Well, I've got time, don't I?" Her
voice wobbled. "They won, didn't they? They've made my
clinic a war zone and they've murdered my daughter and I
don't have anything left to fight with. Tomorrow. Tomorrow and then the day after, and then, after the conference,
I will no longer require your services, Mr. Kodiak."

She turned her head to look at me, meeting my eyes, and
then she looked back out the window. "I am to be added
to the growing list of defeated doctors," she said. "But at
least I'm still out alive. I at least have that, don't I?" She
said the last with an edge that could have cut a diamond.

"Abortion. Abortion. Abortion." She lit another cigarette. "It's the only word I know that doesn't turn into
nothing when you say it over and over. Oh, my God, they
killed my daughter because of what I do . . . because I
believe . . . oh, God . . . oh, my dear dear God. . . ."

The cigarette dropped from between her fingers, bouncing on the floor, showering red flares into the darkness
that flashed and disappeared, extinguished as if they had
never been.

Natalie and Rubin returned a little before midnight. Felice was asleep, and Dale and I moved quietly to let the
others in, unwilling to disturb her rest. For a while it had
seemed she would never sleep again, but when she had
calmed I'd led her back to the blanket, saying, "Tomorrow
will be better."

"No," she had said. "Tomorrow will be the same."

After everyone was inside we gathered at the far end of
the room, away from where the doctor slept, and huddled
like a football team planning defensive strategy. Rubin
looked better for the rest he had received, as did Natalie,

and frankly I was overjoyed to see them. From thirty blocks away I could hear my bed calling.

"I really want to move her," I said to Natalie. "So if the safe apartment Sentinel has frees up early, let me know."

"If we can't get it until late, you want to take her back to Gold Street, return her to familiar surroundings?"

I nodded. "I'll be back by eight. One of you can go down to her apartment and check it out then."

"We can get police protection, can't we?" Dale asked.

"Cops," Natalie said. "No damn good."

"But better than nothing," he said.

"Felice doesn't want us being replaced," I told them. "So we're going to have to work with the marshals when they show, because they certainly won't go away. That may be for the best, getting them to do some extra coverage."

Everybody nodded, and we got ready to leave. Before Dale and I left, I walked over to where Felice was sleeping and spent a minute or two watching her.

She slept with grief as her lover.

CHAPTER SEVENTEEN

My futon was waiting like an escort service's best bet, comfortable and almost comforting. I was pulling back the sheets when the phone in the kitchen rang.

I didn't swear too much.

It was Alison. She said, "Hey, you. How you doing?"

"I'm all right," I said. It was a lie, but I didn't think it mattered.

"I'm so sorry, Atticus. I am so sorry for you and for the doctor. I called around eight and Rubin said you'd be back before one, so . . . well, I wanted to talk to you."

I sat on the windowsill. The apartment was pleasantly cool. I liked the darkness. "I'm glad," I said. "I tried to return your call this afternoon but you were at lunch."

"Yeah," she said.

It seemed like she wanted me to say something more, but I was too tired to come up with anything. I let the silence grow for a while, then said, "How are you doing?"

Alison made a clicking noise, then said, "I'm okay, I'm . . . no, I'm lying. I really need to talk to you, but this isn't . . . well, this doesn't seem like the best time."

"No, it's all right," I said, looking down at the alley. "What's up?"

She sighed, and that's when I realized exactly what was happening on her end of the phone. A squadron of stunt butterflies started aerial maneuvers in my stomach.

"I've been thinking about us," Alison said. "Jesus, this is . . . this isn't how I wanted to do this. I've been thinking about us, Atticus, and I don't think . . . I mean, I don't want us to see each other anymore. Not like we have been."

The pause sat there like roadkill for almost a minute before I said, "I'm sorry if I haven't been there for you, Alison. If that's—"

"That's not it," she said. "I mean, it's not just the abortion, it's that . . . I like you a lot, you know that. I even love you, you know, but after the abortion I started thinking about us, I mean, really about us. I couldn't see a future together, you know? Us as parents? You and me? And I realized that . . . that you're not the man I'm going to spend the rest of my life with."

"Oh," I said.

"I'm really sorry," Alison said. "This isn't how I wanted to do this."

"Yeah, your timing leaves a lot to be desired."

"You said you were doing fine."

"I lied," I said.

We shared the silence for a few more seconds. Then Alison said, "I had to tell you this, you understand, don't you? You wouldn't want me to lie to you, not about this."

"No, I wouldn't."

"I'm sorry."

"Me, too, Alison."

More silence.

"You can give me a call, you know? Whenever you want. We're still friends."

"You bet," I said.

She caught the tone, and hers changed, too. She said, "Well, good night, then. You take care."

"You, too."

I listened to the dial tone. Then I rose and replaced the receiver in its cradle. I looked at where the phone sat on the table, next to the answering machine, next to where I had dropped my pager and my gun. The phone was matte black, nothing more than a shadow in the darkened room.

I picked up the unit and threw it against the wall as hard as I could. The cord snapped, the cable whipping back and clattering on the table. The unit itself hit the wall at an angle, first the base, then the receiver. Then it fell to the floor.

From the next apartment, somebody shouted at me to knock it the fuck off.

"I own a gun," I said loudly.

Then I went to bed.

Sleep was elusive. I spent a long time staring at my ceiling and listening to the city. The caffeine I'd ingested had run its course hours before, but still my pulse bucked and, try as I could, it seemed I would never sleep.

Then I was dreaming.

I come through the door of Crowell's apartment with the HK in my hand, low, careful, knowing that I am going to shoot somebody. But it's also Romero's apartment, the way locations can be only in dreams, and as I start up the stairs to the main floor I hear a step. Crowell turns onto the landing above me, raising his right hand. There's a book in his other hand. I sight and fire three shots, a simple line from his stomach to his throat, and he dies with the book falling from his hand, bouncing each step to my feet, where it lies open. It's a Bible, but it's a story about

the Incredible Hulk. Katie's voice calls, " 'Cus? 'Cus?''
There's another sound I can't identify, a thin curl of sound
like music.

I continue up, and at the main floor hear movement
from the landing above and swing my gun without looking, firing another shot. I keep going, I don't care. Out of
the kitchen comes Barry and I shoot him before he can
throw anything at me. He dies gracefully, without bleeding, without pain.

The plate-glass door has been replaced, and the curtains
are drawn. I see movement on the patio, a silhouette, and
fire another two shots, feeling the gun kick pleasantly in
my hand, hearing the spent shells eject cleanly and bounce
off the wall and table. Special Agent Fowler falls through
the door, shocked that he's suddenly dead. I didn't want to
kill him, I realize, I thought that would be Rich.

But I'll get over it.

But something nags at me. Who did I shoot in the living
room, then? Turning around to check, Dr. Romero is right
behind me. She's entirely unafraid of the gun or me, she
doesn't flinch when I bring the barrel up to her.

Dr. Romero says, "Look what you've done." She points
to the landing above her.

I go up the stairs with her watching me, but she doesn't
move. As I'm climbing, I hear the door open downstairs,
and watch Natalie and Dale and Rubin all come to surround the doctor. Good, I think. They're doing their job.

Bridgett Logan is sitting at the top of the stairs. She
doesn't look at me as I go past, but offers me a Wint-O-
Green Life Saver from the roll in her hand saying, "Nice
shot, stud."

Katie Romero is sitting on the floor, the Walkman headphones on her ears, pieces of paper with crippled drawings
in bright crayon surrounding her. She looks fine, except
that there's a perfect entrance wound in her left eye from
my shot, and a chunk of her face is gone.

Madonna squeals from the headphones that hang on what's left of her head.

Then the alarm was beeping and I was trying to turn it off. Neurons finally began hitting their receptors, and I realized the alarm didn't beep, it buzzed, it was my pager that beeped, so the way to make the noise stop was to answer the page. I lurched to the kitchen, dragging my sweaty sheets after me, tripping over them. I shut off the pager and looked at the number that had been sent, but didn't recognize it. I reached for the phone and then remembered where I had put it.

There was a black mark on the wall from the impact.

I shuffled down the hall to Rubin's room and used his phone.

"Yeah?" Bridgett said.

"Morning," I said. The clock over Rubin's bed said that it was five after seven.

"Did I wake you? You weren't answering your phone."

I thought about explaining that the phone nearest my room was broken, and that Rubin's was too far away to hear, but decided against it. I rubbed my eyes and said, "No, you didn't wake me. What's up?"

"I'm reading letters. A real education in anatomy, let me tell you."

"Where'd you get the copies?"

"I talked to Lozano in person, got replacements. He was very accommodating."

"How'd that go?" I asked, sitting on Rubin's bed. One of Natalie's shirts was draped over the bedpost.

"He wanted to know if I thought you were doing all right."

"What'd you tell him?"

"I told him you were off your twig. No, I said you were fine."

"So he doesn't think I was stalking Barry?"

"If he does, he didn't share his suspicion with me. Anyway, I'm looking over all the threats again, and I'm wondering if you can give me a hand. There's a lot to go through."

"I've got to go cover Romero, see if we can move her. If we get settled into a new location and secured I'll give you a call."

"Do that. One more thing—Barry is being arraigned this morning. As far as I could tell, he didn't tell Lozano that you skipped a groove yesterday."

"Decent of him," I said.

"Yeah, he's the salt of the earth. Talk to you later, stud."

I hung up the phone. For some reason there was no hot water in the building, which led to me taking a very short shower. I dressed, affixed holster and pager to my belt, grabbed a jacket, and hit the street. I stopped long enough for a cup of coffee and a bagel at a bodega on the way to the subway station, finished them both on the platform, and made it to the studio by eight on the dot, certain that I hadn't been followed.

Nothing much had changed. Dale arrived a few minutes after I did, at which point Natalie called her father and determined that we wouldn't be able to access the safe apartment until late that afternoon. I relayed that information to Felice.

"I'd like to go home," she said softly. "I'd like a chance to clean up and get my papers and things for the conference."

"You're certain? I can send someone to get your things."

Her eyes were puffy behind her glasses this morning. She put a hand on my forearm. "I want to go home," she said. "Just for a little bit."

I didn't have the heart to argue.

I dispatched Dale to get the car and sent Natalie to the Gold Street apartment to secure it, then called Fowler to tell him that we would be taking Romero back to her place for a little while.

"I'll let NYPD know," he said. "You planning on staying there long?"

"Not if we can help it."

"Good," he said. "She's still going to Common Ground?"

"We haven't talked about it. But the answer is probably yes."

He sighed. "Not good," he said. "Katie's death has pushed the news national, Atticus. We've got people from D.C. down here now. That conference is going to be a five-ring media circus."

"I haven't seen the papers."

"It's everywhere," Scott said. "And it's only going to lure more nutcases out of the woodwork."

"We'll deal with it," I told him. "Marshals on scene yet?"

"They're already covering the clinic, waiting to hear from Romero. I explained that they weren't going to be needed for close coverage, but that didn't sit too well with the deputy who's running the show."

"I talked to Felice about it," I said. "She wants us to remain on duty."

"I'll pass that along. They won't like it."

"I can deal with bruising a few egos."

"Let's hope that's the only bruising that'll happen."

Natalie was waiting when we arrived at the Romero apartment, and as I closed the door she helped the doctor out of the bulletproof vest. We walked up the short flight of stairs to the main floor, Natalie and Dale in front of Felice, Rubin and me behind her.

When she reached the top of the stairs, Dr. Romero stopped, wavered. I put a hand on her shoulder to support her if she fainted, but she didn't.

"Oh, my God," she said. "Oh, Atticus, look at what they've done to my home."

There were toner stains on the kitchen counter and around the remains of the sliding door from where the CSU technicians had tried to lift fingerprints. On the floor were torn wrappers from all sorts of equipment, both forensic and medical. The spilled orange juice had dried to a sticky stain on the linoleum, and the whole room stank of juice and blood and chemicals, and just the memory of perfume. The bloodstain on the sofa where Katie had fallen had dried dark, and the smear from where I'd pulled her into the kitchen looked like a drunk had dragged a giant paintbrush across the floor.

"This . . . this was a bad idea," Felice said.

I put an arm around her and led her to her bedroom. At least that room was untouched. Once beyond that door, Dr. Romero went straight to the bed and sat down.

"We can take you back to the studio," I said.

She shook her head, and her mouth was clamped shut so tightly the blood left her lips, draining them white.

"You want me to leave you alone for a couple of minutes?" That earned a nod, and I said, "You just call my name, okay, Felice?"

Another nod.

I closed the door as I went out.

Dale, Natalie, and Rubin were all looking at me.

"She's right," Dale told me. "This was a bad idea."

I nodded.

"What were you thinking?"

"She wanted to come home," I said.

They all kept watching me, until finally Natalie turned her head and looked the apartment over again. She sighed, said, "Let's get this place cleaned up."

We got to work, and it wasn't until I was moving furniture back in place by the bedroom door that I heard her crying. It was a soft and lonely sound, and it wanted no company.

After we finished, Natalie got on the phone to her father again, spoke quietly to him, and then hung up. She simply shook her head at me and went back to her seat on the sofa beside Rubin, who had started reading a magazine. Dale sat at the table, idly sliding the salt and pepper shakers back and forth. I tried not to pace.

Then Felice screamed, high and terrified, and I ran into the bedroom and saw only her clothes, folded neatly on the bed. Pivoting to my left as Dale came in after me, I went to her bathroom door and tried the handle; it was locked. Felice screamed again. I kicked the door just below the knob, and it flew open, rebounding back off the wall so I had to stop it from shutting again with my right hand.

She was standing in her bathrobe with a pool of bloody water spreading around her feet from where it was flowing out of the toilet. The water looked pink as it spilled past the white porcelain, then went to red on the darker floor. Dale said something as I reached for Romero, pulling her to me. Felice turned to me as I drew her in, shutting her mouth, cutting off her scream, and her eyes were wide and uncomprehending. I lifted her up in my arms and Dale moved aside as I carried her out of the bathroom, past Natalie and Rubin at the doorway, back to her bed.

Felice wouldn't let go of me, and I had to pry one hand free to reach into my pocket. I held out the business card Bridgett had given me and said, "Natalie, call her, ask her if we can use her place, bring Dr. Romero over there *now*. Then call Fowler and Lozano."

Natalie took the card and I turned my head to look back into the bathroom. Dale had removed the top of the toilet tank and was reaching inside, trying to stop the flow of bloody water. I looked to Rubin and said, "Get a bag together for the doctor—clothes, stuff like that."

"Right," he said, and headed for her closet.

I knelt down beside the bed, pulling a corner of her bathrobe back over Felice's legs.

"It's okay," I told her. "It's just water, somebody just backed up the pipes. It's okay."

Her mouth was still open, her lower jaw shaking, her whole body trembling. But her eyes came back to me from wherever she had been looking. I stroked her hair and repeated, "It's okay, Felice, it's just water, it's just water."

She put her other hand back around me and pulled her face to my chest, hiding and crying.

Natalie came back. She said, "Bridgett'll be waiting for us."

I nodded and told her to keep an eye on the door until the police came.

I heard Dale say to Rubin, "Cruel motherfuckers who did this, very cruel."

After the police arrived, I left Natalie alone with Dr. Romero and gave Dale and Rubin their brief. Natalie had copied Bridgett's home address onto a piece of paper, and I handed it to Dale, saying, "You'll take Felice to Logan's place, and you'll lock it down. Take the car. Natalie and I'll catch up after we're done here. Call if anything happens, if anything turns up. Make sure Felice gets whatever she needs, but do not let her out of your sight."

Normally, one of the two of them would have given me a smart-ass answer—"What do you think we are, stupid?"—or along those lines. But this time neither of them did. Dale collared one of the cops, and the two of them went down to the car. Scott Fowler came in as they were leaving, and he took the stairs up slowly, looking around.

"You didn't clean the apartment, did you?" he asked.

"Yeah."

"Shit," he said.

"Yeah," I said. By being conscientious, we had effectively destroyed any forensic evidence.

Fowler went to talk to the officer in charge of the scene, and a few minutes after that Dale came back without the cop. He grabbed the vest off the coatrack before he came up the stairs, handing it to me as he said, "I've got the cop watching the car."

Then the bedroom door opened and Felice came out, Natalie with her. Fowler and the cops stopped speaking when the door opened, turning to look, then politely turning back away. Dr. Romero was dressed now, a pair of blue jeans and a white T-shirt, holding a leather briefcase with both hands.

"Ready?" I asked her.

"Yes," she said.

I held up the vest, and Felice handed her briefcase to Natalie. She slipped into the Kevlar and I made certain it was securely fastened. After she had her briefcase back, Felice said to me, "Thank you."

Fowler and two other cops helped us with the egress, and we got her in the car without trouble. Rubin and a cop sat on either side of the doctor in the backseat, with another uniform in the front next to Dale.

"Call me when you get secure," I told him.

"Understood," Dale said. I shut his door and backed away. Felice was looking at me as the car pulled out.

I stopped to get her mail on the way back upstairs, and amongst the bills and mailers, saw an envelope that looked all too familiar. I showed it to Fowler and he took it and bagged it without bothering to open the envelope.

"We'll read it at the lab," he said. "Maybe get a better chance of working some useful information off it."

"Have you pulled DNA off any of them?" Natalie asked.

"Not off these latest ones. Whoever's doing it is using a sponge or washcloth to wet the glue, not their tongue." Scott pulled his cellular and made a quick call, asking for a courier. "Who knows?" he told us after he hung up. "Maybe this one'll be different."

"Only if our luck changes," I said.

———

The police didn't find anything significant. The toilet had been backed up with butcher's cuttings and blood, and forensics determined the blood wasn't human, and surmised that the cuttings were from pigs. Other than that, there was nothing. Best guess was that whoever had clogged the pipes had come in through the broken terrace door.

Two hours after Dale called to tell us they were in, Natalie and I left to join them at Bridgett's. Fowler said he'd call us when he had details on the latest letter. We said thank you, and then took the stairs down to the street. It was nearly eleven in the morning, Friday.

On the subway, Natalie said, "Conference is tomorrow."

"Yeah."

"You been to the Elysium yet?"

"I'll go over there this afternoon, do a walk-through," I said.

She took her notepad from her jacket pocket, pulled out a folded sheet, and handed it to me. "You'll need this. It's the convention schedule."

I glanced over the sheet. It listed panels and talks by title, but didn't tell where the events were going to be held in the hotel. "When'd you pick this up?"

"Couple days ago," she said. "Romero had a stack of them at the clinic. When you're done with the walk-through, give me a list of the changes you'll want and I'll make sure my father gets them done."

"It'd be easier if you came along."

"Maybe," Natalie said. "But one of us should stay on the principal from now until the conference is over, and it'd be better if that's me."

"Yeah?"

"Felice is starting to rely a little too heavily on you," she said. "And you know how that can affect the op. She can't forget that there are other guards around her."

It took me a second to recognize how correct she was. "I wasn't seeing it," I said. "But you're right."

"Transference is normal, Atticus, you know that. It's one of the by-products of our job. Yesterday she hated you, today you're her salvation."

"I thought it was because I'm so roguishly handsome," I said.

"And witty," Natalie said. "It's not too bad yet, but we might want to head it off."

"Sort of flattering, really."

"I wouldn't rely on it as a method of meeting women," she said.

CHAPTER EIGHTEEN

Bridgett's apartment was in a small brownstone in Chelsea on the fifth floor. The building was recently renovated, clean, and the stairs didn't creak. Natalie knocked on the door, saying, "It's us."

Several locks turned and Rubin pulled the door back, letting us through. The door opened into a hall that ran to the left to a tiny living room. After Rubin locked up he led us down the hall.

It was a comfortable, if cramped, apartment, with photographs framed on the walls and a lot of old, perhaps antique, wooden furniture. There was a lumpy easy chair and a faded sofa arranged facing one wall in the living room, a small television and VCR unit that sat on an oak bureau. The television was tuned to CNN.

Dr. Romero was on the couch, her briefcase open beside her, a legal pad on her lap. She said, "Atticus," when I came in, and tried a smile that almost worked, but never reached her eyes. Dale rose from where he was filling the easy chair.

"You're feeling better?" I asked Dr. Romero.

"Showered and had some food," she said. "Working on the funeral preparations. It'll be Monday, the day after the conference. It's keeping my mind busy, you see."

"Good."

"I'm . . . I'm sorry about the apartment."

"That's nothing you should apologize for," I told her.

"If you say so."

"I do," I said. I looked around at everyone. "Let's have a powwow."

Natalie and Rubin joined Felice on the couch, and I motioned Dale back to the easy chair. Bridgett came in from another hall, past the kitchen. She was wearing a black T-shirt and torn black jeans today, flashing skin at thighs and knees, and she said, "Hey, stud. This private?"

"No, stay. You should hear this, too."

"Bitchin'," she said, and leaned against the door frame.

"The conference is tomorrow," I said. "And the threat is still active. It may come from SOS, it may come from another quarter entirely, but I think everyone can agree that an attempt will probably be made. Security for the conference will be good, but that is no guarantee; it never is.

"Do you still plan to attend?" I asked Felice.

She capped her pen and set it on her legal pad. "I've got to go," she said. "They killed my little girl trying to keep me quiet, trying to keep me still. They've won enough off me; I won't give them another victory."

Bridgett shook her head. "Excuse me, but if they kill you, isn't that their final victory? At least in this battle?"

"If they kill me," Felice said.

Bridgett pulled the tin of Altoids from her hip pocket and popped a mint, offering the container around. Natalie and Rubin each took one.

"I'm going to attend," Felice said. "Damn them."

"All right," I said. "Then you will do the following, to the letter, until after the conference. From now until tomorrow night, you go nowhere, do nothing, without at least one other guard with you at all times. This means everything, from sleeping to showering to eating." I looked at my crew. "This means one of you is on her at all times, no excuses."

"When are we going hot?" Rubin asked.

"The conference starts at ten-hundred tomorrow morning," Natalie said. She pulled her notepad out of her jacket pocket and flipped a couple of pages, then found the entry she wanted. "It's scheduled to run until twenty-hundred." She asked Dr. Romero, "When do you plan to arrive?"

"I'm speaking at the opening with Veronica," Felice said. "Then I'm scheduled for a panel at noon and a talk at three. The talk should finish by five."

"Do you know the locations of those talks?" I asked her.

"The panel will be in the Imperial Ballroom, and my talk is to be held in the New York Room," she said. As she spoke, Natalie wrote this new information down. "I believe that Veronica and I are to speak in the Imperial, as well."

Natalie tore the sheet from her pad and handed it to me. I folded it and put it in my pocket next to the schedule. "We're going to need a general briefing with all the agencies involved," I said. "And the only time I see when we'll have a chance to do that is before the conference itself starts. Figure we'll go hot at oh-seven-hundred. Transport at oh-seven-thirty, and we place Dr. Romero in the command post by oh-eight-hundred. We'll hold the general briefing there at oh-eight-thirty. Egress at seventeen-hundred if possible. We return to normal coverage only after Dr. Romero is secured at the safe apartment tomorrow night." While I was speaking, my pager went off, and I silenced it, then checked the number.

"How are we covering in the hot zone?" Dale asked.

"When Dr. Romero is speaking or in any group, all of us. Otherwise I'll be on the principal unless needed elsewhere, in which case one of you will sub in. Dale, you'll be responsible for evac and exits," I said. "Rubin will cover entrances, and Natalie will be the floater. As always, the chain of command will run from me to Natalie to Dale to Rubin."

"Joy," Rubin said.

"Understood?" I asked.

Everyone gave me a nod, even Bridgett.

"Good," I said, and checked my watch. It was almost twelve-thirty. "I'm going to head over to the Elysium now, do the walk-through, and plan the routes."

Bridgett pushed off the door frame and said, "You need a phone? Use the one in my office."

I followed her down the hall. The floor was hardwood, highly polished. She guided me through a door on her right into a small office with an oak desk in a corner. The desk was huge, and I wondered how she had fit it into the room. Its surface was covered with papers, a Macintosh computer stuck in one corner, cables running from it to the printer on the floor. She pointed me to the chair in front of it, pulling a seat for herself from the corner. Both of the chairs were backless, the kind where you rested your knees on pads below the seat. I picked up the phone and dialed.

"Who you calling?" she asked.

"Fowler," I said.

She made a face, then said, "I've got a friend, a reporter. Did some digging for me. You know that Veronica Selby has published four books about abortion and how to protest it?"

"She'd mentioned as much to me."

"Lectures, articles—she's very busy."

"And?"

"She and Crowell were at one point engaged."

Fowler answered his phone before I could respond further, and Bridgett just grinned at my shock.

"Got a preliminary report on the letter," Scott told me. "It reads: 'Dear Butcher Bitch, two down, one to go. Not twins, not triplets. Murdered babies, punished mothers. I will have justice.' That's it."

"Read it again," I said, and grabbed a pen and one of the scraps of paper on Bridgett's desk. Fowler read the letter again and I copied it down, then handed it to her to read, saying to Scott, "Did you find anything on the letter?"

"That's the good news," he said. "The lab pulled fiber traces from the envelope, blue. Could have been carried inside a coat pocket or something. It's not a lot, but it's progress. I'm still waiting for the lab to finish."

"Not a mail carrier's jacket?" I asked.

"No, definitely not. That was the first check we ran. What do you make of the letter, that 'two down' business?"

"No idea."

"Sounds like the writer is Katie's murderer," Fowler said.

"Then who's the second victim?"

"That's a good question. Felice have any other children, anything like that?"

"No."

"Maybe Katie was pregnant?"

"Are you kidding? Absolutely not," I said. "Besides, she was having her period when she was shot."

Bridgett's eyebrows rose. I shrugged at her.

"I'm just theorizing," Fowler said.

"Well, trash that particular theory. Is that it?"

"No, there's one other thing. Barry is out on bail."

Twice the bastard had been caught dead to rights, and twice he had been set free. "How?" I fought to keep my voice level.

"He made bail, Atticus. All he was charged with was

aggravated harassment for the phone call and criminal possession of a weapon for the gun. The call itself is only a misdemeanor, it's the CPW charge that's a felony. He walked on fifty thousand, cash or bond."

"Where'd the money come from?"

"Crowell."

"Barry needs to be in custody," I said. "He's our prime suspect, Scott, and the conference is tomorrow."

"I know. NYPD has been following him since he got out. They'll pull him back in if he gives them cause."

"They better not lose him."

"I know."

"I mean it, Scott."

"Watch your tone, Atticus," he said. "Everybody's doing the best they can."

"Bullshit," I said, and hung up.

Bridgett was looking at me, expectant.

"Barry got out," I told her. "That motherfucker is walking the streets again."

"Tough break, stud," she said.

"Would you stop with that?"

"You don't like being called stud?"

"Not particularly, no."

"Too bad . . . stud," she said, and popped another Altoid.

I got up and headed back into the hall, mostly hoping to find a safe outlet for my anger. And I was angry now, could feel it rumbling. I was having a hard enough time trying to protect Romero as it was without legal loopholes, incompetents, and liars getting in my way.

"Where you going?" Bridgett asked, coming after me.

"Out. I've got to do the walk-through."

"I'll come with you."

"Can I stop you?"

"Maybe with your gun, but I don't think you're that kind of boy," she said.

"You have no idea what kind of boy I am," I said.

"But I'm learning."

We entered the living room. "Bridgett and I are going out. We'll be back about four for the transport," I told Natalie.

"We'll be ready."

Bridgett grabbed her leather jacket from the counter between the living room and the kitchen, slipping into it. Felice stopped what she was doing with her papers to watch us go, and when her eyes found me I discovered that I couldn't look at her. I went to the front door, out of sight, to wait.

No, Felice didn't hate me today. Maybe she didn't even blame me. Natalie was probably correct; I had gone from failure to savior in under twenty-four hours, and as I watched Bridgett Logan come down the hall, her car keys in her hand, I wasn't certain which position I liked better.

CHAPTER NINETEEN

We got into Bridgett's Porsche, and I told her we were going to Park Avenue first.

"The Elysium's on Fifty-third, isn't it? Between Sixth and Seventh?"

"We're making a stop. Unless you're unwilling, in which case I'll just take a cab," I said.

"Whoa, easy, stud. We can make a stop first, sure. So, where am I headed?" I told her to drive uptown and she nodded and ran the Porsche like a demon. "So, whose place are we going to?"

"Veronica Selby's."

The doorman who looked like a royal guard stopped us from entering, and gave us the evil eye while he called Selby on the house phone. He said my last name like it was a disease. It didn't help my mood.

"You can go ahead," the doorman told Bridgett.

I led the way, knocked on the door twice, and was about to rap it again when it was opened by the same woman who had let me in before.

"Veronica is in the living room," she said, and then led us down the hall, then retreated and disappeared as she had before.

Selby was wearing khakis and a white T-shirt today. Her wheelchair was positioned in front of her computer. As we entered she turned and smiled, saying, "This is a surprise, Mr. Kodiak. . . ." Then her smile faded as she read my face.

"Time to confess," I said.

"Excuse me?"

"You held back last time I was here, and I didn't push, because it didn't seem necessary. But now it's out of control, and I want to know everything you know about Crowell, SOS, and his plans."

She drew herself up in the wheelchair. "Are you implying—"

"Goddamnit, stop it," I said. "I know that you were engaged to the man."

That put the brakes on. She looked away from me to a point on the wall. "I was," Veronica Selby said. "But that doesn't mean that I know anything—"

I interrupted again. "No, don't try playing that hand. Katie Romero is in the morgue with holes where her heart should be. Her mother is attending Common Ground tomorrow knowing that she may die, too. Now, you stop with this innocent bullshit now, and you tell me the truth, or I swear to God that Felice won't show tomorrow, and you'll be going it alone."

She turned her head, showing me that lovely neck again, and still not showing me her eyes. "It was a long time ago."

"How long?"

"Five years, no—six. I met him in Albany and I

was . . . I was discouraged, do you understand?" Selby finally looked up at me. "He was charming, and he got things done, or so I thought. And I was tired, so tired of fighting and losing all the time."

"And Crowell is your idea of a winner?"

"He was . . . I thought he was getting things done." She touched the gold cross at her throat. "But he wasn't. He was making things worse."

"You should have told me, you should have told me when I first talked to you. I only found out because Ms. Logan here did a check on Crowell's past."

Selby looked at Bridgett, tilting her chin in a greeting. "Pleased to meet you," she said softly. Her accent was stronger now, southern grace rising to the occasion.

"The pleasure is mine," Bridgett said.

"Why didn't you tell me?" I asked.

Selby went back to worrying the cross, her fingers tracing its shape over and over. "I was ashamed. I was seduced by him, and I was terribly ashamed. Won't you both sit down? Please?"

Bridgett sat on the couch and slid over, making room for me beside her. I positioned myself on the edge of the cushion. Selby rolled closer to us, stopping at the end of the coffee table, folding her hands in her lap.

"It wasn't seduction of the flesh, exactly," she said. "What Jonathan Crowell seduced was my spirit and faith. I've . . . Mr. Kodiak, I think I am a weak person, and I don't know if you can understand that. I conceived when I was only fifteen, and I had an abortion. I aborted my daughter with a coat hanger after drinking a bottle of gin.

"The difficult thing, the right thing, would have been to carry my baby to term, to let her live. But I was a coward and I was weak, and so I murdered her. I nearly died myself as a result, both inside and out. When I left the hospital, my legs were . . ." Her hands strayed to the wheels of the chair, then back to her lap.

"This is my life, Mr. Kodiak. I believe from the bottom

of my soul and with all my heart that abortion is murder, and that murder is wrong. But I believe more that Jesus Christ is my salvation." She stopped speaking for a moment, looking past me. I turned, and the woman who had let us in was standing in the archway.

"It's all right, Madeline," Selby said. "Perhaps you could bring us some tea?"

"Certainly, Ronnie," Madeline said. She hesitated, watching me, then went back down the hall.

Selby continued, "What Jonathan Crowell said to me, fundamentally, absolutely, I agree with to this day. To abort a child is to murder a child. And I heard him say what I felt, except say it more eloquently, and I heard him say it at a time when I was succumbing to weakness again. I had lost my faith, and I thought that through Jonathan I could find it again."

"You didn't," I said.

She almost smiled. "It took me a while. It took me long enough to have accepted one ring from him, and to want a second. But then I realized exactly what he was doing."

"Which is?"

" 'He that sayeth I know Him, and keepeth not His commandments, is a liar, and the truth is not in him,' " she said. "Jonathan Crowell claims to act in the name of Our Lord, to do His bidding. Jonathan has claimed His authority, but refuses to submit to the same. And that is a sin, Mr. Kodiak. That is a terrible, almost unforgivable sin."

Madeline returned with a silver tray. There were three glasses and a pitcher of iced tea on it. She set the tray on the coffee table and then put a hand on Selby's shoulder, eyeing Bridgett and me. Selby said, "Thank you."

Madeline nodded, then left, and I poured three glasses.

"I should have told you," Selby said after accepting her glass. "But you reacted so strongly when you saw his name on the list, and I was terrified that Felice wouldn't come, that you wouldn't let her attend Common Ground."

"Do you think Crowell is behind Katie's murder?" Bridgett asked.

"I hope not, I hope . . . he's certainly responsible for some of the letters," Selby said. "Indirectly, at least. Jonathan would never write them himself; instead, he would encourage others to do that work for him."

"And what about Dr. Romero?" I asked. "Do you think he is trying to kill her?"

"I don't know if Jonathan is trying to kill Felice," she said. "But I think he is capable of justifying such a murder. He has assumed that authority. Whether he would actually try to do it, I don't know."

"Do you know Clarence Barry?"

She frowned. "Clarence Barry? I knew him through Jonathan."

"Would he murder a sixteen-year-old retarded girl?"

Selby said, "Clarence Barry is so full of hate he could do anything. He used to make jokes about . . . Let's just say he speculated about what Jonathan and I would do in bed, had we gotten married. His speculation wasn't kind, and centered on the fact that I have very little movement in my legs." She emptied her glass, turning it in her hand and watching the ice slide before setting it on the tray with a gentle click. "I'll make certain that Jonathan isn't admitted to the conference," she said.

"Is he a martyr?" I asked.

"Jonathan? It's one of the parts he plays, but it isn't anything more than an act."

"Then don't bar him from attending," I said. "If we keep him from coming, we create a martyr. If he comes, we'll be able to keep tabs on him. And if he's not willing to sacrifice himself to his cause, then Felice may actually be safer if he is there."

"I see," Selby said.

I stood. "We've got to go."

Bridgett set her glass down. "Thanks for the tea," she said, rising.

"Certainly." Selby turned her chair slightly toward me, so we were facing, and offered her hand. I took it. "Will you allow Felice to attend?" she asked.

"She'll attend," I said. "We'll see you tomorrow morning."

"Tomorrow will be a good day," she said.

Madeline showed us out.

We parked in the garage provided by the Elysium, and before we went up into the hotel, I asked the attendant what the security was like around the cars.

"Cameras," he said. "We check for new plates every evening."

"Is that all?"

He shrugged.

I thanked him and then Bridgett and I went up to the lobby. "Let's hope nobody wants to take out the whole building," I said.

"You think they'd use a car bomb?" Bridgett asked.

"They're in vogue," I said.

"That would be totally sprung."

"And murdering doctors isn't?"

We came in from the garage, near the center of the lobby. It was beautifully appointed, broad, heavily carpeted, decorated in browns and golds. Quite stylish. The front entrance was actually on the west side of the building, allowing one to enter near a variety of services, from a sports bar and café to the south and a bar and lounge to the north. After a moment to look around and count the cameras, I took Bridgett to the bar. We each bought a Coke and had a seat.

"What are you doing?" she asked.

"Just looking. How many guards do you see?"

She downed a handful of complimentary mixed nuts, chewing thoughtfully. After a minute of watching the lobby, Bridgett said, "I count three. They're the ones in the blazer-and-slack combos, right?"

I nodded. "There are five," I said, and pointed them out. "Then there are those two, house detectives, probably." Both were in plainclothes, and one was actually lurking near us. I smiled at him and he looked hard at Bridgett and me, then moved on.

"Thinks I'm tricking," Bridgett said. "Guess I should've worn my nice clothes, huh?"

"Or one less nose ring," I said.

We finished our sodas and then walked over to the reader board. The board was electronic, with announcements scrolling past in bright red LED. A pediatrics convention was in town; so was a technical writers' symposium. The board listed "Common Ground: Abortion in the United States" near the end of its cycle, noting that registration began at eight the next morning. I looked over the schedule Natalie had given me, then handed it to Bridgett.

"Let's check the rooms," I said.

The Imperial Ballroom was almost large enough to earn its name, but apart from that, didn't look as if it would pose a problem. There were three sets of doors off the hallway that led into the room, but two of those could easily be sealed to control the access. On the south side of the west wall was another door, and when I opened that I was in a service hallway.

"Are we allowed back here?" Bridgett asked me.

"That's half the point," I told her.

We followed the hall along and passed several storerooms, two kitchens, and twelve staff people. Not one person stopped us or asked what we were doing. The hall ended on a loading dock, and a camera was positioned there to watch whoever came in or out. I gave it the finger. Hopefully, somebody was awake in the control room, and flipped me off in return.

"This isn't good, is it?" Bridgett asked.

"It's not too bad, actually," I said. "This is all single access. Sentinel will put one person here, in a uniform. As long as the instructions are simple and clear, there shouldn't be a problem." I pushed the door back open and we headed back the way we had come.

Two men were waiting for us at the end of the hall. About ten feet away from them, the elder of the two said, "You're still wearing those damn earrings, Kodiak."

I grinned and tugged on the two hoops in my left earlobe. "So I don't lose my head," I said. "Makes it easy to hold."

"Hate to have those yanked in a fight," the other one said. I didn't know him, but his voice was wonderfully distinctive, rich and with an accent.

"Bridgett Logan," I said, indicating the first man, "this is Elliot Trent, Natalie's father."

"We've met," Bridgett said.

"Yes, we have," Trent said. "I assume you've since replaced your camera?"

Bridgett grinned. "Oh, yeah. The agency's still waiting to be reimbursed."

"An oversight," Trent said. "I'll have a check cut to you today." He went so far as to make note of it in the leather portfolio he was carrying. Then he closed the portfolio and said, "Why don't we go upstairs, so I can give you an operations brief?"

We followed Trent and the other man up to the third floor, where the New York Room was. This was the room where Romero would give her talk, and it was already laid out for the event. According to the sign on the wall, the room could seat five hundred people. Elliot Trent took us up to the front of the room, and sat on the edge of the stage, in front of the table. Bridgett and I took seats, and the other man stood for a moment longer, then sat on the opposite side of the aisle. Like Trent, he was dressed conservatively, in that style of dress that seems to linger long after the wearer has left government employ. His skin was very tan, and his hair and eyes were very brown.

"You haven't met Yossi, have you?" Trent asked me.

"No," I said, and extended my hand.

He took it and gave me a firm shake, saying, "Yossi Sella."

"Yossi is fresh from the Shin Bet," Trent said. "Their Executive Protection Squad. We've stolen him away. Much as you've done with my daughter, I might add."

"You mean he's dating your best friend?" I said.

Trent looked appalled, but Sella laughed.

"Let's get to work, shall we?" Trent said.

He had maps of each floor of the conference, showing the rooms that were going to be used, the rooms that were scheduled to be empty, and all the service routes that led to the conference areas. Marked on the maps were security checkpoints, guard posts, and camera emplacements.

"I want restricted access here," I told him. "The elevator should be the only way up, and I want to control the flow into the room."

"There's an escalator onto this floor," Sella said. "And two stairwells."

"The escalator will have to be locked off."

Trent nodded. "We'll put a guard in uniform at the top, just in case. There'll also be one uniform at each stairway."

"What are the cameras like?" I asked.

"They've got good people in their security room," Sella answered. "Not the best, but they pay attention. That's how we saw you in the hallway, on the cameras." He smiled and raised his middle finger at me. Bridgett laughed.

"Can we have a Sentinel uniform in there?" I asked Trent.

Trent shook his head. "But that'll be covered by the marshals."

"How's the communication?"

His frown deepened. "Not great. Because of the publicity, every agency wants to be seen as responding to the best of their ability."

"We're being crowded," Sella said. "But we'll manage."

"I want a general briefing for eight-thirty in the morning," I told Trent. "Where we can make introductions, set up the pecking order, so on. Can you arrange that?"

He nodded and made another note on his pad. "I already discussed the importance of a briefing with Ms. Selby, so she's prepared for the eventuality."

I got up and started walking around the room. "This is the only place Dr. Romero will speak solo," I said. "If there's a try, my instinct is it'll be here."

Trent pointed to a door in the corner. "That leads to the kitchen. No refreshments are being served, so we'll lock it down before her talk begins."

About five feet from the doors into the room were a series of switches mounted on the wall, sliders and buttons. One of the buttons was square and red, and I pressed it.

All the lights went out, and the room was completely dark.

"Well, that's definitely not good," I heard Bridgett say.

I pressed it again.

"We need to cover this up," I said, when the lights came back on.

Trent made another note. "Anything else you can think of, Atticus?" he asked.

"Couple more things. First of all, I want a designated watcher outside each event Dr. Romero attends. Make sure that person has photographs of Barry, Rich, and Crowell, and make sure the only job they have is to look for those faces. I want to know if they show.

"Second, at each event Romero attends, nobody carries anything in. They check their bags, purses, whatever. Additionally, I want all attendees run through a metal detector."

"We'll be doing spot searches at the registration desk," Trent said. "That's where the metal detector will be set up."

"Then get somebody with a hand-held," I said. "No way I want anything snuck into a room where Romero is speaking."

"We can't demand that people check their bags," he objected. "Too much flack."

"I don't give a shit about flack, Elliot."

"No, you wouldn't. But how we look does matter. My agency is the marquee name here."

"Listen. I don't give a shit," I said again. "It's my principal."

"We should be certain," Sella told Trent.

"We can search bags," Trent said. "But we cannot check them. Logistically, that's more than we can handle."

"Thorough searches," I said.

"Of course," he said. He checked his watch and then looked at me. "Is that all?"

"One last thing. I want a room for Romero to stay in while she's not speaking. Nothing fancy, just someplace she can be comfortable until she's on."

Sella smiled. "We've already taken care of that. The command post is in a large suite, and one of the adjoining rooms has already been designated for Dr. Romero."

"Then that's it," I said to Trent. "I'll have Natalie phone you tonight with any additions and details on Romero's transport."

Trent closed his leather portfolio and rose, rebuttoning his jacket. "We'll see you tomorrow, then. The apartment should be clear by now, so if you want to move the doctor, go right ahead."

"We will. Thanks for the loan."

Trent nodded. He knew he was doing me a favor; we both knew eventually I'd be asked to pay it back.

Sella got up and we shook once more, then he took

Bridgett's hand and crooned, "I hope we'll be seeing each other again."

"I'm sure I'll see you tomorrow," Bridgett said.

He released her hand, saying, "Until then."

We watched them go. She was paying, it seemed to me, particular attention to Sella as he departed.

"Cute ass on that one," she said to me after the door shut.

"Tomorrow you can ask for a close-up."

"Tomorrow maybe I will."

We headed out of the room, taking the stairs down to the lobby. "What's the deal with the camera?" I asked.

"Sentinel was hired to protect an oil exec," Bridgett told me. "Agra and Donnovan was hired by said exec's wife shortly thereafter to prove the gentleman was engaging in extramarital recreation. This was at the end of my apprenticeship, before I got licensed, about a year ago. Anyway, I got pictures of this fellow romping with a brunette at a hotel in Boston."

"You beat Sentinel security?" I asked.

"It took time and money and me dressing up in a maid's uniform, but yes. Rigged a couple of distractions and managed to get in and click away. And on my way out I ran into Natalie and another guard."

"And she took the camera?"

"No, the other one did. Stomped it to pieces. Took the whole thing very personally, unlike Natalie, who thought it was funny. I don't think she liked the client." We were at the garage and she handed the attendant our parking stub. He disappeared to find the car.

"How much money were you out?"

Bridgett laughed. "We weren't. It was all expenses, and we got a bonus for completion."

"You lost the pictures."

She popped a Life Saver into her mouth. "Who said there was only one camera, stud?"

CHAPTER TWENTY

Dale drove us to the safe apartment, with Rubin in the front seat and Felice sandwiched in her Kevlar between Natalie and myself. The drive took thirty minutes, with Dale winding his way along the streets. The apartment was in the Upper West Side, only two blocks from where Alison lived. When I thought about that, I felt the emptiness again, and felt too the rage that had possessed me to smash a phone against a wall.

Bridgett and I had returned to her place shortly after five. We'd found Dr. Romero ready to go.

"You're coming along, aren't you?" Felice asked me.

"I'll be riding with you."

Romero gathered her stuff together and Natalie gave me an I-told-you-so look. I shrugged, then arranged to meet Bridgett back at her place before eight.

The apartment was on the ground floor on a quiet street, and we were met by a Sentinel employee who handed Natalie the keys and showed her how to disarm the alarm. It was nicely furnished inside, classic styling that oozed money and power, designed to make Sentinel's clients feel as if they were at their new home-away-from-home. The air had a slightly antiseptic tang from the rushed cleaning it had gotten before being turned over to us.

All five of us made a quick walk-through. The kitchen was fully outfitted, all the cupboards crammed with canned goods and other foodstuffs. The two bedrooms were small, each decorated with classic prints of English country foxhunts. We ended our tour in the living room. It wasn't particularly spacious, but it was certainly comfortable, and there were no bloodstains on the carpet. Dr. Romero sat at the desk there and went back to her papers.

Dale asked, "We're all sleeping here?"

"You three and Felice will," I said. "I'll be back here early tomorrow before the transport."

"I'll need to go home before then," he told me. "Get a change of clothes and some stuff."

Rubin said, "I'd like some clean underwear myself."

I looked at Natalie and said, "You willing to go down to just two for a while tonight?"

"That's our minimum," she said. "We're good here. The glass is bulletproof, the doors are almost unbreachable, and we've got everything we could want."

"Dale, you go home, get what you need, and get back here by ten tonight," I said. "Rubin'll go after you get back." I asked Natalie what she wanted to do about herself.

"What time are you planning on getting here tomorrow morning?" she asked.

"I was thinking seven or so."

"Make it six and I'll run home, then meet you back here."

"Deal," I said. "One other thing before I go. Give your

father a call, see if we can get Dr. Romero a Kevlar dress shirt for tomorrow."

Felice looked up from where she was writing. "I don't want to wear the vest at the conference."

"This'll look and feel mostly like an ordinary shirt," I told her.

"Mostly?"

"Well, it's not silk, let's put it that way."

She stared at me, unsmiling, and said, "If you think that's best."

"Will white be okay?" Natalie asked her.

"I have a choice?"

"A rainbow of colors to choose from," she said.

"White will be fine, thank you."

Natalie looked at me and said, "They actually do a nice blouse, believe it or not. I'll have some options brought by for her to look at."

"Fashion show," Rubin snorted.

I noted the phone number of the apartment, told everyone I'd see them tomorrow, and left.

Bridgett said, "The thing is, I can't find anything to tie these directly to Crowell."

I looked at her over the coffee table in her living room, then looked back at the pile of letters she had set there. Yellow tabs of Post-Its stuck out from various letters, and she had filled several pages of a college rule notebook with her notes on what she had found. The apartment was dark now, and the only light came from a lamp in the corner.

"Then we're just not seeing it," I said.

She fussed with her nose ring, then sat back in the easy chair. "Well, stud, I'm open to suggestions."

I looked at the piles. "How are these arranged?"

"The big pile, those are from organizations other than SOS. Anything that claimed affiliation with some right-to-life group. Not necessarily threats in the SOS sense, but possibly dangerous. The second one, medium there, that's SOS."

I looked at the pile she meant. It was easily three hundred pages. "All of it?"

"If it had the emblem, you know, that cross and barbed-wire thing, or the letterhead, or mention of either Crowell or the organization, it went into that pile." She arched her hips in the chair, pulling the tin of Altoids from her back pocket and then relaxing again. She dropped three of them in her mouth, one after the other. "Last pile, that's just the letters that didn't have any clear association."

"And the latest ones, those are in that pile?"

"Bingo."

I picked up that pile, found the handwritten transcript of the letter Fowler had read to me, then the two others of the same style and read them again, in the order received. *'Dear Butcher Bitch, two down, one to go. Not twins, not triplets. Murdered babies, punished mothers. I will have Justice.'* The only SOS connection was in the letter writer's desire for justice, a sentiment Crowell had shared with the crowd outside of the clinic.

And in that crowd, anybody could have written these letters, I thought.

The answer clicked fast and solid and I knew, intuitively knew, the answer was correct. At the same time, I realized exactly how much trouble we were in, all of us, me, the squad, and most of all, Felice Romero.

"What? What are you thinking?" Bridgett asked.

"It's not Crowell," I said. "We've been blind, we've been focusing on him because he's big and he's using the conference, and we haven't even considered that the threats could be coming from somebody who doesn't care about Common Ground at all."

"Then why try to kill Felice?"

"You're assuming that Katie's murder was an accident. What if it wasn't, what if somebody was gunning for her specifically?"

"But killing Katie serves only one purpose, stud; it keeps Romero from attending Common Ground."

"But it doesn't," I said. "I mean, look, Katie's dead and Felice is still going."

"Then what's the motive?"

"Revenge." I handed her the letters. "We're looking for a man who knows a woman who had an abortion. This is all about revenge. Why else kill Katie?"

Bridgett read the letters, marking them with her black felt-tip pen. For five minutes we didn't speak, me thinking of the possibilities, and Bridgett trying to find a hole in my logic. She set down the pen finally, took a handful of her hair, and tugged, saying, "Fuck a duck."

"No Crowell," I said.

"This doesn't rule him out," Bridgett objected. "He could still be connected to this."

"I don't think so," I said. "It's got to be some guy who's wife or girlfriend or mother or whoever had an abortion."

"That doesn't absolve SOS or Crowell," Bridgett said, and her voice climbed slightly, pressing her point.

"Look at the letters," I said. "There's no reference to the organization. On these other ones," and I pointed at the medium-sized pile, "you said there was the SOS emblem, some sort of signifier. But on these new ones, nothing."

She pushed her hair back into place, then began gnawing on her bottom lip. "It explains the letter at the clinic yesterday," she conceded. "The writer was shooting at Katie, not Romero, so he knew Romero would get the letter."

"Makes the writer and the shooter one and the same," I said. "And that goes to revenge. He's telling Felice what he's doing, because if she doesn't know why he killed Katie, why he's going to kill her, there's no point. He writes these letters to let her know."

"But they're obtuse, stud. I mean, if that's what this guy wants, why not just say, 'Dr. Romero, you killed my wife's baby, and I'm going to kill you'?"

"He wants her to suffer. Why else kill Katie?"

"You murdered my child, I'll murder yours?" she said.

"Yes."

Once again, she reread the letters. "So you're saying that we've been looking in the wrong place."

"That's what I'm saying." I pulled my glasses off and rubbed my eyes.

"So you've been trying to protect Dr. Romero from a threat that's coming from a different direction entirely?"

I nodded.

"You're fucked," she said softly.

I nodded again.

"Okay," Bridgett said. "Let's work the problem, right? If it's revenge, then the abortion in question had to be through the clinic. The author has claimed two bodies, and we know one of them is Katie, so the other is who?"

"Not Romero," I said.

"No, not Romero. Not if your theory is correct, anyway. He won't claim her until she's dead. It's got to be the mother, then, right? The woman who had the abortion. He's killed the mother for having the abortion, and he's killed Katie because Romero performed the abortion, to let her know what it felt like."

"So it's a question of finding the man who impregnated a woman who went to the Women's LifeCare Clinic in the last year or so and who had an abortion," I said. "That can't be too hard, right? Only one, maybe two thousand candidates?"

"No, we're looking for a dead woman," Bridgett said. "And these letters started only a couple of weeks ago, so it's got to be a patient that died fairly recently." She got up and went to the phone on the kitchen counter. "I'll call Dr. Faisall, see if I can get access to the patient files."

"It may not be worth it," I said. "Common Ground is tomorrow, Bridgett."

Without stopping her dialing, she said, "You're being awfully defeatist." Then she was talking to Dr. Faisall, explaining our theory and asking if she could please look at the patient records of the last few months. The inactive records, Bridgett specified, people who were no longer coming in for one reason or another.

I put my glasses back on and then my pager went off. I silenced it and held it up for Bridgett to see. She nodded, told Dr. Faisall she would be by the clinic in the morning, then hung up and stepped out of the way for me at the phone.

It was Fowler. There was significant background noise over the phone, multiple voices and what sounded like radios crackling.

"Atticus, is Romero secure?"

"Very," I said.

"Barry lost his tail," Fowler said. "He went to see Crowell, left there, and headed to Grand Central. Took the shuttle to Times Square. NYPD lost him near Port Authority. We think he's left the city."

"But you don't know?"

"No, we don't. A bench warrant's been issued, and there's an APB out on him. I interviewed Crowell after we heard Barry had bugged, and he was convincingly surprised. Crowell told me that he had fired Barry."

"Hold on," I said, and relayed the information to Bridgett.

"Ask Fowler if he knows about Barry's personal life," she said.

I ran that one at him and Scott said, "What? Why?"

"He ever been married? Have a girlfriend, siblings, anything?"

"No girlfriend," Fowler said. "No known acquaintances except Crowell. He's got two sisters in Tennessee. We think that may be where he's headed. Look, I've got to go, coordinate this thing with NYPD. It's a monkey-show over here."

"Sounds like it was from the beginning. You never should have lost him."

"Fuck you," he said cheerfully, and banged the phone down.

Bridgett had gone down the hall, and now came back, fastening a shoulder holster into place, a Sig Sauer P220 now riding under her right arm. She reached for her jacket, saying, "Let's go."

"You think we're going to find Barry?" I said.

Bridgett shook her head. "But I can think of a good place to start looking."

She parked off Fulton, about a block from Romero's apartment. The streetlights shone on all the people out for a Friday night walk to the South Street Seaport, holding hands or clustered in groups that we had to step around.

"I want to see the apartment," Bridgett had said once we were in the Porsche.

"The police have—"

"I know," she said. "But I haven't."

"We don't know if Barry is the shooter," I said.

"I doubt he is. But the shooter backed up the pipes, under our current theory. I want to see if he left anything behind."

"Anything that the police and FBI might have missed, you mean," I said.

"Do you have a better idea?" she shot back.

"We could go to Crowell's and beat him within an inch of his life," I said.

"No, we couldn't. You'd end up in jail, and what would Romero do without you?"

"What's that supposed to mean?"

"Nothing. Here, have a mint, stud."

I took the mint and crunched on it, and neither of us spoke for the rest of the drive.

Philippe was at the door and I remembered I owed him twenty bucks, so I gave him the money before we went past. Bridgett watched the exchange of currency without comment. We took the stairs to the second floor, passing a young man I didn't recognize as we started down Romero's hall. Bridgett stayed ahead of me and didn't stop. When we'd instituted security for Romero, I had made a point of getting to know each face on the doctor's floor.

This guy wasn't one of them.

Could be anybody, I thought.

But I stopped and turned around and said, "Hey, excuse me?"

He had opened the door to the stairwell, and he turned his head. His hair was buzz-cut short, dirty blond, and his arms were thick and powerful. A pair of brown leather gloves were thrust into the back pocket of his jeans. His face was that of a boy. His eyes were hazel, and they met mine.

Gloves, I thought. In summer.

Then he ran.

"Bridgett!" I shouted and started after him, yanking the door to the stairwell back in time to see him exiting into the lobby. I swung over the railing, and felt my left ankle twist and then give as I came down on the last step. I sprawled forward through the door before it swung shut completely.

"Stop that man!" I shouted to Philippe.

He took a second to react, then pivoted, putting his body between the other man and the door, but the other man didn't stop, just bent low and then blasted forward like a linebacker after a quarterback when the blitz is on. Philippe went through the glass door backward, hitting the cement sidewalk hard, the glass showering about them both. The other man regained his footing almost immediately and kept going.

Bridgett ran past me as I got up, and I was ten feet behind her when we hit the street. Philippe was coughing as I went past, struggling to his feet, and I assumed he was fine.

Bridgett had pulled up, looking frantically both ways, growling, "Where's that pest-bastard?"

There was a ripple in the Friday-night crowd, heading south toward the Seaport. I started that way, Bridgett following me. I'm not much for running, only when chased, I suppose, but I am quick.

This guy was, too, and he had the lead on us.

We hit the open promenade of the Seaport in time to see him push through a crowd that had surrounded a fire-eater. My left ankle was killing me, protesting with sincere pain every time I came down on it. Bridgett cut left around the crowd, and I went right, and we met up again on the other side, each scanning. The crowd was bubbly, liquid, shifting easily now, and with a lot of noise, conversation, patter, laughter.

He was nowhere to be seen.

"Fuck!" Bridgett shouted. "Fuck fuck fuck!"

A young couple pulled their son away from us, and the crowd thinned near where we stood.

"Son of a bitch," Bridgett said breathlessly. "Mother of . . . oh, I'm so mad I could just—what the fuck are you looking at?" The last was directed at a young woman wearing a Fordham T-shirt.

"Whoa," the woman said, and backed away with her friends.

"Preppy bitch," Bridgett said.

"I know who he is," I said.

"What?"

"That guy, I know where I've seen him before. Outside the clinic, the day the bottle was thrown. He was with Barry, he was wearing a Columbia University sweatshirt."

"You're sure it's the same guy?"

"It's the same guy."

"Good, okay, good, that means we can find his name," she said. "That means we can find out who he is."

"No."

"What do you mean, no?"

"He wasn't arrested."

She squeezed her eyes closed, putting both her hands to her head and sliding them up into her dark hair. Her hair fell back and she exhaled sharply, then opened her eyes and said, "He was in her apartment, wasn't he?"

"Maybe," I said. "Probably."

"We'll get prints off her door. I've got a kit in the Porsche."

I shook my head. "No, he had gloves. He must have worn them in the apartment."

"The stairwell!" Bridgett said.

We gave the crowd one last look-over, but it was futile. Then we turned and started back up the street.

"Quit limping," she told me.

"Fuck you," I said sweetly.

Philippe was on the phone when we got back to the building. Bridgett continued on to her car for her print kit. I waited until he hung up. "Just ordered a new door," he said. "Who the hell was that guy?"

"An athlete," I said.

"No shit?" He brushed specks of glass from his uniform, muttering.

"You're okay?"

"Didn't get cut, if that's what you mean. Don't know how."

"Lucky."

"You get him?"

I shook my head.

He went to get a broom, saying, "Should I call the police?"

"We'll handle it," I told him.

Bridgett dusted the doors to the stairwell, both front and back, and then worked the railing. She pulled numerous useless prints, but got a portion of a palm off the inside of the first-floor door where we figured University had pushed it open.

"It's a nice partial," she said, blowing gently on the toner.

She prepared the cards and I used the doorman's phone to call Fowler's cellular. I told him what happened, that I recognized the man from outside the clinic, and that Bridgett had pulled a possible print. Fowler said he'd get there as soon as he could, and told us not to disturb anything more.

"Let us do our job," he said. "You protect Romero: That's what you do. I find clues and bad guys: That's what I do. Got it?"

"We'll be in the apartment," I said.

"No, you won't," he said. "Don't even go near it. You'll destroy evidence."

"We'll wait in the lobby," I said.

"That's a good boy. Keep it up and you'll get a puppy treat."

I barked at him before he hung up.

Bridgett didn't want to wait in the lobby. "I just want to look around," she said.

"We wait."

She grumbled and checked her pockets for more candy, coming up empty and heading to a deli next door to restock. The first patrol car pulled up as she returned, starting in on the first roll. The CSU arrived a few minutes later. Bridgett was starting on a new roll, Spear-O-Mint, when Fowler showed up and told us to wait in the lobby. We followed him up to Romero's apartment.

It would have been funny, I think, if the situation was different. But walking into the apartment again, taking the flight of stairs onto the main floor, and seeing, again, the whole living room in forensic disarray, a pressure built behind my eyes. While Bridgett dogged Fowler through the apartment, I stood by the stairs, and watched the technicians work. This wasn't the same as when Katie died, I knew that, but it was hard to get past it, and my dream from the night before came back sharply.

Cops and techs coming up the stairs kept brushing past me. The third time the same officer bumped me I snapped, "Watch what the hell you're doing."

The patrolman turned and said, "You got a problem?"

"You can stop fucking pushing me every time you come up the stairs, that's my problem."

He shoved his face to mine, leaving half an inch of hostile air separating us. "You can wait outside, or you can shut up, but you're at a crime scene and you've got no rights, asshole."

I almost put my fist in his stomach, but Bridgett got to me first, saying, "Come here, would you?" and pulling me by the arm. The cop and I kept eye contact until Bridgett nudged me into the bedroom.

"What the fuck's your problem?" she asked.

"No problem," I said. "I just don't like being pushed."

"You don't like . . ." She shook her head. "Try the decaf, stud, calm down."

"Don't call me stud."

"Sit down, stud," Bridgett told me.

I glared at her and she pushed my chest with her index finger firmly. "Sit." I took a seat on the bed, watching while the CSU analyzed the stained footprints on the carpet by the bathroom. One of the techs asked me to take off my sneakers so she could run a comparison, and I complied without comment. My ankle was starting to swell, and it hurt to remove my shoe.

"Five sets," I heard her tell Fowler. "I can tell you that already. One of them's his," and she pointed the toe of my Reebok at me. "I assume we've got matches for the others at the lab. But we do have a fresh one."

"You didn't come in here before we arrived?" Fowler asked me.

"No."

The CSU tech gave me my sneakers back, and after that, feeling claustrophobic, I limped back down to the lobby. I thought about calling the safe apartment to check on everything, decided against it. There was a bench out front of the building, so I sat on that and waited. The doorman was fussing at the workmen who were replacing the broken door.

Bridgett came out ten minutes later and said, "Mint?"

I took one, looked at it, then threw it across the street.

"That was a waste of a perfectly good mint," she said. "You hungry?"

"I suppose," I said.

"I know a great place. Come on."

Bridgett parked against the curb on Third Avenue and we walked back to the Abbey Tavern. It was dim inside and fairly busy, the bar full. Bridgett turned a sharp right and was greeted by a gray-haired man wearing a subdued suit.

"Bridie, it's been how long?"

She said, "Two months, I think, Chris."

"And those holes, dear Lord, look! Your parents would scream if they saw what you've done to that beautiful face. And how many have you added since I saw you last?"

"Two more," Bridgett said.

"You're mad."

It might have been me, but I could have sworn I heard an accent creeping into her speech.

Chris grabbed two menus and walked us to a booth. After we were seated he said, "I'll send Shannon right over." He gave me a smile, then left the table.

Bridgett shook hair out of her eyes. "You're not Irish, are you?"

"Not unless it's a well-kept family secret," I said.

Our waitress Shannon was short and slender, and gave Bridgett a hug when she reached our table. I was introduced, and Shannon gave Bridgett an approving look, then told us the specials. I picked the lamb stew; Bridgett ordered a large salad. We both ordered pints of Guinness.

"Come here a lot, do you?" I asked.

She nodded and grinned. "My people. And yours?"

"I'm a mutt. Some Czech, some Russian, some Polish."

Our food arrived and we bent to the task. The stew was substantial, and it came with a basket of soda bread that made for perfect company. I cleaned out my bowl and sat back, finishing my stout. "Good choice," I said.

"You want some of this?"

"No, thanks."

She pushed her greens around some more, then set down her fork and knife and pulled out another mint. "So?" she asked. "You want to talk about it?"

"I don't know, actually."

"Fair enough."

Shannon returned and shook her head at Bridgett's bowl. "You'll waste into nothing," she said as she cleared the table. Then she returned and gave us each a cup of coffee.

"Were you going to belt that cop?" Bridgett asked me.

"I might've."

"Dumb."

"I know."

She tapped the side of her cup with a fingernail. Her nails were short, but clean and unpainted. I wondered if she went for manicures.

"Have you ever had an abortion?" I asked her.

"No," Bridgett said. "No, never an abortion."

"The woman I was seeing, she had one. That's how I met Romero."

"Alison?"

"That's her," I said. "We've been seeing each other for about seven months, and she called me when I got in last night, told me that I wasn't the man she wanted to grow old with."

Bridgett raised her eyebrows.

"Not in those words," I amended. "Close, but not those words."

"Her timing is for shit."

"I told her that."

Shannon returned and refilled our coffee cups. Bridgett waited until she was gone, then said, "This because of her abortion?"

"I think in part. If nothing else, it made her take another look at me. And I hadn't been around—I wasn't super supportive after the fact. I was working for Romero."

"You don't sound too certain about the decision."

"No, it was the right thing to do, I really believe that. I can't be a father yet, and Alison sure as hell didn't want to be a mother. It's just that working for Romero, in a way it was an easy excuse. Made the abortion something I didn't have to deal with."

"Not anymore."

"No," I said. "And Katie's dead, and that is so wrong and it makes me so angry . . . shouldn't our child mean the same thing?" I toyed with my coffee cup, watching the way the liquid sloshed along the sides. It made me think of the bloody water pouring from the toilet in Romero's bathroom. "I look at people like Veronica Selby, even Crowell, for God's sake, and I wonder."

"Don't give Crowell that much credit. He doesn't see sanctity of life, he sees a road to attention."

"I think he's a son of a bitch, don't worry. I can't imagine what would be left of him if I got him alone in an alley for a few minutes."

"Him or Barry?"

"Both," I said.

"Romero's still alive."

"Tell me that tomorrow night," I said.

"It's a date," she said as Shannon slipped the check onto the table. Bridgett picked it up before I could, saying, "It's on me."

"Next one's mine," I told her.

"Then I'll pick somewhere extremely expensive tomorrow night," she said. "I don't know what to tell you, Atticus. You're not necessarily talking to the right person, here. I respect Selby, everything I know about her. But I disagree with her fundamental argument. This sounds harsh, but that fetus Alison aborted wasn't anything more than a parasite. It could never have survived without a host, and it was giving nothing in return. Equating that to the murder of Katie Romero, that's only going to fuck with your head, because they are absolutely two different things. Katie Romero, even if she suffered from Down's syndrome, was never a parasite. Her potential was realized, and continued to grow."

"A bastard with a rifle cut that short."

She put some bills on the table and we stood up, stopping to say good night to Chris on the way out. "Don't be gone so long next time," he said to Bridgett. "We've been missing you."

"Promise," she said.

We walked back to her car.

"Get in, stud," Bridgett said. "I'll take you home."

CHAPTER TWENTY-ONE

We drove in silence, each of us thinking, I'm sure, about what exactly she and I were doing, and, perhaps, were going to do back at my apartment. She was very attractive to me that night, we both knew it. But if Bridgett came upstairs, I wouldn't want her to stay, and part of me was preparing what I wanted to say to her if it came to that.

When we reached Thompson, Bridgett couldn't find a place to park. Even the illegal spaces were taken, including the red zone right in front of the hydrant by my building.

"You can just drop me off."

"Let me walk you home."

"You're a perfect gentleman," I told her.

"A foxy chick like yourself shouldn't be walking the streets alone this time of night."

She parked on MacDougal, and together we walked back toward Thompson. It was well after one: Bleecker had few people on it and Thompson was empty. We went into the little entrance cubicle to my lobby, and I unlocked the interior door, and held it open so Bridgett could slide past. I shut the door and she waited for me to get back in front of her, since the hallway was too tight to walk comfortably side by side.

He was waiting on the stairs, and I guess he was expecting only me. As I put my foot on the first step he came around the landing above, and then I was forced back off the steps and into the wall, a baseball bat pressed horizontally against my throat. It was a good hard press, and I couldn't breathe. Barry finished the move by bringing his face close to mine, saying, "Motherfucker, this time I'll make you piss your pants, motherfucker."

Which was a mistake, because Bridgett put her pistol to his temple and said, "Drop it, shithead." She cocked the Sig for emphasis.

He debated the decision for a moment; it was clearly in his eyes as they moved from me to his left, trying to see her. His pressure didn't let up, and my vision began to cloud with dots moving in from the periphery.

"Now," Bridgett said. "Or I'll paint the wall in Early Neanderthal Brain. That means you, Clarence."

Barry looked back in my eyes, the same mad-hatred look he had pointed at me when Lozano led him away, and then took a step back. Bridgett let the barrel leave his temple, but kept the gun trained on him. As the bat cleared my chin, I brought my head down and began coughing, trying to find my breath.

"Drop the bat," Bridgett said.

Barry was still looking at me, the bat now at waist level, held lengthwise with both hands. "Fucker lost me my job," he said. "Fucker ruining my life, thinks he can make me some faggot pussy, making people laugh at me."

"Drop the fucking bat now, Clarence," Bridgett said.

"Yeah, I'll drop it, cunt," he said, and then he jabbed the bat sharply to his left, catching her hard in the chest with the end. Bridgett staggered, losing her aim, and went down on one knee. Barry brought the bat up again and around, zeroing once more on me. This time I was ready for it, and blocked his arm with my left forearm, shunting his swing off to the side. As the blow came down I snapped my forehead into his nose, felt it give, and pulled back to grab the bat. He brought his free hand up to my face, clawing my glasses off, and we both went back against the wall again. I got a second hand on the bat, twisted, and slammed his wrist against the banister. He dropped the bat, and caught me with a backhand that made my head ring. I lost my grip on him entirely, and staggered back into Bridgett.

Barry took a look at Bridgett where she was coming back up with her gun, then turned and went out the side door into the alley.

"Bastards never finish what they start," Bridgett said as she pushed me after him. Her voice was breathy and strained from the blow. I took the short stairs out to the alley in one jump, landing in time to hear garbage cans ahead of us clang and fall. Bridgett came out right behind me, her gun in her right hand, and we turned in time to see Barry start over the fence.

"Stop or I'll shoot," Bridgett shouted at him, bringing her weapon up.

Barry didn't stop and he didn't look back and she brought the gun back down as I tried to make it to the fence. I jumped at the last moment, and my ankle wailed in pain. Barry pulled his foot clear, and I got a handful of nothing, scrabbling at the blurred chain links on the fence. Barry dropped and sprinted through the common courtyard between buildings, then out the alley onto MacDougal.

"This has not been a good night for chases," Bridgett said.

I went back to get my glasses.

———

Barry hadn't bothered with my apartment. Rubin had reconnected the phone in the kitchen while he had been home, so, while Bridgett dumped her coat and holster on the floor, then headed to the bathroom, I called Fowler's cellular and told him the good news.

"So he didn't leave town," Fowler said.

"Very astute of you," I told him, sitting on the window-sill and trying to work my sneaker off without causing my ankle any more damage.

"You want somebody to come by?"

"And do what?" I said. My ankle stabbed a pain up my leg and I decided trying to remove the shoe was probably a bad idea for now. "Bridgett and I both saw him. You pick him up, we'll identify him. There's no point. He's not coming back tonight."

"How can you be so sure?"

"He's not that dumb," I said. "He's crazy, but not dumb. I'm here, Bridgett's here, we've both got guns. He'd have to be absolutely insane to want to risk it."

"Logan's spending the night?"

"Shut up," I told him.

"You could be receiving other visitors," Fowler said. "If Barry found you, it can't be that hard for anyone else. You've been seen around the clinic."

"If somebody else was planning on coming by, they would have done it a while ago, Scott," I said. "My ex-girlfriend and I were photographed going into and out of the clinic on our first visit. I'm sure there's a file on each of us somewhere."

"With your names, addresses, so on."

"Exactly," I said.

"Why's Barry after you?" Fowler asked. "Romero I understand, you don't make much sense."

"I embarrassed him," I said.

"You embarrass a lot of people."

"Thank you, Scott. I know you mean that in the nicest possible way."

"What did you do to him, particularly?"

"I scared him," I said as Bridgett came out of the hallway from the bathroom. She was pulling on her shirt, and I saw another ring, this one through the top of her navel. The ring reflected with the same deep emerald green of her bra, making her skin seem delicate and radiant. I looked out onto the alley before I could see anything else.

"You scared him enough to make him come after you?" Fowler asked.

"The impression I get is that he's blaming me for losing his job."

Fowler was quiet for a moment, and I risked looking back at Bridgett. She had finished with her shirt and was opening the refrigerator. "Beer?" she asked.

I nodded.

Fowler said, "Hate to say this, but if he's after you, maybe that's a good thing. That means he's got less time for Romero."

"That still leaves the gentleman from earlier this evening."

"We're running the prints. We should have something by tomorrow."

We said our good-byes, and Bridgett handed me a bottle of Anchor Steam, taking one for herself. I had some of the beer, then put the bottle on the table and tried again to get my sneaker off. It was easier to do with two hands and no phone. Then I limped to the sink and grabbed a dish towel. With ice from the freezer I made a pack, then went back to the table.

"Elevate your foot," Bridgett told me.

I grunted and swung my leg onto the table, and she took the ice pack and set it around my ankle. I put the beer bottle against my left cheek, where Barry had connected below my eye.

Bridgett slid her chair back against the wall, stretching her legs out in front of her.

"Are you okay?" I asked.

"The bat caught me smack in the middle of the breast-bone," Bridgett said, and indicated the spot between her breasts. "Missed my tits, which is good, but it's going to be a lovely bruise. Nicer than the one you're going to have."

"This will be a mighty fine bruise," I told her, pulling the bottle back to give her a look.

"Amateur stuff."

We finished our beers, and Bridgett said, "I should go. We've both got an early day tomorrow."

"You going to come by the conference?"

"I'm going to the clinic first, look at those inactive files. I'll try to come by in the early afternoon. Will you have any time if I find something out?"

"Probably not, but we'll see."

She rose and put her holster back on, not bothering to stabilize it to her belt. As she slipped into her leather jacket I got my leg off the table and stood up, then went with her to the door.

"Be careful on your way home," I told her.

She gave me a look and then it softened, and she said, "Don't worry about me, stud."

We looked at each other a moment longer, and I got that rush in my stomach, a mixture of anxiety and anticipation.

"Good night," Bridgett said, and she remained in the doorway.

"Night," I said. My pulse was racing faster than it had when Barry attacked in the lobby.

Her mouth turned into a small smile, and for a moment she looked all of fifteen. Then she stepped into the hall, and I watched her go to the stairs, start down them.

I shut the door and set all the locks and got ready for bed. Before I turned off the lights, I put my gun beside my futon. It wouldn't do anything to my dreams, but it would sure as hell slow Barry down.

———

In my dream, we're escorting Romero to the conference, Natalie on point, Rubin and Dale at each flanking position, and me on Romero. We're taking her downstairs, to a panel, and as we get to the floor where she is to speak, the crowd surges in our direction. We try to fall back and keep our zone intact, but it fractures, and I pull Romero back behind me, pushing her up the stairs. I'm keying my palm button, shouting for assistance into the mike on my lapel, but there's nothing; my radio's dead.

Romero is clear behind me, and I start to turn to cover the rest of her retreat, and I see a man with a gun.

I've never seen this man before. He looks like Barry, but not quite. He looks like Crowell, but not quite. He looks mostly like the man in the hall, the one from Columbia.

But not quite.

The gun is a semiautomatic, a Browning, and I do the one thing left for me to do, the one thing it's always been about.

I put myself between the gun and Romero, and the pistol fires, and I feel the slug hit me dead in the middle of the sternum, feel the shock of impact rattle through my body. As I go down, Natalie, Dale, and Rubin all fall on the shooter, swarming and crushing him to the floor. He's out of the picture.

His threat, as they say, has been eliminated.

I put my right hand on my chest, where I've been shot, and I'm afraid to look, but I do anyway.

My hand is clean.

Looking around, behind me, I see Dr. Romero. She's fallen, sprawled over the steps, and there is a hole in her chest where there should be one in mine, there is blood spilling from her mouth where there should be some in mine.

I was up again before dawn.

CHAPTER TWENTY-TWO

We took Dr. Romero in through the service entrance at a quarter past eight in the morning, Natalie leading on point, Dale on the left flank, Rubin on the right, and me in the rear a half-step behind Romero to the right. We had been cleared all the way in, a marshal radioing me before we left the car that an escort would meet us at the end of the hall.

Uniformed NYPD officers, holding paper cups of coffee and looking almost awake, had covered the entrance. Dale stayed behind the wheel while we got out, pulling out when we were clear of the car and then quickly backing into place. It would save us time if we had to leave in a hurry. But if things got that bad, it probably wouldn't matter.

I keyed the small button on my left palm and said, "Pogo is in." All of us were wearing radios with roughly the same setup. The unit sat on my belt, black metal and plastic about the size of a pack of cigarettes, with three wires running off it. The first went down my left sleeve, my off hand, and ended in the transmit button. The second ran up the back of my shirt to my right ear, ending in the receiver. The third ran along the inside of my coat to the lapel, where the mike rested. The mike was small, and very sensitive, easily picking up conversation when the button was keyed.

In my ear I heard the dispatcher announce our arrival to all units. *"Confirmed, Pogo is on scene."*

Dale was back in the fourth position by the time we entered the hallway. The cops moved only to let us pass, and as we walked down the concrete corridor, more like a bunker's than a hotel's, we passed two other guards in the black and gold of Sentinel's security uniforms. The hall ended with doors on the right, where two men in blue marshal's jackets waited for us. One of them went to the door on the right, preparing to open it.

The dispatcher said, *"Pogo is clear through the Imperial Room."*

"That's a negative," I said. "Pogo will not, repeat not, enter through the Imperial Room. Pogo will proceed to the CP by an alternate route."

Natalie put her hand over the marshal's, pushing the door shut again and saying, "What the fuck are you doing?"

He looked confused. The second marshal pulled his radio and began speaking into it.

The dispatcher came back at me saying, *"South stairwell clear to third floor."*

"Ten-four," I said. "Natalie, proceed."

She dropped her arm and looked at the man in front of her, and he looked at the other marshal, who was listening to his radio. The marshal on the radio nodded to his partner, and they opened the door ahead of us. We collapsed a little closer about Felice as we started up. The radio traffic as we moved was mostly minor. Our frequency was secured for just the protection detail, limited to my crew, the dispatcher in the command post, and myself. If there was news happening on another channel, it was up to the dispatcher to inform us.

As we got to the third floor, the dispatcher came back on, saying, *"Pogo is clear all the way in."*

The marshals opened the door onto the hall, each stepping out on either side of us, and we went through, from the concrete to the carpet. The command post was two doors down on the left, and we passed two more guards in Sentinel uniforms on our way, and another NYPD uniform.

One of the marshals opened the door for us, and we stepped inside. The large suite was quiet: that would change once the conference got going. The curtains had been drawn over the windows, and all the lights in the room were on. A large table at one end of the suite was covered with papers and maps, and copies of the Common Ground schedule were taped to the wall in four separate places.

Fowler, Trent, and Lozano were all there, as well as two other men I didn't recognize. A woman wearing a black headset over her short blond hair was seated at a desk, scribbling notes onto a pad. She was hooked to one radio via the headset, and had another at hand. She turned to look at us as we entered, then keyed her headset and said, *"Dispatch to all units, Pogo is secure."* A man in NYPD uniform and sergeant's stripes looked at us when she did, then spoke into his radio, too.

Elliot Trent turned from where he was standing behind the dispatcher and said, "This way," then led us into a bedroom on the side.

"Five minutes until the briefing," he said. "I've ordered coffee and Danish."

"Fine," I said.

Trent nodded and went back out, shutting the door behind him.

Felice dropped her briefcase on the bed, then went after the buttons on her overcoat. The overcoat looked like a Burberry, but was layered Kevlar, much like the blouse she was wearing, but stronger. With the coat and blouse, she would survive just about any shot, if the blunt trauma didn't kill her.

No guarantees.

Felice put the overcoat on the bed, then sat down, smoothing her skirt and looking at me. The skirt was light brown, and fell to just above her ankles. She was wearing flats, and the blouse that Natalie had found was pearl white and looked quite nice on her.

"Now what?" she asked. Her face was drawn, and her makeup did nothing to hide her fatigue.

"Now you wait," I said. "We'll have a general briefing that you'll want to attend, just so everyone can identify you. Otherwise, there's nothing for you to do but try and relax."

Dr. Romero nodded, then reached for her briefcase and opened it, returning to her papers.

People began arriving for the briefing about five minutes later, Veronica Selby and Madeline among them. Selby and Romero spoke quietly to each other for a few moments before we actually began, Selby holding both of Felice's hands in her lap while the two women talked.

By the time we were ready to start, the main room of the command post was crammed with people, among them several federal marshals, FBI agents, NYPD brass, and Sentinel personnel. Elliot Trent made a brief welcome, then introduced Selby. She didn't speak for long, mostly thanking everyone for their assistance and participation thus far, and emphasizing the need for the conference to be peaceful. Then we went around the room, introducing ourselves and stating our agency.

There wasn't a whole lot more to say. Everyone present

knew that the threat against Romero was legitimate. Everyone present knew that Barry, Rich, and Crowell were all to be considered possible trouble. Fowler circulated a description of the man Bridgett and I had encountered the night before, saying that if anyone matching the description was seen doing anything suspicious, he and I were to be notified ASAP.

By the time we were finished, the coffeepots were empty, and there wasn't a Danish to be seen.

I took Romero back to her room, accompanied by Selby and Madeline, then told Rubin to stay with them while I went back out to finish speaking with the others.

Fowler was speaking to his supervisor, who shook my hand and then, after looking around, nodded once and said, "Looks like things are well in hand." Then he headed for the door, stopping to chat with the two NYPD captains who had attended the briefing. Lozano was with them, and he backed off when the new arrival came.

"Christopher 'Big Man' Carter," Fowler told me. "Special Agent in Charge, Manhattan. Wouldn't know it to look at him."

"As long as he stays out of the way."

"Come on," Fowler said. "You should meet Pascal."

He led me to a substantial tower of a man who hadn't spoken during the briefing. His hair was gray and cut neatly and close, and his eyes were brown, and very hard. He had his marshal's badge hanging from a chain around his neck.

"Burt Pascal, this is Atticus Kodiak," Fowler said.

"When do we take over?" Pascal asked me, gripping my hand.

"When Dr. Romero says so," I said.

He shook his head, saying, "Poor woman." He gave a polite smile to both Natalie and Dale, then moved on to talk to more of his people.

As Pascal left, one of the two captains detached from

where he had been cornered by the SAIC, and came over to us. Lozano came with him.

"Captain Harner," he introduced himself. "Donald Harner, Midtown North." He wore glasses, and was almost entirely bald, with worry lines etched from his mouth to his forehead. "SOS sent us a copy of a press release they're going to deliver when this thing starts. They're boycotting, claiming that the whole conference is a sham."

"What a shock," Natalie said.

"I'm going to have my people stay outside mostly, deal with the protesters. They're already gathering out in front of the hotel," Captain Harner said.

"Keep an eye on them," I said.

"Peaceful protest," Harner told me. "We won't be able to move them if they follow the rules and behave." Then his radio went off and he excused himself.

"I'm going to do a walk," Natalie told me, adjusting the wire that ran to her palm. "See how it looks down there."

I grabbed Dale and told him to double-check our egress routes. "Make sure the guards know what's what," I told him. "Anybody comes running down those routes not shouting the password, they're to stop and detain them."

"And the password of the day is?" Dale asked.

"Wolf," I said.

He repeated it. "You sure that's not too hard for them?" Dale asked. "I mean, if they're given the chance they'll totally fuck it up."

Trent, who was listening, said, "My people know their job."

"Take Rubin with you," I told Dale.

I waited in the bedroom with Dr. Romero. Selby and Madeline had left shortly after Dale. Selby said she wanted to make certain things were proceeding well at the registration desk.

"I'll see you in about two hours," she told Felice before she left. "We're really going to do this."

"We really are," Dr. Romero said, and the two women hugged.

They left, and Felice went back to her briefcase, and I sat on the couch, because there was only so much securing of the command post I could do. After a while, she gave up on her papers and went to the television, turning it on and then sitting beside me on the couch. We still had an hour before she and Selby were to speak, and the difficulty of the wait showed in her posture and manner. I had left the door open to the other room, and occasionally the noise filtered in suddenly louder, and Felice would turn first in the direction of the noise, then to me.

"I'm nervous," she said softly, as if making confession. "I don't know what worries me more. Speaking in front of all these people, or . . . I mean it's silly, isn't it? I should be more terrified of dying than of having to talk in front of a crowd, but I'm not."

"You'll be fine," I said.

CNN carried a story on Katie's death. Various political figures were seen decrying the violence, and two sound bites were played, one of the president, who broadly condemned the action, and another of a southern senator who admitted it was a tragedy, but then went on to say that abortion was the issue that needed to be addressed, and implied that the horror in Katie's murder lay there rather than with the person who had fired the rifle. Footage followed of a protest outside the Women's LifeCare Clinic. The reporter closed by mentioning Common Ground, and said there would be more information later in the hour.

We watched the report in silence, and then Felice said, "We'll be burying her in Westchester, have a small service at the graveside. There's a plot there, my husband's family. She will love a green place, I think."

"A lot of people will want to attend," I said.

"I don't want that. Just the people that knew her. That's

the most important thing," she said. "I'd like you and the others to be there."

"We'll be there, Felice. You've got us until you say otherwise. Certainly through tomorrow."

"And after that?"

I shifted on the couch, trying to keep the base of my radio from digging into my hip. "The purpose of the threats was to keep you from coming here today," I said. "To keep Common Ground from happening."

"So tomorrow, I'm no longer worth killing?"

"Perhaps."

"I hope so," Felice said, softly. "I really do hope so." She smoothed her skirt with both hands, playing with one of the pleats. "You know what frightens me more than anything? That I won't say the right things. That nothing will change after all this, that it will all just continue as before . . . that my daughter will have died for nothing."

Fowler came in with Lozano, and we talked briefly. Neither had any good news.

"Still waiting on the prints," Fowler told me. "We should have them by the end of the day."

"After the conference," I said.

"Well, you heard the briefing. The description's been given out to everyone here. It's the best we can do until we have a name on this guy."

"Let's hope it's enough."

Lozano said, "Nobody's seen Barry, Rich, or Crowell. Not outside, not inside."

"Crowell's supposed to speak," I said.

"One o'clock panel. About the limits of legal protest," Fowler said. "I can't wait."

"He hasn't canceled?" I asked.

"Not as far as I know," Lozano said. "I'll check again with Selby."

From the couch, Dr. Romero said, "He won't cancel.

It's a performance like any other for that man. He'll arrive at the last minute, as if he's doing us all a favor. The boycott is just to emphasize his contempt for all of us here. Just wait. He'll show."

Roughly a half hour before Romero and Selby were to deliver the opening address, Natalie radioed me. *"I'm sending Rubin up to cover you. I need you down at registration."*

"Got it."

Rubin came into the CP about three minutes after that, saying, "It's a clusterfuck down there."

Dr. Romero looked over at me as I got up and put my suit coat back on. "I'll be right back," I told her, then went out and took the stairs down to the lobby, straightening my tie as I went.

Natalie was arguing with SAIC Carter by the metal detector. Her father stood beside her, clearly wishing he was somewhere else.

The detector had been set up in the open area outside the Imperial Ballroom, with ropes running from either side of it to the walls to keep people from bypassing the checkpoint. The registration desk was beyond the detector, and several people were already entering the ballroom, wearing red, white, and blue convention tags on their jackets or shirts.

On the other side of the detector, leading into the lobby, people were crammed wall-to-wall, and getting impatient.

"Change the goddamn setting," the Special Agent in Charge was saying.

"It wasn't me who only brought in one metal detector," Natalie responded, and cast a pointed look at her father.

"It's broken," Trent said. "We're bringing people over with hand-helds."

"What's the problem?" I asked Natalie.

"The problem is that the head Fed here wants us to change the setting," she told me. Her eyes were blazing.

"It's going off at everything," Carter said. "Take it down a quarter turn, you'll still catch anything coming through."

I checked the dial on the side of the metal detector. It was cranked all the way to the right.

"It doesn't take a whole hell of a lot of metal to make a bomb," Natalie insisted. "Guns aren't the only things we're worried about."

"It's going off on goddamn bobby pins," Carter said. "And right now we're filling the lobby with people who can't get where they are going. You listen to me, there's as great a risk in the fucking lobby as in the fucking ballroom at this point. A bomb will do as much damage in both places. All of these people are potential victims, and the longer they wait the more at risk they become."

"How long until the hand-helds get here?" I asked Trent.

"Fifteen minutes at the most," he said. "We've got two here already, we can hand-scan some of these people."

"That's not good enough," Natalie said.

"Jesus H. Christ," Carter said. "What do you want, to cavity-search them, too?"

"If it'll catch a weapon," Natalie said. "You bet your ass."

"It'll catch a weapon, damnit," Carter said. "It's catching on fillings." He appealed to me. "Turn it down."

"Wait a minute," I said.

"Turn the fucking thing down," he said. He reached around the side of the detector and turned the knob down a notch. "There. That wasn't so hard, was it, honey?" he said to Natalie.

"Pompous son of a—" Natalie started.

I grabbed her, turning to Trent and saying, "We'll work with it. Make sure that everyone gets at least one pass with either the detector or the hand-helds."

Natalie pulled herself away from me, and I pointed her over to a corner, away from Carter. As we did that, I heard Trent call two Sentinel uniforms down to give him a hand at the detector. They began processing people through again.

"They're fucking our security," she said to me.

"I know," I told her.

She brushed her hair back over her right ear with an angry hand, nearly yanking her earpiece free. She turned her head to look back at the SAIC, who was now clearly king of his domain, then looked at me again. "I hate that guy," she said. "Asshole feeb."

"Yeah," I said.

"It makes our job harder, Atticus." She took a couple more deep breaths, then said, "I'm fine. Really, I'm fine."

"You sure?"

"Oh, yeah. I've dealt with sexist assholes before, why should he be any different?"

"No reason."

"Exactly," Natalie said. "No reason." She looked at where the crowd was now flowing toward registration. "Son of a bitch."

"Give me twenty minutes or so," I said. "Radio when it's clear to bring her down."

"Understood." She turned back to me and said, "It's just tension, I know. You know and I know, just tension. I'm fine now. Just had to blow off some steam."

"Made your father's day."

"Think I embarrassed him enough?"

"Close, maybe."

"See you soon," she said, and with a bitter little smile headed back to the metal detector.

I sat beside Romero on the raised platform at the south end of the Imperial Ballroom, trying to look inconspicuous. Also on the platform were Veronica Selby, a city councilman, a pastor from a church in Buffalo, a doctor from Mount Zion, and a nun.

The room was packed for the opening, faces and faces and faces, each with a pair of hands, always moving. Dale was on the door to the west, scanning the crowd and ready to secure our escape if it came to that, while Rubin stood by the entrance, watching everyone as they came in. Between Rubin and myself, we had a full view of the room. Natalie was outside, floating, and I could hear her commentary in my ear.

"No sign SOS . . . no sign Crowell . . . Rubin, black jacket, baseball cap, watch him . . . nothing at registration . . . crowd's stable out front. . . ."

When Selby went to speak, she parked her wheelchair just in front of the podium, and the nun handed her the microphone. She was greeted with applause, and began by thanking people for coming.

That was the last clear thing I heard her say before her voice turned into a background noise against Natalie's commentary. I kept my eyes moving over the crowd, listening to Natalie's hot wash of information, and wished I could stand up, roam, move, instead of needing to pretend I was a panelist.

In my ear, I heard Rubin say, *"Baseball cap, hands clear."*

Dale said, *"Third row, fifth from center, bouquet of flowers."*

"A lot of people carrying flowers," Rubin said.

A man with light brown hair moved a red backpack onto his lap in the second row.

"Second row, third from left, backpack on lap," I said softly.

Rubin took six steps, saying, *"Looking . . . looks like a program."*

The backpack returned to the floor.

A lot of applause filled my ears, and Selby was rolling back to her place on the podium.

"Pogo's up," I said.

Dr. Romero rose and her right hand brushed my shoulder as she went to the podium.

"Confirmed," Natalie said.

"Movement on the aisle, eighth row," Dale said.

"Camera," Rubin said.

"Fucking reporters."

"Another one," Rubin said.

"News crew in the lobby," Natalie said. *"I'll hold them."*

There were several flashes as pictures were taken.

". . . compelled to be doctors, lawyers, police officers, or bodyguards," Romero was saying. "We make a choice, and we make it with the same joy, trepidation, and fear as we make all the other choices in our lives. . . ."

"Eleventh row, red skirt getting up," Dale said.

"Moving . . . heading your way," Rubin said.

I heard a woman ask Dale directions to the bathroom. He directed her out past Rubin, then said, *"I'm clear."*

"Clear," Rubin agreed.

". . . disagree? Witness Drs. Britton and Gunn," Romero said. "Witness the women shot while working in a clinic in Boston, or the individual who is confined to a wheelchair for simply managing a clinic in Springfield. Witness my daughter, whose only crime was that I was her mother. . . ."

"All units, we have an altercation at the west entrance," the dispatcher said in my ear. *"NYPD responding, all other posts hold steady."*

"Confirmed," I said softly.

"I've got a visual on that," Natalie said. *"Three women, NYPD on scene. They're breaking it up."*

"Bald man, last row, west side aisle, reaching for something," Rubin said. *"Wrapped in cloth, whatever it is. . . ."*

I tried to figure the fastest way to take Romero down to the floor. I couldn't see the person Rubin was referring to, and tried to shift in my seat without making too much of a distraction.

"*I see him,*" Dale said. "*Can't get a make on what's in his hands, moving.*"

". . . result of cooperation, of two very different ideologies finding a common ground for discussion, and through that, for hope. . . ."

"What is it?" I asked.

". . . *can't see,*" Rubin said. ". . . *unwrapping . . . , well, fuck. It's a sweater.*"

"*Confirmed. He's putting on a sweater,*" Dale said.

I started breathing again.

"*Air conditioner's on too high,*" Rubin said.

". . . if one of us can, then we all will profit. No one need change sides. . . ."

"She's wrapping up," I said.

"*Understood,*" Rubin said.

"*Coming back,*" Natalie said.

". . . instead, agree on how we will fight one another, if fighting is what we must do. But let us remember the white flag of truce. Let us remember that flag is flying here, now. Thank you very much for coming," Dr. Romero said. She took a step back as the crowd began to applaud, then stopped as the ovation turned standing.

"*They're going to their feet,*" Dale said.

I rose as the crowd did, and they continued to applaud. Felice Romero looked around some more, stunned more than anything else, and I moved forward to her. The crowd rising was nice for her, but it made my job hell.

"Natalie, get in here," I said. "All others, stay on post."

"*Confirmed,*" Natalie said.

"*Confirmed,*" Rubin said, then Dale.

From the front row four women came to the platform, offering Romero a bouquet of flowers. Felice started to reach for them, then looked over at me. I nodded and she took them. In her ear I said, "Hand them to me."

She nodded and handed me the bouquet, and I set it on my chair.

"The flowers are for Pogo," I said to my lapel.

"Understood."

Natalie emerged from the surging crowd, below the platform and in front of Felice. Dr. Romero handed me another bouquet, this one with an attached card. More people were coming forward, offering flowers or envelopes, though one held up a box covered in wrapping paper. I stepped forward for that and took it.

"I'll make sure she gets this," I told the man. He was old and gray and smelled of patchouli. The box felt light for its size, and nothing shifted as I put it on the chair. The man smiled and nodded at me, then backed into the crowd.

The flowers kept coming.

CHAPTER TWENTY-THREE

Felice sat on the couch in the command post. The lunch room service had brought sat untouched on the cart in front of her, as she read yet another card and tried to stop crying. Dozens of flowers were in the room, standing in glasses of water and lying on the table and bed. Roses, daisies, carnations, and even some lilies. Most were white, though some of the flowers were pale pink or yellow.

We had screened all the sealed envelopes and the one box for explosives and metal and had come up negative. Felice had held the first envelope without opening it, and I knew she was afraid of what they might call her this time.

But she had opened the envelope anyway and found not a threat or condemnation, but a condolence card.

Dear Doctor Romero:
Please accept our sincerest sympathies for the loss of your daughter. Our prayers are with you at this

*time, and although we know your pain will never go
away entirely, we wish you memories of joy.*
                              Sincerely,
                              Christian Mothers for Life

Over twenty-five signatures were on the card in different color inks.

Every card was a variation on the first, some longer,
some shorter, but all offering support for Dr. Romero's
loss from both the pro-life and pro-choice sides. Additionally, some praised her courage with words of admiration
that made her blush when she read them. She opened the
box to find a white scarf that had been hand-knitted, em-
broidered with the words "Common Ground." His card
had said, simply, "May this warm you when you are cold."
The scarf smelled of patchouli, too.

Felice read the last card and set it carefully with the
others, saying, "I'd forgotten, you know?" She wiped her
eyes with a napkin from the cart, removing her glasses
first. Then she blew her nose. "I absolutely did not expect
this."

"This'll probably happen again at your panel and at
your talk," I said. "When they bring you gifts, hand them
directly to me. If it isn't wrapped, if it's anything they want
you to open then and there, let me handle it."

"I will," she said.

Natalie said in my ear, *"We're ready in the Imperial."*

"Crowell shown up?"

"That's a negative," she said. *"No sign of him. Don't
think he's coming."*

"We're going to take a few minutes to get down there,"
I said.

"All right. Then I'll check three."

I grinned. It was our code for using the bathroom. That
way if anyone was listening, they wouldn't know we were
suddenly short one person on our detail. "Confirmed," I
said.

"The panel?" Felice asked me.

"It's time."

She wiped her eyes again, then put her glasses back on. I helped her into her blazer, and she took my hand when she slipped into it, turning to face me. She said, "Thank you, Atticus."

"It's not over yet," I said.

"I know. But I haven't ever thanked you, I don't think. And I want you to know."

"You're welcome," I said. "You're doing fine."

"Am I?"

"Yes. Katie would be proud."

Natalie came back on, saying, *"I'm check four."*

"Confirmed. Pogo is on the move."

The panel was titled, "Abortion and Reproductive Rights: Means of Family Planning." Six people were on the panel, and it was moderated by none other than Madeline, whose last name turned out to be Schramm. It also turned out that she was a full professor of Ethics at NYU. The table on the dais was long, set five feet back from the edge of the platform, with the panelists all seated facing the room. Each person had a microphone, a pad of paper, a pencil, and a glass of water. A full pitcher was placed on either side of the moderator for refills. Dr. Romero sat second in from the left, beside the director of Planned Parenthood for Manhattan on one side, and a man from Social Services on the other. On the other side of Madeline sat Veronica Selby, a professor of religion from some seminary upstate, and an author from Vermont.

I stood about four feet behind Romero, a little to the left. This time, my view of the room was unobstructed, and I could see just about everything. Again Dale and Rubin were covering the exit and entrance, and again, Natalie was floating outside.

The room was packed. People stood at the back and sat

on the floor in front of the platform. Before we had started, two Sentinel uniforms had walked through at our request and made certain all the aisles were clear. So far, they had remained that way, and the crowd was remarkably still, paying careful attention.

The dispatcher came over my radio shortly after Romero was seated, saying, *"Mr. Kodiak, be advised we have confirmation of one Sean Rich at the west entrance."*

"What's he doing?" I said.

There was a pause, then the dispatcher came back on. *"Working with the protesters. NYPD is watching him. Detective Lozano is here with me. He says Rich appears to be alone."*

"Keep me informed," I said.

"Ten-four."

"All guards," I said. "Confirm receipt of last conversation."

Natalie, Rubin, and Dale called in order, each saying they had heard.

"Be on the lookout," I said.

"Like we're not already?" Rubin said. He said it softly enough that the mike almost didn't pick it up.

"Rubin, repeat please?"

There was a pause. *"Uh, negative, Atticus. Was just giving some guy directions. I'm clear."*

Forty minutes into the panel, when Madeline was taking questions from the audience, a man in the sixth row suddenly struck the person in the seat next to him.

"Fight," I said to my mike, and moved directly behind Romero's seat.

"Got it," said Rubin.

The dispatcher came on, *"Units responding."*

Natalie appeared in the doorway, then started working her way down the aisle. Two Sentinel units followed her in about three seconds later, converging on where the two men were grappling. The people on either side of them had risen and recoiled. No one left the room.

"Gentlemen!" Madeline said. "Gentlemen, stop it!"

Not surprisingly, the two men continued to pummel and tear at each other and then they were being pulled apart by the guards, Natalie supervising. I heard her tell the uniforms to eject the men from the conference.

"NYPD responding," the dispatcher said in my ear.

From my left I saw the door behind Dale open and I brought my hands down onto Felice's shoulders, preparing to sweep the chair out from under her with my foot. Rich with a gun, I thought. Perfect.

"Dale, door," I said.

He turned and his right hand started back for his gun before he realized he was looking at a cop.

"What the fuck are you doing?" I heard him say.

The police officer said he was responding to the fight.

"Not through this door you don't," Dale told him. He jerked the cop into the room, then slammed the door. *"Nothing,"* he told me.

"I see," I said.

"Going to have to chat with the guards in the hallway," he said.

"After Pogo's secure."

"Of course."

I watched the policeman meet up with the two Sentinel uniforms and their angry charges. Spontaneous applause broke out in the audience when they were evicted from the room.

"It's unfortunate," Madeline told the crowd. "I think we were all hoping we could make it through this day without any violence. Let's hope that's all we'll have to worry about."

I let my hands slide off Felice and took two steps back, resuming my position.

———

Rubin, Dale, and I were walking Felice back to the command post when Natalie came over my radio.

"Atticus, be advised that I've been informed by NYPD that Rich left the premises over an hour ago."

"Why the hell wasn't I notified?"

"Lozano just found out," Natalie said. *"Apparently some sergeant on the ground thought that his arrival was the only important thing."*

"Wonderful."

We entered the CP, and I walked Felice to the bedroom, where she poured herself a cup of coffee and lit a cigarette. Fowler followed us in from the main room.

Dale said, "I'm going to go yell at the guards."

"You do that."

Rubin said, "I'm going to watch him yell at the guards."

"You do that, too."

They both left, and I sat on the sofa and removed my glasses. I got myself a glass of water from the room service cart, pulled four ibuprofen from my coat, and swallowed them. Shortly after the two pugilists had been dragged from the room, I'd felt the beginnings of a headache start at each of my temples. The ache had slid its way to my forehead by the time we were ready to remove Dr. Romero, and now it was enough to distract me from my sore ankle.

"How you holding up?" Fowler asked me.

I made a face.

He took his notepad out of a pocket and flipped it open, then waited for me to put my glasses back on. He said, "The prints on the stairwell came back. I've got an identification for you. Name is Paul Grant. No record, found his prints through the California DMV. Twenty years old, six feet three, two hundred and fourteen pounds. Blue eyes, blond hair. They're faxing a picture."

"I don't know the name," I said. "Sounds like the right guy, though."

"There's no record of a Grant with SOS. We're looking

for other information, and the Bureau office in Los Angeles is sending someone out to his home in Irvine to talk to his parents. Should have more information by the end of the day."

I nodded and rubbed my temples, thinking. Then I said, "Can you make sure that description gets passed to all the guards, everybody, along with the previous one?"

Fowler nodded. "I'll do that now."

"Crowell never showed?" I asked him.

"Not as far as I know. Guess he backed down."

I didn't like that. Crowell not showing worried me. Felice's analysis of his personality had seemed correct. If he was missing as great an opportunity as this, there had to be a good reason. And for Crowell, it seemed to me, a good reason and self-preservation would be identical.

Something was going to come down, I was certain. Grant or no, Bridgett's theories about SOS aside, Crowell wasn't going to let this convention end without leaving his mark on it somehow.

Fowler asked, "That all?"

"For now. Thanks."

He stopped at the door. "You're almost through this thing," he said. "Try to relax."

I didn't bother to respond.

". . . simply, a woman's right to reproductive services. In the deluge of media attention the abortion issue has attracted since *Roe* v. *Wade,* many of us have lost sight of this core point," Dr. Romero said. "The clinic I run provides a full range of family planning services, from education and counseling to medical services and AIDS testing.

"Yes, we perform abortions.

"As we also provide a full range of birth control methods, prenatal care, Pap smears, STD testing, pregnancy planning . . ."

We were in the New York Room now, Dr. Romero on

the platform, leaning intently toward the microphone. Her speech was in front of her on the speaker's podium, but she was hardly referring to it, glancing down at the yellow legal sheets occasionally only for reference. She spoke clearly, committed to having her words heard and understood.

And again, I was on the platform, four feet back from her, off to the right, listening to Natalie's hot wash in my ear, letting my eyes scan the crowd. Of the five hundred seats that had been set up, all of them were filled, and again people stood at the back of the room and sat on the floor, away from the aisles. The metal cover to the light switches I'd noticed the day before had been replaced, and Rubin stood beside it at his post by the entrance.

This crowd had busy hands, though, many of the people taking notes. Rubin had noted four reporters, and, again, there were multiple photographers. Veronica Selby was in the audience, also, her chair parked on the outside of the second row on my right, the side nearest the entrance.

"Looks like the SOS protest is breaking up outside," Natalie said in my ear.

"Confirmed," I said.

"I'm working back to the second floor," she said. *"First floor clear."*

"Black coat, black tie, ninth row, near the aisle," Dale said. *"Reaching in bag . . ."*

I shifted my gaze, saw the man Dale meant. He was young, blond hair, but not big enough to be Grant and too big to be Barry.

"Photographer," Dale said. *"He's changing lenses on his camera."*

I looked away, letting my eyes sweep back to the right quadrant of the room, and then saw a face I knew.

"Mary Werthin is in the audience," I said softly. "Fourth row, fifth from left, blue floral print dress."

"Looking . . ." Rubin said. *"Hands are clear."*

"Confirm, hands are clear," Dale said. *"She has a purse."*

"Watch her," I said. "Dispatch, advise Detective Lozano that Mary Werthin is in the audience."

"Will do," the dispatcher said.

"Want me back?" Natalie asked.

"Negative. Continue float."

"Confirmed."

Mary Werthin was watching Romero, but it didn't seem that she was listening. Her hair was tied back, and she looked quite young. My immediate concern was more for Felice. As far as I could tell, she hadn't seen Werthin yet.

". . . cannot say it is simply an issue of family. It is an unstable word, treacherous and constantly changing," Dr. Romero was saying. "To maintain that the only family of merit is, by definition, one husband, one wife, and a minimum of one child is ludicrous in this day and age. More to the point, perhaps, it is impractical. The need for family planning services, then . . ."

"Lozano's here," Rubin said.

Sure enough, the detective was standing just inside the door, next to Rubin, who indicated Werthin's position.

"He wants to know if she should be removed."

"No need yet," I said.

I watched Rubin relay that to the detective, who nodded, made brief eye contact with me. He remained by the door.

I resumed scanning, trying to concentrate on the crowd, trying to keep tabs on Mary Werthin. She didn't move much, barely reacting to Romero's speech, even when the crowd applauded something. But she flinched every time Felice said the word "abortion."

Cute effect, I thought.

"Atticus," It was Natalie. *"Bridgett Logan is on her way up to the New York Room."*

"Confirmed."

"She says she needs to talk to you."

"It'll have to wait."

"Obviously."

A man seated on the floor by the front row moved suddenly, and I zeroed in on him. "Movement, floor left, front row," I said.

"Responding," Rubin said, and I saw him step forward in my periphery. The man reached for a pocket and I started calculating my takedown, then stopped when I saw he had removed a handkerchief from his pocket. He blew his nose quietly, checked the cloth, then folded it again and returned it to his coat.

"Hands clear," Rubin said.

"Confirmed."

"Logan's here," he said.

I glanced over at the door and saw Bridgett standing there, and we made eye contact and she grinned. She looked amazingly out of place, and a couple of heads turned and stared at her. After a moment, she started down the aisle to where Selby was parked.

I went back to scanning the crowd, listening to the traffic in my ear.

". . . will not change. This right of self-determination will not go away," Dr. Romero said. "It has existed for thousands of years. Abortion is only a small part of it. The battle over the right to one's own body will continue. Making any of these services illegal, restricting them through claims of immorality or decadence, will do nothing to remove the inherent right of freedom of choice."

She stopped speaking. For a moment she just looked over her audience. Then she said, "That's my talk. I want to thank you for coming, for listening with open minds. I've only one more thing to add.

"The last several weeks leading up to this conference I can say, honestly, have been the most difficult of my life. Certain organizations, certain individuals, were determined that I should not speak today.

"I do not know why I was singled out among all the

doctors and clinics in Manhattan. It's an arbitrariness that cost the life of my daughter, Katherine. It's an arbitrariness that has revealed all the worst about the human spirit to me. Frequently in the last few days, I reconsidered my decision to attend. There hardly seemed a point."

Dr. Romero stopped long enough to take a drink of water from the paper cup on the podium.

"When I resolved I would still attend today, I did so simply to spite those people who had worked so hard to keep me from coming," she said. "I did it as an act of defiance, which I told myself was for the memory of my daughter.

"Arriving here this morning, surrounded by policemen and bodyguards, I expected the worst.

"When I read the first card given to me this morning, I feared what it would say. The letters I've received in the past have been hardly kind.

"This card offered sympathy and condolences.

"The card was from an organization called Christian Mothers for Life. An antiabortion group, a pro-life group, call it what you will.

"It made me weep.

"I had forgotten, you see? I had forgotten exactly what this conference was about. My motive in attending had changed. I did not arrive this morning wanting peace. I wanted vindication. Victory.

"And this card made me see that I had become exactly the kind of person this conference was designed to reach out to," Felice said. "If I can be reached, after all that has happened, if I can see moderation and hope, then we all can.

"Thank you again."

"They're going to their feet," Rubin said in my ear.

He needn't have bothered with the transmission. They were up before he had finished speaking, applauding so loud that I almost lost what he was saying. I saw Veronica Selby beaming, her smile radiant, clapping with the rest of the crowd. Bridgett stood behind her, shaking her head slowly from side to side.

And I didn't see Mary Werthin.

"I've lost sight of Werthin," I said.

"Can't see her," Dale said. *"Too much traffic."*

People were starting to push forward in the aisles, and I saw more flowers being held up, more cards. The crowd was a mass of noise, still applauding, now cheering. Felice took a step to the edge of the platform, taking someone's offered pen and program, and she was blushing as she autographed it. I moved in closer to her, scanning like mad as too many people pushed toward us. Romero began handing me cards and bouquets, and I began dropping them in a pile behind me just as quickly.

"Natalie, get in here," I said.

"Confirmed."

". . . see her," Rubin came in. *"I see her, she's got something in her hands."*

"Repeat?" I said.

"Werthin's got something in her hands, it's not her purse. . . ."

"I can't see her," Dale said.

"What's in her hands?" I asked Rubin.

". . . something, looks like a book. . . ."

"Where?" I said.

"Just fantastic," a young black woman was saying to Dr. Romero. "God bless you, Doctor. . . ."

"She's in the crush, I've lost her, I can't see her," Rubin said.

I pulled Felice back a half step, further from the edge, but she went right back, taking another card and transfering it to me, thanking the couple that handed it to her. Then she stepped off the platform, taking another offered pen and program, scribbling her name. I dropped off after her, trying to stay tight.

"Pogo's off the platform," I said.

". . . her," Dale said. *"Ten feet up, center aisle."*

I couldn't see anything in the crowd. "Hands?"

"Can't see them. No purse."

"Rubin?"

"Nothing, boss, shit," he said.

"She's moving up," Dale said. *"No, damnit, I've got to move in."*

"Hold your position," I told him, taking another bunch of carnations and dropping them behind me.

"Confirmed."

A woman with silver hair held up a wicker basket for Romero to take, a shiny white bow on the handle. I flinched as Felice grabbed it, taking it from her as gently as I could and setting it on the platform beside me. Turning back around, I saw Mary Werthin at the front of the line, holding a pen and a hardcover book.

Abortuaries and the Death of America, by Jonathan Crowell.

Felice was leaning to take the book, but then she recognized Werthin and stopped long enough for me to move forward and intercept. "I'll give it to her," I said.

"I want her to sign it," Werthin said. "She has to sign it." She pushed the book forward, trying to get it around me.

I blocked her arm with my body, and she drew the book back. "I'll give it to her," I said once more. Under the edge of the cover, opposite the spine, a sliver of blue fabric jutted free. The edge looked rough and curly. I took the book with my right hand, Werthin still holding it.

It was too heavy.

She tried to jerk the book back, saying, "She has to sign it!"

Then the adrenaline dumped and I thought a lot at once. Velcro, I thought. Velcro keeping the book shut and the book's too heavy and it's not a gun inside this book, no, it's a bomb.

I keyed my transmitter, and as I did it I knew that the bomb wasn't radio-controlled, couldn't be with all the radio traffic in the hotel, or else it would've gone off as soon as Werthin arrived. Wasn't motion-sensitive, or else it would've gone off as she brought it through the crowd. Must be a timer, must be a timer or a switch. I swung my left foot around and behind Werthin's legs, jerking the book toward me with my right.

She's pregnant, I remembered.

Then I hit her in the middle of the sternum with the palm of my left hand, sending her back over my leg, into the crowd of people still milling there, looking shocked. She released the book when she fell.

And I said, "Bomb."

The adrenaline made it come out far louder than I would've liked.

People began backing away, and then someone screamed, and almost en masse, they turned and ran for the door.

"Dale, get over here," I yelled, and he was already halfway to me, climbing over the seats as I turned and pulled Felice back onto the platform, away from the people, out of the crowd. Most of the people were packed into the far side of the room already, pushing for the exit, and I heard Rubin try to transmit and then give up as he was washed out by the panic.

"Evac," I said. I said it three times, and tried to make it clear.

"*En route,*" Natalie said.

Dr. Romero's eyes were wide and on mine and then she looked at my right hand and took a quick step back, her left shoe knocking the wicker basket over. A stuffed bear fell out onto the floor. The bear had a yellow hat and a blue jacket, and something was pinned to its coat.

I'm holding a bomb, I realized.

Bridgett shouted, "What do I do?"

"Hold her," I said, indicating Werthin with my head. Dale had made the platform and had already drawn his weapon, scanning for a secondary threat. I looked, too, and saw Veronica Selby still seated in her wheelchair, eyes on us. She was bone-white.

That was it. The crowd was still pushing out the door with one mind.

Bridgett went down and grabbed Werthin, who was trying to slide away on her rump. Dale went down to help her.

"You can't do this, you pushed me, you bastard," Werthin kept screaming.

"Natalie, where the fuck are you?" I asked.

"En route, goddamnit," she said.

"All units, repeat, we are evacuating, we are evacuating," I said. "Get Pogo the hell out of here, now."

I saw Natalie push through the doorway, running to us, followed by Rubin and Lozano. As soon as Dale saw them, he went to the side door. He opened it with a sharp push, stepping back, then looked down the corridor, his gun leading.

Bridgett was telling Werthin that she had the option to stop moving voluntarily or to become permanently disabled.

"Rubin, get Selby out of here," I shouted to him, and he veered off from heading to us and went to her wheelchair. Lozano made straight for Werthin. He reached her as Natalie finally made the platform, grabbing Felice with both arms.

"Do exactly what I tell you," Natalie said to the doctor.

"But Veronica—"

"Rubin's handling it," I said. "Get out of here. Now!"

She started to say something more but Natalie lifted her off the platform and then ran her to where Dale stood by the exit. Rubin had Selby almost to the door, and they were practically bowled over by three more men coming in, one marshal, Fowler, and an NYPD uniform. The uniform took over on Selby's wheelchair and Rubin headed back toward me.

"No," I yelled at him. "Not me. Go with Pogo, damnit."

He stopped, looked at me, then turned and followed in the direction Natalie and Dale had gone.

Lozano was cuffing Werthin, who screamed that he was trying to kill her baby.

"You're under arrest," he said, pulling her to her feet.

"What kind is it?" I asked her, showing her the book.

"Rot in hell, you bastard, you tried to—"

"What kind of bomb is it?" I asked her again.

Her mouth stayed open but she issued no sound, and all that was in her eyes before turned to panic. She tried to run for the door, but Lozano had a good grip, and the marshal helped him hold her. She said, "Oh my God, oh my God, that's why I wasn't supposed to open it, oh sweet Jesus—"

"Who gave this to you?"

"It's—oh God, I swear I didn't know," she said, turning her head from me to Bridgett to Fowler to the marshal, trying to convince all of us at once. "He gave it to me, I swear—"

"Who?" Bridgett asked her.

"Mr. Rich, he gave it to me, he told me to have the butcher sign it, oh my God."

"Get her out of here," Fowler said, pulling his radio. He keyed it and said, "All units, search the immediate area for Sean Rich. Consider him armed and extremely dangerous. He's wanted for questioning."

The marshal helped Lozano remove Werthin from the room. At this point it wasn't truly necessary; she had become almost docile.

"I didn't know, oh God, I swear I didn't know. . . ." she kept saying.

"The bomb squad should be here any moment," Fowler said to me. He said it very gently, as if he was talking to a child.

"Oh, good," I said.

"You want to put the book down now, Atticus?" he said.

I looked at the book in my right hand, watched a drop of sweat from my forehead hit the cover, heard it splat on the glossy surface. "Yeah, I'd like that, Scott," I said.

"Go ahead, then," he said.

I looked at the book. I looked at him. I looked at Bridgett. "Maybe you guys should leave the room," I said.

"Not without you," Bridgett said.

"See," I said. "I don't know what the mechanism is, and if it's a timer, it could go off any moment. So better that there's just me here, you see?"

"And you'll do what, exactly?"

"I'm going to put the book down," I said. "Then I'm going to lay the podium over the book, to tamp the blast. Then I'm going to run away. Very fast."

"Sounds like a plan," Fowler said softly.

"See you in a minute," I said.

Scott started to back out of the room. Bridgett didn't move.

"Go," I said.

She didn't move.

"Bridgett, please. Go away."

She held my eyes for a moment, then took three or four steps back. Then she stopped.

"Dinner's at eight, stud," she said.

Then she turned and ran with Fowler to the exit.

When they were out the door, I stepped back onto the platform. I figured the bomb was plastique, and it didn't feel more than six or seven pounds. More than enough to make finding all my pieces a true challenge were it to go off. At the center of the platform I knelt down, setting the book beside where the teddy bear had fallen from the basket.

The note pinned to the bear's coat read, "Please look after this bear."

It took some effort to get my fingers off the book. I held my breath when I let go, as if that would have made a damn bit of difference.

The book didn't do anything.

I stood, grabbed the podium, and pulled it toward the center of the platform. Romero's speech fluttered off the stand, and her cup of water fell over. My hands were sweating, and my grip slipped when the cup hit the ground, the noise scaring the hell out of me. I caught the podium before it fell, then lowered it over the book. It wouldn't do much, but it was something.

I scooped up the bear on the way out.

CHAPTER TWENTY-FOUR

I ran like hell.

The second floor had been evacuated, and I jumped the rope that had been strung over the end of the escalator and went down it faster than my hurt ankle would have liked, and still too slow for my taste. The metal detector shrieked at me when I ran through it, but I didn't stop, sprinting through the empty lobby and out onto Fifty-third Street, where the evacuees had gathered.

Evacuating an entire hotel into a Manhattan street on a summer's evening is truly a sight to behold. People were everywhere, most with dazed looks, some pissed at having their lives disrupted, some enjoying the confusion. I wondered how many of them knew exactly what was going on.

I moved off to the other side of the street, then keyed my radio. "Natalie?" I said. "Come in."

She came in faint, cut with static. *"Atticus? Are you all right?"*

"I'm fine. How's Pogo?"

"We've almost gotten her home."

"Confirmed. I'll be in touch," I said. Then I looked around, trying to find a face I recognized. There wasn't one. After a few minutes of looking, I saw a man in a Sentinel uniform and cornered him, asking to use his radio. He relinquished it reluctantly. I guess he didn't trust my teddy bear.

"This is Kodiak. Somebody come in," I said.

Trent came on. *"Atticus? Where are you?"*

"North side of the building."

"Come around to the west."

I told him I would and handed the radio back to the guard. He checked it carefully, making certain I hadn't hurt it.

The bomb squad was entering the building as I came around the corner onto Seventh Avenue. The fire department had already arrived, and was cordoning off the street. I worked through the crowd and found Trent in a cluster of people, with Selby, Madeline, and Bridgett.

"You're all right?" Selby asked when she saw me. "You're fine?"

I nodded. Selby touched my hand, and said, "And Felice, she's all right, too?"

"She's safe," I said.

Bridgett put her hand on my arm and brought her mouth to my free ear, saying, "NYPD found Rich."

"Where?"

"He was parked in the garage. When the evacuation started, he couldn't get out of the lot. Fowler and the rest took him and Werthin to Midtown North."

"Let's go," I said.

"I'm just waiting for you, stud."

———

In her Porsche, I examined the teddy bear carefully. It was the real thing, not stuffed with anything more dangerous than wadding.

"Cute," Bridgett said.

"I'll get you one."

"I'd die first."

I set the bear on the floor, then shut off my radio and began removing my wires.

"Did Fowler get an ID on the fellow we ran into yesterday?" she asked.

"His name is Paul Grant," I said. "No record. That's about all he got."

She pursed her lips for a moment, then reached into her jacket pocket and pulled out a sheaf of papers, folded in half. She handed them to me, saying, "This is what I got at the clinic. All the inactive files of the last year. I haven't had a chance to sort them yet."

I looked them over. It looked to be over one hundred names, and they were listed alphabetically. There was no Grant.

"Sorry," I said.

"Stab in the dark," Bridgett said. "You okay?"

"I'm waiting for my heart to start beating normally," I said.

"Patience."

One of the marshals who had worked the conference was at the Midtown North front desk, talking to a cop, when we arrived, and he escorted us to the room that had been commandeered for the combined agencies. Lozano was the only person inside I recognized.

"Hey, it's the hero," he said when he saw me. "Let me buy you a cup of caffeine. Have a seat."

Bridgett and I sat down and Lozano poured two cups of coffee from the urn on the stand in the corner, asking, "Either of you want it doctored?"

We both said no.

He brought us our coffee and sat down at the table, watching as we sipped.

"God almighty," Bridgett said, and set down her cup. "This is obscene."

Lozano chuckled and lit a cigarette. "They're making me sit it out," he said. "Not my precinct."

"Rich's in interrogation?" I asked.

"Yeah. Captain Harner and Fowler are running at him right now."

"Was it a bomb?" I asked.

He raised his eyebrows at me. "Be a bit anticlimactic if it wasn't, huh? Yeah, it was a bomb. They disarmed it about fifteen minutes ago, said it was a real simple device. They're running it over to forensics now, doing a rush job. We'll see what they get off it."

"I want to know how she got it into the conference," I said.

"Well, I don't know how it got past the detectors, all that," Lozano said. "But Werthin gave a full statement. Says she was protesting outside, and Rich showed up about noon. She saw him asking if anyone had seen Crowell. She says he left shortly after that, but came back around three. Rich called her over—he knew her from the paint incident, he was the one who told her to do it, she says—handed her the book, and said that Mr. Crowell wanted her to take it in and get it autographed by Romero. Says that Rich told her it would be a perfect reminder of exactly what a mockery Common Ground is, or words to that effect."

"And whatever you do, don't open it?" I said.

"Yeah. She didn't think it was odd, figured there was something inside, maybe some fish guts, she says. He told her to hide it in her dress, since she was pregnant and all."

"Christ, is that woman stupid," Bridgett said.

"She's committed," Lozano said. "That's not the same thing."

"In this case, Detective, it is."

He shrugged, put his cigarette out in his coffee, then stood. "I'll tell the captain you're here." He left without looking at Bridgett.

I loosened my tie, then got up and threw the rest of my coffee into the trash can.

"How's the pulse?" Bridgett asked.

"Better," I said. There was a phone in the room, and I used it to call the safe apartment. Rubin answered, and I asked him how things looked.

"We're fine here," he said. "Nobody followed us, and we've locked down. Felice is a bit shaky, but that's it."

"Good work," I said.

"Yeah? You're fucking nuts, you asshole," Rubin said, and there was true anger in his voice. "What were you going to do? Disarm it yourself?"

"I had to make sure it didn't go off while anybody else was there."

"I kept imagining what I'd tell your parents. 'Dear Mr. and Mrs. Kodiak, I'm sorry but your little boy Atticus got himself blown up.' That would have been quite a phone call," he said, still mad.

"Not one you need to make."

"For now. So, what's next?"

"I'm at Midtown North. They found Rich at the scene, and he's in interrogation. I'm going to stick here for a bit, see what's what."

Rubin said that sounded fine to him, and then I asked to talk to Natalie. I double-checked that Felice was all right, then told her I'd try to come back sometime that evening.

"Romero's writing the check," Natalie said.

"Guess that means we're out of a job," I said.

"Day after tomorrow, she says. Wants us until the funeral, I think."

"It's her choice."

"And the client is almost always right," Natalie said. "We did it. Got her in and out in one piece."

"I owe you a drink," I said. "You did good work today."

"Yeah, I did."

"Don't let it go to your head."

"We've got an all-points out for Crowell and Barry," Fowler told me. "He won't tell us where they are, says he doesn't know."

He gestured to the one-way mirror, and I looked in on Rich in the interrogation room. He was seated at the desk, a paper cup in front of him. He was wearing jeans, no holes, and a red button-up shirt. He had cowboy boots on, too, crocodile skin. He didn't look worried.

"Has he lawyered up?" Bridgett asked.

"Not yet," Fowler said.

"You serious?"

He nodded, eyes on Rich. "I don't understand it, either. He knows his Miranda, says he doesn't want a lawyer. Not even when Harner showed him a copy of the CSU prelim on the bomb. His prints were all over it."

"Tell me about the device," I said.

"Six pounds of Semtex tied to a variation of a mouse-trap switch," Fowler said. "Spaced the wires so the mass of the metal was diffused. The detector didn't pick it up."

"It would've if Carter hadn't lowered the setting," I said.

Scott shrugged. "Thing is, Semtex is a professional's explosive, like plastique. I mean, it's not that hard to get, relatively speaking. The IRA bought tons of it off the Czechs a few years back, then brought it into the country."

"In the spirit of capitalism," Bridgett said.

"Give the lady a cigar," Fowler said. "They sold it to anyone who had the cash. It's been popping up everywhere."

"Where'd he get it?" I asked.

"Won't say. Won't say if there's any more of it, either."

"Can we talk to him?"

Fowler looked back through the mirror, then nodded. "Hand over your weapons, first," he said.

We gave him our guns and he let us into the room.

When Rich saw me, he grinned. "Hey, boy," he said. "You're one lucky son of a bitch, aren't you?"

"Blessed," I said.

"Well, God works in mysterious ways," Rich said, and laughed.

I pulled a chair and sat down. Bridgett leaned against the wall.

"You're a pretty one," Rich told her. "Come sit on my lap."

She snorted and pulled a quarter from her pocket. "Here's twenty-five cents; buy yourself a new line." She tossed the coin over to him and Rich batted it out of the air, knocking it to the floor with a jingle.

"Cunt," he said.

"My, you're a regular Oscar Wilde," Bridgett said. "That was a shitty piece of work."

"What are you talking about?"

"Your bomb," she said. "It stank."

"Now, why do you go and say a thing like that, hon? There's no need to be mean."

"Just stating a fact, Sean," Bridgett said. "That was shoddy work. I mean, it didn't even go off, and your prints were all over it."

"Well, see, sweetheart, thing with a bomb is, when it goes off, you don't have a whole lot to look for prints on."

"But it didn't go off," I said.

He looked at me. "It would have, boy. It would have blown her to hell without breaking a sweat."

"And Mary Werthin, too," Bridgett said.

"She'd have gone to heaven, hon. She'd have gone to heaven."

"And Mary Werthin's baby?" I asked.

There was a pause. Rich kept his eyes on Bridgett.

"Would her unborn baby have gone to heaven?" I
asked.

"You bet your ass."

I sighed. "She's right, Sean. That was sloppy work. You
were so hard to kill Dr. Romero, you'd have killed a baby
to do it."

"You don't know what the fuck you're talking about,
boy."

"I'm talking about your firecracker," I said.

"Where's Crowell?" Bridgett asked.

"I don't know," Rich said.

"Did he know you made that bomb? That you were
going to kill a baby to kill Dr. Romero?" I asked.

"Or is that just the way it works?" Bridgett asked.
"Like killing Katie."

"That's probably it," I told her. "He builds bombs to
kill babies with."

"I didn't have anything to do—" Rich said.

"You're a liar," Bridgett told him.

"About as good a liar as a demolitions man," I said.

"Well, I'm a damn good demolitions man," he said.
"And I'm not lying."

"Then who killed Katie Romero?" Bridgett asked.

"Shut up, bitch."

She smiled. "Who's Paul Grant?"

"Never heard of him," Rich said.

There was a knock on the mirror, and then the door
opened and Fowler said, "All right, that's enough."

"We were just getting started," Rich told him.

"Don't worry, Sean. You'll have more company soon."

"He was lying about Grant," Bridgett said. "He knows
him."

Scott nodded.

"How do you know?" I asked.

"He was taking his time on everything else, except when

we were pressing him," she told me. "On that one, he had the time, and he rushed. Trust me."

"It may not matter," Fowler said. "We get Crowell in for questioning, I'm certain one of them will roll on the other."

"Nobody's brought him in yet?" I asked.

"We can't find him," Scott said.

"First Barry, then Crowell."

"They probably left town. If the bomb had gone off, they'd have been at the top of our suspect list."

"So they left in anticipation," Bridgett said.

He nodded. "Rich thinks he's buying them time. We'll give him a little while to stew on it, then hit him with Katie's murder, see what else breaks loose. He's already confessed to building the bomb, so he's got to know that his options are diminishing. He'll break, and when he does, we'll know who killed Katie."

We went to a bar near the precinct house. Bridgett had a pint of Guinness and I had a Scotch.

"He's wrong about Rich and Katie," Bridgett said. "There's no link there to Romero, no revenge motive."

"None that we've found," I said. "Does this mean you buy my theory?"

"At this point, yes. Look at the list. Is there a Rich anywhere on it?"

I pulled it out and flipped to the last page, looking. "Rafael, Rodriguez, Rossi, Ruez," I said. "No Rich."

"Sigh and double sigh," she said, and drank some of her Guinness.

I put the papers on the bar and sipped my Scotch, thinking. The names on the list were in small print, in four columns, starting with the last name, then the first, then a date, and then a number.

"The dates are for what?" I asked Bridgett.

"When the file went inactive," she told me. "Lynn explained it to me. If a patient misses three follow-ups, moves, has their records transferred, or dies, they close the file. The last number is the actual file code."

I finished my drink, looking at the dates on the first page. A couple of them were recent, in the last month. One of them only ten days ago. "Baechler, Melanie," I said.

"She on there?"

"Closed out about a week before Katie died. Melanie Baechler," I said, and then it hit me, and I read it again.

"What?"

"Katie," I said. "Oh, yes, that's it, that's got to be it. Katie knew her. Melanie B. Melanie Baechler. Katie knew her."

Bridgett turned on the stool and looked closely at me. "What are you talking about?"

"Why's she on the list?" I asked her. "It doesn't say."

"I don't know. I told you, she could have moved or missed a follow-up or—"

"She's dead," I said. "That's got to be it."

"Explain it to me," Bridgett demanded.

I ordered a cup of coffee and did just that. Then I asked the bartender if he would let me see his white pages. I found the address I wanted, and Bridgett and I paid and left.

CHAPTER TWENTY-FIVE

Melanie Baechler's apartment was up on West 124th off Claremont, directly north of the Columbia campus, one of the many buildings consisting entirely of apartments rented to students, and it showed. Clean, well-lit, and fairly secure, but not so nice as to buck the average rent in the area. The first floor of the building on the south side had been converted into a bodega, so access to the interior was limited from the west. Standard New York fare, the same two-door setup that allowed entrance into my apartment building in the Village. The building was prewar design, gray with orange and blue art deco tiles around the trim. The tiles looked original, faded and weathered, and had a pleasant sheen in the fading light of dusk.

I held the door of the building for Bridgett and we stepped into the foyer, searching the intercom listing. Next to the button for 4A were the names "Baechler & Scarrio."

"You or me?" Bridgett asked.

"You," I said. "Your melodic voice and gentle manner will immediately put whoever answers at ease."

She gave me the finger and a smile and pressed the button.

After a few seconds we got a garbled voice saying, "Yes?"

"My name is Bridgett Logan. I was wondering if I could speak with you about Melanie Baechler?"

"She, uh . . . I'm sorry, but she . . . she passed away about a week and a half ago." Even with the distortion of the intercom, you could hear that the wound was still fresh.

"This is in connection with her death," Bridgett said. "I'm wondering if you would answer a few questions."

There was a long moment, filled with just the sound of the traffic on the street, and I wondered if this wasn't a wild goose chase after all. Melanie B. wasn't a real person. Katie had probably been referring to a character from a television show.

There was another click and the voice said, "All right." The intercom clicked off and the door buzzed. I pushed it open and we walked into a large and brightly lit lobby. There was a fern in the corner by the elevator, and it looked real, but I get fooled by the plastic ones a lot. A flight of broad stairs started at the left of the plant. We took them up. From over the rail I could see that the next floor, and the stairs, too, were well-illuminated. Security-conscious management, I suppose. It would be hard to take anyone by surprise around here. Maybe the owners could talk to my building's management.

At the end of the fourth-floor hall, opposite 4F, was 4A. The door was metal and painted white with no other markings upon it but for the peephole. Bridgett pressed the buzzer. The door opened immediately and a woman, perhaps in her early twenties, stood there.

"Are you the police?" she asked, looking at each of us

suspiciously. We were quite the couple, I admit, with Bridgett in her leather jacket and nose rings and me in my Brooks Brothers suit.

"No." Bridgett reached into a coat pocket. She produced a business card and handed it to the woman. "Private."

The woman glanced at the card, then asked, "What can I do for you?"

"We have some questions about Melanie Baechler," I said.

"Did Melanie's family hire you?" she asked. "The police haven't found the guy yet. They probably never will."

Bridgett said, "This is in relation to something else. Miss—?"

"Scarrio, Francine Scarrio." Francine had curly black hair, glossy and wild, wrapping her head and shoulders. She was wearing either a perfume or hair spray that smelled like strawberries and made my nose itch. Tugging a curl, Francine looked us both over again, then moved out of the way to let us in. We stepped onto a throw rug with blue-and-black five-pointed stars stitched into the weave. Francine Scarrio closed the door behind us, then slipped past in the narrow hallway and said, "Why don't you have a seat in here?"

"Here" was a combination office/living room/dining room, with a short hallway leading to the left and a galley kitchen off to the right. The walls had posters of different musicians and bands mounted with green thumbtacks, ranging from Melissa Etheridge to Miles Davis, and I counted six separate shoes, each without an apparent mate, as we walked into the main room. A table was positioned flush against the wall, and on it were a pile of envelopes, a roll of stamps, and a stack of stationery. The envelopes and stationery matched, each with a drawing of unicorns in the lower left corner. Scarrio took a chair from under the table, saying, "I was writing letters." It sounded like a guilty pleasure. She gestured to a small brown love seat and companion chair, saying, "Please."

Bridgett took the chair while I took the love seat. Scarrio was looking at the business card again. I looked at her. She had on a tight navy blue top, short-sleeved and low-cut, just above the swell of her breasts, and she had on white shorts and no shoes. Her skin was tanned, and she projected that collegiate vitality I'd seen in Alison when we first met. I wondered if anyone had ever complained about Francine's perfume.

She looked up at me and said, "Who are you?"

"My name's Kodiak."

"Are you both private eyes?" She didn't wait for an answer, but said, "What's this about?"

"Have you heard of the Women's LifeCare Clinic on Amsterdam and One Thirty-fifth?" I asked her.

"I've even been over there a couple of times—NARAL and clinic defense stuff. You know, demonstrations."

"When was the last time you were there?"

"Couple weeks ago, I think. Why?"

"You know about Katie Romero's murder?" Bridgett asked.

"The retarded girl?" Francine nodded, and her curls bounced on her shoulders.

"Did you know Katie?" I asked.

"I spoke to her once or twice."

Bridgett rolled her shoulders and looked around the room. "Baechler was your roommate?"

"Yes. What does this have to do with the clinic?"

"What can you tell us about Melanie's death?"

Francine frowned. "Melanie got mugged. She was coming back from dinner and she was mugged, some guy stole her purse and stuff. The police told me they think it's some crackhead, but they haven't found the guy." She picked at her nails for a moment. "He beat her to death."

"When was this?" I asked.

"Wednesday before last," Francine said, softly. "She'd

gone out to the library and then went to dinner off campus, at Kowloon's, and she got mugged on her way back. The guy beat her to death," she said again. "I had to identify her." She had a broad face with heavy freckles, and the lines around her eyes suddenly became vivid with the memory. "She's from Cincinnati, see? And her parents couldn't arrive until the next day."

"Were you close friends?"

She nodded.

"I'm sorry."

"I don't even know why she went out. We had done all this shopping the day before," Francine said. "We had all this food and she wanted to make a shepherd's pie."

Bridgett asked, "Did she have any boyfriends? Anything like that? Anyone she might have been out to eat with?"

"Melanie had a lot of friends, some were guys, if that's what you mean, but, like, she wasn't sleeping around."

"Both of you used the clinic, right?"

"We'd both been there."

"But inside?" Bridgett asked.

"No."

"How'd you meet Katie?" I asked.

Scarrio blinked. "She was outside once or twice."

"She didn't normally go out."

"It was at a demonstration."

"Francine," Bridgett said. "We don't really care what you've done at Women's LifeCare. We're just trying to figure out what Melanie's relationship to the clinic was."

She bit her lip. "We went there for our checkups."

"Columbia has a health service."

"We couldn't get the doctor we wanted," she said. She looked directly at Bridgett. "It's stupid, but I don't like having a male OB/GYN, you know. And Melanie didn't either, so this one time we went to the clinic and got examined there."

"There must be a female OB/GYN connected with the school," Bridgett said. "Why didn't you use her?"

"Dr. Lucas, the one we normally use, she's not here during the summer session. I was embarrassed. We'd made the appointment, found out it was Dr. Ferrer, he's this old guy, really nice, but just, you know? And I got all embarrassed. So I told Melanie and we decided to go to the clinic. We only went inside that one time. We didn't have abortions, if that's what you're trying to find out." She kept her eyes on Bridgett.

"That's where you met Katie?"

"She was just wandering around the building with, like, this Walkman on and the cord had gotten all tangled. Melanie asked her if she could help and they started talking about music."

"Madonna?" I asked.

"No, Cyndi Lauper, I think. Yeah, that's it, because we all sang a couple verses of 'Girls Just Want to Have Fun.' She couldn't sing very well. She was sweet."

"Anything else happen?"

She shrugged. This was ancient history and it was already cold for her. "We had to wait for a couple of hours before they could see us; they were busy, because there were protesters outside that day. Not many, but it was distracting. We spent a lot of that time talking to Katie. She couldn't pronounce my last name really well, so I told her to just call me Fran and she said she should know my last name so we settled on S. Fran S. So she was Katie R. and I was Fran S."

And Melanie was Melanie B.

"Melanie had no boyfriends?" Bridgett asked again, a little more insistently.

"She'd just broken up with a guy. They'd been seeing each other for maybe a month at the most. No big thing."

"When'd that happen?"

"The breakup? End of the term, would've been last week of May, I think."

"Why'd she stop seeing him?" I asked.

"Dunno. Melanie said he was hard to talk to, real old-fashioned."

"And she didn't see him after that?"

"No. I mean, if she saw Paul again, she didn't tell me about it."

There is a God, I thought.

"Could you describe Paul Grant?" I asked.

She stared at me a second as if she hadn't truly noticed me before, then got up, saying, "There's a picture of them." She disappeared into the last door on the hall, returning quickly with a Polaroid. She handed it to me. "I took that at a Yankee game we went to. That was the beginning of May."

Melanie Baechler was wearing a navy-and-white Yankee cap, pale hair spilling out around a thin face. She wasn't a big girl. My memory of Grant put him at over my height, and Melanie came to above his elbow in the photograph. She was smiling for the camera.

There was no question that the man holding Melanie's hand was the same one I'd seen outside the clinic, the same one Bridgett and I had chased out of Romero's building the previous night.

I handed the picture to Bridgett, asking Francine, "May we keep this?"

She hesitated, then nodded. "Sure."

"Where's he live?" Bridgett asked.

"I don't know."

"Did he ever go to the clinic?"

"Paul? Why would he?" Francine asked. She was looking bewildered and now just a bit scared. Her fingers tugged at one of her curls. "Do you think he knows something about Melanie's death?"

I looked at Bridgett, and she looked at the picture, then back to me. Then she said to Francine, "There's a chance that he may have murdered Melanie, as well as Katie Romero."

"What? What are you saying?"

"Francine—did Melanie have an abortion?"

"No! She didn't sleep around, I keep telling you, and besides that she was on the pill. We both were. That's why we had to go to the clinic, we had to get our prescriptions filled."

Bridgett stood up and I followed her lead. "Thank you," she said. "Keep the card. Maybe you'll remember something and give me a call, all right?"

"Wait, what do you mean he killed her? Why would he do that?"

Bridgett said, "Because he saw her enter the clinic. We know Grant was attending SOS demonstrations there. He saw her go into the clinic to abort his baby."

Francine shook her head, saying, "No, that's not right. We went for a Pap smear. She never had an abortion."

Bridgett didn't say anything.

"It's not right," Francine said. "You're not making sense. It's not right. That's crazy."

Out on the street Bridgett popped another mint. It was dark now, and the sodium lamp over the bodega made her hair shine. "Poor kid," she said.

"Francine and Melanie both," I said. "What do you think happened?"

"I think Baechler and Grant slept together, and when he saw her going into the clinic, he jumped to the conclusion that she was there to abort their child."

"And he killed her for it."

"And he killed Katie believing that he was balancing the scales, I guess. Romero took his child, so Grant took hers," she said. "They both died because Melanie Baechler needed a Pap smear."

We were getting into the car when my pager went off. I got back out and used a pay phone by the bodega.

"We've found Barry," Fowler said. "He's at your place."

"My place?"

"Asshole's threatening to blow the building up."

CHAPTER TWENTY-SIX

"I was making a circuit of the building," the patrolman said. There were sweat stains under his armpits, and around his collar. "Came around through the alley on Sullivan into the courtyard here, saw this guy up on the fire escape on the sixth floor. For a moment I thought, I don't know, I thought it was just some fuck trying a little B and E. He was toting a duffel bag, big blue-and-green thing. So I called backup and we went around, left my partner at the bottom of the fire escape in case he tried to come down that way. We're halfway up the stairs when my partner calls us back. Says he'd been made, said the shithead swears he has a bomb and is going to blow the place up. I got up to the sixth floor and Barry—and it's him, he gave his name—said if anyone comes any closer he is going to start shooting. Says he has a gun and a bomb.

"Then the circus came to town." The patrolman waved

his arm around the courtyard, smiled apologetically at me, then asked Lozano if that was all.

"That's all," the detective told him.

Lozano, Bridgett, and I stood on the outer perimeter line, at least twenty-five uniforms between us and the inner perimeter, where the commanding officers were assembled. There was no radio traffic, that had been disallowed the moment it was suspected that Barry might have a bomb, but the racket was still considerable, mostly from the crowd that had gathered. The media was still arriving, camera crews and photographers and reporters, and then there were the spectators, a lot of them kids freed for summer, with nothing better to do it seemed than to take bets on whether my home would be going up in a ball of flame.

Floodlights were up and running, bathing the building in halogen light. The courtyard spread in a perfect square at the back of all four buildings, with my apartment on the east side, sixth floor. Barry had pulled the blinds in Rubin's bedroom, preventing prying eyes from seeing just what he was up to. Facing that window, from the opposite building's roof, was one ESU sniper, poised and set with his rifle sighted on the bedroom window. Snipers waited on other roofs, covering all the possible angles of attack. There were really only two shots they could take, the first through Rubin's bedroom window and the second across the alley, and the snipers would take the shot only if Barry started gunning for lives.

Or if Barry was really serious, if he was really going to burn the place down.

And the cop was right. It was a circus.

Bridgett and I had arrived only seconds after the Manhattan North Emergency Service Unit team. Manhattan South had already been there, in position, for five minutes. They used to be called SWAT teams, but the title was changed to something less provocative, I guess, and now there were roughly forty ESU personnel milling about outside and inside the buildings. Only eight of them were snipers, the rest devoted to other tasks I could only guess at.

The Sixth Precinct commander was already on scene when we arrived, but he was quickly replaced by some inspector from One Police Plaza; I don't know what he did, either, but everybody deferred to him until the Chief of Detectives arrived and started commiserating with SAIC Carter, who showed up at roughly the same time, that is, about three minutes after we got there. Fowler was already there, and joined Carter when he saw him. Scott and I hadn't had a chance to speak, and I knew we wouldn't get one. Not now.

Then there was the Bomb Squad supervisor and one of his technicians, and a TARU guy, though nobody seemed to know what exactly he was supposed to do, but he was working closely with the hostage negotiator and all the personnel under the HN's command. That was just the police, mind: I'm not even talking about the fire units or the EMS units or the press, or all the units that had been evacuating the building. Everybody inside the perimeter wore heavy ballistic vests, the kind that would stop a .44 bullet, and consequently everyone was sweating like pigs. The night had cooled things a bit, but the humidity was rough. At least the snipers were comfortable; they don't wear the vests—hinders their movement, don't you know.

The hostage negotiator was on the phone when we arrived, talking carefully, but I couldn't hear a damn thing he was saying. He was talking to Barry, though, I knew that, because the negotiator kept watching the windows as he spoke.

So that was the circus, all gathered to see a little man from the Appalachians try to blow up my home because I scared him enough to wet his pants.

Lozano had his badge out, hung off his belt, and he wandered around inside the outer perimeter, and then returned to tell Bridgett and me what was going on, tugging at his vest like it pinched him. They wouldn't let us through; civilians had no place here. Bridgett ate Life Savers and I stood beside her in a corner of the courtyard, in a patch of shade, my hands in my pockets. It was a beautiful night, the sky deep and dark, no clouds, nothing to cut the depth. Every so often Bridgett would lean in and whisper something in my ear.

"They've cut the power and the water to the apartment," she would say.

Or, "See that guy? He's taking high-res photos. They'll develop them here and see if they show anything going on inside."

Or, "Looks like Barry cut the phone, they're going to have to use bullhorns now."

Lozano came back, sweat beaded like glass pebbles across his brow. "He wants you to go up," he told me. "He's demanding you go up, and then he wants safe passage to La Guardia and a flight to fuck knows where. Or else he blasts the building. He says he's got fifteen pounds of Semtex and he's holding the detonator."

Bridgett said to Lozano, "He's not going up there." It took me a second to realize she meant me.

"Of course he isn't," Lozano said. "You think we're nuts?"

"You got a phone I can use?" I asked him.

He pulled a cellular out of his jacket. "He pulled the line to your apartment."

"Yeah," I said, and dialed the safe apartment.

Rubin answered on the first ring. "What's up?"

"How's it look there?" I asked him.

"Dale and the doctor are napping, Natalie and me are just hanging loose. Why?"

"You got the television on?"

"Not yet. Hold on. Any channel?"

"Pick one."

I waited while he turned on the TV, watching the crowd. There was activity inside the perimeter now, the ESU commander having a heated debate with the negotiator. Lozano lit a cigarette.

"Fuck me," Rubin said.

"Yeah. I'm outside right now."

"Barry is in there?"

"Yeah."

"Oh, fuck me. Atticus, all of our stuff . . ."

"It's just stuff," I said. It came out flat.

"The cocksucking motherfucking pimple-gnawing son of a bitch," Rubin said softly. "What does he want? The TV isn't saying what he wants."

"He wants me to go in there, I think."

Rubin didn't ask why. He didn't need to ask why. Instead he said, "How's it look?"

"Barry just killed the phone connection, they've evacuated the building and the neighboring ones, too, and I have no idea how this is going to jump. He's nuts. He's gone around the bend."

"I'm coming over."

"Come around on Sullivan. Bridgett and I are in the southwest corner of the courtyard." I handed the phone back to Lozano in time to see two women who lived across the alley from me get escorted firmly away from the perimeter line by a uniform. One of them saw me and said something to her friend and pointed and they both looked at me like I was Evil Incarnate.

Lozano was asking me what was in my apartment, if there were any weapons or things like that.

"Kitchen stuff, knives. No guns, but there's about one hundred rounds of nine-millimeter ammunition in the lockbox in my room," I told him. "There's a bottle of lighter fluid for my old Zippo, and Rubin's got some turpentine, paint thinner, you know. That's about it. Nothing much there."

He nodded, and tried to readjust his vest.

Up on the roof two ESU guys were setting rappelling lines to jump down onto the fire escape if it came to that.

"We sent a team up there with the fiber-optic camera," Lozano told us. "He's lying about the amount of Semtex, apparently, not more than one or two pounds. He's got some gasoline spilled around, too. He's pretty much trashed the place."

"What's the procedure?" Bridgett asked. She hadn't said anything in a while.

"We want him alive, if he's willing, but we're not too sold on that happening. When he saw the sniper across the alley Barry freaked, that's when he cut the phone connection."

"I don't believe this," I said, and sat down with my back to the wall, looking up at the window. "I just don't believe this. This just isn't fucking happening."

Lozano stepped on his cigarette, then headed back to the command post, and Bridgett knelt beside me. She put a hand on my shoulder, resting it there for only a moment, then withdrawing it.

She didn't have anything to say, I guess.

"Clarence, can you hear me?"

The bullhorn's sound echoed and reverberated off the buildings, and the negotiator's voice bounced around the courtyard like a Super Ball.

No movement at the window.

"Clarence, can you hear me?" the negotiator called again. "Clarence, we've been talking about what you want and we're working on it, but you've got to understand we can't send a civilian inside, you know that, don't you?"

Nothing.

"Clarence, I think maybe we should talk about this, try to work something out, okay?"

Just the echoes.

"Clarence? If you don't talk to me we can't—"

And from an open window, "Fuck you, you nigger, give me Kodiak, you cocksucking ape, give me Kodiak or I'll turn the whole block into rubble!"

The negotiator lowered his bullhorn, and even from where I was I could see him struggling for control, for the right words, the words that wouldn't act like a match to Barry's anger. He raised the bullhorn back to his lips and said, "We can't send him inside, Clarence. Why don't we talk about what we can do?"

All the snipers were motionless.

There was a slight breeze now, smelling of exhaust.

"I'm going to fucking do this place, damn you!"

Rubin showed, working his way through the crowd and then pushing over to me, looking wound up and a little ill. He had changed out of his suit, at least, now in jeans and a T-shirt, both black. He sat beside me on my right, Bridgett on my left. It was almost nine, and some of the crowd had dispersed, but other people had shown up, had heard about it on the news and commuted in from wherever they had been to watch the show.

"Sorry it took me so long," Rubin said.

"No problem."

"What's he said?"

"Nothing for about an hour. He wants me to go in there or he's going to set off the bomb."

"You're not thinking about doing it, are you?"

"What do you think?" I asked him.

"Stupid question, sorry."

We were quiet for a while, watching the cops, watching the crowd. Then Bridgett said, "I think he's realized he's not getting out of this free and clear. I think he's realized he's gonna die."

———

She was right. About twenty-five minutes later a new negotiator, this one white, tried one last dialogue with Barry via the bullhorn and that ended with Barry shouting that he either got me to kill or that was it, end of block, end of story.

Lozano came over shortly after that and was telling us that ESU was probably going to try to take him, break through the wall from the next-door apartment, when Barry stuck his hand out of Rubin's window and started firing.

It happened really quick.

He was using a .357 revolver and the reports were loud. His first or second shot hit one of the ESU personnel on the ground, punching hard into the vest and knocking the cop down. Barry kept firing, but that was the only person he hit, and he sent bullets whistling in ricochets off the brick and brownstone, and everybody dove for the ground with the exception of Rubin, Bridgett, and me, and maybe a couple of others who felt secure under their cover. Which is why most of the people missed what happened next.

Barry's first or second shot must have sparked the gasoline he had spilled. By the third shot, a blossom of fire already licked out the window. Barry's hand was visible for less than a second, but the snipers had been waiting with a green light, and that second was all they needed. They're professionals, they know their job, and from the angle of a hand they can estimate where the rest of the body is. The two working the west rooftops fired at the same time, high-velocity rounds that flew supersonic. Barry fell through the blinds face first, on fire, onto the fire escape landing. He screamed once as he fell to the metal grate, but that was it, and he was probably dead by the time he hit the landing. The gasoline must have gotten into his clothes, though, because he continued to burn outside while our apartment went up. The detonator fell with him, clattering on the metal, then falling until the wires running off it went taut. It swung in the air, maybe fifteen feet under the landing where Barry burned.

The Bomb Squad went in immediately and pulled the device out, disarming it, while the fire department got the blaze under control. There was no explosion, much to the crowd's disappointment. Worse, from the crowd's point of view, the fire didn't spread out of our apartment.

But the apartment and Barry, both were a total loss.

CHAPTER TWENTY-SEVEN

It was after eleven that evening before Rubin and I could get into the apartment, and even then we got only a quick look around. It was depressingly straightforward. Barry had soaked everything he could with the gasoline, and when it went, it went fast. Some things caught, like the futons, and kept going, others smoldered and died. The bathroom had survived relatively unscathed. My room was a distant second as it was furthest from Rubin's, where the fire had ignited. But Barry had ripped, shredded, and otherwise destroyed everything identifiable as mine. Some of my clothing was dry and had escaped the fire, and I thought maybe I'd have some changes of underwear, but they hadn't escaped Barry, either. Each shirt had been sliced up the back, and he had pissed and defecated on my underwear. Every book I owned he had stacked in the kitchen, along with every book Rubin had owned, including his six thousand comic books, and they were nothing more than wet ash. That made me feel it most, what he had done to our books, our things. I loved my books, many of them gifts, many of them prized possessions I had haunted used bookstores for or had picked up in library sales or when I was with the service.

All of Rubin's art supplies, all of his drawings, all of his paintings, were ash. As he moved through the wreckage, Rubin trailed his hands alongside him, lightly brushing each blackened object, tears shining in his eyes.

We were out about five minutes after going in, and none of our neighbors said anything to us, but their accusing stares dug at our spirits as much as our backs when we descended the steps.

Natalie was waiting for us outside, having come over when Rubin called her. Dale was with Dr. Romero, and for now it seemed that one-person coverage would be enough. Bridgett stood with her. When Natalie saw Rubin, she went to give him a hug, and I watched them as they held each other.

"It's so fucking stupid," Rubin said. "It's just . . . stuff . . . it's just stuff and it's nothing. . . ."

"It was your stuff," Natalie told him.

They held each other. Then Rubin pulled back and turned to me. "So, what now?"

The question surprised me a bit. "We think we know who killed Katie," I said. "Bridgett and I need to find Fowler, let him know what we've found."

"Is Felice still in danger?"

"Barry is dead, Rich is in custody, and Crowell has probably bugged out," I said. "With everybody looking for Grant, I think the threat's diminished considerably."

"I'll go back to post," Rubin said. "Natalie and I will go."

I looked at him, at the fatigue and grief in his eyes, and I knew he would be useless.

"No," I said. "Natalie, call your father, see if we can get some of his people to cover for us tonight. I'll call the marshals, let them assist. Then you both go home, get some food, something."

"She's expecting us to cover at the funeral," Natalie said. "I think she really wants us there."

"Monday morning, day after tomorrow, we'll resume coverage," I told them. "We'll meet at the apartment before the funeral."

They seemed okay with that, and Rubin and I talked about the insurance and stuff for a little bit, and we were covered, and that was good, and it could have been worse, it could have been one of us, and I said yeah, and he said yeah.

"Get some rest," I told him.

"Practice what you preach," he told me.

I called Fowler's cellular from a pay phone by the drugstore on the corner, asking him to get me in touch with Deputy Marshal Pascal. He gave me the number and I dropped another quarter while Bridgett went into a bodega for more Life Savers and some coffee. I was put on hold at the marshals' office, then told that Pascal was out, and did I want to leave a message?

"My name's Kodiak. I'm the guy who's been running Dr. Felice Romero's protection."

The woman I spoke to said she would transfer me. I waited, watching the street. Saturday night in the Village, and people had things to do. There was a newspaper machine holding a copy of *Newsday*, and I could see a tag line about a story on page two regarding Katie and the hunt for her murderer. A homeless woman reclined on a large piece of cardboard in front of a toy store down the block, singing Billie Holiday. Even over the traffic I could hear her voice, clear and clean. An invisible woman singing a dead lady's song.

Pascal came on, saying, "Kodiak? What is up?"

"My people are done in," I said. "We're bringing in

some guards from Sentinel for the night to take over. I was wondering if you wanted some of your folks there."

"Until the morning?"

"Tomorrow, too. We'll resume coverage for the funeral."

"When do you need them?"

"As soon as possible. I've only got one person covering her right now."

"I'll send two men over. Where's she at?"

I gave him the address of the safe apartment, then got off the phone. Bridgett was sitting on the front fender of her Porsche, watching me. I crossed Bleecker to where she was, taking the cup she held out for me.

"Black and sweet," she said.

"Thank you," I said. "Can you give me a lift to the safe house?"

"Sure."

As we drove, she asked, "Where are you sleeping tonight?"

"I thought I'd stay at the safe apartment."

She signaled a turn, sliding over a lane. "You're staying at my place, and if you offer one word of argument, I swear I'll kick your ass so hard you'll never walk right again."

"Yes, ma'am," I said. I took the teddy bear off the floor and put it in my lap.

The marshals and Sentinel had beaten us to the safe apartment. They were inside with Dale when we arrived.

"They say they're taking over," Dale said, eyeing one of the Sentinel bodyguards. "What's that mean, they're taking over?"

" 'Til Monday morning," I said. "Go home, get sleep, be back at seven Monday."

He looked at the marshals and the guards, weighing their worth, then said, "I'm out of here." Before he went to the door he put a big hand on my arm, saying, "I'm sorry about your place."

"See you."

The new crew settled in easily enough, and although I didn't have a whole lot of faith in the marshals as bodyguards, they paid attention to what I told them. It's not that I don't like the Federal Marshals Service; it's more that I just don't see how apprehending fugitives qualifies them as personal protection specialists.

Done with them, I went to look in on Felice. She was asleep. I debated for a moment by the side of the bed, then called her name. The third time I said it, she stirred, reaching for the light. It came on to reveal her disheveled, her hair stuck straight up on one side of her head. She found her glasses, put them on, then sat up, pulling the sheets around her.

"There are two federal marshals here," I told her. "And some people from Sentinel. They're going to stay with you tonight and tomorrow. We'll be back Monday, early."

"You're done?" she asked.

"Not until after Katie's funeral. We'll be there. But we all need rest. You'll be okay with the marshals until then."

She nodded, her hands moving to her hair, trying to smooth it. "I survived," Felice said.

I handed her the teddy bear. "I'll see you Monday, okay, Doctor?"

"The last day," she said.

CHAPTER TWENTY-EIGHT

Lozano was thrilled to see me. "What the hell are you doing back here?" he asked.

"I want to talk to him again," I said. "I want some answers from that son of a bitch."

"Go home, Kodiak," Lozano said, and then probably realized how impossible that was. He started to say something else, then changed his mind and scowled.

"Where's Fowler?" I asked.

"He's in the box with Rich."

I turned around and walked out of the room, heading back to the cubicle where earlier we had watched Rich in interrogation. Bridgett came with me. Lozano followed, grumbling.

"You can't just walk in there," he said.

"I know."

We passed a couple of uniforms, then went into the

observation room. Pascal was inside, watching the proceedings through the glass.

"I thought you were done for the night," Pascal said.

"He say anything more?" I asked.

He shook his head. "But he doesn't know about Barry yet. Fowler's still playing him." He reached over and clicked the switch on the speaker, so we could hear the conversation inside.

". . . got to know who this guy is, Sean. We know you know him," Fowler was saying.

"Maybe I do. Might have seen him before," Rich said. "We have a lot of members." He looked wilted now, tired. But the energy in his voice was still there.

Scott played with the stud in his ear, then shook his head. He looked better than Rich, but not much.

"I don't think you see your situation, here," Fowler said. "Let me explain it to you clearly. You're dead-to-rights on the bomb, and that's not only state, that's federal. I've got you for conspiracy, possession, harassment, three counts of attempted murder, and one successful straight-up—"

"I keep telling you, I didn't kill the retard."

"Maybe you didn't pull the trigger, but accessories are tried just the same as murderers, Sean. And now that New York has the death penalty, you might just want to think about how a plea could help you. . . ."

Pascal switched the speaker off. He sighed, rubbed his chin. "It's been like that since Fowler went in there. Real illuminating."

I shifted my weight off my sore ankle. "Can you get Scott out for a few minutes? We've got some information that may help."

"Like what?" Lozano said.

Bridgett said, "We can link Grant to Dr. Romero."

"How?"

"Call the Two-six," she said. "See what you can find on

the murder of Melanie Baechler. Paul Grant and she were going out." She spelled out "Baechler" for him.

"And?"

"Baechler was murdered ten days ago," I said. "Katie knew her."

We were in the box with Rich. On the table in front of him lay the photograph that Francine had taken of Grant and Baechler at the Yankee game. Beside it were photographs of Baechler's body at the crime scene, and a copy of the autopsy report. The photographs showed ugly bruises around her neck. The left rear portion of her skull was caved in.

Rich sniffed the air. "Now that smells like gasoline." He looked at each of us, then settled on me. "Have an accident, boy?"

I pictured what his eye would look like with a pencil through it and smiled.

"Look at the photographs, Sean," Fowler said.

He did, then asked, "Who's the bitch?"

"Melanie Baechler. She's dead," Fowler told him. "Grant beat her to death."

Rich shrugged.

"You know why he killed her?"

"Tell me," Rich said.

"He beat her to death because she aborted his baby," Scott said.

Rich looked at Bridgett. He smiled. "Sound like the gash got just what she deserved."

Bridgett cuffed him at the back of his head. Her eyes were like glacial ice. "Be polite, Sean," she said softly.

"Funny thing, though," Scott said. "Melanie wasn't even pregnant." He tapped the autopsy report. "See? Says so right there. Wasn't pregnant, no sign of an abortion."

Rich's smile stayed on his face. "Then the report's a lie,

but that isn't a surprise, now, is it? All them doctors are in it together, changing the facts and spreading lies."

"No lie, Sean," Bridgett said. "She never had an abortion."

"You say."

"Grant murdered her," Fowler said. "And he murdered Katie Romero, and he wants to murder Felice Romero. With your help."

"He still might," Rich said. His eyes were on me. "You don't have this guy, do you? Whoever he is?"

"He won't be able to do it," I said.

"He's not alone. The army still marches on."

"You mean Barry? Crowell?" Bridgett asked.

Rich kept looking at me. "Like that."

"Barry is dead," Fowler said. "Got himself shot at Mr. Kodiak's apartment."

Rich's smile flickered.

"He was about as good with demolitions as you are," I said. "Hope you didn't need that Semtex."

"It's easy to get."

"Not where you're going."

He sniffed the air again and I felt my anger start to rise. "Well, maybe Clarence didn't need the Semtex? Your apartment? What happened, boy, did he torch it? Is that why you smell like a truck stop?" He leaned forward in his chair. "Did he torch your little nest, boy? Did you lose again, like you lost when the retard got capped?"

I was over the table before Fowler or Bridgett could move, driving Rich out of his chair and back into the wall with both my hands on his neck. I was pulling back, preparing to start slamming his skull against the concrete, when Fowler caught my arm, and then Bridgett had her arms around me, pulling me back.

Rich was laughing.

The door to the box flew open and Lozano came in, grabbed me, and with Bridgett, got me out of the room.

The look Fowler gave me as I went through the door was one of disgust.

Rich kept laughing. I heard it all the way out into the hall. I heard it when Lozano told me to go home and get some rest. I heard it when Bridgett and I got our gear back, and again when she disarmed the alarm on the Porsche.

Sisters of Mercy screaming on her tape deck did little to shut it out.

CHAPTER TWENTY-NINE

We had stopped for groceries and to buy me clean underwear, and after we unpacked, Bridgett told me to stay out of her way, she was going to make dinner. I sat on the old couch and tried to watch the television. A framed photograph hung over the bureau, a picture of a lighthouse with the mother of all waves crashing about from the far side. In the photograph you could see a person, either a man or a woman, it was impossible to tell, standing in the little doorway of the lighthouse. The wave threatened to swamp him or her, to wrap around the pillar of light and toss the little person off into the maelstrom. It was a beautiful picture, though sad, and I stared at it, trying to understand what I was feeling.

I thought about calling my parents or my brother or Alison, letting them know what had happened, but I didn't.

Bridgett brought two bowls of soup over to the coffee

table, and a bottle of beer for each of us. "Fresh from the can," she said. She sat in the chair by the couch, took her bowl into her lap and then put her feet up on the coffee table. Her shoes were off. She knocked over a stack of magazines, mostly periodicals but one or two literary journals, too, and I saw *Time, Harper's, The Advocate,* and *On Our Backs.*

We watched CNN and ate the soup. They ran a short piece about the fire, without identifying Barry as a member of SOS, then followed it with a seemingly unrelated piece about the bomb scare at Common Ground that afternoon. They ended with a reminder that no arrests had taken place in the search for Katie Romero's murderer, but that the FBI had someone who was "assisting in their inquiry."

"That Rich, he's so helpful," Bridgett said.

By the time they started talking sports, we'd finished our soup and beer. I took the dishes into the kitchen, washed the bowls, then washed the pot Bridgett had made the soup in.

"You don't have to do that," she said.

"I know."

"You want a drink? There's Scotch in the far cabinet. You drink Scotch, right?"

"Scotch is good."

"Pour me one, too."

She had a bottle of Glenlivet, so I poured two glasses, then returned to the couch. Bridgett flipped channels, and I looked around the apartment some more. On the wall by the bathroom door were two pictures, one of a young woman that I took to be Bridgett, her black hair cropped short. The other was of Bridgett looking much like she did now, her arm slung around the shoulder of a man in his fifties, and a woman of roughly the same age. All were smiling.

"Who's that?" I asked her.

She followed my finger and said, "That's my ma and da." She pointed at another framed photograph, this one by the door to her office, and said, "And that's my baby sister."

Her sister looked to be about Bridgett's height, maybe a little shorter, but there was no practical reference in the photograph to really give scale. She was very beautiful. She was wearing a heavy winter coat in the photograph and a stocking cap, and was looking out of the frame at something that made her laugh.

"What's her name?"

"Cashell. You have siblings?"

"A younger brother. Alex. He's in grad school."

I looked around for other photographs and didn't see any that looked to be of friends or relatives. She had an Ansel Adams shot of Half-Dome in a black frame, but that was about it. I looked back at the picture of her parents. "What does he do for a living?"

"He was a cop," she said. "A Good Irish Cop. He died two years ago. Lung cancer. And Ma was a Good Irish Cop's Wife."

She opened a tin of Altoids and sucked on one. She smiled to herself, one of those smiles that you know means whoever is doing it has gone inside and is amused by what they see there. She sipped her drink, then shook her head and said, "Two tastes that don't mix well at all." She swallowed the mint, then set her glass back on the table and looked at me. "How are you holding up?"

"I'm tired."

"That's not what I meant."

"I know," I said. "I wanted to rip his throat out with my hands, Bridgett." I emptied my glass, looked at it. "He went right for my buttons and I took off like a rocket. I don't know what's wrong with me, I don't know what's going on in my head. Since before Katie died . . . I've been having nightmares."

"About the shooting?"

"Maybe, I don't know. In one of them, I'm on a killing spree, I . . . it's the same feeling I had when I saw Crowell at the hospital, the same feeling as when I was holding Barry's gun. And now Rich, and he's nothing, he's fucking nothing, and I let him set me off like that."

"Some of it may be fatigue," she said softly.

"Yeah."

"You want a refill?"

I looked at the glass again, thought about nodding. She went and retrieved the bottle, refilled my glass, refreshed hers.

"I've got no home," I said. "I keep thinking about how I'm guilty, here, how I've done this to myself. I couldn't protect Katie. I pushed Barry too far and I didn't need to push him at all."

"Barry was waiting for an excuse," she said. "Don't flatter yourself."

I finished my drink and stared at the glass. Eventually she got to her feet and turned off the television.

"There's clean towels in the bathroom," she said. "I bought you a toothbrush. Go take a shower and I'll make up the bed."

She had a good shower, plenty of water pressure, and the head was high enough for me to stand under without stooping. There was a bar of oatmeal soap in the dish in the shower, and I used that and managed to get the smell of burning out of my nose and mouth. Her selection of shampoos was generous, and I sampled the organic one made in Australia. It made me smell like a mango, but that got the gasoline stench out of my hair.

The mirror was covered with condensation when I shut off the water, the clouds of steam hanging in the room, sticking to the plaster and tile. I turned on the overhead fan, realizing I should have done so before taking the shower, and dried myself off with one of the thick, clean, fresh towels. My ankle throbbed when I touched it.

I put on my glasses and looked at my face, and it

brought me down. Pale brown eyes and too-long hair and a shadow of stubble and lines starting to find permanent homes about my mouth, eyes, and forehead. The bruise on my cheek was turning yellow-green. And I thought, I'm twenty-eight years old, and I'm in the wrong line of work.

I opened the new toothbrush and cleaned my teeth, and then, with the towel wrapped around me, I left the bathroom, heading back to the couch where Bridgett had made a very passable bed. It was a long couch, and it would hold me. She came in from the kitchen and looked me over. Then she said, "Sit down," and went into the bathroom. I heard her rattling around and took the opportunity to put on a new pair of boxers.

She came back out with an Ace wrap and tape and told me to lean back on the sofa. She began to wrap my ankle. She sat on the couch to do it, her back to me, leaning forward to my legs. Each time she touched me I felt it, a little stroke, the caress of her hair, and it made me think about her, it made me very aware of her.

When she finished she said, "That better?" and I said, "Yes," and she nodded and moved into me, one hand lightly on my shoulder, the other slowly tracing its way up my neck, and I put my arms around her, lost my fingers in her hair, and we kissed.

She tasted of her mints and the Glenlivet, and her first kiss was kind. Her second was safe and reassuring, gliding into a rising passion at the third that I fell into gratefully. Her grip on me tightened, and she fit into me, her skin pleasantly hot, and we moved slightly. I brought my mouth from hers, and with her hands now in my hair, she guided me to her neck, and I tasted her skin at the hollow of her throat.

That was all I could do.

I stopped, and she held me against her, and I could feel her heart beating against my chest, feel my breath as it bounced back from her skin. We lay like that, neither of us moving, just my breathing and her heart, and then the sounds of traffic. She began to stroke the back of my neck.

"I can't," I said.

She kept her hands in my hair and on my neck, moving them gently. For a while my mind fumbled for more words but then just gave up, gave out, unable and unwilling to work to label emotions that wouldn't keep in line and that I couldn't properly articulate.

Bridgett slid her hands to my shoulders, and I brought my head back to face her. She brushed my lips with hers and then shifted off the sofa, standing, her hands still on me. "Lie down," she said. When I did, she covered me with the blanket and took my glasses off my face and set them on the coffee table. I watched her walk away, heard water running from the bathroom, the sounds of her brushing her teeth and washing her face. They were enduring noises, and they lulled me closer to sleep, and my eyes closed and shut out the light. I opened them when the water stopped, hearing her move from the bathroom to her bedroom, and I shut them again, thinking that was all.

But she came back, and I opened my eyes to see her looking at me lying on her sofa, and now she wore a man's nightshirt that fell to the middle of her calf and made her legs seem very long, blue-and-white pinstripes with an old-fashioned short collar, and the stripes blended into one shimmering smear. She pulled the blanket back and lay down against me, and somehow we fit on that little sofa, and that was how we slept, together, the first time.

Barry is a blackened corpse, with an insane grin from the contraction of his muscles during the fire that ate him alive. He's standing beside Rich, at attention, and both are wearing uniforms that look like a cross between something the Klan wears to rallies and desert fatigues. They have military insignia on their collars, and their left breasts are laden with medals, pips for meritorious service.

Each pip is a tiny enameled carving of a fetus.

Crowell is standing before them, and through a megaphone he says, "For service above and beyond the call of duty . . ." and he opens a wooden box, and resting on the pink satin inside is a large medallion on a black ribbon. Engraved on its surface is Melanie Baechler's head in profile, the side that collapsed when she was beaten. Crowell lifts the medallion and on the other side is carved Katie Romero, an artist's interpretation of how she looked when she fell.

The artist has made her look like a monkey.

Crowell offers the medal to me.

In my dream, I think that if I take it, I'll be close enough to kill him, and that'll end this whole damn thing once and for all. That's what I think.

But between Crowell and me stands Felice Romero. She's dressed all in mourning and she's holding a stuffed bear. I have to push past her to reach him. When I do, Felice falls down, shatters into pieces.

Barry and Rich applaud.

I start toward Crowell again, but now there's Bridgett. I try to push past her, but she won't be moved so easily. She pushes back, and is joined by Rubin, and Natalie, and finally Dale. All try to restrain me. In my frenzy to reach Crowell, I start struggling violently, thrashing against them. I kick Rubin in the leg, and he flails, loses me. I strike Natalie with the back of a hand and gouge at Dale's eyes. As Dale falls away from me, I grab his revolver, trying to train it on Crowell.

But of course, he's gone, and I shoot Bridgett instead.

CHAPTER THIRTY

When I opened my eyes, Bridgett was watching me. For a moment I thought I was still dreaming, and I started, almost falling off the couch. She put an arm out on me, guiding me back to safety. I was pulling deep breaths, and she settled back against me, resting her head on my shoulder. Her hair smelled of green apples.

"Relax, stud. You're okay."

"I shot you."

"No, you didn't," she said. "That was a dream." Her fingers went to my brow, then my hair, smoothing it. "You're okay, stud. Just you and me here. You're okay."

She made me think of Romero, the way she said it, made me think of how I had spoken to her when the toilet had overflowed. After a moment I nodded, felt myself relaxing against the cushions of the couch.

Bridgett pressed her mouth delicately to mine, let the tip

of her tongue stroke my lips lightly. Then she put her head back on my chest.

I fell back asleep.

When I woke I felt better. I shouldn't have, I suppose. Four hours on a lumpy couch and nightmares to boot, but the sunlight was reflecting off the photograph of the lighthouse, as if the keeper there had thrown the switch on. Storm warning, Atticus, he or she was saying from high in that slender tower. Fog's coming in. Here's a light, follow it; see what you can; go where you must.

Bridgett stirred against me as I reached for my glasses, and her weight was a pleasure, the way she was pressed between me and the back of the sofa, one strong leg wrapped around mine. I put the glasses on and tried to negotiate a way off the sofa, but it wasn't going to be possible without disturbing her. Then her eyes were open, looking at me, her face blank. She raised a hand and patted my head and then pushed herself off me so she was on her knees. She jerked the hem of the nightshirt down from where it had climbed to her waist, getting off the couch. She said, "Make coffee," and headed for the bathroom.

I found everything and made coffee. The clock by the stove said seven-fifteen. I rang the safe apartment and spoke to the marshal who answered the phone for a few minutes, getting a rundown on the previous night.

"Nothing happened," the marshal told me. His tone said he hadn't expected anything to.

"Just keep sharp," I said. "Crowell and Grant are still wandering around out there. When Romero gets up, ask her to call me with the funeral details." I gave him Bridgett's number and hung up.

The shower was running in the bathroom so I poured myself a mug. I turned on the television and listened to the mindless babble of some morning show about what a won-

derful summer day it would be in New York City while I
stripped the blankets and sheets from the couch and
cleaned up. Bridgett came out of the bathroom in a robe,
wet hair clinging to her face, her nightshirt bunched in her
hand. She tossed the shirt through the open door into her
bedroom, went into the kitchen and poured herself some
coffee.

"Hot damn," she said after a sip. "This is passable,
stud. Keep it up and I might even let you stick around."

"Don't make offers like that to a homeless man," I said,
and went to use the bathroom.

She was dressed in black jeans and a black sleeveless
T-shirt, her shoes in one hand and the telephone in the
other, when I came out. When she saw me she said, "It's
Fowler. He paged you."

I nodded and she went back to talking with Scott while I
pulled on my pants from the previous day and a T-shirt we
had bought the night before.

"That's none of your business," Bridgett said. "No, he
isn't . . . Wait, wait . . ." She pressed the receiver
against her shirt and said, "He wants to talk to you."

I took the phone. "Scott? What's up?"

"Have a nice night?"

"Delicious. What?"

"Nothing so far on Crowell or Grant. We searched
Grant's rooms this morning, found a pair of gloves that
tested positive for blood. Nothing else."

"Baechler's blood?"

"Probable match. NYPD is going over everything
again."

"What about Crowell's place?"

"He's not there."

"No, I meant, what did you find?"

"We haven't looked." He said it patiently. "No warrant,
no probable cause to search the location. We need to wait

for him to turn up, or to be listed as missing, and we can't list him as a missing person until tonight. We've got somebody watching the building."

"You might want to ask Veronica Selby if she knows where he is," I said.

"Why? Since when did she become involved?"

"No, not like that, but she was engaged to Crowell at one point. She might have an idea where he'd go."

"I'll talk to Selby, then," Fowler said. "You know funeral details?"

"Not yet. Romero said that Katie'll be buried in Westchester."

"There going to be a Mass?"

"I imagine so. Don't know where yet, but I've got a call in to Felice and she'll let me know."

"And you will pass that information along like a good soldier, right?"

"You can't see it, Scott, but I'm saluting you as we speak."

He chuckled and I put the phone down. Bridgett was seated on the couch, pulling on her shoes. "What was that about Crowell's apartment?" she asked.

"He hasn't returned to it," I said. "They're watching the place."

"What did they find there?"

"They haven't gone in yet. No warrant."

She just looked at me, her blue eyes waiting. I knew what she was thinking.

"Somebody's watching the place," I told her.

"So? They're watching for Crowell, not us."

"You're talking about breaking and entering."

"Like you've never done anything illegal before, stud." I kept my mouth shut and she leaned back against the couch and grinned like she knew my darkest secrets. "You're not all Boy Scout, are you? You've got the naughty streak in there somewhere."

"You're a bad girl," I said.

"Thank you."

I went back to the kitchen and poured myself another cup of coffee. "I'm waiting for Felice to call," I said.

"Hey, we've got all day, right? Nothing else on the agenda?" Bridgett turned and found the remote control, snapped on the television, and started surfing channels. "I like the idea of breaking and entering for our first date," she said.

Around ten Felice called, told me that the Mass for Katie would be held at St. James at nine the next morning, followed by a drive to the cemetery in Westchester for the burial. I asked who she had invited.

"Not many people. Colleagues. Most of the clinic staff will be there, I expect."

"Your husband?"

She blew smoke into the receiver, and the sound rustled like newspaper in my ear. "Marcus can't make it." I listened to her inhale and exhale again. "I want you all to sit with me. You were Katie's closest friends when she died, and I want you to sit with me, please."

"Felice—" I started.

"Yes, my safety, yes, my protection, I know. That's not why I invited you, Atticus. You're coming because you knew Katie. There will be marshals and FBI and the National Guard, too, for all I know. Let them protect me. I want you to sit with me. Katie would have wanted it."

"I'll see you tomorrow morning," I told her.

"For the last time." Her voice was sealed with irony.

I watched the phone for a minute after hanging up. From down the hall I could hear the television, and then Bridgett's laugh over the dialogue from the set.

I called Alison. She was surprised to hear from me, I

think. "I wanted to know if you had thought about attending Katie Romero's funeral."

"No," she said.

"No you hadn't thought about it, or no you're not attending?"

"I don't think I could handle it, Atticus," Alison said. "I just don't think I can deal with another dead child."

"Interesting equation."

"Perhaps." I heard her moving over the line, pictured her in the kitchen, putting dishes away. Then she said, "I saw your apartment on the news last night. I thought about calling you and then realized I didn't even know where you were."

"You could have paged me."

"Yes, I could have, I suppose," Alison said. "But I . . . I wasn't sure you wanted to hear from me, you know? After what had happened."

I thought, after breaking up with me the same day that Katie was murdered, you mean. "I'm staying at a friend's," I told her. "You want the number?"

She said yes and I gave her the number. "That Dale's place?" Alison asked.

"No, Bridgett Logan's. You haven't met her."

"Bridgett Logan." She tried the name thoughtfully. "Cute name."

"Oh, believe me, she's not cute."

"No, I don't suppose she is."

"Look, Alison, I just called to see if you were going to the funeral. I'd like it if you were there, but if you're not going, fine, whatever. I'll talk to you soon."

"I'm not planning on going."

"So you've said. That's it, that's all I wanted to say. Have a good day, all right? Take care."

"You, too."

Just before I put the phone down, I heard her voice, shrunken over the wires. I think she said, "I'm sorry."

Bridgett drove the Porsche twice around the block, then parked up the street from Crowell's building. The same doorman from our first visit was on duty.

"He'll remember us," I said. "He got reamed for not stopping us the last time."

"No way," Bridgett said. "You think he even knew what Crowell was yelling at him about?"

"There was a time when all doormen knew the tenants in their building."

"There was a time when a gallon of gas cost a nickel, but I don't remember that either," she said. She reached around onto the backseat and found a short crowbar, which she stowed inside her jacket.

We got out and walked along the sidewalk, her arm around my waist. She slipped in front of me just before we reached the awning, turned, kissed me, then said, "Call me a name."

"Bitch," I said.

She slapped me hard and then turned and ran into the building, covering her face, calling me a bastard.

It took me a moment, but then I said, "Honey, wait!" and ran after her. She had already hit the elevator button, but it was on the third floor and descending. So she turned around and slapped me again.

"Bastard," she repeated.

I straightened my glasses and rubbed my jaw, watching the doorman's reflection on the marble. He was sneaking curious glances our way, but nothing more. Bridgett mouthed "sorry," then turned her back on me again just before the elevator arrived. I went in after her, blocking her body from the doorman's view as she turned to push fourteen.

When the doors had closed, I said, "You might've warned me."

"Method acting," Bridgett said. "You're very good."

"Thank you. Now I know what to do if this bodyguarding thing doesn't pan out."

The fourteenth floor was empty when we arrived, and we walked to Crowell's door and knocked loudly three times. Nothing happened. Bridgett handed me the crowbar and then got down on her hands and knees, pressing her nose to the space between the bottom of the door and the floor.

"Can't smell anything. Don't think there's a corpse."

"The air conditioner could be on."

"True." She took hold of my belt and pulled herself up so her nose was nearly touching mine. "I love this shit," she said, then turned to shield me from the elevator. "Go to it, stud."

I worked the crowbar into the jamb. It took some good muscling, and I tried to remember how many locks I'd seen when we'd been inside before. Most New York apartments are locked up so tight one needs a diamond-bit drill to crack them rather than a crowbar, and I didn't have much faith that this was going to be successful. Just as I thought that, though, the wood tore with a snap and the door flew open. We went inside, closed the door after us.

The apartment looked exactly the same. Clean and still, devoid of any life. We took a few steps into the open room where Crowell had received us, looking around, listening hard. The air conditioner hummed, but that was the only sound.

Bridgett headed down the hall, and I went to the kitchen. I heard her opening doors as I checked the refrigerator. It was nearly full, bottles of mineral water and fresh fruit, some hot dogs, eggs, cottage cheese. I closed the door and then put my palm on the stove. It was cool.

I looked back at the door. There were four locks mounted on the frame. None of them had been closed. I walked over and checked the knob, and saw that, in fact,

the crowbar had been unnecessary; the door was unlocked.

"Atticus?" Bridgett called. "Come take a look at this."

She's just used my name, I thought. She must have
found a corpse.

And, lo and behold, she had done exactly that.

CHAPTER THIRTY-ONE

Jonathan Crowell lay on the carpeted floor of his office, flat on his back, three holes in his chest. Black powder burns radiated from the wounds in his linen jacket. He looked like a discarded rag doll, limp and with the stuffing exposed; except for the holes in his chest, the image might have offered some comfort. His blood had soaked the carpet, turning it from gray to black.

"Can't say I'm broken up about this," Bridgett said, staring down at the body.

"Fowler is going to love us."

"It's just jealousy. It's because we're having all the fun."

"It's jealousy all right."

She shrugged, knelt down beside the body. "He's got a nasty scrape on his cheek, here, and some bruising. Looks like he took a punch or two."

"Grant," I said.

She craned her neck my way. "Well, possibly, yeah. But why?"

Now I shrugged. "Is there a reason one of us isn't using the phone?"

"I want to nose around some more first."

"You'll contaminate their crime scene."

"Fuck their crime scene." She got up and frowned at Crowell's body, then turned away and opened the closet. I counted seven briefcases inside, vinyl and fake leather, all roughly the same size and color. I grabbed one and opened it. It was empty.

All of them were empty.

"Who needs seven briefcases?" Bridgett asked.

"Seven attorneys for seven prenups for seven brothers?"

"That's very clever," she said approvingly.

On the floor of the closet was a yellow-and-green molded plastic tackle box. Inside we found three spools of wire, some tools, pieces of electric equipment, a radio speaker, stuff like that.

I went over to the desk. In a letter holder were two white business envelopes, stamped and sealed. I pulled them, saw they were both addressed to the clinic. I handed one to Bridgett, then tore open the other.

The letter inside was identical in format to the ones we figured were sent by Grant. It read:

DOCTORS OF DEATH—
MY BABY'S IN A BOX.
HER MOMMA'S IN A BOX.
ANOTHER CHILD IN A BOX.
HER MOTHER GOING TO THE BOX.
TIME TO FINISH WITH A BANG.
NO MORE BUTCHERS.
MY JUSTICE.

It was, as always, unsigned. "It's like the others," I said to Bridgett. "It's another veiled threat about Romero and—"

"Read this one, stud," she said.

We traded letters.

To Whom It May Concern,

This is my final letter. I have finished my work now, and now the world knows. No more tricks, no need for games. We are both dead, and I am now to be judged by the only Law that matters.

I did what I've done because Dr. Felice Romero murdered my child. Her punishment was something I am glad to give my life for. Common Ground has failed.

I did what my Lord wished. I have no regrets.

Paul J. Grant

"It's a suicide note," I said.

"An unmailed suicide note," Bridgett said. "Grant was supposed to carry the bomb to the conference. These should have been mailed yesterday, or even the day before."

"But he didn't show at the conference," I said. "And the letters are here."

Bridgett scowled at Crowell's body. "So Crowell knew what Grant was going to do. Rich made the bomb on Crowell's orders, and Grant was supposed to deliver it."

"But he didn't. For some reason he didn't."

"No. So Rich used Mary Werthin as a backup when neither Grant nor Crowell showed at the conference."

"Grant had killed Crowell," I said. "That's why Crowell didn't attend."

"Why, though? What's Grant's motive? Baechler, we've got that, but why kill Crowell?"

"Grant never wrote the letters Felice was getting," I said. "Crowell did. He was setting Grant up. Somehow Crowell or Rich or Barry, one of them, found out that

Grant murdered Baechler, and they decided to use that to get Grant to kill Felice."

"And they never knew he wanted to kill Katie, too?"

"I don't think so, no."

Bridgett opened her Altoids, dropped the remaining mints into her mouth. "One of us should call Scott."

"You can," I said. "He's got a crush on you."

"I know," she said, and went to find a phone.

Scott tore each of us a new asshole, threatened to have us arrested, and then, when he arrived, threw us out of the apartment.

"Go back to Logan's and stay there or I swear to God I'll shoot you both," he said when we were in the hallway.

"I like a man who shows his anger," Bridgett told him.

"Then you're falling in love with me," Scott said, and slammed the door on us.

"Whatever gets you through the night," she told the closed door, then hooked her arm through mine and led me to the elevator.

In the lobby, the doorman finally asked us if we lived here or not.

"Sure do," I told him. "We're the McKennas in fifteen-G."

"But I'm not his wife," Bridgett said, patting my hand. "I'm his mistress. Maybe you recognize me? I'm Kim Basinger."

The doorman politely asked us to leave.

We went out arm in arm.

Bridgett decided she was hungry and that we should stop for brunch before going back to her place. I had no objections to that, so we ended up at a diner off Tenth near a taxi depot, both sides of the street outside lined with yellow cabs in various states of health. I had a bowl of oatmeal with some brown sugar, and Bridgett had a plate of steak and eggs. She didn't clean her plate.

My punchiness wore off over the meal, and when we were back in the Porsche, heading to her place, she said, "All right, stud, spill it."

"Where's Grant?" I asked.

"Fuck if I know."

"My point exactly. He hasn't left town."

"You don't think so? He missed the conference, he's got three bodies to his name. He's got to know that the FBI, the NYPD, and the marshals are all looking for him."

"He hasn't finished the job," I said. "He wants Romero."

"Maybe, stud. But he's run out of opportunities."

"There's the funeral."

She pursed her lips for a moment. "Yeah, there is. But then again, that's what you're for, right? And he knows by this point that you're no slouch."

"I take the compliment as it comes."

"Take it however you find it."

Bridgett went out to rent a couple of videos, and while she was gone I called Dale and gave him a quick brief over the phone about the funeral. After that I called Natalie's place. Rubin picked up.

"Enjoying your time together?" I asked him.

"A night of rarefied bliss, my friend," Rubin said. "I can almost forget that my *Cerebus* issue-one went up in smoke."

"You lie."

"I do," he said. "I'll mourn that issue forever. But I'm trying."

"Crowell's dead," I told him, and then ran it down.

"So tomorrow we worry about Grant?"

"Most likely. I expect Fowler will call to confirm that one way or another. But the funeral will be well covered,

let's face it. All of us, cops, Feds, what more could we ask
for?"

"Close air support?"

I laughed.

"So, what's the deal with you and Logan?" he asked.

"She's like her car," I said. "A wild ride that pushes the
envelope."

"That's an awfully sexual metaphor. Are you speaking
from experience?"

"No," I said.

"But?"

"But what?"

"Remember who you're talking to, buddy-boy," he said.

"It's crossed my mind," I admitted. "We came close last
night."

"What stopped you?"

"An inability to perform."

"You had that problem, too?"

"Oh, yeah."

"Thank God," he said. "I thought it might've been
something I ate."

I heard the front door opening and said, "I'm going to
go. See you at the safe apartment tomorrow, all right? Tell
Natalie to get there by seven."

"Will do," Rubin said.

We were finishing the third of the four Jackie Chan movies Bridgett had rented when Fowler called. She answered,
then handed off to me.

"Grant's prints were at the scene," Scott said.

"Did he shoot Crowell?"

"That's how it looks, but we're not certain yet. We
found some interesting stuff in Crowell's files, though.
Your address and a couple of photographs of you with a
young woman, both going in and coming out of the
clinic."

"That would be Alison."

"There were lots of other photos, too. I just bring this to your attention because I know you, you understand. Nice to know that you were under surveillance just for going to the clinic. There's something else, though . . ."

"The tackle box and the briefcases," I said. "I know."

"What do you want to do about it?"

"Who's going to be covering at the funeral?" I asked him.

"We'll have local NYPD and marshals at the church. Sheriffs and marshals in Westchester. We'll run dogs at both locations," Scott said. "Grant may have just taken it and run. He doesn't necessarily know where the Mass or the cemetery service are going to be held."

"Do you really think he can't find out?"

"No, but I don't know what more we can do, dude. We've got people checking hotels in Westchester in case he's already up there, but you and I both know they're not going to find jack-shit. We'll just have to keep a sharp eye and hope he's decided not to risk it."

We had pizza for dinner, and I told Bridgett about the bomb.

"It's a better one, not like that piece of crap that Rich threw together for the conference," I told her. "This one, the original bomb, is Rich's masterpiece. That's why he was so fucking smug. It's in a briefcase or something like that, and it's radio-controlled."

She folded her slice lengthwise and dripped grease onto the wax paper at the bottom of the pizza box. "You mean Grant can plant it tonight and then just sit back somewhere with the detonator?"

"Yes and no. Theoretically, he could do that, but he won't risk it going off too early. The longer the bomb stays armed, the greater the chance of some stray transmission detonating it by accident, and he probably knows that," I said. "He'll plant it tomorrow morning, most likely at the cemetery, and he'll wait."

"A trap."

I wiped my hands with a paper napkin and Bridgett closed the pizza box, took it to the refrigerator. She put it inside and came out with two bottles of Samuel Adams, which she opened. "Considering what you've just told me, you're remarkably calm," she said.

"The optimal way to deal with the threat would be to find Grant, and I don't even know where to look. Best to leave that to the Feds and the police. Tomorrow, both the church and the cemetery will be swept with electronics and dogs, and we'll have done everything short of forbidding Felice to attend. And that last is clearly not an option."

"And that'll be enough?"

I shook my head. "No. That'll be the best we can do."

She brought me my beer and sat down beside me on the floor. We were both leaning with our backs against the couch. "Can you get to St. James by yourself tomorrow?" she asked.

"You're not going?"

"I've got to go early for confession if I want to take communion."

"I pity the priest," I said.

She elbowed me. "You going to put an arm around me or what?"

I put my arm around her shoulders and she put her free hand on my thigh, leaning against me. We each drank some of our beers.

"It's going to take you and Rubin at least a week or two before you boys can find another apartment," Bridgett said. "I'm thinking that you're welcome to stay here until then."

"You sure? That's a hell of a nice offer and you strike me as someone who values her privacy."

"True. But you're a friend in need." She took another swig from her bottle. "Ready for the last flick?"

"Shoot."

She reached for the remote control and we watched the final installment in our Jackie Chan fest, my arm around her, her head against my shoulder. We killed another beer each before it ended, and when the film was done, she rewound the tape and helped me set up the sheets on the couch.

"You're going it alone on the couch tonight, stud," she said. "Think you can handle that?"

"I may roll off but I imagine I can survive the fall."

"Good thing, 'cause my back can only take so much of that action." She took the empty bottles and headed to the kitchen, dropping them in her recycling bin under the sink.

"Night, stud," she said, and headed for her room.

"Good night, Bridgett."

She stopped, pivoted on a toe, and came back. With no preamble she put her arms around my neck and kissed me, holding me to her mouth for the duration. She released me with a crooked smile.

"You can call me Bridie," she said, and then went back down the hall.

The photograph on the wall, the one of the lighthouse, bounced blue light from the street to where I lay on the couch, alone. I listened to Bridgett down the hall, where she was sleeping with her door open. She talked in her sleep, soft and incoherent, and I gained no insight trying to decipher her mumbled words, instead falling into visions of Grant lurking in the Westchester woods with Rich's bomb. The imagined images taunted me until sleep came.

No dreams.

CHAPTER THIRTY-TWO

It was the hole in the ground that I kept returning to, earth cleanly pared away to hold the white casket that had traveled from the city to the sloping and grassy hills of this cemetery, that turned me from observer into mourner. In the hot and humid air, I kept finding the smell of wet earth on the breeze, and my eyes went back to the grave again and again between sweeps of the area.

Felice sat between Natalie and me, slim and stoic in her black dress, hard as coal. Dale and Rubin sat in the chairs behind her, and the other mourners spread from there, familiar faces from the clinic staff and others I didn't recognize. Veronica Selby sat in her wheelchair with Madeline beside her, both their faces fixed in granite sorrow. Bridgett sat on my left, her hands in her lap, focusing on the coffin, her emotion unreadable. All of us on the gray metal folding chairs, listening to the breeze, or the birds, or the sobs, or the priest.

"We gather here to commend our sister Katherine Louisa Romero to God our Father . . ."

A radio crackled, its volume turned down low, and a sheriff's deputy turned away to answer it. Transmissions were being made with less care now that the sweep had been completed. No signs of a bomb or Grant, no signs of danger or distress. I watched the deputy listen to the transmission, radio a response, and take the ten steps to where Fowler stood at the end of our row. They put their heads together briefly, and then the deputy stepped away again, sent another transmission.

". . . says the Lord, inherit the kingdom prepared for you . . ."

The earth in the grave looked soft, and I imagined it sweet, perhaps comfortable. The casket had been open at the Mass. Inside it, Katie's face was still kind, the smile fixed and clearly not her own. I'd looked at her face and seen only the expression she had when shot, the tears pooling in her eyes and the turn of her mouth as she asked for her mother.

Now the casket was sealed, set on a platform beneath an evergreen. When the breeze moved a branch, sunlight would grace the coffin, the white metal impossibly smooth and shiny.

A marshal stood beside a sheriff's van in the distance, helping the deputies there load the dogs back inside. The dogs made no noise, wouldn't unless they caught the scent of an explosive.

"Grant that our sister may sleep here in peace until You awaken her to glory, for You are the resurrection and the life," the priest said. He was in his thirties, and his voice was full and strong enough to carry clearly. He spoke with sincerity and faith. He spoke the way Crowell pretended to speak. "Then she will see You face to face and in Your light will see light and know the splendor of God, for You live and reign forever and ever."

"Amen." I heard Bridgett say it clearly, but Felice

seemed to only mouth the word. She took off her glasses, set them in her lap. Somewhere behind us, I heard someone crying.

A woman stopped at a headstone some fifteen feet away, holding a fresh and simple bouquet. She unbuttoned her blazer before kneeling and then she offered the flowers to the deceased. Her head pitched forward with tears then, and I looked away.

The van pulled out, passing the line of parked cars that had been our procession out of the city. The road was one hundred yards from where we now sat, perhaps further. The marshal looked our way, wiping sweat from his forehead. He turned and walked back along the line of cars, stopping to check the Sentinel Ford that Dale had driven. The marshal dropped to his knees and looked under the vehicle, then rose and continued, passing a groundskeeper in brown coveralls who was pulling a black trash bag of cuttings beside the road. The lawn had been freshly cut this morning, and the smell of the grass was thick.

". . . when the love of Christ, which conquers all things, destroys even death itself," the priest said. He looked up from his book at us and added, "We will pray silently."

Heads bowed. At the far end of our row, in the last seat, Alison looked my way and offered me a smile. She was wearing a white blouse and a black skirt, and I moved my eyes back to the grave, wondering what the smile meant.

During the silence, Felice shuddered once and began to weep.

The priest moved to the coffin, sprinkling the glossy surface with holy water. Another radio crackled. The groundskeeper hoisted his bag and then dropped it, bending to clean the spilled cuttings. He adjusted his cap and looked around, embarrassed.

The priest began to read the Gospel, Matthew.

"Blessed are the poor in spirit . . ."

Alison had come after all, had changed her mind. I wondered why she had done it, what had happened to make the funeral become something she felt she could attend.

". . . for they will inherit the land. Blessed are they who hunger and thirst for righteousness . . ."

It was confusing that she had changed her mind. Had she come for me or herself? Or was this, for her, more about our aborted child?

The priest began the Song of Farewell, and again I heard Bridgett's voice clearly amongst all the others. She knew the words, and sang with the confidence of someone who's had voice lessons.

Natalie had put an arm around Felice's shoulders. Her eyes were on me, sympathetic for my loss.

Catalogue of losses, I thought. Home, child, and child again. Felice had said that no matter where you stood on the line, somebody always got hurt, and she had taken the worst of it. What could be worse than outliving your own child?

I looked at Alison again, and she was still looking at me, now only serious and concerned. She'd never been one to change her mind, and if she was playing games, if this was some guilt maneuver, I wanted no part of it.

The priest began the Prayer of Commendation as I turned away from her, seeing the groundskeeper get back to his feet, the spill cleaned up, on his way down the road and away from our car.

". . . console us and gently wipe every tear from our eyes: in the name of the Father, and of the Son, and of the Holy Spirit," the priest said.

"Amen." Chorused, and I imagined Alison adding her voice to the rest.

"Go in the peace of Christ."

"Thanks be to God," and that was the only time I heard Felice clearly. Then she was rising, taking my hand as I stood beside her. Dale, Rubin, and Natalie closed around her, too, and we stood with her as she accepted condolences, as if we were part of the same family. Bridgett waited, looking sculpted and immovable. She was wearing a white vest under a black double-breasted jacket and tux-edo pants, and she made them work, made them seem the most appropriate clothes possible for mourning Katie. I had arrived with her, and I would leave with her when the time was right.

Because the job was over, now.

Madeline guided Selby's chair to Felice, and waited while Veronica spoke softly to Dr. Romero, holding her hands as she had before the conference. Then Selby re-leased them, wiped her eyes, and said to Madeline, "We should be going."

Madeline nodded once and began pushing the chair toward the road.

Lynn Delfleur gave Felice a hug. There were tears in her eyes.

"Katie was a princess," Lynn said. "Perfect."

Felice kissed her cheek, then pulled away, turning to the consolations of another mourner. Lynn stood still for a moment, looking at each of us, then touched Dale's arm before heading toward the road.

Fowler caught my eye, held his hands open in an empty gesture. Nothing. I nodded, and he moved to speak to one of the marshals. Most of the law enforcement types were heading to the cars. Already one of the sheriff's vehicles had pulled away.

Rubin asked, "How're you feeling?"

"I don't know."

He worked a thin smile up, then sighed. "Me, too. It's over, I guess, huh?"

"I guess."

"It wasn't our fault, was it? Katie?"

That seemed the most important question, suddenly, and I could say only what I had told him before. "We did everything we could, Rubin. It wasn't our fault."

"You don't believe it, though. You haven't forgiven yourself."

The woman with the blazer and the flowers rose from the headstone she had been tending, and I watched her walk away, wondering. "Have you?" I asked.

He shook his head. "But I'm trying to."

I focused on the grave again, heard Rubin move off a few steps.

When I brought my eyes back up, Bridgett had moved beside me and the mourners had withdrawn. Alison was taking Felice's hand.

"I'm so sorry for your loss," Alison said. "I wish I could say more."

Felice accepted the sentiment with a little nod. "And you, Miss Wallace? You're well?"

"I'm well."

"I'm glad." Felice was watching the casket now. "It's always a difficult choice to make."

Alison looked at me, at Bridgett, then withdrew a few steps near the evergreen, waiting. Only she was left now. Even the priest had withdrawn, leaving us, and a grounds-keeper to clean up.

"Why don't you guys take her back to the car," I said to Natalie. "I'll catch up."

"I'm having a reception at my apartment," Felice said. "Will you and Bridgett come?"

"We'll come," Bridgett told her.

They started toward the car, Rubin in front, Natalie in the primary position behind Felice, and Dale behind her.

"Alison," I said, "this is Bridgett. Bridgett, Alison."

"That's a nice outfit," Alison said.

"Thank you," Bridgett said. She patted my elbow. "I'll leave you two alone."

After Bridgett had left us, Alison asked, "How are you doing?"

"Reasonably well, I suppose."

She looked over her shoulder at Bridgett. "She doesn't seem your type."

"I don't know if she is," I said. "I'm surprised you came, you said you weren't going to attend."

"I hadn't planned to." She put a hand out on the casket, feeling the metal. "But we got off the phone and I felt guilty, and then that FBI agent called about the guest list and asked if I was coming. I told him no, and he said that you really wanted me here."

"Fowler said that?" I asked. Beyond the tree about fifty feet I saw Bridgett stop, turn back to watch us. Another forty yards or so down I could see Rubin leading the squad to the car.

"No, that wasn't his name, it was Burgess, I think. Did you really want—"

Grant must have taken the file on Alison from Crowell's office, I realized, and I was already stepping forward when I heard her suck quick air, saw the color leech from her face.

"Don't take another step. Just turn around. Turn around or I'll shoot."

Bridgett had her hands on her hips, waiting, but I knew we were too far apart, that she couldn't see my expression. My gun was at my hip, and even at my fastest I couldn't index it and fire in time.

I turned and Grant was only six feet away across Katie's grave, the same young face captured in the photograph, the same face I had seen in the crowd, looking just as much the groundskeeper now as when he had slipped the bomb under the car. He appeared almost serene, but that broke with the burn in his eyes. At his waist he held a service .45, pointed at my middle.

And in his left hand he held the small black plastic box Rich had made from radio components. The antenna was tiny, but more than enough to do the job. His thumb rested on the toggle switch.

"I'm going to finish this," Grant told me. "If you move, if you try to warn anyone, I'll shoot." He craned his neck to look past us, and I imagined the squad slowly making their way to the car. Maybe twenty yards left before Grant flipped the switch.

Alison swayed in my periphery, her right hand going to the casket for support.

"You're doing this for no reason, Paul," I told Grant. "Melanie never had an abortion—"

"She went to the clinic," he said.

"For a checkup, for a Pap smear. You killed her and she was innocent."

"Don't lie to me. Crowell lied to me. Barry lied to me. Now you're trying to lie to me," Grant said. He craned his neck again and I took the chance to move my hand to my belt, nearer my weapon, hoping Bridgett would see the movement, wonder why Alison and I were so suddenly enthralled by a rubbernecking groundskeeper.

Grant looked back at me. "I won't be used. I'm going to finish this." He saw my hand and cocked the pistol. I stopped moving. "You think I'm joking?" Grant asked.

"You fire and they'll know exactly what's up."

Perspiration had soaked onto the bill of his baseball cap. He exhaled sharply, then trained the gun on Alison, canting the barrel at an angle to put the bullet through her head. "You willing to sacrifice her? After all, she murdered your baby, too. Or don't you see it like that? This is all about choice, right? So you make a choice."

I pictured Felice walking with Natalie almost on top of her. Maybe ten yards from the car, maybe thirty feet. I wondered what the blast radius was. Alison was breathing rapidly, short breaths, close to hyperventilating, her eyes fixed on the gun. That was why Grant got her here, I realized. To hold her life in one hand, Felice's in the other. And the longer I took to decide, the less my decision would matter.

He tilted his head to look again and I made my choice, swung my left arm out and shoved Alison down hard as I sprang forward. Grant fired almost immediately on my movement, but I was across the grave, scrabbling at the dirt and grabbing at his arm and I couldn't tell if he had missed or not, if I had killed Alison or not. I got one hand on his gun, pushing it down, and was fumbling for the transmitter in his left hand when I heard the blast, felt the air shudder with the concussion.

Then Grant was on top of me, and we were falling into the grave, my head bumping against dirt all six feet down. He landed on me, flat, pushing my air out, still struggling to regain control of the gun. I punched him quick and hard twice in the face, tearing my knuckles on his mouth with the second blow, and he pulled back, but wouldn't let go of the gun. His left hand came down and I twisted, caught a piece of the blow on my jaw.

"Wrong choice," he was screaming at me, over and over.

I got a hand up and threw the edge of it at his throat and he turned his head, presenting neck instead. It was enough, and he went back against the opposite wall of the grave, releasing the gun. I felt for the handle of the .45, swinging it between us as he started for me again, when three shots punched Grant in the chest.

He slumped back, his legs digging furrows in the loose earth of the grave. His eyes opened wide with the shock and then pain, and his mouth moved once more, but only rattling air escaped.

I pulled myself to my feet, turned, and found Bridgett's left hand reaching into the grave for me, the Sig still in her right. She helped me up, and I saw Alison standing with her back against the tree, very much alive. Grant's bullet had torn bark three inches from her head.

Then I was running across the grass, Bridgett at my heels, pounding toward the circle of marshals and deputies and the blazing car. Fowler caught me outside the ring, tried to push me out, saying my name. I elbowed past him, past Selby in her chair and Madeline frozen at her side.

I saw the body then, Natalie standing over it, went down on my knees on the clean grass.

She didn't look at me.

In my mind I could see what had happened, see it so clear and clean that I thought I could feel the wound.

Grant fired his gun, and the squad, knowing only that the shot had come from behind them, not able to take the time and find the shooter, did an immediate takedown. Natalie knocked out Romero's knees with her own, pressing the doctor flat and then following with her own body. Dale had done the same, drawing as he fell, turning to find his shot.

Rubin, in the lead, had spun and drawn, and when the car exploded, he'd taken the force of the blast in his back.

Felice had rolled him face up to work on him, Rubin's life flowing out from beneath his torn body. There was too much trauma and now her hands were stained with blood that clung to the grass, shining in the sunlight.

I looked at my friend. His eyes were open and his mouth, and my first thought was that I would never hear his voice again. He still had his gun in his hand, fingers darkened with old ink frozen around the butt. Cut grass clung to his face. A single blade had stuck to his right cornea, a sliver of green cutting the brown into two mismatched halves.

Patrol cars were sliding onto the lawn, their doors swinging wide even before they stopped. Deputies ran in all directions, some reaching for fire extinguishers to fight the dying flames of the car. Alison still stood beside the grave where Grant had fallen, staring at me, still not moving, and some of the cops were making their way toward her now, too. The air tasted of charred upholstery, gasoline, and soot, and black smoke from the burning rubber spilled to the sky.

"Evac Pogo," I said.

I was afraid she would make me repeat the order, but Natalie nodded slowly once, her eyes still on Rubin. She holstered her weapon and stepped around to Felice, reaching a hand for Dr. Romero's shoulder. Dale moved after her, offering assistance, and I saw he was crying, silently. They helped the doctor stand, and she was staring at me even as each of them took an arm. Fowler guided them to a car, holding the door open and then slamming it shut once they were all inside. Felice never took her eyes off me, sharing our new bond.

When the car was out of sight, I sat down on the grass next to Rubin and waited for the rest.

FINDER

This is for Jennifer

ACKNOWLEDGMENTS

Thanks go out to the following people for their assistance and aid in making this book possible:

As always, the President of Executive Security and Protection International (ESPI), Inc., Gerard "Jerry" Hennelly, for service above and beyond the call of duty *and* friendship.

Jonathan Rollins, for telling me more than I could ever want to know about the clubs of Manhattan, both for firearms and B/D; Officer William "Bill" Conway of the NYPD, for legal points and procedural accuracy; Elizabeth Rogers, NY EMS Paramedic, for advice about wounds; Paul Biddle of Dorsett, for fact checking and accuracy via long distance.

Benjamin Toro, for telling me that who dares wins.

Special thanks to: Kate, Peter, Amanda, Mike, Nic, Daria, Nunzio, Joaquin, Veil, and Tut. The debts are great, and the thanks not nearly enough.

Some kill their love when they are young,
And some when they are old;
Some strangle with the hands of Lust,
Some with the hands of Gold:
The kindest use a knife, because
The dead so soon grow cold.

Some love too little, some too long,
Some sell, and others buy;
Some do the deed with many tears,
And some without a sigh:
For each man kills the thing he loves,
Yet each man does not die.

Oscar Wilde, *The Ballad of Reading Gaol*, st. 8 and 9

CHAPTER ONE

She was lost.

I only saw her because I was doing my job, just looking for trouble, and I must have missed him when he came in, because I didn't see him enter. He was a white male in his early thirties, neat in his clothes and precise in his movement, and he clearly wasn't with the scene, the way he lurked in the corners of the club floor. The Strap had been built in an abandoned warehouse, the walls painted pit-black and the lights positioned to make shadows rather than eliminate them. For people who were serious about the scene, The Strap wasn't a club of choice, and if they showed at all, it wasn't until after midnight, when the wannabes had gone to greener pastures or to bed.

Bouncing is a people-watching job, a process of regard and/or discard. You look for potential trouble; you isolate potential trouble; then you wait, because you can't react until you're certain what you've got really will be trouble.

I was waiting, watching him as he looked for her, as he weaved around the tops and bottoms playing their passion scenes. It was after two now, and the serious players had arrived, a detachment of leather- and PVC-clad types who took their playing very seriously indeed. Now and again, over the industrial thud of the music, the slap of a whip hitting skin, or a moan, or a laugh, would make it to my ears.

Trouble stopped to watch a chubby woman in her fifties get bound onto a St. Andrew's Cross, black rubber straps twisted around her wrists and ankles, making her skin fold and roll over the restraints. His hands stayed in his coat pockets, and I saw that he was sweating in the party lights.

Maybe cruising.

His manner was wrong, though, and when the woman's top offered him his cat-o'-nine-tails, Trouble fixed him with a level stare that was heavy with threat. The top shrugged a quick apology, then went back to work. Trouble cracked a smile, so fast it was almost a facial tic, then turned and headed for the bar.

It wasn't a nice smile.

Hard case, I thought.

I followed him with my eyes, then let him go for a minute to watch two new entrants. As the newcomers came onto the floor a woman cut loose with a pathetic wail, loud enough to clear the music, and the younger of the two stopped and stared in her direction. Both men were dark brown, with skin that looked tar-black where the calculated shadows hit them. The younger looked like a shorter, slighter version of the older, right down to their crew cuts. Both were dressed for watching, not for playing, and the younger couldn't have been much over twenty-one, just legal enough to get inside. His companion was older, in his forties. He shook his head at the younger man's reaction, said something I couldn't hear, and as they began moving off again, I looked back to the bar.

Trouble had ordered a soda from Jacob, the bartender. The Strap was a licensed club, and since there was nudity on the premises, it couldn't serve alcohol. Trouble paid with a wallet he pulled from inside his jacket, and when he put it back, the hem of his coat swung clear enough for me to see a clip hooked over his left front pants pocket. The clip was blacked, the kind used to secure a pager, or perhaps a knife.

So maybe he's a dealer, I thought. Waiting to meet someone, ready to make a deal.

Or he really is trouble.

He sipped his soda, licked his lips, began scanning again with the same hard look. A man and a woman crawled past me on all fours, each wearing a dog collar, followed by a dominatrix clad in red PVC. She held their leashes in one hand, a riding crop in the other, and gave me a smile.

"Aren't they lovely?" she asked.

"Paper trained?"

"Soon," she said.

Trouble had turned, looking down at the other end of the bar, and I followed his gaze, and that's when I saw Erika.

She wore a black leather miniskirt, torn fishnet stockings, and shiny black boots with Fuck-Me heels. Her top was black lace, also torn, showing skin beneath. Her hair was long, a gold like unfinished oak. The club lights made it darker and almost hid the stiff leather collar she wore, almost obscured the glint from the D ring mounted at the collar's center.

She was brutally beautiful.

She was just like her mother.

She was only fifteen.

Trouble and I watched her light a cigarette, tap ash into her plastic soda cup while watching the scenes play around her. She looked carefully bored, meeting gazes easily as she found them, no change in her expression.

The pitch and yaw in my stomach settled, and I took a breath, wondered if it really was Erika, wondered what the hell I was supposed to do now.

Trouble finished his soda and moved, settling beside her, his lips parting in an opening line. She didn't react and didn't look away, and he spoke again, resting his left arm on the bar, his right in his lap.

Erika cocked her head at him, then turned away on her stool, tossing her hair so it slapped him in the face.

He responded by grabbing her with his left hand, taking hold of her shoulder and spinning her back to face him, and that's when I started moving.

Erika tried to shrug his hand off, but he didn't let go, and I was close enough now to hear her saying, "Fucking fuck off, asshole."

"We're going," he told her.

Jacob had turned behind the bar, figuring maybe to break them up, but Trouble's right went to his pocket, and it wasn't a pager he'd been carrying, but a knife. He thumbed the blade out and it left a trail of silver in the light, like water streaming in a horizontal arc, and he casually swiped at the bartender's eyes. Jacob snapped his head back, both hands coming up for defense. Trouble kept the point on him over the countertop, his other hand still on Erika, and I arrived to hear him saying, "Don't be a hero." He had an accent, British and broad.

His back was to me, but Erika saw me coming, her mouth falling open with surprise and recognition as I brought my left forearm down on Trouble's wrist, pinning it to the bar. The surprise of the blow made him lose the blade, and it skidded over the edge, landing in a sink full of ice. It was a nice-looking knife, with a chiseled tanto point, the blade about three and a half inches long, and Jacob went for it immediately as Trouble started swearing. I felt him shift to move, and I snapped my right elbow back as he was bringing his free hand around for my head. I hit first, catching him in the face, and I came off his pinned arm, turning, to see him staggering back. He had released Erika, and had one hand to his nose.

She said my name.

"Erika," I said, still looking at Trouble. If he had reacted with any pain or surprise, I'd missed it, because now his hand was down and he was smiling at me. He looked at Erika for an instant, then back to me, and I took the opportunity to check his stance.

He knew what he was doing. He knew how to fight.

Blood flowed over his upper lip, and the smile turned bigger, and I could see dark pink around his teeth.

"You want me to show you out?" I asked him.

Trouble shook his head, and the smile blossomed into a grin.

"You took my knife," he said. The lighting made the blood from his nose look black. "That's a fucking precious knife, and you took it."

"You didn't have a knife. If you had a knife, you would have just committed a felony, and we'd have to call the cops."

"Fuck that," Jacob said. "I *am* calling the cops." I heard the rattle of plastic on metal as he reached for the phone.

Trouble shifted his weight, settling and coiling, wanting the fight, and I took a step to the side, putting myself between him and Erika, figuring that if I was about to get beaten, at least he'd walk away without her. His hands were up and ready, and his breathing was under control.

If he was a serious martial artist, I was deep in the shit. Despite my chosen profession, I don't like pain, and at seven-fifty an hour, I'm not getting paid enough to change that fact.

"You've no idea the world of hurt you've bought," Trouble said, showing me his teeth. His eyes moved from me to see beyond my shoulder, and then everything changed. His glee vanished with the grin, face turning into a battle mask, and he spat blood onto the floor.

I wondered how much this was going to hurt.

His hips began to torque, and I thought he was starting with a kick, prepped myself to block it.

But the leg didn't launch.

Instead he turned, breaking for the fire door, pushing through the people who had stopped to watch this different scene being played, knocking over the PVC woman with the leashes. She went backward, falling onto her slaves, crying out, and he kept going.

I went after him, trying to be more polite about my pursuit, but the fire door had already swung shut by the time I reached it. I slammed the release bar down and pushed, stepped out into the alley, checking left and then right, spotting him as he reached Tenth Avenue, then turned the corner.

By the time I could make the avenue, he'd be gone.

I thought about going after him anyway, then decided I'd gotten off easily and had better not push my luck. My breath was condensing in the mid-November air, and it was cold out, and getting colder. There was a wind blowing, too, floating the smells of alcohol, urine, and exhaust down the alley.

I heard the rubber seal at the base of the fire door scraping the ground, saw Erika stepping out to look past me to the avenue. The door swung shut slowly, and I heard the latch click.

"You broke his fucking nose," she declared.

"Probably," I said. "What'd you do?"

"Me? I didn't do anything."

"Something scared him off," I said. "What did he want?"

"He wanted to top me."

"With a knife?"

She shrugged, faked a shiver, and said, "I'm going back inside."

"The hell you are."

Erika stopped, turned her head and tossed her hair much as she had done to Trouble. "What?"

"You're fifteen, Erika. Isn't that right?"

"Twenty-one," she said immediately.

"You got some proof of that?"

"Atticus. You know who I am."

"Exactly."

She waited for more, and then realized that was my whole argument.

"Fuck you," she said, finally, then spun on one of her too-high heels, making to go back inside. I let her, because she couldn't get far. It was a fire door, after all, and there was no handle on the outside. Great for exiting the building in a hurry, not so good for a return trip.

It took her a second to come to the same conclusion. "I'll go through the front. No problem. I've done it before." She brushed past me, heading down the alley.

"I'll make sure you're carded."

"I've got ID."

"I'll tell them it's fake," I said.

That stopped her once more. Without turning, she said, "I fucking hate you."

"Nice to see you, too."

"Go to hell," Erika snarled. She turned and pointed a finger at me. "Where the fuck am I going to sleep tonight?"

"At home."

"You are so wrong." She threw her hands out as if to ward me off, then began shaking her head and muttering. The wind kicked up, gusted down the dark street, and I felt its teeth through my jacket. Erika had goose bumps on her skin, and the cheap lace of her top made her pale breasts stand out in contrast. I looked toward Tenth Avenue, feeling like a dirty old man.

She certainly wasn't dressing fifteen.

"Why the fuck are you doing this?" Erika demanded.

I took off my jacket and offered it to her.

She ignored it. "Where the hell do you get off telling me I can't go back in there? What's your fucking problem, huh?"

"You're underage, Erika," I said. "Will you put this on?"

"So fucking what?"

"So it's illegal, that's so fucking what. How'd you get in there?"

"None of your business."

"Will you please put this on?"

"Why?"

"Because I can see your nipples and they're erect and I embarrass easily," I said.

Erika checked her front, then grabbed a breast in each hand and looked at me. "That's the point, asshole," she said, squeezing, her thumbs and forefingers pinching flesh.

"Put on the goddamn jacket, Erika."

She grabbed my coat and put it on.

"Thank you," I said.

"You're a fucking asshole," she said.

I began heading toward Tenth Avenue, walking slowly, hoping she'd join me. After five steps, she did, falling in on my left.

We were almost to the corner when Erika asked, "How you been?" She asked it like I'd seen her yesterday and we'd maybe just caught a movie, then done some window-shopping at Macy's.

"I've been better. Why aren't you at home? Why aren't you in D.C.?"

Erika laughed. "The Colonel retired, lives in Garrison, now. I don't even live with him."

"So where do you live?"

"Wherever I find a bed, dipshit." She stopped, checked her tone, then continued, more patiently. "That's why I need to get back in there, Atticus. That's where I'm going to find my shelter for the night."

This time, I stopped. "You're tricking?"

"Sometimes, I guess. Sure."

"What the hell's happened? Why aren't you living at home?"

Erika took an impatient breath and looked off past my shoulder, shoving her hands into the pockets of my army jacket. The gesture revealed her age, the jacket much too big for her, the miniskirt almost entirely swallowed by its hem. The light on the street wasn't fantastic, but I could see her eyes clearly, and they looked fine, her pupils equal. She didn't seem to be on anything. I waited.

Erika said, "They got a divorce, you know that, right?"

"I heard a rumor."

She ran a knuckle over the bridge of her nose, wiping imaginary club grime away. "Yeah, well, the rumor is true. Maybe a year after you left, Mom took off. They've been fighting since then, over money, over me, you name it. It all went final about a year ago. I don't even know where she is these days, and frankly I don't fucking care. So, I live with the Colonel, just him and me . . . and he doesn't go out much anymore, you know?" She was still watching something beyond me, keeping her gaze distant. "He sort of sees me . . . he sort of sees me as in-home entertainment. So I don't like to be around the house that much."

In-home entertainment. I swallowed, felt a little sick as all of the implications of that phrase hit home.

An NYPD sector car turned off the avenue and headed down the street, passing us. Erika watched its progress, and when it stopped in front of the warehouse, she said, "Guess somebody called the cops, huh?"

"How long has it been going on, Erika?"

She shrugged, picking a spot on the pavement that interested her. "He retired a little before it went final, brought me home from school; I was going to boarding school in Vermont." She rubbed her hands against her upper arms, making friction for heat. "You going to take me home now? I'm fucking freezing my tits off."

CHAPTER TWO

After my old apartment in the Village had been trashed in a fire, I'd spent a month searching for a new place to live, trying to reconcile my love of space with the real estate prices in Manhattan. The same friend who'd found me the bouncing job at The Strap had hooked me up with a rental agency, and the end result was that I now had a four-room apartment in Murray Hill all to myself. In exchange for this, I handled the building's security and did consulting for the realtors, pro bono. I couldn't complain. I had a home, which is more than a lot of people in this city can say.

More than Erika could say, it seemed.

I unlocked the door to my apartment, hit the lights, and let her inside. She took a few steps in, looking around.

"Cool," she said.

"Glad you like it."

I'd had the apartment for two months and her approval mattered simply because I still wasn't certain

what I thought of the place. Everything I owned had
been turned to ashes, and with the arrival of my insurance check, I'd begun the process of rebuilding the
trappings of my life. My shopping so far had been hap-
hazard. The kitchen and bedroom were pretty much
furnished, now. Both the spare and living rooms still
needed work.

I locked the door as Erika began walking through the
space, exploring her way through the bedroom, then
the kitchen, then the bathroom, the spare room, and
finally the living room. She shook her head at the cheap
couch I had backed against one wall, opposite the radiator. It had been left by the previous tenants, and I
hadn't bothered to haul it outside and down the four
flights of stairs to the street yet. Besides, it was a surprisingly comfortable couch.

"That is pathetic," she said.

"But comfy."

In another corner were some painter's supplies, three
rolled canvases, a folded easel, two stained palettes, and
a box of paints. I had shared the apartment in the Village with a friend, Rubin, and all of his belongings were
ash now, too. He had kept a studio in Chelsea, though,
and when I had cleared it out, Rubin's things had come
home with me. The only other object worth attention in
the room was an oil painting that hung on the wall
opposite the window, almost cartoonish, done in two
frames. The first depicted a well-kept hand holding a
ridiculously complex semiautomatic pistol. It had been
painted in the act of firing, complete with the ejecting
shell. The pistol pointed to the second frame, showing a
frontal view of a very surprised face. The bullet exited
on the opposite side of the frame, a wake of gaudy
blood and matter following. Most of my friends thought
the painting was morbid, but I sort of liked it. The expression on the victim was one of frustration more than
anything else, as if he was saying, well, this is *just* what
I needed.

Sometimes, I knew that feeling exactly.

Erika stopped in the center of the empty room and shrugged my jacket off, tossed it down and sat on the couch, curling her feet beneath her. The skirt climbed a bit, but she didn't move to adjust the hem. She looked at the painting. "That is so cool."

"Hungry?"

"Sure."

I brought the jacket to the kitchen and hung it off the coat hook I'd put in the wall earlier that week, then began foraging in the refrigerator. I found a container of cold chicken chow mein and a soda, got a fork from the appropriate drawer, and carried them back to the living room.

"I don't have a whole lot of food," I told her. "Need to do some shopping."

She took them, saying, "Thanks," and began to eat. I went back for a paper towel so she could use it for a napkin. After she took it, I sat down on the floor by the radiator, facing her.

Erika wiped her mouth with the paper towel, then pointed at the painting with the fork and said, "Rubin do that one?"

"Yes," I said. It surprised me that she remembered him. She hadn't met him more than once, and that would have been four years back.

"How's he doing?"

"He's dead," I said.

She gave me a look like she thought I was joking, then dropped it when she saw my face. "When did he die?"

"About three months ago. Closer to four."

"How?"

"We were on a job, protecting a woman. Some guy put a bomb under a car, and when it went off, Rubin took most of the blast."

It wasn't something I wanted to talk about, and Erika seemed to understand, hunting the carton with the fork for a minute in silence, spearing pieces of chicken and

chewing on them thoughtfully. "He was a nice guy,"
she said.

"Yeah, he was. I'm surprised you remember him."

She smiled into the carton. "He made an impression."

"We need to talk about you."

Erika shook her head, and her hair swung from side
to side, coming dangerously close to meeting the chow
mein.

"Erika, if your father's molesting you—"

"I don't want to get into this right now."

"We need to find a place for you to stay. I don't want
you on the street, and I don't want you tricking for a
place to sleep."

"I'll stay here." She looked at me and, before I could
respond, asked, "You don't want me to stay here?"

"No, you can stay for as long as you need to,
Erika—"

"Why that look, then, huh? You don't want me?"

"I'm not sure this is the best place for you to be," I
said. "That's all I meant."

"This is as good a place as any, Atticus. Come on, it'll
be like in Maryland. You and me, that big brother, little
sister thing we had going. It'll be fun, just like before,
except no Mom. But that's okay, right? We don't need
her."

She was so earnest and she again seemed so young
that her words made me smile, made me realize how
glad I was to see her again. She saw it, and that led to
one in return, generous and warm, much like I remembered her mother's.

"See? You like the idea. You and me. Think about
how much fun we could have."

"There's this little thing called life," I told her. "As
in, you have one. Minor things like school, and so on."

"We can work that out."

I shook my head. "This is serious shit, kiddo, you
know that. All the fun you and I might have, it still

won't make your problem go away. We're still going to have to deal with the Colonel."

"The Colonel doesn't matter," Erika said. "He's doing his own thing, he's the same as always, and you know what that's like. Anyway, what the fuck are you going to do? Break his nose like you did that guy tonight? Let me stay here, Atticus. It'll be fine." She peered into the empty carton, set it on the floor, and took a drink from the can of pop, looking around. "You look like you could use the company."

"Do I?"

"We'll have to get some furniture in the spare room of yours. It's fucking empty in there."

"There's a desk," I said.

"And no chair. No, we'll fix that one up, and it can be my room. Get a futon or a bed in there, a decent sofa out here. God, you don't even have a television, do you?"

"As a matter of fact, no, I don't."

"And we can move the stereo in your room out here so we can share it. Is it a good one?"

"It's a good one," I admitted.

"All right, so we're not totally fucked up, then. And we'll get a TV and a VCR."

"And some clothes for you."

"You don't like what I'm wearing? Oh, yeah, I forgot." She pinched her nipples once more.

I shook my head.

"What do you think? Pretty nice, huh? Just like Mom's." She stood and planted her feet in a broad stance, raising her hands over her head, and then cocking her hips. She did it as if stretching, showing off her muscles, her body. Beneath the lace, her breasts looked crushed. "Just like Mom," she said again. Her eyes were hazel, flecked with gold, and they watched me the whole time.

I reached for the empty carton and the paper towel, then got up.

She dropped the pose, asking, "Are you blushing? Is Atticus blushing?"

"Atticus is going to put this stuff in the trash," I said, heading back to the kitchen. "And you are going to get some sleep."

"You *are* blushing." She came down the hall after me. "Why?"

"Because I'm a prude. You want a glass of water or something before you go to bed?"

"You are so not a prude. That's not it." She hopped up on the counter while I dumped the garbage in the trash can under the sink. "Do you think I'm pretty?" She probed a tear in her fishnets with an index finger.

I rolled my eyes at her.

"No, I'm serious. Do you?"

"Yes, I think you're pretty, Erika."

"Do you want to fuck me?"

I put the can back and shut the door, straightening up to look at her. Sitting on the counter, she was about my height. The look in her eyes was stone serious.

"No," I said.

"Why not?"

"Aside from your age?"

"Sure, if that's an excuse."

"I don't think of you in that way."

"You could."

"No, I couldn't."

She considered, then slipped off the counter and stepped to the middle of the room, turning her back to me. She pressed her ankles together, as if she were standing to salute, and then knelt. Once on her knees, she crossed her wrists at her lower back, her palms facing me, tossed her hair over her shoulder, and then pressed her left cheek gently against the hardwood floor. Her leather collar looked hard in contrast to her hair and skin, and the D ring had turned on its mount, easily accessible. "I'm told I'm pretty good," Erika said.

"Not funny," I said.

"You could just take me like this." She pulled her knees in tighter, raising herself up another inch or so.

"Get up." It was a position of absolute submission, of one animal awaiting the entry of another, and I didn't like her in it at all. I especially didn't like her using it on me.

She licked her lips as if in a movie, looking at me over her shoulder and upturned rear. "Is that an order, Master?"

There was a knock at the door.

"I'm making you hard, aren't I, Master?"

"Erika, get up."

"Make me," she requested. Her leather skirt was secured with a button and zipper at the waist. She unfastened the button and started to pull the zipper as there was another knock. "Shall I answer that, Master?"

"No, Erika, now would you please—"

She turned her head to face down the hall and shouted, "We're busy!" She gave me a smile, finished tugging her zipper down.

I went to the door, unlocking it as noisily as possible. Maybe a fear of embarrassment would keep her skirt on. I doubted it.

"You're busy?" Bridgett Logan asked me when the door opened. She looked like she should have been in bed.

"That wasn't me," I said, getting out of the way. I could smell her shampoo as she went past. "I've got a houseguest."

"So I gathered."

Erika was where I'd left her, the skirt still on but open at the back. She had black panties on and they didn't cover enough. Faded welts marked her skin. "Shall I serve her, too, Master?" Erika asked.

Bridgett looked at me for an explanation.

"Bridgett Logan, this is Erika Wyatt," I said. "Erika Wyatt, Bridgett Logan."

"Charmed," Bridgett said.

"Do I have permission to speak, Master?" Erika asked.

"Does she?" Bridgett asked.

"You're not helping," I told her.

"He's just beginning to discipline me," Erika told Bridgett proudly.

"Enough," I said, and reached down, taking her by one arm. She got to her feet, keeping her eyes on the floor. The skirt stayed on, clinging to her hips.

"Will you beat me, Master?" she asked, and there was hope in her voice. "Punish me? Have I disobeyed?"

Bridgett grinned, went to the refrigerator, and pulled out a beer. "I'll wait in the living room," she said, then went down the hall. "Take your time."

I guided Erika to my bedroom, and pointed her to a corner while I turned down the bed.

"That your girlfriend?" Erika asked.

"My friend," I said. Compared to the living room, the bedroom was crowded, and Erika positioned herself between my bureau and the closet door while I pulled back the sheets and turned on the nightstand lamp. There were three pillows on the bed, and I took one and a blanket from the closet. I've worked hard to void most of my Army-conditioned habits, but I still make a very neat bed. The extra pillows are a luxury.

"You going to join me when she's gone?"

"I'm going to sleep on the pathetic couch. There are towels in the bathroom, and you can help yourself to anything in the kitchen. We'll go out to breakfast tomorrow, if you like, but we're going to have a long talk."

She sat on the bed and started unlacing her boots. "Are you mad at me?"

"We'll talk tomorrow." I folded my blanket and went to the door.

"Hey, Atticus?"

I sighed. "What?"

"I've missed you."

"I'll see you in the morning. I've missed you, too," I told Diana's daughter.

Bridgett had placed herself in the same spot that Erika had chosen earlier, sunken back on the couch with her long legs fully extended to the floor. I took a second to look at her before coming the rest of the way into the room, enjoying the hum her presence set off in my stomach. She caught me at it and gave me a grin.

"Isn't she a bit young for you?"

"It's a long story."

"Well, I've got a story for you, too, actually, that's why I'm here. Why do *you* think I'm here, Atticus?"

"I think you're here because Burton called you from The Strap and said that the bouncer you told him to hire bugged out after a fight tonight," I said.

Bridgett tapped the hoop that ran through her left nostril and said, "On the nosey. Apparently your departure preceded an absolute flood toward the exits."

I sat back on the floor, in my corner by the radiator, putting the pillow and blanket beside me.

"Am I correct in assuming that your altercation at the club had something to do with the provocatively dressed nymphet who was offering herself to you when I arrived?" Bridgett asked.

"Yes."

She ran a hand through her glossy black hair and gave me a serious looking-over, so I returned it, because there are many things worse than looking at Bridgett. Bridgett is twenty-eight, my age, roughly the same height, but leaner, not as bulky as I am. Her face is a beautiful oval, with a small mouth and full lips, a stubborn jaw, and the bluest eyes I've ever seen. Both her ears are multiply pierced, hoops that run from the lobes to the high cartilage on each side. The hoop she wears through her left nostril is the thinnest and smallest of the bunch, and it somehow makes her face all the prettier. She's got another one through her navel, and the few times I've seen it, the effect on her torso is much the same. Bridgett was wearing gray sweatpants and a Stanford sweatshirt under her biker jacket, and a pair of Reebok high-tops, and I knew that Burton's call had gotten her out of bed.

She looked lovely anyway.

"He told me to tell you not to show up for work tomorrow night," Bridgett said finally.

"I'm fired?"

"Like a cannon." She rapped her fingernails on the brown glass of the beer bottle. I liked her hands; her fingers were long and slim. "You want me to talk to him?"

"Don't bother."

"What are you going to do for work?"

"I'll find something," I said.

Bridgett made a noise that was almost a snort.

"What?" I asked.

"Another bouncing job?"

"Maybe, if that's what I find."

"You're distressing me," Bridgett said. "Why aren't you out trying to drum up some real work, out there protecting people?"

"Because I don't feel like it."

"You're a PSA, and yet you haven't taken a job since Rubin died. Isn't it time you climbed back on the horse that threw you?" She was looking at the painting supplies when she said it.

"I'm just not interested in protecting anyone right now."

Bridgett shifted her eyes, now studying the double panels of the painting on the wall. "If this is some way of punishing yourself because he died, it's stupid."

"If it was, yes, it would be. But it isn't."

"No?"

"No."

She shook her head, not quite believing me, but not willing to call me a liar. "You leave the club because of her? Erika?"

"Yeah, she was trying to get back inside."

"I thought you were okay with this," Bridgett said. "That you didn't have a problem with the scene."

"I don't have a problem with the scene. She's fifteen. I don't know how she got past the door, but she was insistent about going back in, and I couldn't let her do that."

"Then you should have put her in a cab home, and gone back to work."

"Ease up," I said. "She won't go home. I didn't bug out because I wanted to. I've got a loyalty to Erika, and she needed my help."

Bridgett turned her head to look back at my bedroom. "Did you say fifteen?"

"Uh-huh."

"Doesn't look it."

"I know."

She looked back at me. "So, who is she?"

"Her father was a colonel at the Pentagon. I protected him and his family. Erika says he's retired now. She also tells me that he's molesting her, and that she's run away from home."

Bridgett raised her eyebrows. "Is he?"

"I don't know. The Colonel was a true son of a bitch, and we didn't get along, but I'm certain he never touched her when I was assigned to him. If Doug Wyatt is molesting her, it started after he divorced her mother."

"Where's her mother?"

"God knows. Erika says she doesn't know and doesn't care."

Bridgett finished the beer, examined the art on the label. "I know some people in Social Services. Also a really good children's advocate if you need names."

"I'll handle it. Figure she'll stay here until I find out what's going on."

"Sounds like a plan. You're certain you don't want me to talk to Burton?"

"I'm certain. I think he's overreacting, but then again, someone pulled a knife in his place tonight, so he's got a reason to be angry."

"Then I'll head home, go back to sleep."

Bridgett handed me the bottle, and after I'd disposed of the empty, I took her to the door. She stepped out into the hall, then turned and wrapped her arms around me, kissing me. It caught me by surprise, but I recovered quickly, and kissed back. Bridgett broke off, slid a fingertip over my nose and mouth.

"I'll call you tomorrow, stud," she said. "Maybe we can have dinner later this week?"

"I'd like that."

"I bet you would." She grinned, and I watched as she went to the top of the stairs. She gave me one last smile, then ran down the steps, her sneakers squeaking on the turns.

I fixed all the locks on the door, debated about looking in on Erika, and then went back to the living room, turning off lights as I went. The street illumination was enough to see by, and I made my bed, turned on the radiator, and took off my shoes and pants. It was risky, perhaps, but I didn't think Erika would see boxers as a sign of dominance. I put my glasses under the couch so I wouldn't step on them in the morning and lay down on my back.

The radiator hissed and banged, and I waited for sleep, thinking about how much I'd like to have dinner with Bridgett. We'd been close to becoming very close when Rubin died, and after the fire, I had stayed at her apartment until she had helped me find this place. Since then, we'd been trying to regain the ground his death had lost us, trying to discover what we meant to one another and what we wanted to mean.

Then I was remembering the Army, when I had met Erika, when I knew her mother and her father. I had served with some good people, one of them Rubin, and inevitably he dominated my thoughts again, like he had every night since he died, and once again I found myself missing him, wondering if I'd ever get over getting him killed.

CHAPTER THREE

She had left a message, scribbled on a piece of paper from my desk and left on the pillow that still held the memory of where she'd rested her head.

DID YOU FUCK HER??? the note read.

And if that's not a great way to start a day, I don't know what is.

I read the note a few more times, searching for hidden meanings, then crumpled it and dropped it in the trash. I cleaned up my room, then changed into my sweats and headed out to the East River jogging path. I ran for four miles, went home, did my sit-ups and push-ups and all the little things that were supposed to clear my head, although none did. When I showered, I checked the towels, and noted that none of them were wet. Erika had skipped bathing, maybe to keep from waking me.

I dressed and went down to the street, walking the half block to my bodega on the corner of Third Avenue. The bodega was run by a Korean family, and the youngest son, perhaps seventeen, was working the register. He gave me a thumbs-up and a grin, saying, "Plain bagel and coffee black, right?"

"Right," I said, giving him my money.

"Bitching cold out there today," he said. "Winter's coming early."

I nodded. "Did you see a girl this morning—pretty, blond hair? She would have been wearing a leather skirt and boots?"

He gave me my change, thinking, then said, "Really pretty?"

"Yeah."

"No. I would have remembered that."

I thanked him, took my coffee and bagel, and returned to the apartment building, doing my walkthrough as I ate my breakfast. It was a four-story building wedged between two larger ones, and the three pretty much made up all the structures running between Second and Third Avenues. I didn't see any of the tenants or the super, and I saw no signs that the building had been broken into during the night. I checked the garage carefully, paying special attention to Bridgett's car. She owns a beautiful dark green Porsche 911, her pride and joy, and she uses my allotted parking space to keep from paying for one of her own. The extra security doesn't hurt, either. I don't mind, as I've no intention of ever buying a car; I hate cars.

I finished my walk on the roof, finishing the bagel at the same time. An empty bottle of Mad Dog 20/20, raspberry flavored, lay near an air vent, but nothing else. During the late summer, when I first moved in, some homeless people had camped up on the roof, having climbed down from a neighboring building. The roof was tar, and retained the summer heat, and I suppose it had been a pleasant and safe enough place to spend the night. I'd kicked them off anyway, feeling rotten about policy.

Since then, nobody had camped on the roof.

I threw the bottle in the recycling bin on the ground

floor, then went back up the four flights of stairs to my apartment, finished my coffee, and threw the cup out. My answering machine and telephone sat on a corner of the kitchen counter. There were no messages, but I hadn't expected any.

The bondage scene has slang for those who dominate and those who serve, calls them tops and bottoms. Last night at the club, and more so when I brought her home, Erika had been performing like a bottom. The maneuver in the kitchen spun that, turned her submission into a particularly subtle form of topping. It had been impossible for me to react without, in some way, validating her behavior. Sort of like asking the Senator if he's stopped beating his wife.

Now Erika had gone, leaving spite on my pillow for me to find. I wasn't certain if I was still playing her game or not; she was no fool, and she knew I would look for her.

Metro-North runs trains from Grand Central up the Hudson, and I caught an express to Poughkeepsie at a little before ten, taking a seat on the left side of the carriage to watch the river as we worked upstate. The sky was overcast and the tint of the windows made everything outside look gloomier, hinting that winter was closer than any of us mortals suspected. The coach was empty except for two elderly black women, seated side by side, reading paperbacks. I didn't have anything to read, so I just kept staring out the window.

According to NYNEX information there were three Wyatts in the Garrison phone book, and although there wasn't a Douglas listed, there was a "D." The operator had been kind enough to give me the address, and I appreciated that, because if she hadn't I would have had to go through the New York State DMV, and I didn't have an in there. That would have required calling Bridgett for help, which in turn would have led to her asserting her right to accompany me on this trip, no debate allowed.

I needed to see the Colonel alone.

Garrison sits on the opposite side of the Hudson River from West Point, maybe four stops south of Poughkeepsie. West Point rises from the river, steely and grim, as if it has always been there and always will be. The academy looks like what it is: a military school dedicated to the art of war, where cadets are turned into leaders devoted to country and God. I've never actually been inside, only seen it from a distance, but each time I do I feel the same strange twinge of history and foreboding. The place frankly gives me the creeps.

The train left me on the platform to get my bearings while zipping up my coat. The cold was working on my hands, and I felt my fingers resisting me slightly when I moved them. The platform itself looked more appropriate to a spaghetti western than to the Hudson River valley, with a closed restaurant and an information shack, both made out of wood. There was only the barest of covering to shelter under in case of rain or snow, and it didn't look like it would do much good. A display case hung on one side of the shack. Sun-faded copies of the Metro-North schedule and a street map of Garrison were tacked up inside. I checked the map against the address I had, then decided I could use the walk. It didn't look far.

It took twenty minutes, walking along the shoulder of the two-lane road that paralleled the river, keeping my hands deep in my pockets. The Hudson was a muddy gray, choppy, and there were no boats out. I passed a few houses, each spaced generously apart from its nearest neighbor. Smoke trickled from their chimneys, and the scent of burning wood made me wish I was indoors or, at least, warmer. Inside was comfort. Outside was solitude.

The house was two stories with a gravel driveway leading to the garage. The place looked beaten into submission by weather and age. A new Chevy pickup truck, navy-blue, was parked in the driveway, dusty and water-spotted. There was a chimney here, too, but no smoke, and looking at the windows, it was hard to tell if there was anyone at home. No lights shone from inside.

I crunched my way up the drive, crossed over the dead grass on the corner of the lawn, and knocked on the front door. My hand was cold enough that the contact hurt, and I shoved it back into a pocket so it could recover, thinking that a smart man would buy himself a pair of gloves, what with winter coming and all.

Nothing happened. I listened, and heard no noise from inside, only traffic in the distance and some gulls crying out overhead, and under it all the Hudson slapping the shore. I quite possibly had the wrong house. I considered peeking through one of the windows, and instead knocked again.

From inside came the sound of steps working slowly down the hall. They stopped at the door and I heard the bolts turning, two locks, one after the other. The door opened inward, swung back, and I saw Colonel Wyatt standing there, one hand still on the knob as if using it for support.

His other hand was pointed at my forehead, and in it he held a gun.

CHAPTER FOUR

I think he was almost as surprised as I, his thumb back on the hammer and his finger resting on the tail of the trigger. When he got over being shocked, he relaxed, drawing his finger to the side of the barrel, not committed to the firing any longer.

"Sergeant Kodiak." The sound of his voice was surprising, hoarser than I remembered, almost wheezy. He didn't bother to move the gun.

"Colonel." The barrel looked deep and clean, and it wavered only fractionally in front of my eyes. It looked like a Colt .45, the traditional officer's side arm, although a lot of them now carry Berettas. I had been in the service when the debate had started as to which weapon was better, arguments about stopping power and reliability, and so on. Personally, I preferred the Beretta. The Colonel, it seemed, was a traditionalist.

Funny what you think about when someone's got a gun pointed at your face.

"She's not here," Wyatt said. "We're divorced."

"I know." His face looked drawn and yet flaccid, like he had lost a lot of weight and had lost it quickly, his skin sagging with the change, unable to keep up. Shadows hung tight to each cheek, and a white crust stuck to the corners of his mouth. I could see the same color on his tongue when he spoke.

"I'm wondering why I shouldn't drive a hollow point through that NCO brain of yours," Wyatt said. "Sort of like God's given me an opportunity to get some payback, that's what I'm thinking."

"I saw Erika last night."

He licked his lips again. "Where?"

"You want to lower the gun?"

"Where'd you see her?"

"In the city."

The Colonel brought the weapon down, flicked the safety, leaving it cocked but locked. The act seemed to tire him immensely. On the ring finger of his right hand was his class band from West Point, and it slid to his knuckle when he lowered the gun.

"Lock it behind you," he said, and turned away.

I stepped in and shut the door, threw the locks, then followed him down the hall. The rooms were dim, and Wyatt moved slowly, leading me into the kitchen. He stopped at the stove and picked up the kettle. Steam drifted from the spout. He stuck the gun in his waistband, then made himself a cup of tea, carefully pouring the water into a mug. He had been taller in my memory, and I realized that, in fact, I had as much as three inches on him. Both his pants and sweater looked too large, as if mimicking the skin around his skull. There was a smell, too, a little saccharine and cloying, tinged with vomit and urine, and it permeated the whole house. It was the smell hospitals try to disguise with bleach and air fresheners.

The place was very clean, but cramped, filled with all the items Wyatt and Diana and Erika had collected while moving through the years from post to post. A sunken den had been built beyond where the kitchen opened into a breakfast nook, and from the different shades of wood marking the spaces, I assumed the den was a recent addition. A couch and two easy chairs marked the space, facing the large window that ran across the wall. Through it I could see the unkempt backyard, then the Hudson, then The Point. Around one of the chairs were grouped three space heaters, their electric coils glowing orange.

Wyatt put lemon into the tea, then honey, then broke into a fit of coughing that required him to hold on to the counter for support. The coughs were dry and harsh, and when they ended he had to wipe tears from his eyes. He turned, leaving the mug, and walked past me into the den, saying, "Get that for me." He took the pistol out of his pants and set it on the folding metal television tray beside his easy chair. A red and black flannel blanket was draped over one arm, and he spread it out, covering his legs with it after sitting. Even from where I was, I could feel the warmth from the space heaters.

I brought him his tea.

"No, put it on the tray, Sergeant."

The television tray had the New York Giants logo on it, and I set the tea next to his gun.

"You want a fucking tip?" he said. "Sit down."

I unzipped my jacket and took the other chair, being careful not to kick any of the heaters. I was already beginning to sweat.

Colonel Wyatt took a sip, then cradled the mug in his hands against his chest, drawing in the steam. "Ask me if I'm enjoying retirement," he said.

"Are you enjoying retirement, Colonel?"

"No, but thank you for asking. And you? How are you?"

"I'm fine."

"You've been out for how long, now?"

"Three years."

"I always knew you would bug out."

"I wasn't a lifer, Colonel. Never pretended to be."

"I fucking hate retirement," Wyatt told his tea.

"What's with the gun?" I asked.

He looked at the weapon. "Fucking kids keep coming by, ringing the bell and running off. Thought I'd teach them a lesson."

I took off my jacket, wiped some sweat from my forehead.

"So you saw Erika," he said.

"Last night."

"Did you fuck her, too? Is that why you're here, you've come to gloat?"

"No." It was a cheap shot, but not entirely unexpected.

"No, you're not here to gloat? No, you didn't fuck her? No, *what*, Sergeant?"

He barked it out as if I were still in uniform, and I had to bite back the urge to respond appropriately. It was difficult enough to not add "sir" to everything that came out of my mouth; three years free and the conditioning was still in place. Instead, I asked, "Do you know where she is?"

Wyatt looked into his tea again. "She's gone down to Manhattan to stay with some friends."

"When was the last time you saw her, Colonel?"

"Tuesday. She'll be back by the weekend, usually is. Why are you asking me this?"

"I was bouncing at a club last night. A place called The Strap. It's a bondage club—"

Wyatt laughed. "No shit? Well, it's rough all over, isn't it, Sergeant? My mighty security officer reduced to baby-sitting perverts while they party. I like that, I like that a lot."

"—that's where I found her," I finished.

He didn't find that quite as amusing. "You're full of shit."

"Why would I lie to you?"

"Because you always lied to me, Sergeant."

"She told me she'd run away from home, Colonel. I

watched a man pull a knife on her because she wouldn't
play with him."

His gaze was level, and he thought before saying it.
"You are a goddamn liar."

I shook my head, looked out the window. If it didn't
get warmer, it'd be snowing by nightfall.

"She goes to visit friends," the Colonel said. "She
doesn't want to be around here, and I don't blame her."

"She's homeless," I said. "She's turning tricks in exchange for a place to sleep."

"Shut up, you shut up," he ordered, and it started
him coughing again, strangling, rasping barks. The mug
swung in his hands, hot tea splashing over the lip. I got
up and took it from him, and Wyatt was coughing too
hard to even resent my help. I set the mug down, picked
up his gun and unloaded it, making it safe. I didn't
think he would shoot me, but I didn't know how he
would react to my next statement. I put the gun down,
but didn't move from beside his seat.

The coughing ended, leaving him drained, his head
back against the chair, his eyes staring at me. "I never
liked you, Sergeant. Even before you slept with my
wife, I never liked you. You're arrogant and you're too
damn proud for your own good."

I nodded. It wasn't a unique observation. "Erika tells
me that you're molesting her," I said.

His eyes had held steel when I knew him in D.C.,
when I worked for him at the Pentagon. His eyes
seemed so much smaller now, but steel came back to
them all the same, and he started up from the chair,
screaming, "You son of a bitch. You son of a bitch, how
dare you?"

"Are you?"

The blanket dropped to the floor, and he punched at
me slow, already winded. I let him land it, and he connected with the left side of my cheek like a drunken
mosquito. There was no muscle behind it, only rage,
and when the punch didn't move me, he prepared to
throw another one, bringing his right back, then stop-

ping. It was too much effort for too little result; we both knew it. He dropped his arm and relaxed his fists, turned away from me, looking out the window.

"She wouldn't say that," he said, finally.

"She said it."

"And that's why you're here? Because you figure I could be that kind of monster? You think I could hurt my daughter like that?"

"I don't know what goes on in your head, Colonel. I never did." My shirt was sticking from the heat.

He sat again, and it took effort for him to reach the blanket, but I knew better than to help. When he had covered himself once more he sagged back into the faded chair.

"Sit down," he said. When I had, he pointed to the corners of his mouth. "You know what this shit is, Sergeant? It's called thrush, that's what it is, and it's a fucking yeast infection, it's what women get in their cunts, except I've got it in my goddamn mouth. Do you know why I've got it in my mouth, Sergeant? Can you field that one?"

"You have AIDS," I said.

"That's right, I have AIDS. I can't fight off a fucking yeast infection, I've got shit in my mouth, my body is turning to crap, I need a nurse to come in every fucking day just to clean me. I am dying, do you understand, and it's as inevitable as the river out there. I am a walking dead man." He ran out of breath and stopped, his chest heaving, then reached for his mug. When his breathing had slowed, he sipped some of the tea.

I looked at his pistol, wondered why he hadn't used it on himself.

"Erika is my life," Wyatt told me. "Erika matters more to me than anything I've ever had. I would never hurt her. So, you're accusing me of infecting my daughter, murdering her, that's what you're accusing me of. How do I respond to that?"

"I don't know," I answered.

"You don't know." He laughed, and I expected him

to start coughing again, but he didn't. Sleet started to pelt the glass. Neither of us moved. The sleet and the river, it reduced the world to just us, just two men in this room on the Hudson, with three space heaters and a whole lot of history.

Erika had lied about her father. She had substituted incest for AIDS, and it made sense. No one would question her decision to run away from abuse; running away from someone who was terminally ill, that was a different story. The problem was, the lie threw everything she had said into question. One lie leads to another, and now I didn't know what to believe.

"They made me retire, because soldiers don't get a faggot's disease," Wyatt said softly. "It was easy, I got to keep my goodies. I left and bought this place so I could look at where it started, to look at The Point, and I brought my baby home because she's all I have left. She's out in the middle of nowhere, her father is broken and dying, her mother is fuck knows where, so why the hell should she stay here? Why the hell should she sit in a dark house on a cold river with her dying father? Would you?"

"I had to ask."

"You had to ask . . . and you hoped it was true."

"I didn't."

"No? You never liked me, either, Sergeant, I know that."

I didn't say anything.

"Now Diana's gone, and I'm dying of AIDS."

"The irony hasn't escaped me."

"No, it wouldn't have," he said. "All of the fucking around I did, I guess this is how it caught up to me."

"Do you know how you caught it?"

"No. Could have been any one of a hundred women." He knuckled his eyes. "Don't think I gave it to Diana, though, so you're probably clear. Have you seen her?"

"No."

"Not once since then?"

"I heard about the divorce through the grapevine," I told him. "That's all I knew about you two."

He rubbed at the corners of his mouth, swore at the flakes that came away on his fingertips. "I would have thought with me out of the way, Diana would have gone straight to you."

"I haven't seen her," I said.

He took his mug again, finished the tea. "She left, and a year later filed for divorce, started fighting for money and Erika and everything else I had. Three years of fighting, and she didn't even try to see us, just let her lawyer do all the talking."

"She didn't see Erika at all?"

"Once or twice."

"She wouldn't do that," I said.

"You knew her that well?"

"Well enough."

"Get out of my house," he ordered.

I got to my feet and waited for him to rise, and as he did, we both heard the front door open. The thrush at his mouth cracked with his sudden smile, and he hurried past me to the hall, kicking over one of the space heaters, calling, "Erika?"

I bent and fixed the heater, heard her voice, and then another's, and the sound of the front door closing. I came down the hall to see Wyatt facing another man and Erika standing in the entranceway. She looked haggard, and it seemed to me frightened, but otherwise healthy.

"I told you not to," Wyatt was saying. "Dammit, Robert, I told you—"

"Easy, Colonel," the other man said, and his accent was British, and I was thinking that it couldn't be coincidence when I got a look at his face, and began to worry.

Not Trouble, not the man who had pulled the knife, but instead I was looking at one of the two men I'd seen enter before the fight at The Strap had started, the older of the two. His skin was a beautiful, rich brown, and his tight crew cut was peppered with gray. It was absolutely the same man from the night before. Maybe six feet tall, and with muscle, wearing a dark red polo shirt under his anorak and his very blue jeans.

"We just gave her a ride home," the man continued telling the Colonel. "Isn't that right, luv?"

"Is that true?" Wyatt asked his daughter.

"Yeah, that's right." Erika wouldn't look at any of us, staring at the baseboard. She still wore the miniskirt, stockings, and boots, but had covered her top with a gray sweatshirt that I recognized as mine. I wondered if she had taken anything else from my home.

"Robert Moore," the man said to me, extending a hand and a smile. "You a friend of the Colonel's?"

I shook his hand, saying, "Atticus Kodiak. I'm an acquaintance."

Moore went for strength in his grip, but not for the crush, smiling like he'd known me forever. If he recognized me at all, he was covering it well, but the smile never made his eyes, and they were professional, assessing me. When he had seen enough he dropped my hand, and I spotted the lump of a holster at his hip under the anorak. Like Trouble, Moore also had the same black tongue hanging over his pants pocket, also was carrying a knife.

"They're a great family," Robert Moore told me.

"Yes, they are."

"You close to them?"

"I was."

"Army?"

"Yes."

Moore nodded, then turned back to the Colonel, whose voice was controlled, but fraying, when he said, "Damn you. I told you not to do this."

Moore's eyes flicked to me, then went back to the Colonel. "Are you certain we want to talk about this here, sir?" he asked softly.

Wyatt coughed once into his hands, then looked at his daughter, who continued to look at the floor. He took a deep breath, and even where I stood I heard the rattle in his chest, like wind running through a field of weeds.

"Walk Atticus out," Wyatt told Erika.

Her posture changed slightly, all at once, and I knew her father had just let her down. She spun, went straight to the door. "Come on," she muttered.

"Take care of yourself," Moore said to me.

"I can stick around," I told the Colonel.

"You'll miss your train."

"I can get another."

Wyatt brushed his fingers through his hair, wiped the oil on his shirt. "You don't want to be late," he said.

"It's been a pleasure," Moore said.

"I'll see you," I told the Colonel, then stepped past Moore and out the door.

Erika came out behind me, shutting the door with a slam and then going straight to the porch railing. She crossed her arms and pressed her hands into her armpits for warmth.

I zipped up my jacket, wishing she would look at me. The wind was slapping the sleet down in cold gusts, but we were safe from the spray where we stood under the overhang. Erika began to shift from one foot to the other, doing a lazy hop to keep her legs warm.

"So, who is he?" I asked her.

"Some guy," she said. "Why are you here?"

"Just some guy?"

"Yeah, just some guy the Colonel knows."

"Where'd you meet him?"

"It's like he said, okay? They picked me up. I told you, Dad knows him." Erika uncrossed her arms and cupped her hands together, blowing on them.

"What does that mean, they picked you up? Off the street? At my place?"

"At the train station, okay? Jesus fucking Christ, it doesn't matter."

"It does matter."

"Why are you here?"

"I was looking for you."

"Yeah?" she asked, clearly not believing me. "Why were you looking for me?"

"You were gone when I got up," I said.

"So?"

"I was worried."

"You wanted me to leave."

"I never said that."

"You wanted to be alone with what's-her-face," Erika said.

"Bridgett, and no, I didn't say that, either." I didn't sound exasperated at all.

She shrugged, kept looking at the empty road and blowing on her hands. "You didn't say it, but you wanted to. You're in love with her. She totally wants you, too. She was dripping for you. She's a slut."

A black Cherokee was parked in the driveway, beside the Chevy. Moore's car, I assumed, and inside I could see two men, both sitting in the backseat, watching us through the sleet. There was no way to make out their faces, but I had an idea who they were. Trouble and the other man from the club, the young one, most likely. The plates were New York, and a rental tag was stuck in the corner of the front window.

They hadn't picked her up at the train station, I realized. She was dry and there had been no shelter to speak of at the platform. With the sleet coming down, she should have been soaked through.

Another lie.

"Who are they?" I asked, looking at the Cherokee.

"Friends of his."

"All Brits?"

"Sure."

"One of them the guy who pulled the knife last night?"

She looked honestly surprised. "No."

Neither of the men inside the car had moved, or even

acknowledged my gaze. They were waiting, and they were waiting like professionals—no fidgets, no shifting around in their seats. They didn't even appear to be talking to one another.

"I think you're lying to me," I said to Erika. "You lied to me last night and you're lying to me now."

"Yeah?"

"You lied about your father."

"So fucking what?" she asked.

I exhaled, watched the steam cloud and then whip away with a gust of wind. "It's a serious thing to accuse your father of doing."

Erika shrugged again and gave up on trying to warm her hands with her breath, instead rubbing her palms together.

"Erika."

"Okay," she said. "He's not fucking me. There. Okay? What more do you want?"

"What do I want? Jesus, Erika, I want to know that you're all right, that you're not sleeping in the streets or in strange beds, that you're not in trouble. I want to know if Moore hurt you. I want you to tell me the truth, dammit. What I want is a little of your trust."

Her head came around to look at me, chin out and mouth tight, full of anger. She was laughing at first, but tears were welling in her eyes, and as she spoke, the tears started spilling down her cheeks, and the laughing turned to crying. "You fucker! You motherfucker! Trust you? You want—you want me to—where were you, huh? Where were you? You said we were friends! You said I was like your sister, that you wouldn't forget, but you left, you left and you don't care, don't pretend that you do. It was all her, and when you couldn't fuck her anymore, you didn't care, so don't pretend—" And then the sobs caught up to her, and she was biting her lip to stop them, pressing both her palms to her eyes as if that would dam the tears.

I watched her, feeling small and embarrassed and

then, mostly, like a scoundrel who had been caught breaking into someone's heart.

The sobs racked Erika and I reached to hold her, but she flailed at my arm angrily and backed away until she was against the railing, saying, "Don't touch me, you don't fucking touch me. Go away, just go away, get out of our house." She put her back to me again, crying hard.

In my pocket I found my pen and the receipt for my train ticket and wrote my phone number on the back of the slip. I walked over to where she stood crying, held the paper out past her shoulder. She saw it and grabbed the paper with one hand, wiping her nose with the other while reading it.

"Call me if you need anything," I told her.

She crumpled the ticket and flung it away. The wind snatched it and blew it into a corner of the porch.

"I didn't know you knew," I said. "I'm sorry, Erika."

Then I turned up my collar, and started off the stoop to the road, walking past the Cherokee and the two men who were watching me go, beginning the long walk back to the train station.

CHAPTER FIVE

After ten minutes I was soaked and frozen and angry, and almost blind, fighting to keep my balance on the rapidly forming skin of ice, and swearing at the driver of the last car who hadn't bothered to avoid a puddle. My glasses were almost entirely coated with sleet, and I swiped at them with my fingers, clearing the lenses, as I heard another car coming behind me. I ducked my head to my chest, brought my arm up as a shield. Sure enough, another blast of ice and water hit me.

I swore and looked up and saw it was Moore's Cherokee, and that it was pulling onto the shoulder twenty yards ahead.

Fuck, I thought, and stopped.

None of the doors opened. The exhaust from the car clung to the asphalt where it trickled from the muffler.

I started forward again, and when I was even with the car, the passenger door swung open, and I could see Robert Moore leaning across the seat at me, dry and warm.

"Get in, mate," he said. "You're going hypothermic."

I swiped at the ice in my hair, looking into the backseat where the two other men were seated. The one behind Moore's seat I recognized as the young man who had been with him at The Strap, and the young man looked at me with a smile, then turned in his seat to look back down the road the way they had come. I decided he was twenty-one at the most.

The other one was taller, older, perhaps thirty, with brown hair and disconcerting eyes that were fixed patiently on mine. It took a second for me to realize exactly what was throwing me off—his right eye was blue; his left was brown.

Both were dressed similarly to Moore, comfortably and casually, jeans and sweaters and coats, and all were very neat, very healthy, and I realized it was a carload of soldiers.

A carload of British soldiers.

"You're letting the hot air out," Moore told me. "Come on, get in. We don't bite."

The one with different colored eyes laughed. "Denny does," he said.

Denny was the young one. He turned and slugged the speaker in the arm lightly. "Fuck you, Terry." He sounded as upset as any soldier gets at allegations of homosexuality.

"Don't think you're his type, though," Terry told me.

"You getting in or not?" Moore asked.

What the hell, I thought. Whoever they were, if they wanted me in the car, there were enough of them to make certain they got their way. And maybe they'd tell me what was going on.

"I'd wear the seat belt," Moore said after I'd closed the door. "These fucking roads, doesn't matter how good a driver you are, you know?"

I snapped the belt across my lap. The defroster was on full, blasting hot air, and the ice was already melting into cold trickles down my face and neck. I took a mo-

ment to clean off my glasses, searching for something
dry to use as a towel, and settling for an almost dry
corner of my shirt.

"Where you headed?" Moore asked.

"Train."

He looked over at me, almost adding a second question, then checked his mirrors and pulled back onto the
road.

"Thanks," I said.

"Ah, it's not a problem. Soldiers have to look out for
one another. The Colonel tells me you were his bodyguard, that right?"

"That's right."

He nodded. "Fucking hard work, that. Muck that up,
the brass comes down on you like a ton. Ever happen to
you?"

"No."

"God bless you for it," Moore said. "Mind if I
smoke?"

"It's your rental."

"That it is." He pulled a pack of red Dunhills from
his pocket, fed one into his mouth. The car slid a bit on
an easy turn, but he held the wheel with one hand,
lighting up with the other. Behind me I heard Terry
move, and the flick of another lighter. The defroster
made the cigarette smoke tango.

"We can take you farther," Moore said, exhaling two
streams from his nostrils. "Down to the city."

"The train is fine."

"Your choice, mate."

I looked in the rearview mirror, watching the reflection of Denny in the backseat. His eyes met mine, crinkled into a grin. He looked very friendly, so I turned
around in my seat and looked at both men, saying, "Hi,
I'm Atticus."

Moore said, "Fuck, where are my manners?"

"I was going to ask, boss," Denny said.

"Atticus Kodiak, the young fellow is Trooper Edward

Denny, and the man behind you is Trooper Terrence Knowles. Say hello to Atticus, boys."

Both Denny and Knowles said hello, and we all shook hands. They were wearing guns, too, and had knives clipped to their pockets. Both were wearing Rolexes, and I tried to remember if I had seen one on Moore's wrist.

"Can I see your knife?" I asked Denny.

He hesitated, and then Moore said, "What's he going to do with it, boy? You can hand it over."

Denny shot me a sheepish look and handed over the knife. I turned back to face the road and examined it, and it was exactly what I thought it was, and that didn't make me happy at all.

Knives are fetish objects for most professional soldiers, and the higher trained the person, the more knife choice matters. It's not simply that they're looking for a knife that can cut well; it's a multipurpose tool that needs to be as rugged as, in theory, the soldier himself. What's the point of carrying a knife that won't open after you've slogged through a swamp, or rusts if you take it under water, or loses its edge once you've cut a throat to the bone?

The knife Denny had handed me, and the knife that Trouble had pulled at The Strap, and I assumed the knives that both Moore and Knowles were carrying, were all the same model, one called the Emerson CQC-6. CQC stands for "close quarter combat." It's a folding knife that can be opened with one hand. The blade is aggressive, very sharp, and the tanto point makes it ideal for cutting, thrusting, or chopping. Good for chopping kindling, or killing, depending on your preference.

It's a knife that the special forces community covets, the way they covet Rolex watches; they always want the best equipment. Like the Rolex, it's a lodge pin of sorts—you have one, you're a member of the club. You have both, you've been paying your dues.

So I was sitting in a car with three special forces-trained soldiers. The only question was which group, and I already didn't like the answer to that one.

I closed the knife and handed it back to Denny, saying, " 'Who dares wins.' "

Denny reverted to his sheepish look. Knowles examined his cuticles.

"Figured it out, huh?" Moore asked.

"You're all SAS?" I asked, and there was no way the question could sound casual, but I tried anyway.

"Badged members in good standing."

I went back to looking out the window.

It meant a couple of things. It meant that if they wanted me dead, I was dead. There were three of them in the Cherokee, and they could take me with their bare hands without breaking a sweat. It explained why Trouble had been so gleeful at the thought of tearing me apart the previous night; on a good day, I might have given him a run for his money, but it was the challenge that he was responding to, and the odds would have been in his favor.

It explained a lot. But it raised a thousand other questions.

Moore slowed the car carefully for another easy turn, and I felt the wheels slip before finding traction again.

"You're a sergeant, too?" Denny asked.

"I *was* a sergeant," I said.

"Well, you never really leave it behind, do you?" Moore said, rolling his cigarette from the right corner of his mouth to the left.

I didn't answer.

Moore pulled the Cherokee carefully into the lot across from the train platform, shutting off the engine but keeping the defroster blowing. Even with the hot air being pushed out, the windows kept a steady blanket of condensation. The world outside of the car seemed to recede behind the mask of fog.

"Sure you don't want a ride into the city?" Moore asked.

"I'm sure."

"Well, we'll wait, if you like. Don't want you freezing your prick off in this weather."

"It's bad," I agreed.

"Fuck, yeah. Like maneuvers in the North Sea. Ever been out that way?"

"I did some exercises in Alaska," I said. "That's the nastiest weather I ever had to deal with."

"Now, that's fucking beautiful country," Knowles said from behind me.

"They're going to rape it blind, though," Moore added. "Just like the North Sea. They've got these fucking oil derricks out there now, blowing shit into water and ruining the view."

"Let me ask you a question, Sergeant Moore," I said.

"You can ask me whatever the fuck you like, but you'll have to call me Robert. They're the ones who have to call me Sergeant." He gestured toward the backseat.

Knowles said, "Among other things."

Denny laughed.

"Robert," I asked, "why is an SAS brick after Erika Wyatt?"

He let the cigarette dangle from his bottom lip, then took it between his fingers and crushed it out in the ashtray. "What do you mean?"

"I mean you picked her up outside of my apartment this morning, didn't you? Which means you followed us home last night. Both you and Denny were at The Strap, and that other fellow, the one who wanted to fight. What stopped him? Did you warn him off when my back was to you?"

But for the defroster, the car became very quiet.

"I don't think anybody followed you last night," Moore said evenly.

"So, you're saying that meeting her at the train was just good luck?"

"Yeah, I guess that's what I'm saying, Atticus."

I looked around the interior of the car, at the backseat, at where both Denny and Knowles were focused on me. Their friendliness had gone. Knowles was staring at my throat, probably wondering what it would look like with his hand through it.

Three SAS-trained men versus one fifteen-year-old girl. It wouldn't have been much of a contest. My memory didn't reveal any marks on Erika when she had stood on the porch, but there didn't have to be any. If they had wanted to hurt her, they could have done it without leaving so much as a blemish on the outside.

I looked back at Moore. Pissing off members of Britain's Special Air Service is never intelligent no matter how well trained you might be. The SAS is to Great Britain what the SEAL teams and Detachment Delta and the greenies are to the USA, although many would say they're even better. In 1980, the Iranian Embassy in London was taken over by terrorists opposed to the Ayatollah Ruholla Khomeini. After five days of negotiations, the terrorists killed a hostage, and the SAS went in, black balaclavas and all. It took them eleven minutes to clear the Embassy; they killed five of the six terrorists, and freed twenty-two hostages. All on national television.

Apparently, of the five terrorists killed, all had thrown down their weapons before being shot.

In the great pyramid of soldiering, if the SAS isn't the top, they're only one step down. They're hyper-trained, hyper-committed, and exceptionally gifted at all the arts of war.

Which only meant that Moore and Company could have grabbed Erika, put her through an emotional and physical wringer, and then brought her home to Daddy. To what end they would do such a thing, I had no idea.

In fact, I had no idea what was going on at all. I looked out the window again. Wyatt, Erika, Moore. They're all lying to me, I thought.

What the fuck does it matter anyway?

"Never mind," I said, reaching for the door handle.

"Erika's all right, though, isn't she?" Moore asked. "Home safe and sound?"

I got out of the car. "Thanks for the ride."

Moore nodded, pulling another cigarette out of his pack. "We'll see you around, mate."

"You probably will."

I slammed the door and went onto the platform, pressing myself under the tiny awning that hung over the board where I'd read the map earlier. The sleet kept coming down, and the shelter was useless. Moore's Cherokee pulled away, splashing through new puddles, then turning on the road and heading out of sight.

Both Denny and Knowles watched me as they went.

CHAPTER SIX

The sleet had stopped by the time I returned to the city, and I came out of Grand Central Terminal to see patches of blue sky. It was still cold, but the weather had turned docile, and I decided to walk back to my apartment in Murray Hill, arriving in time to catch the mail carrier filling the tenants' boxes. I waited until he was done, then took my mail with me upstairs.

There were a lot of bills.

I changed out of my damp clothes and into some dry ones, putting Moore and Wyatt and, most of all, Erika out of my mind with a more pressing concern: money. The insurance check from the fire had been robust enough when it had arrived, but now seemed positively anemic. The job at The Strap hadn't paid well, but it had paid enough to keep me warm and dry.

After some thought, I went to the living room and sorted through Rubin's old canvases, finding the painting of Natalie Trent. In my opinion, it was the best piece he'd ever done, about as far from the cartoon style of

Gun and Head as possible. He'd captured Natalie the way an artist is supposed to capture beauty, with passion and precision and hope. Her face was tilted skyward, toward her raised hands, kind and strong, framed by red hair like the corona around the sun.

When Rubin had died, I'd been working with two other bodyguards, Dale Matsui and Natalie Trent. Dale was another Army buddy, like myself a graduate of the JFK SpecWar Center's School for Executive Protection. We'd met doing the course, and had both been posted to the Pentagon at the same time, although Dale had covered a one-star who worked in the NATO office, and I'd covered Wyatt, who'd been appointed the President's Advisor on Far East Terrorism.

Natalie I knew through her father, who ran Manhattan's biggest security firm, Sentinel Guards. Elliot Trent was ex–Secret Service, and had worked the Presidential Detail for Carter and, for a while, Reagan. He'd trained Natalie, and she was damn good, my second whenever I needed someone to check my work and watch my back. Natalie had been my friend, and it was she who had introduced me to Bridgett.

Rubin I had trained myself. He'd never done the course at JFK, he'd never protected a president. He had been at the Pentagon, too, but as a driver for a light colonel who worked across the hall from Wyatt.

Rubin and Natalie had been in love.

His painting of her wasn't something I could look at for too long. I felt like a spy.

There was a poster tube among the supplies from the studio, so I slid the canvas inside and sealed it up, then grabbed my jacket and headed outside and uptown, to Sentinel Guards.

I made it to the offices on Madison, guarding the poster tube from pedestrians and other standard Manhattan street hazards. The blue sky had disappeared quickly, and it was gray above once more, threatening rain or perhaps more sleet. It took me twenty minutes, and I arrived a little after four, walking into the marble lobby of the building and striding boldly past the reception desk. One of the attendants called after me to stop.

I raised the tube so he could see it, and without breaking stride said, "Artistic License, we're on Forty-seventh. Delivery for Natalie Trent." I continued to the elevator, got in, and punched the button for the eighth floor, wondering if the attendant had any training at all.

He hadn't, it seemed, because when I got out on eight, no one waited for me. I went down the hall to the double glass doors and stepped into the reception room. The receptionist was a tiny blonde in her forties wearing a starched white blouse and lipstick so red it looked like a magnesium flare had gone off in her mouth. She frowned when she saw me, I suppose at the way I was dressed. Sentinel's clients are the Fortune 500 brigade, decked in Armani suits and Ferragamos. I was wearing dark green corduroys and a black sweater and my army jacket. Under the sweater was a T-shirt, but I didn't think the receptionist could see that. My feet were clad in Reebok high-tops, but I didn't think she could see those, either, from where she was seated. What she could see was that I stood a little over six feet with 190 pounds behind it and had two small hoops hanging from my left earlobe.

One of these things is not like the other, I thought.

"Atticus Kodiak," I told her. "I'm here to see Natalie Trent."

"Is Ms. Trent expecting you?"

"No."

The receptionist picked up her pen and made a small mark on her desktop blotter. "Ms. Trent's extremely busy."

"I'm a friend of hers. Would you tell her I'm here?"

She made another mark beside the first, and then a third, and I realized the receptionist was drawing herself a tic-tac-toe board. "She's in with a client, Mr. . . . ?"

"Kodiak," I said.

"Mr. Kodiak, yes. Ms. Trent is in with a client right now and has asked not to be disturbed."

"I'll wait until—"

From down the hall we heard someone shout, "Kodiak? Is that you?" Both the receptionist and I turned to see Yossi Sella coming at us, straightening his tie and grinning broadly. He looked sleek and handsome, with hair and eyes so brown they appear black. Yossi's a born-and-bred Israeli whom Natalie's father wooed away from the Shin Bet's Executive Protection Squad, and though his English is flawless, he speaks with the rich Israeli accent that sounds like gravel being sifted through silk.

He had his hand out and I transferred the tube to my left, giving him my right. The shake was firm, dry, and quick. "Are you slumming?" Yossi asked.

"I'm here to see Natalie," I said.

"We should have had you come in the service entrance."

"Probably."

He turned to the receptionist. "Mr. Kodiak's with me, Tina, don't worry about him."

"Certainly," Tina said, and gave me a glare, then logged my arrival and went back to her game of tic-tac-toe.

Yossi clapped my shoulder, guided me down the hall. The carpet was gray, thick enough to eat footsteps, and I felt like I was in a doctor's office, which is the way I always feel when visiting Sentinel. Natalie used to say that the decor was to project professionalism; to me, it projects sterility.

The door to his offices was oak, with an engraved brass nameplate centered on it that read MAJ. YOSSI SELLA and beneath it EXECUTIVE THREAT ANALYSIS.

"Major?" I said.

Yossi shrugged, opening the door. "Trent thinks it makes me sound more authoritative."

"And he would know."

That earned another chuckle, and he led me through

the front room past his secretary. "Peter, hold my calls," he said.

Peter was typing at a computer and didn't turn his head. "Consider them held."

Yossi grinned at me. "I love saying that."

"It shows."

"Don't you have work to do?" Peter asked, head still bent, fingers flying over the keyboard. He was a demon typist.

Yossi chuckled some more and held the door to the inner office open for me. "I have a secretary," he said, clearly delighted.

"I noticed."

"Peter's the best," Yossi said, pointing me to a chair. I sat and rested the tube against my knee. He closed the door, then went to the coffee machine and poured us two mugs. His office was nice, with a leather couch and solid wooden desk. The chairs were leather, too, the sort one imagines in a gentlemen's club. He had a computer on the desk, a telephone, and several manila folders with neatly typed labels. Three photographs hung on the wall, one of Yossi standing alone in uniform, one of him with his unit. The last one was smallest of the three, and showed Yossi shaking hands with Yitzhak Rabin. If you wanted to get Yossi in a fury, all you needed to do was mention the security around Rabin when the Israeli Prime Minister was assassinated.

"You take anything in your coffee?" he asked.

"Black as my heart," I said.

" 'And death will fear you, because you have the heart of a lion,' " he said, doctoring his mug with sugar and cream. "That's an Arab proverb, you know? I like that one."

"It's a good one."

He handed me my mug. It was a glossy black with the gold Sentinel Guards logo printed on it, a Roman soldier standing behind a tall buckler, looking fierce and possessive. Yossi sat behind the desk, opened a drawer on the side, and leaned back, resting his feet on the new extension. He tasted his coffee, then asked, "What can we do for you?"

I said, "I was thinking I should talk to Natalie."

He shook his head. "That's not so good, my friend. Natalie doesn't want much to do with you, I think."

"Is she here?"

"She's in the office today, yes. Some movie hotshot wants protection, Natalie's doing the interview." Yossi pointed at the tube. "That's for her?"

I nodded.

"I'm sorry about your friend," he said. "The doctor you were protecting, have you heard from her?"

"She's working in Florida. That's all I know."

"Brave woman." He assessed me some more, then asked, "Aside from Natalie, why are you here?"

"How do you know I want something more?"

"I didn't." He grinned, his teeth lightly yellowed from years of cigarettes and coffee. "Out with it." When I didn't immediately speak, he asked, "You looking for work?"

"Either you're reading my mind or my face, and I like to think I'm not such an open book in either case," I said.

Yossi chuckled some more, washed down his mirth with a deep drink of his sweetened coffee. "There are only two reasons for you to be here, Atticus. The first is to see Natalie. The second is to find employment. You've already admitted to the first, and you're still here."

"I could just be acting polite," I said.

"Sure, you could."

"If I were looking for some pickup work . . . ?"

"Can't promise anything. Trent's scaling back for the fiscal quarter, and there's a rumor floating about layoffs. I do wish I could tell you more. I'll certainly keep you in mind."

I shrugged. "That's all I ask."

His intercom buzzed as Yossi was about to apologize

further, and Peter said, "Your four-thirty is here, Major."

"I should take this," Yossi told me.

"Certainly, Major." I rose and saluted and he laughed. He took the mug from me and I retrieved the poster tube, and then Yossi again put a hand on my shoulder, walking me out.

A beautiful African-American woman was waiting by Peter's desk, dressed in shredded blue jeans showing long johns beneath, a black halter top, and two flannel shirts. Tina hadn't given her any flack, though, because she was also wearing a long rope of pearls looped twice about her neck. The pearls made it plain that this woman could wear whatever she liked, although she was more than attractive enough to wear tinfoil and make it work.

"I'll call you if something comes up," Yossi told me, taking the new arrival's hand. The charm was already in full force by the time the door closed, and I found myself grinning as I walked back to reception. Yossi could be very smooth, indeed.

Of course, it had to happen.

I was halfway down the hall to Tina's desk when the door to Natalie's office opened, and she came out laughing at something the man with her had said. I recognized him, too. Not quite an actor; more a movie star in the making. And it's true what they say: He was a lot shorter in person.

"Monday," Natalie told him. "You'll be picked up at the airport by two guards, then come back here, and we'll start the detail then."

He faced her, gazing intently. "I can hardly wait."

I don't know if he thought the attempted seduction would work or not, but I understood why he felt the need to try. If Bridgett is at the top of The Most Beautiful Women I Know list, Natalie runs a close second. Her hair is fire-red—not carrot, almost burgundy. She was wearing her professional clothes, a black cashmere blazer and black skirt, low-heeled shoes. Natalie paid her way through college on the money she had made modeling during high school, and it would probably still be a feasible career for her if she wasn't so old. She's twenty-seven, after all.

At the reception desk, Tina said, "Ms. Trent, that man is waiting to see you." She pointed an accusing pen at me.

Natalie turned, and her professional smile crumbled to a fixed line as her eyes met mine. I thought she'd react in some other way, move or speak, but she gave me nothing more. She just stared the cold stare she'd discovered over Rubin's body.

"I can hardly wait," the actor said again. Perhaps he thought she'd missed her cue.

Natalie's eyes were as gray as the sky outside.

The actor looked over at me, back to her, then shrugged and said, "Whatever. See you Monday."

After he was out the glass doors, I said, "Hey, Natalie."

Nothing.

I hefted the poster tube, then walked the ten feet between us until I was close enough to hand it over. "I've been meaning to give this to you."

She looked at the cardboard as if I were offering her nothing but air, then resumed staring at me.

"It was at the studio," I said.

Natalie licked her lips, then said, "Tina?"

From the desk, Tina said, "Yes, Ms. Trent?"

"Mr. Kyle will be needing an appointment on Monday, about three in the afternoon," Natalie said. She kept looking at me. "And tell Mossen and Herrera I'll want them to pick him up. He's flying into JFK on United from LAX, arriving at thirteen twenty-one hours."

There was a pause that I interpreted as Tina writing Natalie's orders down, and then Tina said, "I'll make sure they know."

"Thank you," Natalie said.

"He would have wanted you to have it, Natalie," I said.

Nothing.

I offered her the tube again. "Please. It was for you."

Natalie's eyes changed, shifted slightly as if she was finally, after all this time, focusing on me. Her mouth moved a fraction, making me think she would acknowledge me, either a curse or a greeting. Instead, she turned and went back into her office. The door closed gently after her.

CHAPTER SEVEN

"Happy birthday," Bridgett told me when she came through the door.

"It's not my birthday."

She kissed me fiercely, then handed over one of the two paper shopping bags she had brought with her. "No, but I missed your last one, so I'm making up for lost time. And you remembered mine, so this is karmic balancing, that's what this is."

"You didn't know me on my last birthday."

"You're a gracious bastard," Bridgett said, blowing past me to the living room. "You're holding the salad fixings."

"And you're holding?"

"You'll find out."

I took the bag she had handed me into the kitchen, placing its contents on the counter. After folding the bag and putting it away, I pulled my new colander off its hook by the fridge and began washing lettuce. Bridgett returned, sniffing the air.

"You baked bread."

I nodded.

"I love fresh bread," Bridgett said. Her lipstick was the brown of dried blood. "If it's any good, I may swoon."

"Oh, it's good, I promise. I learned from the best."

She elbowed me gently away from the sink, saying, "I'll do that."

I relinquished the colander and set the table, then opened us both a beer. She was still shredding and chopping when I had finished, so I sat down and watched her, listening to Joe Jackson playing on the stereo in my room. Today, Bridgett was wearing black tights and a short black pleated skirt and a black turtleneck under a black sweater, and her hair was loose, ink-black that reached for her shoulder blades. Gemstones of water shone in her hair from the rain that was pouring outside. The temperature had risen in the two days since I'd seen the Colonel, but the weather was still miserable, and my radio was forecasting snow by the end of the week.

When the salad was done she sat down and I checked the lasagna in the oven, then the bread.

"How we doing?" Bridgett asked.

"Another fifteen minutes."

She took a pull of beer from her bottle, pushed the unused chair from under the side of the table with the toe of her boot, and then swung her legs up. I sat back down and she asked me about Erika and what had happened, and I told her about the visit to Garrison, about Moore and Company showing up, about how I'd seen him and Denny at The Strap. I glossed over the conversation with Wyatt, since that would have required an explanation of my relationship with Diana, and I didn't want to slide down that slippery slope yet.

"She called me a slut?" Bridgett asked, amazed.

"A dripping slut."

She laughed. "What the hell's her problem with me?"

"You're a strong female. You threaten her."

"That must be it. You have any idea who the fuck Moore is? Not somebody from your jarhead days?"

"Those are marines. I was a grunt, sometimes called a swinging dick. No, never met him before. All I know is that he's SAS."

"*The* SAS?"

"All three of them. Trouble, too, probably."

"Bastards." She practically spat it.

"Don't much care for the Special Air Service?" I asked.

She didn't like the levity. "Let me tell you about the illustrious Special Air Service. They work undercover in Northern Ireland. They're suspected of running death squads there. They're suspected of employing a shoot-to-kill policy when dealing with the Irish."

"Any of that proven?"

She snorted. "Of course not. You think the British government is going to cop to that?"

"Your politics are showing," I told her. "If they're fighting the IRA, they're fighting a terrorist organization. You can't really condone one over the other."

"Watch me," Bridgett said. "I'll tell you a story. In 1988 the SAS gunned down three IRA members in Gibraltar. They thought they were planting a bomb, see? So the SAS starts following these three, and then one of the IRA turns around, looks right at some trooper. The trooper panics, figures he's been made, pulls out his Browning, and starts pumping bullets. His partner does the same thing to the other one, a woman, shoots her in the back. They fire something like twelve shots into these two. The third guy, young fellow named Sean Savage, understandably turns around at all the noise, he gets shot fifteen times by the guy who's following him. He shoots Savage fifteen times, and four of those shots are into his head once he's on the ground.

"The kicker is that none of the three were armed, none of the three had a detonator, and there was no bomb found anywhere on Gibraltar. Lo and behold, though, when the public finds out and the outcry starts, the SAS finds a car loaded with Semtex days later."

"You think the car was planted?"

"I think the SAS enjoys firing their guns a little too much, that's what I think. They should have arrested the three, not have gunned them down." Bridgett rubbed her eyes. "That's only one incident, mind you. There are others." She sighed heavily enough to make her chair creak.

"And how was your day, honey?" I asked.

She winced at the "honey." "I closed the infidelity case I've been working. The client is coming in tomorrow at eleven, and I'll have a set of glossies for her." Bridgett ran fingers through her hair, separating wet strands. She'd been working for Agra & Donnovan Investigations for as long as she'd been licensed, and had plans of one day turning the firm into Agra, Donnovan & Logan Investigations.

"Glad it's over?"

Bridgett shrugged. "Some man or woman starts screwing around on the side, they don't have the courage to tell their significant other that it's going on, that's abuse, in my book."

"Depends why they're having the affair, doesn't it? Could be that they're in love with this new person, or that this new person is providing something their partner is denying them."

"In which case, they should tell the abused partner it's going on and not skulk around like high school kids. I'm not saying it isn't understandable, Atticus. I absolutely understand desire. There are times when I don't give a flying fuck who's cheating on who, both partners are rotten, and all I think is good riddance."

"This case isn't one of those."

Bridgett shook her head. "The problem with this case is that this woman is devoted to her husband." She stopped to drink some more of her beer and look out the window at the rain. The runoff gutter on this side of the roof was broken, and water was pouring into the alley with a steady slap.

Bridgett continued, "Sometimes, a client will come in, man or woman, doesn't matter, and they'll hem and haw and then say, 'I think my wife/husband/lover is having an affair. I need to know.' And the pain is so obvious. They *already* know. They just want the proof. And I always say, 'If you're right, and I find the proof, you know that won't solve the problem.'

"And they look in my eyes, and they nod, and they tell me to do it anyway." She turned away from the rain, faced me again. "That's what I get to do tomorrow."

"I can't tell if you don't like the work or the result."

"I don't like the pain."

The lasagna was done and I pulled it from the oven and set it on the counter to settle, served the salad with some of my freshly baked bread. When she tried the bread, Bridgett swooned theatrically. We each had another Anchor Steam and ate, and then Bridgett said, "I saw Natalie last night. We went out for dinner."

"How's she doing?"

"She's better. She told me you came by the office, tried to give her one of Rubin's paintings."

"I'm surprised she told you. She didn't speak word one to me, and we were face-to-face. She acted like I wasn't there."

"She told me she didn't know what to say to you."

" 'Hello' would have been nice for starters. 'How you been?' Any of the small-talk standards would have worked, instead of a silence that said 'Fuck off and die.' "

Bridgett tore the heel of the loaf in half, took a small bite. "I doubt that's what she was thinking."

"I'm pretty sure it was. I'm pretty sure she hates my guts."

"Natalie doesn't hate you, Atticus."

I gnawed on the other half of the heel before saying,

"She belted me at the funeral. She ignored me yesterday. She wouldn't even take the goddamn painting."

"And you can forgive that, can't you?" Bridgett asked. "Grief and all."

"She hasn't spoken to me once."

"You confronted her at work, in front of a client, as I understand it. Not the best timing. The phone works two ways, you know. You should have called her first, asked if you two could get together."

I took my empty plate to the sink, rinsed it quickly, and put it in the dish drainer. When I went back for Bridgett's, she put her hand on mine. "You're painful for her to be around, Atticus. You were his best friend, you two were a package. Natalie doesn't know how to know you without Rubin."

I nodded and she moved her hand, and I washed off her dish, then served the lasagna.

"It'll pass in time," Bridgett said. "You can't be impatient about this."

"Rubin's dying really fucked up my world," I said, and it came out far more bitter than I had intended.

After we cleaned up the table, we made a pot of coffee, and once we'd filled our mugs, Bridgett led me by the hand into the living room. Three boxes lay on the floor in front of the couch, gift-wrapped, one large and two small, laid out in descending order, right to left. Bridgett kissed my cheek, then stepped over the boxes and sat on the couch.

"You didn't have to do this," I said.

"You took me to dinner and a movie and you gave me a case of mixed Life Savers on my birthday," Bridgett said. "Just pretend this is yours, okay?"

"But I didn't get you anything."

"It's not *my* birthday."

"That's sort of my point."

Bridgett shook her head, playing exasperation. "Just

open them. This one first." She indicated the largest box.

I picked it up. The same paper decorated each box, cute bear cubs wearing pointed party hats and holding balloons. I gave the box an experimental turn, didn't hear anything shifting inside. It weighed maybe four pounds.

"What is it?" I asked.

"It's called 'a present.' You see, in some cultures, when one person likes another person, and they want to do something nice for said individual, they spend money on them in the form of commercial items for the sheer pleasure of giving the gift. It's an ancient and revered capitalist tradition."

"Thank you, Margaret Mead," I said.

She bounced her knees up and down impatiently, holding her coffee mug in both hands. "Come on, you're killing me here."

I found the seam where the paper had been joined, began working the first bit of tape free.

Bridgett started knocking her boot heels together. "Just rip the goddamn paper, dammit."

It was a toy X-wing fighter.

Bridgett laughed with glee. "Isn't it *great*?" she demanded. "Isn't it fucking great? Open that one next."

It was a Luke Skywalker doll.

Bridgett giggled, grabbed her jacket from where she'd left it on the arm of the couch, and took out a package of four AA batteries. "I saw them and I just couldn't resist."

"Uh," I said, because no words were springing to mind.

Bridgett gave me a wonderful smile. "I got you, didn't I? You *like* this."

I nodded, felt myself grinning without meaning to. "Should I open the last one?"

"Depends if you want to play with the X-wing first or not," she said mysteriously. "You open that one, there's no going back."

I picked up the smallest box. It was very light, roughly the width of a cassette tape, but longer and taller. Bridgett watched me for a moment, then shifted her attention to the toys.

"Cocaine?" I asked.

"Gift-wrapped. You got me." Her smile was broad and dazzling.

I tore the paper off, and found myself holding a package of thirty-six condoms.

"They're a little big for Luke," I said, indicating my new doll.

"I didn't buy them for Luke."

I turned the package in my hand. We'd been dancing around this moment forever.

"What do you think?" Bridgett asked.

"I think that you were right."

"Yeah?"

"There's no going back."

I stood, and Bridgett set her mug on the floor, then rose, too.

"Happy birthday," she said as she put her arms around me.

We didn't do a lot more talking after that.

The weather the next morning was fucking awful, rattling rain and sleet, and I decided to skip running to stay in bed with Bridgett. The box of condoms sat on my nightstand, and there were plenty left, so we made love again, taking our time, and then Bridgett said that she had to go to work, and I said that I'd make coffee, and she said that would be good. She didn't bother to reach for my robe when she got out of bed, just walked on out of the room and headed down the hall. I watched her go, looking at the tattoo of a rose on her left calf as she went.

Yet another discovery from the previous night.

I made coffee and, when Bridgett got out of the bathroom, went to take my turn, showering slowly. The muscles in my thighs trembled while I let the water run off me, and I liked the feeling. I liked everything I was feeling. I was very happy that Bridgett had stayed the night.

When I got out, I dried off, put my robe back on, and headed back to the kitchen.

Wyatt was seated at the table, scowling.

Before I could open my mouth he said, "Ditch the bitch, Sergeant. We need to talk."

Bridgett stood in the corner by the coffeemaker, and she calmly offered me a mug. Once I'd taken it, she asked me, "Can I shoot this arrogant cocksucker?"

I shook my head.

"Get rid of her, Sergeant," Wyatt ordered.

"You let him in?" I asked Bridgett.

"If I had known, I'd have made him wait outside."

"Yeah, yeah, yeah," Wyatt said. "You two can fuck anytime. I need to talk to him now."

Bridgett leaked air out of her mouth in a soft hiss, decompressing. Her eyes were closer to gray than blue now, and her lips were pressed together hard. But the question was there, clear.

"I'll walk you to the door," I told her.

She nodded, finished the contents of her mug.

"Nice meeting you," Wyatt said.

"Eat me," Bridgett told him.

I unlocked the door and she gave me a very nice kiss before stepping into the hall, and when she broke it to pull away, I tugged her back in, holding her close and tight. I held on to her for a good thirty seconds, pushing my face into her hair, feeling my heart beating, enjoying our new intimacy. I was falling in love with her hair.

"Thank you for a wonderful birthday," I whispered.

She laughed low in her throat, then sighed, kissed me again. "If you need help disposing of his body, call me at the office."

"I'll talk to you tonight."

I locked the door again, went into my room, and dressed quickly. As I pulled on my clothes, I could hear the Colonel moving in the kitchen, opening and closing the cupboard doors. When I came back into the kitchen, he was looking in the refrigerator, and I ignored him, went to the coffeemaker, and poured myself another mug. After a second to think about it, I put on a kettle for tea, too. No need to stoop to his level, I thought.

He shut the refrigerator door firmly, looked at me, then sat back down at the table. "Nice-looking cunt," Colonel Wyatt said.

I pivoted and covered the space between us. "You talk about Bridgett like that again, I'll throw you out the window, Colonel."

"You're a fucking hypocrite, Sergeant. You know that?" He smiled, and the yeast scent rose off him sweet and sticky.

"I'm not married."

"Is she?"

I shook my head and went back to the stove. "I'm not cheating on anyone. Must be hard for you to swallow that, huh?"

He muttered something I didn't catch, unwrapping his scarf from around his neck. He was wearing a fat down winter coat, unzipped, and beneath it I could see a thick navy-blue sweater, wool. A black stocking cap stuck from the pocket on the jacket's left side.

"You want tea?" I asked him.

"If you're going to the trouble."

I pulled a box of tea bags from a cupboard, got another mug out. "The water will take a few minutes."

"Thank you."

We looked at each other. Wyatt broke the stare to examine the calendar of jazz greats I had hanging on the wall. This month's picture was of Thelonius Monk. He shook his head, then checked his watch.

"Can I have a glass of water?" His tone made it seem like I'd already said no.

I filled a glass and put it on the table, and Colonel Wyatt pulled several bottles of pills from his pockets, opening them one at a time, laying out his dosages. I counted eight bottles before I went back to the stove, watched as he began putting pills in his mouth, shooting water down after them.

"What are you taking?" I asked.

"Every fucking drug they make." He grimaced, took another pill. "AZT, DDI, Bactrim, you name it. Vitamins, too. Fuckload of vitamins." He finished his last pill and emptied the glass.

"Are they helping?"

"Do you think they're helping, Sergeant? There's no cure for the disease, right? All they do is fuck with my system, that's it."

He held the empty glass for me to take, and I brought it to the sink, and had a paranoid fit that I should maybe throw the glass out instead of just washing it. But I wasn't going to get AIDS from Colonel Wyatt, not unless we ended up exchanging fluids somehow. I made certain the water was very hot, though, in spite of myself.

The kettle started to rattle, and I turned off the heat, poured the Colonel a cup, then brought the mug to the table with a bottle of honey and a spoon. I didn't have any lemon.

"I've got to go out of town for a while," the Colonel said after he had dropped a dollop of honey in his mug. The thrush at his mouth fell like snowflakes onto the tabletop as he spoke. "Johns Hopkins has an HIV program, they've got a treatment I've been selected for, and I'm leaving tomorrow. Could be gone for a week or two, I don't know. I want you to watch Erika while I'm gone."

"No."

"I was thinking she could stay here, with you," he continued, ignoring me. "I'll bring her down in the morning, before I go to the airport, and you can keep an eye on her, take her out, whatever. Just so she has somebody with her."

"I said no, Colonel."

"I heard what you said. I want you to watch her for me."

"I'm not a baby-sitter."

He turned in the chair, sighing. "You want me to fucking blow you, Sergeant? I need you to watch her. I don't have anyone else."

"You and Moore seem chummy," I said. "Why not ask him or some of his boys?"

"It's not their bag."

"And it's mine?"

"It's closer to what you do."

"I protect people, Colonel. You know that."

"When you're not bouncing, you mean."

I let it slide, dumped the remaining coffee in my mug down the drain.

"She needs to be protected," Wyatt said.

"Yeah?" I thought about the SAS, about Trouble and his knife. "From whom?"

I heard his down jacket rustle with a shrug, and turned back to see he was still facing me.

"I think your friend Moore and his crew are a little more than casually interested in your daughter," I said. "I think they've been following her, and that maybe they're prepping to grab her. I think that's why he brought her back to your place the other day, just to show you how easily he could do it."

"That's what you think?"

"It's a theory."

"Moore wouldn't hurt Erika," Wyatt told me. "He's a professional, like you and me."

"How do you know him?"

"Same way I know you. The Army."

"And?"

"And what, Sergeant?"

"And what's going on? What's your relationship with him? Why was he at the house? You can answer any of those."

Wyatt started to respond, then bent with a rapid series of coughs. These sounded thicker, wetter, than they had in Garrison, and it occurred to me that it was stupid for him to be out on a day like today, to have come into the city in weather like this. His system couldn't defend against the environment, and traveling in the wet and the cold would get him nothing but a quick and lethal case of pneumonia.

I waited.

Wyatt finally got enough breath back to say, "Moore's a good man, and a good soldier. He wouldn't hurt Erika."

"Somebody tried to."

"Then let her stay here while I'm gone, Sergeant. You can protect her. I know you can do that. I'm asking for your help."

I just looked at him, trying to think of a way to refuse.

"You owe me this," he said. "Diana left because of you—"

"Diana left because you were sticking your cock into any and every thing that moved. Diana left because you were a fucking awful husband, and you treated her like shit. Sir."

His eyes narrowed at me. People didn't talk to him like that, I knew, and he was contemplating his response. Finally, he decided to go on as if I hadn't spoken, saying, "And Erika, she was devoted to you. You abandoned her. You never wrote. You told her you would. You didn't. You never called. You betrayed my trust, and you betrayed the trust of my daughter. Now I'm asking you for help, here. I'm asking you for this, and I've never asked you for anything before. Do this for me, Sergeant. Watch her. Let her stay here with you."

This wasn't right. He should have upped and walked out by now. He should have thrown my insults right back at me. But instead he just sat in his huge coat, looking diminished, and his expression did nothing but support his words.

"What's going on?" I asked.

"I told you, I've got to go down to Baltimore for treatment."

"If you don't tell me what the threat is, I can't protect Erika," I said.

He almost smiled. I'd turned the corner, was on his street, now. He considered, then said, "Just keep an eye out for a rogue brick."

"I could use more information."

"That's all I can give you," he said. "I'll be by tomorrow before nine with Erika. I'll leave a number where you can reach me. How much do you charge?"

I hesitated.

"They're the SAS," Colonel Wyatt said. "You'll need help, and help will cost."

"A couple hundred will do."

He knew I was going low. "I don't want any of your fucking charity, Sergeant. I'll pay what you're worth." He got up, wrapping his scarf around his neck, and the discussion was obviously over. I walked him to the door, and he went on out without saying anything else, without looking back. His steps were slow going down the stairs, and the echoes rang back in my apartment, even after I had closed and locked the door.

I spent fifteen minutes cleaning up the apartment, the kitchen and my bedroom in particular, and when I caught a whiff of Bridgett on the bedsheets, my stomach did a quick flip, and I felt stupidly giddy. Then I put on my jacket and went to do my walk-through of the building.

A rogue brick, the Colonel had said. Watch out for a rogue brick, meaning watch out for a group of SAS. Or, watch out for Moore and his crew.

There are three regiments of the SAS, the 21, 22, and 23, though only the 22 is active military; the other two are reserve units. The 22 SAS is referred to as, simply, The Regiment, and has somewhere between 550 and 750 troopers assigned to it. Troopers are subsequently broken down into smaller units, or troops, and those troops are divided into bricks, which are units of three to eight men, normally assigned to specific functions— counterterrorism, mountain operations, vehicle operations, training, or whatever.

Unlike the United States military, where if you join the Rangers or the Green Berets, say, you stay, most SAS troopers are "temporary." Soldiers volunteer from other units, go through a hellish selection process, and then, if they're accepted, are badged as members of the regiment. They serve something like three years, and then return to their parent regiment. That's most of them; others are permanently badged, soldiers who are accepted into the SAS, and there they remain.

Moore had said they were all permanently badged, referring literally to the insignia that the regiment wears, and that meant these guys were on top of their game. No lag-time to dull the lessons they'd learned. If Moore was leading a brick, he could have as many as seven more highly trained soldiers at his beck and call. So far, including Trouble, I'd met four of them.

And they were rogue, which meant that whatever they were doing, they were doing it without sanction from their government. Possibly as mercenaries, possibly for motives entirely of their own.

It was enough to make me regret agreeing to watch Erika.

The Colonel had been absolutely correct; not only would I need help, I'd need a lot of it.

I spent the rest of the morning in my apartment, cleaning and installing, putting cup hooks in the bottom of one of my cupboard shelves. I consider my apartment pretty secure, but if I was going to keep Erika in it, it also had to be defensible, and that meant that I had more shopping to do. About noon I went out to a hardware store and bought supplies, including a new front door, and paid for same-day delivery and installation. The person who took my money told me they could have it at my place by four, but I'd be paying time-and-a-half if they had to stay past six for the installation. I smiled sweetly.

Next I went shopping for a cellular phone, and ended up buying a no-frills model for only seventy dollars, plus an additional activation fee. The phone was probably hot, but that didn't much matter to me. I was going to use it only in emergencies.

My last stop before returning home was at a furniture store, and I bought a queen-sized futon and frame that would fold up into a not unattractive couch. When the cashier ran my credit card through the reader, I winced, fully expecting the purchase to be bounced back. It went through, though, so I guess I wasn't over my limit yet.

I returned home, and set about hardening my defenses. This was mundane stuff for the most part, just installing another set of sliding dead bolts on the front door and getting the still-mostly-empty spare room ready for Erika. The futon and frame arrived first, and I had just finished putting it together when my intercom buzzed, telling me my front door was at my front door. I helped the delivery men bring it up, then directed them to the office.

"You want it here?" the older of the two asked. He was in his late fifties and looked cheerful, if confused.

"Right there. Take the other one out, put that one in."

He looked at the interior door, then at the new one leaning against the wall, then at me. "This is a front door," he said. "You know that, right?"

I nodded and he smiled at me, the way someone smiles at a dog they're not certain is going to bite them. I thought about explaining that I was trying to create a hard room, a place I could retreat to with Erika if the apartment was breached, but figured such information would only confuse him more.

I left them to their work and went to the phone in the kitchen, called Dale Matsui at his home. It took seven rings, and he answered with a "Yo?"

"Dale? It's Atticus."

"Atticus!" He sounded overjoyed. "Jesus, I was going to call you today, see if you wanted to go bar-hopping tonight, try to corrupt the youth of America."

I laughed. Since Rubin's funeral, I'd pretty much avoided everyone but Bridgett. Somehow, Dale made my guilt at avoidance irrelevant. "How you doing?" I asked him.

"Still got all my fingers and toes," he said. "So, what do you think about tonight?"

"Actually, I wanted to see if you could come over here around seven or eight," I told him. "I've got a job, and I need help."

"How long?"

"Looks like two weeks, maybe less. Local. Starts tomorrow."

"Is it glamorous?"

"It's watching a fifteen-year-old girl. Erika Wyatt."

"Colonel Doug 'If-It-Moves, Fuck-It' Wyatt's daughter?"

"You remember her?" I asked.

"Of course," Dale said. "How could I not? You were sleeping with her mom, for God's sake."

My pause said it all.

"You think I didn't know?"

"Yeah," I said, finding my voice again. "I thought you didn't know."

Dale got a good chuckle out of that. "Rubin told me about Diana. And I was out at the house a couple of times, don't forget. You had that family vibe when you were out there. And you and Mrs. Wyatt, watching you two practically required insulin."

"We weren't that bad."

"Maybe not around the Colonel, but yes, you were. I'm surprised the kid didn't know."

"Ah, well, it turns out she did."

"Everyone in the E-ring knew Wyatt was a horn-dog. I personally thought you had drawn a raw deal, having to protect him. I mean, how do you keep the man secure when he's sleeping with a different woman every night?"

"You don't," I said. "When I tried, he ordered me to leave him alone. That's how I met Diana—the Colonel ordered me to secure his home because he didn't want me following him on weekends. I can't believe Rubin told you."

"Well, he was happy for you, if a bit jealous of the time you were spending with her. Said you were in love." He said "in love" like he was Barry White crooning into a microphone.

"That's five years old," I said.

"Of course it is. And now you've got Bridgett, and that's moving up in the world, at least in my book."

"What?"

"You and Bridgett," Dale said patiently, and I imagined his self-satisfied grin, the one he wears when he knows he's got a secret.

"How'd you hear about that?"

"Bridgett called Natalie this morning, Nat called me."

"What'd she have to say about it?"

"Nat? She was happy for you."

Somehow I didn't believe that. "I have no secrets, do I?"

"None," Dale said, pleased. "I think it's great, by the way. You and Bridgett balance each other well."

"You think so?"

"Shit, yes. You're practically made for each other."

"Like oil and water."

"I was thinking like Stan and Ollie," Dale said. "So, why does Erika Wyatt need protection?"

"Some rogue SAS types have designs on her," I said.

There was a brief pause, and then Dale gave me the dum-de-dum-dum sting from *Dragnet*.

"Yeah," I said.

"Who else are you getting?" Dale asked.

"I'm going to call Yossi next, and Bridgett."

"That's it?"

"That'll be four, including me."

"You should call Natalie," he said, as if scolding a child.

"I'll think about it. How's eight tonight?"

"I'll be there with bells on," Dale said.

"Bring your gear. We're going to use my place as the safe house."

He said he'd be sure to, and we chitchatted for a couple more minutes, with Dale telling me about the work he was doing on his place. The storm windows on his house were giving him grief, but his garden was prepared for the winter. Before I got off the phone, he said, "It's good that you're working again."

I said thanks and hung up, wondering that if it was so good for me to be working again, why didn't I feel more confident about going up against the SAS.

CHAPTER NINE

By a quarter past eight, Dale, Yossi, and Bridgett were gathered in my living room, worshiping around pizza boxes. Yossi and Bridgett had taken the couch, and I sat by the radiator. Dale sat beneath the window, playing with the X-wing between bites of his slice. He's a big guy of Japanese descent, with about two inches on me and another forty pounds, all muscle. If you saw him coming at you down a dark alley, you'd swear you were a dead man. But that's his mask; in truth, Dale's one of the most gentle people I know. He had taken it visibly harder than any of us when Rubin died, and perhaps that was why he had seemed to recover sooner and faster.

"Give us the brief," Yossi said, when everyone had finished their last slice of pizza.

I laid it out, giving all the details I could, and trying to explain the situation as I knew it. None of them liked the fact that I was vague on the threat.

"They're trying to kidnap the girl?" Yossi asked.

"That's what it looks like."

"But it could be a hit," Dale said.

"It could be, but I doubt it."

"We better hope to God not," Yossi said. "If there's one thing those SAS boys know how to do, they know how to kill. They won't hesitate to put bullets into us to get to their target."

"We'll defend her to the best of our ability," I said. "It's just like any other operation."

"Where are you keeping her?" Bridgett asked.

"Here."

"You certain that's wise? If they picked Erika up outside of here, Moore knows where you live."

"It's a hardened location," Yossi interjected. "They can know she's here, doesn't mean they'll be able to breach the defenses. Better to keep your principal in a place that you know than one that you don't."

Bridgett looked at him, perhaps amused, perhaps alarmed, then switched back to me, saying, "Do you really want a firefight in your apartment?"

"If they want to come in after her, they'll have to do a recon," I said. "And we can make this place look pretty hard to crack. There are four of us, remember."

Dale pressed the button on the X-wing, and the sound effect of lasers squealed twice, then stopped abruptly. "Natalie said no?"

"I didn't call her."

All three of them looked at me. Dale made a scolding noise, and Yossi just shook his head.

Bridgett said, "Well, you're going to have to call her, stud. I've got to go to Jersey tomorrow with one of the bosses, and I'm going to be out of the city all day."

"We need at least four guards at all times," Yossi said. "And one of them should be a woman, so she can stick with the kid in the bathroom, and so on."

He sounded a little patronizing to me, and I almost responded to it before reason intervened. They were still all looking at me, and I realized they were absolutely right, that I would have to make my peace with Natalie.

"I'll talk to her tonight."

Everyone smiled, and Bridgett leaned forward and patted my knee. "That's my boy."

"He learns quick," Dale said.

"I understand he's actually quite bright," Yossi added.

"College boy."

"That so?"

"Sure. Cambridge, Yale, Harvard, all of the fancy ones."

"You're embarrassing him," Bridgett said.

I showed them all a tight smile.

"What are the positions?" Dale asked me.

"If Natalie agrees, she'll work my second, and we'll alternate close cover on Erika. You'll handle driving and egress routes, and Yossi will be the perimeter man. Bridgett can float when she's available."

"How many cars will we have?" Yossi asked.

"One," I answered. "We'll use Dale's."

Yossi shook his head. "We should have two. One to follow."

"He's right," Dale agreed.

"It's too easy to ambush a car," I objected.

"All the more reason to have two."

"I hate cars."

"Too bad."

"He hates cars?" Yossi asked Dale.

Dale just nodded.

Yossi looked at me for an explanation.

"I just don't like cars," I said.

"We can use mine. It's a company car, good for light work."

"That'll be fine."

"I'll bring it when I come over tomorrow," Yossi said.

"That'll be fine," I repeated. It occurred to me that I should say something about their challenging the authority of the team leader, but knew that wasn't really what was going on. If we were in the field, it would be different, but as of now, the protective effort had not officially begun.

We spent another hour going over details, checking the safe room and the rest of the apartment, and by ten everyone but Bridgett had left, saying they would be by tomorrow between seven and nine in the morning. As I ushered them out, Bridgett was using the phone. I traded my last good-byes with Yossi and Dale, shut the door, and bumped into Bridgett who was standing behind me, holding my coat.

"Going out?" I asked.

She shook her head. "You are. I called Natalie, she's expecting you."

"If I'm not back by midnight, she's killed me."

"If you're not back by midnight, it went exceptionally well, and you're reminiscing."

"You'll be here?"

"I'll be here."

I took the subway up to Eighty-sixth Street and headed for her apartment on East End Avenue. The doorman was pushing seventy, with two rows of brass buttons on his jacket running from throat to his bulging waist. I could see my face reflected in each of the buttons as I identified myself and asked him to ring Natalie Trent's apartment.

The doorman went to the house phone, dialed, and said I was downstairs. There was an interminable wait of only five seconds before he hung up again and said, "You can go up."

I went through the lobby to the elevators, pressed the button. There was a small marble-topped table with a pink flower arrangement opposite the elevator door, and behind it hung a mirror. The reflection made it seem as if I were holding the vase of flowers.

The car arrived and I rode it up to seventeen. Her hall

was empty and quiet, and I walked to her door,
knocked twice. She opened it almost immediately, then
turned and left me standing there.

I stepped inside and shut the door.

Natalie's apartment was big, almost unreasonably
spacious for someone her age living in Manhattan, and
the door opened into a living room with a hallway running from the left that led to the bedrooms and bath.
The living room had two large windows through which
you could admire the city, and a sliding-glass door that
led onto a patio with a high railing. I could see scattered
lights from other buildings, and as I looked, it started to
snow.

Natalie went to the stereo and switched off the music, loud rock sung by an angry woman. Then she went
to look out the patio door, maybe at the view, maybe at
the snow, or maybe just my mute reflection in the glass.

A Persian rug covered the wood floor. Between book-
cases on one wall was a display cabinet, with small stat-
ues arranged inside, some of bronze, others of crystal.
Her books ranged from college editions of the classics
to trades on security, electronics, and firearms to mod-
ern novels and short-story collections. On the seat of
one of her chairs was a copy of Gerald Posner's *Case
Closed*. The bookmark peeking out of it had a red tas-
sel. She looked to be about halfway through.

Inside the display case, beside a miniature replica De-
gas sculpture, was a framed photograph, and at first I
thought I was looking at Natalie, but the clothes were
nearly twenty years out-of-date. The closer I looked the
more I could see differences in the features, and I realized this was the first time I had seen a picture of Natalie's mother. Rubin had told me that she had died while
Elliot Trent was still in the Secret Service. Natalie had
been eleven or twelve at the time.

Natalie hadn't moved, and over her shoulder I could
see three wooden planter boxes, arranged against the
railing. I could also see her reflection, watching me,
and I watched back, and so she turned and fixed the

stare on me, folding her arms across her chest. Her hair
was down and loose, and she wore a long-sleeved white
T-shirt and blue jeans. She had lost some weight since
Rubin died.

"Thanks for letting me come up," I said.

Natalie brushed some of her red hair behind her right
ear, then crossed her arms again. Just as I was thinking
she'd be giving me the same silent treatment, she said,
"Could I have stopped you?"

It wasn't much of a question.

"I appreciate it," I said.

"I probably shouldn't have let you in."

"Yeah, but you did, and I'm here now."

"Yes, you are," Natalie said. After a second more,
she went to a cabinet beneath the display case, opened
it, pulled out a decanter and a lowball glass. She poured
herself something golden and put the stopper back in
the decanter hard, and the edge of it rang on the crystal,
a low note. The sound depressed me.

"What do you want?" she asked.

"I need your help."

"Out of cannon fodder, are you? Need another
corpse to cover your mistakes?"

I couldn't find a response that wouldn't make things
worse.

"Help doing what?" Natalie asked when I didn't say
anything.

"I've signed on to protect a kid, fifteen years old.
She's got a rogue SAS brick after her."

"You are full of shit."

"I'm not making this up."

"The SAS is after this kid?"

"No, just one brick, maybe eight guys. They're
rogue."

"Why are they after her?"

"I don't know."

She looked downright disgusted. "Who hired you?"

"Her father."

"And he didn't tell you?"

"No."

"They want to snatch or whack?"

"I think snatch. But both are possible."

"Who have you got?"

"Yossi, Dale, and Bridgett," I said. "But Bridgett's got to go out of town tomorrow, so we'll be short one."

"You're short anyway," Natalie said. "You can't defend against a brick with only four people."

"I could with five."

"No, you couldn't."

"What do you want me to say, Natalie?" I asked. "I'm here because I need your help."

Natalie looked down into her glass, decided she didn't want to take a drink just yet. "What would you want me to do?"

"Work as my second, provide close cover for Erika. I want somebody with her at all times, and that'd be a hell of a lot easier if one of the guards was female."

"You don't have any right to *ask* for my help," Natalie said. "I don't want anything to do with you."

"I let this girl down once. I can't do it again, and I can't protect her without you."

"So the burden is on me? I don't help you, you're fucked?"

"Yes."

Natalie set her glass on the shelf, gently, took three steps to where I stood, and punched me in the mouth. It was a good punch, and my vision blurred for a couple of seconds. My lip began leaking blood immediately, and my hand came away with a smear on my palm. I wiped the blood off on the thigh of my jeans, focusing on her again. She stayed in front of me, ready to throw another.

"You are a son of a bitch," Natalie said, and her voice shook. "How dare you lay any guilt on me, come into my home and unload that shit on me."

I checked my lip again. It'd start swelling soon. "I deserved that," I told her. "But only that. Nothing more."

"You deserve a lot more. You deserve shrapnel tearing open your back and snapping your spine."

"Is this about the girl or about Rubin?"

"It's about you. It's about you being negligent and dangerous, about how you let members of your team get killed."

"I didn't let Rubin get killed." I was trying not to shout. "He was doing his job, and it was a job he had volunteered to do. Nobody forced him into the detail, nobody ordered him to the front of the formation."

"He was an *artist*, for God's sake!" Natalie cried. "He wasn't a PSA, he never should have been a PSA. He shouldn't have been on scene in the first place."

"He was exactly where he should have been, doing exactly what he needed to do. He saved the principal's life, Natalie."

"You are responsible!"

"Yes, I am. I don't deny that. And I hate it that he's dead, and I feel guilt every time I think about it. But that doesn't make me guilty."

"You got him killed."

"What is it, Natalie? You have to blame me to find a way past this? You can't blame the guy who made the bomb, the guy who held the detonator?"

"You were in charge," she spat.

"You were my second. If you saw holes, why didn't you say so? If you're so certain it was my fault, why the fuck didn't you tell me we had a problem? If he shouldn't have been leading formation, why didn't you do something about it?"

Natalie's mouth went tight, and I knew that one had hit home and hit hard, and I figured she was going to punch me again. Instead, she went back to the shelf and I thought she was going for her drink, but she didn't, just dipped her head to look at the floor. Then her hand came up, pushing her fallen hair back, and with it, her head upright. To my reflection in the glass, she said, "Because I didn't think of it."

"None of us did."

"But we should have. You and I, we should have."

"The PSA's job is to protect their principal. The nature of what we do for a living is that people like us *do* lead the formation, that we're in the right place at the wrong time."

"I should have been leading."

"You were on the principal, where you were supposed to be. If anyone was out of formation, it was me, and that was because a madman had a gun pointed at my head."

Somewhere in the room I could hear the motor running on a clock, and the sounds of traffic on the street far below. It wasn't much past eleven, and yet it felt far later, as if we were pushing toward morning with no rest and no sleep.

"Tomorrow's a Friday, you know? We used to spend Friday nights at your place."

"You two used to kick me out to get some privacy," I said.

"Yeah." In the reflection on the window, I could see her eyes close, her breath condensing on the glass. "Where and when?"

"We're keeping her at my place, starting tomorrow," I said. "It's only supposed to take two weeks, tops. Yossi and Dale will be coming over by nine."

She nodded.

"Thanks, Natalie."

"You can thank me after," she said. "If no one dies."

CHAPTER TEN

Natalie and Yossi arrived together around eight, just as Bridgett was preparing to leave. We all said good morning, and Natalie kept her tone level, rather than sincere. Yossi and I unloaded their gear in the living room while the two women talked in the doorway. I couldn't hear what they were saying, and Yossi caught me straining to listen.

"Cut it out," he said. "You're worse than a kid in school."

"And if they were talking about you, you wouldn't want to know what they were saying?" I asked.

"Kid in school," Yossi repeated, opening one of the bags and removing four radio sets.

Bridgett called my name and I went down the hall, moving out of Natalie's way as she brushed past.

"I won't be back in the city until at least eight tonight," Bridgett told me. "You want to get together then?"

"If you're up to it, that'd be great."

"Then I'll call when I get in."

We kissed good-bye and I shut the door, went back into the living room to find Natalie loading a shotgun. "Where does this go?" she asked.

"In the spare room," I said.

"Show me," she said, and I realized this was the first time she'd been in my new apartment. I led her to the office, and she looked the room over carefully, checking the window and the view out onto the street, before setting the weapon in the corner by the door. She closed the door, threw the bolts, and then turned the knob and gave it a good sharp tug. The door didn't budge. She checked the spyhole next, then stepped back.

I waited, wondering if this was how Rubin had felt when a critic reviewed his work.

"Looks good," Natalie said, finally.

"I had it installed yesterday."

She searched the room again with her pro gaze, then put her hands on her hips. "Where's the secondary phone?"

I pulled the cellular from where I had stowed it under the futon.

"They can block that," she objected.

"There wasn't enough time to have NYNEX install another line. This was the best I could do."

"The first thing they'll do is cut the phone lines," Natalie said. "Then they'll cut the power. Then they'll blow through the front door or one of the interior walls."

"I know."

In fact, that was the entire motive for having purchased the cellular in the first place. The room we stood in served two purposes as far as the protective effort was concerned. Primarily it would serve as Erika's space, where she could keep her things and sleep at night. Its secondary purpose was as our room of Last Stand; if Moore and his men broke in, this was where we would retreat with Erika, and pray we could hold them at bay. The phone was simply for calling the police, in the hope that they could arrive in time.

"Visibility to the street is good," Natalie said. "At least we'll be able to see the cavalry if they ever arrive."

"Passive/aggressive behavior doesn't suit you," I said.

She whipped her head around at me, and her ponytail lashed out like blood in the air. "You want me to second you or not?" Natalie asked.

"I want you to second me, absolutely, but if you're going to sound that pessimistic when the principal arrives, I'd recommend keeping your mouth shut. You make it sound like she's already dead and buried."

"I'm pointing out potential problems and weaknesses in your security."

"And I'm telling you that I'm aware of them."

We stood and glared at each other, and then I heard the intercom buzz out in the hall. "That's them," I said.

Without a word, she took a step back, letting me unlock the door. I hurried down the hall, pressed the talk button on the intercom panel, and asked, "Yes?"

"We're here," the Colonel said. Through the grille, his voice sounded like it had gone through a food processor.

"Come on up," I said, and buzzed them through.

They took their time on the stairs, and I waited with the door open for almost three minutes before Erika appeared, her father right behind. He was clearly winded from the climb, and she looked half-asleep, in jeans and my sweatshirt.

"Morning," I said.

Erika ignored my greeting, walking straight to the living room with her duffel bag and backpack. I heard Yossi greet her, then Natalie, and she ignored them, too.

"We had an argument on the way down," Wyatt confided in me, handing over a thick plain white envelope.

"I don't need this much." I tried to hand it back.

"You don't know what it fucking is, Sergeant." He

had cleaned himself up, shaved, and the thrush around his mouth was diminished, but it still appeared on his tongue; his breath was still sweet and cloying.

"This is too much."

"No, it's not." He went after Erika, and I looked at the envelope in my hand, then dropped it on the kitchen table and followed.

Colonel Wyatt had finished shaking hands with Natalie and Yossi, and was now facing his daughter, saying, "I'm going now, sweetheart. I'll see you in a week or two. You listen to Atticus and his friends, do what they say, all right?"

Erika folded her arms across her chest and looked at her father, then at me. "Sure."

"I'll be in touch."

"Yeah."

Wyatt took another step toward her, put his hands on her shoulders. He looked large again, the way I had remembered him, with his hands like two mammoth paws on Erika. He kissed the top of her head lightly and awkwardly.

She unfolded her arms and wrapped them around his middle, hugging tight. Her fingers barely met at the small of his back.

Wyatt pulled away. "I left the number where I'll be staying in the envelope. You take care of her, Sergeant."

"I will."

"Good."

I locked the door after him, went into the kitchen, and opened the envelope. Inside was a piece of paper with a phone number written on it, and I recognized the area code for Baltimore. The rest of the envelope was stuffed with money, twenty thousand dollars by my quick count.

Too much money.

Erika had followed me. "She's not here, is she?" she asked.

"Who?"

"What's-her-name."

"Bridgett?"

"Yeah, slut-girl."

"Don't call her that, Erika."

She mocked a sharp intake of breath. "Is Atticus in love with the slut-girl? Did I hurt Atticus's feelings?"

"You don't know Bridgett well enough to be calling her names," I said.

"I know her. I see women like her all the time. She's trying to act tougher than she is. She's attitude and nothing else, Atticus."

I didn't say anything about pots and kettles.

"What about the redhead?" she asked. "Total babe, huh?"

"Let's put your stuff in your room," I said, and led her back into the living room. Yossi was seated with his back to the wall, his gym bag open beside him and its contents arrayed carefully on the floor. He had six spare magazines, two boxes of ammunition, two semiautomatic pistols, five grenades—smoke and CS—and an assault rifle. Yossi's position on the team was as the perimeter man, which meant he had to be quick, and he had to have the firepower to cover a retreat, or lay down suppression, if it was necessary. For that purpose he had chosen the civilian model of the M-16, the assault rifle the U.S. military normally uses.

"Holy fuck," Erika said.

I nodded. It was an awful lot of hardware, and even I found it somewhat disconcerting. Yossi grinned up at us, enjoying his work.

"You going to war?" Erika asked him.

"Anybody tries to hurt you, angel, you bet your cute ass."

I gave him a warning look, and Yossi shrugged, went back to loading his magazines. Charming or no, I didn't want him flirting with Erika, even in jest.

She stifled a laugh. "So if I get shoved on the subway, you're going to open fire?"

"If you get shoved on the subway, I'll shove back,"

Yossi answered without looking up. "Anybody tries to really hurt you . . . he's dead."

"Really hurt me how?"

"Points a gun at you," Natalie said. "Threatens your life."

Erika looked us all over, ending her pan on me. "You'd kill someone who pointed a gun at me?"

"We all would. Our first duty is to protect you," I said.

Erika watched Yossi load for several seconds longer. "He's crazy," she finally declared.

"He's an Israeli," Natalie explained. "He won't take any chances with you."

Erika examined Natalie before asking, "What about you?"

"Me? I get to be with you whenever Atticus isn't."

"Yeah?"

Natalie nodded, and there was a hint of a smile.

"What happens if I don't like you?"

"Then I get to be with you whenever Atticus isn't." The hint turned into a confirmation. "But I think you'll like me."

"Oh, yeah?"

"Yeah."

"How do you know?"

"My dad's a pain in my ass, too."

"What about your mom?"

"I don't have one."

"Bullshit. Everyone has a mom."

"She died when I was twelve."

"You lie."

"Absolutely not."

Erika went quiet, then glanced over to where Yossi was still clicking rounds into place. She brought her eyes to mine, said, "Show me my room."

We took her bags into the office, and after they were set down, Erika turned and went to the door, shutting it. She put her back against it and leaned, looking me over, then said, "They're all right."

"There's one other guy coming, too. Dale. He was at the Pentagon around the same time I was working for your father."

Her brow was a couple more years from having serious creases, but she furrowed it all the same, then said, "He protected General Vogt, right? Big Asian guy?"

"That's him."

"He was okay. What happened to your mouth?"

I touched the swollen lump from where Natalie had hit me the night before. "I got rapped in the mouth."

"Yeah? Who did it?"

"Natalie," I said.

"Liar."

I shook my head.

Erika looked over at the shotgun. "That for me?"

"No, you're not to touch that. It's loaded, and we need to keep it in here, in case there's trouble. Are you going to have a problem with that?"

"I know how to treat guns. Dad taught me."

"I want your word that you won't touch it, Erika. Otherwise I'm going to have to move it into another room."

She elaborately crossed her heart. "Hope to die," Erika said.

"You want me to help you unpack?"

"I can do it. Besides, if you stay in here much longer, they'll think we're fucking or something."

"I doubt it."

"You totally don't want me, do you?"

"I totally don't," I agreed.

Her gaze went past me, to the window, and her expression had turned neutral. Then she made the briefest nod, grabbed her backpack, and headed for the futon. "It's not like I have to stay in this room, is it?"

"No, you can have the whole apartment. If you want to go out or anything, though, we'll have to talk about that."

"I told Dad that you didn't have a television. He said he gave you enough money to buy one."

"When Dale gets here, I'll send someone out for one."

"And a VCR."

"Sure."

Erika removed a laptop computer and its power cables from her backpack, then began hunting for an outlet. I pointed her to the one beneath the desk, and she got down on her hands and knees to plug in the cord. Unlike the last time she had crawled on my floor, Erika was quite matter-of-fact about it.

"You seen Moore or any of his buddies?" I asked her when she was back on the futon.

"Not since you were at the house."

"Are you going to tell me what happened?"

"Nothing happened. They just picked me up, that's all."

"At the train station."

"That's what I said, isn't it?"

"You were awful dry for a lady who'd stood on that platform in a storm," I said.

"They had the heat turned way up in their car."

I sat beside her on the futon, rubbed my eyes behind my glasses. Erika tapped on the keyboard a couple of times, brought up a game of solitaire, and began to play. Down the hall the intercom sounded, and Natalie went to answer it. It was probably Dale. If it wasn't, she'd get me. I listened and didn't hear her come back down the hall, but I did hear her opening the front door. Definitely Dale, then.

"Did they hurt you?" I asked Erika.

She answered immediately without looking up from her game. "Would it matter?"

I needed a second before I could say, "Of course it would matter. Yossi isn't the only one who doesn't want to see you hurt."

"Yeah? Who else?"

"Your father, for one," I said. "Me."

"You?"

"Me."

She twisted her mouth as if chewing on lemon rind. "Sure."

"I should have been there for you, and I wasn't, and I'm sorry, Erika. I was a bad friend. All I can say is that I made a mistake, and I'm trying to earn a second chance at your trust."

Erika clicked the top of the computer shut and turned on the futon so she could look directly at me. "No," she said.

"Please," I said.

She smiled at me, and it was an old person's smile, sad and deeply tired. "I've given second chances, and it gets me nothing. Nothing fucking at all. I trusted you, Atticus, and you didn't even care. Mom's pussy ran dry so you forgot about me, you just forgot. No letter. No call. All the things you said you'd do, you didn't do them. You had your chance, and you fucked it up."

She had leaned forward, kept her voice low and gentle with the weary smile still in place as she spoke. This was worse than her tears on the porch, in a way, because she was so calm. I was guilty as she'd charged, and we both knew it, and although what she suspected were my motives and the truth were different, they weren't so different that her words didn't strike and stick.

I had been twenty-four, she had been eleven, and she was right; I'd thought of her as my baby sister, but I'd forgotten her when Diana turned me away.

Erika put her hands in her hair, pulling it up and away until she held strands like sheets of gold. Then she shook her head, as if dismissing the whole speech. She leaned back against the futon, staring out the window to where the snow that had started last night was still falling.

She said, "You know what the sick fucking thing is? Everyone does it. Everyone. Mom did it, the same thing, and she's supposed to love me, but instead she just left and never said another word.

"And then there's Dad, the lovely fucking Colonel

who was fucking everyone but his own wife, who sent
me away to school after school because he didn't know
what the hell to do with me. And then they had the
nerve to fight over me, to each claim that they were the
better parent. And when it was all over, and the Colonel had won, he said he wanted me home, wanted me
near him, and I find out it was only because he's going
to croak. It's not that easy, Atticus. You can't just undo
it."

"I know."

"Then don't expect me to be like you, okay? 'Cause
I'm not. I can't be."

"Like me?"

"You trust everybody. You trust me. You shouldn't,
but you do. You trust Dad, and you shouldn't, but you
do. Fuck, you should be in the bondage scene, you trust
so much."

"Am I that bad?"

"Your best friend could have totally betrayed you,
you would never have known it," Erika said. "Because
you wouldn't even consider the possibility that he *could*
betray you. He could've been a total fucking lying bastard, you would have just kept on going in total blissful
ignorance."

"Rubin and I didn't keep secrets," I told her. "And
I'd appreciate it if you didn't talk like that about him."

"That's exactly what I mean."

"I'm serious, Erika. That's enough."

"Fine." She picked up her computer and put it on the
desk, then went back into the living room, leaving me
alone. I could hear Natalie introducing her to Dale, and
Erika said that she remembered him, and they all
started chatting happily, like the best of friends. Even
Yossi joined in, and between him and Dale, they had
Erika in stitches.

I sat on the futon for another five minutes, thinking
about what Erika had said, then decided I was being
antisocial, and joined them in the living room. For the
next hour, Dale, Yossi, Natalie, and I went over the

security procedures with Erika, making certain she understood what each of us did, and what each of us wanted to do if things went bad. She was attentive, and made no visible reaction when I mentioned the possibility of Moore and his men trying to grab her, remaining carefully indifferent to her fate; Erika perked up when we started talking about vehicle operations, excited at the prospect of going out.

"When?" she asked.

"Maybe tomorrow," I said. "Where would you like to go?"

"Anywhere," she said, and then focused on Yossi's gym bag. "Can we go to a range?"

Yossi told her, "I like you."

"Can we?"

Natalie brushed stray strands into place while thinking it over, then asked me, "City Hall Rifle and Gun?"

I nodded.

"It's one of the more secure places in the city."

She was right. All of the ranges in Manhattan were exceptionally secure, and the City Hall Rifle and Gun Club was one of the best.

"You know how to shoot?" I asked Erika.

"The Colonel taught me, I already told you. After Mom left he tried to make it a father/daughter thing. When I was home on breaks he'd take me to the range."

"You'll have to behave."

Erika looked hurt. "I'm not stupid. I know how to treat guns." She shut her eyes and used her fingers to tick off points. "Treat every gun as loaded unless you have personally checked that it ain't; don't ever point a gun at anything you're not willing to destroy, ever; keep your finger away from the trigger until you're ready to shoot; always control where the weapon is pointing at all times; and never shoot at water or another hard surface, so you prevent ricochets." She opened her eyes as Dale and Yossi both gave her a small round of applause.

"Very good," Dale said.

"Please?" Erika asked me. "Can we go shooting?"

"All right, we'll go tomorrow."

That made Erika happy, and I left her alone with Dale and Yossi, taking Natalie with me on a walk of the building. We each took a radio so we could stay in contact, and we each took our personal weapon, for me my HK and for Nat her Glock. I doubted we were in any danger in the building, at least right now, but from the moment Erika had arrived, we were all obligated to be in full paranoia mode.

We started in the garage and worked up, staying silent for the most part, as we didn't have much to say to each other. Bridgett had taken her Porsche for the day, so my parking spot was empty. Dale, Natalie, and Yossi had all driven, but none of them had used the garage, which was probably just as well. If the building was being watched, then the garage was being watched, and there was only one way in and out of the space. Moore and Company would have no problem spotting any new cars. As it was, they were probably logging all the comings and goings from the building, putting us under surveillance and constructing a timetable, evaluating when would be the best time to strike.

"Which vehicles are we using tomorrow?" Natalie asked as we were checking the boiler-room door. It was locked, as were the other rooms in the basement, but we were checking each anyway.

"Your car is wired for communications?"

"Both Yossi and I are wired, handheld and vox," she answered.

"Then we'll use those. He's got a sedan, right?"

"Yeah."

"That'll be the principal's car."

Both Natalie and Yossi used their cars for business, and they had been modified accordingly. Most people imagine a protective vehicle as some sort of James Bond car—bulletproof everything with tear gas dispensers hidden in the boot. In fact, some are, but those are rare vehicles, and aside from the obvious expense such modifications require, there are downsides. Such vehicles are very heavy on the road, often sluggish to handle, and like all things, the more moving parts they contain, the greater the chance that something will go wrong. For their work with Sentinel Guards, Natalie and Yossi really only needed lights and sirens, a hands-free radio setup, and, perhaps, tire inserts to keep the wheels going if the rubber went flat.

We'd use Yossi's car to move Erika, with Dale driving. Either Natalie or myself would ride along, and then Natalie's car would follow, driven by whoever wasn't on top of Erika. Yossi would literally ride shotgun in the follow vehicle.

Natalie and I worked our way up to the roof, and stood in the falling snow for a minute, scanning the surrounding rooftops and the street. It felt in the high twenties, chilly enough to make me want to head back inside. The pack on the roof was undisturbed, which I took as a good sign; no one was lurking around above my apartment.

"I'm not seeing any watchers," Natalie told me.

Nothing looked out of the ordinary, just pedestrians walking below in the snow. As I watched, an elderly man slipped on the near corner of Third Avenue, by my bodega. A passerby saw the fall begin and shot out an arm as she went past, catching the man by the elbow and keeping him from hitting the concrete. Once the man was upright, each of them continued in their chosen directions. It didn't look like they exchanged any words.

Other than that, the traffic flow looked entirely normal. Cars were parked on the opposite side of the street, some covered with snow, others cleared off. I looked over the adjoining and opposite roofs once more, didn't see anything that looked like a surveillance blind. Still no movement.

"Neither am I," I said.

"I don't like your roof," Natalie announced. "It's too

easy to access from either of the neighboring buildings."

"You want to put someone up here?"

"I want to get a motion alarm, like they sell for travelers to use in hotel rooms. We should hang it off the inside of the door to the stairs. That way, if someone comes in from above, we'll hear it."

"Good idea."

She put her hands in her pockets, turned in a slow circle, scanning, and finally settled on me. "What's the plan for the rest of the day?"

"Keep Erika happy and occupied. When Bridgett gets back we'll talk about giving someone time off tonight."

"Bridgett's willing to come over and stay with Erika?"

"I don't know. You have plans for tonight?"

"Don't you?" Natalie asked.

"What?"

"Don't you have plans for tonight?"

"I'm planning on staying here," I said, slowly. "With my principal."

"Good." She was keeping her eyes on mine. "You ready to go back down?"

"After you."

I followed her back to the apartment, wondering if she really thought I would bag my watch to sneak off with Bridgett.

At two that afternoon, I sent Dale out with five hundred of the Colonel's dollars to do some grocery shopping, pick up a motion alarm, and purchase a television and VCR. Before he left, he asked Erika, Yossi, and Natalie if they wanted anything specific, and that led to Erika deciding she wanted to cook us hot sesame chicken salad for dinner. She went through my kitchen quickly, and gave Dale a list of all the ingredients she needed, which turned out to be everything but spaghetti. He told her he'd do his best, and I walked him down to the front door. Dale went off, and I scanned, thinking I'd just make a quick check, then head back up.

Trooper Edward Denny was sitting in a rented blue Chevy coupe across the street, seven cars down from my left.

I keyed my radio. "We've got a watcher," I said.

"*How many?*" Natalie came back immediately.

I checked the length of the block carefully. "Just the one."

"*What do you want to do?*"

Denny was eating a sandwich, and he looked over my way. After a pause, he made an apologetic shrug, and took another bite out of his meal.

"I'm going to talk to him," I said.

Natalie took a second. "*You want support?*"

"Negative. You guys stay put. I'll be in touch."

I stowed my radio and made my way across the street, avoiding the traffic that came slaloming past. Denny had his window rolled down, and when he was sure I was coming, he got out of the car and went around to the sidewalk, to wait for me.

"Good afternoon, Sergeant Kodiak," he said. He had black cargo pants on, an anorak much like Moore's, and a pair of black leather gloves. He offered me his hand and I ignored it.

"What are you doing?"

"Just watching your place." There was an almost innocent edge in Denny's voice, as if he wanted approval. "Not in the way, am I?"

"Well, actually, Mr. Denny—"

"Oh, you can call me Ed. Everyone calls me Ed. Except Terry, but Terry likes to tease, you know how people like that are."

"Actually, Ed, I'd like it if you moved," I said.

He rubbed his chin, as if checking his last shaving job. By my guess, he was a couple years away from having to worry about stubble.

"Can't," Denny said. "Sorry."

"Why not?"

"Orders."

"Why are you out here?"

He looked up at my building, and his jaw tightened a fraction, and I realized that most of what he was giving me had to be an act. The SAS is brutal to its recruits. Nobody who was as aw-shucks as all this would have ever survived their basic course.

"She's in there, is she?" Denny asked.

I sighed, scanned the street once more. No sign of Moore or Knowles or Trouble. He seemed to be entirely alone. I looked back at him, and he had put the smile on again, eager and friendly. "Either you move, or I'll call the police, and have you moved."

"Don't see how you can do that," Denny said.

I moved around him to get a look in the car. On the backseat was a large duffel bag, another smaller bag beside it. Then I took a look at the license plate of the car.

"Why don't you just go back inside, Sergeant? Get back to what you were doing," Denny suggested.

"No," I said. "See, Ed, what I'm going to do is call in this vehicle as stolen. And then the police will come and they'll arrest you—"

"They'll arrest you, too, filing a false report."

"No, they won't. Because when they arrest you, they'll find your gun and your knife and whatever else you've got stashed in the backseat, there, and I'm betting none of your guns are licensed."

He frowned.

"Criminal possession of a firearm is a felony in Manhattan," I said. "You'll be held at Rikers Island until trial. And when I'm questioned, I'll tell the police about Sergeant Moore and Trooper Knowles and Trooper I-Don't-Know-His-Name who pulled a knife on me, and you'll pretty much be shut down for a while."

Denny scratched his chin again, then kicked some snow, before heading back to the driver's side of the car. I watched him climb behind the wheel, and he started the engine. Before he pulled out, he said, "Well, look, you have a nice day all the same, all right, Sergeant?"

I smiled and waved good-bye. When he was out of sight, I keyed my radio. "Nat?"

"Problem?"

"None at all."

Dale was gone for almost two hours, during which time Erika played *Doom* on her laptop, the explosions, growls, and gunshots echoing out of the spare room. Natalie played with her for a while, while Yossi and I kept watch; then Yossi played, and Natalie and I kept watch. Erika invited me to play, and I tried to watch the first-person perspective as it blurred past, but discovered that it was making me motion sick, so instead kept an eye on the window and the snowy street down below.

Denny did not return, and no replacement appeared. At least, none that I could see.

Then Dale buzzed us from the lobby to say that he had returned victorious in his hunt for both electronics and ingredients, and would we please open the fucking door and let him in, his arms were killing him. Natalie went down to the lobby while Yossi and I waited with Erika, and they came up together in under two minutes, carrying a box with the Sony label on it, and two grocery bags. Natalie immediately found the motion alarm in one of the bags and went to set it up on the door to the roof.

I stayed with Erika as she proceeded to make a mess out of my kitchen, cutting, crushing, and spicing with abandon. Dale had purchased an integrated television-VCR unit, and he set it up quickly, then returned to the kitchen to tell us he had taken the liberty of renting some movies, and would Erika like to watch them after dinner. She told him yes, and we brought bowls to everybody in the living room. Yossi waited until we had finished before having his dinner. After everyone had eaten, Erika went from person to person making certain we liked her cooking. We assured her that was, indeed, the case. Dale started a movie on the VCR while I went to wash up, and Natalie took her radio and went on another walk-through.

It was five of ten when Bridgett called. "Sorry I'm late. Just got back into the city."

"I was beginning to wonder," I said. "Did you bring the car back?"

"No, I parked it at a garage by the office."

"How'd it go?"

"The agency took the job, and then Donnovan put me on it as lead. Should only take one day, but that means I can't lend a hand tomorrow." I heard her put a candy into her mouth, click it against her teeth. "How's your end?"

"We're settled. They're watching a film on our new television, and Erika seems content. She's been good all day."

"You lie."

"No," I said. "We're going to go out tomorrow, and I think that's made it easier on her. She and Natalie are getting along fine."

"And you and Nat?"

"We're getting along."

"Fine?" Bridgett asked.

I ignored the bait. "You coming over?"

"I was sort of hoping you could come over here, leave the baby with the sitter, stuff like that."

"I can't do that," I said.

"I thought I was going to see you tonight."

"I thought I was going to see you, too, but I can't leave here."

She crunched the candy. "Are you going to give any of them time off?"

"I'll probably send Yossi home for the night."

"So he gets to go off shift, but you're working twenty-four/seven."

"He has to be fresh tomorrow. Vehicle work is hardest on the perimeter man."

"And if not Yossi, you'll send Dale, or Nat, right?"

"Probably."

"Listen, stud, you and I both know that you're going to have to take a break at some point, or else you'll burn out."

"True," I said. "But I can't take one yet."

"Why not?"

From the living room, I could hear the movie playing on the VCR, the voices from the soundtrack. Erika, Natalie, Dale, Yossi, they were all quiet, listening—either to the movie or to me, I didn't know which.

If I was protecting anyone else but Erika, I'd happily take a night off for myself. I'd just work myself into the rotation along with the other members of the squad, and when my turn came, I'd get out of the way. It's what I would allow Yossi and Dale and Natalie to do. It's not simply an issue of kindness, either, Bridgett was correct: it's necessary to give all the guards time to do something other than guarding, to let the brain and body rest from the concentration that's been required. No PSA in his right mind stays on a long rotation without a break, for no other reason than that it ultimately does more harm than good. It's one of the reasons true protection requires teamwork.

But Erika had already said she didn't trust me, had said it point-blank, and I knew she meant it. If I left her alone with Natalie and Dale and Yossi she would probably be safe, but I'd have run out on her again. And, if I went to Bridgett's, that would be adding insult to injury.

In a week, perhaps, I could take a night off. But maybe not, and certainly not now, not on the first day of the job.

"Is it because of the nymphet?" Bridgett asked.

"In part."

I heard her put another candy in her mouth.

"I don't know what to tell you," I said.

"Yeah, well, I can't think of anything, either. I want to see you, you can't see me, and it sounds like this is going to be status quo until her shithead father gets back. I'll lump it, but you should know that I'm feeling a tad shafted here."

"I don't like it, either."

"Yes, but you're not willing to do anything about it. Two nights ago we started something that I'd like to continue."

"I would, too."

She didn't say anything.

"I don't have a choice, Bridie," I said. "I have to do it this way."

Her sigh was loud in my ear. "You know where I'll be. Call me if you have the time."

She hung up before I could respond.

CHAPTER ELEVEN

We took both cars downtown a little before eleven the next morning, Dale driving Yossi's blue Saab with me in the backseat beside Erika. Natalie drove her car behind us, a black Lexus sport coupe, with Yossi seated at her right in the front, his gym bag at his feet. We all had our side arms, and each car had its radio set to voice-operation, so Dale and Natalie could communicate. In addition to my pistol, I'd brought another bag with my range equipment.

We'd checked the street carefully before bussing out, and there had been no signs of an SAS presence. Of course, that meant nothing, and it made me nervous. If I'd had it my way, we wouldn't be going out at all, but Erika had made it plain she was going to make us miserable if she didn't get out of my apartment.

After getting off the phone with Bridgett, I'd sent Yossi home and told Natalie and Dale that they'd be spending the night at my place. Erika had taken that as tacit permission for a slumber party of sorts, and it was almost one before she had gone to bed, Dale and I following suit. Natalie had awakened me a little after five to spell her, and she had taken my bed after I'd showered and dressed. Yossi returned at eight, by which time Dale had risen, and the two of them watched the apartment while I went to make my rounds. Nothing had really changed, although the snow on the roof was now considerably deeper.

I'd returned to find Natalie showering, and Dale watching Erika sleep. I made everyone breakfast, and we kept our silent vigil until Erika woke up just before ten. She went through the morning ritual quickly, refusing breakfast, saying, "I want to go shoot."

So shooting we would go.

The traffic was normal for late-morning Manhattan, and the snow had stopped during the night, so visibility was good. Erika sat quietly while I tried to see everything around us as we went, convinced that I was missing more than I caught. Every PSA I've ever known has their own pet paranoia, something that worries them above all else when they're working, that gives them their nightmares. For some, like Natalie, it's snipers, and the knowledge of how hard it is to stop a man with a rifle if he knows what he's doing. For others, like Yossi, it's bombs, and the fear of a single sprung mind driving a truck loaded with two hundred pounds of TNT straight into a bus queue. Dale just hates crowds.

Every guard has his or her own ghost.

Mine's cars, or, more precisely, being ambushed in a car. Even before Rubin died, I didn't like them. Now, I felt more justified than ever in avoiding vehicles whenever possible. The way I see it, from a car, you have almost no control over your variables, over your environment. With a sniper, you can stay in cover, work in a tight formation, deny the shooter their shot. With a bomber, you can harden your target, misdirect, even jam or flood frequencies, trying to prevent detonation or cause a premature explosion. In a crowd, you close ranks, run surveillance, use decoys.

But there are just too many ways to take out a car. You can use a mine, or a rocket launcher, or a roadblock, or another car. You can caltrop the road and blow out the tires, or put a bullet through the engine. You can scoot up on a Vespa, and just open fire with a submachine gun. And there are too many other fucking people on the road, and each of them is in their own little universe, oblivious of yours, just trying to get from A to B with all due speed. You're in their way, and that makes them mad.

Yet, if you need to move your principal, you must use a car. You can't really transfer the protective effort to a bus, or cab. So it's a necessary evil, and that makes me like it even less.

My tension must have rubbed off on Erika, and she was silent for the drive, listening to the communication between Dale and Natalie.

"You've got a cab coming up on your right, he's weaving," Natalie said.

"Got him."

I looked and saw the car speed past, brake hard, and then cut two lanes left to get to an opening behind another cab. Three people were crammed together in the backseat, and two of them looked terrified. Probably tourists.

"We're coming up on a yellow," Dale said. "I'm stopping."

"Right with you."

I put a hand on Erika's shoulder, ready to send her to the floorboards. Our back was covered by Natalie and Yossi, but our flank was badly exposed, and either of the neighboring vehicles could hold a threat. The only escape route would be forward, into the cross traffic, and that would probably get us killed.

But nothing happened, and the light changed, and Dale said, "Going."

"You're clear."

"Relax," Dale told me, glancing in his mirrors. "We're fine. Almost there."

I ignored him and kept watching the Mazda pickup that had turned onto the street behind us. It was hanging a couple cars back behind Natalie, and kept swerving slightly from side to side. Either looking for an opening, or the driver was drunk.

"There's a red Mazda pickup back there," I said to Dale. "I don't like it."

"You catch that, Nat?" Dale asked.

"*Confirmed. You want me to close up?*"

"No, keep your distance."

I heard Yossi start laughing over the radio, say something to Natalie that I couldn't understand. She chuckled, said, "*The Mazda's all right. Yossi says the driver is trying to change the cassette in his deck.*"

"Nothing to worry about," Dale said.

"Shut up and drive," I said.

"Driving."

Dale dropped us off in front of the club entrance on Chambers Street, Natalie pulling in right behind, and then getting out. Yossi slid over to take the wheel, and then pulled away after Dale. They would park the cars together, and then stay with the vehicles while we were gone. When we were ready to leave the club, we'd radio them, and they'd drive back to get us.

The City Hall Rifle and Gun Club is all but unmarked, innocuous, and secure. New York City is reasonably paranoid about firearms, and the security at the Club is very tight. Access is controlled by a glass security door that leads into a foyer, another door beyond it. The glass is heavy ballistic stuff, made to take some savage punishment. A security camera in the foyer is pointed outside.

"This is a range?" Erika complained as we stood looking in through the door. "Doesn't look like much."

"It's a range," I assured her, pressing the bell and hearing nothing. After five seconds there was a buzz, and I pushed the first door open, guiding Erika past me, followed by Natalie, to the second. We went through it together, then down a flight of steps, walking side by side, into the hallway. There were no decorations on any of the walls, and there was almost no noise. Natalie took the lead at the next door, and we started down a second flight of stairs, this one very steep and very narrow. Erika stayed between Natalie and me.

We emptied into the outer room of the basement, and from behind the counter, I heard a man say, "Kodiak, Trent. You brought a guest."

"Lonny, this is Erika," Natalie said.

Lonny was leaning on the glass case, casting a shadow over the weapons on display. Lonny is five feet three, built like an oil drum, and entirely bald, but gets the height he needs for the shadow effect by standing on a footstool that he keeps behind the counter. He always carries a cocked and locked .45 on his right hip while working; like Colonel Wyatt, Lonny's a traditionalist.

Over his shoulder on the wall were three video monitors, one showing the view of the outside we'd been checked through on, one showing the first-floor landing, and one showing a view of the final set of stairs. The security was designed to turn that final flight into a fatal funnel if anyone was stupid or crazy enough to try to rob the place.

"Erika," Lonny said, extending a hand. She took it, then winced at his grip. "Nice to make your acquaintance."

"Nice to meet you, too."

I turned to look through the Plexiglas window, and noted that there was nobody on any of the shooting points. The range was empty.

"Slow day," Lonny told us. "How many points you all want?"

Natalie looked at me for an answer, so I said, "We'll take one."

"You're twenty-one, aren't you, Erika?" Lonny asked her.

"Turned twenty-one at the end of September," she said easily.

"Sure," Lonny said to me.

"She's responsible," I told him, getting out my wallet. "We need two sets of eyes and ears, and twenty-five Q targets."

Lonny raised an eyebrow, then grunted, took my money, and disappeared behind the counter. Erika looked happily from Natalie to me, and when Lonny came back up to hand them their eye and ear protectors, she thanked him.

"Pick your point," he told me, handing over the targets.

I led the way through the two sets of double doors, and then out onto the range, walking down to the last shooting point, eight. Erika stood with her back to the glass while I unpacked my goggles and ear protectors, but she came forward to help me load my spare magazines. When I was finished, Natalie prepped her gear, then hit the button on the side of the cubby. She clipped the first target onto the hanger, then sent it back out to ten yards. When that was done, Natalie stepped back.

I unloaded my gun, checked it, and then slipped in a magazine of the cheap ammunition. I set the gun on the counter, barrel pointing out, and stepped back, pulling on my ear protectors.

"Go ahead," I told Erika.

She glanced at me, then stepped up to the point, taking the gun carefully.

"There's no hammer," I told her. "You cock it by squeezing the lever in the grip. Keep it held down and fire away."

She nodded, and I heard the click as she raised the gun. Her stance was good, and she took her time before taking her first shot. Then the report came, and the target wavered, and I could see over her shoulder the hole she had put through the shaded paper.

"Good."

She nodded again, not looking away, and methodically fired off the rest of the magazine, one shot at a time. She missed once out of the thirteen shots, on the last one, but that was because she rushed. When the gun was empty, she set it down and looked back at me.

"It's different," Erika said. "I like it. It's fun."

"I'm glad. You want to shoot again?"

Erika looked at Natalie. "Can I try yours?"

"Certainly." Natalie waited until I reloaded, then checked her weapon. She handed the gun over and moved in behind Erika to give her pointers on the Glock. Erika fired like she had before, hitting the target cleanly, and when she was empty, she handed the weapon back to Natalie.

"You guys can go."

"We'll wait until you're done," I said.

"Can I shoot yours again?" she asked Natalie.

Natalie said yes, and handed her a fresh magazine. I took the spent ones and set about reloading while Erika continued to shoot. She went through another six magazines and another target, taking about thirty minutes to do so, having fun with it, but never getting sloppy. Her muzzle control was good, and I could see where the Colonel had drilled his respect for firearms into his daughter. She was a responsible shooter.

With her last magazine empty, she brought the target back and the three of us looked it over together.

"Nice groups," I told her.

"You think so? That's Dad. Taught me how to shoot and how to sleep around."

Natalie raised an eyebrow.

"Your placement is better than mine," I told Erika.

"Really?"

"Oh, yeah."

"It is," Natalie confirmed.

Erika looked at the target in her hands, then at us. "You're lying."

Natalie shook her head.

"You guys shoot. Then we'll compare." She stepped

back to watch as I put up a clean target and held the button down until it hung roughly seven yards away. The targets could be automatically sent out to the fixed distances of ten, twenty-five, and fifty yards, but since those fixed ranges weren't that relevant to my or Natalie's work, I didn't drill at them, and neither did she. Most engagements take place at seven yards or closer, and that's what I needed to be prepared for if things ever went so bad on a job I had to start shooting.

But if things ever got that bad, the odds were I wouldn't even get my weapon out.

Natalie and I took turns, and between us we fired off almost two hundred rounds in about an hour, doing our drills. We started with double-taps, firing two shots as fast as possible, then switched to vertical tracking where we would work our way up the target. We'd start with the gun either in its holster or in the hands at what's called the low-ready position. Then we switched to one-hand drills, first the strong hand, then the weak one, firing off shots again and again, five or six from each presentation position in each drill, and changing the targets for the different exercises.

When the papers would come back, we'd hand them over to Erika, asking her to circle where we'd missed the shading with a pen from my bag. The Q targets we were using are the same ones the FBI utilizes for qualifying work, and the shaded portion on them represents the human central nervous system. Shots to different areas net different results. In vertical tracking, for instance, the goal is to draw a line up the body, starting at the abdomen, with the hope of taking out the CNS. If it works, the target goes down and doesn't get up again. End of problem. Shots to the pelvic girdle, on the other hand, are motor shots, used to cripple a target, to keep him or her from moving. Shots to the cardiovascular system are bleed-out shots. They'll put the target down, but it can take up to fifteen minutes, sometimes longer. They're not much use in our line of work.

Natalie and I finished up by sending a target out to

fifty yards and taking some aimed shots with our good ammunition. When I'd emptied the magazine, I started to pull the target back in, but Erika stopped me.

"Can I try?"

"Sure," I said. I reloaded the magazine, set the gun down, and stepped back.

She made certain her goggles were in place and took the weapon, sighted, and cracked off a shot, looking back my way almost immediately. "What happened?"

"Different ammunition. You were firing some cheap stuff before. Now you're firing the stuff we use at work. It's a faster bullet."

"Kicks more."

"Yeah."

She readjusted, then emptied the gun. I cleared the weapon, reloaded it with the good stuff, then put it back in my holster while Erika called the target back from downrange and took it off its hanger. The three of us spent another ten minutes cleaning up, picking up our spent brass and dropping it in the buckets that were left for collection purposes.

We returned the eyes and ears to Lonny, and Erika thanked him again.

"You had fun?" he asked her.

"It was great."

"You can bring her back anytime," he told us. "She's a good little shooter."

We waited for Dale in the lobby, with Erika going over the targets while Natalie and I kept watch.

"You were right," Erika told us. "I did group better. Why is that? You guys shoot more often than I do."

"You're taking more time and you're using the sights more," Natalie said. "When we shoot, we're just trying to hit the target as best we can. We don't worry about the placement."

"The emphasis is on speed," I said.

"Don't you worry about where you hit, though? I

mean, you shoot some bad guy, you want him to fall down."

"Exactly," Natalie said. "We want him to fall down as soon as possible. So if Atticus can get two shots in, even if one of them just takes out his shoulder, he's probably going to fall down and go boom."

"Fall down and go boom?"

"That's the professional term," Natalie said. "All of us pros use it." Then her radio went off.

"*Ready,*" Dale said.

"I want to ride with Natalie," Erika told me.

"You're sure?" I asked. It would mean I'd have to drive the Lexus, because Yossi couldn't do it and keep his hands free.

"Nothing personal," Erika said. "You're just way too fucking nervous."

"He's always nervous," Natalie said. "It's what he does."

"It's what I get paid to do," I said.

"Well, you can relax," Erika told me.

The SAS hit us twelve minutes later.

CHAPTER TWELVE

It was textbook perfect, a final exam A plus, and the only thing that saved our ass was that they didn't know there was a follow car.

We'd just cleared the transition on Third Avenue at Twenty-fourth, where the street changes from running two ways to only going one-way, north. They made their move in the flurry of cars trying to fill the new gap, coming up on either side, Gray on the left, Black on the right.

I caught the movement in the mirrors, radioed to Dale, saying, "Left and right."

"*Got it,*" he said.

The gray car shot past, its passenger window open, and in the mirror I saw revealed a van, dark blue, following it. Delivery van, I thought.

"Van."

"*Confirmed.*"

"Too much fucking traffic," Yossi said.

The window was open, I thought.

The two cars were already passing Dale as the van came parallel to me. I started to glance over when the brake lights flashed on the gray car, just a flicker of a foot on a pedal, and Yossi and I realized what was going on at the same time, but it was already too late, and all we could do was hold on as I started to brake.

Gray and Black had cleared the front of the Saab, the van coming along its left side. Then, perfectly synchronized, the two cars went right and left, slamming together and skidding into a stop that blocked all four lanes. It looked like a fender bender, it looked like two people trying to merge into the same lane at the same time. Dale's curse cracked over the radio, and he stomped on his brakes as we were coming to a stop. The Lexus skidded only slightly, and I felt the shoulder harness lock and hold me steady. The Saab slid farther, started to turn, but Dale got control of the skid, and they came to a halt just shy of the new roadblock. The van had braked also, and now was perfectly parallel with the Saab.

"It's a fucking stopper," Yossi said to me, already going into his gym bag.

Dale came over the radio, *"We're all right, we're all right—"*

Natalie's voice, saying, *"Fuck, oh, fuck, it's an ambush, we've got two men with MP5s, they're zeroed."*

"Don't move," I said.

"We're blocked on the left," she said.

"Don't fucking move!"

I saw Natalie shoving Erika down in the backseat. Other than that, both she and Dale were motionless. Beside me, Yossi was slamming the bolt back on his rifle. Then he began pulling spare magazines from the bag, stuffing them into his pockets.

Gray had turned in its collision with Black, so that the open window was now fronted toward the Saab. The driver was still seated, but I could see his weapon raised and steady, pointed at Dale. Gray was a white man, with curly black hair, but I couldn't make out his face.

From Black had emerged another man, also white, with brown hair tied in a ponytail, and he was edging along the side of his car to flank the Saab, his weapon leveled at Natalie.

Both men held submachine guns. Both men could hose the car with enough bullets to kill all three of its occupants. If either Dale or Natalie moved, tried to raise a weapon, it would be all over.

The side door of the van slid open, and over the radio, I heard Erika ask what was going on. Natalie silenced her.

Trouble came out of the van, sliding a gas mask over his face. He held a large canister in one hand with a hose that ran from the spout coiled in the other. Slung across his back was another MP5, and he had a pistol in the holster at his waist. Before the black rubber and plastic hid his expression, I saw the tic of his smile.

Over his shoulder, barely visible from my angle, was a fourth man, crouched, holding an automatic rifle steady on the Saab. The rifle looked like the same model Yossi had locked and loaded.

It was quiet, and I thought that Lexus made a very nice engine, that I could barely hear it, that I wasn't even certain we hadn't stalled out.

Ten seconds had passed, at the most. Behind us, in the stopped traffic, a couple of horns began sounding.

Whatever was in the canister, Trouble was going to pipe it into the Saab. Maybe tear gas, maybe pepper, it didn't matter. He'd just punch the needle through the seal around one of the windows, fill the car, and then, with Natalie and Dale out of the way, grab Erika and go.

"*They're going to gas us out,*" Natalie said. "*They're going to gas us.*" She sounded very calm, now, and I knew she was afraid.

"*Orders?*" Dale asked.

If they moved, they were dead.

Yossi shifted beside me.

"You have smoke?" I asked him, unfastening my seat belt. It would save me a second or two later, although I already knew I'd be paying for it.

Yossi nodded, and out of my peripheral vision, I saw his left hand open as he showed me the grenade.

"You know what to do?" My switchblade was in my coat pocket, and I got the knife out, held it tight in my hand.

"It's the only thing to do," he said.

Trouble was running one hand along the seam of the rear driver's side window, looking for a good spot.

"*Orders?*" Dale repeated.

Gray was steady and still. Black was edging closer to the Saab, his weapon canted to shoot down through the tinted windows.

Yossi had pulled the pin on the grenade. "See you on the other side."

Trouble was raising the needle to punch the seal.

We are going to die, I thought, moving the gearshift into first. The stick felt awkward under my palm, pressed against my knife.

"*Jesus, Atticus, what are our orders?*" Natalie asked.

"Now," I told Yossi, and he went, out the door, his rifle in one hand, throwing the grenade forward in the other, and I stomped on the gas, came off the clutch. "Brace for impact," I told the radio.

It took perhaps four seconds to cover the distance between myself and the Saab, and it was eternal, and I heard the shots, heard Natalie saying, Oh, fuck me, heard Dale shouting for everyone to hold on. Yossi was shooting somewhere behind me, firing his first volley at Gray, five shots that cracked back-to-back, and Black was breaking for cover, diving over the hood of his car. From the van, the man covering Trouble's back got off one shot, and a window in the Lexus broke, glass dancing onto the upholstery.

Stupid Things You Think When the Adrenaline Dumps #92: I hope Natalie's insured.

Then I rammed the back of the Saab.

The cars met with a crunch of metal, and the inertia went straight to me, throwing me forward, and just before I hit the dash, the airbag caught me, threw me back. My left knee hit the console and I thought it was louder than the sound of the metal twisting, of the glass breaking, of the shots. The windshield shattered, chunks of safety glass raining down as the hood buckled, and my head was aching, my neck sore, my left hand throbbing from deep in the bone. For a horrible second, I had no idea where I was, what I needed to do.

The smell of the smoke caught me, sweet in the throat, and I saw that we were through. Yossi's grenade was spilling a gray cloud out around the Saab.

Somehow, I'd held on to the knife. I popped the blade, then drove it into the bottom of the airbag, feeling the balloon collapse. I hit the switch again, put the blade away, and rolled out of the car.

The collision had spun both the gray and black cars almost 180 degrees. It was less than ten feet to the back of the Saab, and I broke cover and ran for it, hearing shots behind me. Each step with my left leg felt like my knee rested on splinters. To my right, on the ground, I could see Black, blood running from his head. His car must have hit him when the collision came, and all I thought was, good, maybe he'll stay down. Behind him, on the sidewalk, I could see people hiding in doorways, behind cars, trying to remain safe while trying to see what was happening before them.

I went down at the back of the car, drawing my gun and turning again to face the van. Yossi was firing another volley and Trouble had gone for cover inside the vehicle. The Cover Man with the rifle was returning fire, and I opened up with my pistol, trying to suppress.

It worked. The Cover Man pulled back, and Yossi dropped the magazine from his gun onto the ground, slapped in a replacement, and then began working his way toward me in a running crouch. I emptied my clip at the van, pulled back against the side of the Saab, and reloaded. I only had one spare left.

Yossi was crossing the line made by Gray and Black when the Cover Man ducked out of the van and lay down another return burst. He was firing on automatic, and the burst scattered off the wrecked Lexus as Yossi went past. I fired two double-taps as Yossi returned fire, and the Cover Man fell, and I saw that Yossi had gone down, too, and I was certain that both men were dead.

Then Yossi was scrambling to his feet again, blood running down his forehead, snapping shots at the van. On my left, I heard the side doors of the Saab open, Natalie shouting, "Get in, you bastard, get in!"

I waited until Yossi was inside, then followed, ending half on Natalie and facing the wrong way, out the rear window. Trouble was getting out of the van, and I saw him poke the Cover Man with his foot before Dale accelerated away, and the scene disappeared behind us in smoke.

Yossi was leaning low against his seat, reloading the rifle. Blood coursed down the side of his face, flowing heavily over his jaw, his neck, onto his white shirt. Erika had taken Dale's coat off the front seat and was applying it against Yossi's temple.

"Head for my place," Natalie told Dale, moving Erika out of the way to tend Yossi. She shot a glance over her shoulder my way, for confirmation, and I nodded, finished my reloading.

"No," Yossi said.

"We've had a strike," Natalie told him. "We can't go back to the primary location."

"We know his place," Yossi said. "We don't know yours. We know how to defend at the primary—"

"We're going to Natalie's," I said. "How's it look?"

"He got lucky," Natalie said. "A graze."

"Ricochet," Yossi said.

"He'll be all right?" Erika's voice was thick.

"I'll be fine, angel," Yossi told her. "I told you we'd shoot anyone who tried to hurt you."

Erika looked at me.

"He'll be fine," I assured her.

"Are you fine?" Erika asked me.

"I'm all right. Bumps and bruises, that's all."

"You want a hospital first?" Dale asked me.

"We secure the principal first," I said. "Then I'll take Yossi to the hospital."

"Confirmed."

I told Natalie, "When you get in, see if you can raise Bridgett, tell her what happened. Tell her we could use her help."

"I'll call the office, too," Natalie said. "See if I can get one or two of the guards on our roster to come over and assist."

"Good."

Everyone fell silent, then, with Dale driving quickly and carefully, and the four of us crammed into the backseat of the Saab, with the smell of blood, sweat, and gunpowder. The blood from Yossi's wound had slowed to a steady trickle. I was covered in a fine white powder, like sand, and I assumed it had come from the airbag. My index and middle fingers on my left hand were swollen, and already looked bruised, and I figured they were broken. My left knee felt like I'd rammed it into a brick wall.

Erika put her arms around me.

CHAPTER THIRTEEN

"What I don't like, see, is people shooting at each other on Third Avenue in broad daylight." Detective Third Grade Ellen Morgan was in her early thirties, five-eight at the most, with a leanness that made me think of a greyhound. Her hair was cut short and blunt, and she wore glasses with lenses so thin I wondered if she actually needed them. Her skin was the rich brown of dark beer.

I asked, "As opposed to shooting at each other in the dead of night?"

"Excuse me, do you think this is funny?"

"Sorry."

Morgan sat down in the chair opposite my end of the table. The interrogation room was NYPD-standard, probably built in the forties, and smelled of fear, cigarettes, Lysol. The mirror at the far end, behind her back, was smudged and dirty. I wondered who was watching us from the other side. Detective Morgan pulled a cigarette out of her pocket, lit it with a chrome

Zippo, all while consulting her notepad. By my watch, it was almost eight in the evening. Yossi and I had been in custody for almost three hours now.

"My attorney here yet?" I asked Morgan.

She didn't look up from her notes. "Not yet. You want to stop?"

I had waived my right to silence early; there was no sense in antagonizing Morgan and her partner. Our actions today had been defensible and, in my opinion, correct, but that didn't change the fact that shots had been exchanged in downtown, and somebody needed to be held accountable.

It also didn't change the fact that despite being certain I was in the clear, I was nervous as hell.

Morgan looked at me, and repeated, "Do you want to stop?" She kept it casual.

"No," I said. "Ask whatever you want."

We had hustled Erika inside at Natalie's place. I'd stuck around just long enough to make certain we were secure, before Natalie told me to get Yossi to the fucking hospital. I'd departed, driven the bullet-pocked and body-bent Saab over to Lenox Hill, and taken us both into the emergency room. Yossi had been lucid, but quiet.

It took over an hour before we were treated, I for my nasty bruises and two broken fingers, Yossi for his head wound. The doctor had wanted to put a cast on my arm, and I'd refused, forcing him to settle for a tape-up job with a metal splint. He'd had to do much the same on my knee, which was swollen, but functional.

Yossi didn't make it any easier on the man.

"What happened?" the doctor wanted to know.

"I was at a late lunch with clients," Yossi said. "You know the rich—they eat, they drink, they drink, and they drink some more. We were leaving the restaurant, there's a flight of stairs, and, well, all that snow and ice, whoops. Hell of a fall. Ouch." He turned his winning smile on. "Too many martinis."

The doctor sighed, nodded, and finished stitching up

the wound on Yossi's forehead. We left before the police arrived.

When we'd gotten back to the Saab, Yossi had pulled his cellular phone and handed it to me, saying, "You're in charge. The honor is yours."

I called the 13th Precinct, got a duty sergeant, and said, "A friend and I were involved in the shoot-out on Third Avenue around Twenty-fourth this afternoon. We'd like to come in and make a statement."

The duty sergeant could hardly contain his excitement, told me that would be great, and when could he expect us?

"Half an hour," I said, and hung up, dialed Natalie's apartment.

She answered after two rings, and I told her what we were going to do. "You'll need a lawyer," Natalie said.

"You're right." I gave her my attorney's number. "Call her and see if she's free for the evening."

"You make it sound like a date," Natalie said.

"They're going to hold us overnight, at the least. You have coverage?"

"Herrera from the office is here, and I touched base with Bridgett. She'll be over by eight. She wasn't happy."

"She's rarely happy," I said.

"I wouldn't know. Tell Yossi I'll have the house counsel meet you at the station. It's the One-Three, right?"

I handed the phone back to Yossi, and we got back into his Saab, with me once again driving. I went carefully, granting right of way, not taking chances. The drivetrain was off on the car, jarred by the collision, probably, and it handled like a drunk cat.

"You're going to have to get the car repaired," I told Yossi.

He was idly rubbing the gauze square that had been taped over his stitches. "No, no, no repairs. You owe me a new car."

For some reason, we both thought that was the funniest thing anyone had ever said, and we laughed for al-most two minutes, amused at the brilliance of the line. Then our laughter died, and we heard the road, and the traffic, and the engine, and all of the sounds were dis-tinct, as if set in relief against the rest of the world.

"Scared the hell out of me," Yossi finally said.

"Yes."

"How many did you count?"

"I only saw four, but there had to be one driving the van," I said. "Figure five."

"One went down."

"All right, four."

"Was that you or me?"

"I think it was you."

Yossi shut his eyes for a moment, and I saw him gri-mace. "Any of them that Moore fellow? Or the other one you saw?"

"Denny, and no. The one with the gas, though, I've seen him before." I tried to remember the faces, the bodies. "The gasser, he was the only one I recognized."

Yossi scratched the edge of the tape with his finger-nail.

"Stop picking," I snapped.

He pulled his hand back with a guilty grin. "It itches," Yossi said. "They split the brick. Five men for the hit."

"That's how it looked."

"Where were the other three? On surveillance?"

"It's possible. Or securing their safe house, or pre-paring the escape route."

"SAS works eight-man teams, right?"

"I think it depends on the mission."

Yossi sighed, looking out his window at the Datsun passing us. The driver was a woman, maybe in her thir-ties, pretty. "If they had all been there, we would have died."

"I know."

"I appreciate what you did."

"It's mutual."

He turned his head back. "Sure, yeah, but it's something I feel the need to say, you know?"

I knew, and we didn't say anything more until we reached the precinct house. We were booked, our weapons taken, and then two uniforms escorted us up to the detectives' squad room to wait. The detectives were busy, we were told, working a crime scene out on Third Avenue. After fifteen minutes, Yossi's attorney showed up, and the two of them went off with the only detective present to have their interview. Twenty minutes after that, the Special Victim Squad was summoned, and Detectives Morgan and Hower arrived to take control of our interviews.

Ellen Morgan asked, "Where's her parents?"

"I don't know where her mother is. Erika's father is in Maryland, at Johns Hopkins. He left a number with me."

Morgan looked at me patiently.

"It's at home," I told her.

She nodded and wrote something in her notepad. "And these men, the SAS, they were going to do what to her?"

"Looked like a kidnapping attempt to me," I said.

"Why?"

"I don't know."

"Her father's not active military anymore, is he? You said he'd retired."

"That's correct."

"I've been working a lot, so maybe I missed this," Morgan said apologetically, and flicked ash onto the table. She used her fingernail on the filter, and the sound it made was like a cockroach crossing a kitchen floor. "We're not suddenly at war with that Green and Pleasant Land, are we?"

"They're rogue, I already said."

"Yeah, you said they were a, uh, 'rogue brick,' that right?"

"That's what I was told."

"By her father?"

"Yes."

Morgan took a drag and left her cigarette hanging in the corner of her mouth. She gave me a good look, head to toe, then flipped her notebook shut, got up, and went out of the room, saying, "I'll be right back."

"Right back" took fifteen minutes, and according to my watch, brought us to eight-oh-eight at night. She returned with my attorney.

"I'd like five minutes alone with him, if that's all right," Miranda Glaser told Detective Morgan.

Detective Morgan gave her a huge smile, and shut the door behind her as she left.

"What'd you do this time?" Miranda asked me.

"Hi to you, too," I said.

She shook her head, sat down in the chair that Morgan had used, one hand waving at the smoke that still hung in the air. Miranda's in her early thirties, slender, with short black hair and smart brown eyes that today were blue. She was wearing an ivory-colored turtleneck and burgundy-colored corduroys, and it was the most casual I'd ever seen her.

"Nice contacts," I said. "Blue suits you."

"I like them."

"Where were you?"

"I had a date."

"Dressed like that? Cheap date."

Miranda gave me the finger. "Spill it, Kodiak."

I spilled and she listened, her chin resting on her hands, her elbows parked on the edge of the table. She has an eidetic memory, and I've heard her quote entire conversations verbatim weeks after they occurred, much to the chagrin of other, opposing, attorneys. I like Miranda. She's always done well by me.

When I had finished, she said, "Good, it's a positive defense. You acted within your rights and according to the law. I'll be right back."

I sat at the table and looked at my left hand, tried to

move the fingers experimentally. The metal of the splint caught the light, and I tried to bounce the reflection onto the observation mirror at the far wall.

This time I was only alone six minutes, and Miranda returned with both Morgan and Hower in tow. Standing beside Morgan, Hower looked like a giant albino, with straw-blond hair framing a bald patch on his scalp, and watery blue eyes. He had a good twenty years on his partner, as well as seventy pounds, minimum.

"You and Mr. Sella are going to spend the night in custody," Miranda told me. "I just spoke to his attorney and with the detectives, here, and we all agree you and Mr. Sella acted within your rights. The D.A. will probably see it that way, too. But you'll have to stay in custody until your arraignment tomorrow."

"And then?" I asked.

"You'll enter a not-guilty, it'll go to the Grand Jury, and the case will be dismissed, because the Grand Jury won't indict."

"Sounds good," I said.

"It is good," Morgan said flatly.

"I need to use a phone."

"I'll call Miss Trent," Miranda told me. "Just give me the number."

I told her the number and Miranda went off to use the phone. Morgan resumed her seat at the table, with Hower looking at his reflection in the glass. After she had lit another cigarette, Morgan said, "We called Johns Hopkins. They have no record of Colonel Douglas Wyatt being admitted. In fact, they told me they have no special AIDS project at all. Just standard treatment."

That rat-fuck son of a bitch, I thought.

I shrugged.

"I thought you said he was verbal?" Hower asked his partner, and his voice was deep enough to make the table vibrate.

"He was verbal. You're scaring him," Morgan said.

"He lied to me," I said. "That's all I can tell you."

"Why would he do that?"

"I don't know."

"Do you know anything at all?" Hower asked.

"I know that five men tried to kidnap the teenage girl I've been hired to protect. I know that we barely got away. I know that a whole lot of shots were fired."

Morgan checked her pad. "And one man was killed."

"That's how it looked."

"Which of you did it?"

"Haven't the foggiest," I said.

"CSU found blood spatter at the scene," Detective Hower said, stroking his bald spot. "But no body. They probably put him back in the van."

"Did you get anything off the cars?" I asked.

Morgan enjoyed a drag off her cigarette before deciding to answer. "Both were stolen within the last twenty-four hours."

I nodded. No surprise in that. "What now?"

"Like your lawyer said, you go to Central Booking."

Hower turned around and leaned back against the glass, putting both big hands in his pockets. "Your buddy is a pain in the ass," he said.

"Yossi?"

"Went on and on about how in any other country but this one, what happened on Third Avenue today wouldn't be an issue."

"He was joking," I said, hoping he had been.

Hower grunted. "He showed me the stitches in his head, said he got it from a ricochet, said that I should appreciate the fact that he was the only professional there. Apparently, Mr. Sella was doing the citizens of New York City a great service by only firing those special bullets of his, those dynamite noble—"

"Dynamit-Nobel," I said.

"Whatever the fuck they are. Says they're training rounds?"

"That's right."

"So I should be grateful he's only killing people with training rounds?"

"Well, it's a range thing," I said. "The bullet is pretty much spent after a hundred feet or so."

Hower used both hands on his bald spot, as if polishing it. "Oh! I get it. He was only killing people in the twenty-four-hundred block. He didn't have enough bang to hit the twenty-five."

"Something like that."

Miranda returned, and said, "We're all set."

Somehow or other, perhaps because we had taken responsibility for the shooting and had made it relatively easy on the cops, Yossi and I got to share a cell at Central Booking. We handed over all our personal belongings, but they let me keep my earrings, for some reason. We received receipts, and were brought to a moldy cell in a noisy hall, where the winter chill seemed to work its way through the floor and walls, despite the strained heating system.

"That Hower fellow, he just doesn't understand brilliance," Yossi said. "No one got hit by one of *my* ricochets." I watched him tear the gauze from his forehead, then wad the cotton and tape into a ball and toss it at me, saying, "Catch!"

I caught the bandage.

"Want to play catch?"

"You're a sick, sick individual," I said, and threw the bandage back to him. "And you need professional help."

Yossi laughed, and we played catch until bedtime.

We were arraigned together the next morning, standing in the criminal court with an attorney flanking both of us. Miranda was all business today, power suit in place, and we were run through the system efficiently and according to plan. The judge asked for the charge, Miranda and Yossi's attorney entered our pleas, the A.D.A. said that as far as his office was concerned, we weren't a risk to ourselves or the community, and we were told we could go home.

"I'll get in touch with you before the Grand Jury date," Miranda told me, and then disappeared with Yossi's attorney to chat up the A.D.A.

Yossi and I went back to Central Booking to retrieve our things, and we checked them carefully against the receipts. Nothing was missing, although the NYPD hadn't finished testing our weapons. The guns would stay at the ballistics lab until they were certain neither had been used in another shooting. We'd get them back eventually.

We walked outside together, into a clear and cold day, with a bright blue sky and sunlight that bounced from the melting snow. I felt filthy and stiff, my fingers throbbing in time with my heartbeat. Yossi didn't look much better. The blood around his stitches had dried black and hard.

"I'm going home, get cleaned up," he told me. "Meet you at Nat's?"

My watch said it was ten of ten. "I'll see you there at two," I told him.

"You should shower. You smell."

"And you're a bouquet of roses."

Yossi grinned, clapped me hard and painfully on the shoulder, and then bounded to the street, hailing a cab.

I went for a pay phone and called Natalie's place. Dale answered.

"We're out," I told him. "How's it there?"

"Locked down. Erika just woke up."

"How is she?"

He paused. "Quiet. I think yesterday spooked her but good."

"Did me, too."

"When can we expect you?"

"Give me three hours. I want to head home, get some clean clothes and something to eat. Yossi's already gone off to do the same."

"We'll be waiting."

The shower was lovely, the clean clothes were better, and the bagel and coffee I grabbed at the bodega were downright divine. I went back to my place to finish eating, and found the number Wyatt had given me before he left. I dialed it and waited.

After two rings, a voice came on saying, "Hardee's, can I help you?"

You rat-fuck son of a bitch, I thought once more.

"Hello?" the voice said. "Is anybody there?"

"Yeah. Is Doug Wyatt there?"

"I'll check, hold on."

I held, and it took a minute before the voice returned to my ear, saying, "No, sorry."

"What's your address?" I asked.

"We're off Belair Road at I-695. Take exit 32." He hung up.

I dialed again, making certain I got the number Wyatt had given me correct. Benefit of the doubt, you know.

After one ring, the same voice answered, and I hung up before he could offer to help me.

The Colonel had known I'd recognize the Baltimore area code. So instead of just giving me a fake number, he went to the trouble of finding me a real one.

Yet another why. And I was getting tired of not knowing any of the becauses.

I went to my room and took out my spare HK, giving it a once-over. I loaded it and two extra magazines, put the gun in my holster on my hip, and the clips in the pocket of my army jacket. Then I made my way to Natalie's apartment, where the rotund doorman recognized me and waved me through.

By my watch, it was a quarter of twelve when I knocked on the door.

No answer.

I knocked again, harder.

Still no answer.

I listened, and heard nothing.

The air smelled of smoke.

I tried the knob. The door was unlocked.

My stomach began shrinking, and I drew my weapon while letting the door swing open. Of all the possible reasons to worry, this was the worst.

The door should absolutely not be unlocked.

Natalie never would have left the door unlocked.

I listened for another half a minute, then took a breath and went through the doorway.

From outside, I heard the wind whistling against the glass doors. Wisps of smoke hung in the air, turning gently, and the smell of a cooking fire flowed into my nose, down my throat.

Smells like bacon, I thought.

"Natalie?"

The main room was empty and quiet. The doors onto the patio were closed. On the dining table by the kitchen entrance, place mats, glasses, and utensils were laid out. More smoke drifted from the kitchen.

I heard the footsteps coming from the hall, several sets, running. I turned, bringing my weapon up, thinking that I didn't want to be shooting again, that there had been enough of guns already.

Natalie came into the doorway, Dale right behind her, and a third man I'd seen at Sentinel. Herrera, I thought.

I managed not to fire. "What the hell is—"

"She bolted," Natalie said.

CHAPTER FOURTEEN

"She wanted to make us breakfast," Natalie told me. "She wanted to make breakfast, so I went to shower, and Corry was setting the table, and Dale was in the kitchen with her."

"Eggs," Dale said. "I was beating the eggs."

"She was cooking the bacon," Natalie said. "And either it happened by accident or she started it herself, but there was a grease fire."

The four of us were in the main room, Natalie seated on the couch, Dale standing by the patio doors, and Corry Herrera in the reading chair. Herrera was short, handsome, with straight black hair and quick eyes, dressed in black jeans and a brown sweater. His face had the lines of a man who likes to smile.

"She meant to do it," Dale said. "She shrieked, and I saw the flames, and I thought she was trying to beat them out. She grabbed a glass of water she had filled—she was thirsty—and tossed half of it on the fire before I could stop her. By that time Corry had come in, and he got her out of the kitchen, then came back in with me. It took us a minute to get the flames out, and Corry went back to get Erika, told me she was gone."

"The door was wide open," Corry Herrera said softly. "She must have run the moment I left her to go back into the kitchen. Took the stairs, probably went out the back."

Natalie's mouth was shut tight, and her eyes were on mine. Strands of wet hair stuck to her cheeks and neck. Still heavy with water, it made the color closer to brown than red.

"We checked the building," Dale said. "No sign of her. Asked the doorman if he'd seen her, nothing."

"She could be anywhere," Corry said.

I nodded, still watching Natalie, waiting for her to speak. The silence was spreading like oil.

She clenched her fists at her sides. "I fucked up," Natalie said.

I nodded again.

"What do you want to do?" Dale asked me.

"We have to find her," I said. "And in this city, that's going to be next to impossible."

"We can get police help."

"I'll call Morgan and Hower," I said. "They'll be delighted. Did anything happen while I was gone?"

"Like what?"

"Like a fight. Like somebody maybe did or said something to upset her."

"I think the gunfight yesterday was probably enough to upset anyone," Natalie shot back at me.

"So that's a no?"

"Correct."

"Not even when Bridgett was here?" I asked.

Dale said, "They tossed some insults back and forth."

"Like?"

"Erika made a comment about Bridgett's relationship with you. Bridgett hit back."

"How hard?"

There was a moment for memory, or decision, and then Corry answered. "Logan said that Erika ought to get over having tits, and try having a brain, instead."

"She got us, Atticus," Dale said. "There was nothing we could do to stop her. No way we could have seen it coming."

Corry Herrera leaned forward in his seat and asked, "Do you have any idea where she would go? Maybe home?"

"Not home," I said. "She knows it isn't safe."

"We have to contact her father," Natalie said.

"We can't. I don't know where he is."

"He gave you a contact number."

"It's bullshit. It's the number of a Hardee's in Baltimore. NYPD tried to reach him through Johns Hopkins, came up empty."

"Why the hell did he do that?" Dale asked.

"I don't know, and it doesn't matter right now. What matters is finding Erika. We've got a city of eight million some odd, and she could be anywhere in it with an SAS brick coming after her, hard."

"Maybe she left the city," Corry suggested. "Her parents are divorced, right? Maybe she's looking for mom."

"It's possible," I said. "Check your wallets, see if you're short cash."

Dale and Corry both went to where their coats were hung on the stand near the door, and Natalie went to her room. I felt the tension coming off her, bottled and rising. She didn't like being made a fool of, and I suspected she liked it even less in my presence.

Dale said, "Motherfuck."

"She tapped you?"

"Cleaned me out, almost one hundred and fifty bucks," he said. "I had change from the shopping. She left my cards and papers, though."

"One-fifty, she could catch a bus or train, even a short flight," Corry said.

"She's still in the city," Natalie said tersely. "She won't leave the city."

"How do you know?" I asked.

"She won't leave the city," she repeated, and then headed for her coat. "I'll start checking the immediate area, see if she just ducked into a park, anything like that. Dale and Corry can check the terminals." Though Natalie had said their names, she directed the last at me.

"Check Grand Central, first," I told them. "I may be wrong. She might have decided to try going back to Garrison after all."

I waited while everyone got ready, and then we stepped out of the apartment. Natalie locked up, and we went down to the lobby in a silent group. When we hit the street, we split.

"Watch your back," I told them.

After two tries, I found a pay phone that worked, and got ahold of Detective Morgan, told her what had happened.

"Jesus Christ," Morgan said. "I'll have some units head over, do a search of the area. We'll have to report this to the local precinct."

"I appreciate it."

"She ran? She wasn't taken?"

"Ran."

"Why?"

"Hell if I know," I said.

"We'll notify you if we find her," Morgan told me, and hung up.

I dropped another quarter and caught Yossi before he left his apartment. He listened to the rundown, made the appropriate noises of frustration and concern, and then said he'd come by Natalie's and give her a hand.

"I'll bet she's livid," Yossi said.

"Natalie? Livid might describe it."

"And how are you?"

"I feel sick," I said.

"Erika will be all right. She's a smart kid."

I dialed Bridgett next, got her at her desk, and she sounded good.

"Hey, it's me," I said.

"Hey, you! I've been sitting here, having lascivious thoughts and hoping you'd call. Wazzup?"

"Erika bolted."

"What are you talking about?"

"A little before noon," I said, and explained what had happened.

"Clever maneuver," Bridgett said when I'd finished. "Didn't think she had it in her."

"Yeah, I heard about that."

She caught the tone. "Oh, come on. You can't seriously be blaming me for her running off."

"No, I can't, and I don't, but I don't think it was bright to antagonize her."

"Me?" Bridgett said, and I heard her chair creaking over the phone, could picture her straightening in her seat. "That nymphet has the manners of a spoiled cat. She's going to claw at me, I'm going to claw back, stud."

"She's fifteen."

"And should therefore know better. Don't come down on me because she ran away from you."

"That a singular or a plural 'you'?"

"Take your pick."

I took a breath, watched traffic whiz past. This was getting us nowhere, and I didn't want to fight. What I wanted was to find Erika, and fast. Most of all, I wanted the lump in my gut to disappear.

I said, "Natalie, Dale, and Corry Herrera are all out looking for her. Yossi's on his way over. I'm going to start poking around, but the problem is there's no reference point, nowhere to start."

"The bondage scene." Bridgett said it immediately.

"You think she's looking for some action?"

"Jesus, relax, Atticus. The kid's into the scene, then

that's what she knows in the city. She'll go to a club. The entire principle of bondage is trust. She figures she's safe there.''

"That's a hell of an assumption," I said.

"It's the same assumption the SAS was making, you got to figure. Explains that guy with the knife." There was a moment's pause while she put something in her mouth. Probably a Life Saver. "That's where I'd look."

"The Strap," I said. "Can you lend a hand?"

She sucked on the candy in her mouth. "I'll meet you there at ten."

"I was hoping sooner."

"I can't sooner. I'm working."

"See you at ten, then."

"Good luck."

I hung up and it took a while, it took an hour of fruitless searching, with the panic in my gut rising, and no sign of Erika, before I realized that I was angry at Bridgett.

I wasn't sure why.

CHAPTER FIFTEEN

I was outside The Strap at a quarter to nine that night, alone. Our search party had reconvened at Natalie's apartment at seven to share results, and we'd each come up with the same nothing as everyone else had. Dale and Corry decided to drive to Garrison and check with the local police, just to be certain that Erika wasn't hiding at home, and after they left, Natalie got the idea to check the youth hostels in town. Yossi went with her. Everyone said they'd call me in the morning.

I'd gone home after that for food and some warmer clothes. The clear blue sky of the day had disappeared behind clouds even before sunset, and the temperature had taken a nosedive. I fixed myself a bowl of oatmeal, didn't eat it, put on my gun and my coat, and headed down to the street and started walking. After three blocks, it began to snow.

Jacob was working the door instead of the bar when I arrived, and he wouldn't let me in, saying, "Uh, no, Atticus. You've been banned. Burton's orders."

"I'll pay," I said. "Just like any other customer."

His face tightened in a pained expression, thinking, and I could see that Jacob wanted to let me in, but that he also wanted to keep his job. It was that last that did it for him, too, I think. After all, I'd been fired, so there was no question it couldn't happen to him.

Jacob shook his head. "Sorry, can't do it."

"Is Burton here?" I asked.

"He's up in the sound booth, setting up the tapes."

"Let me talk to him."

That he could do, and so Jacob turned and asked one of the cashiers at the door to fetch Burton, bring him down to the front. I backed off and waited beside the door, using the palm of my right hand to shield my glasses from the falling snow. There was a short line of people already waiting to get inside, most outfitted for light bondage and the rest dressed as if this was just another club, which, ultimately, I supposed it was. I saw a couple I recognized, a man and a woman who tended to play in a corner by themselves. A very pretty Hispanic woman with a small hoop through the left corner of her lower lip and wearing tight black leather pants gave me a careful sizing up, then a smile. She was wearing a bright orange quilted ski jacket, zipped, and was keeping her hands in her pockets for warmth. I tried to recall if I knew her or not. I didn't think so.

Burton stuck his head out the door. "What?"

"I need to get inside," I told him.

He folded his arms across his chest, and the gesture made me immediately think of Erika. Burton is an average-looking guy in all ways, and he dresses like a neat Connecticut preppy, pure WASP. You'd never know by looking at him that people paid Burton hundreds of dollars for the pleasure of being bound and beaten at his hands. Despite that, even Burton admits that his club is barely in the scene.

Burton surveyed me slowly, lingering on my swollen lip and splinted fingers before saying, "Absolutely not, Atticus."

"Will you hear me out?" I asked.

He nodded.

"A young woman I was taking care of ran away this afternoon. Her name is Erika. She's the girl that had the knife pulled on her last week, the night you fired me. She's got some hard people after her, one of them is the guy who pulled that knife."

"You think she's hiding here?" Burton asked, confused.

"No, but Bridgett thinks she's hiding in the scene, and there's a chance that somebody here might know Erika, maybe even know where she's gone. I just want to get inside and ask some questions. I'll be good, I promise."

Burton thought, putting his right thumbnail in his mouth and scraping it against his bottom teeth. Someone in the line greeted him—the Hispanic woman who had approved of my form, in fact—and he gave her a nod and smile, then stepped out of the doorway to get closer to me.

"You're putting me in a bad position," Burton said softly. "I believe you, I believe what you're saying, but I can't let you into the club, you've got to understand that."

"Why not?"

He put his hands together as if about to pray, pointing the steepled end in my direction. "I had a fight here a week ago. I had a man pull a knife on an employee *and* a customer. This is a sensitive scene, and I know you understand that. People were here that night, they saw what happened. How is it going to look if I let you back inside? They know you've been fired, they know why you've been fired. If I let you in, it looks like I'm going back on my word, that I'm not committed to protecting my clients."

"I think that puts more of the blame for the fight on my shoulders than I deserve," I said, carefully calm.

"It does. I know you didn't start it. But a knife came out in my establishment, was brandished openly, and that's the damage. If it's any consolation, I can assure you that neither the girl nor the guy who had the knife are in here tonight. They've been banned, too." He watched my reaction, hoping I understood. "I am sorry. It's not personal."

"I know." He was starting to head back in when I asked, "Will you let Bridie inside?"

When he smiled, he looked like a benevolent priest. "Yes, I'd let Bridgett inside."

It was almost ten-thirty when she arrived, and she was dressed for the scene, black jeans, black boots, and her biker jacket. Her top was black, too, but from the collar to the swell of her breasts was a thin mesh instead of solid fabric. It wasn't the cheap lace Erika had worn, more an expensive optical illusion, showing skin only if the light caught the cloth right. Bridgett's hair was pulled back, and she'd removed all of the studs from her ears, replacing each with surgical steel hoops. Her lipstick was burnt red.

"Cute," I said, and my anger came back as I said it.

"If I'm canvassing, I don't want to look out of place."

"Aren't you cold?"

"It's going to be hot inside."

"Burton won't let me in," I told her. "I'll wait out here."

"Where can I find you?"

"By the fire exit. I don't want to scare off business by standing out front."

"You can go home, you know."

"I'd prefer to wait here."

"This could take a while."

"I'll wait."

Bridgett dropped a red Life Saver in her mouth, then put the pack away in a jacket pocket. "Your choice. See you in a bit."

"Good luck," I said.

She headed past me and cut to the front of the line.

Before anyone could protest, Jacob had waved her through, and I watched her go out of sight, pushing through the black masking that had been hung inside the entrance to block the view.

I walked up to the alley and then turned left, going on until I reached the fire exit. Several cardboard boxes had been stacked by the Dumpster, and I discovered a couple that had yet to be touched by the snow. I experimented for a few minutes with placement, finally finding a way to stack them so they could hold my weight, and then sat down, putting my back to the wall.

The snow was falling more slowly, large and heavy flakes that floated like trim feathers. The ground had been clear and wet until now, but with this snowfall the dirty concrete and asphalt dissolved away under smooth fresh white. It would be pitted and brown by morning, polluted, frozen ice rather than soft powder. The temperature felt in the mid-twenties.

Through the wall I could feel more than hear the thud of the music playing in the club. I couldn't recognize the tune. There was noise from the street, traffic and voices, people coming and going. At the far end of the alley, yellow cabs were going in and out of their depot. I could hear the sounds of the cars being washed as cabbies went off shift. The cars would remain clean for maybe thirty seconds after they hit the street.

A hard winter, I thought.

Near eleven a group of people came through the fire exit, five of them, men and women, club-hoppers rather than scene players. They ignored me and moved like a rugby scrum toward Tenth Avenue, discussing where they should head next. One of them suggested his home, and that began a loud debate. They were out of earshot before reaching a conclusion.

A homeless man came my way forty minutes or so later. I gave him five dollars, and then he asked for my cardboard boxes. I handed them over, and he left happy.

That's me, Atticus Kodiak, harbinger of sweetness and light.

Bridgett came back out at seven after one, her arm around the waist of the Hispanic woman I'd seen earlier. Both were laughing, and I'd have thought that maybe both were drunk, too, but knew that wasn't possible. Burton's soda was potent, but not that potent.

"Atticus, this is Elana," Bridgett said, introducing me.

"Oh, so this is the guy," she said, grinning. "Elana Corres." She offered me her left hand. Her right remained around Bridgett's waist.

I took it and said hello. Corres was an attractive woman, and I put her close to my age, perhaps twenty-nine. Her hair was long and black, tied into a single braid that ran down her back. She had her orange ski jacket open, and aside from the leather pants, I could see she was wearing a black leather vest. The vest was short, showing cleavage at the top, and her navel at the bottom. She had a stud through her belly button, and I wondered if she knew that Bridgett wore a hoop through hers, too.

Elana Corres released my hand and then reached into an inside pocket, coming out with a long, thin cigar. Bridgett and she separated, and Elana took a double-bladed cutting tool from the same pocket, began to slice the end of the smoke.

Bridgett said, "Elana knows Erika."

"You do?"

Elana didn't look up from her work on the cigar. "In passing. Nice kid. Can't believe she's only fifteen."

"How do you know her?" I asked.

"Elana's a writer," Bridgett answered, leaning back against the wall. "Scribbles for a variety of magazines and journals, isn't that right?"

Elana blew on the cut end of her cigar. "I do all right,

cover the club scene for the *Free Press* and rags like that." She slid the cutter back in her pocket.

"And the *Voice*," Bridgett added.

"And the *Voice*." Elana lit up, rotating the cigar in her mouth until the end was going well. "I met Erika about a month ago, maybe," she said between puffs. "Kept seeing her at all these different clubs—Paddles, The Vault, Spankers—and we just started chatting one night. Smart girl. Real pretty."

"You take her home?" I asked, and that's when I was certain I was jealous.

Elana blew out smoke and laughed, stowing the lighter. Bridgett gave me a look that was more than a warning. I gave her one back that asked what was going on.

"No," Elana said. "I wasn't interested. She tried, though. She did try."

"You got another one of those?" Bridgett asked her.

Elana held up the cigar, then offered it to Bridgett, saying, "Certainly, pet."

Bridgett took it and began smoking, saying, "There's more. Tell him."

Elana took a second cigar out of her pocket, offering it to me. I shook my head, and she set to work on it, saying, "Well, Bridie says that you're also looking for some men, maybe men who have been lurking in clubs looking for—" She swung her head to look at Bridgett. "What is it you called her?"

"Lolita," Bridgett said, puffing.

"Like you've read Nabokov."

"Like you have."

"Bitch."

"Tramp."

Both of them laughed, and I shifted in the snow, glancing down to see it crushing beneath my shoes. My feet were cold.

"Yes, well," Elana said, glancing at me and acting more serious, "I haven't seen all of the men described, but I've seen one of them, I think. A Brit, about five feet ten, black hair, mean. Looks in his thirties?"

I nodded. Trouble.

"He was at Spankers two weeks ago, asking around about Lolita. Erika. Offering money. He got thrown out of the place."

"Have you seen him since then?" I asked.

She put the cigar in her mouth, saying, "Couple days ago he was at an underground club I sometimes hit, up in Harlem. Looked like his nose had been broken. He had modified the approach, but the vibe I got off him was that he was still on the prowl for your little girl."

"Anything else?"

Elana shook her head. *"Lo siento."*

"I may need you to talk to the police, just have you tell them what you've told me," I said. "Would you be able to do that?"

"Sure." She lit her cigar, looked over at Bridgett, who was watching us, puffing quietly. "Rose there knows where to find me."

I thought of the red flower on Bridgett's left calf, didn't say anything. I switched my eyes over to Bridgett. She suddenly seemed unhappy, and I realized she wasn't looking at either of us anymore, but past us, down the alley. Then her eyes came to me, then to Elana, focusing.

"Thanks," Bridgett said.

"It's no problem. I hope you two find her. Like I said, she's a smart kid. I liked her." Elana checked her watch. "I've got to go." She turned and offered me her hand again, saying, "Nice meeting you, Atticus."

"Thanks for your help."

She smiled and turned back to Bridgett, leaned in to give her a kiss on the cheek, holding her cigar at arm's length. "See you around. Don't be a stranger."

"You, too."

We both watched as Elana walked down toward Tenth Avenue. When she made the turn, Bridgett sighed, looking down at the cigar in her hand. She dropped it in the snow, crushed the end with the heel of her boot. The odor from the tobacco intensified, sour.

"We used to go out," she told me.

"So I'd gathered."

"The rose comment gave it away?"

"That, and the fact that she calls you Bridie."

"We stopped seeing each other in May," Bridgett said.

"How long had you been going out?"

"Eight months."

"Serious?"

"I was in love with her." Bridgett zipped up her jacket. "You want to go get a drink or a cup of joe?"

"I was thinking I'd go home."

She heard the contrariness in my voice. "Does it bother you?"

"It doesn't bother me that you were involved with another woman, if that's what you're asking," I said. "I'd have preferred to find out you were bi another way, though."

"Oh, yeah? How? A threesome? You, me, and Elana, maybe?"

I watched my breath float away before I said, "You could have told me."

"You never asked, Atticus."

"She the last person you were involved with?"

"Yeah. I went from her to you. I'm just batting a thousand so far, aren't I?"

"What?"

"Nothing. Never mind," Bridgett said. "You think I should have told you about her?"

I nodded, knowing that even that was a mistake.

"Right. Sorry. I didn't realize that we had to do postmortems of all our past liaisons before we could sleep together. I mean, you've been so forthcoming and all about your past, for fuck's sake."

I still didn't say anything.

"I'm going home," Bridgett said. "You know where

you can find me." She looked at me for a second longer, and when I didn't move or speak, she turned and went.

The streets were as near to empty as they get in Manhattan, and the few people who were out had come to enjoy the weather, walking alone or in couples, watching the snowfall. It was a beautiful night, the island lit by a canopy of light reflected from the falling flakes. It was the sort of night to look up and open your mouth and catch what you could, and to be happy you could catch anything at all. It was a good night for children and lovers.

I didn't look up.

When Bridgett had introduced Elana to me, it'd seemed that she was getting some payback for our argument the night before last, and for the way I'd sounded when she'd arrived at The Strap this night. It was petty, but no more than I had been, and it should have been something from which we could both recover. Yet it had only gotten worse. When they had come outside together, I'd felt an inner alarm go off, but now I couldn't tell if I was honestly jealous about Elana or not. I'd told Bridgett the truth. Elana could have been a purple Amish woodsmith, and I wouldn't have cared. Love has always seemed like love to me—gender, race, religion, none of those things matter when on that playing field.

But I was bothered and, again, vaguely scared, and it wasn't until I was coming down Twenty-eighth Street that I realized why. It wasn't that she hadn't told me about Elana; it was that I sensed she'd deliberately withheld the information.

And that's when the guilt hit but good, because what the fuck was I doing, if not the exact same thing?

My shoes were soaked through and my toes and fingers felt like marble when I unlocked the door to the building. I went to the stairs, heading up to the sound of my feet going squish-squeak-squish. A spineless sound, I decided. Apropos.

I reached the top, fourth floor, and turned, and there was a rustle from outside my door, someone standing up in the shadow, and I thought, it's the SAS. Idiot, Atticus, idiot, so busy, so concerned, and your mind was elsewhere, and now they've got you dead to rights, and you're screwed, you're absolutely screwed.

My gun was clearing the holster when I realized it was a woman who was coming toward me, and I stopped and I stared.

"Atticus?" The light hit her, and it wasn't Bridgett.

It wasn't Erika, either.

No, this time, it was the real thing, and I felt my stomach tighten, the anxiety ache giving way to a different kind of nervousness entirely.

"It's not too late for you to invite me in for a cup of coffee, is it?" Diana Wyatt asked. "I've been waiting out here all night."

CHAPTER SIXTEEN

She looked lovely, a little older perhaps, and that made her more attractive. She was forty-one now, and the lines at her eyes and mouth had gone a tad deeper, more definite, but the face was the same, the body the same, the voice the same. Just seeing her was enough to take my breath and hide it, leaving me speechless.

Or maybe that was just the surprise.

Either way, I just stood there, trying to cope, one hand on my gun, gun in its holster. Jaw on the floor.

Diana stopped, amused, and then her arms came up and around me in a hug and the top of her head grazed my chin. She smelled just the same, and all of it came back with that, the memories, the emotions, and I almost didn't hear her saying, "It's good to see you. God, I've missed you. It's so good to see you."

"Diana," I said.

She tilted her head up, her smile wonderful, her arms still around me. "Atticus," she said easily, and that was the way she always said my name when we were alone, no Colonel, no Erika, just her and me, like I was comfortable, and hers.

Then we would kiss, and even as I thought it, I felt her hand sliding up my back, going to my neck. I let her tug me down, and I put my lips against her cheek, caught the scent of her perfume. She accepted the change, turned her mouth away, let the kiss rest where I set it, and then she pulled back.

"Late night?" Diana asked. "It's nearly two-thirty."

"Have you been waiting out here long?"

"A couple of hours," she said. "I should have called first, but I wanted to surprise you."

"You did," I said.

She laughed, following me into the apartment as I unlocked the door and turned on lights. I stopped in the kitchen, saw that the indicator on my answering machine was blinking red. The apartment was quiet, and looked undisturbed. Snow fell past my window.

"Do you really want coffee?" I asked.

"I'd really like a drink," Diana said.

"I've got beer and some harder stuff, that's about it."

"Scotch?"

"I have scotch."

"Neat, please."

I fixed her a drink, and she took it with a thank you, then began looking around the apartment as I poured myself a glass. When she was out of the kitchen, I hit the play button on the answering machine, hoping the message was good news.

It was Bridgett.

"Hi. I guess you're not home, yet. Wanted to talk. I'll . . . I'll try to reach you later. Maybe tomorrow." The machine beeped and clicked, and erased the message.

I removed my coat and gun, then went with my drink to find Diana. She was standing in the living room, examining Rubin's painting.

"Gruesome," Diana Wyatt said.

"I suppose."

"Hold this?" She offered me the glass of scotch, and I took it, watched while she took off her coat and draped it carefully over the arm of the sofa. It was made from lamb's wool, navy-blue, and beneath it she wore a ribbed mock turtleneck top the color of Spanish moss, and light gray wool pants. Her belt was thin and black, and her shoes were black, too, leather ankle boots that looked soft and expensive.

Diana sat on the couch and after I'd handed her drink back, she asked, "Surprised?"

"Stunned," I said.

"Pleasantly, though?"

I nodded.

"I got into town this evening," Diana said. "Somewhere I'd heard you were in New York, so I looked and there was your name in the book. It's been five years?"

"Four."

"Still too long." She took another small sip from the glass, caught me looking at her left hand. Smiling again, she wiggled her bare fingers at me. "Free at last, free at last."

"I noticed."

"Two years now," Diana said. "That goatfucker fought it every step of the way. Got himself a fancy lawyer, stuck me with nothing, and left me with less. I barely won visitation rights." Her eyes narrowed when she spoke of the Colonel, and the hazel there darkened to brown. "He won't even let me see my own daughter."

I nodded, but kept quiet, still not quite believing it was her. My stomach was beginning to settle, but the anxiety and excitement remained, and it was awkward, trying to determine what I still felt.

I took a seat against the wall, and we went silent. Finally, Diana asked, "Nothing to say?"

"I'm trying. I'm really trying."

"You can keep staring at me. I don't mind."

I laughed and looked away, saw the X-wing lying in a corner.

"How's Rubin?" Diana asked. "Did you two ever link up again after the service?"

"Yeah, we did," I said. "He died three months ago."

That surprised her, and she was quiet for several seconds, trying to think of what to say. When she spoke, she used the traditional "I'm very sorry."

I nodded. "What brings you to New York?"

"Not the weather."

"No."

"Doug has AIDS," Diana said.

"I know."

"You've seen him?"

"We've been in contact."

"I've been tested," she said quickly. "I'm clean."

"I'm glad to hear it."

"Not like I had much chance to get it from him. The last time he and I made love, Reagan was in his first term." The bitterness was sharp in her voice. "The son of a bitch deserves it. How long do you give him?"

"I don't know. He's not well. Maybe six months. Maybe more."

Diana almost smiled. "Then I'll finally get my daughter back."

"Is that why you're here?"

She looked surprised, but knocked it down. "I lied," Diana said. "Erika called me a couple days ago, said she was staying with you."

"Erika called you?"

Diana nodded.

"She told me she didn't know how to contact you," I said. "That she hadn't talked to you since the divorce."

"Then she lied, too," Diana explained. "Doug doesn't want her talking to me, Atticus. He's forbidden her from doing it, and you remember how he is when he gets in a rage. Erika called from his house once, while he was sleeping or out or something, and when the bill came, he discovered what she'd done. She told me he hit her. She's been calling from pay phones ever since. Is she here?"

"No," I said.

"Did she go back to Garrison?"

"What'd she say when she called you?" I asked.

She wanted me to answer first, but I kept quiet. Before the silence got entirely awkward, Diana said, "Just that she was staying with you while Doug went out of town and that everything was fine. I got off the phone and thought I'd fly out—I've been living in Chicago—and surprise the two of you. Finally have a chance to spend some time with my daughter, and maybe do some catching up with you. Bad idea?"

"You missed her," I said, thinking that somebody was lying, here. For the last three days, at least until this afternoon, Erika hadn't been alone long enough to make any calls, long distance or otherwise. She could have used the cellular I'd put in her room, but I doubted it; one of us would have heard her talking. It was just possible that she could have reached out to her mother after bolting from Natalie's, and perhaps, out of fear and with nowhere to go, that's what she had done. Diana could have rushed to catch the first flight available to come to her daughter's aid, but if that was the case, why was she here?

Just too much coincidence, Diana arriving the same day Erika ran away.

"Doug came and picked her up?" Diana asked.

"When did she call you?"

Diana looked at me, again wanting my answer first, and again I waited her out. "Yesterday evening," she said finally. "I flew out today after I got off work. Did she go back to Garrison with her father, Atticus?"

"She's staying at a friend's," I said.

"Do you have a number? I'd like to see her before Doug makes that impossible."

"I'll get it for you," I said, and headed back to the kitchen where I wrote a random number down on a pad. It wasn't much of a lie, but it would buy me enough time to think. The clock on the coffeemaker read twelve minutes past three. I doubted Diana would call to check tonight.

She followed me, carrying her coat. She put her empty glass in the sink and then took the sheet of paper from me, folding it precisely and putting it into her pocket.

"I'll call her tomorrow," Diana said. "We can plan something for the three of us."

"That'd be nice."

"It would," she said. "Time for bed?"

"I need to get some sleep."

"You look like it. What happened to your hand?"

"I got in a car accident."

Diana put a hand out to my face, slipped it down to the side of my neck. Her palm was warm. "I can stay," she said.

"I don't think you should."

"I've missed making love with you."

I shook my head, and after a second she removed her hand and grabbed her coat.

"I'll call you tomorrow," Diana said.

"Yes," I said. "You will."

CHAPTER SEVENTEEN

Sometime after four, I fell asleep. I was up again before seven.

It was still snowing.

After my walk-through, I made calls to Natalie, Yossi, and Dale. The calls were pretty much the same: no, I hadn't found her, and no, they hadn't either, and yes, we'd all keep looking. Natalie and Yossi were going to work Times Square, and Dale and Corry were going to try Port Authority. They said they'd call in the afternoon, after they met up again.

Good luck, I thought, knowing full well we wouldn't find Erika at any of those places.

I went down to the diner on the corner for breakfast. Diana would be calling before ten, I was certain, demanding to know what the hell I was playing at, and where her daughter was. I still didn't know what I would tell her. Gee, Di, great to see you, and by the way, until yesterday afternoon, I was protecting Erika from an SAS brick. Then she ran away. No, I have no idea where she is now. Yes, nice to see you, too.

I got myself a copy of the *Times*, ordered myself a bowl of oatmeal, and tried to clear my head over breakfast. I don't know how I got on the oatmeal kick; as a kid I'd hated the stuff, but the last few days, I'd been craving it. Maybe it had something to do with the change in the weather.

The bell over the door jingled, and I glanced up and saw Moore, Denny, and Knowles enter, all pulling off gloves and watch caps. The gloves and watch caps were black, but otherwise, they were dressed the same as when they'd given me a ride to the train station six days ago. They looked at me, and then Moore said something and the other two picked a booth against the wall so they could keep an eye on the door and on me. Moore came straight to my booth, smiling a greeting. I forced one out in return, then checked the street through the window. Traffic was moving normally. I didn't see the rest of the brick, but that meant nothing.

"Always sit with your back to a wall, do you?" Moore slid in on the vinyl seat, waved at the waiter, saying, "Coffee."

"What do you want?" I asked him.

"I was thinking breakfast. What's good?"

"I like their oatmeal."

"Porridge," he told the waiter, then explained, "oatmeal."

The waiter grunted.

Moore moved his cap and gloves from his hands into a pocket, then unzipped his anorak. I could see the edge of his gun in its holster, but if they had come to shoot, I'd have been dead already. In their booth, Denny and Knowles were examining the menu.

"What do you want, Sergeant?" I asked again.

"Did the Lady Wyatt visit you last night?"

"You're still watching my place?"

"Did she?"

"Where's Erika?"

"Don't you have her?" Moore asked. His smile was cheerful and condescending.

"Is she with you or not?"

"I don't have her."

"I don't think I believe you, Sergeant."

"Robert," he corrected. "You should. What did Diana tell you, mate?"

I ignored him, began looking at the sports page.

"Whatever she told you, ten to one she's lying, Atticus," Moore said. "I know you have a history with her, but if you're placing loyalty with that woman, it's a grand mistake. She ran out on her husband and her kid."

"She ran out on a miserable marriage," I said. "Colonel Wyatt was a rotten spouse, and I saw that first-hand."

"Every kid needs a mother."

"You should run for office," I told him. "Family values are very vogue right now, what with the millennium coming and all."

"I'm not on about the decline of western morality," Moore said. "I just want to know what she said to you and where she is."

"You didn't follow her when she left?"

"Let's say we had a run of bad luck and lost her, shall we?"

"That sucks, Robert. Sorry to hear it."

"Traffic in this city is a bitch."

I put the paper down. "Do you have Erika?"

"No."

The waiter came, set the bowl of oatmeal and coffee on the table. "Same check?"

"Sure," I said.

When the waiter had retreated, Moore grinned. "I like you, Atticus. You don't trust me, you don't even like me, and you're willing to front me breakfast."

"You're paying," I said, and went back to the paper.

He chuckled, and I heard him pouring sugar into his coffee, the clink of the spoon as he stirred. Moore asked, "You know what it is that I really like about you?"

"My ability to fire three rounds a minute in any weather?"

That earned a full-bore laugh, loud enough to draw attention. Both Denny and Knowles looked our way, and they raised their hands to me in greeting. I waved back. We were a polite bunch of killers, and Moore certainly didn't seem worried about being spotted with me.

"No, it's that you're a professional like me," Moore said easily, answering his own question. "You're still carrying the burdens of your rank, your honor, your sense of loyalty."

His eyes were on mine, crow's-feet crinkling with his smile. It seemed to me that if he thought I was so honorable and so loyal, he didn't know the full story about Diana. He certainly didn't know about Bridgett.

"But your loyalty's misplaced," he went on. "The Lady Diana don't deserve it. Come on, now, tell me what she said to you last night."

"Why is an SAS brick after Erika Wyatt?"

Moore sighed. "An SAS brick isn't after Erika Wyatt, Atticus. You've got to believe me. I mean little Erika no ill will. She's safe with me, as far as that goes. I've no interest in her whatsoever. It's her mother I'm concerned with."

"If you're so sweet on Erika, why'd you have some of your boys try to snatch her away from me and my people two days ago?"

"I didn't."

"Yes, you did, Robert. I know you did. I was there. I've got the broken fingers and the knee brace to prove it."

We stared at each other for a full fifteen seconds before he turned his head, looked out the window onto the snowy street. Denny and Knowles were both eating their breakfasts, shoveling food as if they were in a mess tent.

"I don't want to go toe-to-toe with you," Robert
Moore said. "I could take you, and I know that sure as
the sun rises, but it wouldn't be easy, and we could do
one another a lot of hurt before it was over. We don't
have to be at odds, mate. I'd prefer to work this out
amenably."

"I would have, too," I said. "But that passed when
five of your boys started shooting at me and mine."

"And if the boys who shot weren't mine at all? If
Erika is in absolutely no danger from me? If she's
safe?"

"Then I want to know who they were, and I want to
know where she is."

"What did Lady Di say to you?"

"Do you have Erika?"

"You tell me where Diana Wyatt is, you tell me what
she said to you, I'll give you an answer."

"No," I said. "I want Erika. That's all I want. I want
to know where she is, if she's all right, if she's safe. If
you've got her, I want her back. If you don't give her
back, I'll find a way to take her back. And until she's
with me I've got nothing more to say to you."

"Atticus—"

"I'm not finished," I said. "If you or any of your boys
harm her in any way, I will kill you."

"You know what you're saying?"

"I know perfectly what I'm saying. And who I'm saying it to."

"We don't have to do it this way," Moore said.

I folded the paper and slid it over to him, getting up.
"Thanks for breakfast. If you've got the time, there's a
nice article on A-12 about special-forces involvement in
Korea."

"Don't do this, Atticus."

"You have a good day, Robert."

While I was unlocking my door, the phone in the
kitchen started ringing. By the time I was inside and

reaching for the receiver, the answering machine had picked up, and when that happened, the caller disconnected. The indicator light was blinking rapidly, and I hit play, listened to the string of messages. Four of them, all from Diana, all wanting me to call her.

As the last message ended, the phone rang again.

"The number you gave me was wrong," Diana said. She didn't say hello. She sounded frustrated.

"Good morning, Diana. I know."

"Where's Erika? I want to talk to my daughter."

"We need to meet," I said.

"You lied to me last night, didn't you?" Diana asked in a hot rush. "You lied to me. Why'd you do that?"

"It's a long story. We meet, we can talk it over."

"I'm at the Bonnaventure," she said. "Registered as Diana Bourne. Come over."

"False name?" I asked.

"Maiden name."

"It'll be at least an hour, maybe more," I told her.

"Just get over here and tell me where my daughter is."

The Bonnaventure is off the Avenue of the Americas, near Rockefeller Plaza. From my apartment, it normally takes upward of fifteen minutes to get to the hotel, closer to thirty if you walk. I took two hours, foot, cab, train, and bus, until I was certain that none of Moore's company was dogging my trail. I didn't know why Moore wanted Diana so badly, but for once I felt I had the advantage, knew something that he didn't, and I wasn't about to blow it.

Big mistake.

It was noon when I reached the house phone and asked the operator for the room of Diana Bourne.

"What the hell kept you?" she asked.

"I wanted to make certain I wasn't followed. You want me to come up?"

"Room eleven thirty-three."

"Be right there."

The snow I'd accumulated on my clothes and in my hair was melting by the time I reached the elevators. The bandage around my splint was soggy, and my broken fingers ached from the cold. My knee was acting up, too, irritated by all the running around I'd been doing. I unzipped my coat, unwrapped my scarf, and, on the eleventh floor, made my way to room 1133. The dark green carpet was spongy and my shoes sank with each step. The hall was empty.

I knocked and Diana said, "Atticus?"

"It's me."

"Come on in."

The room was nice as far as hotels go, and large, with a window that afforded a view of skyscrapers to the west, and then, through the cracks that were the streets, a shiny sliver of the Hudson River. The bathroom was on the left as I came in, a closet on the right, and both doors were shut. Diana stood at the foot of her bed, wearing a black sweater and ocean-blue corduroy pants, no makeup.

I shut the door, then headed into the room, and as I came around the corner of the bathroom, Trouble hit me in the stomach. The strike caught me completely, and I felt my air blow out my mouth and nose, my gorge rise even as he yanked me upright again. There was another one, the man with curly black hair who had driven the gray car. The skin on the right side of his neck was puckered and discolored, like a cancer had grown there once upon a time. As Trouble pulled me up, the other man put two more quick rights into my stomach, then a last left to my jaw.

Then there was disorientation and pain, and I felt hands on me, and heard Diana saying that was enough, that was more than enough, to leave me alone, and I was being dragged to my feet.

Trouble had my gun, and I watched while he worked the slide, ejected each bullet unspent onto the carpet.

When the gun was empty he tossed it at Diana, saying, "Hold on to that."

She caught the pistol, shoved it into the waistband of her pants, and then pulled her pretty sweater down over it.

"Hold him still, Glenn," Trouble said. "He's liable to elbow you something fierce."

Glenn pulled me up a little higher, his grip around my throat tight. I felt my breakfast spasm and try to climb out, but managed to keep it down. Somehow, my glasses had remained on my face.

Diana kept watching all of us, her arms folded across her chest, and her face drawn.

"Where's the girl, then?" Trouble asked me.

I didn't say anything, mostly because I didn't have the air required.

Trouble pointed to his nose. "I owe you for this, see. You tapped me, and I don't like that. You made me lose my knife, and I don't like that either. You slotted one of my boys, and I like that least of all. Now, where's the fucking girl?"

I wanted to sound defiant when I said, "Rot in hell." Instead, I sounded weak and tired.

Trouble looked at Glenn, and Glenn slammed my head against the wall. It hurt. A lot.

"What I will like, though," Trouble informed me, "is beating you bloody."

Clever guy, I thought.

"That's enough, Mark," Diana said.

Trouble looked back at her. "He knows where your kid is."

"Let me talk to him."

"He already lied to you once."

"He didn't know what was going on," Diana told him. "Let me talk to him. Let him go, Glenn."

I couldn't see Glenn's reaction, but Mark—Trouble—gave him a nod, and the pressure around my neck went away, and I tried to keep my feet, and instead fell forward, coughing. The oatmeal came up, too.

"You're not good," Mark told me. "You're not even lucky."

Very clever, I thought.

"Go. Let me talk to him," Diana repeated.

Mark cleared his throat and spat on the back of my head, then said, "Come on." Glenn followed him out the door.

My breath was coming back, now, and with it my orientation, and Diana gave me a hand, helped me up and around onto the far side of the queen-sized bed. Out the window, the city was pewter, snow falling like sugar from a shaker. It still felt as if Glenn had his hand around my throat. Diana went into the bathroom, and I heard her running water. I straightened my spectacles, got myself upright as she returned and handed me a glass.

"I'm sorry about that," Diana said. She went back to the bureau by the television, took my gun from her waistband. She considered what to do with it for a moment, finally dropping it next to the ice bucket.

I drank the water and looked at her. The sour taste melted slightly, but my throat still felt tight. I put the glass on the nightstand. The nightstand had a digital clock on it. Another nightstand, on the other side of the bed, had a telephone.

"They work for me," she said. "I hired them to get Erika away from her father. I guess he hired you to keep me from doing that."

"I guess so."

"He's brainwashed her, Atticus. He's made my own daughter hate me. This was my only choice."

"Bullshit," I said.

"They're rough men."

"Hadn't noticed." My stomach trembled with the water, but didn't rise.

"They were out of line. Sterritt's angry at you. He says you killed one of his partners. Mark gets rougher than the rest," Diana said, as if that would apologize for the beating, explain away the pain.

"You know who they are?" I asked.

Diana nodded.

"You know they're SAS?"

"Former, but yes." She was matter-of-fact about it, as if there was no difference between SAS and PTA.

"These are very bad men, Di. Hard men. These are not men you want near your daughter."

"This is the only option I have left."

I shook my head.

Diana frowned. "I don't like using them. If I had a choice, I wouldn't. But Doug's taken every other option away from me. He's turned my own daughter against me, made her hate me. I can't get close to her. And he's going to keep her until he dies, and that's torture. He hates me so much he's willing to torture Erika. This is the only way I can get her back."

I would have laughed, but didn't trust my stomach enough to try. "How's it going?"

"Poorly. Doug hired you to protect Erika, didn't he?"

I nodded.

"He figured it out, I don't know how, but he figured out that I had hired Sterritt and his people, so he hired you to protect Erika. You see what he's done? Now he's turned us—you and me—against each other. We're fighting each other."

"Maybe," I said. "How many men does Sterritt have?"

"Three others. He had four, but your people killed one of them." Diana pulled an attaché case from the floor and set it on the bureau, opening it. The case was black and elegant, and inside I could see a lot of money. She took a stack of bills and held them for me to see.

"This is ten thousand dollars," Diana said. "Unmarked, untraceable, tax-free legal tender." She dropped the bundle back into the case, but left it open, to make certain I could see.

"A lot of green."

"There's two hundred thousand dollars right here," she said. "I can get you another three hundred thousand in stones, diamonds and emeralds. You can have it all if you take me to my daughter."

"Where'd you get the money?" I asked.

"It's not important."

I looked down the hallway at the door to the room. Sterritt and Glenn were probably standing right outside, listening as best they could. At least two more men were lurking nearby, too. SAS-trained mercenaries. They would be very expensive. Very expensive indeed.

"I'm offering you five hundred thousand dollars, Atticus. It's money for nothing. You don't owe Doug anything. He split us up. It was you and me and Erika, and he destroyed that like he destroyed our marriage."

"If I don't tell you?" I asked. "What then? You hand me back to Sterritt and let him finish his beating?"

"They'll torture you."

"And you'd let them."

"I want my daughter back."

I rubbed my neck, felt the soreness around my Adam's apple. "I don't know where she is," I said.

Diana pushed air through her nose. "Don't lie to me again. You lied to me last night, don't do it again. I don't have time."

"I don't know where she is, Di," I said. "Honest to God. She ran away from me and my people yesterday afternoon."

"I don't believe you."

"Then we have a problem, because they won't either, and I don't fancy getting tortured."

Diana reached into the attaché case and came out this time with a gun. It was a small gun, a holdout weapon, exactly the kind of pistol designed to be concealed in a case full of money.

She pointed the gun at my head.

"Don't do that," I said. It looked like a Beretta. Maybe the Jetfire.

She cocked the gun.

I could feel my pulse throbbing in my broken fingers. "You're going to shoot me?" I asked.

"Atticus, tell me where you're keeping my daughter."
She adjusted her grip on the gun, supporting it with
both hands. In her fingers it looked ridiculously small.

"You're really going to shoot me, Di?"

"Goddammit, Atticus, you tell me where she is!"

"I don't know."

"Stop fucking lying to me!" She was almost screaming. "Damn you! Damn you, I will shoot you, do you
understand? I will shoot you if you don't tell me!"

"I don't know!" I shouted back. "Ask Moore. Maybe
he's got her."

That stopped her.

"She ran away from us, Di," I said. "She could be
anywhere."

"Moore?" The gun dipped slightly, but not enough to
keep me from being hit if she decided to fire.

"Sergeant Robert Moore, of the 22 SAS. Didn't your
pal Mark tell you about him? I assumed they were all
mates."

"Were you followed here?" she asked. She was very
pale.

"I don't know. I don't think so."

"You don't know?"

"Moore and a couple of his men leaned on me at
breakfast, wanted to know where you were."

Diana shouted, "Mark!"

The door opened immediately, and Sterritt came in,
Glenn right behind him. Both men had their Brownings
drawn.

"Moore's here," Diana told them. "He's got men
with him."

"Yeah, I know," Sterritt said, eyefucking me all the
while. "Knowles and some new brat. Looking for us."

"You *knew*?"

Sterritt nodded. "Figured they followed the paper.
It's all right, they're way behind us."

"You idiot," Diana snapped. "Moore had breakfast
with him this morning." She used the pistol to indicate
me. "He might have been followed."

They didn't like that. "We're fucking leaving now," Sterritt said. "Get the boys."

Glenn went to get the boys.

"You're packed?" Sterritt asked Diana.

"Yes."

"Kill him," Sterritt said.

"What?"

"You have to kill him. He can connect all of us. If he tells Moore or the Feds, it's all over."

"We can take him with us."

Sterritt grinned. "Nah, we can't. Too dangerous, isn't it? We've got to leave him here."

Diana began to shake her head.

"You don't fucking do it, I will," Sterritt said, and he started to bring the Browning in his hand up, and I figured if I was going to die, I'd rather go with my fingers in his skull, and I moved, and then there was the shot, and my legs cut out, as if they no longer existed. I hit the bed, saw the red stain from where my middle had hit the mattress, and then my knees were on the floor. I had swallowed fire, it was living inside me, starting to catch and spread, and I fell back, felt the glass of the window icy cold on my head.

Both of them were looking at me. Mark Sterritt had let his gun drop to his side, and his mouth was wide with a smile.

Diana still had the gun pointed at me.

I tried to say something and it felt as if Glenn had his hands at my throat once more. I tried to move, and my legs just didn't listen.

Diana took three steps to where I was propped against the wall, and with her right foot, she pushed me over, onto my back, and I was lying between the bed and the window, and I thought it was a strange grave.

"Good," I heard Sterritt saying. "Put one in his head and make damn sure."

She stepped in beside me and looked down, and her eyes were empty and far away. Her hair fell along her face, a light brown with yellow. It made her seem far away, too. Diana raised the gun once more, in both hands, and the barrel was over my right eye.

"Don't," I said.

Then she pulled the trigger.

◼ CHAPTER EIGHTEEN ◼

I waited, and it was the hardest thing I've ever done, and I don't know how much time I lost, I don't know when the pain made me go away, or when it made me come back.

They're gone now, I thought. Time to get up. Rise and shine.

I took a breath and tried to sit, and the world pirouetted, flipped, and any sense of direction or gravity went with the dance. The fire in my stomach burst into open flame, and I went back hard, gasping for air, suddenly queasy, and managed to turn before I started puking. The heaves were dry, and each one hurt my gut, and when the fit passed, I was fetal on my side, my hands around my abdomen, looking at where the last shot had gone.

The bullet hole in the carpet was neat and small. It didn't look like a hole that size could do much, really. Not much at all.

Except if Diana had put that hole in my head, I wouldn't be around to wonder at it.

Tears had filled my eyes, and I tried to wipe them away, saw my hands wet and red. My shirt and jeans were sodden with blood, and I realized I was lying in it, and that it was my own.

She'd hit once, though. She'd gut-shot me.

My legs hurt, muscle-sore, and now that I remembered, the pain in my abdomen cut loose, rolling free, and I stayed on my side, trying to keep control. My legs were shaking, and I could hear a keening that was either myself or the winter wind.

I hoped to God it was the wind.

I thought I could hear my blood falling.

All those shots. Someone will be here. Someone will come. It's a hotel, after all, and you never can get the privacy you want in a hotel.

I'm losing blood. I'm dying, here.

Moore's on his way. He'll find me. He and smiling young Trooper Denny and old Trooper Knowles, they'll find me.

Dead.

How professional of me. How honorable, how loyal. Yeah, I'm a fucking sterling troop, that's me. I'm doing what soldiers have always been trained to do. I'm dying.

The nightstand was above me, dark wood with shiny handles and a lamp on high that shone too bright. I reached, and the muscles in my belly tore, and I stopped reaching.

Where was the phone? Which nightstand? This one? The other one. The one on the other side of the bed.

Might as well be in Tahiti.

I'm bleeding, I thought.

Gut wounds are the worst. You die so slow, you die with a perforated bowel and shit filling your stomach, touring in your blood. For fuck's sake, if she had to shoot me, why couldn't she have done it right? Why couldn't she have shot me through the eye?

Oh.

Right.

For fuck's sake. Jesus, I sound like Bridie, here.

I realized I was talking out loud, and decided that that was good, that meant I was still conscious.

A muscle spasmed in my belly, and I brought my legs in tight, my arms back around, driving my teeth together to stay silent. The muscles stopped, and I relaxed again, wheezing for air.

Male.

Stupid bullshit asshole male.

Go ahead and scream. People will hear.

People will hear you and come.

I think I shouted for help.

I think time passed, and no one came.

Figure only four, five hundred feet to the top of the bed. The bedspread was a washed-out blue with randomly spaced squares of green on it. The pattern stung my eyes. I reached for it with my left, used it to pull myself sitting, making noise as I went up.

Nothing.

Go.

It took both hands and my legs to make it up on the bed, and my broken fingers hardly mattered, because I was crying by that time from the pain in my middle. I made it to the top, twisting as I sprawled across, trying to shield my stomach. Tears had fallen from my eyes onto my glasses, warping my vision.

Go.

Go, dammit. At least don't die on the bed. How will that look?

And then Dale will tell Bridie about Diana, and Bridie will think I was fucking Diana, that I didn't care. Bridie will think that I didn't care, and that I didn't trust her, and that I died that way.

Go for the phone, asshole. It's not that far away.

Nice mattress. Firm. Comfortable.

I'm bleeding all over the bedspread.

That'll never come out. They'll have to bill Di and Mark and Glenn. They'll have to bill Di and Mark and

Glenn and then they'll pay in diamonds and emeralds and other precious stones.

Go. Go go go go don't stop. Don't rest. Go.

It's actually quite nice here, on the bed.

No, it's not nice.

Quit fucking slacking and pull yourself to the other nightstand, and get the damn phone. Go on, get the phone.

Go.

The receiver slipped out of my hand when I pulled it from its cradle. There should have been noise when it banged against the nightstand, when it fell to the floor. I didn't hear any.

Oops.

Dropped it.

Just forget about the receiver for now, no, don't reach for it, don't stretch, you still have to dial. Dial first, then you get the receiver. Dialing first, receiving later.

Go, asshole.

Press zero. The one at the bottom, in the middle. Zero.

Okay.

Now, off the bed. Just roll off the bed.

Right.

Atticus, meet gravity. Gravity, meet Atticus.

Atticus, meet floor.

Go.

Get the receiver.

Go.

Say, "I've been shot and I don't want to die, please. I really don't want to die."

Stop.

CHAPTER NINETEEN

I came up for air to find Detectives Morgan and Hower waiting for me. She came to my side, leaning in. Her features were pleasantly fuzzy and kind, and then she slid my glasses on me, and her expression resolved, and I saw that it was neither of those things. Angry and tired, perhaps; not fuzzy, and most definitely not kind.

"You rotten little shit," Detective Morgan said, by way of greeting. "Ben, he's awake."

Hower looked down on me. "Howdy," he said, drawing it out. "How you doing, cowboy?"

I croaked at them. My throat was stripped raw, and my stomach felt full of broken glass. But all my fingers and toes seemed in place, even the broken ones. I decided I was alive.

"He probably wants water," Hower said. "The anesthetic dries you out."

"That so?" Morgan said, sounding genuinely curious.

"Absolutely. Plus the blood loss, this guy is probably

one desiccated husk of a citizen. That's why he's on two IVs, see, because he's so damn drained."

"Desiccated. That's a nice word."

"Yeah, I like it. It was on my calendar this morning."

They both looked down at me some more.

"You should offer him a cup of water, something like that," Hower told Morgan.

"Not my job. Besides, let him desiccate away, I don't give a fuck."

"Yeah, but if you want him to talk, he's going to need some sort of, ah, lubrication for his vocal cords."

"I doubt he's got anything to say."

"Well, you won't know until you ask him."

Morgan considered that, pursing her lips. She leaned in so she was directly over my face, and asked, "You got something to say to us?" Her voice seemed very loud.

I winced.

"See?" Hower said. "Give the poor cowboy some water."

"You do it. I don't want to have to touch him."

Hower buffed his bald spot, then moved to the stand beside the bed, poured water from the supplied pitcher into a plastic cup. Both the cup and the pitcher were an ugly brown. Hower took the cup, helped me sit, and put the drink in my hands. The tubes running from my IVs had been taped to my arms, and my splint had been removed and replaced with a new one, nice and shiny and tight, and it made my left hand all but useless. I had to support the cup from its bottom. There was a tightness in my gut, too, a strange soreness as if I had overextended my abdominals. I tried a swallow, felt the tepid water slide past a lump in my throat, or maybe it was a grapefruit.

"That better?" Hower asked.

I winced again.

"Thought you said he wanted to talk to us," Morgan said. "He's making faces, Ben. That's not verbal communication."

"You're the one who said he was verbal."

"So I was wrong. Shoot me."

I finished the water, and the grapefruit shrank to an orange. Hower took the cup, and I lay back again.

"Give him a second, Ellen," Hower said.

Ellen Morgan looked at her watch, then down at me. She said, "Okay, talk."

"Fuck you." My voice skidded over sandpaper before coming out.

"I'm going to kill him," Detective Morgan said to Detective Hower. "I'm going to kill him right here."

"Well, see, he's irritable, now. He got shot, after all."

"Oh, that's right. He got shot. I forgot. Funny how that happened, what with him and his friends running through my city, shooting at people in my streets, leaving bodies that have no papers or names for us to find."

I had started to drift during her monologue, but that hooked me and yanked me back. "Bodies?" I croaked.

"Just the one," Hower said. "John Doe, found in the back of a bullet-riddled van near the Riverside Parkway. That's what the papers called it, 'bullet-riddled.' Guy was shot with your buddy's fancy bullets. Those training rounds kill pretty good, don't they?"

"That's all?" I asked, getting anxious.

"Well, there could be more," Morgan said. "We just haven't found them yet."

Not Erika. Not Diana. Not the Colonel.

I closed my eyes.

"Where're you going?" Morgan snarled.

"He's tired. Let him sleep."

"Where am I?" I asked, my eyes still closed.

"Roosevelt," Hower said. "You came out of surgery four hours ago."

"How . . . ?"

"How, what?"

"He wants to know how he got here," Morgan said. "Isn't that right?"

I nodded. At least, I think I nodded.

"Apparently, you called the front desk at the Bonnaventure Hotel and asked for an ambulance."

I didn't remember doing it.

"Who is Diana Bourne?" Morgan asked.

"Her mother," I said. I had to say it twice, because the first time it didn't sound like English.

"Erika's mother?"

"Yes."

"Who shot you, Atticus?" Hower was doing the asking.

"Her mother."

"Erika's mother? The kid's mother?"

"Yes-s-s . . . I think so. . . ."

"Can you give us a description?"

I was fading fast. They had to ask me about her hair color three times, and finally, I felt my glasses being tugged off, and heard Morgan gripe, "Jesus, you're useless. Just heal, would you? We'll be back tomorrow."

I was out again before they left the room.

It was light when I opened my eyes again. An analog clock hung over the door, and it read either shortly after ten or eleven. I couldn't tell without my glasses. I tried to roll and reach for the nightstand, when I heard Bridgett ask, "What are you doing?"

She was seated in the far corner of the room, long legs extended, slouching in her jacket. She pushed herself up using the armrests, saying, "I'll get it. You after water?"

"My glasses," I said.

Bridgett handed my glasses to me, and once I'd taken them, moved her hand, pressing her fingertips against my forearm. It was a light touch, and it seemed to embarrass her, and by the time I'd put my spectacles on my face, she had started for the door.

"I'll call a nurse," she said.

"I think I'm okay."

"Yeah, you're great, but I'll get a nurse anyway."

The door squeaked shut, and I lay on my back, taking inventory. The IV in my left arm had been removed, and the bandage over the incision itched. I thought about scratching it, wondered how Yossi was doing with his stitches. My head felt much clearer, but it seemed there was nothing wrong with lying in bed, admiring the acoustic tile above me, maybe never moving ever again.

It took twelve minutes for Bridgett to return, leading a slender nurse in her fifties who reminded me of my grandmother. The nurse checked my chart while Bridgett went back to the chair in the corner and began popping Life Savers.

"Mr. Kodiak, I'm Renee. How are you feeling?"

"Sore."

Renee the nurse nodded. "Dr. Vollath will be by later on his rounds, and you can talk to him then. How's your head?"

"Sore."

Renee nodded again, apparently pleased by this response. When she checked the stitching in my belly I winced, but got my first look at the wound. The line of sutures was black. Renee checked my eyes, my blood pressure, my pulse, my breathing, and my orientation. After I had told her what year it was and the name of the President, she patted my arm.

"Get your rest." To Bridgett, she said, "Don't tire him out."

"Shucks," Bridgett said dryly, then waited for the door to close. Once it had, she said, "You stupid fucking idiot."

I fumbled around for the controls to the bed, raised myself up so I could get a better look at her. Bridgett had left the chair and was now pushing the curtains away from the window. The curtains were a bleached light blue. I couldn't see the view from the window.

"I'm not certain how to apologize for getting shot," I said. "It wasn't something I meant to do."

"Morgan and Hower, neither of them will tell me what's going on." She was keeping her voice low and level, and I knew her well enough to know she was very angry. "I asked Nat and Dale, and they don't know either. You were supposed to meet them yesterday afternoon, you never showed."

"I was detained."

"Oh, that's funny, that's really very funny," she said, turning to look at me. "Did those SAS fucks do this to you?"

"No . . . I don't think so."

She waited for an explanation.

"I need you to do something for me," I said.

"Who shot you?"

"Erika's mother. Diana."

"When did Diana enter the picture?"

"She was waiting for me when I got back from The Strap, night before last. I went to meet Diana yesterday at the hotel she was staying at, and it all went downhill from there."

"She shot you?"

"Yes."

"What the fuck were you thinking? Why didn't you have backup? Dale, or Natalie? Or, heaven forbid, even me?"

"I didn't think of it."

She snorted.

I went to rub my eyes, hit the lenses with my splint, realized there was no way I could use my left hand for the task, gave it up. "It looks like there are two teams of these SAS guys. One of them is working for Diana. She's paid them to get Erika away from the Colonel. She says her ex-husband has brainwashed their daughter into hating her, and this is the only way to save Erika. She said it was torture to permit Erika to live with the Colonel until he died."

"And hiring killers to kidnap the girl isn't?"

"She wasn't rational."

"No kidding. Two teams?"

"I think Moore's leading one, and the guy who pulled the knife, his name is Sterritt. Mark Sterritt. He's in charge of the other group. Sterritt's working for Diana."

"They're mercenaries? This woman hired mercenaries to grab her own kid?"

"She's got a lot of money, and I don't know how she got it, but she's willing to spend it. She offered me five hundred grand to take her to Erika."

Bridgett came over to the bed, sat on the end. She was careful not to touch me. "Colonel Bad Attitude knew this?"

"I think that's why he hired me."

She snorted. "That whole family needs to be put against a wall and shot."

"Not Erika."

"No, Lolita just needs therapy. A couple decades of it."

"She's a good kid," I said. "She's confused and she's being yanked from all sides. Cut her some slack."

Bridgett started to retort, but instead grabbed for the roll of Life Savers in her pocket. She put a red one in her mouth, and then, after a thought, took a second one, green, off the roll with her fingers and handed it to me.

"I need you to do something for me," I said again.

"Find Lolita?"

"Yes."

"Sort of figured that would be the next move."

"Get Natalie and Dale and everyone, tell them to give you a hand. Moore told me that he didn't want Erika, that he wouldn't hurt her. Even if he is telling the truth, if Sterritt and Diana get to Erika first, we'll probably never see her again. We need to find her."

Bridgett moved the red Life Saver around with her tongue, and I could see the shape pressed against her lips, then cheek. "All right. They're pretty steamed at you, too, you know. Natalie went ballistic."

"Probably angry she didn't get to do it herself," I said.

"Knock it off," Bridgett said. "We'll start searching

the scene tonight. It's going to be impossible to find her."

"Call your friend Elana. Maybe she'll help," I said.

"Maybe I will." Bridgett rose.

"Have fun."

She looked at me, angry, and I saw that I'd spiked a nerve. Before I could apologize, she was out of the room.

I slept until mid-afternoon, only to be awakened by the arrival of Dr. Vollath. He didn't look much older than I, sporting a neatly trimmed black beard that failed to make him look either older or more distinguished. He checked my chart, prodded my belly, listened to my chest, sighed deeply, and then explained why I was the luckiest man in Manhattan.

"You exercise, don't you? Sit-ups, run maybe?"

"Yes."

He nodded. "Saved your life. You were shot with a twenty-five, and it didn't have enough energy to break the muscle wall. If it had penetrated to the bowel we'd have lost you. Even if we hadn't, you'd have been fitted for a colostomy bag."

That was an image I didn't want to pursue. "So when can I go?"

"We want you to stay here another day or two, at least. After that you can go on home, get some rest. You're going to be muscle-sore for a while. If you don't push yourself, you should be fine."

"Can I leave tomorrow?"

"Two days," Dr. Vollath said. "And don't try to figure out how to leave sooner. We don't want any complications. You tear your bowel, you'll be in septic shock before the end of the week."

I promised I'd be a good patient, and Dr. Vollath told me not to lie to him, he knew a good patient when he saw one, and I clearly didn't qualify. He left, saying he'd be back to check on me sometime tomorrow.

Morgan and Hower returned just after dark to have me go over the story once more, and to bring me up to speed. There wasn't a lot to say, really, only that Erika was still missing, and that they had found no signs of her, her mother, or the men who'd worked me over. The detectives took their frustration with them when they went, and left me with my fear.

I tried calling Dale, then Natalie, then Yossi, and then, finally, Bridgett, and not one of them was home. I left messages, and no one called back.

All I could think was that I'd let Erika down, again, that she was gone, either on her own or with her mother. Neither option was good, and neither made it easy to lie still and memorize the holes in the acoustic tile while the night passed.

Once again, Erika was lost.

CHAPTER TWENTY

Neither Renee nor Dr. Vollath liked the fact that I was discharging myself.

"I knew you would do this." Vollath tugged at his beard, saddened by my predictability.

"I didn't want to disappoint you."

"You go easy. Nothing strenuous or you'll tear that wound open again."

"I'm going to go home and sleep," I told him.

"Liar," he said as Renee handed me a pile of forms to sign. When I had finished, Vollath added, "You have any seepage, any infection, you get your fanny back here, pronto."

"Pronto," I repeated. Now he was reminding me of my grandmother.

Renee gave me what was left of my clothes. My pants were intact and clean, having been sent through the hospital wash, but my coat was bloodstained. There was no sign of the shirt I'd been wearing. They'd probably cut it off me when I arrived in the ER.

Getting my shoes on proved difficult, and I took my
time with them, bending slowly. My abdomen was tight
and sore. I struggled with the shoelaces, too, my
splinted fingers getting in the way. It took me twenty
minutes to get everything on and tied, and I was zipping
up my coat when Bridgett came in, smelling like an
ashtray that someone had filled with beer. Her eyes
were puffy, and her black hair tangled, and she looked
very pale, very tired. She was wearing a T-shirt and
leather pants, both in her traditional black, and held her
jacket in one hand.

"I'll give you a ride home," she said, then turned on
her heel and left the room, returning in under a minute
with a wheelchair from the nurse's station.

I got into the chair carefully, and Bridgett pushed me
out of the room and down the hall to the elevator.
While we waited for the doors to open, she took a stub
of mint Life Savers from a coat pocket, crunched down
three of them. That was the closest we came to conversation.

When we reached the garage, Bridgett rolled me to
the side of the Porsche, took her keys from one of her
pockets, and the alarm chirped on the car. I tried to
stand, using the Porsche as support, and managed to
get upright without undue pain. She returned the
wheelchair to a rack by the elevator, and as she came
back, I asked, "You get any sleep?"

"No," Bridgett said. She opened my door, then
headed for hers while I climbed inside. Getting into the
seat wasn't one of my smoother performances, but I
was having less pain from the movement than I'd have
thought.

She buckled up, started the car, and pulled out. It
was snowing again, and the roads were dusted with
slush and powder.

"How you doing?" I asked.

"I spent all night looking for your little Lolita in
places where questions are unwelcome at best."
Bridgett didn't look at me when she answered. "Ten

clubs in twelve hours, wading through smoke, sweat, and drama, and I come back here to find you're on your way out the door. How do you think I'm doing? I haven't been home in days, I haven't been to sleep, I feel like shit, and I smell like the bottom of a very sleazy bar."

"I'm sorry."

"I don't want your damn apology. Not for that, at least." She floored the Porsche suddenly, scooting us around a moving van parked on an angle on Forty-second Street. The Porsche slid only slightly, shooting spray away from the sides of the car.

"Elana help you out?" I asked.

"Elana knows what Erika looks like. We don't have a photo of her, remember? Of course she helped me out."

"How are things with her?"

Bridgett stopped hard at a light. "The same. If you're worried about something happening between me and her, you can stop. We broke up."

"So you said."

The light changed, and she shifted up, racing past an NYPD sector car on the right. If she was afraid of getting a ticket, it didn't show. "She was cheating on me."

That muzzled me.

"We'd been going out eight months," Bridgett continued. "I thought we were serious about each other. And then I found out she'd been cheating on me for three of those eight. Maybe even longer. This was shortly after Da died, and I didn't take it well."

"Bridgett," I said. "I'm sorry."

"You and your damn apologies. I don't get involved lightly, do you understand that? Whatever is going on between us, however much of an asshole you've been or I've been, I've made a commitment here, and I'm not planning on bugging out."

My stomach hurt, and it wasn't the stitches, and I didn't open my stupid mouth again until we'd reached my apartment building and Bridgett had pulled the

Porsche into its slot. I watched her hand as she killed the engine, pulling the keys out and then rattling them in her palm.

"What you said yesterday. You're right. I was a stupid fucking idiot," I said.

"You've been that a lot lately."

"I had an affair with her, when I was in the Army. When I was working for her husband."

She used the mirror to look at my face. Her eyes were very blue, waiting.

"Wyatt was cheating on her. Everyone at the Pentagon knew it. It's one of the reasons he never rose past Colonel. The Army likes their officers to be good family folk, and Wyatt didn't even pretend."

"So you figured it was all right to jump on that train?"

"He used to go out, pick up women. I'd try to cover him, and it just wasn't possible. I told him what I thought and he told me to leave him the fuck alone, I was getting in the way of his fun. So I ended up at his house, watching Diana and Erika. That's how it happened."

She kept silent. Nothing changed in her eyes.

"I was twenty-three, twenty-four, and I thought I was in love. After six months Wyatt found out, and I got transferred. Overseas for a while, then to the CID."

"You ever see her again?"

"Four days ago was the first time I'd seen her since then."

She looked away from me, from the mirror, rattling the keys in her palm. "Love."

"At the time."

"When she was at your door the night I introduced you to Elana, did you invite her in?"

"Yes."

"Did you sleep with her?"

"No."

Bridgett looked at the keys in her hand. "So," she said.

"Yeah."

She got out of the car, and after a time, I did, too. She came around to the passenger's side, leaned against the car's body.

"I should have told you about Diana earlier," I said. "I should have told you when Erika first showed up."

"Maybe." Her voice was hard to hear. "I didn't tell you about Elana."

"It's not the same."

"Sure it is. We both have secrets. It's a question of trusting one another enough to share them," Bridgett said. "Let's get you upstairs and back into bed. You shouldn't be up and around yet."

"We need to find Erika."

"We've got nowhere to go until night falls. The clubs are all closed."

"We're past this?" I asked.

She let her breath out in a little hiss. "Do you want to be?"

"Yes."

"Then we're past this. Now you should kiss me."

So I kissed her.

We slept half of the daylight away, wrapped side by side for warmth. I woke twice briefly, each time surprised Bridgett was still beside me, and the second time my fear for Erika was so strong I couldn't get back to sleep. I'd dreamt about her, I realized, and as I worked myself upright and out of bed, pulling my glasses on, I remembered that in my dream, Erika had died.

I had turned on the heat and started making tea when Bridgett emerged from the bedroom. She was in her underwear and T-shirt, and I was about to ask if she was cold, when the intercom buzzed. She was nearer the grille than I, and so she turned and punched the button and asked, "What?"

The Colonel's voice came through the grille, demanding that we let him inside.

"You're supposed to be looking for my daughter, not fucking your whore." Colonel Wyatt pushed past me before I could respond, and that was just as well, because AIDS or no, I believe I would have punched him had he stopped moving.

I shut and locked the front door, followed him into the kitchen where Bridgett was fixing herself a mug of tea at the counter. She had pulled on her leather pants, and the Colonel took a seat at the table, looking her over. "I'll take one of those, sweetheart."

She smiled benignly at him and began fixing another cup of tea while I asked, "Where the hell have you been?"

Colonel Wyatt began unwrapping the scarf from around his neck. "Chicago. Baltimore." He heaped the scarf on the table, still watching Bridgett. "Like I said before, Sergeant, you've got taste."

"He means you," I told Bridgett.

"Go figure," she said, turning to offer me the mug of tea she'd finished preparing. To Wyatt, she said, "I'm looking forward to the day you finally die." Her smile was still in place.

Wyatt searched for a retort, failed, and went to the standard backup. "Fuck you."

Bridgett pouted her lips like a little girl. Then she laughed at him.

Wyatt turned to me and said, "So the bitch shot you." His voice was reedier than before. The wet weather was probably wreaking havoc on his system.

"If you mean Diana, yes."

To Bridgett, he said, "He was fucking my wife. You know that?"

Bridgett nodded.

He looked surprised that I'd ruined his surprise. "Watch yourself. He'll fuck you over, too."

"Why didn't you tell me where you were going?" I asked the Colonel.

"Because I was looking for Diana, dipshit. You're fine?"

"I got lucky."

"Purple Heart." He sounded disgusted.

"Erika's gone," I said. "She ran away."

"I know."

"How?"

"You're a fucking moron, Sergeant. Moore has her. She's all right."

"Moore's working for you?" Bridgett asked.

"With me. He's got his own agenda."

"You should have told me what was going on," I said.

"If I had told you my ex-wife—your ex-fuck—had hired mercs to snatch my daughter, would you have believed me? Until that two-faced cunt tried to cap your ass, you were still in love with her." He turned his head down to the floor and coughed, covering his mouth.

I looked at Bridgett. She was staring at the top of Wyatt's bent head, mouth curled in disgust.

When the fit had passed, the Colonel wiped his hands on his scarf, but said nothing.

"I want an explanation," I said.

"Of what, Sergeant?"

"Diana shouldn't be hiring mercs, Colonel. She shouldn't know how to contact them, let alone afford them. There's an SAS brick running around downtown, and it looks like you and Diana are right in the middle of it. What's really going on here?"

He rasped air. "What makes you think I know?"

Bridgett laughed curtly. "You are *such* an asshole."

Wyatt stabbed a finger at Bridgett. "She doesn't need to hear this."

"Yes, she does," I said.

Bridgett leaned back against the counter and looked satisfied.

He scratched at the corner of his mouth with a fingernail, deciding. Then he grunted. "Maybe five years before you came on at the Pentagon, I put together an

intelligence op with some boys from the SAS. Moore
was one of them. This was just after I'd started as the
PAOFET—"

"PAOFET?" Bridgett asked.

"President's Advisor on Far East Terrorism," Wyatt
and I said at once.

"Ah."

"Can I continue?" Wyatt asked her.

"If you've got the air, be my guest."

The Colonel grunted again, eyes cold. "There was a
need to gather hard intelligence on terrorist groups in
the Far East. You know how terrorists are, they'll sell
their own dicks if the price is right. So Moore and his
brick handled recruitment, located contacts, offered
them pretty paychecks and whatever goodies got them
all hard, then brought them in and baby-sat during debriefing. All the contacts had to do was provide good
intel."

Wyatt had been PAOFET for several years before I'd
arrived at the Pentagon to protect him. That dated him
to the early eighties, after the failed attempt by Detachment Delta to rescue the hostages in Iran. One of the
things that failure had created was a military within the
military, an environment where Oliver North could ex-
ist, and where soldiers could take actions that the
public, and the Congress, never even heard whispered
about.

"Superblack," I said.

"Of course. Off the books. Entirely unauthorized. No
oversight committees, no receipts. No paper at all."

"Illegal."

He held out his right hand, tilted it from side to side
as if balancing scales. "It was off the books. We were
acting in the country's best interest."

"How in heaven's sweet name can you say that if the
country didn't know about it?" Bridgett asked.

He shot her a look that said women should be seen
and never heard. "You don't understand."

"I don't understand that arrogance," she agreed. "So clearly, I don't understand you."

"Is she going to shut up?" Wyatt asked me.

"Where'd you get the funding?" I asked him.

"Wherever we could, through a slush fund. Standard skimming, you know. It was an expensive op. We were handing out six, seven million dollars a year for a while. Not just cash. Some of these guys got paid in dope, weapons, cars. Whatever. You following?"

"Jesus," Bridgett muttered. The disgust was rolling off her like waves.

"I'm following," I told the Colonel. I was, too, and beginning to get nervous at the thought of where this road was going.

"Set all this up in the States, you understand. We couldn't keep the money and dope in a bank, and besides, we needed safe houses for debriefing, and so on. The SAS didn't have anybody they were willing to use at the start. They wanted to keep it as quiet as we did, and they didn't want to get hit by the shit if it went wrong. But I knew it wouldn't go wrong, you see?"

It was like being shot again, and Bridgett hit it as I did, and she said, "You used your wife?"

The Colonel cracked a smile that gave us both a good look at the thrush on his teeth and tongue. "Think about it. I was a full bird. I couldn't be seen hopping around, flying here and there, signing leases and contracts under false names. Would have been fucking unbecoming of an officer. But Diana was high speed."

"You used your own wife to set up a superblack intelligence operation," I said.

"Yeah." He was smug, either with the memory of his brilliance, or with our reactions. Probably with both. "She had travel clearance, could go anywhere, no questions asked, or, at least, no questions asked that couldn't be reasonably answered. Erika was a kid. All Diana had to do was leave her with a sitter and take the next flight to Switzerland. It took some work, but between Moore and myself, we turned her into a pretty

fine spook. She couriered for us, messages and mer-
chandise, set up the safe houses. We had places all
along the Eastern Seaboard. There was a great place in
Providence, right on the water. Always impressed the
ladies."

Bridgett muttered something I didn't catch, and Wyatt's smile grew.

"She set up your cache?" I asked.

"We had a place in Baltimore that we used," Wyatt
confirmed. "One of those high-tech operations where
the storage rooms move around underground."

"Diana knew where your slush fund was?" Bridgett
asked.

Colonel Wyatt nodded.

"And that's why you were in Baltimore," I said. "To
check on the cache."

The Colonel nodded again.

"And?"

"I'll get to it. Thing is, by the time you came on
board, Sergeant, the operation had been running nice
and smooth for a while. We weren't using Diana anymore. We didn't need her. So we cut her out."

I thought about Diana, at their home in Gaithersburg, alone while an eleven-year-old Erika was at
school, while her husband was at the Pentagon. How
had she felt knowing that the Colonel was bedding yet
another nameless woman in an apartment that Diana
herself had rented? Knowing she had been a convenient
tool, nothing more.

"Then we had a change of presidents," Wyatt went
on. "New administration, new agenda, and we shut the
whole thing down."

"But you kept the money," Bridgett said, and she
made certain the Colonel heard the contempt in her
voice.

"What the fuck was I supposed to do with it? Give it
back? Nobody fucking even knew it was gone. I figured
to hold on to it, and when I got sick, I used it to buy the

house. The rest is for Erika, to make sure she goes to college, gets the life she deserves."

It was clear, finally, the lies all falling away at last to reveal a tiny truth, hard and sharp.

"How much did she take?" I asked.

"Two million in cash," the Colonel said. "Another four million in gold and platinum. Left the dope and guns."

"Any gems?"

"No. You take a loss on the exchange. We stuck with metals."

"You're certain?"

"It was my fucking cache, of course I'm fucking certain. We never used stones. Why?"

"Curiosity," I said. She'd offered me gems, and showed me cash, and that meant either Diana had lied or she was converting the metal for transport. Even at roughly four hundred dollars an ounce, four million dollars in gold would be too heavy to move quickly or easily. "Does Moore know about the money?" I asked.

"Moore doesn't care. That's not why he's here. He's after Sterritt and the rest of those fucks. They were all the same brick, you see? Moore was Sterritt's sergeant."

"And that's how Diana knows Sterritt."

"Right."

"So Sterritt knows about the six million?"

"Probably."

"Why didn't you move it?" Bridgett asked.

Wyatt coughed instead of answering. This was a rough bout, and it made me remember Diana asking how long I thought her husband had left. Less than before, time forfeited by trips to Chicago and Baltimore, by coming here now.

"When your wife left, why didn't you empty the cache out, find a new location?"

"I made a mistake," the Colonel finally admitted. "I never figured she'd go there. I'd convinced myself that she'd forgotten she was ever part of the op."

Bridgett rolled her eyes at me, reeling from the Colonel's arrogance.

"Bit me in the ass. She's got me, now."

We went into silence, thinking. I thought about how Wyatt had destroyed Diana. I thought about how she knew where to get the money to fund her revenge. I heard a television snap on in the apartment below mine, the rumble of reproduced voices. "Why are you telling me this now?" I asked.

"I want you and your people to take over my daughter's protection," the Colonel said. "Free Moore up to resume his hunt."

"What about your wife?"

"I don't give a flying fuck about my wife."

Liar, I thought. "Have you explained this to Erika? That her mother has hired mercenaries to kidnap her?"

"No."

"Not at all?"

"Moore explained the situation to her."

"Jesus," I said, feeling disgusted.

"Will you do it?" the Colonel asked.

Something ugly reared inside me, opening its eyes. "You haven't thought about your daughter once in all of this, have you? Not once. You haven't stopped to consider Erika."

Wyatt began to growl a response, then choked. His face stayed bone-white, and he lurched from the chair, spat into the sink. Bridgett moved to one side, never taking her eyes from him.

"It's like it was in Gaithersburg," I said. "You and Diana still slicing pieces out of one another. Still using Erika as the sharp edge."

"No, not anymore," the Colonel said. "Not anymore. I've changed. That's what Di's trying to do, but it's not my game."

"Bullshit," I said.

He faced me, made certain I was looking in his eyes. "I was a rotten father, I admit that, but I've changed, Sergeant. My time's running out. I'm doing all this for

Erika, don't you see? The money was always for her, all of this is for her. I can't let her go with her mother."

"Hey, dumbfuck," Bridgett said. "You're dying, remember? What happens after you croak? What does your daughter do then? What if she wants to go with her mother then?"

"Then that's her choice. I just hope she'll choose better." The Colonel's voice was sour. "All that bitch had to do was wait, a year at the most, and Diana could have had Erika all to herself. But instead she does this, she buys mercs and fucking declares war. Well, I'm not going down without a fight."

The Battle for Erika. Not something they teach at West Point.

"You've got the whole story, now," Wyatt said, when I stayed silent. "Will you protect my daughter, let Moore take Sterritt down?"

I wished I could actually think about what he was asking me to do, that I could justify deliberating. But there was no decision to make, really. It didn't matter if the Colonel was telling me the truth, if I could trust him, if he had changed, if he did this for his daughter or for himself. At the core, I didn't care what he wanted, what Moore wanted. And what Diana wanted had nearly killed me.

"Where's Erika?" I asked.

Wyatt went back to the table for his scarf, saying, "Get your coat. I'll take you to her."

"No," I said. "You're going home. Give me the address and a phone number, I'll call Moore and tell him I'm coming over with my people, but you're going to stay the hell out of the way."

"I'm involved in this, Sergeant."

"You show up at the safe house, I'll have one of my people carry you all the way back to Garrison if I have to," I told him. "You're going to stay out of my way."

He stood by the table, holding his scarf, glaring at me. Then he reached into his pocket and pulled out a folded square of paper, which he threw on the table. "She's my wife. You can't cut me out."

"She *was* your wife. And I can and I will. You're sick, Colonel."

"Of course I'm sick. What sort of shithead observation is that?"

"We'll notify you if anything happens," I said.

Colonel Wyatt wheezed into his hands, his skin going papery. "I know what I'm doing, Sergeant."

"So do I," I said. "You're trying to get yourself killed, but you're not willing to take the responsibility for it. You never took responsibility for your actions. You're hoping the weather or maybe Sterritt will do it for you. You go home, or I won't take the job."

Color began to leach into the Colonel's cheeks, and he drew one ragged breath after another while we stood face-to-face and Bridgett watched. And then the Colonel shoved past me, to the door, and I watched him snap the locks back, yank on the handle. He stormed to the stairs, and I could hear his coughs echo down the hall as he disappeared.

Bridgett said, "You know he won't go home."

"I know," I said, and went to the phone to make the calls that would tell Natalie, Dale, and Yossi that we were back in business.

CHAPTER TWENTY-ONE

The safe house was off Christopher Street in the Village, a quiet block with quiet homes. Bridgett parked the Porsche around the corner, and together we walked back, each of us carrying one of the bags Erika had left at my apartment. It was shortly after three, and the snow that was falling was thin and light, abused by the wind, and hard to see in the fading light.

A short set of concrete steps led to the front door, a hardwood monster with a spyhole set high in its center. Windows onto the street were positioned on the left and right, the curtains drawn. The house looked empty.

"We the first to show?" Bridgett asked me.

"Dale and Natalie should've arrived here an hour ago." I'd reached each of them immediately after the Colonel had left my apartment, my calls dragging them from their rest. I'd told them where to go and who to see, asked them to contact Yossi and Corry. Then I'd called Moore.

"I'm coming in to take over the security," I told him.

"About bloody time," he said. "Don't be followed."

I'd taken the admonition to heart. Of all the people involved, I was the one most likely to be tailed. If there was any way to possibly help it, I wasn't going to be the man to lead Sterritt to Erika. Bridgett and I had left my apartment separately, I on foot and she in her car, each of us heading in our different directions, and after an hour we'd met up outside the main branch of the public library. We'd been clean then, but spent another thirty minutes making certain before coming the rest of the way to Christopher Street.

I rang the bell, and after he was certain it was me, Corry unlocked the door and let me inside. Dale stood at the far end of the hall, his weapon out, and he holstered it with a goofy grin, as if apologizing for being careful.

"Who's here?" I asked him.

"All of us but Yossi," Corry answered without looking away from the street.

"Moore?"

"He went out after we got here, to join the others. On the hunt." He shrugged.

"Where's Erika?"

"She's in her room," Dale said. "Napping. Nat's watching the door. I get the impression the kid hasn't been getting a lot of sleep."

"Show me around, then," I said.

Dale walked Bridgett and me through the house. Someone had done a good job of locking the place down, and the space was secure, although not a fortress. The furniture was mixed, with a butler's table that looked authentically antique, and a fair number of what could only be described as disposable pieces put together with a screwdriver and some white glue. The walls had movie posters tacked up, B films I'd never heard of, and, inexplicably, a poster from the last Cézanne exhibit at the Met. In the living room, someone had hung a picture of the centerfold from this year's *Sports Illustrated* swimsuit issue.

"That's lovely," Bridgett said, not meaning it.

"It was here when we arrived," Dale said. "One of Moore's boys must've put it up."

"Moore picked the place?" I asked, dropping Erika's bag on the couch. The room smelled of Chinese food and cigarettes. The ashtray on the coffee table had several butts in it, Dunhills.

"Through a rental agency, yeah," Dale confirmed. "He assured me there's no paper trail for the Bad Men to follow."

Bridgett took the pinup off the wall, and looked around. Not finding a trash can, she dropped it on the floor and nudged it under the couch with her toe.

"What does Nat think?" I asked.

"She likes it for the most part," Dale answered. "Thinks that the street's too quiet, and I agree with her there, but otherwise, we've got a nice view on all sides."

"Did Moore say when they'd be back?"

"Sometime tonight, depending." He showed us into the kitchen, offered us coffee. We each took a mug, and he said, "I'll go relieve Natalie and you guys can brief."

"I'll go," Bridgett said. "After all, you three are the security pros. I'm just a lowly P.I."

Dale shrugged and looked at me and I said, "Don't antagonize Erika. She's having a rough time."

"I'll be Emily Post," Bridgett told me.

I tried my coffee and wished I hadn't. It was industrial stuff, and I figured it had been sitting on the burner for most of the day. I dumped the mug down the drain and turned off the pot, began cleaning it out. "Has Erika said anything about her mother and father?" I asked Dale.

"Nothing at all. She doesn't know that Mrs. Wyatt shot you, either, FYI." He smiled softly. "We didn't want to scare her any more than she already is."

"When's Yossi coming in?"

"He was working at Sentinel today. Figure he'll be

here by six tonight. Natalie wants to send Corry home when Yossi comes on post."

"How's he working out?"

"Corry? He knows his stuff. Young, though."

"Pedigree?"

"Sentinel. Been with them about a year."

"One of Trent's," I said.

"One of Trent's what?" Natalie asked, coming into the room.

"We're talking about Corry," I said.

"Is there a problem?"

"I don't think so," Dale replied.

Natalie looked at me.

"I just asked how he's working out," I said.

"He knows his stuff. Dad trained him."

"Then there's no problem. Let's brief."

Dale propped himself against the wall by the oven, and Natalie remained standing, and we spent the next half hour talking about the situation as we knew it. Bridgett had relayed most of the information about the shooting already, and between what Wyatt had told me, and what Moore had told them, the picture was now pretty complete. Neither Natalie nor Dale had anything to say about my getting shot.

"Do you believe him?" Natalie asked me when I was done.

"Wyatt? I'm not sure. The superblack story is all too possible, and it does explain Diana's connection to Sterritt, Moore, and the money."

"But you don't believe Wyatt?"

"I think Wyatt's got his own agenda, and I'm afraid his daughter is incidental to it, at best."

"Special Agent Dude?" Dale suggested. He meant Scott Fowler.

Natalie almost smiled, then caught herself.

"Yeah," I said. "I'm thinking I'll reach out to him today, see what he thinks."

"You think Moore's going to be happy you're contacting the FBI?" Natalie asked.

"No," I said. "Neither will Wyatt."

"So you're going behind their backs."

"Our concern is Erika's safety. Everyone and everything else can go screw."

Natalie folded her arms across her chest, and considered before asking, "When?"

"I'll call Scott when we're done, see if he'll meet with me," I said. "How are we here?"

"Fine. I don't want to go lower than three guards at any time, though."

"I agree. Dale said you wanted to send Corry home?"

"He was up all last night, like the rest of us," Natalie said, "looking for Erika."

"When Erika wakes up, he can go."

"She's up already. She was getting into the shower when Bridgett relieved me."

"Then let Corry walk, have him back by ten tonight. That way one of you can get some sleep."

"I'll stay," Natalie said.

Dale shrugged. "No skin off my nose. I like sleep."

"There's one last thing," I said. "I need a gun."

They both looked at me as if I'd said I needed clean underwear. Dale asked, "What happened to yours?"

"I lost my backup when I got shot," I said.

"Any flavor in particular?"

"What have we got?"

Dale looked over at Natalie, and she pushed hair back behind her shoulders, sighing. "There's a Smith & Wesson in my bag," she said.

"Be right back," Dale said, and went to fetch the gun. When he went through the door back to the living room, I heard a snatch of voices, probably the television.

Natalie said, "Don't worry about Corry."

"I'm not. If you say he's good, he's good."

She pushed off from the counter, where she had been resting, and her expression was flat. "He is."

"I trust you."

Natalie thought that over, then headed out the door, saying, "I'll tell Corry he's free."

I made a fresh pot of coffee, thinking that while the stuff may be the water of life for the protective effort, Natalie ought to cut down a little. I trusted her absolutely. If she didn't believe me when I said as much, there was nothing I could do about it.

When the coffee began dripping, I made a call to the FBI offices in Manhattan, asking for Special Agent Fowler. I was told Fowler was out of the office for the day, but I could leave a message. I did so, asking that he call me as soon as he got a chance.

Erika was on the couch in the living room, her legs tucked beneath her, her backpack in her lap. Dale sat beside her, clicking bullets into a clip. Bridgett had pulled one of the chairs from the dining table by the far wall and was straddling it, watching both of them. The television against the wall had been tuned to a shopping network, and a middle-aged man was hawking food dehydrators from the screen. Erika looked fine, clean and healthy, wearing blue jeans and my sweatshirt. She finally looked her age, too; just a kid watching TV.

She saw me enter and knocked the backpack off her lap, hitting Dale with it, then popped off the couch as if she'd been sitting on springs. She didn't say anything at first, just came straight to me and then stopped short. She put her right hand out to touch me.

"You're okay?" she asked.

I looked over her to Bridgett, wondering if she had spilled the beans, and she made a slight shake of her head. "I'm all right," I told Erika.

"I was scared stiff about you."

"Is that why you ran from Natalie's place?"

That earned a nod.

"You scared us pretty good," I said.

"You fucking scared me first! I thought you were going to die, Atticus. And then Yossi got shot, and you were both in the car, and then . . ." She shook her head. "You scared me first."

"I know."

"Well, that's why I ran, okay?"

"How'd you find Moore?"

Erika went back to the couch slowly, tugging the sleeves of the sweatshirt down into her palms and balling her fists. "He told me something might happen, that these men were going to try to get me, maybe, and I thought he was just trying to scare me. He gave me a number and told me to call him if I got in trouble. So I called him after I left Natalie's apartment."

"When did you talk to him?"

Her look clearly questioned my intelligence. "They gave me a ride that day," Erika said. "You know? The day you were at the house when I got home?"

Dale slipped the full clip into the pistol on the coffee table, then held the loaded weapon out for me. I took it, put it into my holster. It was a double-action semi, no safety, just point and shoot. I wondered briefly how long I'd be able to hold on to this one.

"They're going to try for me again, aren't they?" Erika asked, watching me stow the gun.

"Maybe," Bridgett said.

"You're a rotten liar," Erika told her without turning her head. To me, she repeated, "They're going to try again."

"Yes," I said.

Erika sank back against the cushions of the couch, stared at the television screen, and didn't say anything more.

CHAPTER TWENTY-TWO

Yossi arrived at half past six. Bridgett headed home for a shower and a change of clothes, saying she'd be back by eight. Erika watched her departure closely, and I couldn't read her expression. As far as I'd observed, they'd had nothing to say to each other.

Neither Moore nor his men returned, and at seven I cut Dale loose, standing post by the door with Yossi while Natalie and Erika played Scrabble in the living room. We checked the windows, trying to stay aware of what was happening beyond our four walls. The stitches on Yossi's forehead had been cleaned up, and the line looked neat, the skin pink and healthy. I showed him my scar.

"Mine's better," he told me.

"Everything's a competition with you."

"I'm just saying, mine's better."

From the living room came the sound of something clattering onto the floor. Erika shouted, "Quit it!"

I told Yossi to stay put and went to find Erika on the

couch, knees drawn to her chest, Natalie in the chair opposite her looking stunned. The Scrabble board was facedown on the floor, tiles scattered as far as the wall.

"You're cheating," Erika said. Her breathing was fast, and she looked at Natalie as if she hated her.

"I'm not—"

"You're throwing the fucking game, you're fucking cheating. I don't want to play if you're going to fucking cheat."

Natalie looked at me, shaking her head slightly.

"Stand with Yossi," I told her.

Natalie left the room. Erika didn't move.

I waited a couple of seconds, then picked up the board and began collecting tiles. "What happened?"

"She was cheating. She was letting me win."

"How do you know?"

"She played 'tomb' and then she played 'tone' and there was only one square between them, and it was a triple-word-score."

"Were they legal?"

"Of course they were legal! But she knew I had an 's,' okay? She knew I had it and she set it up anyway!"

I dropped a handful of tiles into the draw bag. "Maybe she didn't realize what she'd given you."

"She knew."

I pulled the drawstring and shut the bag, then sat in the chair Natalie had used.

"I'm not stupid," Erika said through a clenched jaw. "I know what's going on."

"No, you're not stupid."

"Mom hired those men," Erika declared. "Because she wants me back."

"Yes."

"It's the same thing, see? Like I don't have a choice, like I can't make a decision on my own, like I don't *know*. It's the same thing as trying to make me spell 'tombstone,' like I can't handle myself, make my own fucking moves."

"It would have been a nice play," I said.

Erika swore.

"You don't want to go with your mother?" I asked.

"Do you?"

"No."

"Even if she wanted you back?"

"No," I said.

"Not even if she said she still loved you?"

"No."

Erika was silent.

Bridgett returned at seven after eight with a case of soda and six sandwiches from the deli near her place.

"Hey, slut," Erika said when Bridgett came in.

I tensed.

"Hey, brat," Bridgett responded.

Erika smiled, and it occurred to me then that neither of them meant what they had just said. Erika followed Bridgett into the kitchen, and I heard them trading insults, and then I heard them both laugh.

"What just happened?" I asked Natalie.

She answered with a look that said there were mysteries between women I'd never understand.

"You want to head home?" I asked her.

"I can stay," she replied.

"How long you been awake?"

"Since yesterday. I'm fine."

Yossi made clucking noises with his tongue. Natalie glared at him.

"I want you to go home," I told her. "Get some rest. Come back tomorrow around ten."

"I can stand."

"I know you can stand, but now's a good time to rest. Go home. Be fresh tomorrow."

Natalie wavered, and I was afraid she'd fight me on this, too, but then she nodded. "I'll be back at eight."

"Fine."

She scribbled Corry's number on a slip of paper, stuck her head into the kitchen to say good night, and then went to the door. Yossi and I covered her exit, waited until she was off the street, and then went back to post. After that, Erika and Bridgett came out of the kitchen, and all of us had sandwiches and soda. I put on more coffee after the meal, and Bridgett left Erika to watch television, following me into the kitchen where we snuck a kiss.

"Been a while since we did that," she said.

"At least ten hours," I said. "What's with you and Erika?"

"We're getting along a little better."

"So I see. Who called the truce?"

"When we got here this morning and I went to watch her room, she started snipping at me, so we had it out. I told her everything I didn't like about her, and she told me everything she didn't like about me. She thinks I'm a poseur, you know that?"

"She'd mentioned something to that effect."

Bridgett took a tin of Altoids out of her pocket, giving the container a shake. The mints rattled against the tin. "I'm a poseur and a fake, and I'm all attitude. The attitude bit I don't dispute." She opened the box and put four or five of the mints into her mouth.

"What'd you say about her?"

"That she was selfish, self-pitying, way too interested in her power as a sexual creature, and that if she was jealous of my relationship with you, too fucking bad, because she's fifteen and I'm not."

"And because of that you two are trading insults like endearments?"

"It's taken her all day to decide, but, what can I say? Honesty is the best policy."

Around nine Bridgett asked if Erika wanted to play Scrabble, and Erika said yes. Corry returned at ten, and we were about to discuss arrangements for the rest of the night when Yossi drew his pistol and said, "Car pulling up. Two exiting, driver still set."

Corry drew and moved without a word to cover at the end of the hall, and I pulled back to find Bridgett putting an arm around Erika.

"Where does she go?" Bridgett asked me.

"The bathroom."

"It's just Sergeant Moore," Erika protested.

I nodded and told Bridgett to take Erika to the bathroom anyway.

Corry was using a corner of the wall as a brace, setting up his shot with both hands, and I went past him, saw Yossi waiting off to the side, near one of the windows looking out. There was a pounding on the door, a clenched fist, rapid. Yossi held up a hand and I nodded, drew my gun, and went to the door, being careful to stay out of the line of sight from the spyhole. Whoever was outside probably couldn't see us inside, but if I blocked the light to the hole, he or she would know where I was standing. All it would take then would be a trigger pull.

The Smith & Wesson felt big, its butt thicker than I was used to. I held it in both hands, my splinted fingers only getting in the way. I really didn't want to have to shoot. Yossi was still watching me, waiting on my signal. Doors are funny things, and people universally treat them the same way. Ask a question from behind a closed one, and the responder will direct their answer straight to it.

"Who is it?" I asked.

"It's Moore, damn you. I've got Denny with me. Open up."

I nodded to Yossi, and he took the glance past the curtains.

"Fucking let us in, we're in a hurry."

Yossi nodded at me, lowered his gun.

I threw the locks back and stepped away, saying, "It's open."

The door swung inside, and Sergeant Robert Moore came in right after it, Trooper Denny on his heels. Outside, I could see the Cherokee parked at the curb, lights off, Knowles waiting behind the wheel. Denny bolted down the hall, ignoring Corry and his weapon. Moore turned to me, his features sharp with excitement. "We found the bastards," he said.

"Where?"

"They're staying at an apartment in TriBeCa, one of those short-term places. We're going to take them down." He said the last with a smile verging on glee.

"You're certain?"

"Wyatt did a recce, says that Diana and—"

I shook my head. "Wyatt?"

"Yeah, I don't know how he did it, but he found them, and gave me a call."

Denny came back, two large duffel bags slung over his shoulders. "All set, boss."

"Put it in the car," Moore told him. "You and Knowles check and load."

Denny nodded, hustled out of the house. He was smiling, too.

"Wyatt still there?"

Moore nodded. "He's sitting on them, making certain they don't take air."

"And Diana's there?"

"They're all fucking there! Sterritt, Perkins, Cox, Hardy, Diana, it's bloody pay dirt, Atticus." He said it impatiently, like I was being thick.

Shit, I thought.

Moore was turning to go, already out the door, and I looked at Yossi, and he just shook his head, because he knew what was going to happen. Moore and Denny and Knowles would infiltrate the building, find the apartment, wait until everyone was in the nest. Then they'd blow the door and go in firing. And they'd kill everyone they found.

Including Diana, and I couldn't let that happen to Erika's mother.

"Call Dale, get him down here," I told Yossi. "Keep Erika secure. Anybody you don't know tries to get in, shoot them."

Then I ran after Moore.

CHAPTER TWENTY-THREE

A film of mucus shone between the Colonel's nose and upper lip, shining in the streetlight. The night turned his pallor cyanotic, and he kept coughing and wheezing to catch his breath. But if his physical condition was sapping him, he was wired emotionally, sitting impatiently in the back of the Cherokee while Knowles, Denny, and Moore quickly set their gear and loaded their weapons.

The apartment building was a big one, thirty floors with a doorman and a manned security desk, both visible when Knowles had made his initial drive-by. A sign over the awning advertised executive suites—a home away from home for weary business travelers. Long-term rates were posted for single, double, and triple occupancy rooms, all expensive. We were parked a block away, in the shadows, but Colonel Wyatt hadn't taken his eyes from the building, proud of himself, still watching the entrance, still bragging.

"I got the bitch. I got her. You asked me if we had

any gems, and the only reason you would've asked me that was if that cunt had some, if she had been selling off the metal. She had to be converting them. I called around. Fucking direct hit with Credit Suisse on Broadway. See, she had to use her name, she had to use her real name so they could cut her the check, and she had to warn them she was coming, or else the exchange would've taken forever. So the stupid cooze told them she was coming, and they told me. Fucking showed up at three with two of the mercs and a fucking hand truck. I followed them from the bank. They thought they were clean."

"Or they made you and are trying to reel us all in," I pointed out.

Moore looked up momentarily from where he was stripping his Browning, and cast a glance at Wyatt.

The Colonel shook his head violently. "The fuck they did. I was careful and I was slow, and they didn't look back once. They split up after the bank, and I stayed on the slut, and she led me right back here. Couple hours later, the other two returned. Nobody's been in or out since."

"How many exits to the building?" I asked.

"Two."

"Then you don't know if they're all in there, you don't even know which floor they're fucking on."

"Twenty-six," the Colonel said immediately. "I saw Diana take the elevator."

Moore had gone back to assembling his gun, and I watched him slip a clip into the Browning and rack the slide.

"You can't be serious about this," I said to him. "You don't even know which apartment you need to hit."

"Fucking pussy," the Colonel told me, wiping his nose.

Moore ignored us both, turning to Knowles. "I'm giving you twenty minutes," he told him. "Set the line cutters to take out the phones and lights at 2340, not a bloody moment before. We'll meet you on twenty-five at 2335."

"They won't even know I was there, boss," Knowles said, and then he and his duffel bag were out of the Cherokee and disappearing into the cold shadows across the street.

Denny was singing softly to himself, contented.

Moore turned in the front seat to face me. "You're going to get us inside," he said.

I said nothing, knowing my silence was saying it all.

"They're rental suites, for businessmen," Moore said. "Turnover has to be high, then, doesn't it? Means the fucking doorman hasn't a fuckin' clue who's supposed to be there and who isn't. But the bloke at the security desk, now he's supposed to know faces, so you're going to lead us in like you belong there, and he'll be a good puppy and not bark."

"You don't need me for that," I said.

"Both Denny and I got the wrong skin color," Moore said. "Security will stop us as a matter of course. We need your white face to do this. Once we're on twenty-five, we'll break out the weapons, get to work."

"Have you not heard a thing I've said?" I asked him. "This is not Prince's Gate. You don't know what apartment they're in, you don't know if they've made the Colonel or not, you don't even know if they're all fucking there, Robert."

"This is not an extraction, this is a hit," Moore said, patiently. "We just find them, point, and go to work."

"You're planning on going room to room?"

Moore smiled wide. "No, I'm planning on watching you use a little social engineering. You're a fucking bodyguard, Atticus, you're a professional sneaky bugger. You'll figure out a way to get the information."

I pushed my glasses back up my nose, knowing that he was right. I could think of at least three ways to get the guy on the security desk talking. It wasn't that hard to do. It didn't matter that I didn't want to do it.

"And we find the room, and you three start killing," I said.

"Right."

"Including Diana?"

Moore hesitated, and in that space the Colonel broke in, saying, "Fucking pussy bullshit limp-dick crapola. Leave him in the fucking car, Robert, I'll get you through the door."

"You're staying here," Moore told Wyatt.

"You can't trust Kodiak. He's still popping chubbies over my wife, you don't want him covering your back."

Moore appraised me for a second, then looked back at the Colonel. "She tried to slot him. I figure that pretty much ended the relationship."

"I need to be there," the Colonel wheezed, angry and choking up.

"You'll fucking wait in the car," Moore bellowed, and I suddenly knew how he must've sounded while training his troops. "You're sick, you're slow, and you're bloody useless to us. If I had my way, I wouldn't use either of you, you're both fucking sub-par. But I need Atticus to get inside, and he's coming with us."

"You can't trust him," Wyatt insisted.

Moore looked at me when he answered. "Yes, I can. I figure he doesn't want to get shot again."

It was depressingly easy to get into the building, as Moore had predicted. We left an angry Wyatt in the Cherokee, hailed a cab, and had it take us around the block and drop us in front of the building. The trip cost twenty dollars, and the cabby thought twenty was more than enough to make up for any weirdness in our request. The doorman looked us all over as we got out, me leading, Moore carrying the duffel bag right behind me, Denny at his side.

Before we were all out of the cab, the doorman had opened the doors for us, and the three of us walked into a large open foyer with linoleum on the floor that was supposed to look like marble. In the center of the foyer was the security desk, a black plastic crescent shape with its points directed to the back of the space, at the elevators. The man behind the console was maybe in his early twenties, wearing a navy blazer with the building's logo over his heart. As we approached I could see the telephones and monitors mounted on the console, but the guard hadn't been paying attention to those; he'd been watching one of the late night talk shows on a small portable television.

He saw us enter, though, and I headed his way before he could rise.

"Excuse—"

"Jesus, I was so hammered last night," I told him. "I don't even remember—" and I turned my head to Moore and said, "Bobby, who the hell did those guys work for?"

"London CompCom," Moore said, and he pushed his accent, and he didn't miss a beat.

"Oh, yeah, the Brits," the guard told me. "They're in twenty-six oh-eight."

"Thanks." I slowed down to let Denny and Moore pass me on the way to the elevator, then leaned in to the guard and gave him my best virile male smile. "You know that babe last night?"

His eyes flickered, desperate for a memory.

"Did her."

"Yeah, she was sweet," the guard agreed.

There were two cars for the elevator, and one of them had been parked on the ground floor, because the door was opening as I joined Moore and Denny. We got into the car, and Moore hit the button for 26, then for 25. The doors slid shut.

"Brilliant," Moore said, patting me on the back.

Denny, who had yet to stop singing to himself, raised the volume a bit, and gave me a wink. I could finally make out the lyrics. He was singing "Born in the USA."

"This is not going to work," I said.

"Sure it will," Moore soothed, checking his watch. "We've got eight minutes, still."

The car stopped, and the doors whispered open.

"Hold the car," Moore told Denny, and stepped out onto the hall carpet. It was wall-to-wall, light blue with red checks. Denny reached for the DOOR OPEN button and held it down, and we waited. I wondered if the guard downstairs was watching the elevators, if he'd noticed we were on the wrong floor. It didn't matter; even if he did spot the discrepancy, he'd just think we'd hit the wrong button by mistake.

Moore was back in ten seconds, saying, "Okay, we get out here." He pulled the duffel bag halfway out into the hall, so it would block the elevator doors, then moved aside to let us out.

The hall was quiet, and wide enough for the three of us to stand abreast if we wanted to. The door to the stairs was marked with an EXIT sign and emergency lights, and on the wall beside it was a fire alarm and extinguisher. There were eight other doors on the hall, leading to different apartments, and it took a moment for my ears to make out the muted sounds of a stereo playing in one of the nearby rooms.

Denny unzipped the duffel and both men removed their jackets, then began grabbing gear. Moore told Denny, "The stairway doors are all one way, so we'll have to ride the elevator up to 26."

Denny nodded, producing one HK MP5 from the duffel bag. He checked the weapon quickly, slapped the bolt down, and slung it over his shoulder. "Does he get one?" he asked Moore. He didn't look at me. I might have been part of the wall-to-wall carpet.

Moore nodded. Denny removed a second machine gun from the bag, handed it to me. It was an identical model, banana clip already in place, with a second clip inverted and duct-taped to the first to make for a faster reload.

"Robert, I can't let you kill Diana," I said.

He didn't look up from where he was busying himself

with the duffel bag. "Jesus, don't tell me the Colonel was right. You're not still harboring hopes of dipping your wick, are you?"

"The only hope I'm harboring is for Erika. I can't let you murder her mother."

Moore straightened up, adjusting the MP5 on his shoulder. He checked his watch, then jerked his thumb toward the door to the stairway. Denny went wordlessly, I assumed to wait for Knowles.

"Listen to me, Atticus," Moore said. "If the woman's in the way when the bullets start, I'm sorry, too fucking bad, it's the price she pays for picking the wrong team. I'm here to do a job, and I'm going to bloody well do it."

"I can't let you—"

His hands came up fast and grabbed my jacket, and then I was being pinned against the wall. His voice was steady, and the hint of the smile had returned. He said, "Yes you can let me, because you've only got two choices. Either I trust you to cover our asses and not fucking interfere, or I put a bullet in you here and now. Makes no difference to me either way, lad. No difference at all. Understand?"

Denny was opening the door to the stairway, and I could just make out Knowles as he emerged. Denny closed the door carefully, and together the two of them trotted lightly down the hall to us. They made no noise as they came.

"You understand?" Moore repeated.

I nodded.

He made a clicking noise with his tongue and released me. Denny handed me a gas mask.

"You may need it, Sarge," he said. "The wankers'll pop the CS if we give them the chance."

"Thanks," I muttered.

Denny resumed singing. Knowles was telling Moore something about the cutters, that they'd be going off in four minutes. "I set two on each line," Knowles said. "Just in case one of them misfires."

"That's my boy," Moore said. "Let's get to work."

We all got into the elevator and Denny pulled the duffel back into the car, pressed the still-illuminated twenty-six, and the doors slid shut.

We're four men standing in a Manhattan elevator with machine guns and gas masks, I thought. Ding. Twenty-fifth floor, guns, ammo, SAS. Ding. Twenty-sixth floor, mayhem, blood, murder.

Everybody out.

Moore turned to me after the doors opened, saying, "Take the bag, put it against the wall. When we go in, if any of them make it past us, I expect you to take care of it."

The layout was identical to 25, with 2608 at the opposite end of the hall from the stairway. I dropped the duffel against the wall between the elevator doors. Denny tapped my shoulder and motioned me to pull my mask down, and as I did, I saw the up arrow mounted on the wall for the second car light up, and I pointed. All three men dropped into a crouch, pulling their masks into place and unslinging their weapons, moving to surround the door when it opened.

There was another soft ding as the car arrived, and I thought, oh fuck, it's one of them, it's Sterritt or Hardy or whoever, come back from searching for Erika. They're doing what we were doing, they're hitting the clubs, they're working at night.

Then I saw the gun, the cocked and locked Colt, and I knew it was the Colonel.

CHAPTER TWENTY-FOUR

"Get the fuck out of here," Moore hissed at the Colonel. Through the mask, his whisper sounded ethereal and frightening.

"Go screw yourself," the Colonel spat back. "I'm part of this action, I'm involved, and I'm going to be here to see it through. You wouldn't be here if it wasn't for me."

Moore started to respond, but Knowles caught his eye by tapping his watch. Moore nodded, the mask bobbing strangely.

"I'll hang back," the Colonel said. "You go in, do whatever you need. I'll hang back."

It was too late to get rid of him, I realized. We could put the Colonel back in the elevator, but it wouldn't matter, because when the power went out, he'd be caught between floors. We could try to send him down the stairs, but unless one of us went with him, there was no way to guarantee he wouldn't just double back. His timing couldn't have been worse. Or better.

Moore realized the same thing. "Stay the fuck out of the way," he said.

Wyatt grinned and took up position opposite me, holding his Colt. Moore began leading his men down the hall, again in their crouch.

They were almost at the door when Wyatt started coughing, and I glanced over to see him fighting it, his face white as a bleached bone. Moore, Denny, and Knowles froze.

Room 2608 knows we're here, I thought.

The Colonel swallowed hard, but didn't make any other noise. Trapped in the gas mask, I could hear my own breathing, too loud, feel the way the rubber was sticking to my skin. Sweat had already started down my face, slicking the bridge of my nose.

Great, I thought. My glasses slide down my face and I won't be able to see. I adjusted the MP5, trying to grip it firmly with my good hand, only using my splinted one for support.

They had reached the end of the hall, passing 2606 on their right. Outside the door to 2608, Moore and Denny went to the left of the doorway, Knowles to the right. Moore held up a fist.

And the lights went out, and the whole world went black.

All around us, in all of the apartments, people began to move.

The emergency lights clicked on, dim and ineffective illumination filling the hall, and Moore's fist came down, and Knowles's boot hit the door, and for a moment there was nothing to do but watch and appreciate the beauty of it all. They had rehearsed this entry a thousand times, perhaps a hundred thousand times, and all three of them moved in a special-forces ballet, with each of them knowing their place and their duty, and doing it flawlessly.

Knowles put the sole of his boot just above the doorknob, and the blow shattered the plate, the door snapping back on its hinges with a pop and a crack, the

security chain jangling as it broke free from its housing.
And even as Knowles was stepping back from his kick,
turning again to get out of the doorway, Denny was
moving in, slipping low in a crouch across the thresh-
old, crossing from outside on the left to inside on the
right, the MP5 steady before him. Before he had come
to a stop, Moore followed suit, staying tight on the wall,
his left shoulder against the door frame as he swiveled
around from the hallway to the apartment.

Cross buttonhook, I thought, very nice, and I waited
for Knowles to finish the move by filling the gap, waited
for the shooting to begin.

But Wyatt ruined it all, lurching forward before
Knowles could move, rushing past the three men and
into the darkened apartment, screaming for someone to
fucking take a pop at him, for the cunt to give him her
best shot.

I was aware of the noise from the apartment, aware
that the door to 2606 was opening as I went forward,
but I didn't stop and I didn't think. I just sprinted full
and jumped for the Colonel, feeling the stitches in my
belly pull and tear. He was screaming that his wife was
a slut, that she should fucking kill him now, and I got
my hands on his shoulders, and I rode him all the way
down, hitting furniture, hearing him still shouting, and
then hearing gunfire.

The apartment was barely lit and I rolled onto my
back, looking for the threat, and saw the shapes of
Moore and Knowles diving down for cover in the apartment, and a muzzle flash beyond the doorway coming
from the hall. Denny had managed to pivot in cover,
and he fired back as a second burst cut loose and I
heard Moore swear. Glass above and behind me shattered, and in the emergency lights shining above the
door to the stairway, I saw Diana being shoved into the
well by Hardy. Sterritt was covering their retreat and I
tried to bring my weapon to bear as he fired again, but
the Colonel caught my arm, cursing, wheezing, club-

bing me with his free hand. I saw Sterritt reach for the
fire alarm, tug the bar down, and the klaxons filled the
building, painfully loud.

And Sterritt was through the door and they were
gone.

CHAPTER TWENTY-FIVE

The building was in mayhem, and that's the only reason we got out without being stopped, arrested, or shot. With the rush of people for the exits, we'd been able to stow the gear back in the duffel bag and join the crowd on our way out. In making good their escape, Sterritt had made it easy on us. Not that any of that mattered to Moore; all he knew was that when we reached the street Sterritt and the rest had gone, and with them, Moore's best chance at bringing them down.

For a second, among the crowd in the lobby, Moore pulled up, saying curtly, "We need to separate."

"I'll stick with you," the Colonel told him.

The rage in his voice was impossible to hide. "You'll fucking not," Moore said. "Terry, take the Colonel to the train, and fucking ride with him all the way fucking home. Make sure he stays there. If he gives you any trouble, blow the slag's bloody kneecaps off."

Terry put a hand on the Colonel's shoulder. "See you tomorrow, then," he told Moore.

We watched them slip into the stream, make for the front door. Denny went next, turning left onto the street. The security guard looked directly at Moore and me as we passed his station, his phone to his ear, and he nodded an acknowledgment to us.

Wonderful night, I had to agree.

We broke track outside, heading away from where the Cherokee had been parked and walking in a five-block loop back to the vehicle. Moore carried the duffel bag with him, and he didn't say a word until we were in sight of the car. Then he stopped short, dropping the duffel bag and grabbing for my jacket to pull me back.

"You didn't fucking tip them off somehow, did you, Atticus?" he asked. His right hand was on his hip, resting on the butt of the Browning.

"How would I have done that, Robert?" I asked.

He searched my eyes. Then he let go of me, let his hand drop from where he wore his gun. "No, you couldn't have done."

"They were adjoining apartments," I said. "There's no way we could have known they had free access to both."

"Better intel."

I didn't say anything to that. None of us had gotten a good look at the space, but the one thing we'd all been able to determine was that 2608 and 2606 were adjoining apartments. The spaces were rented to suits in town on prolonged business, after all, so it was only logical that the layout would be something akin to a hotel's. If we'd taken more time before going in, one of us would have realized that fact.

But we hadn't, and Moore knew that was where we'd stepped wrong; or, rather, that was one of the places we had stepped wrong.

It was five minutes to one when we got back. Dale was on the door, and he let us in with Yossi covering from the far end of the hall. Denny went straight for the room he, Moore, and Knowles had been using for their quarters. Moore and I went into the living room, to find Bridgett and Erika there, facing off over the Scrabble board. Erika was setting down the tiles for "sleazy" with a blank for the "z."

"How'd it go?" Bridgett asked.

I just shook my head while Moore smiled benevolently at Erika, then gave Bridgett a long looking-over. I realized that this was the first time they'd met.

"Sergeant Robert Moore," he told her. "A pleasure."

"SAS?" Bridgett asked sweetly.

No, not tonight, I thought.

"Yes, ma'am."

"Go step on a mine." Bridgett shook the tile bag and offered it to Erika. "Draw."

Moore looked at me, so I said, "This is Bridgett Logan. She's helping us out."

"Logan," Moore said. "Irish?"

"Irish," she said.

"Ah, fuck. It's not true, whatever you've heard."

"What have I heard?"

"All the bullshit about the Regiment slotting their way around Ireland," Moore said, rubbing his eyes. "It's shit, it's just propaganda."

"No kidding?" Bridgett said. "God, I am relieved to hear you say that. So, Gibraltar was just propaganda, too?"

"Gibraltar was unfortunate."

"Loughall?"

"The IRA was trying to blow up a police station," Moore said, and the edge he'd used on Wyatt came back a bit. I wanted to tell him that it wouldn't work on Bridgett, but knew it wouldn't do any good.

Bridgett dropped her smile and said, to me, "The 'Regiment' killed nine people that day. One of them was some poor son of a bitch motorist who just happened to be driving by."

"They had a fucking bulldozer loaded with explosives, darling," Moore said, and I could see Bridgett's shoulders tense at the endearment. "Five hundred fucking pounds, and they slammed it into the RUC station. The plan was to send those constables straight to fucking heaven."

"It was an ambush," Bridgett said, still talking to me. "They evacuated the police station, had forty-some-odd men with guns hiding in the fields. They waited until the bulldozer hit the police station before even moving, and when they did, it was a bloodbath. Ten minutes of shooting everything in sight." When she said "they," it was clear she meant Moore. "Easier to execute those men than to arrest them."

Erika turned her head to Moore, waiting for his response. She was listening closely with a handful of tiles, not certain if she should be alarmed.

"I'll not fucking talk about this," Moore said. "Your kind is all the same. The poor fucking IRA. What about the poor fucking men and women you'd murdered that year, or the years before, or the years since? Or maybe you think the '84 bombing in Brighton was justified politically, or maybe you think mortar attacks on Royal Ulster Constabulary are reasonable? Maybe killing innocent people doesn't bother you at all?"

"Explain to me the difference between what the SAS did in Loughall and what you condemn the IRA for," Bridgett retorted, color climbing her cheeks.

Moore looked at me for help. "Who the fuck is this woman?"

Bridgett said, "Explain to me how death squads are any better than what you're calling terrorism?"

It was as if she'd verbally kicked him between the legs. "There are no death squads!"

Bridgett smiled at him, the face of a murderous angel. Erika quietly began pulling tiles from the letter bag. There was the sound of a car passing on the street, and I heard Yossi telling Dale that everything looked clear.

Moore pivoted with a sharp squeak of his boot and went into the kitchen, shutting the door with a slam that made the Scrabble tiles jump.

"I win," Bridgett told me, pleased with herself.

"Congratulations. Now do me a favor and cut him some slack."

She shook her head. "We can work together, I'll swallow that, but I will not be on the same side as that son of a bitch."

"If you can't get along with him, you're going to have to leave," I said.

The pleasure of victory dissipated some. "I'm not going to kiss up."

"I'm not asking you to kiss up, Bridie. I'm asking you to work together."

Erika had finished placing her tiles in her rack. "I'd like it if you stayed," she said, pushing the bag across the board. "It's your turn."

"Fine," Bridgett said. Whether it was to me or to Erika, I wasn't certain, but I decided to take it as both, and headed into the kitchen after Moore. As I left, I heard Erika asking what exactly Loughall was.

"Loughall is the reason to never trust the SAS," I heard Bridgett say.

Sergeant Moore had opened himself a beer and was drinking it while looking in the sink. The sink, as far as I could tell, was empty. Moore had removed his anorak and bundled it onto the counter. Gun and knife were still in place.

"Fucking bitch," he said to me.

"I think of her as spirited."

"It's bullshit, you know that?"

"What is?"

"Death squads."

"She doesn't think so."

"Nobody fucking thinks so. There's this son of a bitch in England, wrote a book, and in it he claims he was a member of the Regiment, and that he'd been part of some secret death squad in Northern Ireland. Detailed all of these murders he and others in the squad had committed in the early seventies. And the book becomes a fucking bestseller, and everyone is jumping up and down saying look what the SAS has done. Regimental command is screaming that it's all bullshit, nobody fucking listens. Seven months this book is out there, and then finally the Royal Ulster Constabulary arrests this guy, the one who wrote it, and they bring him up to Belfast, and they sit him down, and they say, listen, mate, if it's true, you're going to be done for murder.

"And this guy, he immediately says, nah, it's not true, none of it's true. Made the whole thing up, see?" Moore looked at me. "And none of the book fucking checks out. He's got bits in there where he's detailing the date and time he's offing someone, and the RUC finds out that, in fact, he wasn't in fucking Belfast at all, but down at the dentist's in Dorset, some such. So none of it's true, not one word."

Moore finished the beer, set the bottle by the sink, began pushing it in a circle with his fingers. The countertop was an aquamarine tile, and the glass bottle left a smear of condensation that made the green seem darker.

"I've been SAS for over twenty years," Moore said. "I was in the Falklands, on the ground, blowing supply lines and aircraft. I was on the second pagoda team at Prince's Gate. We're the best damn soldiers in the fucking world."

"The SAS summarily executed five unarmed terrorists at Prince's Gate," I said. I didn't add that Moore had almost pulled a repeat of that move tonight.

"Tell me you don't know how that happened, that you can't imagine what it was like in there."

"That's what the government wanted?"

"Soldiers are an instrument of politics. Soldiers do what they're told. That's all I can say."

Not all soldiers, I thought.

"And then there're bastards like Mark Sterritt, and they take our good name and they take the skills we taught them, and they drag it all down into the shit, so deep you can't even see it."

"There's a huge difference between SAS and ex-SAS," I said.

"You think so? You really think if the press knew all about Sterritt, they'd not care that he and his boys all learned their killing at my knee?"

"Maybe not."

"Maybe not. But probably so. Just another nail in the coffin of the SAS."

The kitchen door opened, and Erika came in, saying, "Do we have any popcorn?"

Moore said, "Denny bought some of that microwave kind, it's in the pantry." He sounded sullen.

"You two should come back out," Erika said, opening the pantry door. "You're being antisocial."

"You should go to bed," I said.

She stuck her tongue out at me. "What're you doing?"

"We were talking," I said.

"Duh." She found the popcorn and put it in the microwave. "It's more fun if there's more of us out there."

"You think this is supposed to be fun?"

"Look, I'm the one who's stuck here. If I want to try and have fun, you should be helping me out." She was patient with her explanation, as if giving me a basic lesson in maturity.

"She's got you there," Moore told me.

"You, too," Erika said to him. "Bridgett will be nice. I had a talk with her." She absently reached for her left earlobe, and I saw she now had two hoops hanging there.

"She gave you those?" I asked.

Erika grinned. "Said I could borrow them." To Moore, she added, "Bridgett just wanted to let you know where she stood, that's all."

"She did that just fine," Moore said.

"Then quit hiding in here and come out. Bring the popcorn."

We watched her go out of the kitchen. The micro-wave beeped at us and Moore moved to fetch the bag.

"You go on point," he said. "That way I can dive for cover."

I found a bowl to serve the popcorn in, and we re-turned to the living room. Yossi and Dale were still on the door, and I heard one of them murmur something about the smell of hot popcorn. Bridgett greeted Moore with a look cut from the ice outside, and as I set the bowl down on the table, she transferred the look to my middle.

"Atticus," she said softly.

It took me a second, and then I looked down at my stomach, saw the bloodstain on my T-shirt from where my stitches had torn during my dive for the Colonel. "It's minor," I said.

"What?" Erika asked, and then she saw it, and she said, "Oh my God, you're bleeding. Why are you bleed-ing, what happened?"

"It's nothing."

"What do you mean it's nothing, your stomach is bleeding, that's not nothing."

"Oh, come on," Moore said. "It's not like he got shot again."

We all heard the penny drop.

Erika's face went flat. "Again?" She asked it softly.

"It's okay," I said.

She slid off the couch and walked over to me. "You got shot? When? Tonight?"

"Couple of days ago."

"And no one told me?"

"We didn't want to worry you," Bridgett said, glaring at Moore.

Erika ignored her. "Why didn't you tell me?" She kept her voice soft, asking a reasonable question. "Don't lie to me, Atticus."

"I'm all right," I said, and right after I said it, I saw her make the leap, put together the pieces we'd let slip.

"Mom shot you?" Her hands stayed at her sides, fingers curled into her palms. "It was my mom who did this?"

I didn't say anything, but that was enough for her. She knew.

"Let me see," Erika said.

I looked over at Bridgett, who shook her head slightly. Easy for her to say. I pulled up my shirt, thinking about Lyndon Johnson and feeling embarrassed. The bruising was beginning to fade around my stitches, and the bleeding had already stopped, but it didn't look pretty.

Erika didn't move.

I lowered my shirt, tucking it back in, and the movement made my stitches itch.

"That bitch," Erika said. "That bitch."

"I agree," Bridgett said.

Erika turned on her. "You don't know! You don't fucking know! She shot him! My mom shot him!"

Down the hall, I heard Yossi and Corry responding to the shouting, and I held up a hand, waving them back to their posts.

"Do you know what that means?" Erika was demanding shrilly.

"It means I got lucky," I said. "She could have killed me."

Erika spun back around, and now I could see her rage, and it was frightening. "Lucky! Because she didn't kill you? Everything else she did to you, and you think you're lucky? She's a fucking *liar*, she's a goddamn fucking *liar* and she shoots you and you think you're *lucky*?"

"Sterritt wanted her to kill—"

"*Lucky*? You let her keep hurting you and hurting you and you call that *lucky*?"

"It's not the—"

"She just fucking steps all over you and you call that *lucky*? When she was fucking Rubin, did you call that *lucky*, too?"

I thought, no, I didn't hear that right.

Erika slammed her mouth shut as if she'd swallowed a bug.

The whole house was silent.

I thought: She's lying again. She is lying to you, again, the way she lied about her father molesting her, about how Moore and Denny and Knowles didn't pick her up that day in the city. She's angry and she's upset and she feels betrayed again, and she's just going for the reaction. That's what she's after, the reaction. This is a lie.

Her expression had changed, and she was sucking at the air rapidly, avoiding my eyes. She had bitten her bottom lip so hard I could see teeth marks. "I'm sorry, I didn't mean that, I'm lying, I didn't mean that."

And then I knew she was telling the absolute truth.

Erika turned, put her face in her hands, and started crying.

Without thought, I put my arms around her. I brushed her hair back, stroked it, holding her the way I had in Gaithersburg, when she was eleven, and I was twenty-four, and desperately in love with her mother.

CHAPTER TWENTY-SIX

"The thing is," I told Bridgett, "it makes sense. It makes such perfect fucking sense. I'm a goddamn fool. I can look back, and I can see all the things that I read the wrong way, all the things I used to ignore—my evasions, his lame lies. It was goddamn fucking obvious, right under my nose, and I denied it because he would have told me. He was my best friend, and he would have told me."

Bridgett sat watching me from her chair, silent. Listening.

I looked around the room, down the hall at where Moore and Dale were standing post. It was quiet. Erika was maybe asleep in her chosen room, Yossi outside her door. It was just Bridgett and me, with me trying to explain why I was so angry.

"He knew," I said. "That's the thing that gets me, right now, that's the thing that makes me want to dig him up and spit on him. He knew I was seeing Diana, he knew how I felt, and he was screwing her anyway."

Bridgett nodded.

"He made a choice. He made a choice to betray me. And he took this little secret of his to the grave."

"Are you angry that he did it? Or that he never told you?"

"Who the fuck cares which one I'm angry about?"

She nodded again, and I wished she would stop doing that. It made me feel as if I were talking to a paid therapist.

"He left the Army before I did, you know? And when I was getting out, it was Rubin's idea for me to move in with him, for us to live in New York together. His idea. He was the best friend I ever had, he was the person I told everything to, every fucking little thing. And he didn't tell me. He turned our friendship into a sham."

"But it wasn't a sham," Bridgett said. "I didn't know him long, but I knew enough about the two of you to know that your friendship was mutual."

"Then why not tell me about her? Why hide it?"

"Fear, maybe. If he thought you would take it badly, if he thought it would threaten the friendship. He didn't have many people, did he?"

"I can understand him not saying anything when I first moved in. I can accept fear as a reason to be silent. But he died never having told me, Bridie. He died hoping it would never come out, that I would never know. And that's cowardice. It's unbecoming of him. It's fucking unbecoming."

"But you don't know what would have happened if he had lived," she insisted. "I've lost people before, too, and I've learned one thing from it if nothing else. You can't look back and speak to the things the dead didn't do. It's pointless, it gets you nowhere. You can have your own regrets, but you can't know what Rubin would have done had he lived, Atticus."

I stayed quiet, my throat raw with angry tears I was never going to shed.

"Everybody betrays us, in the end," Bridgett said. "Make your peace with it, Atticus. Grow up."

I couldn't answer that, and we sat in silence while I tried to sort my thoughts and feelings. But there was no clarity, everything in a jumble.

I got up, grabbed my coat. "I'm going home," I said. "I'm no fucking good here right now, I'm going to be in the way, and I need some time for myself. Give Natalie a call, have her come in."

"You want to wait until she gets here? I can go with you."

"No. No, I think I really need to be alone."

"All right. I'll make the call. Are you going to be okay?"

"Oh, yeah. I'm going to walk in the general direction of my apartment, hope that somebody tries to start something. Then I'll beat the fuck out of them. That's my plan."

"Take a cab."

"Go to hell," I said, and left.

In the Army, Rubin could get anything.

Early on he had discovered the hidden market, had mastered the barter system and become one of the long line of soldiers who could play the game of supply-and-demand as an expert. When we were on maneuvers during Advanced Infantry Training, he was the guy who got us beer in the field. When another soldier we both knew was getting short, Rubin made him a military ID that wouldn't expire until the next century. He'd create false identities for sport, with credit card applications and forged transfer letters from the New York State DMV. He had copies of every official form he had ever laid eyes on, and if you gave him a photocopier, he could create a letter that you would swear was signed by the Provost Marshal himself. It was what he did, and while it was often illegal, it was rarely harmful. He had been billeted to the Pentagon as a driver at about the same time I'd been assigned to Colonel Wyatt, but that was just Rubin's work.

His job was making deals, earning favors and then calling them in. And his first law was, "In this man's Army, you never get something for nothing."

His second law was, "And I'm the man who can get anything for anyone."

"Here," Rubin said, handing me an envelope. "Diana called last week, asked me to get this for Erika's birthday."

I was packing for a weekend at the house in Gaithersburg. The Colonel was off on another of his fuck-and-suck missions, and the only reason it was especially appalling this time was that Erika was turning eleven on Sunday. He had already told her and his wife that he wouldn't be back in time. A conference, he had claimed, but both Diana and I knew otherwise.

"What is it?" I asked, slipping the envelope into a pocket.

Rubin grinned. "You'll find out. See you Sunday night. Try not to get any hickeys."

"You're a crass motherfucker," I said.

Erika was at the door when I pulled up and she came down the driveway, running to the driver's side door and pressing her face against the window. With her features mashed against the glass, she looked like a demented Muppet. She made a face and I made one in return, and Erika was giggling when I got out of the car.

"Need help?" she asked, motioning to my bag.

"No, I think I got it."

She indicated the wrapped present on the passenger seat. "That for me?"

"Maybe."

She eyed the box while I picked it up, then said, "Mom told me we're going to a movie tonight. Is she lying?"

"Would your mother lie to you?"

Erika gave me a look that said my answer was totally beside the point. "Are we?"

"Lying?"

"Stupid." She made another face, this one a direct and unfavorable assessment of my intellect. "No. Going to a movie, doof."

"We are going to a movie." I started up the walk, hefting my duffel over my shoulder, the present under my arm. Diana stood at the open door, watching us both, looking amused.

Erika ran past me and came to a screeching halt in front of her mother, saying, "Atticus says we *are* going to a movie."

"After we go for pizza," Diana said.

"I'm gonna get my coat." Erika scooted past her mother and I heard her running up the stairs to her room.

Diana led me to the guest room. I dropped my bag on the floor, set the gift on the bed, and she kissed me, her hands on my chest. I returned the kiss in kind, my libido kicking like crazy. She pulled back when we heard Erika's feet pounding on the floor overhead as she ran for the stairs again.

"Rubin gave me an envelope, said you called and asked for it," I told Diana.

"Good, he got them."

"What?"

"Hopefully, exactly what Erika wants for her birthday."

We fetched her daughter, then, and went out for pizza and a movie. Erika talked throughout dinner, telling me about her week in detail, describing at length a particular boy in her class named Ryan that she classified as stuck-up.

"When he plays football, when he scores, he walks around with his hands on his hips in front of all the girls," she told us. "He thinks he's so hot."

We got back to the house near ten, and Diana hustled

Erika off to bed, then came back downstairs to join me on the sofa in the living room.

"That kid's got a crush on you," Diana told me.

"How can you tell?"

Diana toyed with the edge of my sleeve, where the fabric ended at my wrist. "Why do you think she kept talking about Ryan at dinner? She wants you to know she's looking at boys."

We kissed, and I very softly assured her that Erika posed no lethal threat to our relationship. We made love in the guest room, quiet and intense, and Diana left me lying there when we were through, returning to her bed upstairs without a word.

Erika's birthday party was attended by six or seven kids, most of them the children of other officers posted to the Pentagon or Quantico or any of the many bases in the D.C. area. The much-talked-about Ryan was in attendance as well, and he didn't seem like such a bad sort to me. Certainly shy. He was, after all, the only boy who had been invited to the party.

Diana had made tacos for lunch, and it was followed with a small cake, purely for the ceremony of song and candles, and then an ice cream sundae buffet, which was an enormous hit. Erika fixed herself a mountain of chocolate and vanilla, soaked in butterscotch and wrapped in whipped cream, crowned with what must have been half the contents from a bottle of maraschino cherries.

"This is going to be hell to clean up," Diana murmured to me while the kids were eating. "But I swear to God it's worth it. Look at her."

"She's going to be sick," I said.

Diana laughed and told me to stop acting like a parent, that I was stealing her thunder.

With the sundaes finished, Erika declared the time had come to open her presents. She began with those brought by her guests, and I remember them as gifts of the day, impersonal for the most part, most likely selected by the other kids' parents; a CD by the Pet Shop Boys; another by U2; a Breyer model horse; a cheap Walkman. Ryan gave her a stuffed plush dragon, purple and blue, and Erika seemed to like it, but also seemed to not want Ryan to know that fact.

The presents from her peers unwrapped and examined, she switched to those gifts coming from the adults. Her father's present first, a set of pearl earrings. The pearls were tiny but real, and a couple of Erika's guests made a big fuss over the jewelry.

"You like them?" Erika asked one girl. "You can have them. Here."

She started to hand them over but Diana moved to intercept, saying firmly, "I'll hold on to these."

Erika shrugged, opening her next present, which was from me. She took her time with the card and the wrapping paper. I'd bought her the boxed set of Madeleine L'Engle books, and she gave me a big smile, saying, "Cool. I can't wait to read these." She set them aside next to the plush dragon.

Finally, Diana handed her daughter the envelope Rubin had asked me to bring.

"What is this?" Erika demanded.

Diana was smiling, made a gesture of keeping her mouth zipped shut.

"Money," one of the guests said. "It's money."

Erika held the envelope to the light. "It better not be a gift certificate, Mom." She tore the envelope open, and out fell four concert tickets. A babble of voices started, asking what show they were for, and Erika gathered them up, reading in disbelief.

Then she let out an almighty shriek of delight, jumping to her feet and dancing in place, chanting, "Joshua Tree, Joshua Tree, Joshua Tree!"

"No way!" one of the girls said.

Erika shoved the tickets in her face. "Take a look! Four tickets to the Joshua Tree tour at RFK Stadium! I'm going to see U2, I'm going to see Bono and the

Edge and Adam and Larry! I'm going to see U2!" She pulled the tickets to her breast, protecting them, spinning, and then headed for her mother, exclaiming, "Thank you, thank you! You're the best, Mom, you're the absolute best!"

"You're sure you like them?" Diana asked, teasing.

"I love them!"

"Because if you don't, we can always return them—"

"I love them, I told you, I love them!" She danced about some more, stepping on wrapping paper, and, incidentally, the dragon Ryan had given her. "How did you get them? The whole tour sold out the day the tickets went on sale."

"I have my ways," Diana said.

Erika hugged her mother. "Thank you so much! This is the best present, the absolute best."

"I love you, baby."

"I love you, too, Mom." Erika studied the tickets once more, then handed them to Diana, saying, "Hold on to them, please."

The party pretty much died after that, with many of the kids gripped by a powerful envy concerning what a great mother Erika Wyatt had. Parents arrived to take their children home, good-byes were made, and Erika ultimately went up to her room to play her new U2 CD very loud. I helped Diana clean up.

"Tell Rubin I said thank you," she said as we were washing dishes. "He must have traded some heavy favors for those tickets."

"I'm sure he did," I said. The Joshua Tree tour tickets were scalping at one hundred dollars a pop, and those were for the nosebleed seats. "How'd you know to go through Rubin?"

"You told me, remember? 'Rubin can get anything for anyone.' That's what you said."

"I said that?"

She kissed me on my nose. Her breath smelled of ice cream and cherries. "Yes, you did."

"I was right."

"I know. Like I said, tell Rubin thank you. I owe him."

———

"You made Erika Wyatt the most popular kid at her school," I told Rubin when I saw him Sunday night. We were in our apartment in D.C., and he was sprawled across the sofa, working with one of his sketch pads. I was sitting on the coffee table, watching him draw. He was working on an idea for a comic book, one featuring a six-gun-wielding young woman who roamed the United States like a cross between Shane and The Man With No Name.

"I'll bet," he said, not looking up from his sketch pad.

"I can't imagine what you had to promise to get those tickets."

"Too much, I'll tell you that."

"You selling missile codes to the Libyans again?"

Rubin capped his pen, rolled onto his side to look at me. "Hey, I can get anything."

"You can't get me a ride on Air Force One to Paris. You can't get me a date with Mary Stuart Masterson."

"Well, I might've been able to until now," he mused. "Those tickets pretty much tapped me."

"Fibber."

"Fibber?" Rubin shook his head. "Nope. Got nothing out of this one. So if you're needing a favor anytime soon, I may not be able to provide, sorry."

"And here I was hoping you could get me some claymores to wire around the Washington Monument."

"You and your penis fixation," he said. "Like you're not getting any."

"Like you are."

He waggled his eyebrows at me, and I laughed, and that was pretty much the last I thought of it.

———

Until tonight.

I had introduced Rubin to Diana. I had even talked to her about his wheeling and dealing.

But I'd never said he could get anything for anyone. I had never said that.

It was an arrogant holdout on my part, and the only reason I refuted his claim was because I didn't believe it. He *couldn't* get me a ride on Air Force One to Paris; he *couldn't* get me a date with Mary Stuart Masterson. Stupid, perhaps, but I wasn't willing to stroke his ego like that, and it hadn't really ever mattered. He would say he could get anything for anyone, and I would always try to trump him, come up with something that was beyond the pale, and that was how it went. It was one of our games, one of the ways we communicated.

"Rubin can get anything for anyone," Diana had said.

She hadn't heard it from me.

And the thing that galled me most now, as I walked down the wet, snowy street to my apartment, as I fumbled my key into the lock, was that I had known something was going on the moment Rubin had handed me that envelope. And I'd ignored it.

Because, ultimately, what right did I have to be jealous? I was having an affair with a married woman. I'd taken a stance on the issue of fidelity, and it certainly wasn't pro the sanctity of marriage.

How could I condemn Rubin for doing to me what I was doing to Colonel Douglas Wyatt?

CHAPTER TWENTY-SEVEN

My coffeemaker told me that it was twenty-seven minutes past two in the morning when I got in, and I didn't bother with the lights, going straight to the radiator in the kitchen and twisting the knob with my good hand until I heard the steam hissing into the pipes. I pulled a chair from the table, tugged off my wet shoes and socks, purposefully bending too far, trying to enjoy the pain that came from my wound. My answering machine was telling me I had a message waiting, and I told my answering machine that it could go fuck itself, by ignoring the little red light.

I removed my coat and gun, then got up and found the bottle of Glenlivet and a clean glass. I poured myself about three fingers, and drank. For a moment, I wished I smoked.

New snowfall, and I watched it spiral past my window, heavy and fast. I poured more scotch. Rubin had loved vodka. Once, he brought me a case of Glenfiddich for covering his ass during a spot inspection. I told him I didn't want it, that he was my friend, and that he would have done the same for me.

"You're right, I would," he said. "But since I didn't, I stole you scotch instead."

It struck me then, dull points seated behind my eyes that made me realize, whatever else I was feeling, that I missed him horribly.

Right now what I wanted was Rubin, here, in this new apartment that I shared with no one but myself. I wanted to read him the riot act, ask what the hell he had thought when he first started seeing Diana. I wanted to ask if he had been in love with her, too, and was he still. I wanted him to tell me why he had kept this secret, and what other secrets he'd taken down with him. I wanted him to tell me if my trust in him was deserved, or if I was as gullible as Erika had called me over a week ago. I wanted to ask if Bridgett was right about my need to grow up.

I wanted to get shit-faced drunk with him, and tell bad jokes about the SAS and getting shot, to try to hide fear and guilt and repeated failure.

I wanted my friend back.

The intercom in the hall buzzed, and I looked at the clock, saw it was almost a quarter to four. There was another buzz, more tentative, and, as I started up from the kitchen table, a third, more insistent. The floor was very cold, and I shifted from one bare foot to the other as I pressed the speaker button. "Who is it?"

"Natalie," the intercom crackled.

I blinked a couple of times, thinking that perhaps I'd had more scotch than I thought. "Nat?"

"God, look, I'm sorry, I thought you were up." Her voice sounded pressured, as if it were being forced through the wires and out the intercom grille.

"No, I was up. I'll buzz you in."

I leaned on the button to unlock the door, counted to three, then came off it and leaned against the opposite wall instead. My feet were still cold, though, so I went to my room for slippers, and had pulled them on when I heard her knock. I checked through the spyhole first, confirmed that I was looking at Natalie Trent outside my door, and unfastened the locks.

"I'm sorry," Natalie said. "I didn't mean to wake you."

"You didn't. I was up. I've been drinking."

"You, too?" she asked. "The bars are closed."

I chuckled, led her inside, flipping the light switch on the kitchen wall as I headed for the cupboard. I had to squint while finding her a glass, but by the time I turned back to face her, my vision had adjusted, and I got a good look at her.

Natalie stood by the table, wearing jeans and a thick wool sweater, her gray pea coat on, but open. She had no gloves, no hat, and her hair was soaked from the snow. Flakes melted down her forehead and cheeks. Her eyes were red, and I thought it was irritation, but the rest of her face didn't sell it.

"Hey," I said. "Hey, what's the matter, Nat?"

Her mouth moved a fraction, as if she couldn't control it. She shook her head. She shut her eyes.

I put the glass on the table. "Natalie?"

When she opened her eyes, they were wet.

"I miss him," Natalie said.

It was still dark and still snowing when we finished the Glenlivet and moved on to the Maker's Mark, and by that time I had told her all about my night, about Rubin's affair with Diana and my affair with Diana and the whole damn thing. She had listened closely, getting good and angry along with me, then launching into a tirade about what a rotten bastard he'd been, and how he had made her miserable by dying. It had to be nearing five in the morning, now, but the only clock in the living room was the one on the TV/VCR Dale had bought, and he hadn't bothered to set it. As far as Sony was concerned, it was always an insistent midnight.

On the floor, unrolled, was Rubin's painting of Natalie, and she stood looking down at it, bourbon in her hand. He had painted her nude, on one knee, her arms above her head, fingers splayed, palms flat, reaching for something that either wasn't supposed to be there, or hadn't yet been painted. The muscles in her arms and legs were taut, and I wondered how much of her had been imagined and idealized in Rubin's mind.

"I hate it," Natalie whispered, staring at it.

"No, you don't. It's one of the best he ever did, ever."

"I hate it. I hate it absolutely." Her enunciation became precise.

I drank from my glass, watching as she tried to kneel on the floor. She had to put her left hand out for support, and ended up placing it smack on top of the X-wing. She yelped, yanked her hand back, and ended up on her rear.

All without spilling her drink.

"Bridgett gave you this?" Natalie asked, poking the toy.

"For my birthday."

"I missed your birthday?"

I waved a hand to dismiss her concern. "It's pretty cool, though. It makes noise."

"Noise is good," Natalie decided. She pushed the X-wing along the floor with her index finger. "I thought maybe you'd be over there. At Bridgett's, I mean."

"Not tonight."

She made a silent "oh," then asked, "How's your mouth?"

"My mouth?"

"Your lip."

I reached to check, surprised myself with the coldness of the splint. The swelling had gone down almost entirely. "It's fine."

"I hit you," she said.

"I remember."

"It's fine?"

"Yeah. I forgot about it."

She drank some more, then glanced back at the painting. "I hate him."

"I do, too," I said.

Her hair fell across her face when she tried to look at me. Natalie blew at it to clear her vision. "You don't really hate him."

"No," I agreed. "I lied."

She pointed her glass at me. "I *do*. I really really do."

"Why?"

Natalie looked back at the painting, evaluating it carefully. "Because he made me look fat."

I laughed, and Natalie began laughing, too, getting to her feet and coming back to join me on the couch. She flopped down, finishing her bourbon and then reaching for the bottle. I handed it over, and she refilled her glass, then refilled mine.

"They're looking for them?" Natalie asked, out of the blue.

"Who?"

"Moore."

"Tomorrow."

"I hope they find them."

"I do, too."

"Yeah. And those other ones. And Diana."

"Sure."

"They should find them."

"They should," I agreed, not entirely certain what we were talking about. There was only an inch left of the bourbon.

"And then we can protect Erika," Natalie said. "What time is it?"

I checked my watch, realized I'd taken it off. "Watch's in the kitchen," I told her. "Hold on."

"I'll come with you," she suggested.

Each of us emptied our glasses down the kitchen

drain. The coffeemaker clock read twenty-two minutes past five.

"I should go home and get some sleep," Natalie sighed. "I have to be at the safe house at eight."

"Yeah, me, too," I said.

She reached for her coat and I realized she'd left the painting in the living room, so I asked her to wait and went back for it, rolling the canvas quickly and slipping it into its poster tube.

"You almost forgot this," I said, trying to hand her the tube.

"I don't want it."

"Sure you do. Just to have it. You don't have to hang it anywhere or anything like that, but it's yours, and you should have it. He loved you."

Natalie looked at the tube in my hand, and there was an odd expression on her face, like for a moment she'd forgotten where she was, and then her breath got ragged, like something inside her had just broken.

I rested the tube against the wall, went to hold her. She pressed her face against my shoulder, and I could feel her cheek on my neck, her skin hot and flushed against mine, her face slick with tears. She put her arms around me, tight, shaking. She snuffled at the air, trying to clear her nose, and her hands turned against my back, her short nails digging through my shirt.

"I hate him," Natalie sobbed.

I put my good hand on her head, my fingers slipping through her hair, and the other on her back. She shifted against my body, and as Natalie moved I became aware of exactly how she felt against me, of the way her legs rubbed against mine, the press of her breasts to my chest. She turned her head in from my shoulder, and her breath hit my throat, and I could feel her tears on me, and she pushed harder against me. Her back felt strong, and I moved my hand, could feel the muscles that Rubin had painted.

Natalie tilted her head to see me looking at her, to see my expression. Her eyelashes were matted, tears shiny

on her face. She said my name and her hands moved up
my back, and she drew me in as I leaned to her.

Her mouth, like her skin, was hot, salty, and we were
pulling at each other, trying to climb, to make one
body. I felt a hand leave my neck, pulling at my shirt,
and then her other hand followed it, and her fingers
were on my skin. We were pulling at clothes, our lips
still together, separating just long enough to remove
our shirts, wanting to feel more of each other. I put my
mouth to her shoulder, then lower, moving over her
chest, and Natalie gripped my head with both hands,
guiding and driving. She said my name again, and she
was still crying, but that had changed, too, a different
pitch, a different kind of flood. She pushed my head
back with one hand, the other trailing down my chest,
skimming over the stitches on my belly, until she
reached my belt and began tugging it free.

Our remaining clothes landed on the floor near the
shirts, and we put our arms around each other again,
and I felt wonderful skin, soft and hot. She gasped
when the splint touched her, laughed, pressed herself
back against me. I couldn't get enough of her, I couldn't
feel enough of her. I knew what was going on, I knew I
could stop it, that I could pull away, that I could quit,
but I didn't. I didn't want to.

And so neither of us did.

CHAPTER TWENTY-EIGHT

The phone woke me, the third ring before the answering machine clicked on, and I pulled myself out of bed, my stomach muscles throbbing when I sat up, the headache kicking in immediately. Natalie pulled the covers back over her, still asleep, and I stumbled to the machine to turn it off, but by then the beep had come, and Scott Fowler's voice filled the room.

"Atticus, call me. Call me. Call me now. Call me as soon as you get this message."

I stumbled back into my room for my robe and glasses, stepping over the clothes we had strewn in the hall. Natalie's bra was twisted on top of one of my slippers. The bra was a pearl-gray color, silk, very simple, very pretty. I imagined Natalie looked very nice in it, but I couldn't quite remember. She hadn't moved, eyes closed, breathing even and deep. My alarm clock said it was exactly nine in the morning.

I drank two glasses of water back to back, then swallowed four aspirin and a vitamin C with a third. My stomach felt stable, the muscle ache on the outside rather than within. I started coffee brewing, picked up our clothes, brought them back into my room. I put mine in the laundry bag. I folded hers, and set them on top of my bureau. She had rolled onto her stomach, and I watched her sleep for a while before heading back to the kitchen and calling Scott.

He answered immediately, asking, "Don't you ever check your messages?"

"We need to talk," I told him.

"I know," he said.

"You know?"

"I read the papers, Atticus. You have a shootout in downtown, you expect the city not to notice?"

"It made the papers?"

Scott expired air into the phone. "Are you at your place?"

"Yeah."

"I'll be there in twenty."

"Give me an hour."

"One hour," he said, and hung up.

Natalie woke at ten of ten, and came out in my robe to find me seated in the kitchen, dressed, drinking coffee and staring at Thelonius Monk. I pointed to where I had filled a glass of water for her beside the bottle of aspirin, and she went to it, then saw the clock and said, "Shit. Did you call them?"

"No," I said.

She reached for the phone, dialed. "Bridgett? Hi, it's Nat . . . yes, I know . . . I know, how's it look? . . . I overslept . . . Very funny. Give me an hour . . ." She looked at me. "No, I haven't talked to him . . . Fine . . . we're . . . Bridgett, we're getting along fine . . . I'll talk to you when I get there."

She hung up, took the glass and the aspirin, and went into the bathroom, carrying them. She showered quickly, emerged once more wearing my robe, headed back into my room. I got up and fixed her a cup of coffee, considered bringing it to her.

Better to wait until she was dressed.

I went back to the table, and she came out again, sitting in the other chair, her hands going to the mug, then to where I had laid the poster tube on the table.

"What do you want to tell her?" she asked finally.

"The truth." My mouth felt filled with broken glass. "I don't know what I was thinking last night. I didn't mean—"

"I know. Neither did I." I drank some of my coffee. My head felt too small for my brain, but the aspirin was finally kicking in.

"We can just forget it ever happened," Natalie said.

"Is that what you want?"

"We were drunk, we were grieving. Why make it more than that?" Natalie looked at me, then repeated, "Why make it more than that?"

"That's all it was?"

"That's all it should have been."

Both of us had nothing to say, then.

"Rubin's wake," I said.

Natalie turned on a small smile. "Well, we never did have one, did we?"

"No."

"I'll talk to Bridgett, tell her what happened," Natalie said. "All of it."

"I should do it."

"No, let me. I'm her friend, I've been her friend for a long time. Let me tell her. You can talk to her after."

It wouldn't matter which one of us it came from, I knew. The damage was done. Either a friend or a lover had betrayed her. I gave Natalie a nod.

She emptied her mug and got up, saying, "I'll tell her when I get there. Maybe you . . ."

"I've got to wait here for Fowler to come by," I said. "It'll be at least another hour before I get to the safe house. That should give you enough time."

I was out of the shower and dressed when Scott buzzed, and I told him I'd be right down. I pulled on my jacket and my gun, locked up, and took the stairs as fast as I could without exacerbating my stomach. My abdominals were killing me.

"Dude," Scott said as I came outside. "You look like shit."

"Thank you, Scott. And might I say, the new earring suits you."

He smoothed his tie and then brought the same hand to his left ear to twist the new stud. It was a small gold stem, set a quarter of an inch above his old earring. "Prepping for undercover work," Special Agent Fowler said.

"They must hate you down at the Bureau."

"Most of them think I'm queer." He grinned. "They haze me out, I'll sue their asses for discrimination."

I laughed, and it only made my stomach hurt more. I considered Scott Fowler a friend. He'd been there when Rubin died, working the Federal side of the job. We got along, perhaps because he seems determined not to appear as what he is—a competent and professional agent of the FBI. He is three or four years older than me, and always manages to look like a California surfer, even in his conservative suits. It didn't matter that we were bearing into a vicious winter, he was still evenly tanned. His hair is the color of dried straw, and his eyes are blue. He was wearing contacts today, instead of his glasses.

Rubin used to call him Special Agent Dude, or SAD for short.

Thinking about it made me smile.

"It wasn't that funny," Scott chided.

"Something else entirely."

The smile faded to a more serious appraisal. "So, where we going?"

"Let's walk," I said, and started for Lexington Avenue.

Scott reached into his pockets for a pair of black leather gloves, and slipped them on as we began walking. The pedestrian traffic was light. Not many people wanted to be walking in the falling snow today, it seemed.

"How you doing?" Scott asked.

"Aside from being shot?"

"In spite of being shot. Why'd you call me?"

"What do you know about the SAS?" I asked, and then told him all of it. He listened, occasionally trying to catch snow in his gloved hands, and we were down to Twelfth Street before I'd finished.

"That fits with what we've got," Scott said.

"Which is?"

"I need you to put me in touch with Moore."

"I doubt he'll want to talk to you."

"He doesn't want to talk to me. He's avoiding me."

"Why?"

"What Wyatt told you is correct, to a point. Moore's here officially, with Knowles and Denny, to help bring down Sterritt."

"It's official?"

"To a point. It was the Brits who told us Sterritt and his crew were in New York, but their condition on sharing that information was that we allow Moore to assist us in the pursuit and arrest. The State Department said okey dokey, told Justice, Justice told us, and we swallowed it. Problem is, the moment Moore and his two hit the dirt, they were running, and they left us in the dust. He doesn't want to share with the FBI."

"How is it Sterritt warrants such special treatment from both governments?" I asked. "What's he done?"

Scott stopped, tilted his head back to catch some snow in his mouth. After he'd caught a few flakes, he said, "Tastes like shit."

"That's the sulfuric acid," I said. "You going to answer my question?"

"Yeah, Sterritt and his team, they've been in business since the late eighties, when they got booted from the SAS. They've been connected with three abductions in Italy between 1989 and '90, nine throughout the rest of Europe, mostly in the former Soviet states, and then a whole spate of them in Colombia lasting until a year ago."

I knocked snow out of my hair. "But why the FBI?"

"Three of the snatches were of American foreign nationals." Scott scooped up snow and began packing it into a ball between his palms. "They work for themselves, and they take contracts. Rumor is you get the squad for a flat million. If ransom's involved, there's probably a cut of that, too. Their record isn't very pretty."

"How many returns?" I asked.

"Less than twenty percent. Victims who make it back tend to need immediate medical care. Women fare much worse than men. Sexual abuse. Torture." He scowled at his snowball, then threw it to the ground, where it burst. "Those who come back go straight to therapy."

"And the rest?"

"The bodies aren't always recovered."

And these are the people Diana has hired to kidnap her daughter, I thought.

"Where's Moore?" Scott asked.

"Right now, I honestly don't know. Maybe at the safe house."

"Can you take me to him?"

"I need to pave the way," I said.

"Atticus, I've got to talk to Moore. We'd lost him, you understand? The first proof we had that any of them were still around was when the NYPD found Ennis's body in that van."

"Ennis?"

"One of Sterritt's crew. There are three others— Glenn Hardy, Evan Cox, and Michael Perkins. The one Yossi capped was Paul Ennis. According to the paper

the Brits sent over, they're all hard-core bastards."
Scott stopped, facing me. "Moore fucked us over good
when he ditched us. Like I said, we had squat, and then
Ennis turns up, the NYPD is telling me about an attempted kidnapping on Third Avenue, and all of a sudden, I'm looking at connections to my good friend
Atticus, who hasn't been returning my calls."

"Sorry about that."

"Uh-huh. Where were you last night?"

"The safe house, then my place."

"I called your place. You didn't answer."

"I didn't get in until late."

Scott shook his head, sad that I wasn't telling him the
truth. "You didn't go with Moore and his boys to a
building in TriBeCa last night, did you?"

"Why?"

"These men are dangerous, Atticus. You're going to
need help if you want to keep your principal safe, and
that means my help."

I had to agree. "I'll talk to Moore, see if I can put you
two together."

"Do that. Your principal, Erika. How secure is she?"

"Normally I'd say very, but they're SAS-trained, and
they know how to infiltrate. As long as Sterritt can't
find her, we'll be all right."

"Don't be counting on Moore to help you protect
her."

"He seems straight."

Scott stuck out his arm to hail a cab, and we stepped
back from the curb as one jerked over, spitting up slush
and water from beneath its wheels. "Moore wants Sterritt and the others, and he wants them so bad he can
taste it. Your principal is incidental to him, at best."

"He's done a good job protecting Erika so far," I
argued.

"That's because Erika's his bait." Scott climbed into
the back of the cab.

I said nothing.

"You make damn sure Moore calls me." He pulled his door closed, and the cab pulled away.

I watched it go, then made for the subway station at Union Square, wondering how I could convince Moore to talk to the FBI. He wouldn't listen to me, I knew. What he wanted was Sterritt, hell or high water, as the previous night had proven, and Scott Fowler would only get in the way of that.

Erika was his bait, Fowler had said.

And bait gets eaten.

CHAPTER TWENTY-NINE

Bridgett had left for work when I arrived at the safe house, Dale and Natalie letting me inside. I was informed that Moore, Knowles, and Denny had all departed before dawn, and that Yossi had gone in search of his bed soon after. Corry sat with Erika in the living room, both reading magazines, or pretending to. Natalie led me in and then gave me a slight shake of the head, and I knew what it meant, I knew she hadn't told Bridgett. I gave her the rundown on my meeting with Scott, and we each took up our posts.

The morning passed without incident, the house filling with a localized tension that was for the most part invisible. It showed only in paranoia, sensitivity to noise; the way we all tensed up when we heard a car sliding down the snowy street; the way Erika jumped when I dropped the remote control out of my splinted hand.

"When are they coming for me?" Erika asked at one point.

"I don't know."

"But they'll come?"

"There are a lot of people looking for them," I said. "The NYPD, the FBI."

"Looking for Mom?"

"And Sterritt and his guys."

Erika tugged the sleeves of my sweatshirt down around her hands, balling the fabric in her fists. "I hate this," she said. "It's making my stomach hurt."

"Mine, too," I said, truthfully, and then my pager went off, and both of us jumped. I silenced it, checked the number.

"Who is it?" Erika asked. "Is it my father?"

I shook my head. "A fellow I know at the FBI."

"Oh."

I got up to go to the phone, then stopped. "The Colonel still hasn't talked to you?"

"No."

"You want me to call him?"

"I don't care."

"I'll be right back," I said, and headed into the kitchen to find Natalie on her way out. I went to the phone, and she touched the back of my hand before returning to the living room.

Just a touch.

I called Scott.

"What's going on?" Fowler demanded.

"They haven't come back."

"When do you expect them?"

"I don't know," I said.

"I've got brass all over my back. Not to mention two detectives from the NYPD that you might remember from the Special Victim Squad," Scott said. "I need to talk to Moore."

"Are you tracing this call?" I asked.

"Are you kidding?"

"Well, pretend you are," I said, and gave him the address of the safe house. "Moore and his people are not here right now, but if you want to come over this evening, you'll probably find one of them."

"See you tonight," Fowler said, and hung up.

I called the Colonel next, and he was coughing when he answered the phone, and continued to cough for almost a minute longer after we were connected. He sounded awful, and the coughs, even over the phone, were savage and ineffective. When he finally spoke, I could barely make him out.

"What the fuck's happened?" he rasped.

"Nothing more. They've resumed the search."

"I've been waiting to hear from you. Where the hell are you?"

"The safe house."

"Still secure?"

"For now. They'll find us eventually."

"If Moore doesn't find them first."

"It's a big if, Colonel."

"How's Erika?"

"She's scared," I told him. "She's holding out. You ought to talk to her."

"No."

"She'd like to hear from you, Colonel."

"It's not necessary."

"For you, maybe."

He raised his voice, what might have been a shout not too long ago. "I've got nothing to say to her."

"Talk to your daughter, Colonel," I said. "At least let her know you're worried for her."

"She's not with the cunt, that's all that matters."

"You're a son of a bitch," I said, hearing my voice climb. "I almost believed you, you know that? But you're still the same selfish rat-fuck son of a bitch you were four years ago."

"Just do your job, Sergeant. Keep my daughter secure." He hung up.

I slammed down the phone, turned, and saw Erika in the doorway. I knew from her face that she had heard the whole thing.

"I just wanted a Coke," she said softly.

"He's worried about you," I said.

She took a can of soda from the refrigerator, closed the door quietly. "Sure."

"He told me to tell you he loves you."

"You don't have to lie for him. He's not paying you for that."

"He's sick and he's scared, Erika," I said. "He doesn't like being out of control. He doesn't like not being here with you."

"Sure," she said tonelessly, and went back to the couch and her unread magazine.

At two I sent Corry home, telling him to be back before midnight, and at four Yossi returned, so I cut Dale loose, giving him until the next morning. None of Moore's crew returned or called, either, but I didn't expect them to. I told Yossi and Natalie to keep an eye open for Fowler, and not to panic if they saw him lurking in the street.

Shortly after six, Bridgett arrived with two pizza boxes and a gym bag, and her appearance sparked Erika, lifting the gloom that had filled the house during the day. It was her manner, mostly, but the effect was immediate, and it made me very glad to see her.

"Hey, brat!"

Erika didn't miss a beat. "Hey, slut!"

Bridgett dropped the pizzas on the coffee table, turned into my arms, and gave me a kiss. It was hard and brief and unexpectedly sweet and she let me go quickly, but not before the guilt kicked me hard below my heart. She flopped down on the couch beside Erika and began opening her gym bag. "Figure I'll be spending the night here again, so I brought some stuff to keep us from going fucking nuts."

"Anything good?"

"Probably not," Bridgett said, reaching into the bag

and pulling out paperback books. "I wasn't certain you could read, you know?"

"Eat me," Erika said.

"Not on your life. See if there's anything you like and leave the rest for me." Bridgett pushed the duffel onto the floor, grabbed the pizzas, and went into the kitchen, saying, "I'll start serving up."

The kitchen door swung shut, and Erika began going through the books. I thought about telling Natalie she was free to go, then wondered if that was honestly what I needed to do, or just an attempt to assuage my guilt.

"Hey, look at this." Erika held up a copy of *A Wrinkle in Time*. "You gave me this for my birthday one year."

"I remember," I said.

"I'm a little old for it." She tossed the book carelessly onto the table. "Everybody else gave me crap that year, but I remember you gave me the whole series."

"Your mother gave you U2 tickets," I reminded her.

It took her a second, and then Erika said, "Shit, right. That was the Joshua Tree tour."

"How was the show?"

"I didn't go."

"What? You went crazy over those tickets, I remember."

"I know. I wanted to, but there were all these people who knew I had tickets, and they kept asking if I'd take them. There was a boy I liked, his name was Ryan, I think, and I wanted to go with him and you and Mom. And that was just before you left, and then Mom said she was too busy that night, so I ended up giving them away."

She shrugged, then said, "I didn't even tell her I hadn't gone. I remember that. I'd been over at somebody's house instead, and when I got home Mom asked how the show was and I totally lied, told her that it was amazing, and that I'd done pot and fooled around with some guy I'd met during the concert." Erika laughed. "She grounded me for a month."

"I'll bet."

Bridgett stuck her head out of the kitchen and asked, "Should I bring Nat and Yossi slices or should they come in here?"

"You can bring it to them," I said. "Just stay with them while they eat."

"No problem. You two might want to grab some food before it gets cold."

Erika and I went to get our slices while Bridgett took two plates to the front. I heard Natalie saying thank you, and everything sounded normal and fine, and I was certain she felt as guilty as I.

"You want a pepperoni slice?" Erika asked me.

"I'm not hungry."

"What's the deal with you and Natalie?"

She reads minds, I thought. "What do you mean?"

"I mean, what's going on between the two of you? Why have you been trying not to look at each other all day?"

"You don't miss much," I said.

She shook her head, agreeing with me, then licking pizza grease from her fingers.

I thought about denying it. Instead, I said, "Natalie and Rubin were going out when he died. When I got home last night, she came by, and we started talking about him. I was pretty upset because of what you'd told me. We had a lot to drink, and we ended up sleeping together." I wondered if this was the kind of confession you should make to a fifteen-year-old. I wondered whose questions I was answering in telling her.

Erika lowered her voice and raised her eyebrows. "You mean fucking?"

I hesitated before answering. The voices from the front were low, and I couldn't make out words, only tone. The tone sounded comfortable. I nodded.

Erika frowned, considering this revelation. "Was it an accident?"

"I don't know. We could have stopped, we knew exactly what we were doing, but we didn't. In part we were lashing out at Rubin, I think."

"In part?"

I took a moment to try to articulate some of what I was feeling.

"Natalie and Bridgett are friends, aren't they?" Erika asked, when I didn't answer. "They talk like they've known each other a long time."

"They're friends. Natalie introduced me to Bridgett."

The kitchen door swung open and Bridgett came back in, saying, "They want soda. Do we have any left?"

"In the fridge," Erika said.

Bridgett stopped and looked at us. "What are you two plotting?"

"Nothing," Erika said.

"Nothing?" Bridgett asked me.

"We're admiring your choice in pizzas," I said.

She went to the fridge and got three cans of soda, saying, "You two had better behave."

We were quiet until we heard the voices at the end of the hall start again. I shouldn't be doing this, I thought. Bridgett's distracting them from their posts.

"You're in trouble," Erika said in a soft playground singsong.

"I know."

"You haven't told her, have you?"

"Not yet."

Erika folded her slice and looked at it, not me. "Natalie's better for you," she said.

I didn't say anything.

"Well, she is," Erika said, as if I'd spoken, as if her reasons were obvious. "I mean, you don't have to prove anything with her, do you? She's like you, in a way."

"You get all this from having known Natalie for how long?"

"One week. And I don't miss much, remember. That's what you said. Right?"

"Right. I forgot."

She brought her head back around with a frown. "I won't tell Bridgett, if that's what you're worried about. That would be totally cruel, so don't think I'd do that, because I wouldn't."

"Bridgett told me that you two are getting along now."

"She's still a pain, but she's not really such a bitch as I thought she was." She picked up her plate. "We'd better go back out there. She'll wonder what we're up to."

"She already does," I said.

Moore and Knowles returned a little past eight, and the two of them finished the remaining pizza and soda. I'd sent Natalie home after dinner, and we'd exchanged silent looks that commiserated in guilt and anxiety, and desire. It was the desire that confused me most of all, that made the guilt worse. That she was feeling it too didn't help matters any.

Knowles went to join Yossi at the door after eating, leaving Moore, Bridgett, Erika, and me in the living room. Erika was reading on the couch, Bridgett beside her, listening to my conversation with Moore at the dining table. There had been no sign of Fowler on the street, and if he was out there, he was being either very patient or very discreet. Or perhaps he wanted all three of them—Moore, Knowles, and Denny.

"We're heading out again in an hour or so," Moore told me.

"Where?"

"We've chased paper to the Bronx, think they may be holed up there."

"The Bronx is a big place."

"So I've heard." Moore rubbed his eyes, and I could see the redness around his corneas. "Have you heard from Denny?"

"No."

"We split up this morning. He was trying to figure

where Sterritt's getting his gear, got a lead on a fellow in Brooklyn. If he calls or comes by, tell him to hold tight here. I don't like splitting the brick this way."

"You can wait until he shows," I said.

Moore shook his head, dismissing the suggestion.

"I talked to the Colonel this afternoon about contacting the FBI," I lied.

"No," Moore said. "No way. This is mine, this hunt is mine."

"I know the lead Fed on this end," I said. "He's a good guy, stand-up. He won't cut you out."

"Fuck that, Atticus. Sterritt's mine, they're all mine. I don't want to have to explain it to some stuffed-shirt civil servant limp-dick who's worried about puckering up to his superior's arse."

"Fowler's not like that."

"That his name? Fowler? I don't care what—"

Then the explosions started.

CHAPTER THIRTY

There were two of them, one on top of the other, terrifyingly loud, and maybe I heard the glass breaking before the explosions, but maybe that was just my mind filling in the sounds I'd missed. The flashes were brilliant and blinding, pure white, caught in my periphery down the hall, and my ears were already ringing. I heard Yossi yelling, inarticulate, in pain, and perhaps Knowles, too, but I was in motion already, going for Erika.

Grenades. They'd come with grenades. Stun grenades, probably, flash bang, and if that was all they were using, we were lucky, because that meant that Yossi and Knowles were still alive.

Bridgett had already grabbed Erika in her arms, and I heard the shots next as we went to the hand-off, pulling Erika to me with my bad left hand. I caught a whiff of explosive powder from down the hall.

The front door came down hard onto the floor of the hallway, the impact echoing down the hall, and I heard the sound of a spoon flying from another grenade. I wrapped my arms around Erika and dropped to the deck, hearing Moore shouting out, hearing the sound of something small and heavy hitting the floor and then, immediately, another detonation, loud enough to shake the room.

From behind the couch, I saw Bridgett fall with a cry, and my heart stopped as rubber shot ricocheted off the walls and ceiling, raining down, stinging me through my clothes.

My gun was in my right hand, I didn't even remember drawing it.

Erika was trembling beneath me.

I rolled, and came around to see the muzzle of a submachine gun pointed at my face. The man holding it was tall, broad-shouldered, wearing a black balaclava. A Browning was on his hip, and the Emerson knife was clipped to his left pocket. Too tall to be Sterritt. Maybe Hardy.

Beyond him, on the floor against the wall, Moore was doubled over in the fetal position, whimpering.

"Lose the gun," Hardy said.

I could hear Bridgett moaning in pain.

They had come with masks and stun grenades. They had thrown a stinger when they could have thrown a frag.

They didn't want to kill us. And that meant that all of us were still alive, in pain, maybe, but still alive. Because if one of us died, they wouldn't hesitate to pull the trigger on the rest. The difference between one count of felony murder and six counts felony murder is academic; after all, the State can only execute you once.

If I started shooting, even if I managed to get a bead and fire before he pumped thirty bullets into me, the others would kill us all.

It was simple, really.

They'd already won.

I put the gun on the floor.

"Push it away," he said.

I gave the Smith & Wesson a good shove, and it slid into the wall, scattering pellets of rubber buckshot as it went.

"Over here," he said, and motioned me off Erika. "Let me have a turn with her."

I hesitated, but it didn't matter, because another one came around from the other side and yanked Erika to her feet, threw her over the edge of the couch. She didn't make any noise when he moved her, and I could look into her face from where I was on the floor.

Whatever she saw in my eyes, it made her start to cry.

"Here, now," the other one said, and I knew the voice, and I knew it was Sterritt. "None of that."

The one on me motioned me back and up, saying, "Slowly."

"We'll treat you nice," Sterritt was saying. "You may even decide you like me." He'd pulled a roll of duct tape from somewhere on his person, and was done wrapping Erika's ankles, and apparently he had found another Emerson knife, because he was using it to cut the strips. He bound her arms behind her back, then took a handful of hair to pull her head up, and placed one last strip over her mouth.

Erika kept crying, kept looking at me.

The last piece of tape in place, Sterritt shoved the roll back into his jacket, folded his knife and slipped it back into his pocket, and then pushed Erika down over the back of the couch once more. "How we doing back there?" he shouted.

"Clear!"

"Take her," he told the one who'd been covering me, and the two changed positions quickly, giving me no chance, no opening.

Hardy hefted Erika over his shoulder. She was limp, not resisting, but she held her head so she could still see me. I thought she was going to hyperventilate, if she kept crying like that, what with the duct tape over her mouth. Her wet eyes pleaded with me to help her, to do something.

"I'll find you," I said to her.

She was carried down the hall, out the door.

Bridgett tried to move, then gave up, doubling herself over. Red welts were on her face and hands. Some bled. Moore had the same marks, caught by the direct blast from the last grenade, and he continued to rock in his fetal position, blood streaking his face, teeth clenched, eyes watching.

Sterritt looked down at me. "You're supposed to be dead."

"I got lucky," I said.

From behind the balaclava, he laughed sourly.

Down the hall, one of the men shouted, "Let's go!"

"Coming!" Sterritt looked at the submachine gun in his hands, then back at me. "Sarge told us never to do this, but I owe you, so here goes."

The muzzle hit me on the right side of my cheek, catching my glasses and knocking them off my face, the metal tearing into my skin. The blow was stunningly painful, and I went down on my hands and knees, my vision liquid and unsteady.

"Don't try to come after us," he said, and then he put his foot in my stomach, and I felt my stitches pop and tear, and I was on my back, on rubber shot, and he was gone.

I rolled the rest of the way onto my stomach, tried to use my hands to get up. I heard Bridgett and Moore getting to their feet, and they each gave me a hand, and then we were standing behind the couch, looking down the hall. Two men, both clad in black, balaclavas in place, were ushering Knowles and Yossi into the living room. They gave them a good shove, then began backing away. Yossi and Knowles managed to keep their footing, but they were unsteady, deafened from the blasts, still having trouble with their vision.

The last two men backed to the front door. One pulled another grenade from his belt. "Nice meeting you all," he said, then pulled the pin, tossed the grenade underhand at us.

Both Moore and Bridgett let go of me, diving for Knowles and Yossi respectively, and I saw them go down as I fell again, heard the jingle of the spoon hitting the ground, and then the pop of primer.

There was no explosion, and I thought, strange, there should be a boom, a really big boom.

The odor that poured into the family room was sweet and sticky.

"Smoker," I heard Moore say.

The smoke billowed into the room, dense and white and thick like smog and foul exhaust. I tried to get up again, heard either Bridgett or Moore moving, and then the burning started, and my head felt sealed in a plastic bag, and I tried to pull deeper and deeper breaths, and it only got worse, my whole chest contracting with pressure from all sides, cinders flying into my lungs and eyes and mouth, a sharp pain pushing straight to my heart. I coughed, crawled, felt something snap and break under my right knee, and knew I'd just destroyed my glasses. Something was running down my face, and my skin stung everywhere, eyes, lips, hands, neck—everything hurt, and I just didn't want to be hurt anymore.

Bridgett choked out my name, and I tried to locate the sound. Liquid ran down over my mouth, salty, and I thought it was blood and swiped at it. My fingers came back sticky and coated with mucus.

I felt a hand on my arm, and I reached, caught her, and she pulled me toward her. Through the tears and smoke I could barely make her out, and she looked like shit, snot running in thick streams from her nose, tears tracking down her face.

"Ah fuck, this hurts," Bridgett managed, coughing.

She reached up to my face, pulled herself in closer, and then gave up.

I did, too.

———

The first cops who arrived came in a sector car that was summoned by the neighbors, scared shitless by all of the noise. Two officers blundered blindly in through the smoke and got taken down just as we all had been. The cloud had spread through the whole house by then, and when Bridgett and I weren't coughing or spitting up snot, I could hear Moore or Knowles or Yossi fighting the effects of the tear gas, too.

It took forever to make it outside, suffering all the way, with Bridgett leading me along on hands and knees until we hit the fresh night air, cold and almost painfully clean, falling into the snow that had gathered on the steps. We lay there, tangled together, leaking blood and mucus.

Two EMTs found us that way, leaned down to help us up, and Bridgett croaked out, "There are others inside."

I couldn't speak.

One of them nodded, went back for his mask, while the remaining technician helped us to the rear of their rig, and began giving us oxygen. We sat with blankets around our shoulders, masks on our faces, while the tech tried to stop the bleeding from my cheek. He went through three gauze pads, and on the fourth I remembered something about facial wounds bleeding a lot, and tried to take comfort in that.

Then the tech saw my shirt and said, "Holy shit." He moved me up onto the gurney, and got out a pair of clothing shears and all I could think was that I didn't want to lose another shirt. I have no idea why I thought that; it was just a gray T-shirt, but I was adamant he not cut it off. He tried to bring the scissors in and I pushed him away, struggled to get my shirt off myself, and finally, with his help, succeeded.

The incision in my abdomen had opened, the stitches tearing through healthy skin to create another injury altogether. The tech tried to question me about the stitches, but I was still finding it difficult to breathe, let alone speak. The tear gas had pretty much cleared

Bridgett's system by then, though, and she offered answers as best she could.

Another rig arrived, then another police car, their lights painting the street and flashing bright inside the ambulance. I heard Yossi and the others being brought out, heard officers asking technicians what had happened, if the house was clear. Bridgett leaned down to look at me, past the technician's shoulder, and she had removed her mask, and I thought she was the most wonderful woman I had ever seen.

I said, "I'm sorry."

The mask kept my voice far away.

"Hey, don't worry," Bridgett said. Her voice sounded raw. "I'm going to talk to the cops, fill them in. Okay?"

I nodded and she gave my head a pat, then hopped out of the rig as the tech left my side, began hooking up a bag of ringers. He used a pocketknife on a nasal cannula, then attached the air line to the IV, turning it into a makeshift eyewash. It helped, and for some reason, that made it easier to breathe.

Eventually, I heard voices I recognized, though it took me a moment. Then Detective Hower was stooping to fit into the rig, saying, "Jesus, cowboy, you do like your punishment, don't you?" He looked at the tech. "Where you taking him?"

"Vincent's," the EMT said.

"How's he doing?"

"It's mostly superficial. The gas got him good, whatever it was."

"Tear gas," I managed.

The tech didn't hear me, saying, "He needs his right cheek stitched up, and the wound in his abdomen."

"We'll see you there," Hower said. "The lady wants to ride with him."

"All aboard."

The ambulance ride and the police presence guaranteed a quick trip to St. Vincent's emergency room. I was put on an examination bed at a suture station and had a moment to glance around me, to see the motion and count heads to determine that all were present and accounted for, before the privacy curtain was drawn around me. I'd been in St. Vincent's ER once before, with Rubin, after a bar fight that he had started by calling a racist Guido from Queens a racist Guido from Queens.

The memory of that and of him gave way to the full realization of what had happened.

The last time I'd been in an ER, it had been at Bellevue, and one of my principals had died. Now I'd lost another.

But Erika wasn't dead, not yet. If Sterritt honored his deals, she was already with her mother.

If he didn't honor his deals, the chances were high nobody would ever see her again.

Nothing good ever comes from visiting the ER, I decided.

Bridgett stood by the bed, checking her wounds. Some of the welts seemed to be fading, but I knew others would stay with her for a while. I was off the oxygen, now, and my vision had reverted to the familiar blur of no corrective lenses.

"That was mean," Bridgett said, her voice still raspy. She blew her nose on some Kleenex. "That was just mean."

"It got them what they wanted." My throat still burned, but I sounded clear to my ears.

"Hurt like a motherfuck. I thought we were dead."

"They didn't want to kill us."

"So they used riot grenades and smoke."

"And tear gas."

She took some fresh Kleenex from the box. "Talk about overkill."

"They threw it after the smoker so we wouldn't know it was there. The tear gas bonds to the smoke, hides it perfectly. It's a military trick. You have no idea what you're running into until it's too late."

She blew her nose again. "Like I said, it's mean."

"It gives us hope. They didn't want any bodies."

"You think they'll hurt her?"

I didn't say anything.

"Do you think they'll hurt Erika?" Bridgett asked again, and she was insistent.

"She's no good to them dead," I said.

"That's not what I meant."

We both knew what she meant.

A doctor rolled back the privacy curtain around us and came in, followed by Morgan and Hower. She gave me a local in my stomach, and that hurt, too, and then started sewing there while the Q&A began with Morgan and Hower. They had gotten a lot of what they were after from the others already. I was just a courtesy interview, used to verify descriptions and accounts. Moore had been able to identify both of the men who'd entered the living room by their voices, and Morgan confirmed it was Mark Sterritt and Glenn Hardy.

"Have you called Colonel Wyatt?" I asked.

Hower grunted. "We've sent a unit up to Garrison to get him. Didn't want to give him the news over the phone. Where do you think they've taken the kid?"

"Hopefully, to her mother."

"Hopefully?" Morgan asked. "If she's with her mother, they're already out of the city."

"If she's with her mother, she's safe, Detective," I said.

"You think those guys are planning to double-cross Diana Wyatt?"

"Maybe."

"As I understand it, the way these contracts work, they've only received half of their money so far. If they want the rest, they have to hand over the girl."

"If that's all they want," Bridgett said.

"What more is there?" Morgan demanded, like she knew we'd been keeping secrets from her.

Bridgett shrugged, so the detectives looked at me. I decided I didn't want to get into slush funds and super-blacks right now, so I shrugged, too. "Where the hell is Fowler?" I asked. "He was supposed to be watching the safe house, waiting for a chance to talk to Moore."

"Oh, was he?" Hower sniped. "Was the pretty Fed trying to cut us out?"

"All I know is that we talked today," I said. "Fowler wanted to see Moore, and I figured the best way for him to do that would be to come by."

"Nice to be in the loop," Morgan muttered.

The doctor was tying off on my stomach, and because of the local, it felt very strange, as if she were tugging on skin that had fallen asleep. She seemed entirely oblivious to, or uninterested in, our conversation, just dropped the needle she had used in the biohazard bin and then moved her stool over so she could work on my face.

"You want a local for your cheek?" she asked.

"Will he be able to talk?" Hower asked.

"If he wants me to punch through to his mouth, sure."

"I'll take the local," I said.

Morgan and Hower said they'd talk to me some more when the doctor was done.

Bridgett had been alert enough to grab my T-shirt out of the rig, and after I was sewed up I put it back on, then went with her and a couple of officers to the 6th Precinct. Morgan and Hower rode along separately, with Yossi, Moore, and Knowles all shipped in other cars. It took a good hour and a half for Morgan and Hower to square everything with the local detectives, then we all went through the night again, this time with forms being filled out. I caught some time with no one asking me questions, found a phone, and called Dale.

"I'm not supposed to be there until midnight," he said after I identified myself.

"We lost her," I told him.

"Oh, God, no. What happened?"

I ran it down in shorthand, then asked Dale to call Corry and Natalie. "Tell them the cops may be calling, just to get all the facts."

"I'll tell them. What are we going to do?"

"Hell if I know," I said, and hung up.

Coming up the precinct stairs was Colonel Wyatt, followed by two officers. He was bundled up for warmth, a dark red scarf around his throat, and his chin was sunk deep into the fabric. Without my glasses, he looked almost cuddly to me. Neither cop offered him assistance as he struggled with the stairs. Both looked like they'd probably learned the hard way how he responded to such treatment. When he finally reached the landing one of the cops detached, went to look for a detective, and Wyatt saw me.

"You pussy-fucking cocksucker," he spat. "First last night, now this. You've ruined everything." It was a blatant accusation, and although he wasn't very clear, or even very loud, I heard everything he put into the statement. "You lost her."

"Yes."

"I knew you couldn't be trusted. What were you doing, huh? Getting a tongue-bath from your girlfriend? You're fucking worthless, Sergeant. You're no damn fucking good at all."

I had nothing to say to that.

"Now Diana has her, so now Diana wins, and you helped her do it. I knew I shouldn't have trusted you with her." He made his way to an old wooden bench along the wall, sat down hard. The skin around his mouth looked coated with a white blur, as if someone had applied correction fluid there, but not enough.

There's one ultimate truth of protection, and that truth is, simply, it's impossible to protect anyone absolutely. It just can't be done. All a bodyguard can do is reduce the odds, take precautions, and try to be sneakier than the opposition. That's it. Because, in the end, time and everything else is on the side of the other team. They can wait, they can plan, they can invest time

and money, research and people that the protective effort will never be able to muster, and that, when it's all
done, that's what will make the difference.

I knew that. I knew that there was no way I'd win
going up against the SAS. I knew that the moment Sterritt and Hardy had come through the door, it had been
all over.

It didn't make me feel better.

All of the knowledge, the rationalizations, the reason-
ing aside, I felt that Colonel Wyatt was right, and because of that, I felt like shit.

Detective Morgan appeared, introduced herself to
Wyatt. She gave him space to let him stand up, then led
him away, saying, "We need to go over what happened
tonight, Colonel. Maybe you can help us."

"Diana won, that's what happened," Wyatt told her.
He was looking at me. "Diana won."

Fowler arrived just before eleven, bags growing beneath his eyes, his perfect tan looking sallow in the precinct lights. He cut past me quickly, barely giving me
time to ask where the fuck he'd been, why he hadn't
shown up. His only response was a look over his shoulder at me, and his eyes were cold and tired, and I realized the rest of him probably was, too. Scott took a
second, then motioned me and Bridgett to follow him.
He found Moore, then an empty interrogation room,
and when all of us were inside, he introduced himself to
Moore.

"Nice to finally meet you," Scott said. He didn't
sound like he meant it.

Moore looked him over. "You're a Fed? You don't
fucking look like a Fed."

"Yeah, I'm a Fed."

"Piss off," Moore said. "Atticus, who is this guy?"

"He's the FBI agent I was telling you about."

"Yes, I'm the FBI agent he was telling you about,"
Scott said. "And I'm too tired to play the aren't-you-

a-little-young, aren't-you-a-little-tan, what's-with-the-earrings-are-you-queer games, Sergeant. If you had fucking honored your agreement with our government, I wouldn't have to be here."

Moore leaned back in his chair and glared at Scott, and for a moment I thought it was a ludicrous situation. Physically, Moore was a monster compared to Scott. He certainly looked like he could tear the younger man in two. "Don't fucking blow hard on me, boy."

"You had two other men with you when you arrived," Scott told him. "One of them's here. Where's the other one?"

"Denny's been out of touch all day. And if you're thinking it was an inside job and he set us up, you're a fucking idiot. Denny's a good troop."

Scott reached into his coat pocket and removed three Polaroids. He set the photographs on the table in front of Moore, but both Bridgett and I could see them.

"Mother of God," Bridgett murmured.

The photographs were crime scene shots of a body, stuffed naked into the trunk of a car. A line of lacerated flesh ran in what looked like a circle about the dead man's scalp, where skin had been peeled up. His face showed serious bruising, shattered teeth, a broken nose, set on a head that wasn't quite centered on the neck. Another of the shots showed his right hand, three fingers missing after the second knuckle. The flash on the camera had made the photos studies of light and dark, but the wounds on Denny's body were clear and devastating.

"Is that Edward Denny?" Fowler asked. There was a strain in his voice that I'd never heard before.

"Oh, Jesus," Moore said.

"Is that him?"

Moore picked up the photographs one at a time, looking at each picture hard and long, boring the image into his memory. Then he handed them back to Scott. "That's Eddy," Moore said.

"The body was discovered around six this evening," Scott said.

"That's how they found the safe house." Bridgett said it softly. "They tortured him."

"The autopsy hasn't been completed, yet, but the preliminary evaluation is that the injuries were all inflicted prior to death."

"How'd he die?" Moore asked. "They know that, don't they? They know how he died?"

"We can't be certain, but it looks like they broke his neck."

Moore closed his eyes, preserving the pictures in his mind.

"I'll leave you alone," Scott told him. "You might want to tell your other man."

Moore moved his head in a nod.

We started out of the room, me following behind Fowler and Bridgett, and as I was reaching the door, Moore said, "Kodiak—I want to talk to you."

I told the others I'd catch up.

"Close the door."

I closed the door.

When I turned, Moore's face had gone to its battle mask, hard and cruel. It was a disturbing look.

"We find them," he said quietly, "Sterritt's mine."

I held his look. "Erika comes first," I said. "We get her back, you can do whatever you like with Sterritt. Erika has to come first."

Moore nodded, saying, "Of course," and I knew he was lying to me.

CHAPTER THIRTY-ONE

They cut us loose at one that morning, sending Colonel Wyatt to a hotel and the rest of us home. Moore and Knowles left together, after another long meeting with Fowler. There wasn't much anyone could say at that point, no new information to be revealed, and I left the precinct feeling empty and numb, Bridgett beside me. There'd been no word of Erika. She'd been gone five hours. The NYPD had retrieved some of our gear from the safe house. I asked about the Smith & Wesson, and was told that it was being held for its owner, Natalie Trent.

Third gun down, I thought.

We didn't talk about it, just went back to my apartment together, and after I'd locked us inside, Bridgett put her gym bag in my room and started undressing, saying that she wanted a shower. I took out my spare set of glasses, and with the world back in focus, made my way to the phone and checked the messages on my machine. There were two, both from Natalie, sounding concerned, saying that Dale had called her and asking if I knew where Bridgett was, asking me to call when I got in.

I put the kettle on, then went through the apartment, turning on the heat. By the time the water was boiling, Bridgett was out of the shower and back in my room, and I was pouring into two mugs when she emerged, dressed, and the phone rang.

"Should I get that?" Bridgett asked.

I nodded.

It was Natalie. They only talked for five minutes or so, during which time I settled at the table with my mug. The tea tasted bitter, and I wondered if I'd steeped the leaves for too long.

"No, we're both fine," Bridgett was saying. "I look like I've been attacked by rabid ball bearings, and Atticus looks like crap, but everybody came through in one piece . . . I don't know. . . . You want to talk to him? . . . I'll tell him . . . probably tomorrow. We'll call you . . . you, too."

"How is she?" I asked when Bridgett had hung up.

"She's worried, sounds guilty as hell. I think she thinks she should have been there." Bridgett took her mug and joined me at the table. "I asked if she wanted to talk to you, she said no."

The look she gave me was sympathetic, and I realized she thought Natalie and I still weren't getting along. I wanted to tell her then, took a breath to do just that, and then Bridgett was getting up from the table, dumping her mug down the drain.

"I'm fucking exhausted," she said. "And you are, too. Let's get some sleep. We'll need it tomorrow."

"And what are we doing tomorrow?"

"Finding Erika, boy-o."

For a very long time I found I couldn't sleep, and ended up just looking at her beside me. Bridgett breathed softly, the blankets pulled to her shoulders.

When she slept, her face relaxed, and her mouth hinted at a smile. She cradled the pillow to her head like a child holding on to a parent, and at the crook of her left arm, near me, I could see a scar on her skin, what looked like a skin graft. She'd stripped to just T-shirt and underwear, and I could feel the warmth coming off her skin. The radiator hissed, banged erratically, and the noise didn't touch her, and it was easy to imagine that nothing could.

But I knew better.

It was after ten when I awoke, could hear Bridgett moving in the kitchen. I got myself out of bed, made my way to the shower, and bathed quickly. I thought about shaving, decided that it would be an exercise in futility and pain. One hand and one cheek, I could almost see the blood flying.

I dressed, made my way back to the kitchen, and found Bridgett reading the paper.

"Coffee's on," she said.

I mumbled thanks and poured myself a mug.

"Scott called," Bridgett said. "An hour ago."

I'd never heard the phone ring. "What'd he say?"

"That they've got squat. He left a number for Moore, though. It's a service. I called and left a message. Hopefully he'll call back."

I drank my coffee, looking out the window. It was clear outside, and looked cold. Most of the snow had been cleaned from the streets. I sat down at the table.

"How'd you sleep?" she asked.

"Like shit."

"Yeah, I sort of figured."

"I've got something I need to tell you," I said. My voice sounded slighter, more distant, and my stomach-ache returned.

She put down the paper. "This sounds ominous." She smiled.

I nodded, tried to find my voice. Watching me,

Bridgett sensed it, then saw that something was coming, and her smile faded. "What?"

"I slept with Natalie," I told her. "Night before last, she came over after I got home, and we were drinking, and we ended up in bed together."

The skin at the outside of her eyes crinkled, and her mouth moved slightly, lips coming tighter together. Then her jaw started to relax, and I knew what she was thinking, could hear the excuse she was forming for me, and I had to stop her before she said it, I had to get there first.

"I knew what I was doing," I said. "I wanted to do it."

She breathed slowly.

"I wanted to do it," I repeated.

"You son of a bitch," she said.

I nodded.

Bridgett's face changed, the muscles going slack. Her chest rose and fell with her breath, and then she got up, went to the sink, then pivoted on her heel and looked back at me. Her look was as accusatory as the Colonel's had been the night before, as hard, and in it I saw pain. She held the look until it snapped, then turned her head away, tilting her chin down, letting her hair conceal her face. When she spoke, the anger in her voice was cold. "You no-good bastard."

I nodded again, knowing she wouldn't see it.

"That hurts. That really hurts," she said softly. I saw the muscles in her jaw flex as she bit against her teeth. "You knew about Elana, you knew how I felt about things like this."

I couldn't have hurt her more if I had tried, and I knew that was exactly what I had done. Tried to get out of the relationship before I wanted to stay in it, tried to get out before she could hurt me, before another Elana fell in love with her, before she could go away and break my heart.

So I'd done it myself, instead.

All I wanted was to take the pain away, to not hurt

her anymore, to never hurt her again. I would have given anything to do that.

"Why?" Bridgett asked.

It took me a while to answer. "Because I'm a fool. Because I'm terrified of being with you."

Her head bent down, her black hair almost touching the rim of the sink, and then she jerked her head back, her hands coming up, and she rounded on me, and she laughed, bitter and loud. "Bastard."

"I'm sorry, Bridgett," I said. "I know it's worth nothing, but I am sorry."

The floor creaked as she moved, stepping closer to me. "You can keep your fucking apology," she said softly. "You can give it to Natalie, you can give it to Rubin's memory, whoever the fuck you like, but don't try to hand it to me. I trusted you with something I've given only to two other people in my life, and you broke it, you just fucking broke it."

Her face was close to mine, and when I tried to meet her eyes, she moved away again, denying me, going to grab her jacket from the hook on the wall. Her left arm caught in the sleeve, and she tugged hard, twice, before getting it through.

In the alley below, I heard somebody laughing.

"I was afraid I'd lose you," I said.

"You have."

I closed my eyes, remembered to breathe. I made each word as clear as possible when I spoke. "You are precious to me," I said. "And I have lost precious things. A fire took the objects. A bomb took a friend. It took me too long to realize what you mean to me, and when I did, the thought of another loss, that loss . . . I didn't want that again."

I opened my eyes. Bridgett had a roll of Life Savers in her hand, was picking at the foil.

"Why didn't you trust me?" she asked. "Why didn't you tell me?"

"I didn't know what I felt. And then, when I did, when I knew, it was too late. I'd done the damage."

She looked down at the roll of candy in her hand, then flung it hard into the wall. The Life Savers shattered, flew free of their wrapping, pelting the floor.

"I gave you my heart," she said.

I was silent.

"We're no longer lovers," Bridgett said, finally. "We may not even be friends. I can't trust you with anything but business now. I can't trust you, do you understand?"

"Yes," I said.

"We see this out, that's it. I don't want to talk to you anymore. I don't want to know you for a while. I don't think I want to know you at all."

She looked past me, her mouth closed and jaw set, and the hurt I'd inflicted was so clear, and there was nothing I could do about it. She was right. There was nothing more to say, not even that I'd never loved her more.

Then the intercom went off, and Diana was begging me to let her inside.

CHAPTER THIRTY-TWO

We could hear her running up the stairs, and a second later she came off the landing, making straight for us in the doorway. It wasn't an all-out run, closer to a stagger, but when she saw us she came faster, saying, "God, I didn't know if you'd be here, I didn't know where to go."

I moved back, let her into the apartment, and Diana came inside, ignoring Bridgett, just stopping in the hall. I shut the door and looked at her. She had black corduroy pants on and a blue crewneck beneath her coat. The cold had brought a flush to her cheeks, but aside from that, she was almost bone-pale.

She was holding a brown cardboard box, not bigger than a loaf of bread.

"I got it this morning, it was delivered to my room, some girl just handed it to me and left." She was breathless, and not from exertion.

I took the box. It was unmarked, clean, just a strip of clear strapping tape running over the flaps at the top.

The tape had already been cut. When I opened the box, Diana turned away.

Inside, on cracked salt, was a piece of meat and cartilage with metal hoops through it. It took another second before I realized the hoops were earrings, and I recognized them, and I wanted to scream.

The bottom half of Erika's left ear.

Bridgett made a choking sound beside me, but didn't move. I felt my pulse kicking at my wrists and temples, and I felt light-headed.

Beneath the piece of ear was a folded sheet of white paper, speckled with blood.

Without a word, I went to the kitchen table and set the box down. Diana stayed still, standing motionless in the hall, as if the power that propelled her had been suddenly switched off.

When I removed the paper, I could hear the chunks of salt falling onto the tabletop and the floor.

The instructions had been typed. They were very simple. There was a time in military notation: 2000 hours. There was a location: a spot on the Harlem River in the South Bronx. There was a demand: four million dollars. There was a caution: no police, no Moore, no SAS, nobody but Diana.

And there was an ultimatum:

Do not call the police, or the Feds, or your husband, or anyone at all.

Money at 2000 and she's in your arms at 2001.

Fuck with us, and she's dead.

Bridgett turned on Diana, grabbed her by the shoulder, snarling, "Were you followed?"

"I don't know."

"Fuck, motherfuck." Bridgett pulled her gun and headed to the door, saying, "I'm going down to check. Don't go anywhere without me."

I folded the note again, put it back in the box, covering the ear. Then I took hold of Diana and put her in one of the chairs at the table. She let me move her without resistance, but her eyes went to the box the moment she was seated, and they stayed there.

"We need to call the police," I said.

Diana shook her head.

"Diana, we have to call the police. It's the only way."

"I can get the money," she said quietly. "It's all I have. I'll give it to them and they'll give her back."

"No, they won't. There's nothing to stop them from killing you and her if you go to the drop."

"They'll kill her if we go to the police!"

"Listen to me," I said. "They are going to kill her anyway. The only way to get Erika back alive is with help."

"I know that! I know that, that's why I'm here!"

To ask me for help. Jesus, Erika was right, I thought. I'm a gullible fool, and I do it with my eyes wide open. "I can't do it alone," I told Diana.

She shook her head, still looking at the box.

I knelt down beside the table, so I could catch her eyes. For an instant she met my gaze, and I took it, speaking softly. "You must trust me. You must let me do this how I think best. There's still a chance to help Erika, to stop them. You have to trust me."

She just stared at me. Finally, she nodded, once.

"Where's the money now?" I asked.

"In storage," Diana said. "A place in Queens."

"Do they know it's there? Sterritt and Hardy?"

"No."

"You're sure?"

"I paid them out of the place in Baltimore and Credit Suisse downtown. Then I moved the money. I moved it, I didn't want them robbing me."

"Okay, you're going to have to go out there and get it, Diana. Go out to Queens, get the damn money, and come back here."

"But—"

"Now," I said. "I'll be here. Just get it and come back."

She shook her head like she was trying to wake up,

focused on me again. Her eyes were dull, as if she hadn't heard anything I'd told her.

"Then we'll go to the drop together," I said.

Diana got up. Her glance snagged one last time on the box. Bridgett was coming back down the hall as I let Diana out.

"It looks clear," Bridgett reported.

"Come right back," I told Diana. "Don't stop anywhere."

"I get her," Diana said suddenly, her voice brittle with hope. "When Erika's back and safe, I get her, right?"

Bridgett looked at me, and her eyes were accusing.

"When she's back and safe," I told Diana, "she's yours."

Diana accepted that with a nod, then continued on. We watched her go to the stairs, and when she was out of sight, I went back into the apartment, heading for the phone.

"Where's she going?"

"To get the money," I said. "I'm going to call Fowler, let him know, see if we can catch the bastards at the drop."

"You're going to let her make the exchange? You're going to let her leave with Erika?"

"I'm going to get Erika back. Then it'll be her decision."

"She won't be in any condition to make that choice," Bridgett said. "You can't let her mother be there, Erika won't be able to say no."

I put down the phone. "We don't even know if we'll be *able* to get her back," I said. "Who she goes with isn't even an issue, yet."

"It is, it's a huge issue. That girl is being bandied between parents like stock options." Bridgett's face was white with anger.

"What do you want me to do?"

"Cut Wyatt in."

"And how do I do that?"

"Tell Fowler that Wyatt has to be at the drop. He can come in after we've got Erika back. Let her make her choice."

"She won't be in any condition to make a choice, you just said so yourself."

"Then Wyatt has to be there, or else it's just another kidnapping under another name." She said it stubbornly.

"You bring him in, then."

"Fine."

I went into my room, fumbled through my stuff, and found my radios. Bridgett stood in the doorway watching me while I took out my two sets. These were my work radios, small units that could be affixed to a belt, with three leads running off them, one to the palm to transmit, one to the lapel as the mike, and one to the ear as the speaker. I hooked all the wires up for one of them, turned it on, and gave it a squelch. The charge looked good, so I shut it off and turned to hand it over to Bridgett.

She was looking at the box of condoms.

"Here, take this," I said, tossing the radio onto the bed. "Don't turn it on until after we've got Erika, or you'll run the battery down. I'll call you when it's clear to bring the Colonel in."

Bridgett picked up the radio without a word, putting it inside her jacket, beside her holstered gun. Then she started out to the front door.

"Where are you going?"

"None of your fucking business. I'll get Wyatt, I'll have him at the drop. That's all you need to know."

"You're just going to leave?"

Bridgett's boot heel left a mark on the floor when she spun to face me. "Yes. I am just going to leave. I don't want to be around you right now. I told you that. I'll call Fowler in a couple of hours, make certain that I know all those important details you won't want ignored."

And then she left.

It took two hours of phone tag to get everything together, starting with the call to Fowler. Scott listened to
me very carefully, and he made it plain that he thought
bringing the Colonel out was a bad idea.

"If it goes wrong, and he's there, he could end up
seeing his daughter killed," Scott said.

"Then let's hope it doesn't go wrong."

There was a moment's pause, and then he said,
"Time's working against us, Atticus. If they've half a
brain, they'll already have staked the drop site out, in
anticipation of this sort of maneuver."

"I'm trying to reach Moore. He trained them. He
knows how they'll be thinking. He can help you position your people."

"If he gets in touch with you."

"He will. He wants to be there for the takedown,
now more than ever. I'll steer him your way."

"You're going to ride out there with her? Mrs. Wyatt?"

"Yes."

"That could tip the whole thing."

"No, I don't think so. Sterritt knows that Diana and I
have a history. He'll accept that she went to me for
help."

Fowler sighed. Then he said, "I'll call Morgan and
Hower, let them know what's happening. They'll want
to be involved."

"Whose people will you use?"

"Probably theirs."

"Make sure they know what's going on," I said. "I
don't want a sniper shooting too early, or putting a
bullet in my back."

"Hell, you've already been shot once in the front,"
Scott said. "Do you figure another wound will stop
you?"

"I don't want to find out."

We made arrangements for someone to come over

and get the box for evidence, and the courier had just left my apartment when the phone started ringing again.

"Go," Moore said when I picked up.

"We've got a swap," I said.

"The son of a whore tried a double cross, didn't he?"

"This morning. He sent the ultimatum to Diana at her hotel room. He wants four million dollars or Erika's dead."

"Was that all he sent?"

"No," I said, remembering the hoops, how small they had looked.

"A finger."

"Her left ear," I said. "I suppose that was kind."

"He won't be able to die enough," Moore said.

"You need to call Fowler right now," I said. "He's going to contact NYPD about getting coverage, but if they try to move in without knowing what they're up against, it could blow the whole thing."

"They haven't sent anyone out to the drop, have they?" he asked, and the alarm was loud in his voice.

"Not yet. Not that I know of."

"Jesus God, they had better not. What's his number?"

I gave him Scott's number. "Call him now," I said.

"I will, I will," Moore said, and I thought he would hang up, but he didn't, and there was just line silence for a couple of seconds. Then Moore asked, "You remember what I said last night?"

"Yes."

"Can I count on you?"

"Erika first."

"Erika first," Moore confirmed.

I thought about what he was asking, about everything that had happened, about how he had acted the night before, and the night before that. About the cracked salt that was still spilt on my kitchen table.

"Once we get Erika clear, he's all yours," I said.

"See you tonight," Robert Moore said, and he hung up.

Diana didn't return to my apartment until almost two that afternoon, buzzing from outside. I came down to meet her, stuffing my radio into my jacket pocket as I went down the stairs. She was waiting for me at the door, and she looked marginally better, with more color to her skin, more certainty to her movements.

"Where are you parked?" I asked.

She indicated her car, a rented Taurus, dark red, parked down the block. Some kids were lurking in the doorways near the vehicle, and I thought that would just be brilliant, for three street kids to boost a car loaded with four million dollars. I grabbed Diana's elbow and began walking to the Taurus, and she yanked her arm free, almost slipping on the ice. The kids pulled back when we approached.

"Keys," I said to Diana.

"I can drive."

"You'll drive tonight. Give me the keys."

She handed over the keys, and I unlocked the doors, waited until she was inside before sliding behind the wheel myself. My stomach got surly at the motion, and I went slow.

"Buckle up," I said.

Diana complied without objection, and I started the car, pulled out carefully onto the street. Traffic was heavy. A cab shot past us as we did so, and I swore.

"I thought you didn't like to drive," Diana said.

"I don't. What took you so long?"

She produced two plane tickets from her coat pocket. "I had to stop and get these. We're flying out of JFK at ten."

"Where's the money?"

"They won't get to leave with it, will they? I need it. It's for Erika and me."

"No, they won't get to leave with it," I said.

"It's in the trunk, in a briefcase."

Four million dollars in one briefcase, I wondered, and then I remembered her offer at the Bonnaventure, before she had shot me. Diamonds and emeralds. "You converted all of it?"

"Most of it," Diana said. Under her breath, so low I almost missed it, she added, "Just like they taught me."

"What about this car? How'd you get it?"

"Why are you asking all these questions?"

"How'd you rent the car, Di?"

"I used a credit card. Don't worry, it's fake. Mark never saw it."

"Have a lot of fake cards, do you?"

"I've got enough for an emergency."

"Rubin teach you that?"

She looked over at me.

"Yeah," I said. "I know."

"How?"

"Erika told me."

"Erika knew?"

"Erika knew, Di. Erika knew every last detail. You and me, you and Rubin, the Colonel and his whores. She knew it all." I stopped at a light, checking the mirrors. I didn't think we were being followed, but there was no way I could be certain with all of the afternoon traffic. I hoped not. Where we were going, I most certainly hoped not.

"She's a smart young lady," Diana said. She sounded proud.

"Then maybe you ought to let her decide for herself who she wants to be with, you or the Colonel."

Diana laughed. "Smart, I said, not invulnerable. Doug's twisted her mind around, the child can't possibly know what she wants."

"And you do?"

"I know," Diana said.

"Have you talked to her at all?"

"I know."

"Have you?"

"Yes."

"When?"

"A couple of weeks ago."

"She said it'd been a couple of years."

"She lied to you."

"Or you're lying to me."

That set her off. "It doesn't matter when I talked to her!" Diana shouted. "Doug shouldn't have her, Atticus! I'm her mother. I'm the better parent, I'm the one she needs, the one who cared for her, the one who isn't dying because he couldn't keep his dick in his pants!"

She fell silent, maybe because she'd said too much, or because she realized where we had stopped. She looked at all the squad cars lined up outside the 13th Precinct. I turned off the engine, began getting out of the car.

"What the hell are you doing?" Diana demanded.

I just shook my head.

"You said you were going to just call them." She made it sound as if I had been the one to cut off Erika's ear.

"Come on."

"Absolutely not. There's an APB out on me. I'm wanted, remember?"

"Oddly enough, I do. They won't arrest you."

"I'm not going in there."

And that was it, and without warning I heard myself shouting at her. "Get out of the fucking car and get inside the fucking station, now, Diana!"

She blinked, startled, and I realized it was the first time I'd ever raised my voice in her presence, the first time she had ever heard me shout. Diana said softly, "I just want to know—"

"Get out of the fucking car, now!"

Diana got out of the car, her boots sinking into the dirty snow.

"Thank you," I told her.

————

"There's an Emergency Services Unit team already been deployed," Detective Morgan told me. "Fowler, Moore, and Knowles are with them. They've been setting up for the last two hours. ESU is taking advice from Moore, so we should be covered on that end."

"The swap's set for when?" Hower asked.

"Eight tonight," I said.

He checked his watch, whistled softly. "Can you imagine what it must be like to have to stay perfectly still under cover for eight hours?"

I nodded, and he raised an eyebrow, so I said, "I was in the Army."

"So was I. Never had to do that, though."

I shrugged, found a pencil on the desk they had seated me at, and a piece of paper. "Tic-tac-toe?" I asked, drawing the board.

"I'll kick your cowboy ass," Hower said.

"Does she want some coffee?" Morgan asked me, motioning to Diana with her lit cigarette. Some of the ash flicked off when she pointed. "You can answer me, ma'am. It won't be used against you."

Hower chuckled and I looked over at Diana. She was seated beside another detective's desk, staring at me. She hadn't spoken since we'd gone into the station, and although she was well within earshot, hadn't contributed to our conversation. Occasionally, she would check her watch, but otherwise, she'd said nothing.

"Do you want some coffee?" I asked her, handing the pencil to Hower. "It's pretty bad stuff."

"Just bias her, why don't you," Hower grumbled. He considered my opening move, and put an "O" in the upper left corner, then handed the pencil back.

"No," Diana said.

"You ought to try and relax," Detective Morgan told her.

Diana said, "It's not your daughter."

Morgan knocked ash onto the floor, crushed it with her shoe. "No, I guess it isn't."

"Then don't tell me to relax."

The detective sighed, turned back to me and asked, "Where's the money? We need to mark the bills."

"It's at my apartment," I said, passing the pencil back once more. "I didn't want to bring it, leave it in the car."

Diana tilted her chin slightly, almost smiled. I was protecting her investment, after all.

"Your car is not going to get jacked up in front of the One-Three." Hower marked another "O."

"Says you. I've lived in this city for a while now. Stranger things have happened."

He handed the pencil back to me. "You're losing. You had the first move, in the center of the board, and you've managed to lose at tic-tac-toe. I'm truly impressed."

I crossed out the board and began writing on the pad. "How about Hangman?"

Hower looked at what I had written and said, "Sure."

"I'm going to use the bathroom first," I said. "Which way is it?"

Hower gave me directions, and I excused myself, went to the men's room. I used the sink to wash my face, dried off, then took off my shirt and began hooking up my radio. I only used two of the leads, the mike and the transmit button, because I could conceal both of those from Diana. If I ran the speaker to my ear, she'd spot that, and I didn't want her to know that the Colonel had been invited to the party.

It took him five minutes, and then Hower came in with another bundle of wires. "We were going to suggest this, anyway," he said. "Why are you so anxious to wear it?"

"Insurance," I said.

Hower paused to check his bald spot, see if it was still naked and in place.

"I don't know what's going to happen out there tonight. I want a record of it," I said. "And I don't want Diana to know that I'm wired."

He began unwrapping the set, then looked me over and asked, "Two radios?"

"One of them's to keep in touch with Moore. He's on a different frequency."

"He's going to be on the ESU channel. We all will be."

"Moore's SAS," I said. "He's got a different channel for himself and Knowles."

Detective Hower hesitated, his blond eyebrows knitting together, then he began wrapping the new radio around my middle.

"Watch the stitches."

"Yeah, yeah," he muttered. "You're a fucking disaster, you know that? I've seen better-looking bodies after an autopsy."

"At least you don't have to shave my chest," I said.

"Lucky me. You normally go so smooth?"

"They shaved me for the surgery, asshole."

Hower laughed, handed me the new microphone, and helped me tape it to my chest. I pulled on my shirt, then ran my other wires, putting the transmitter down my right arm and wrapping it around my wrist, and finally pinning the mike to the inside of my collar.

"You are just way too technical," Hower said. "We should get back, or Mrs. Wyatt will become nervous."

"Will you be recording?" I asked.

"Anything that plays off our wire will go to tape. You are now acting as an agent of the NYPD."

"I'm a snitch?"

"In a word."

"I need one other thing," I said. "My gun, the one that you guys took after the shoot-out on the street. Can I get that back?"

"You planning on shooting anyone, cowboy?"

I didn't answer.

CHAPTER THIRTY-THREE

Diana stayed silent while she guided the Taurus through the heavy traffic on the Grand Central Parkway, making our way to the Harlem River. I kept my eyes on the mirrors, checking the other vehicles. We were clear.

It was just the two of us, now. Morgan and Hower were following along a different route entirely, and would take up a holding position a good five blocks from the site. The last we heard, Moore and Fowler and the rest were holding steady. Apparently, they hadn't been made.

We were passing Yankee Stadium when Diana asked, abruptly, "Do you remember when he found out about us?"

"The Colonel?"

She nodded, then signaled a lane change. She was a cautious driver; Bridgett would have called her timid, or worse.

"Yes," I said.

"Do you remember what he said?"

"He said he'd ruin me. He chewed me out in the middle of your living room, in front of you, and he said he would have me dishonorably discharged, and that he'd make the rest of my life hell."

She cracked a grin. "And I said, 'You do, and I'll tell everyone in this town that I was fucking him.' He looked like I'd kicked him in the teeth."

"I don't think he expected you to react that way."

"No, he didn't. He thought I was just like him, and that you were nothing to me. And then Doug offered you a posting, anywhere you wanted, and you were gone by the end of the month."

"Is that when you took up with Rubin?"

She cast a glance my way, then went back to looking at the road. "No."

"You'd been seeing him before that." It wasn't a question.

"After you left, we became exclusive. Doug never found out about Rubin."

"Why?" I asked. "I mean, I know this sounds horribly naïve, but I thought you loved me. Was I wrong? Was it Rubin you loved?"

She didn't say anything for the next mile or so. I listened to the engine and the road, felt the tires bumping over the salt and sand and asphalt. The transmitter for my radio was digging into my back, and I tried to ignore it. My stitches itched, and the wire taped to my chest made it hard to breathe.

"Yes and no," Diana finally answered. "I loved you both, and I didn't love either of you."

"Nice paradox."

"I was lonely. You were what I needed, both of you."

"It's good to be needed," I said.

Diana fell silent, turning off the expressway and onto 167th Street. We were now heading toward the water. The digital clock on the radio read 7:43.

"Where will you go?" I asked her.

"California. I've always wanted to live in California," she said. "Which way?"

"Right, here."

She signaled and turned, and we were heading north again. After a mile I told her to make a left, and we ran west for another mile or so, and each block we passed seemed more devastated than the previous one. Economics in the Bronx had led to endless abandoned buildings, and they stood now in decay, waiting in vain for money and interest. It would never happen.

The clock now read 7:50, and Diana stopped for a light. I looked at her, but she kept her eyes on the road.

The light went to green and we started forward once more, and after another two minutes, the Harlem River came into view. The road curved north, following the bend of the choppy water. Along our left were empty lots, abandoned buildings, the whole terrain suddenly looking more like downtown Sarajevo than New York.

It made me scared, not only for myself, but for Erika. Until now, I hadn't allowed myself to believe we were too late, that she might be dead already, but suddenly the possibility was forcing itself to the fore. Sterritt could have killed Erika, assuming that Diana would bring the money to the swap all the same. Once she was on his ground, there was no reason to honor the deal. He could just hope to shoot her, take the money, and run.

Only decency, honor, or caution would keep him from doing so. And I knew he wasn't decent, and I knew he wasn't honorable. But he had seemed cautious, if cocksure, and my hope was that he had kept Erika alive to ensure that the money would come to him. After it was in his hands, then he'd be willing to kill her, but not before, not when she was still good insurance.

The logic seemed fine, but it didn't make me feel better. Sterritt had chosen a site out in the middle of nowhere, away from witnesses and prying eyes. The only reason to pick such a place was if he planned on a lot of killing.

I hoped to God that Moore knew what he was doing, that I could trust him.

"Slow down," I told Diana, and began scanning for the cross street. Cars had been abandoned along the side of the road, and I knew they would make good hiding places for a sneaky SAS bastard to stay in cover and perform recon. This side of the river looked like a junkyard, with trash and machinery left to rot and rust. Crisp snow clung to everything, reflecting light, and making the shadows long and blue.

The lot Sterritt had picked was another four hundred yards north, and as Diana turned into it the headlights lit a form, lumpy and twisted, and for a moment I panicked, thought the whole night was blown, that the ESU and Moore and Fowler and all the cops in the tri-state area had been made.

It was a snowman.

A pathetic-looking, malformed, lumpy snowman, with an empty bottle of some kind of liquor in its right hand.

The clock read 7:59, and as we stopped, it flicked to 8:00.

"Where is he?" Diana asked, not certain if she should panic.

"He's here. He's watching."

She killed the engine, leaving the headlights on. The beams made the snowman look as if he had been frozen in midmelt. I unwrapped the tape from the splint around my fingers, removed the metal, dropped the pieces on the car floor. My fingers hurt when I moved them, but I could use the hand if I had to, and that was what mattered.

"Now what?" Diana asked.

"Now we get out," I said. "And you get the money out of the trunk."

I took my time, going slower than I needed to. One of Sterritt's men would be lookout, I was sure, set somewhere in cover with a radio and a pair of binoculars. If he thought I was below par, that I was slow and no threat, so much the better.

I heard Diana slam the trunk shut, felt the car rock slightly as I got out. She came around to my side as I closed the door. The briefcase was brown leather, with brass clasps and fittings, expensive.

I scanned the surrounding area, looking at the line of buildings and the darkness. The river was audible, barely, flowing fast and nearby. Farther away I could hear traffic, and a distant siren, and then I heard the engine, saw the lights stream over the broken chunks of concrete as it came out of the darkness from across the street and came at us, fast, water and snow sluicing away from its wheels.

Diana and I stepped back, against the side of the Taurus, and the new car came around in a slide, then braked on the opposite side of the snowman, its headlights blinding us.

I winced and thought, nice entrance.

We heard the doors opening, and then they got out, three of them. Hardy had been driving, and he stood behind his opened door, both hands out of sight. In the space between the ground and the bottom of the car door, I saw a piece of fabric dangling, the strap to his submachine gun.

From the passenger side door came another man, the one who had been driving the other car in the shootout, the one with the ponytail. He looked young, and I tried to remember the descriptions Scott had given me, figured it was Perkins. He kept his hands out of sight, too, but it wasn't as if I couldn't guess what he was holding.

And from the back came Mark Sterritt, holding Erika in a headlock against his chest. He had his Browning to her head.

She looked terrible, still wearing the clothes she had been taken in, the blue jeans and my sweatshirt, and I could see the dark stains of blood on the left shoulder, where it had run down the sleeve and front. A strip of duct tape covered her mouth, and her nostrils were flared as she tried to breathe. Another strip had been wrapped around her wrists, and a third to bind her arms to her body. The bloody bandage over her left ear looked black in the night, sodden and useless.

Three of them and Erika. Sterritt, Hardy, and Perkins. Which meant that somewhere out in the darkness lurked Cox with his radio, his binoculars, and probably a high-powered rifle.

Again, I prayed that Moore knew what he was doing, that I could buy enough time for everyone to get into position.

"Hey, Lucky, didn't think we'd be seeing you again," Mark Sterritt called to me.

"Bad luck," I said.

"For you." He took his time looking around, checking the surroundings. "Moore hiding out here, is he?"

"Moore doesn't know we're here," I answered.

"That right? Diana, is that right?"

"That's right," she said. Her voice could have frozen out a furnace.

Sterritt made a noise that sounded like a chuckle, then moved the Browning from Erika to us and then to the snowman. He fired two shots, and snow exploded from the shape, flew away from the malformed head, and the bottle dropped from the frozen hand.

Nothing else.

"Just checking," Sterritt said tightly. He came forward carefully, with Erika still gripped tight, the gun steady under her chin. Hardy and Perkins eased away from the car as he came forward, and I saw the submachine guns in their hands, the MP5s they had used at the safe house. Their move kept Sterritt from blocking their line of fire, and I thought that they were very well trained, indeed.

When Sterritt had reached the front of their Buick, he stopped. Erika's eyes were wide and clear. Good, I thought. She's with us, she's aware. If they had doped her up it would have only made things worse, but instead of drugs to control her, they had relied on fear, and that meant that if she could remember to think, we had another advantage.

Diana took a couple of steps forward, saying, "Baby?"

"Don't. Don't move," Sterritt chided, and made a big show of casually adjusting the position of the barrel beneath Erika's chin. "She's fine, you can see that."

"She's not fine," Diana spat. "She's not fine at all. This wasn't what I paid you for."

"So we modified the arrangement, sue us," Sterritt said.

"I paid you already."

"And we incurred more expenses, and then Lucky there killed one of my men. Think of this as hazard pay. I assume that's the money you're holding in your pretty little hands?"

"Yes."

"Four million?"

"Yes. Cash and jewels."

Sterritt nodded. "Cash and jewels. I love the way that sounds, cash and jewels." He looked over his shoulder, first at Hardy, then at Perkins. "Don't you love the way that sounds, boys?"

Neither answered.

"Toss it over here," Sterritt told Diana.

"Let her go, first," I said, trying to buy time, trying to think of a way to get Erika clear.

Sterritt thought that was very funny. "You figure you're in position to give orders, here?"

Gibraltar, I remembered.

"Can I show you something?" I asked.

"I don't know. Is it small and shriveled?"

I held out my right hand, palm up, so he could see it.

"Don't read palms," Sterritt said.

I held up my left hand, palm out, so he could see that, too.

"Don't do sign language, either."

I moved my left hand to my right wrist, and tugged

the transmit button into my palm. Hardy was on the ball, and he zeroed his MP5 on me, and I said, "I wouldn't."

Sterritt looked at Hardy, then to me, and asked, "Why the fuck not?"

"Because what I just put in my palm is a detonator," I said. "And what I put in our Taurus is fifteen pounds of plastique, give or take an ounce. Just to keep you honest, you understand."

"You're shitting me."

"I'm happy to push the button, let you find out."

Sterritt thought for a moment, readjusting his hold slightly on Erika. Her eyes moved from her mother to me and back, and I knew she was following us, that she was hearing it all.

At my left, Diana was looking at me as if I were crazy. I don't know if she believed me or not, if she thought that I had somehow managed to load explosives into the car, but it didn't matter as long as she didn't blow the bluff.

Sterritt said, "No. No, I don't believe you. You're not that hard. You won't kill the girl."

"If she's going to die anyway," I said, "I'm happier if it's at my hands."

"You're not that good."

"Maybe not, but I am a fast learner."

He thought for another second. "How do I know she hasn't filled that briefcase there with rocks?"

I held out my left hand to Diana, said, "Give me the case."

She hesitated, and I almost asked again, and then she handed me the briefcase. It was heavy, and the pressure of the handle on my sore fingers made it feel as if I had needles pushing into my hand.

"Meet you at the snowman," I told Sterritt.

"Glenn, make the swap." Sterritt said it sharply.

Hardy slid out his Browning, came around the front of the car to Erika's side. He handed the MP5 to Sterritt, who stepped back, then Hardy put his Browning against Erika's ribs, took her shoulder in his free hand.

With Hardy now holding on to their prisoner, Sterritt stepped back, gun trained. "You and Glenn," he told me.

I started forward and Glenn Hardy started forward, and it took each of us about ten paces to be within reaching distance of each other. The snowman, head missing from stubby body, stood to my left like a referee at the start of a nightmarish basketball game.

"Open it," Hardy told me.

I set the briefcase down in the snow, keeping my right hand curled around the button in my palm. I knelt, eyes on Hardy, on the position of his gun. I used my left hand to feel for the clasps, to hit the release tabs, and when both had sprung open, I pulled back the lid.

Hardy looked down, and the gun came away from Erika's side, and then his knees buckled, and he started to fall. The sound followed the bullet, the report echoing across the lot and the concrete and the water, and I was launching already, my gun in my hand. Erika pitched forward, and I caught her on my left shoulder, wrapped my arm around her, and brought her to the ground, firing two shots blind at where Perkins had been standing, and then we were in the snow, me rolling over Erika, covering her with my body. I heard Diana's garbled shouts, the chatter of Sterritt's submachine gun, and more snow spat as the snowman took the shots for us.

I raised my head and my gun, saw that Perkins was already down. Sterritt was backing away from the car. He fired another burst that pinged off the concrete and the vehicles. There was motion on all sides, voices, and pressing Erika down I tried to bead on Sterritt as he retreated into the shadows, when one of the shadows burst out of the snow, and Moore had him by the throat. Sterritt tried to raise the MP5, tried to slam it like a club against his former teacher.

He never had a chance. Moore broke his neck before Sterritt had even begun the downswing.

And it was suddenly deeply quiet, and I realized that I was laughing, and I holstered my gun and pulled Erika up into my arms and said, "This'll hurt," and then tore the tape from her mouth, and she didn't yelp, didn't scream.

She said, "I believed you."

I held on to her with my left, and with my right began feeling over Hardy's body, found his knife in his pocket, where I knew it would be. I snapped the blade out with my thumb, began cutting the tape around her wrists and body, and she winced as I pulled it away, but she put her arms around me when she was free, and I helped her up, my arms around her, and Erika kept saying, "I believed you, I believed you."

She wouldn't let go of me, and I didn't mind that at all, just held her and watched as Fowler and the ESU began clearing the scene, moving around Erika and me as if we were the eye of some human hurricane. Emergency lights appeared, and official vehicles, and an ambulance, and people were talking on radios and to each other, and their words didn't matter. Fowler told me they had caught Cox, that he had surrendered, and that Perkins would live. Sterritt and Hardy were both dead. Scott told me I could relax, and let Erika go. I didn't. He moved off, saying nothing.

Then Diana cleared her throat, and I saw that she was standing over Hardy, and she said, "Erika?"

Erika didn't answer.

"Honey?"

Erika moved her head cautiously, so that her wounded ear wouldn't rest against me, and looked at her mother. The bandage was loose, and I could see the piece of her ear that remained, and it looked painful and infected, thick with dried blood.

"Honey, I want you to come home with me," Diana said. "I want you to come and live with me."

Erika looked up at my face, and in her eyes there was

the question, and the only answer I could think of was to press my transmit button and say softly, "Bring him in."

The Porsche pulled up within seconds, and Erika and I turned to see Bridgett stop the car beside the ESU van. After a moment, Colonel Wyatt climbed out from the passenger side, and then Bridgett emerged. From where he had been standing by Fowler, I saw Moore react to the arrival. He began jogging over to us.

I heard Diana saying, "She's coming with me, Doug. You had her already, now she's mine."

The Colonel ignored his wife, standing slumped beside the car, encased in his winter clothes. Only his face was visible, the rest of his body wrapped in flannel, wool, and Polarfleece. He was breathing heavily, like he was wounded.

"Erika," he said. "Stay with me."

Erika looked from him, to me, to her mother. "No," she said, but I was the only one who heard her, and I understood exactly what she meant.

"I'm taking her with me," Diana said. She was still talking to Wyatt.

"You stupid fucking cunt." Saliva gleamed on the Colonel's chin.

"She's mine. She wants to be with me."

"She wants to be with you so fucking much you had to hire mercs to steal her away from me?"

"To save her!" Diana said it with quiet ferocity.

"Yeah, they did a nice job of that."

"You don't deserve her! You got everything else, but not her, you can't have her!"

"You stupid fucking cunt. You have nothing. You're getting nothing from me. Give it the fuck up. What else can you do?"

She can go for a gun, I thought, and even as I did, Diana was bending to Hardy's body, coming up with his Browning in her hand.

"This," she said.

CHAPTER THIRTY-FOUR

"Are you out of your fucking mind?" Bridgett demanded.

Diana steadied the gun with both hands, put the sight on the Colonel's forehead.

"What are you going to do? Shoot all of us?"

"Just whoever gets in my way." Diana said it flatly.

"Shut up," the Colonel told Bridgett without looking away from his wife. He was grinning.

No, I thought. Not in front of your daughter. No. "Colonel," I said.

"Stay the fuck out of this, Sergeant. It's between her and me."

Bridgett and Moore were still. Erika was staring at her parents, arms still around my waist, and she had started to tremble. Farther off, Fowler and Morgan and Hower were in a tête-à-tête with Knowles and the ESU commander. The ambulance had gone, but the ESU van still remained, and around it milled several of the team personnel, joking and waiting. Their helmets were off, their guns slung, celebrating a job well done.

Not quite.

"Maybe you haven't noticed?" Bridgett said to Diana. "But this place is crawling with cops."

"I noticed," Diana said.

"Everybody shut up!" the Colonel shouted, a command, like in the old days. He began walking toward his wife, ignoring the gun.

The chatting stopped, the joking went dead. It took a second for the team to realize what they were seeing, just a heartbeat, and then people were moving through the snow, and I heard the radios crackle once more, heard orders sent down the line as the ESU quickly redeployed. The river continued its contented burble. I heard Fowler demanding that people hold tight, that they hold their fire.

"Don't move any closer," Diana told her husband.

"What're you going to do?" He didn't break stride. "Shoot me?"

"I hate them," Erika hissed. Talking to herself, maybe just thinking out loud.

The Colonel stopped directly in front of his wife, braced his legs. Diana held the Browning steady, and the hate that ran between the two seemed to melt the snow at their feet.

Colonel Wyatt put his forehead against the barrel of the gun, and told Diana, "I shit on you, you're nothing, you're worthless."

"Dad—" Erika said.

"Less than nothing. I used you, and you let me. I ran you, I made you, and I broke you. Get your payback, whore. Pull the trigger. Get your payback."

Erika jerked forward, and I reached to pull her back to me but she kept going, straight to her parents.

Despite the cold I could see Diana sweating, motionless, staring at her husband, at the end of the gun.

"Colonel," I said. "Stand down."

"What are you waiting for?" he taunted. "Go ahead,

do it. Do something right. Just once, do something right."

The ESU were forming a perimeter around us, with Morgan and Hower and the rest. Guns were out once more, held in the low-ready, sights canted to the ground. It had gone quiet, even the radios were dead. I could hear the river water clearly at my back, and the dry scrape of Bridgett's boots shifting in the snow.

Erika said, "Please stop." It wasn't clear which parent she was addressing.

"Stay out of this, Erika." The Colonel didn't turn his head. His eyes stayed on Diana.

"Daddy, please—"

"I said stay the fuck out of this, little girl!"

Erika took a step back, and one of the ESU men began inching forward, perhaps to reach out and draw Erika away from the line of fire, but it was a mistake, because Diana moved for the first time, cocked the gun. "Don't," she said. "Don't. Anybody moves, I'll blow his head off."

The circle rippled as weapons went from low-ready to zero, as sights locked on to Diana. Fowler told everyone that he wanted them alive, to hold their fire.

"Erika, stay here." Diana's voice was strained and low, and the condensation when she spoke drifted out past the gun, around the Colonel's face.

The Colonel coughed. He moved slightly, as if to turn away. Then he spat into his wife's face.

Diana didn't flinch.

ESU hadn't fired, no one had fired, and that meant they'd made a choice, I knew. It all came down to Erika. She was the goal, she was the reason, hers was the life they had to save, and if she could keep her parents alive, they'd give her the chance.

It all comes down to her.

Erika seemed to know that, and she turned away from her parents, and began heading back to me.

She had gone five feet when her mother said, "Erika, get back here."

"Keep her out of this," the Colonel said. "This time it's just you and me. Leave her out of this."

"Get back here right now!" Diana's voice was thin and a little shrill. "You're coming with me!"

"No," Erika said.

"I'll kill him," Diana said.

Erika stopped, and the look on her face reminded me of her mother, when Diana had stood over me, and not put a bullet in my head.

"Good," Diana whispered, and she moved her left leg back for support. I saw the Colonel brace himself for her shot. "Get the case and bring it over here. Get the case and bring it to me, honey."

Erika spun in the snow, shouting, "Fuck you!" Her voice cracked, then, and the words told me how very young she was.

"Don't you dare talk to me like that!"

"Or what? You'll shoot Dad? You'll shoot me? Why not shoot Atticus again?"

"You get the case right now. You're coming with me, young lady."

"Don't you move, little girl," the Colonel ordered. "Don't you fucking listen to that whore."

Erika's eyes went from her father to her mother, then around the guns on the perimeter.

I wondered if the sniper who had shot Hardy was still in position, if he was setting his sight on the base of Diana's skull.

"This is what I want, Erika," the Colonel said.

Quietly, Erika asked, "What you want?"

"Yes."

She stared at her father.

"This has nothing to do with you. It's what I want."

"I understand."

I heard the anger rattling in her reply.

Erika nodded, then knelt, began closing the clasps on the briefcase. The sound was loud in the silence, like gunfire. When it was shut, she rose once more, taking the case in both hands, holding it in front of her like an oversized lunch pail.

"Is this what *you* want?" Erika asked her mother.

"That's a good girl," Diana said. "Bring it over here, honey, by me. Then we'll go to the car together."

Erika nodded, and the Colonel bit out a curse, and then saw that his daughter was backing away from them. When she reached me, Erika put her right hand out for my left arm, and I felt her fingers grip tight. She continued stepping backward, slow paces to make certain of her footing, the case now in one hand, me held with the other. I went with her.

"What are you doing?" Diana demanded, and I saw her fingers tighten around the Browning. "Bring that over here!"

In my peripheral vision, I saw Erika shake her head. The river was louder now, behind us. Or maybe the silence was just deeper.

"Get over here right now!" Diana shrieked.

Colonel Wyatt laughed at his wife.

Erika stopped, and we were at the water, and she let go of my arm and began unfastening the clasps to the briefcase.

"Get over here or I'll kill him! I swear I'll kill him, I'll do it right now!"

"Go ahead," Erika said, loud and deliberate, and she lifted the case, holding it shut, and dangled it over the water. The strain showed in her face, her neck muscles taut, her jaw clenched. "Go ahead, Mom."

Diana glanced at us, and understood what her daughter was going to do, and at that instant, so did I.

"Don't," I told Erika.

"Yeah," she murmured. "Sorry."

My hand went to my gun.

"No!" Diana screamed.

"This is what *I* want," Erika said, and she let the case fall open, and the diamonds and the emeralds cascaded into the dark water, and the bills took to the air.

*Erika looked us all over, ending her pan on me.
"You'd kill someone who pointed a gun at me?"*

Diana turned, bringing the Browning to bear, crying
for Erika to stop as I shoved her daughter down with
my left hand, brought my weapon up in my right. Wyatt
was diving for the ground.

*"We all would. Our first duty is to protect you," I
said.*

I hit her with two double-taps, a clean vertical track,
the first bullet in the solar plexus, the last just above her
chin.

The ESU personnel who'd had clear shots each fired
once, and hit her seven times more.

All it took was one.

The bullets tore into and through her, and Diana
crumpled into snow that was instantly black with her
blood and her flesh.

I heard a radio crackle. Morgan ran forward to take
Diana's pulse. I knew she wouldn't find one.

A diamond glittered at Erika's feet.

Erika began walking to where her father was pulling
himself up in the snow. With him on his knees, they
were almost eye-to-eye. Erika dropped the empty briefcase in front of him.

"You ruined it," the Colonel said. "You ruined everything."

"Yes, I did."

"I don't know you. You're nothing. Just like your
goddamn mother. Don't bother coming home."

Erika shrugged and went to Bridgett's Porsche.
Moore and Knowles began helping the Colonel to his
feet, and Fowler was guiding the three of them away.
Engines were starting up, cars beginning to pull out.

Erika opened the passenger door and climbed inside,
fastened her seat belt. Then she sat, still and calm, looking out over the hood at all of us, finally looking at me.
Her gaze was strong, level, unapologetic. I hoped I saw
a little sadness there, for herself, or her mother, or for
me. Perhaps it was just my imagination.

She knew what she'd done. She knew what she'd made me do.

Then Erika turned her head away.

Bridgett came over to where I stood, still holding my gun. "I'll get her to a hospital. You want me to tell her anything?"

"Tell her I'll be in touch."

"All right." She held out her hand, and I realized she was offering me the radio set I'd given her, not comfort. I took it, put it into a pocket.

Bridgett looked at Diana's body for a moment. Then she made her way to the car without turning back, and then the engine growled to life, and she and Erika were gone.

The lot felt empty once more. Not for long, I knew. Detectives would descend, soon, and the Crime Scene Unit, with their flashlights and their cameras. The money and the stones would be recovered, if possible, then catalogued. Statements would be taken, interviews conducted. Reports would be filed, all telling the story of what happened here tonight, and none of them getting it quite right.

I turned around and looked at the ground, where Diana lay, waiting for attention. A hundred-dollar bill had caught in the wind, and was pinned against her body.

Tracks in the snow ran across the lot, and they stretched undisturbed ahead of me, almost out of sight to the empty road. I walked forward, then stopped, looking back at the path I had made, the signs of two feet, but no person. Just a ghost or memory or history, a solitary trail.

I resumed heading for the road, wishing that Rubin were with me, or Bridgett; just someone to walk with.

ABOUT THE AUTHOR

GREG RUCKA has worked at a variety of jobs, from theatrical fight choreographer to emergency medical technician. The author of *Critical Space*, *Keeper*, and four previous thrillers, he resides with his wife and two sons in Portland, Oregon, where he is at work on his next Queen & Country novel, which Bantam will publish in 2005.